PRAISE FOR RICH HORTON'S
PREVIOUS YEAR'S BEST ANTHOLOGIES

Fantasy: The Best of the Year, 2006 Edition

"The nineteen excellent short stories in this latest addition to the growing field of annual "best of" fantasy anthologies include works by established stars like Pat Cadigan and Peter S. Beagle. Distinguishing this anthology are many stories that first appeared in small press venues.... Horton has gathered a diverse mix of styles and themes that illustrate the depth and breadth of fantasy writing today."—*Publishers Weekly,* starred review

Science Fiction: The Best of the Year, 2006 Edition

"Horton's elegiac anthology of fifteen mostly hard sf stories illuminates a broad spectrum of grief over love thwarted through time, space, human frailty or alien intervention. This anthology reflects the concerns of the genre today—and the apparent inability of our society to do anything about them."—*Publishers Weekly*

Fantasy: The Best of the Year, 2007 Edition

"Horton's fantasy annual showcases the best short speculative fiction that steps beyond the established boundaries of science. The sixteen selections represent both magic-oriented fantasy and cross-genre slipstream fiction. Their inspired and resourceful authors range from veteran fantasists Geoff Ryman and Peter S. Beagle to such newer voices as Matthew Corradi and Ysabeau Wilce. Fantasy enthusiasts looking for stories that expand the genre's boundaries in unexpected ways will find them in this inventive, enticingly provocative collection."—*Booklist*

Science Fiction: The Best of the Year, 2007 Edition

"What with sf's current high literary standing, there is no shortage of gifted authors striving to produce outstanding short fiction, and editor Horton is more than happy to encourage them via this annual for which he sets no higher criterion than plain good writing. Dedicated genre fans may find some overlap of this with other genre annuals, but given the hours of mind-bending entertainment it provides, they'll hardly resent it."—*Booklist*

continued

continued

The Year's Best Science Fiction and Fantasy, 2010 Edition

"The thirty stories in this annual collection present an outstanding showcase of the year's most distinctive sf and fantasy. A better exposure to current trends in sf and fantasy would be hard to find."—*Library Journal*

"American science fiction magazines are struggling to survive, but Horton easily fills this hefty anthology with stories from original anthologies and online publications. Rather than focusing on a narrow subset of fantastic stories, he attempts to illuminate the entire field."—*Publishers Weekly*

Unplugged: The Web's Best Sci-Fi & Fantasy, 2008 Download

"*Unplugged* aims to showcase the online fiction often neglected in standard best-of-the-year anthologies, and a rousing success it is. The selections come from a truly excellent assortment of venues, including *Tor.com*, *Lone Star Stories*, *Baen's Universe*, and *Farrago's Wainscot*. They constitute a shining example of the good general anthology. Clearly, selecting only online stories imposed no limit on scope, variety, and high quality."—*Booklist*

"A short but superlative substantiation of the quality of speculative fiction being published on the Internet, this exceptional anthology of the best science fiction and fantasy put online in 2008 includes gems by genre luminaries as well as rising stars like Tina Connolly and Beth Bernobich. After reading this fourteen-story compilation, online publishing naysayers may rethink their position."—*Publishers Weekly*, starred review

THE YEAR'S BEST SCIENCE FICTION & FANTASY

2013 EDITION

THE YEAR'S BEST SCIENCE FICTION & FANTASY

2013 EDITION

EDITED BY

RICH HORTON

PRIME BOOKS

THE YEAR'S BEST SCIENCE FICTION
& FANTASY, 2013 EDITION

Prime Books
www.prime-books.com

ISBN: 978-1-60701-392-1

To the supportive and very patient *Locus* editorial team, particularly
my editor Jonathan Strahan, and website editor (and my predecessor as
short fiction reviewer), Mark Kelly, who brought me into the fold.

CONTENTS

CONTENTS

THE YEAR IN FANTASY AND SCIENCE FICTION, 2013

RICH HORTON

Is Science Fiction Exhausted?

It is a truism that for an author (or an editor, in this case) to respond to a review is a mistake. But I find myself convinced that Paul Kincaid's review of last year's edition of this book (along with Gardner Dozois's similar volume, and the Nebula Awards volume) was at the same time sufficiently notorious, and sufficiently well-argued, that it deserves engagement. (For that matter, Kincaid's history as a critic is enough itself to inspire respect and to insist on engagement with his work.) Kincaid's review (in the *L.A. Review of Books*) opened: "The overwhelming sense one gets, working through so many stories that are presented as the very best that science fiction and fantasy have to offer, is exhaustion. . . . it is more as though the genres of the fantastic themselves have reached a state of exhaustion. . . . the genre has become a set of tropes to be repeated and repeated until all meaning has been drained from them."

He's got a point, really. I wouldn't go so far—I don't think that "all meaning has been drained from" the tropes we use, but I do think they are becoming overfamiliar. And I do think that the field of science fiction has to a considerable extent become enamored with explicitly backward-looking ideas, most obviously steampunk, but also alternate-history in general, and, too, stories that overtly refer to earlier stories. Kincaid also complains about the recent tendency for science fiction stories to look like fantasy—I think this is indeed a trend, but I'm not so sure it's a problem. If I say any more I will probably distort his argument (I probably have already), so I will just conclude by suggesting that, even though it's not exactly a positive review of my book (nor of Dozois'), it's well worth finding on the web.

(Kincaid also suggests that this problem of "exhaustion" is more evident in short fiction than in novels—and I would respond that a look at the Hugo nominees for this year might disabuse one of that notion—a generally enjoyable set of books, but hardly cutting edge in form or subject matter.)

So naturally I can't help looking at the contents this year through a sort of Kincaidian lens. Is there steampunk here? Check—Nick Mamatas's "Arbeitskraft" is even from an anthology called **The Mammoth Book of Steampunk**)—but is it exhausted? I don't think so—to me it's as fresh and as politically engaged as anyone could wish. Is there science fiction hard to distinguish from fantasy? Well, there's Gord Sellar's "The Bernoulli War," which isn't fantasy by any reasonable measurement, but which does present a posthuman future nearly incomprehensible (to my mind) in contemporary terms. I think that's rather the point (though at the same time I take Kincaid's point that such estrangement speaks to a certain lack of confidence in the future, or in our ability to engage with it). Is there fairly traditional science fiction, reworking old tropes? I guess there is—Kate Bachus' "Things Greater Than Love," an alien planet mountain climbing story, with its main theme concerning understanding an alien intelligence, is hardly "new," though it's lovely and effective. Likewise Linda Nagata's "Nahiku West" concerns asteroid habitats, matter transmission, and genetic modification—not exactly tired tropes, but not new ones either. But I still found it striking and honest and fresh (even as its plot is rooted in traditional the hard-boiled mystery). Are there stories harkening explicitly to old science fiction—indeed, old TV or film science fiction? Yes, indeed—Sandra McDonald's "The Black Feminist's Guide to Science Fiction Film Editing" is in part a paean to an science fiction film never made based on an science fiction story (**The Ginger Star** by Leigh Brackett) that was consciously old-fashioned on its first publication decades ago. Leonard Richardson's "Four Kinds of Cargo" is about an alien ship captain who is trying to emulate the heroes of movies "she" adores. Never mind that the movies are made by aliens—the echoes here are overtly of **Star Trek** and **Galaxy Quest**. In these two cases I must simply plead "Guilty!" But I still think they are damned fine stories—and at their heart the appeal is not nostalgia, but the use of nostalgia to affect more fundamental human concerns. And is there a vampire story? Well, yes again—but I think Nina Allan's "Sunshine" is as pure an antidote to vampire cliches as one could ask for.

That's enough, though. I think the stories we've collected here are a grand mix—some do, to some extent, look backward. Other are, as they say, ripped from today's headlines (or advertisements, as with Michael Blumlein's "Twenty-Two and You." Science fiction is, these days, a genre established in not just the imaginations of fans but in the general populace, and as such many of its tropes are familiar. And, perhaps more seriously, the entire world is at the same time engaged with the future, confused by it, and afraid of it. Science fiction has possibly failed to engage with the near future as rigorously as we might hope. Much of this book engages with a farther future, or with an altered past. (And much of course is fantasy, for which I make no apology.) I still find it exciting, and I hope you do, too.

One other point Kincaid made was that much of the more exciting new science fiction was by writers not necessarily entrenched in the American/ British tradition. I definitely agree. And again in this book we feature, amid many US or UK writers, a number of writers who were either raised entirely in non-Anglophone cultures (as with the French-Vietnamese writer Aliette de Bodard) or who,even if British or American, have spent much of their life elsewhere (as with Jay Lake or Lavie Tidhar). Here we also feature a translated story by Chinese writer Xia Jia; and a story by Sofia Samatar, a Somali-American writer who has spent considerable time in Sudan.

Other breakdowns? Nearly two-thirds of the stories are by women, a very high total in historical terms, but reflective of a continuing increase in the involvement and acceptance of women writers in the field, especially (one hopes) in science fiction (as opposed to fantasy). I usually strive for a roughly even balance of science fiction and fantasy in this book, but this year, by my count, less than a third of the stories are fantasy. (To be sure, a couple I've put in the science fiction columns are ambiguous.) I think this is a year-to-year anomaly—this year was simply a better year for short science fiction than for short fantasy. Online publications are more and more central to the field— this year fifteen stories, just less than half, are from online sources. (Notably, several of these sources began in print, such as *Eclipse Online* (originally the **Eclipse** series of anthologies) and *Electric Velocipede* (a fine small press 'zine that just recently migrated online).) Only five stories come from original anthologies, and only one story is from a magazine nominally devoted to "mainstream" fiction.

I'll for the most part bypass a broader survey of the field this time around, if only to avoid what Kincaid calls "the traditional threnody of woe" that runs through Gardner Dozois's exhaustive summary of closing markets each year. (With the exception of the loss of **Eclipse** as an original anthology market (alas, followed by the closing of *Eclipse Online* early in 2013), the news in 2012 wasn't really all that bad—though I do regret the closing of a nice newish online site, *Redstone Science Fiction*.) Perhaps the biggest news was the announced retirement of Stanley Schmidt from *Analog* (after roughly as long a career at the helm of that magazine as John W. Campbell). Two promising new online magazines debuted: *Arc* in the UK, and the horror-oriented *Nightmare* (companion to *Lightspeed*) in the US. On the whole, I'd characterize it as a year of "holding patterns." I think more and more short fiction will be found online (after all, even the major print magazines have a large fraction of their distribution in electronic form). But, even if from a certain angle evidence of "exhaustion" can be found, I think the best short science fiction and fantasy remains inspiring and vigorous in 2013.

NAHIKU WEST

LINDA NAGATA

A railcar was ferrying Key Lu across the tether linking Nahiku East and West when a micrometeor popped through the car's canopy, leaving two neat holes that vented the cabin to hard vacuum within seconds. The car continued on the track, but it took over a minute for it to reach the gel lock at Nahiku West and pass through into atmosphere. No one expected to find Key Lu alive, but as soon as the car re-pressurized, he woke up.

Sometimes, it's a crime not to die.

I stepped into the interrogation chamber. Key had been sitting on one of two padded couches, but when he saw me he bolted to his feet. I stood very still, hearing the door lock behind me. Nothing in Key's background indicated he was a violent man, but prisoners sometimes panic. I raised my hand slightly, as a gel ribbon armed with a paralytic spray slid from my forearm to my palm, ready for use if it came to that.

"Please," I said, keeping the ribbon carefully concealed. "Sit down."

Key slowly subsided onto the couch, never taking his frightened eyes off me.

Most of the celestial cities restrict the height and weight of residents to minimize the consumption of volatiles, but Commonwealth police officers are required to be taller and more muscular than the average citizen. I used to be a smaller man, but during my time at the academy adjustments were made. I faced Key Lu with a physical presence optimized to trigger a sense of intimidation in the back brain of a nervous suspect, an effect enhanced by the black fabric of my uniform. Its design was simple—shorts cuffed at the knees and a lightweight pullover with long sleeves that covered the small arsenal of chemical ribbons I carried on my forearms—but its light-swallowing color set me apart from the bright fashions of the celestial cities.

I sat down on the couch opposite Key Lu. He was a well-designed man, nothing eccentric about him, just another good-looking citizen. His hair was presently blond, his eyebrows darker. His balanced face lacked strong features. The only thing notable about him was his injuries. Dark bruises surrounded his eyes and their whites had turned red from burst blood vessels. More bruises discolored swollen tissue beneath his coppery skin.

We studied each other for several seconds, both knowing what was at stake. I was first to speak. "I'm Officer Zeke Choy—"

"I know who you are."

"—of the Commonwealth Police, the watch officer here at Nahiku."

The oldest celestial cities orbited Earth, but Nahiku was newer. It was one in a cluster of three orbital habitats that circled the Sun together, just inside the procession of Venus.

Key Lu addressed me again, with the polite insistence of a desperate man. "I didn't know about the quirk, Officer Choy. I thought I was legal."

The machine voice of a Dull Intelligence whispered into my auditory nerve that he was lying. I already knew that, but I nodded anyway, pretending to believe him.

The DI was housed within my atrium, a neural organ that served as an interface between mind and machine. Atriums are a legal enhancement— they don't change human biology—but Key Lu's quirked physiology that had allowed him to survive short-term exposure to hard vacuum was definitely not.

I was sure his quirk had been done before the age of consent. He'd been born in the Far Reaches among the fragile holdings of the asteroid prospectors, where it must have looked like a reasonable gamble to bioengineer some insurance into his system. Years had passed since then; enforcement had grown stricter. Though Key Lu looked perfectly ordinary, by the law of the Commonwealth, he wasn't even human.

I met his gaze, hoping he was no fool. "Don't tell me anything I don't want to know," I warned him.

I let him consider this for several seconds before I went on. "Your enhancement is illegal under the statutes of the Commonwealth—"

"I understand that, but I didn't know about it."

I nodded my approval of this lie. I needed to maintain the fiction that he hadn't known. It was the only way I could help him. "I'll need your consent to remove it."

A spark of hope ignited in his blooded eyes. "Yes! Yes, of course."

"So recorded." I stood, determined to get the quirk out of his system as soon as possible, before awkward questions could be asked. "Treatment can begin right—"

The door to the interrogation room opened.

I was so startled, I turned with my hand half raised, ready to trigger the ribbon of paralytic still hidden in my palm—only to see Magistrate Glory Mina walk in, flanked by two uniformed cops I'd never seen before.

My DI sent the ribbon retreating back up my forearm while I greeted Glory with a scowl. Nahiku was my territory. I was the only cop assigned to the little city and I was used to having my own way—but with the magistrate's arrival I'd just been overridden.

Goods travel on robotic ships between the celestial cities, but people rarely do. We ghost instead. A ghost—an electronic persona—moves between the data gates at the speed of light. Most ghosts are received on a machine grid or within the virtual reality of a host's atrium, but every city keeps a cold-storage mausoleum. If you have the money—or if you're a cop—you can grow a duplicate body in another city, fully replicated hard copy, ready to roll.

Glory Mina presided over the circuit court based out of Red Star, the primary city in our little cluster. She would have had to put her Red Star body into cold storage before waking up the copy here at Nahiku, but that was hardly more than half an hour's effort. From the eight cops who had husks stashed in the mausoleum, she'd probably pulled two at random to make up the officers for her court.

I was supposed to get a notification anytime a husk in the mausoleum woke up, but obviously she'd overridden that too.

Glory Mina was a small woman with skin the color of cinnamon, and thick, shiny black hair that she kept in a stubble cut. She looked at me curiously, her eyebrows arched. "Officer Choy, I saw the incident report, but I missed your request for a court."

The two cops had positioned themselves on either side of the door.

"I didn't file a request, Magistrate."

"And why not?"

"This is not a criminal case."

No doubt her DI dutifully informed her I was lying—not that she couldn't figure that out for herself. "I don't think that's been determined, Officer Choy. There are records that still need to be considered, which have not made their way into the case file."

I had looked into Key Lu's background. I knew he never translated his persona into an electronic ghost. If he'd ever done so, his illegal quirk would have been detected when he passed through a data gate. I knew he'd never kept a backup record that could be used to restore his body in case of accident. Again, if he'd done so, his quirk would have been revealed. And he never, ever physically left Nahiku, because without a doubt he would have been exposed when he passed through a port gate. The court could use any one of those circumstances to justify interrogation under a coercive drug—which is why I hadn't included any of it in the case file.

"Magistrate, this is a minor case—"

"There are no minor cases, Officer Choy. You're dismissed for now, but please, wait outside."

There was nothing else I could do. I left the room knowing Key Lu was a dead man.

I could have cleaned things up if I'd just had more time. I could have cured Key Lu. I'm a molecular designer and my skills are the reason I was drafted into the Commonwealth police.

Technically, I could have refused to join, but then my home city of Haskins would have been assessed a huge fine—and the city council would have tried to pass the debt on to me. So I consoled myself with the knowledge that I would be working on the cutting edge of molecular research and, swallowing my misgivings, I swore to uphold the laws of the Commonwealth, however arcane and asinine they might be.

I worked hard at my job. I tried to do some good, and though I skirted the boundaries now and then, I made very sure I never went too far because if I got myself fired, the debt for my training would be on me, and the contracts I'd have to take to pay that off didn't bear thinking on.

The magistrate required me to attend the execution, assigning me to stand watch beside the door. I used a mood patch to ensure a proper state of detachment. It's a technique they taught us at the academy, and as I watched the two other officers escort Key Lu into the room, I could tell from their faces they were tranked too, while Key Lu was glassy-eyed, more heavily sedated than the rest of us.

He was guided to a cushioned chair. One of the cops worked an IV into his arm. Five civilians were present, seated in a half circle on either side of the magistrate. One of them was weeping. Her name was Hera Poliu. I knew her because she was a friend of my intimate, Tishembra Indens—but Tishembra had never mentioned that Hera and Key were involved.

The magistrate spoke, summarizing the crime and the sanctity of Commonwealth law, reminding us the law existed to guard society's shared idea of what it means to be human, and that the consequences of violating the law were mandated to be both swift and certain. She nodded at one of the cops, who turned a knob on the IV line, admitting an additional ingredient to the feed. Key Lu slumped and closed his eyes. Hera wept louder, but it was already over.

• • •

Nahiku was justly famed for its vista walls, which transformed blank corridors into fantasy spaces. On Level Seven West, where I lived, the theme was a wilderness maze, enhanced by faint rainforest scents, rustling leaves, bird song, and ghostly puffs of humidity. Apartment doors didn't appear until you asked for them.

The path forked. I went right. Behind me, a woman called my name, "Officer Choy!" Her voice was loud and so vindictive that when the DI whispered in my mind, Hera Poliu, I thought, No way. I knew Hera and she didn't sound like that. I turned fast.

It was Hera all right, but not like I'd ever seen her. Her fists were clenched, her face flushed, her brows knit in a furious scowl. The DI assessed her as rationally angry, but it didn't seem that way to me. When she stepped into my personal space I felt a chill. "I want to file a complaint," she informed me.

Hera was a full head shorter than me, thin and willowy, with rich brown skin and auburn hair wound up in a knot behind her head. Tishembra had invited her over for dinner a few times and we'd all gone drinking together, but as our eyes locked I felt I was looking at a stranger. "What sort of complaint, Hera?"

"Don't patronize me." I saw no sign in her face of the heart-rending grief she'd displayed at the execution. "The Commonwealth police are supposed to protect us from quirks like Key."

"Key never hurt anyone," I said softly.

"He has now! You didn't hear the magistrate's assessment. She's fined the city for every day since Key became a citizen. We can't afford it, Choy. You know Nahiku already has debt problems—"

"I can't help you, Hera. You need to file an appeal with the magistrate—"

"I want to file a complaint! The city can't get fined for harboring quirks if we turn them in. So I'm reporting Tishembra Indens."

I stepped back. A cold sweat broke out across my skin as I looked away.

Hera laughed. "You already know she's a quirk, don't you? You're a cop, Choy! A Commonwealth cop, infatuated with a quirk."

I lost my temper. "What's wrong with you? Tishembra's your friend."

"So was Key. And both of them immigrants."

"I can't randomly scan people because they're immigrants."

"If you don't scan her, I'll go to the magistrate."

I tried to see through her anger, but the Hera I knew wasn't there. "No need to bother the magistrate," I said softly, soothingly. "I'll do it."

She nodded, the corner of her lip lifting a little. "I look forward to hearing the result."

• • •

I stepped into the apartment to find Tishembra's three-year-old son Robin playing on the floor, shaping bridges and wheels out of colorful gel pods. He looked up at me, a handsome boy with his mother's dark skin and her black, glossy curls, but not her reserved manner. I was treated to a mischievous grin and a firm order to, "Watch this!" Then he hurled himself onto his creations, smashing them all back into disks of jelly.

Tishembra stepped out of the bedroom, lean and dark and elegant, her long hair hanging down her back in a lovely chaos of curls. She'd changed from her work clothes into a silky white shift that I knew was only mindless fabric and still somehow it clung in all the right places as if a DI was controlling the fibers. She was a city engineer. Two years ago she'd emigrated to Nahiku, buying citizenship for herself and Robin—right before the city went into massive debt over an investment in a water-bearing asteroid that turned out to have no water. She was bitter over it, more so because the deal had been made before she arrived, but she shared in the loss anyway.

I crossed the room. She met me halfway. I'd been introduced to her on my second day at Nahiku, seven months ago now, and I'd never looked back. Taking her in my arms, I held her close, letting her presence fill me up as it always did. I breathed in her frustration and her fury and for a giddy moment everything else was blotted from my mind. I was addicted to her moods, all of them. Joy and anger were just different aspects of the same enthralling, intoxicating woman—and the more time I spent with her the more deeply she could touch me in that way. It wasn't love alone. Over time I'd come to realize she had a subtle quirk that let her emotions seep out onto the air around her. Tishembra tended to be reserved and distant. I think the quirk helped her connect with people she casually knew, letting her be perceived as more open and likeable, and easing her way as an immigrant into Nahiku's tightly-knit culture—but it wasn't something we could ever talk about.

"You were part of it, weren't you?" she asked me in an angry whisper. "You were part of what happened to Key. Why didn't you stop it?"

Tishembra had taken a terrible chance in getting close to me.

Her fingers dug into my back. "I'm trapped here, Zeke. With the new fine, on top of the old debt . . . Robin and I will be working a hundred years to earn our way free." She looked up at me, her lip curled in a way that reminded me too much of Hera's parting expression. "It's gotten to the point, my best hope is another disaster. If the city is sold off, I could at least start fresh—"

"Tish, that doesn't matter now." I spoke very softly, hoping Robin wouldn't overhear. "I've received a complaint against you."

Her sudden fear was a radiant thing, washing over me, making me want to hold her even closer, comfort her, keep her forever safe.

"It's ridiculous, of course," I murmured. "To think you're a quirk. I mean, you've been through the gates. So you're clean."

Thankfully, my DI never bothered to point out when I was lying.

Tishembra nodded to let me know she understood. She wouldn't tell me anything I didn't want to know; I wouldn't ask her questions—because the less I knew, the better.

My hope rested on the fact that she could not have had the quirk when she came through the port gate into Nahiku. Maybe she'd acquired it in the two years since, or maybe she'd stripped it out when she'd passed through the gate. I was hoping she knew how to strip it again.

"I have to do the scan," I warned her. "Soon. If I don't, the magistrate will send someone who will."

"Tonight?" she asked in a voice devoid of expression. "Or tomorrow?"

I kissed her forehead. "Tomorrow, love. That's soon enough."

Robin was asleep. Tishembra lay beside him on the bed, her eyes half closed, her focus inward as she used her atrium to track the progress of processes I couldn't see. I sat in a chair and watched her. I didn't have to ask if the extraction was working. I knew it was. Her presence was draining away, becoming fainter, weaker, like a memory fading into time.

After a while it got to be too much, waiting for the woman I knew to become someone else altogether. "I'm going out for a while," I said. She didn't answer. Maybe she didn't hear me. I re-armed myself with my chemical arsenal of gel ribbons. Then I put my uniform back on, and I left.

All celestial cities have their own municipal police force. It's often a part-time, amateur operation, but the local force is supposed to investigate traditional crimes like theft, assault, murder—all the heinous things people have done to each other since the beginning of time. The Commonwealth police are involved only when the crime violates statutes involving molecular science, biology, or machine intelligence.

So strictly speaking, I didn't have any legal right or requirement to investigate the original accident that had exposed Key's quirk, but I took the elevator up to Level 1 West anyway, and used my authority to get past the DI that secured the railcar garage.

Nahiku is a twin orbital. Its two inhabited towers are counterweights at opposite ends of a very long carbon-fiber tether that lets them spin around a center point, generating a pseudogravity in the towers. A rail runs the length of the tether, linking Nahiku East and West. The railcar Key Lu had failed to die in was parked in a small repair bay in the West-end garage. Repair work hadn't started on it yet, and the two small holes in its canopy were easy to see.

There was no one around, maybe because it was local-night. That worked for me: I didn't have to concoct a story on why I'd made this my investigation. I started collecting images, measurements, and sample swabs. When the DI picked up traces of explosive residue, I wasn't surprised.

I was inside the car, collecting additional samples from every interior surface, when a faint shift in air pressure warned me a door had opened. Footsteps approached. I don't know who I was expecting. Hera, maybe. Or Tishembra. Not the magistrate.

Glory Mina walked up to the car and, resting her hand on the roof, she bent down to peer at me where I sat on the ruptured upholstery.

"Is there more going on here that I need to know about?" she asked.

I sent her the DI's report. She received it in her atrium, scanned it, and followed my gaze to one of the holes in the canopy. "You're thinking someone tried to kill him."

"Why like this?" I wondered. "Is it coincidence? Or did they know about his quirk?"

"What difference does it make?"

"If the attacker knew about Key, then it was murder by cop."

"And if not, it was just an attempted murder. Either way, it's not your case. This one belongs to the city cops."

I shook my head. I couldn't leave it alone. Maybe that's why my superiors tolerated me. "I like to know what's going on in my city, and the big question I have is why? I'm not buying a coincidence. Whoever blew the canopy had to know about Key—so why not just kill him outright? If he'd died like any normal person, I wouldn't have looked into it, you wouldn't have assessed a fine. Who gains, when everyone loses?"

Even as I said the words my thoughts turned to Tishembra, and what she'd said. It's gotten to the point, my best hope is another disaster. No. I wasn't going to go there. Not with Tishembra. But maybe she wasn't the only one thinking that way?

The magistrate watched me closely, no doubt recording every nuance of my expression. She said, "I saw the complaint against your intimate."

"It's baseless."

"But you'll look into it?"

"I've scheduled a scan."

Glory nodded. "See to that, but stay out of the local case. This one doesn't belong to you."

The apartment felt empty when I returned. I panicked for the few seconds it took me to sprint across the front room to the bedroom door. Tishembra was still lying on the bed, her half-closed eyes blinking sporadically, but I couldn't feel her. Not like before. A sense of abandonment came over me. I knew it was ridiculous, but I felt like she'd walked away.

Robin whimpered in his sleep, turned over, and then awoke. He looked first at Tishembra lying next to him, and then he looked at me. "What happened to mommy?"

"Mommy's okay."

"She's not. She's wrong."

I went over and picked him up. "Hush. Don't ever say that to anyone but me, okay? We need it to be a secret."

He pouted, but he was frightened, and he agreed.

I spent that night in the front room, with Robin cradled in my arm. I didn't sleep much. I couldn't stop thinking about Key and his quirk, and who might have known about it. Maybe someone from his past? Or someone who'd done a legal mod on him? I had the DI import his personal history into my atrium, but there was no record of any bioengineering work being done on him. Maybe it had just been a lucky guess by someone who knew what went on in the Far Reaches? I sent the DI to search the city files for anyone else who'd ever worked out there. Only one name came back to me: Tishembra Indens.

Tishembra and I had never talked much about where we'd come from. I knew circumstances had not been kind to her, but that she'd had to take a contract in the Far Reaches—that shocked me.

My best hope is another disaster.

I deleted the query, I tried to stop thinking, but I couldn't help reflecting that she was an engineer. She had skills. She could work out how to pop the canopy and she'd have access to the supplies to do it.

Eventually I dozed, until Tishembra woke me. I stared at her. I knew her face, but I didn't know her. I couldn't feel her anymore. Her quirk was gone, and she was a stranger to me. I sat up. Robin was still asleep and I cradled his little body against my chest, dreading what would happen when he woke.

"I'm ready," Tishembra said.

I looked away. "I know."

Robin wouldn't let his mother touch him. "You're not you!" he screamed at her with all the fury a three-year-old could muster. Tishembra started to argue with him, but I shook my head, "Deal with it later," and took him into the dining nook, where I got him breakfast and reminded him of our secret.

"I want mommy," he countered with a stubborn pout.

I considered tranking him, but the staff at the day-venture center would notice and they would ask questions, so I did my best to persuade him that mommy was mommy. He remained skeptical. As we left the apartment, he refused to hold Tishembra's hand but ran ahead instead, hiding behind the jungle foliage until we caught up, then running off again. I didn't blame him. In my rotten heart I didn't want to touch her either, but I wasn't three. So the next time he took off, I slipped my arm around Tishembra's waist and hauled her aside into a nook along the path. We didn't ever kiss or hold hands when I was in uniform and besides, I'd surprised her when her mind was fixed on more serious things, so of course she protested. "Zeke, what are you doing?"

"Hush," I said loudly. "Do you want Robin to find us?"

And I kissed her. I didn't want to. She knew it, and resisted, whispering, "You don't need to feel sorry for me."

But I'd gotten a taste of her mouth, and that hadn't changed. I wanted more. She felt it and softened against me, returning my kiss in a way that made me think we needed to go back to the apartment for a time.

Then Robin was pushing against my hip. "No! Stop that kissing stuff. We have to go to day-venture."

I scowled down at him. "Fine, but I'm holding Tishembra's hand."

"No. I am." And to circumvent further argument, he seized her hand and tugged her toward the path. I let her go with a smirk, but her defiant gaze put an end to that.

"I do love you," I insisted. She shrugged and went with Robin, too proud to believe in me just yet.

Day-venture was on Level 5, where there was a prairie vista. On either side of the path we looked out across a vast land of low, grassy hills, where some sort of herd animals fed in the distance. Waist-high grass grew in a nook outside the doorway to the day-venture center. Robin stomped through it, sending a flutter of butterflies spiraling toward a blue sky. The grass sprang back without damage, betraying a biomechanical nature that the butterflies shared. One of them floated back down to land on Tishembra's hand. She started to shoo it away, but Robin shrieked, "Don't flick it!" and he pounced. "It's a message fly." The butterfly's blue wings spread open as it rested in his small palms. A message was written there, shaped out of white scales drained of pigment, but Robin didn't know how to read yet, so he looked to his mother for help. "What does it say?"

Tishembra gave me a dark look. Then she crouched to read the message and I saw a slight uptick in the corner of her lip. "It says Robin and Zeke love Tishembra." Then she ran her finger down the butterfly's back to erase the message, and nudged it, sending it fluttering away.

"It's wrong," Robin told her defiantly. "I don't love Tishembra. I love mommy." Then he threw his arms around her neck and kissed her, before running inside to play with his friends.

Tishembra and I went on to my office, where Glory Mina was waiting for us to arrive.

When Tishembra saw the magistrate she turned to me with a look of desperation. I told her the truth. "It doesn't matter."

A deep scan is performed with an injection of molecular-scale machines called Makers that map the body's component systems. The data is fed directly into police records and there's no way to fake the results. Tishembra should have known that, but she looked at me as if I'd betrayed her. "You don't have to worry," I insisted. "The scan is just a formality, a required response in the face of the baseless complaint filed against you."

Glory Mina watched me with a half smile. Naturally, her DI would have told her I was lying.

I led Tishembra into a small exam room and had her sit in a large, cushioned chair. After Glory came in behind us, the office DI locked the door. I handed Tishembra a packet of Makers and she dutifully inhaled it. At the same time my DI whispered that Hera Poliu had arrived in the outer office. Sensing trouble, I looked at the magistrate. "I need to talk to her."

"Who?" Tishembra asked anxiously. "Zeke, what's going on?"

"Nothing's going on. Everything will be fine."

Glory just watched me. I grunted, realizing she'd come not to observe the scan but to gauge the integrity of her Nahiku watch officer, which she had good cause to doubt. "I'll be right back."

The office DI maintained a continuous surveillance of all rooms. I channeled its feed, keeping one eye on Tishembra and another on Hera as she looked around the front office with an anxious gaze. She appeared timid and unsure—nothing at all like the angry woman who had accosted me yesterday. "Zeke?" she called softly. "Are you here?"

When the door opened ahead of me, she startled.

"Zeke!" Hera's hands were shaking. "Is it true Tishembra's been scheduled for a scan? She didn't have anything to do with Key. You have to know that. She hardly knew him. There's no reason to suspect her. Tishembra is my best engineer and if we lose her this city will never recover . . . Zeke? What is it?"

I think I was standing with my mouth open. "You filed the complaint that initiated the scan!"

"Me? I . . . " Her focus turned inward. "Oh, yesterday . . . I wasn't myself. I took the wrong mood patch. I was out of my head. Is Tishembra . . . ?"

The results of the scan arrived in my atrium. I glanced at them, and closed my eyes briefly in silent thanks. "Tishembra has passed her scan."

Against all expectation I'd made a home at Nahiku. I'd found a woman I loved, I'd made friends, and I'd gained trust—to the point that people would come to me for advice and guidance, knowing I wasn't just another jackboot of the Commonwealth.

In one day all that had been shattered and I wanted to know why.

I sent a DI hunting through the datasphere for background on Key Lu. I sent another searching through Hera Poliu's past. I thought about sending a third after Tishembra—but whatever the DI turned up would go into police records and I was afraid of what it might find.

Tish had used a patch to calm herself, resolved to go into work as if nothing was changed. "I'm fine," she insisted when I said I'd walk with her. She resented my coddling, but there were questions I needed to ask. We took the elevator, stepping out into a corridor enhanced with a seascape. The floor appeared as weathered boardwalk; our feet struck it in hollow thumps. Taking her arm, I gently guided her to a nook where a strong breeze blew, carrying what I'm told is the salt scent of an ocean, and hiding the sound of our voices. "Tish, is there anything you need to tell me?"

Resentment simmered in her eyes. "What exactly are you asking?"

"You spent time in the Far Reaches."

"So?"

"Did you know about Key Lu?"

I deserved the contempt that blossomed in her expression. "There are hundreds of tiny settlements out there, Zeke. Maybe thousands. I didn't know him. I didn't know him here, either."

The DI returned an initial infodump. My focus wavered. Tishembra saw it. "What?" she asked me.

"Key Lu was a city finance officer, one who signed off on the water deal."

"The water deal with no water," she amended bitterly. Crossing her arms, she glared at the ocean.

"Someone tried to kill him," I told her, letting my words blend in with the sea breeze.

She froze, her gaze fixed on the horizon.

"There was never a micrometeor. His railcar was sabotaged."

I couldn't read her face and neither could the DI. Maybe it was the patch she'd used to level her emotions, but her fixed expression frightened me.

She knew what was going on in my head, though. "You're asking yourself who has the skill to do that, aren't you? Who could fake a meteor strike? If it were me, I'd do it with explosive patches, one inside, one outside, to get the trajectory correct. Is that how it was done, Zeke?"

"Yes."

Her gaze was still fixed on the horizon. "It wasn't me."

"Okay."

She turned and looked me in the eye. "It wasn't me."

The DI whispered that she spoke the truth. I smiled my relief and reached for her, but she backed away. "No, Zeke."

"Tish, come on. Don't be mad. This day is making us both crazy."

"I haven't accused you of being a murderer."

"Tish, I'm sorry."

She shook her head. "I remember when we used to trust each other. I think that was yesterday."

The second DI arrived with an initial report on Hera. Like an idiot, I scanned the file. To my surprise, I had a new suspect, but while I was distracted, Tishembra walked away.

Glory Mina was waiting for me when I returned to my office. She'd tracked my DIs and copied herself on their reports. "You should have been a municipal cop," she told me. She sat perched on the arm of a chair, her arms crossed and her eyes twinkling with amusement.

"It's not like I had a choice."

She cocked her head, allowing me the point. Reading from the DI's report, she said, "So Hera Poliu had a brother. Four years ago he was exiled from Nahiku, and a year after that he was arrested and executed for an illegal enhancement."

"Hera lost her brother. She's got to resent it. Maybe she resents anybody who has a—" I caught myself. "Anybody she thinks might have a quirk."

"Maybe," Glory conceded. "And maybe that's why she made a complaint against your intimate, but so what? It's not your case, Zeke. Forward what you've got to whoever had the misfortune to be appointed as the criminal investigator in this little paradise and let it go."

I made compliant noises. She shook her head, not needing the DI to know I wasn't being straight. "Walk with me."

"Where?"

"The mausoleum. I'm going home. But on the way there, you're going to listen to what I have to say about the necessity for boundaries." She crooked her finger at me. I shrugged and followed. As we walked past the vistas she lectured me on the essential but very limited role of the Commonwealth police and warned me that my appointment as watch officer at Nahiku could end at any time. I listened patiently, knowing she would soon be gone.

As we approached the mausoleum, I sent a DI to open the door. Inside was a long hallway with locked doors on either side. Behind the doors were storage chambers, most of them belonging to corporations. The third door on the left secured the police chamber. It opened as we approached, and closed again when we had stepped inside. One wall held clothing lockers. The other, ranks of cold storage drawers stacked four high. "Magistrate Glory Mina,"

Glory said to the room DI. She stripped off her clothes and hung them in one of the lockers while the drawers slid past each other, rearranging themselves. Only two were empty. One was mine. The other descended from the top rank to the second level, where it opened, ready to receive her.

Glory closed the locker door. She was naked and utterly unconcerned about it. She turned to me with a stern gaze. "You tried to pretend Key Lu was a victim. This once, I'm going to pretend you just missed a step in the background investigation. Zeke, as much as you don't like being a cop, being an ex-cop can be a lot worse."

I had no answer for that. I knew she was right.

She climbed into the drawer. As soon as she lay back, the cushions inflated around her, creating a moist interface all across the surface of her skin. The drawer slid shut and locked with a soft snick. Very soon, her ghost would be on its way to Red Star. Once again, I was on my own.

No matter what Glory wanted, there was no way I was going to set this case aside. Key Lu was dead, while Tishembra had been threatened and made into a stranger, both to me and to her own son. I wanted to know who was responsible and why.

Still, I knew how to make concessions. So I set up an appointment with an official who served part-time as a city cop, intending to hand over the case files, if only for the benefit of my personnel record. But before that could happen a roving DI returned to me with the news that the city's auto-defense system had locked down a plague outbreak on Level 5 West. The address was Robin's day-venture center.

It took me ninety seconds to strip off my uniform and wrap on the impermeable hide of a vacuum-capable skinsuit, police black, with gold insignia. Then I grabbed a standard-issue bivouac kit that weighed half as much as I did, and I raced out the door.

We call it plague, but it's not. Each of us is an ecosystem. We're inhabited by a host of Makers. Some repair our bodies and our minds, keeping us young and alert, and some run our atriums. But most of our Makers exist only to defend us against hostile nanotech—the snakes that forever prowl the Garden of Eden, the nightmares devised by twisted minds—and sometimes our defenses fail.

A general alert had not been issued—that was standard policy, to avoid panic—but as soon as I was spotted on the paths wearing my skinsuit, word went out through informal channels that something was wrong. By the time I reached the day-venture center people had already guessed where I was going and a crowd was beginning to form against the backdrop of prairie. The city's emergency response team hadn't arrived yet, so questions were shouted at me. I refused to answer. "Stay back!" I commanded, issuing an order for the center's locked door to open.

In an auto-defense lockdown, a gel barrier is extruded around the suspect zone. The door slid back to reveal a wall of blue-tinged gel behind it. I pulled up the hood of my skinsuit and let it seal. Then I leaned into the gel wall, feeling it give way slowly around me, and after a few seconds I was able to pass through. As soon as I was clear, the door closed and locked behind me.

The staff and children were huddled on one side of the room—six adults and twenty-two kids. They looked frightened, but otherwise okay. Robin wasn't with them. The director started to speak but I couldn't hear him past the skinsuit, so I forced an atrial link to every adult in the room. "Give me your status."

The director spoke again, this time through my atrium. "It's Robin. He was hit hard only a couple of minutes ago. Shakes and sweats. His system's chewing up all his latents and he went down right away. I think it's targeted. No one else has shown any signs."

"Where is he?"

The director looked toward the nap room.

I didn't want to think too hard, I just wanted to get Robin stable, but the director's assessment haunted me. A targeted assault meant that Robin alone was the intended victim; that the hostile Maker had been designed to activate in his unique ecosystem.

I found him on the floor, trembling in the grip of a hypoglycemic seizure, all his blood sugars gone to fuel the reproduction of Makers in his body—both defensive and assault—as the tiny machines ramped up their populations to do battle on a molecular scale. His eyelids fluttered, but I could only see the whites. His black curls were sodden with sweat.

I unrolled the bivouac kit with its thick gel base designed for a much larger patient. Then I lifted his small body, laid him on it, and touched the activation points. The gel folded around him like a cocoon. The bivouac was a portable version of the cold storage drawer that had enfolded Glory. Robin's core temperature plummeted, while an army of defensive Makers swarmed past the barrier of his skin in a frantic effort to stabilize him.

The city's emergency team came in wearing sealed skinsuits. I stood by as they scanned the other kids, the staff, the rooms, and me, finding nothing. Only Robin was affected.

I stripped off my hood. Out in the playroom, the gel membrane was coming down and the kids were going home, but inside the bivouac Robin lay in stasis, his biological processes all but stopped. Even the data on his condition had been pared to a trickle. Still, I'd seen enough to know what was happening: the assault Makers were attacking Robin's neuronal connections, writing chaos into the space where Robin used to be. We would lose him if we allowed him to revive.

I checked city records for the date of his last backup. I couldn't find one. Robin had turned three a few weeks ago. I remembered we'd talked about taking him in to get a backup done . . . but we'd been busy.

The emergency team came back into the nap room with a gurney. Tishembra came with them. One glance at her face told me she'd been heavily tranked.

At first she didn't say anything, just watched with lips slightly parted and an expression of quiet horror on her face as the bivouac was lifted onto the gurney. But as the gurney was rolled away she asked in a defeated voice, "Is he going to die?"

"Of course he's not going to die."

She turned an accusing gaze on me. "My DI says you're lying."

I cursed myself silently and tried again, determined to speak the truth this time. "He's not going to die, because I won't let him."

She nodded, as if I'd got it right. The trank had turned her mood to smooth, hard glass. "I made this happen."

"What are you talking about?"

She turned her right hand palm up. A blue prairie butterfly rested in it, crushed and lifeless. I picked it up; spread its wings open. The message was only a little blurred from handling. On the left wing I read, You lived, and on the right, so he dies.

So someone had watched as we'd dropped Robin off that morning. I looked up at Tishembra. "No," I told her. "That's not the way it's going to work."

The attack on Robin was a molecular crime, which made it my case, and I was prepared to use every resource of the police to solve it.

Tishembra nodded. Then she left, following the gurney.

I could work anywhere, using my atrium, so I stayed for a time. First I packed up every bit of data I had on Robin's condition and sent it to six different police labs, hoping at least one could come up with the design for a Maker that could stop the assault on Robin's brain cells. The odds of success would go up dramatically if I could get the specs of the assault Maker—and the easiest way to do that was to track down the twisted freak who'd designed it.

Easy steps first: I sent a DI into the data-sphere to assemble a list of everyone at Nahiku with extensive molecular design experience. The DI came back with one name: mine.

So I was dealing with a talented hobbyist.

It could be anyone.

I sent the DI out again. No record was kept of butterfly messages—they were designed to be anonymous—but surveillance records were collected on every public path. I instructed the DI to access the records and assemble a list of everyone who'd set foot on Level 5 at any time that day, because the blue prairie butterflies could only be accessed from there. The list that came back was long. Name after name scrolled through my visual field, many that I recognized, but only one stood out in my mind: Hera Poliu.

I summoned the vid attached to her name. It was innocuous. She'd been taking the stairs between levels and had paused briefly on the landing. Still, it bothered me. Hera had been involved with Key Lu, she'd filed the complaint against Tishembra, and now I had her on Level 5. Coincidence maybe . . . but I remembered the chill I'd felt when she accosted me in the corridor . . . and how confused she'd been when I reminded her of the incident.

I went by my office and changed back into my uniform. Then I checked city records for Hera's location. She was at the infirmary, sitting with Tishembra . . . Tishembra, who'd been a quirk just like Hera's brother except she'd eluded punishment while Hera's brother was dead. Maybe it was baseless panic, but I sprinted for the door.

The infirmary had a reception room with a desk, and a hallway behind it with small rooms on either side. The technician at the desk looked up as I burst in. "Robin Indens!" I barked.

"Critical care. End of the hall."

I sprinted past him. A sign identified the room. I touched the door and it snapped open. The bivouac had been set up on a table in the center of the room. Slender feeder lines descending from the ceiling were plugged into its ports. Tishembra and Hera stood alongside the bivouac, Hera with a comforting arm around Tishembra's shoulders. They both looked up as I burst in. "Zeke?" Tishembra asked, with an expression encompassing both hope and dread.

"Tish, it's going to be okay. But I need to talk to Hera. Alone."

They traded a puzzled glance. Then Hera gave Tishembra a quick hug—"I'll be right back"—and stepped past me into the hall. I followed her, closing the door behind us.

Hera turned to face me. She looked gaunt and worn—a woman who had seen too much grief. "I want to thank you, Zeke, for not telling Tishembra who filed that complaint. I wasn't myself when I did it. I don't even remember doing it."

She wasn't lying.

I stumbled over that fact. Had I gotten it wrong? Was there something more going on than a need for misguided revenge?

"When was the last time you had your defensive Makers upgraded?"

She flinched and looked away. "It's been a while."

I sent a DI to check the records. It had been three years. I pulled up an earlier report and cross checked the dates to be sure. She hadn't had an upgrade since her brother's execution. My heart rate jumped as I contemplated a new possibility. No doubt my pupils dilated, but Hera was still looking away and she didn't see it. I sent the DI out again.

We were standing beside an open door to an unoccupied office. I ushered Hera inside. The DI came back with a new set of records even before the door was closed. At my invitation, Hera sat in the guest chair, her hands fidgeting restlessly in her lap. I perched on the edge of the desk, scanning the records, trying to stay calm, but my DI wasn't fooled. It sensed my stress and sent the paralytic ribbon creeping down my arm and into my palm.

"Let's talk about your brother."

Hera's hands froze in her lap. "My brother? You must know already. He's dead . . . he died like Key."

"You used to be a city councilor."

"I resigned from the council."

I nodded. "As a councilor you were required to host visitors . . . but you haven't allowed a ghost in your atrium since your brother's arrest."

"Those things don't matter to me anymore."

"You also haven't upgraded your defensive Makers, and you haven't been scanned—"

"I'm not a criminal, Zeke. I just . . . I just want to do my job and be left alone."

"Hera? You've been harboring your brother's ghost, haven't you? And he didn't like it when you started seeing Key."

The DI showed me the flush of hot and cold across her skin. "No," she whispered. "No. He's dead, and I wouldn't do that."

She was lying. "Hera, is your atrium quirked? To let your brother's ghost take over sometimes?"

She looked away. "Wouldn't that be illegal?"

"Giving up your body to another? Yes, it would be."

Her hands squeezed hard against the armrests of the chair. "It was him, then? That's what you're saying?" She turned to look at me, despair in her eyes. "He filed the complaint against Tish?"

I nodded. "I knew it wasn't you speaking to me that day. I think he also used you to sabotage Key's railcar, knowing I'd have to look into it."

"And Robin?" she asked, her knuckles whitening as she gripped the chair.

"Ask him."

Earlier, I'd asked the DI to bring me a list of all the trained molecular designers in Nahiku, but I'd asked the wrong question. I queried it again, asking for all the designers in the past five years. This time, mine wasn't the only name.

"Ask him for the design of the assault Maker, Hera. Robin doesn't deserve to die."

I crouched in front of her, my hand on hers as I looked up into her stunned eyes. It was a damned stupid position to put myself into.

He took over. It took a fraction of a second. My DI didn't catch it, but I saw it happen. Her expression hardened and her knee came up, driving hard into my chin. As my head snapped back he launched Hera against me. At that point it didn't matter that I outweighed her by forty percent. I was off balance and I went down with her on top of me. Her forehead cracked against my nose, breaking it.

He wasn't trying to escape. There was no way he could. It was only blind rage that drove him. He wanted to kill me, for all the good it would do. I was a cop. I had backups. I couldn't lose more than a few days. But he could still do some damage before he was brought down.

I felt Hera's small hands seize my wrists. He was trying to keep me from using the ribbon arsenal, but Hera wasn't nearly strong enough for that. I tossed her off, and not gently. The back of her head hit the floor, but she got up again almost as fast as I did and scrambled for the door.

I don't know what he intended to do, what final vengeance he hoped for. One more murder, maybe. Tishembra and Robin were both just across the hall.

I grabbed Hera, dragged her back, and slammed her into the chair. Then I raised my hand. The DI controlled the ribbon. Fibers along its length squeezed hard, sending a fine mist across Hera's face. It got in her eyes and in her lungs. She reared back, but then she collapsed, slumping in the chair. I wiped my bloody nose on my sleeve and waited until her head lolled against her chest. Then I sent a DI to Red Star.

I'd need help extracting the data from her quirked atrium, and combing through it for the assault Maker's design file.

It took a few days, but Robin was recovered. When he gets cranky at night he still tells Tishembra she's "wrong," but he's only three. Soon he won't remember what she was like before, while I pretend it doesn't matter to me.

Tishembra knows that isn't true. She complains the laws are too strict, that citizens should be free to make their own choices. Me, I'm just happy Glory Mina let me stay on as Nahiku's watch officer. Glory likes reminding me how lucky I am to have the position. I like to remind her that I've finally turned into the uncompromising jackboot she always knew I could be.

Don't get me wrong. I wanted to help Hera, but she'd been harboring a fugitive for three years. There was nothing I could do for her, but I won't let anyone else in this city step over the line. I don't want to sit through another execution.

Nahiku isn't quite bankrupt yet. Glory assessed a minimal fine for Hera's transgression, laying most of the fault on the police since we'd failed to hunt down all ghosts of a condemned criminal. So the city won't be sold off, and Tishembra will have to wait to get free.

I don't think she minds too much.

Here. Now. This is enough. I only wonder: Can we make it last?

THE GRAVEDIGGER OF KONSTAN SPRING

GENEVIEVE VALENTINE

There was something more civilized about a town that could bury its dead, if they stayed dead, and so Folkvarder Gray put out the notice for a gravedigger.

John the gravedigger was the best in the Nyr Nord Territory. He dug them narrow and he dug them deep, and when he came to Konstan Spring he provided references from Nyr Odin, where he had been called in to exercise his craft after the second English War for the Territory.

Folkvarder Gray looked over the letters, and then he shook John's hand and took the "Gravedigger Wanted" sign out of the window, and felt very satisfied.

The water in Konstan Spring was warm all year, and it ran clear and pure, and once you drank it all your cuts and aches and pains vanished from you as if they were caught up in the current.

The town was young (everything in that country was young) and did no great business. The land around the spring had to be worked to coax any crops from the dirt, and it was so far from the sea or the railroad or the Nations tribal gatherings that there was no profit in hotels or in trading.

The general store and the saloon, the chemist and the town lodge, the blacksmith and the whorehouse, tended to those who lived there; there was little other need. The folkvarder's office, with its little jail cell, stayed empty. There was no trouble to be had; people only found Kostan Spring by accident, and often hurried through on their way to someplace greater.

All the same, some lonesome souls had found their way to Konstan Spring.

It was a town that suited painstaking people, and when the town gathered for meetings to decide if newcomers should be given the water, the votes were orderly, and there was hardly a raised voice in the lodge.

(Mrs. Domar was sometimes louder than most people cared for, but the town was loyal to its own—where else could someone go, who had tasted the water in Konstan Spring?—and no fuss was made about her.)

The only man to bring the water out of Konstan Spring had been Hosiah Frode, the old chemist. Two years back he had written "KONSTAN'S ALE—MIRACLE TONIC" on his wagon and taken three barrels, early one morning before Folkvarder Gray could stop him.

Everyone waited to see what would happen. No one said it, but they all worried—if the gunslingers and the gamblers and the ill-living folk got wind of Konstan's Ale and came looking for the spring, the town might be overrun with greedy sorts, and they would never be rid of them.

It was a dark winter.

But Konstan Spring was a practical town, and even under the shadow of trouble, they all made do. Kit down at the whorehouse hired a few new girls all the way from Odal in case city men had finer tastes, and she taught Anni the blacksmith's daughter how to cook sturdy food so she could work the kitchen when all the rich, sickly gentlemen came looking for the water.

But the water must not have been such good luck to Hosiah Frode, because he never came back, and no rush of travelers ever appeared.

Secretly, Folkvarder Gray suspected Frode had angered a higher power with his thieving, and been struck down by stronger hands than theirs—the water was a great gift, and Frode should have known better than to abuse it.

It was a shame, Gray thought; Frode was a liar and a thief, but he had been a fine chemist, and Gray respected a man who was able with his work.

Frode never returned.

By spring, the men in town had developed fine enough taste to call on the new whorehouse girls from Odal (Kit had chosen the very best), and Kit sent Anni the blacksmith's daughter over to the chemist's.

No one complained about the change; Anni had been a terrible cook.

When he came into town, John the gravedigger took the room above the chemist shop. Anni lived in back of the shop, so the upstairs had been sitting empty.

The best the room had to offer was the view of the fenced-in graveyard past the new-painted lodge.

The flat, empty ground had never been touched; as yet, no one who lived in Konstan Spring had died.

The room above the chemist was small and Anni was an indifferent hostess, but John didn't move quarters. People figured he was sweet on Anni, or that the view of the graveyard was as close as a gravedigger could come to living above his store like an honest man.

No one minded his reasons. Anni needed the money. In Konstan Spring the chemist never did much business.

The first man John buried was Samuel Ness, who got himself on the losing end of a fight with his horse.

The grave appeared one shovel at a time, sharp-edged and deep as a well. There was no denying John was an artist. The priest thanked John for the grave even before he asked God to commend Samuel's soul.

"Won't work," muttered Mrs. Domar.

Mrs. Domar was Samuel's nearest neighbor. She had come to Konstan Spring already a widow; her husband had fallen ill on the road, and died in an Inuit town just twenty miles from the Spring. She persevered, but the stroke of bad luck had turned her into a pessimist.

Samuel had a young orchard at the edge of his property line, and Mrs. Domar knew that if there was a way Nature could work against her inheriting that little grove of apple trees, it would.

It was the usual funeral, except that the priest, after the service, suggested that John fill in a little of the ground before the body went inside it.

John obeyed. He wasn't one to argue with the clergy.

Two days later, Samuel Ness wriggled his way out of the shallow grave and came home to his farm and his orchard.

"I knew it," muttered Mrs. Domar as soon as she saw him coming.

John, if he was surprised, said nothing. He smoothed down the earth after the priest had taken back the headstone, and for a few nights, if you walked all the way from the outlying farms to the chemist's, you could see John sitting at his window, looking out over the sparse graveyard as if deciding what to do.

Everyone worried. They'd feared a gravedigger would lose the will for it in Konstan Spring, and they worried that if he went out into the world there would be questions about his hardiness. They had been lucky with Frode, but luck gave out any time.

People suggested that the folkvarder meet with him and point out the hundred-year contract John had signed. They suggested the priest give him counsel. Some suggested Anni should. If he was sweet on her, her kind face would do some good.

Philip Prain, who minded the general store, was the brave one who finally asked John what his plans might be, now that everything was in the open and John knew that the water wasn't just for one's health.

John said, "Try harder, I reckon." After a moment he asked, "We see a lot of travelers?"

• • •

Folkvarder Gray and Prain and Kit down at the whorehouse held a Town Council meeting to discuss the problem.

They spoke for a long time, and made up their minds on the subject. They planned to put it to a vote before the town, since the town was very strict about having a say, but none of them would object. John was a treasure they couldn't lose, and there were bound to be some drifters coming by sooner or later.

In the normal way of things, strangers would have a drink at the saloon and a girl at the whorehouse and ride out the next day, but there was no record of travelers once they were this far into the wild; not everyone can be missed.

The first drifter came on horseback a few weeks later, before there had been a formal vote.

He ordered liquor all night, and went to bed with one of Kit's girls, and fell asleep without ever having tasted the water from Konstan Spring.

He suffered a horrible attack in his sleep. Some nightmare had troubled him so that he'd twisted his neck up in his blankets and broken it.

Anni brought John the good news.

This time John had a little audience: Folkvarder Gray and Anni came, and Mrs. Domar, who wanted to see how to get that sharp edge in her own flowerbeds.

"You cut the ground so clean," Anni said after a time. "Where'd you learn?"

"Started young," he said. "Buried my ma and pa when I was twelve. Practice."

Anni nodded, and after he was finished they walked home side by side.

She was a quiet sort of girl, and John kept to himself, but Konstan Spring began to lay wagers for the month they'd be married. Anni's father, the old blacksmith, wanted it at once—the gravedigger got a hundred dollars a year. Samuel Ness thought it was too soon for a man to be sure he wanted a wife; he said no one should rightly marry until the spring, when the flowers were out.

Kit at the whorehouse swore they'd never get married, but everyone said it was only because John had never given her any business; she had sour grapes, that was all.

For the whole winter it went on that way. The town welcomed four men, each traveling alone, bound for New Freya or Odin's Lake, and one as far south as Iroquois country. Each one had gotten lost in the dark cold, in the snow or the freezing rain, and found themselves outside the saloon in Konstan Spring.

Each one spent the night at the whorehouse—Kit insisted—and of course it was much better to have a hot mug of mead to burn off the frost of a long ride, so there was no occasion to drink the spring-water.

The next morning John got a knock on his door from the Gerder boy who worked at the post office, or Mary the redhead from the whorehouse, to let him know he had a job to be getting on with.

Four travelers was less than it should be, even in winter, and they all worried that a gravedigger of John's skill would tire of having nothing to do. John, however, seemed happy to dig only one perfect grave a month for that whole winter; each one straight as a ruler, crisp edges, ground as smooth as God had ever made it.

People in Konstan Spring began to warm to him. For all they were patient, they were proud, and it was a comfort that the gravedigger of Konstan Spring knew the importance of a job done right.

Finn and Ivar Halfred were clerks who stumbled into Konstan Spring just before the thaw—the last spoils of winter for John the gravedigger.

They were from Portstown, Ivar told the Gerder boy, who took their horses. The Gerder boy didn't have the sense to ask where they were going (he didn't have the sense God gave an apple), so Gerder the father, who tended the saloon, asked instead.

Most of the people in Konstan Spring came out when strangers came into town. It was always interesting to see new people, no matter how briefly they'd be staying.

Anni and John sat at a little table in a corner, set apart from the crowd and noise of the saloon. At the other tables the wagers about their courtship went up and up and up, even in the midst of looking at the strangers; there was always a place for a friendly bet.

At last, old Gerder asked the brothers, "What brings you to Konstan Spring?"

By that time Ivar was already drunk, and he laughed loudly and said, "We were supposed to head south for Bruntofte, but we turned right instead of left!" which was an old joke that no one paid any mind. It was never hard to tell which of two brothers was the fool.

"Bruntofte isn't very welcoming," Gerder said. "Hope you boys plan to do some trade; they don't like people showing up with empty hands. We all saw what happened to the English, before they got driven out."

After a little pause, Finn sighed and said, "Haven't thought that far ahead. We're just looking to start over in a place that has enough room to be lonely in."

You didn't get as far as Konstan Spring unless you were putting something behind you, so no one was surprised to hear it. But the way he spoke must have struck Anni something awful, because she got up from her seat and took a place next to Finn at the bar.

She'd never been pretty (not compared to whorehouse girls from Odal), but the way she looked at him would have charmed a much less lonely man than Finn Halfred.

They talked until late, until everyone had gone home but Kit from the whorehouse, whose girls were working to bring Ivar back and lighten his pockets. They tried to hook Finn, too, but Anni put her hand on his arm, and the girls respected her claim.

Anni brought Finn home with her when she left that night, his arm linked with hers. The girls from the whorehouse thought it was a scandal, but Kit told them to mind their own business and tend to their customer.

Kit was no fool; she knew how slowly time moved in Konstan Spring, and a girl shouldn't be a bad cook and an indifferent chemist year in and year out without anything else happening inside of her. Anni could have a night with a young clerk if she wanted. (It was the first thing Anni had managed well in a long time. Kit was glad to see something worthy from Anni at last.)

The next morning Anni brought Finn out on the little promenade. She told Kit in passing, "He got thirsty—I gave him some water."

Kit told the town.

They held a meeting (in the lodge, safely away from Anni) to discuss what to tell Finn about his brother's sad accident the night before.

Philip Prain said right off that it was a shame about the wagering pool, but Folkvarder Gray called them back to order; all things in their time, gambling had no place in the lodge. They had to decide what would happen now, with their gravedigger.

John was a steady man, but now they weren't sure who would do for him but old Mrs. Domar, who was a widow and too old to be suitable.

"As if I would," sniffed Mrs. Domar.

The only other girl in town was Gerder's daughter Sue, who was only fourteen and couldn't yet go courting. If she got a little older, then perhaps they could consider, but none of them had been in Konstan Spring long enough to really know if the young ever grew older, or if the grown slowly grew old.

(Konstan Spring hadn't been an early settlement by the Longboaters. It hadn't even been in the eyes of the railroad men. It was a town by accident, because the water was of value; a town because the people in it were slow to want change; a town because it was better to live among the same kind forever than to risk going into the wide new country full of strangers.)

The town was like the Ness orchard, whose little apple trees (always saplings and never older) bent their young branches nearly to snapping just to bear their fruit.

It would be the same with Sue, if they let her go courting too early.

Outside, John had turned his hand to his art for poor Ivar Halfred, and one shovelful of dirt after another bloomed from the ground as he worked.

Folkvarder Gray went himself to break the news.

He told Finn that Ivar had drunk himself to death, and his whorehouse girl hadn't been able to wake him no matter what they did. Finn was sorely grieved, and Folkvarder Gray thought it was best to wait for some other day to explain about the water.

On his way out, the folkvarder tipped his hat to John, who was sharpening the edge of his shovel on a boulder that sat beside a wide grave, sharp-edged and deep as a well. John looked as quiet and calm as ever, but Folkvarder Gray had been disappointed in a woman himself, many years back, on his home shores, and he knew the look of a heartbroken man doing a chore just to keep his hands busy.

"No need for all this, John," Folkvarder Gray said. "It'll be weeks yet before the thaw opens the roads, and no knowing when the next one will come."

Folkvarder Gray looked carefully into the thick dark of the grave. "A little steep, my boy," he said after a moment. The warm damp rose up from the ground, sharp-smelling, and he stepped back. That was no smell for the living.

"It's just for practice," said John, turned the shovel on its edge, slid a slender finger along it until he began to bleed.

After the service on Sunday, Anni and Finn went out walking.

Inside the lodge, Samuel Ness started a new wager that they'd come back that same day and ask the priest to marry them. Mrs. Domar, who didn't approve of such suggestions, went to the window and pretended to be deaf.

From the window Mrs. Domar could see Anni and Finn walking on the lawn behind the lodge, hand in hand toward the chemist's, and John's silhouette in the upper window, looking out toward the graveyard to admire his work.

"Finn will come sniffing around after a job," said Philip Prain. "I could make use of him in the store maybe a month out of the year, but he'll have to make his money some other way, and I don't see much need for a clerk in Konstan Spring."

"We have need for him if he does good work," said Folkvarder Gray. "And who will be the chemist if he takes Anni out to some farm instead of staying in town? We can't do without a chemist. It's not civilized."

"They'll find some way to scrape by," said Kit. "Young fools like that always do."

"It's no good," said Mrs. Domar, watching John look over at the cemetery. No one answered her; Mrs. Domar never saw good in anything.

• • •

The wager, sadly for Samuel, came to nothing.

That evening, Finn and Anni disappeared from Konstan Spring, and if Folkvarder Gray noticed that the chemist's house was quiet, that the boulder in the yard was gone and the wide deep grave was smoothed over, he said nothing to John about it.

No town was run well without some sacrifices. Artists had their ways, and another chemist would be easier to come by than a gravedigger of so much patience and skill.

The question of Anni and Finn trapped in the grave made the folkvarder sorry for Anni's sake, but it was what came sometimes of breaking a good man's heart.

(Not everyone can be missed.)

It was for the best. Anni had never been a good chemist; Konstan Spring deserved better, he knew.

Samuel Ness paid Kit from the whorehouse two dollars, having been wrong about both Anni and John, and Anni and Finn.

Mrs. Domar didn't approve of Kit, but she had never forgiven Samuel for taking back his orchard, and was happy to see him lose a little money.

Kit kept the money in an envelope, for a wedding present in case Anni should ever come home. (She knew Anni must; she wasn't the type to disappear on her own.)

After a month of no word, Kit sent redheaded Mary from Odal over to the shop at the edge of the graveyard.

Mary knew a little about the chemist's, and a little about coaxing the hearts of quiet men, and it would be best, Kit figured, to have the gravedigger of Konstan Spring soon settled with a pretty young wife.

Others did not quite agree; against Kit's complaints, Folkvarder Gray put a CHEMIST WANTED sign in the window of his office, and sent young Gerder to town on horseback with another advertisement for the train station wall.

Folkvarder Gray was confident that sooner or later a wonderful chemist would come across the advertisement, when the time was right. The country was still rough and unknown, and brave artists were hard to come by, but he was prepared—he would take nothing but the best.

Konstan Spring could afford to wait, and Folkvarder Gray knew the importance of a job done right.

UNDER THE EAVES

LAVIE TIDHAR

———◆———

"Meet me tomorrow?" she said.

"Under the eaves." He looked from side to side, too quickly. She took a step back. "Tomorrow night." They were whispering. She gathered courage like cloth. Stepped up to him. Put her hand on his chest. His heart was beating fast, she could feel it through the metal. His smell was of machine oil and sweat.

"Go," he said. 'You must—" the words died, unsaid. His heart was like a chick in her hand, so scared and helpless. She was suddenly aware of power. It excited her. To have power over someone else, like this.

His finger on her cheek, trailing. It was hot, metallic. She shivered. What if someone saw?

"I have to go," he said.

His hand left her. He pulled away and it rent her. "Tomorrow," she whispered. He said, "Under the eaves," and left, with quick steps, out of the shadow of the warehouse, in the direction of the sea.

She watched him go and then she, too, slipped away, into the night.

In early morning, the solitary shrine to St. Cohen of the Others, on the corner of Levinsky, sat solitary and abandoned beside the green. Road cleaners crawled along the roads, sucking up dirt, spraying water and scrubbing, a low hum of gratitude filling the air as they gloried in this greatest of tasks, the momentary holding back of entropy.

By the shrine a solitary figure knelt. Miriam Jones, Mama Jones of Mama Jones' shebeen around the corner, lighting a candle, laying down an offering, a broken electronics circuit as of an ancient television remote control, obsolete and useless.

"Guard us from the Blight and from the Worm, and from the attention of Others," Mama Jones whispered, "and give us the courage to make our own path in the world, St. Cohen."

The shrine did not reply. But then, Mama Jones did not expect it to, either.

She straightened up, slowly. It was becoming more difficult, with the knees. She still had her own kneecaps. She still had most of her original parts. It wasn't anything to be proud of, but it wasn't anything to be ashamed of, either. She stood there, taking in the morning air, the joyous hum of the road cleaning machines, the imagined whistle of aircraft high above, RLVs coming down from orbit, gliding down like parachuting spiders to land on the roof of Central Station.

It was a cool fresh morning. The heat of summer did not yet lie heavy on the ground, choking the very air. She walked away from the shrine and stepped on the green, and it felt good to feel grass under her feet. She remembered the green when she was young, with the others like her, Somali and Sudanese refugees who found themselves in this strange country, having crossed desert and borders, seeking a semblance of peace, only to find themselves unwanted and isolated here, in this enclave of the Jews. She remembered her father waking every morning, and walking to the green and sitting there, with the others, the air of quiet desperation making them immobile. Waiting. Waiting for a man to come in a pickup truck and offer them a labourer's job, waiting for the UN agency bus—or, helplessly, for the Israeli police's special Oz Agency to come and check their papers, with a view towards arrest or deportation . . .

Oz meant 'strength', in Hebrew.

But the real strength wasn't in intimidating helpless people, who had nowhere else to turn. It was in surviving, the way her parents had, the way she had—learning Hebrew, working, making a small, quiet life as past turned to present and present to future, until one day there was only her, still living here, in Central Station.

Now the green was quiet, only a lone robotnik sitting with his back to a tree, asleep or awake she couldn't tell. She turned, and saw Isobel passing by on her bicycle, heading towards the Salameh Road. Already traffic was growing on the roads, the sweepers, with little murmurs of disappointment, moving on. Small cars moved along the road, their solar panels spread like wings. There were solar panels everywhere, on rooftops and the sides of buildings, everyone trying to snatch away some free power in this sunniest of places. Tel Aviv. She knew there were sun farms beyond the city, vast tracts of land where panels stretched across the horizon, sucking in hungrily the sun's rays, converting them into energy that was then fed into central charging stations across the city. She liked the sight of them, and fashion-wise it was all the rage, Mama Jones' own outfit had tiny solar panes sewn into it, and her wide-brimmed hat caught the sun, wasting nothing—it looked very stylish.

Where was Isobel going? She had known the girl since she'd been born, the daughter of Mama Jones' friend and neighbour, Irina Chow, herself the product of a Russian Jewish immigrant who had fallen in love with a Chinese-Filipina woman, one of the many who came seeking work, years before, and stayed. Irina herself was Mama Jones' age, which is to say, she was too old. But the girl was young. Irina had frozen her eggs a long time ago, waiting for security, and when she had Isobel it was the local womb labs that housed her during the nine long months of hatching. Irina was a pastry chef of some renown but had also her wild side: she sometimes hosted Others. It made Mama Jones uncomfortable, she was old fashioned, the idea of body-surfing, like Joining, repelled her. But Irina was her friend.

Where *was* Isobel going? Perhaps she should mention it to the girl's mother, she thought. Then she remembered being young herself, and shook her head, and smiled. When had the young ever listened to the old?

She left the green and crossed the road. It was time to open the shebeen, prepare the sheesha pipes, mix the drinks. There will be customers soon. There always were, in Central Station.

Isobel cycled along the Salameh Road, her bicycle like a butterfly, wings open, sucking up sun, murmuring to her in a happy sleepy voice, nodal connection mixed in with the broadcast of a hundred thousand other voices, channels, music, languages, the high-bandwidth indecipherable *toktok* of Others, weather reports, confessionals, off-world broadcasts time-lagged from Lunar Port and Tong Yun and the Belt, Isobel randomly tuning in and out of that deep and endless stream of what they called the Conversation.

The sounds and sights washed over her: deep space images from a lone spider crashing into a frozen rock in the Oort Cloud, burrowing in to begin converting the asteroid into copies of itself; a re-run episode of the Martian soap *Chains of Assembly*; a Congolese station broadcasting Nuevo Kwasa-Kwasa music; from North Tel Aviv, a talk show on Torah studies, heated; from the side of the street, sudden and alarming, a repeated ping—*Please help. Please donate. Will work for spare parts.*

She slowed down. By the side of the road, on the Arab side, stood a robotnik. It was in bad shape—large patches of rust, a missing eye, one leg dangling uselessly—the robotnik's still-human single eye looked at her, but whether in mute appeal, or indifference, she couldn't tell. It was broadcasting on a wide band, mechanically, helplessly—on a blanket on the ground by its side there was a small pile of spare parts, a near-empty gasoline can—solar didn't do much for robotniks.

No, she couldn't stop. she mustn't. It made her apprehensive. She cycled away but kept looking back, passers-by ignoring the robotnik like it wasn't there, the sun rising fast, it was going to be another hot day. She pinged him back, a small donation, more for her own ease than for him. Robotniks, the lost soldiers of the lost wars of the Jews—mechanized and sent to fight and then, later, when the wars ended, abandoned as they were, left to fend for themselves on the streets, begging for the parts that kept them alive . . .

She knew many of them had emigrated off-world, gone to Tong Yun, on Mars. Others were based in Jerusalem, the Russian Compound made theirs by long occupation. Beggars. You never paid much attention to them.

And they were old. Some of them have fought in wars that didn't even have names, any more.

She cycled away, down Salameh, approaching Jaffa proper—

Security protocols handshaking, negotiating, her ident tag scanned and confirmed as she made the transition from Central Station to Jaffa City—

And approved, and she passed through and cycled to the clock tower, ancient and refurbished, built in honour of the Ottoman Sultan back when the Turks were running things.

The sea before her, the Old City on the left, on top of Jaffa Hill rising above the harbour, a fortress of stone and metal. Around the clock tower coffee shops, the smell of cherry tobacco rising from sheesha pipes, the smell of roasting shawarma, lamb and cumin, and coffee ground with roasted cardamoms. She loved the smell of Jaffa.

To the north, Tel Aviv. East was the Central Station, the huge towering space port where once a megalithic bus station had been. To the south Jaffa, the returning Arabs after the wars had made it their own again, now it rose into the skies, towers of metal and glass amidst which the narrow alleyways still ran. Cycling along the sea wall she saw fishermen standing mutely, as they always had, their lines running into the sea. She cycled past old weathered stone, a Coptic church, past arches set into the stone and into the harbour, where small craft, then as now, bobbed on the water and the air smelled of brine and tar. She parked the bike against a wall and it folded onto itself with a little murmur of content, folding its wings. She climbed the stone steps into the old city, searching for the door amidst the narrow twisting alleyways. In the sky to the south-east modern Jaffa towered, casting its shadow, and the air felt cooler here. She found the door, hesitated, pinged.

"Come in."

The voice spoke directly into her node. The door opened for her. She went inside.

"You seek comfort?"

Cool and dark. A stone room. Candles burning, the smell of wax.

"I want to know."

She laughed at her. An old woman with a golden thumb.

An Other, Joined to human flesh.

St. Cohen of the Others, save us from digital entities and their alien ways . . .

That laugh again. "Do not be afraid."

"I'm not."

The old woman opened her mouth. Old, in this age of unage. The voice that came out was different. Isobel shivered. The Other, speaking.

"You want to know," it said, "about machines."

She whispered, "Yes."

"You know all that you need to know. What you seek is . . . reassurance."

She looked at the golden thumb. It was a rare Other who chose to Join with flesh . . . "Can you feel?" she said.

"Feel?" the Other moved behind the woman's eyes. "With a body I feel. Hormones and nerves are feelings. *You* feel."

"And he?"

The body of the old woman laughed, and it was a human laugh, the Other faded. "You ask if he is capable of feeling? If he is capable of—"

"Love," Isobel whispered.

The room was Conversation-silent, the only traffic running at extreme loads she couldn't follow. *Toktok. Toktok blong Narawan.*

The old woman said, "Love." Flatly.

"Yes," Isobel said, gathering courage.

"Is it not enough," the woman said, "that you do?"

Isobel was silent. The woman smiled, not unkindly. Silence settled on the room in a thick layer, like dust. Time had been locked up in that room.

"I don't know," Isobel said, at last.

The old woman nodded, and when next she spoke it was the Other speaking through her, making Isobel flinch. "Child," it said. "Life, like a binary tree, is full of hard choices."

"What does that mean? What does that even mean?'

"It means," said the old woman, with finality, and the door, at her silent command, opened, letting beams of light into the room, illuminating grains of dust, "that only you can make that choice. There are no certainties."

Isobel cycled back, along the sea wall. Jaffa into Tel Aviv, Arabic changing to Hebrew—beyond, on the sea, solar kites flew, humans with fragile wings racing each other, Ikarus-like, above the waves. She did not know another country.

Tonight, she thought. Under the eaves.

It was only when she turned, away from sun and sea, and began to cycle east, towards the towering edifice of Central Station, that it occurred to her—she had already made her decision. Even before she went to seek the old oracle's help, she had made the choice.

Tonight, she thought, and her heart like a solar kite fluttered in anticipation, waiting to be set free.

Central Station rose out of the maze of old streets, winding roads, shops and apartment blocks and parking lots once abundant with cars powered by internal combustion engines. It was a marvel of engineering, a disaster of design, Futurist and Modernist, Gothic and Moorish, Martian and Baroque.

Others had designed it, but humans had embellished it, each competing to put their own contrasting signatures on the giant space port. It rose into the sky. High above, Reusable Launch Vehicles, old and new, came to land or took off to orbiting stations, and stratospheric planes came and went to Krung Thep and New York and Ulaan-Bataar, Sydney II and Mexico City, passengers coming and going, up and down the giant elevators, past levels full of shops and restaurants, an entire city in and of itself, before departing at ground level, some to Jaffa, some to Tel Aviv, the two cities always warily watching each other . . .

Mama Jones watched it, watched the passengers streaming out, she watched it wondering what it would be like to leave everything behind, to go into the station, to rise high, so high that one passed through clouds—what it would be like to simply *leave*, to somewhere, anywhere else.

But it passed. It always did. She watched the eaves of the station, those edges where the human architects went all out, even though they had a practical purpose, too, they provided shelter from the rain and caught the water, which were recycled inside the building—rain was precious, and not to be wasted.

Nothing should be wasted, she thought, looking up. The shop was being looked after, she had taken a few moments to take the short walk, to stretch her legs. She noticed the girl, Isobel, cycling past. Back from wherever she went. Pinged her a greeting, but the girl didn't stop. Youth. Nothing should be wasted, Mama Jones thought, before turning away. Not even love. Most of all, love.

"How is your father?"

Boris Chong looked up at her. He was sitting at a table by the bar, sipping a Martian Sunset. It was a new drink to Miriam. Boris had taught it to her . . .

It was still strange to her that he was back.

"He's . . . " Boris struggled to find the words. "Coping," he said at last. She nodded.

"Miriam—"

She could almost not remember a time she had been Miriam. For so long she had been Mama Jones. But Boris brought it back to her, the name, a part of her youth. Tall and gangly, a mixture of Russian Jews and Chinese labourers, a child of Central Station just as she was. But he *had* left, had gone up the elevators and into space, to Tong Yun on Mars, and even beyond . . .

Only he was back, now, and she still found it strange. Their bodies had become strangers to each other. And he had an aug, an alien thing bred out of long-dead microscopic Martian life-forms, a thing that was now a part of him, a parasite growth on Boris' neck, inflating and deflating with the beats of Boris' heart . . .

She touched it, tentatively, and Boris smiled. She made herself do it, it was a part of him now, she needed to get used to it. it felt warm, the surface rough, not like Boris' own skin. She knew her touch translated as pleasure in both the aug and Boris' mind.

"What?" she said.

"I missed you today."

She couldn't help it. She smiled. Banality, she thought. We are made so happy by banalities.

We are made happy by not being alone, and by having someone who cares for us.

She went around the counter. Surveyed her small domain. Chairs and tables, the tentacle-junkie in the corner in his tub, smoking a sheesha pipe, looking sleepy and relaxed. The ancient bead curtain instead of a door. A couple of workers from the station sipping arak, mixing it with water, the drink in the glass turning opaque, the colour of milk.

Mama Jones' Shebeen.

She felt a surge of contentment, and it made the room's edges seem softer.

Over the course of the day the sun rose behind the space port and traced an arc across it until it landed at last in the sea. Isobel worked inside Central Station and didn't see the sun at all.

The Level Three concourse offered a mixture of food courts, drone battle-zones, game-worlds, Louis Wu emporiums, nakamals, smokes bars, truflesh and virtual prostitution establishments, and a faith bazaar.

Isobel had heard the greatest faith bazaar was in Tong Yun City, on Mars. The one they had on Level Three *here* was a low key affair—a Church of Robot mission house, a Gorean temple, an Elronite Centre For The Advancement of Humankind, a mosque, a synagogue, a Catholic church, an Armenian church, an Ogko shrine, a Theravada Buddhist temple, and a Baha'i temple.

On her way to work Isobel went to church. She had been raised Catholic, her mother's family, themselves Chinese immigrants to the Philippines, having adopted that religion in another era, another time. Yet she could find no comfort in the hushed quietude of the spacious church, the smell of the candles, the dim light and the painted glass and the sorrowful look of the crucified Jesus.

The church forbids it, she thought, suddenly horrified. The quiet of the church seemed oppressive, the air too still. It was as if every item in the room was looking at her, was *aware* of her. She turned on her heels.

Outside, not looking, she almost bumped into Brother Patch-It.

"Girl, you're *shaking*," R. Patch-It said, compassion in his voice. Like most followers of the Church of Robot, once he'd taken on the robe—so to speak—he had shed his former ident tag and taken on a new one. Usually they were synonyms of "fix." She knew R. Patch-It slightly, he had been a fixture of Central Station (both space port and neighbourhood) her entire life, and the part-time *moyel* for the Jewish residents in the event of the birth of a baby boy.

"I'm fine, really," Isobel said. The robot looked at her from his expressionless face. 'Robot' was male in Hebrew, a gendered language. And most robots had been fashioned without genitalia or breasts, making them appear vaguely male. They had been a mistake, of sort. No one had produced robots for a very long time. They were a missing link, an awkward evolutionary step between human and Other.

"Would you like a cup of tea?" the robot said. "Perhaps cake? Sugar helps human distress, I am told." Somehow R. Patch-It managed to look abashed.

"I'm fine, really," Isobel said again. Then, on an impulse: "Do you believe that . . . can robots . . . I mean to say—"

She faltered. The robot regarded her with his old, expressionless face. A rust scar ran down one cheek, from his left eye to the corner of his mouth. "You can ask me anything," the robot said, gently. Isobel wondered what dead human's voice had been used to synthesise the robot's own.

"Do robots feel love?" she said.

The robot's mouth moved. Perhaps it was meant as a smile. "We feel nothing but love," the robot said.

"How can that be? How can you . . . how can you *feel*?" she was almost shouting. But this was Third Level, no one paid any attention.

"We're anthropomorphised," R. Patch-It said, gently. "We were fashioned human, given physicality, senses. It is the tin man's burden." His voice was sad. "Do you know that poem?"

"No," Isobel said. Then, "What about . . . what about Others?"

The robot shook his head. "Who can tell," he said. "For us, it is unimaginable, to exist as a pure digital entity, to not know physicality. And yet, at the same time, we seek to escape our physical existence, to achieve heaven, knowing it does not exist, that it must be built, the world fixed and patched . . . but what is it really that you ask me, Isobel daughter of Irina?"

"I don't know," she whispered, and she realised her face was wet. "The church—" her head inching, slightly, at the catholic church behind them. The robot nodded, as if it understood.

"Youth feels so strongly," the robot said. His voice was gentle. "Don't be afraid, Isobel. Allow yourself to love."

"I don't know," Isobel said. "I don't know."

"Wait—"

But she had turned away from Brother Patch-It. Blinking back the tears—she didn't know where they came from—she walked away, she was late for work.

Tonight, she thought. Tonight, under the eaves. She wiped away the tears.

With dusk a welcome coolness settled over Central Station. In Mama Jones' shebeen candles were lit and, across the road, the No-Name Nakamal was preparing the evening's kava, and the strong, earthy smell of it—the roots peeled and chopped, the flesh minced and mixed with water, squeezed repeatedly to release its very essence, the kavalactones in the plant—the smell filled the paved street that was the very heart of the neighbourhood.

On the green, robotniks huddled together around a makeshift fire in an upturned drum. Flames reflected in their faces, metal and human mixed artlessly, the still-living debris of long-gone wars. They spoke amidst themselves in that curious Battle Yiddish that had been imprinted on them by some well-meaning army developer—a hushed and secret language no one spoke any more, ensuring their communications would be secure, like the Navajo Code Talkers in the second world war.

On top of Central Station graceful RLVs landed or took off, and on the roofs of the neighbourhood solar panels like flowers began to fold, and residents took to the roofs, those day-time sun-traps, to drink beer or kava or arak, to watch the world below, to smoke a sheesha pipe and take stock of the day, to watch the sun set in the sea or tend their rooftop gardens.

Inside Central Station the passengers dined and drank and played and worked and waited—Lunar traders, Martian Chinese on an Earth holiday package tour, Jews from the asteroid-kibbutzim in the Belt, the hurly burly of a humanity for whom Earth was no longer enough and yet was the centre of the universe, around which all planets and moons and habitats rotated, an Aristotelian model of the world superseding its one-time victor, Copernicus. On Level Three Isobel was embedded inside her work pod, existing simultaneously, like a Schrödinger's Cat, in physical space and the equally real virtuality of the Guilds of Ashkelon universe, where—

She was *the* Isobel Chow, Captain of the *Nine Tailed Cat*, a starship thousands of years old, upgraded and refashioned with each universal cycle, a salvage operation she, Isobel, was captain and commander of, hunting for precious games-world artefacts to sell on the Exchange—

Orbiting Black Betty, a Guilds of Ahskelon universal singularity, where a dead alien race had left behind enigmatic ruins, floating in space in broken rocks, airless asteroids of a once-great galactic empire—

Success there translating to food and water and rent *here*—

But what is here, what is *there*—

Isobel Schrödingering, in the real and the virtual—or in the GoA and in what they call Universe-1—and she was working.

Night fell over Central Station. Lights came alive around the neighbourhood then, floating spheres casting a festive glow. Night was when Central Station came *alive* . . .

Florists packing for the day in the wide sprawling market, and the boy Kranki playing by himself, stems on the ground and wilting dark Lunar roses, hydroponics grown, and none came too close to him, the boy was strange, he had *nakaimas*.

Asteroid pidgin around him as he played, making stems rise and dance before him, black rose heads opening and closing in a silent, graceless dance before the boy. The boy had nakaimas, he had the black magic, he had the quantum curse. Conversation flowing around him, traders closing for the day or opening for the night, the market changing faces, never shutting, people sleeping under their stands or having dinner, and from the food stalls the smells of frying fish, and chilli in vinegar, of soy and garlic frying, of cumin and turmeric and the fine purple powder of sumac, so called because it looks like a blush. The boy played, as boys would. The flowers danced, mutely.

—Yu stap go wea? *Where are you going*?

—Mi stap go bak long haos. *I am going home.*

—Yu no save stap smoltaem, dring smolsmol bia? *Won't you stop for a small beer*?

Laughter. Then—Si, mi save stap smoltaem.

Yes, I could stop for a little while.

Music playing, on numerous feeds and live, too—a young kathoey on an old acoustic guitar, singing, while down the road a tentacle junkie was beating time on multiple drums, adding distortions in real-time and broadcasting, a small voice weaving itself into the complex unending pattern of the Conversation.

—Mi lafem yu!˙

—Awo, yu drong!

Laughter, *I love you—You're drunk!*—a kiss, the two men walk away together, holding hands—

—Wan dei bae mi go long spes, bae mi go lukluk olbaot long ol star.

—Yu kranki we!

One day I will go to space, I will go look around all the planets—
You're crazy!

Laughter, and someone dropping in from virtuality, blinking sleepy eyes, readjusting, someone turns a fish over on the grill, someone yawns, someone smiles, a fight breaks out, lovers meet, the moon on the horizon rises, the shadows of the moving spiders flicker on the surface of the moon.

Under the eaves. Under the eaves. Where it's always dry where it's always dark, under the eaves.

There, under the eaves of Central Station, around the great edifice, was a buffer zone, a separator between space port and neighbourhood. You could buy anything at Central Station and what you couldn't buy you could get there, in the shadows.

Isobel had finished work, she had come back to Universe-1, had left behind captainhood and ship and crew, climbed out of the pod, and on her feet, the sound of her blood in her ears, and when she touched her wrist she felt the blood pulsing there, too, the heart wants what the heart wants, reminding us that we are human, and frail, and weak.

Through a service tunnel she went, between floors, and came out on the north-east corner of the port, facing the Kibbutz Galuyot road and the old interchange.

It was quiet there, and dark, few shops, a Kingdom of Pork and a book binder and warehouses left from days gone by, now turned into sound-proofed clubs and gene clinics and synth emporiums. She waited in the shadow of the port, hugging the walls, they felt warm, the station always felt alive, on heat, the station like a heart, beating. She waited, her node scanning for intruders, for digital signatures and heat, for motion—Isobel was a Central Station girl, she could take care of herself, she had a heat knife, she was cautious but not afraid of the shadows.

She waited, waited for him to come.

"You waited."

She pressed against him. He was warm, she didn't know where the metal of him finished and the organic of him began.

He said, "You came," and there was wonder in the words.

"I had to. I had to see you again."

"I was afraid." His voice was not above a whisper. His hand on her cheek, she turned her head, kissed it, tasting rust like blood.

"We are beggars," he said. "My kind. We are broken machines."

She looked at him, this old abandoned soldier. She knew he had died, that he had been remade, a human mind cyborged onto an alien body, sent out to fight, and to die, again and again. That now he lived on scraps, depending on the charity of others . . .

Robotnik. That old word, meaning *worker*. But said like a curse.

She looked into his eyes. His eyes were almost human.

"I don't remember," he said. "I don't remember who I was, before."

"But you are . . . you are still . . . you are!" she said, as though finding truth, suddenly, and she laughed, she was giddy with laughter and happiness and he leaned and he kissed her, gently at first and then harder, their shared need melding them, Joining them almost like a human is bonded to an Other.

In his strange obsolete Battle Yiddish he said, "Ich lieba dich."

In asteroid pidgin she replied.

—Mi lafem yu.

His finger on her cheek, hot, metallic, his smell of machine oil and gasoline and human sweat. She held him close, there against the wall of Central Station, in the shadows, as a plane high overhead, adorned in light, came in to land from some other and faraway place.

HONEY BEAR

SOFIA SAMATAR

We've decided to take a trip, to see the ocean. I want Honey to see it while she's still a child. That way, it'll be magical. I tell her about it in the car: how big it is, and green, like a sky you can wade in.

"Even you?" she asks.

"Even me."

I duck my head to her hair. She smells fresh, but not sweet at all, like parsley or tea. She's wearing a little white dress. It's almost too short. She pushes her bare toes against the seat in front of her, knuckling it like a cat.

"Can you not do that, Hon?" says Dave.

"Sorry, Dad."

She says "Dad" now. She used to say "Da-Da."

Dave grips the wheel. I can see the tension in his shoulders. Threads of gray wink softly in his dark curls. He still wears his hair long, covering his ears, and I think he's secretly a little bit vain about it. A little bit proud of still having all his hair. I think there's something in this, something valuable, something he could use to get back. You don't cling to personal vanities if you've given up all hope of a normal life. At least, I don't think you do.

"Shit," he says.

"Sweetheart . . . "

He doesn't apologize for swearing in front of Honey. The highway's blocked by a clearance area, gloved hands waving us around. He turns the car so sharply the bags in the passenger seat beside him almost fall off the cooler. In the back seat, I lean into Honey Bear.

"It's okay," I tell Dave.

"No, Karen, it is not okay. The temp in the cooler is going to last until exactly four o'clock. At four o'clock, we need a fridge, which means we need a hotel. If we are five minutes late, it is not going to be okay."

"It looks like a pretty short detour."

"It is impossible for you to see how long it is."

"I'm just thinking, it doesn't look like they've got that much to clear."

"Fine, you can think that. Think what you want. But don't tell me the detour's not long, or give me any other information you don't actually have, okay?"

He's driving faster. I rest my cheek on the top of Honey's head. The clearance area rolls by outside the window. Cranes, loading trucks, figures in orange jumpsuits. Some of the slick has dried: they're peeling it up in transparent sheets, like plate glass.

Honey presses a fingertip to the window. "Poo-poo," she says softly.

I tell her about the time I spent a weekend at the beach. My best friend got so sunburned, her back blistered.

We play the clapping game, "A Sailor Went to Sea-Sea-Sea." It's our favorite.

Dave drives too fast, but we don't get stopped, and we reach the hotel in time. I take my meds, and we put the extra in the hotel fridge. Dave's shirt is dark with sweat, and I wish he'd relax, but he goes straight out to buy ice, and stores it in the freezer so we can fill the cooler tomorrow. Then he takes a shower and lies on the bed and watches the news. I sit on the floor with Honey, looking at books. I read to her every evening before bed; I've never missed a night. Right now, we're reading *The Meadow Fairies* by Dorothy Elizabeth Clark.

This is something I've looked forward to my whole adult life: reading the books I loved as a child with a child of my own. Honey adores *The Meadow Fairies*. She snuggles up to me and traces the pretty winged children with her finger. Daffodil, poppy, pink. When I first brought the book home, and Dave saw us reading it, he asked what the point was, since Honey would never see those flowers. I laughed because I'd never seen them either. "It's about fairies," I told him, "not botany." I don't think I've ever seen a poppy in my life.

> *Smiling, though half-asleep,*
> *The Poppy Fairy passes,*
> *Scarlet, like the sunrise,*
> *Among the meadow grasses.*

Honey chants the words with me. She's so smart, she learns so fast. She can pick up anything that rhymes in minutes. Her hair glints in the lamplight. There's the mysterious, slightly abrasive smell of hotel sheets, a particular hotel darkness between the blinds.

"I love this place," says Honey. "Can we stay here?"

"It's an adventure," I tell her. "Just wait till tomorrow."

On the news, helicopters hover over the sea. It's far away, the Pacific. There's been a huge dump there, over thirty square miles of slick. The effects on marine life are not yet known.

"Will it be fairyland?" Honey asks suddenly.

"What, sweetie?"

"Will it be fairyland, when I'm grown up?"

"Yes," I tell her. My firmest tone.

"Will you be there?"

No hesitation. "Yes."

The camera zooms in on the slick-white sea.

By the time I've given Honey Bear a drink and put her to bed, Dave's eyes are closed. I turn off the TV and the lights and get into bed. Like Honey, I love the hotel. I love the hard, tight sheets and the unfamiliar shapes that emerge around me once I've gotten used to the dark. It's been ages since I slept away from home. The last time was long before Honey. Dave and I visited some college friends in Oregon. They couldn't believe we'd driven all that way. We posed in their driveway, leaning on the car and making the victory sign.

I want the Dave from that photo. That deep suntan, that wide grin.

Maybe he'll come back to me here, away from home and our neighbors, the Simkos. He spends far too much time at their place.

For a moment, I think he's back already.

Then he starts shaking. He does it every night. He's crying in his sleep.

"Ready for the beach?"

"Yes!"

We drive through town to a parking lot dusted with sand. When I step out of the car the warm sea air rolls over me in waves. There's something lively in it, something electric.

Honey jumps up and down. "Is that it? Is that it?"

"You got it, Honey Bear."

The beach is deserted. Far to the left, an empty boardwalk whitens in the sun. I kick off my sandals and scoop them up in my hand. The gray sand sticks to my feet. We lumber down to a spot a few yards from some boulders, lugging bags and towels.

"Can I take my shoes off too? Can I go in the ocean?"

"Sure, but let me take your dress off."

I pull it off over her head, and her lithe, golden body slips free. She's so beautiful, my Bear. I call her Honey because she's my sweetheart, my little love, and I call her Bear for the wildness I dream she will keep always. Honey suits her now, but when she's older she might want us to call her Bear. I would've loved to be named Bear when I was in high school.

"Don't go too deep," I tell her, "just up to your tummy, okay?"

"Okay," she says, and streaks off, kicking up sand behind her.

Dave has laid out the towels. He's weighted the corners with shoes and the cooler so they won't blow away. He's set up the two folding chairs and the umbrella. Now, with nothing to organize or prepare, he's sitting on a chair with his bare feet resting on a towel. He looks lost.

"Not going in?" I ask.

I think for a moment he's going to ignore me, but then he makes an effort. "Not right away," he says.

I slip off my shorts and my halter top and sit in the chair beside him in my suit. Down in the water, Honey jumps up and down and shrieks.

"Look at that."

"Yeah," he says.

"She loves it."

"Yeah."

"I'm so glad we brought her. Thank you." I reach out and give his wrist a squeeze.

"Look at that fucked-up clown on the boardwalk," he says. "It looks like it used to be part of an arcade entrance or something. Probably been there for fifty years."

The clown towers over the boardwalk. It's almost white, but you can see traces of red on the nose and lips, traces of blue on the hair.

"Looks pretty old," I agree.

"Black rocks, filthy gray sand, and a fucked-up arcade clown. That's what we've got. That's the beach."

It comes out before I can stop it: "Okay, Mr. Simko."

Dave looks at me.

"I'm sorry," I say.

He looks at his watch. "I don't want to stay here for more than an hour. I want us to take a break, go back to the hotel and rest for a bit. Then we'll have lunch, and you can take your medication."

"I said I'm sorry."

"You know what?" He looks gray, worn out, beaten down, like something left out in the rain. His eyes wince away from the light. I can't stand it, I can't stand it if he never comes back. "I think," he tells me, "that Mr. Simko is a pretty fucking sensible guy."

I lean back in the chair, watching Honey Bear in the water. I hate the Simkos. Mr. Simko's bent over and never takes off his bathrobe. He sits on his porch drinking highballs all day, and he gets Dave to go over there and drink too. I can hear them when I've got the kitchen window open. Mr. Simko says things like *Après nous le déluge* and "Keep your powder dry and your pecker wet." He tells Dave he wishes he and Mrs. Simko didn't have Mandy. I've heard him say that. "I wish we'd never gone in for it. Broke Linda's heart." Who does he think brings him the whiskey to make his highballs?

Mrs. Simko never comes out of the house except when Mandy comes home. Then she appears on the porch, banging the door behind her. She's bent over like her husband and wears a flowered housedress. Her hair is black fluff, with thin patches here and there, as if she's burned it. "Mandy, Mandy," she croons, while Mandy puts the stuff down on the porch: liquor, chocolate, clothes, all the luxury goods you can't get at the Center. Stuff you can only get from a child who's left home. Mandy never looks at her mother. She hasn't let either of the Simkos touch her since she moved out.

"I'm going down in the water with Honey," I say, but Dave grabs my arm. "Wait. Look."

I turn my head, and there are Fair Folk on the rocks. Six of them, huge and dazzling. Some crouch on the boulders; others swing over the sea on their flexible wings, dipping their toes in the water.

"Honey!" Dave shouts. "Honey! Come here!"

"C'mon, Hon," I call, reassuring.

Honey splashes toward us, glittering in the sun.

"Come *here!*" barks Dave.

"She's coming," I tell him.

He clutches the arms of his chair. I know he's afraid because of the clearance area we passed on the highway, the slick.

"Come here," he repeats as Honey runs up panting. He glances at the Fair Folk. They're looking at us now, lazy and curious.

I get up and dry Honey off with a towel. "What?" she says.

"Just come over here," says Dave, holding out his arms. "Come and sit with Daddy."

Honey walks over and curls up in his lap. I sit in the chair next to them and Dave puts his hand on my shoulder. He's got us. He's holding everyone.

Two of the Fair Folk lift and ripple toward us through the light. There seems to be more light wherever they go. They're fifteen, twenty feet tall, so tall they look slender, attenuated, almost insect-like. You forget how strong they are.

They bend and dip in the air: so close I can see the reds of their eyes.

"It's okay," Dave whispers.

And it is, of course. We've got each other. We're safe.

They gaze at us for a moment, impassive, then turn and glide back to their comrades.

Honey waves at them with both hands. "Bye, fairies!"

On my first visit to the clinic, I went through all the usual drills, the same stuff I go in for every two weeks. Step here, pee here, spit here, breathe in, breathe out, give me your arm. The only difference the first time was the questions.

Are you aware of the gravity of the commitment? I said yes. Have you been informed of the risks, both physical and psychological? Yes. The side effects of the medication? Blood transfusions? Yes. Yes. The decrease in life expectancy? Everything: yes.

That's what you say to life. *Yes.*

"They chose us," I told Dave. Rain lashed the darkened windows. I cradled tiny Honey in my lap. I'd dried her off and wrapped her in a towel, and she was quiet now, exhausted. I'd already named her in my head.

"We can't go back," Dave whispered. "If we say yes, we can't go back."

"I know."

His eyes were wet. "We could run out and put her on somebody else's porch."

He looked ashamed after he'd said it, the way he'd looked when I'd asked him not to introduce me as "my wife, Karen, the children's literature major." When we first moved into the neighborhood he'd introduce me that way and then laugh, as if there was nothing more ridiculous in the world. Children, when almost nobody could have them anymore; literature when all the schools were closed. I told him it bothered me, and he was sorry, but only for hurting me. He wasn't sorry for what he really meant. What he meant was: *No.*

That's wrong. It's like the Simkos, hateful and worn out with saying *No* to Mandy, saying *No* to life.

So many people say no from the beginning. They make it a virtue: "I can't be bought." As if it were all a matter of protection and fancy goods. Of course, most of those who say yes pretend to be heroes: saving the world, if only for a season. That's always struck me as equally wrong, in its own way. Cheap.

I can't help thinking the absence of children has something to do with this withering of the spirit—this pale new way of seeing the world. Children knew better. You always say yes. If you don't, there's no adventure, and you grow old in your ignorance, bitter, bereft of magic. You say yes to what comes, because you belong to the future, whatever it is, and you're sure as hell not going to be left behind in the past. *Do you hear the fairies sing?* You always get up and open the door. You always answer. You always let them in.

The Fair Folk are gone. I'm in the ocean with Honey. I bounce her on my knee. She's so light in the water: soap bubble, floating seed. She clings to my neck and squeals. I think she'll remember this, this morning at the beach, and the memory will be almost exactly like my own memory of childhood. The water, the sun. Even the cooler, the crumpled maps in the car. So many things now are the way they were when I was small. Simpler, in lots of ways. The things that have disappeared—air travel, wireless communication—seem dreamlike, ludicrous, almost not worth thinking about.

I toss Honey up in the air and catch her, getting a mouthful of saltwater in the process. I shoot the water onto her shoulder. "Mama!" she yells. She bends her head to the water and burbles, trying to copy me, but I lift her up again. I don't want her to choke.

"My Bear, my Bear," I murmur against the damp, wet side of her head. "My Honey Bear."

Dave is waving us in. He's pointing at his watch.

I don't know if it's the excitement, or maybe something about the salt water, but as soon as I get Honey up on the beach, she voids.

"Christ," says Dave. "Oh, Christ."

He pulls me away from her. In seconds he's kneeling on our towels, whipping the gloves and aprons out of the bag. He gets his on fast; I fumble with mine. He rips open a packet of wipes with his teeth, tosses it to me, and pulls out a can of spray.

"I thought you said it wasn't time yet," he says.

"I thought it wasn't. It's really early."

Honey stands naked on the sand, slick pouring down her legs. Already she looks hesitant, confused. "Mama?"

"It's okay, Hon. Just let it come. Do you want to lie down?"

"Yes," she says, and crumples.

"Fuck," says Dave. "It's going to hit the water. I have to go make a call. Take this."

He hands me the spray, yanks his loafers on and dashes up the beach. There's a phone in the parking lot, he can call the Service. He's headed for the fence, not the gate, but it doesn't stop him, he seizes the bar and vaults over.

The slick is still coming. So much, it's incredible, as if she's losing her whole body. It astounds me, it frightens me every time. Her eyes are still open, but dazed. Her fine hair is starting to dry in the sun. The slick pours, undulant, catching the light, like molten plastic.

I touch her face with a gloved hand. "Honey Bear."

"Mm," she grunts.

"You're doing a good job, Hon. Just relax, okay? Mama's here."

Dave was right, it's going to reach the water. I scramble down to the waves and spray the sand and even the water in the path of the slick. Probably won't do anything, probably stupid. I run back to Honey just as Dave comes pelting back from the parking lot.

"On their way," he gasps. "Shit! It's almost in the water!"

"Mama," says Honey.

"I know. I tried to spray."

"You sprayed? That's not going to do anything!"

I'm kneeling beside her. "Yes, Honey."

"Help me!" yells Dave. He runs down past the slick and starts digging wildly, hurling gobs of wet sand.

Honey curls her hand around my finger.

"Karen! Get down here! We can dig a trench, we can keep it from hitting the water!"

"This is scary," Honey whispers.

"I know. I know, Hon. I'm sorry. But you don't need to be scared. It's just like when we're at home, okay?"

But it's not, it's not like when we're at home. At home, I usually know when it's going to happen. I've got a chart. I set up buckets, a plastic sheet. I notify the Service of the approximate date. They come right away. We keep the lights down, and I play Honey's favorite CD.

This isn't like that at all. Harsh sunlight, Dave screaming behind us. Then the Service. They're angry: one of them says, "You ought to be fucking fined." They spray Honey, right on her skin. She squeezes my finger. I don't know what to do, except sing to her, a song from her CD.

> *A sailor went to sea-sea-sea*
> *To see what he could see-see-see*
> *But all that he could see-see-see*
> *Was the bottom of the deep blue sea-sea-sea.*

At last, it stops. The Service workers clean Honey up and wrap her in sterile sheets. They take our gloves and aprons away to be cleaned at the local Center. Dave and I wipe ourselves down and bag the dirty wipes for disposal. We're both shaking. He says: "We are not doing this again."

"It was an accident," I tell him. "It's just life."

He turns to face me. "This is not life, Karen," he snarls. "This is *not life*."

"Yes. It is."

I think he sees, then. I think he sees that even though he's the practical one, the realist, I'm the strong one.

I carry Honey up to the car. Dave takes the rest of the stuff. He makes two trips. He gives me an energy bar and then my medication. After that, there's the injection, painkillers and nutrients, because Honey's voided, and she'll be hungry. She'll need more than a quick drink.

He slips the needle out of my arm. He's fast, and gentle, even like this, kneeling in the car in a beach parking lot. He presses the cotton down firmly, puts on a strip of medical tape. He looks up and meets my eyes. His are full of tears.

"Jesus, Karen," he says.

Just like that, in that moment, he's back. He covers his mouth with his fist, holding in laughter. "Did you hear the Service guy?"

"You mean 'You ought to be fucking fined'?"

He bends over, wheezing and crowing. "Christ! I really thought the slick was going in the water."

"But it didn't go in the water?"

"No."

He sits up, wipes his eyes on the back of his hand, then reaches out to smooth my hair away from my face.

"No. It didn't go in. It was fine. Not that it matters, with that giant dump floating in the Pacific."

He reads my face, and raises his hands, palms out. "Okay, okay. No Mr. Simko."

He backs out, shuts the door gently, and gets in the driver's seat. The white clown on the boardwalk watches our car pull out of the lot. We're almost at the hotel when Honey wakes up.

"Mama?" she mumbles. "I'm hungry."

"Okay, sweetie."

I untie the top piece of my suit and pull it down. "Dave? I'm going to feed her in the car."

"Okay. I'll park in the shade. I'll bring you something to eat from inside."

"Thanks."

Honey's wriggling on my lap, fighting the sheets. "Mama, I'm *hungry*."

"Hush. Hush. Here."

She nuzzles at me, quick and greedy, and latches on. Not at the nipple, but in the soft area under the arm. She grips me lightly with her teeth, and then there's the almost electric jolt as her longer, hollow teeth come down and sink in.

"There," I whisper. "There."

Dave gets out and shuts the door. We're alone in the car.

A breeze stirs the leaves outside. Their reflections move in the windows.

I don't know what the future is going to bring. I don't think about it much. It does seem like there won't be a particularly lengthy future, for us. Not with so few human children being born, and the Fair Folk eating all the animals, and so many plant species dying out from the slick. And once we're gone, what will the Fair Folk do? They don't seem able to raise their own children. It's why they came here in the first place. I don't know if they feel sorry for us, but I know they want us to live as long as possible: they're not pure predators, as some people claim. The abductions of the early days, the bodies discovered in caves—that's all over. The terror, too. That was just to show us what they could do. Now they only kill us as punishment, or after they've voided, when they're crazy with hunger. They rarely hurt anyone in the company of a winged child.

Still, even with all their precautions, we won't last forever. I remember the artist in the park, when I took Honey there one day. All of his paintings were white. He said that was the future, a white planet, nothing but slick, and Honey said it looked like fairyland.

Her breathing has slowed. Mine, too. It's partly the meds, and partly some chemical that comes down through the teeth. It makes you drowsy.

Here's what I know about the future. Honey Bear will grow bigger. Her wings will expand. One day she'll take to the sky, and go live with her own kind. Maybe she'll forget human language, the way the Simko's Mandy has, but she'll still bring us presents. She'll still be our piece of the future.

And maybe she won't forget. She might remember. She might remember this day at the beach.

She's still awake. Her eyes glisten, heavy with bliss. Large, slightly protuberant eyes, perfectly black in the centers, and scarlet, like the sunrise, at the edges.

ONE DAY IN TIME CITY

DAVID IRA CLEARY

Joey's in the 60s, about to do a heist. This far uptown, he's arthritic in his hands, sore and knobby-jointed. But his knees and ankles are grand as ever, so he rides his moped.

The moped's sweet. Seven gears, top speed forty, courier backpack fastened to a rack behind the seat. Best of all, its brake pads are new, and stopping's quick.

Like now. The Conquistador 6-by-6 he's behind (three axles, five tons) brakes suddenly. A moped with old pads would flip him backside to the tinted rear window. But the new brakes stop him upright.

He sees himself reflected in the Conquistador's gleaming citrine shell. Blue Pick–Up Boy helmet, eager frightened eyes, smile lines like riverbeds, the smile itself automatic though his gray nostril hairs are trembling.

"Sorry!" shouts the Uppie who's driving.

Joey doesn't quite believe him. Especially given that, as the Conquistador starts up, it becomes clear there was no reason to stop.

He locks his moped to a parking meter at 63rd and Eon. He grabs the courier backpack, and carries it into the Art-Deco-style Very Large Motors office building across the street. The security guard, who knows him, passes him through. The new receptionist on the eleventh floor, who doesn't, is suspicious.

"It's not even nine, bike-tyke."

Joey wouldn't have expected disdain from a chunky guy in a white pony-tail who's wearing an earring and a garish red tie. Dressed like a Downster but acting like an Uppie. Probably a bounder, a guy unhappy with his social class. Joey feigns a hearing problem. "Yeah, you can sign." He pushes the invoice across the desk. "I'll take it to her office myself."

Her being Carla Dakota, Chief Vision Officer for Very Large Motors.

"She's not in yet!"

Joey waves affably as he enters the office area. He hopes the pony-tailed receptionist is green enough he won't call security. He smiles at the one person he sees, a lady with thin hennaed hair enjoying her coffee, sitting in a cube so small she has to be a Downster. Then he reaches Carla Dakota's office.

It's a big corner office, pure Uppie, with a view of the Farlands across the bay. There are framed posters of old ad campaigns on the walls. Models of Sport Utility Cars hang from the ceiling like stuffed birds in a museum.

On the shiny U-shaped desk is the model Joey wants.

It's called the Ghengis Khar. Tri-axled and made of balsa wood, it's a foot long, eight inches high. Small numbers until you consider the scale. 1:35. Seats for ten, with a living area subdivided into two levels.

It seems nothing more than a scaled-up Celestial Adventurer, last year's flagship model. That is, until Joey rips the model off the base and spots the retractable units at both ends of the vehicle. When you touch a lever on the undercarriage, a row of wooden needles springs out from each bumper. Joey pushes them back in. They are sharp enough to hurt his thumb. Like tiny too-sharp toothpicks.

"Whoa-boy!" he says.

Clearly meant to puncture bike tires.

A clock on the desk pings softly. 8:45. Joey packs the Ghengis Khar into his backpack, cushioning it with Styrofoam. He leaves the office.

Spying two security guards approaching the reception desk, he goes the other way.

He strolls. Uptown his mind is fast but his body's slower, more resistant to panic. He follows the perimeter of the floor, cubicles on his left, glass-fronted offices on his right. He's glad this is the 60s, not the 70s. Just a few streets further uptown the offices would be full of white-haired early risers.

He completes the square, passes through the reception area.

"Stop!" shouts Pony-tail. "We got something to ask you!"

Joey presses the down button for the elevator. He waits until he sees Pony-tail hurrying toward him, waving a rolled-up newspaper. "I said stop!"

Joey takes the stairs. Stepping quickly. Here's a surprise: Pony-tail follows him. Shouting, taking his job far too seriously. The guy's heavy steps echo in the cement stairwell so it seems there's more than one of him. Joey maintains his pace. No running. His hips hurt when he turns at the end of each flight.

Pony-tail is suddenly quiet. Joey's alarmed. He imagines the guy clutching his chest, slumping to his knees on a landing. Some guys aren't meant to run. At least not when they're uptown.

Just as he reaches the first floor, he hears Pony-tail shout, "We're going to get you!"

Joey's glad the guy's okay.

• • •

Smooth sailing until he gets to his moped.

It's been torn in half by a Land Yacht. The Yacht's rear bumper caught the frame behind the steering column, pulling it away from the parking meter. Seat and motor and rear wheel are still attached to the meter, which is bent. The front wheel and steering column are still hooked to the bumper. The Yacht's parked a few yards down the street, hazards flashing. Its bumper isn't bent at all.

When Joey pushes the front wheel, it spins freely with a wobble.

He notices the two security guards coming out of the building, Pony-tail behind them.

The passenger-side door on the Yacht is unlocked.

Joey climbs in. He smells leather. He'll be safer in back. Coming around the passenger seat, he bumps his knee on the dashboard food-tray, setting a bowl of oatmeal to quivering.

He crawls down the carpeted aisle, past two rows of seats. The back's a bedroom, with a frilly white bed and chiffon curtains and a Leif Garrett poster on one plaster wall. He hides between the bed and the vanity, burying himself beneath teddy bears and stuffed giraffes.

He hears voices outside, but the Yacht is so well insulated that he can't make out any words.

When he's sure they aren't coming into the Yacht after him, he sits up. He thinks things through. He's grabbed the Model, but has lost his moped. On the street he'd be a pedestrian in a Pick-up Boy uniform. He'd be as conspicuous as a glass tower in kidtown. He could wait until darkness, walk safely down to 43rd Avenue, but it would be hard exchanging the moped for a motorcycle without a moped to produce. Maybe, though, the front half would be acceptable, if he could pry it off the bumper.

He hopes the Yacht owner won't park in front of the VLM building all day.

He pushes animals off his body, stands, then, with a cry of, "Whoa!" falls onto the bed. His kneecap aches where he bumped the tray. No swelling visible, but that will come. He is proud of his legs. They retain their musculature into the 70s, but the joints, the ligaments and cartilage, became fragile much lower.

He limps to the Yacht's little fridge. No ice, but he finds a six pack of Uptown Ale ('You *want* to get old for it'). He sits on the bed and holds the cold cans against his knee and considers the bedroom inside the Yacht. Pink walls, a seven foot stucco ceiling. Too low. He'd get claustrophobic if he had to sleep here. Sometimes he understands why Uppies always want their SUCs bigger.

He's started drinking from one can when the Yacht's horn honks.

He slips down by the animals. A woman gets into the Yacht. "Shit," she says. She sobs for minutes. Joey's nervous she'll never start the Yacht. He finishes the can of ale, which doesn't help the nervousness, but makes him feel he might float to the ceiling along with the animals. In the 60s, he gets drunk easily.

He falls asleep.

When he wakes, the Yacht's moving. In the tight space he feels a claustrophobic panic. He cries out as he pushes himself up.

His wrists hurt like nails have been hammered through them. His left hand is clenched closed. His veins are ropy, his skin spotted like a cheetah's hide. His shorts are loose around his thighs. His knee is an ugly purple.

She's driving the wrong way.

Further uptown.

Groaning, creaking, hips aflame, he moves to the cab. "Where *are* you going?"

She stops the Yacht, looks at him skeptically. White hair in bangs and pale blue eyes and the fine pretty features that some Uppies preserve no matter how far up they go. "Why are you in my car?"

"Look!" He points toward the passenger-side mirror. "You broke my moped."

She squints. "Oh, dear." He sees now she has twin worry lines, deep along the bridge of her nose.

Eyes watering, she turns away.

Joey was expecting harsh words. Or at best money pushed at him. Not *this*.

They are at 88th and Eon. There's a green windowed pyramid in the street in front of them. Part of a mansard roof. Maintenance standards are low this far uptown.

The woman regains her composure. "You should get out."

"But you wrecked my moped. I don't have wheels now."

"These wheels aren't going the way you want to go."

"I just need to get to 43rd."

"Let me rephrase. I'm not going south."

"But—" he points "—nobody goes further uptown than this. You could have a heart attack. You could lose your mind."

"I thought bike boys raced uptown to prove how tough they were."

"Not this far."

"Please get out."

"I'm not walking forty blocks." Joey sits in the passenger seat. "Don't you owe me at least a ride?"

"I'm sorry." She doesn't say about what—the moped, her attitude. She drives around the pyramid. They pass abandoned cars, rusty but intact. Up here few have the strength to lift hubcaps, let alone wheels. She maneuvers around office furniture and broken glass fallen from an International Style tower. At 89th Avenue, she stops. "Get out."

"Are you punishing yourself?" Joey asks. "For wrecking my moped?"

She stiffens. "Get out."

He's hit a nerve. Not that it's the moped. Sometimes Uppies get afflicted with a conscience. They'll drive small SUCs, overtip couriers, even slum it downtown for a day or two. But nothing drastic like this.

"This seat's comfy," Joey says. He doubts she'll go much further if he stays aboard. "I'll ride with you."

She shrugs and crosses 89th.

Joey wonders: why try to save her? Is he soft this far up? Or is it that he thinks she's cute?

A post-modern building's collapsed. He can tell by the rubble blocking the street: the window panes like Fresnel lenses, the curves in the structural beams, the copper gargoyle, whose face is unmistakably Mickey Mantle's. No way past this. She'll have to turn around.

She puts the Yacht into four wheel drive.

She takes them up a slope of bricks and sparkling glass. The bricks shift beneath the Yacht's weight. Joey expects the hill to topple, drop the Yacht then crush it. But she handles the vehicle expertly. They crest the hill then follow the easier far slope down.

Safe on asphalt, they pass 90th.

"Why do this?" Joey asks.

A vein, delicate and green, pulses in her temple.

Joey says, "If something's broken, if something's wrong, you can always go back and fix it."

"No, I can't. It's too late. Life's not just bodies."

"Too late for what?"

Tears brim in her eyes. The nose lines are so deep you wonder if they touch bone.

He pats her shoulder. "Too late for what?"

She blinks. "At VLM. It was gone."

"What?"

"This year's model. The Ghengis Khar!"

Midtown Joey might freak, jump out of the car, but up here his body's slow enough he can think of eight or ten things to say to calm himself before his nerves take over. And things to say to her. "You're in trouble—because it's gone?"

"*I'm* not in trouble. You bike boys are in trouble!"

Is she accusing him? "I don't follow."

"I thought bike boys had spies! I'm the *prototype artist*. I build balsa models. Usually to the specs engineers give me. But this time was different."

"How?"

"Carla Dakota wanted APS! The engineer didn't!"

"APS?"

"The Aggressive Pathway System. Blades that extend from the bumpers. They're going to market them as debris catchers. When it's obvious that what they'll do is slash bike tires and carve up legs!"

"Oh boy," Joey says. Partly because the leg-carving possibility hadn't occurred to him. Partly because he is seeing four women instead of one. "So there was controversy."

"Even some hawks were appalled by the idea. The engineer sent me specs without the blade. But Carla made it clear the model should have it!"

It is his right eye. If he closes it, he just sees one woman. "And so you added the leg-carvers."

"Yes! I added the blades, and delivered the model late Friday. Then I decided I should stand up to Carla!"

Things click for Joey. He has a cataract. And: "You went in because you wanted to take the model back. But it was gone."

"I was going to fix it! I was going to break off the APS units! But Carla must have taken it home!"

"No, she didn't," Joey said.

She stops the Yacht. Intersection of 92nd and Eon. The traffic light is stuck on yellow. A little past the avenue, four trees grow side-by-side in the center of the street. Correction. One tree.

She's weeping. With his clawed left hand Joey touches her shoulder: it's hunched, raised higher than the other. Joey feels tears in his own eyes. God, the indignities of age. "We stole it. Me and another bike boy."

She shakes her head. "Don't believe you."

"We took it this morning. He's got it now."

"You're lying." She pushes his hand away. She's stronger than he is. She drives forward, slowly.

"I'm not. We went in at 8:30 and I grabbed it while my partner talked to the receptionist." Joey's voice is tinny. With his right eye open he sees eight trees. "My partner's got it now. You've got no reason to feel guilty."

"You lie," she says. "I bet he's at 43rd Avenue, isn't he?"

"He's downtown." It was true enough that he and his roommate Wayne lived on 24th Avenue. Their apartment doubled as the City-Wide Headquarters of the Bike Defense League, and Wayne, Chairman of the BDL, was expecting the model.

They're approaching the trees. Joey thinks of kites and picnics and the toothpicks used to hold together club sandwiches. *Toothpicks.* "When you hold it you push a disk and these toothpick things come out."

She cries harder. There's a roar like a waterfall as they reach the trees, and then suddenly she's turning the Yacht around them, all of them at once, and just for a second, at the apex of the turn, Joey sees uptown not just trees but a welcoming green forest.

There's nothing like a drive toward downtown to make you feel better. Joey's eye clears, his hand unclenches, his calves regain definition and he fills his shorts again. He pissed them uptown. He can smell that now.

"You drank my beer," the woman says.

"You wrecked my moped."

"True," she says. She's not weepy anymore. Her nose lines don't cut so deep. She's tough like you expect Uppies to be. But there's also something friendly in her eyes. Gratitude, maybe. "Why steal it?"

"To figure out something protective. We knew VLM was going to put something dangerous on the new model."

She says nothing, but doesn't cry either.

At 67th they hit traffic. Stop 'n' go, cacophony of horns, exhaust fumes so thick they tint the aluminum towers blue. She turns on the Yacht's air filter. She turns off the hazards, which had been blinking the entire ride.

A guy in a Pillager pick-up opens his door as a lane-splitting bike boy approaches it. The bike boy leans hard left, almost falling into the car in the next lane, but passes under the Pillager's door. He recovers to vertical the other side.

"Hey!" Joey says. "Great technique!"

"I'm sorry he had to use it."

"Not your fault."

"You don't know how many times I've given Carla *exactly* the designs she wanted."

"Designs don't matter as much as assholes," Joey says.

At 66th they see why there's a traffic jam so late. Police cruisers are parked in front of VLM.

She turns east onto 66th, follows it to Temporal Park, but instead of joining the traffic going south on Fleet, she drives into the park.

"Wow!" Joey says. She plows through brush, she fords streams, she scrapes the base of the vehicle against stones. They might be the only Yacht in the park, though, as they are driving up a hill of birch trees and crabgrass, they pass a stretch limo with tank tread wheels coming down.

"Shit!" she says.

"What?"

"Executives hate trespassers."

"Let them pout."

"Don't you see? They'll call the cops."

They follow the park to its end at 53rd. Joey's alert and adrenalized. There's no doubt about *why* now. Her hair is turning brown. She's not so thin anymore, especially in the chest. And she's brave and breaks the rules and acts more like a Downster than an Uppie.

Joey leans over and kisses her cheek.

She pushes him away. "Let me drive."

Midtown. Where Uppies and Downsters mingle. Where bounders burn their savings on three-bedroom brownstone flats. Where Uppies down on their luck or desiring to improve their souls by living like a Downster rent those same flats once the bounders are evicted. Where Joey first realizes he might get laid today, if he can get her downtown to his apartment.

But first they go to the Exchange Building, on 43rd. They don't have much choice. The Land Yacht couldn't make most turns south of 40th. And Joey needs a motorcycle.

Joey gives her his address, an address on 24th Avenue, at Tick-Tock Square. "Offices of the BDL. The Bike Defense League. My partner Wayne's got the model. Let's meet there."

He's afraid she'll think he wants to abandon her. But he must be sweating sex hormones by the liter. "Okay," she says. "What are you carrying in that?"

"Floppy disks," he says, putting on the backpack. He gets out of the Yacht so she can join the queue for the valet.

The Exchange Building is a granite Neo-Classical structure fronted by big marble columns. Bike boys and office messengers, word processors and janitors, waitresses and plumbers, are riding their machines (moped, bike, or motorcycle) up a cement ramp toward the building's entrance. Joey takes the staircase. His knee's sore but his calves are bulging. The Exchange's dusty inside smells of fumes and motor oil and is raucous with the sound of motor-cycle engines being gunned. Joey forgoes the lines of people with machines and walks to the end of the long counter, where there's a placard reading special situations.

"I need a motorcycle. My moped was wrecked."

The clerk arches his pierced eyebrow. "I don't see the moped."

"Most of it's uptown. I've got the front wheel outside."

"I need the whole moped for a trade. Unless you want a bike."

Joey takes a sturdy twelve-speed. Coasting down the exit ramp, he passes Pony-tail, who's sitting on the staircase eating his lunch from a paper bag.

"You!"

Joey starts off. Slaloming around other bikes, standing as he pedals because the bike's in a high gear, he follows the ramp down, then rides the sidewalk. He reaches the Land Yacht, which is at the front of the valet line.

The woman's in the cab.

"What are you doing?" she says.

He points back at Pony-tail, who's slim and sprinting after him. He motions for her to get out, and when she doesn't, he opens the passenger door, lifts the bike—"Take it!"—then climbs into the cab.

"What the hell?" she says.

"Why aren't you in a new car?"

"They said they had to notify the insurance adjuster because of the moped wheel."

Pony-tail pounds the window.

"Go! They were probably calling the cops."

"And now they will for sure," she says, starting off.

They take 42nd east, then The Split Second Parkway south. Joey, pressing the bike against the dash so it doesn't fall on him, feels the great energy of the chase and the even greater one of love. He wants to stroke her brown shiny hair, kiss her long-lashed eyelids. She's preoccupied with driving, though. Split Second's the widest road midtown, but still the Yacht's too big for a single lane. She flattens the mirrors of the little SUCs in the lane over, makes a *thump* on Joey's side of the Yacht.

"What was that?"

Joey looks in the mirror. "You just dragged a Scamper out of its parking space. Knocked off my moped wheel too."

"Great. Is that him way back there?"

Joey looks. He has a fine view of the bikes and the SUCs behind them. And there's Pony-tail, on a moped, two blocks behind and gaining.

Ahead a few blocks, Split Second becomes one-way. One way the wrong way: uptown. Most southbound traffic turns west on 31st. 31st can get clogged so Joey says, "Turn here."

"On 35th? It's an alley!"

"You'll fit."

She doesn't. She turns too tight, taking out the signal pole then hitting the Kwik Shoppe grocery on the near corner, bringing down bricks onto a display of half-price cucumbers. The Yacht stops. "Shit!" She puts it into reverse, then into 4WD, but gets only grinding and more bricks. "We're stuck!"

"Let's go on my bike!"

Joey's out of the Yacht. He gets on the twelve speed. He sees the Yacht is blocking the alley. "Get out this side!"

Pony-tail has reached the corner. She's out, climbing onto the handlebars.

Pony-tail jumps off his moped. He starts to climb onto the hood of the Yacht.

"Wait!" she says before Joey starts pedaling.

She throws a wad of bills at the mustached man in a grocer's apron who's just come out of the Kwik Shoppe crying.

They don't lose Pony-tail until 33rd and Eon. The guy's fit in the 30s, a runner, and with the woman sitting on Joey's handlebars, it's hard for Joey to get the bike up to speed.

But at Eon, Joey runs the red light, the Predator pulling a mobile Farmer's Market uptown honking at him. And seeing Pony-tail stop at the red light, as if obeying traffic signals might earn him points towards Uppiehood, Joey gets inspired. "Let's ride the Market!"

The Farmer's Market is a flat trailer, a third the length of a city block, with a greenhouse atop it. It moves less than a mile an hour. Still in the intersection, greenhouse full of dead cornstalks between them and Pony-tail, they climb onto the trailer near its rear wheels, the woman first, Joey handing her the bike.

Then through an access door into the greenhouse itself.

"Keep low," Joey says. They crawl across the furrowed mulch, toward a pile of cornstalks and debris from the last planting cycle. It's humid and warm but all Joey can think about is the fine shape of her gray-skirted buttocks before him.

Recorded thunder crackles from speakers. Cold water from overhead sprinklers douses them. "Shit," she says, when the rain has stopped and they are sitting close to the cornstalks. "Look at me."

Her skirt is muddy, her nylons streaked with grease, and her wet blouse clings to her so that Joey can see the shape of her breasts. The automatic rain has raised a sweet smell of manure but also, from her body, a heady mix of perfume and perspiration and wet hair. Joey is aroused. "I think you're beautiful."

"Why is that guy after you?" she asks.

"He's a bounder."

"You did something to him."

All at once, shoots break through the mulch, like an array of green swordpoints thrust upward from below. One pokes Joey in the butt. He slides off the shoot towards her, but as he moves to embrace her, he catches his backpack on a sharp broken cornstalk. "Oops!" He's stuck. "Don't want to break it!"

"Break what?" she asks.

He pulls his arms out of the straps. "The mod— the floppy— the disks."

Before he can stop her, she has the pack down from the cornstalk. She opens it. "I thought so."

"I can explain," Jocy says. "I wanted to help you."

"My car is wrecked. I've lost my job. I'm sitting in manure. I don't need your explanations." With her hair brown, her blue eyes are startling. "Let's do things my way now."

"Okay."

She takes putty and a utility knife out of her purse. She begins to work on the Ghengis Khar.

As the rows of plants individuate, tomatoes where they sit, stalks of corn in four other rows, Joey wonders how he's going to get the model to Tick-Tock Square.

And he wonders if he has any chance of getting laid.

He watches her finish altering the model. She's already filled the blade holes and cut away the lever and spring for the APS blades. Now with her knife she levers out the units themselves. Even with the tomato plant sending vines around her ankles, her hand is steady, her motions sure. Joey feels the same admiration he'd have for a bike babe who'd trimmed her delivery time by car-roofing down a busy street. There are too many reasons to love her. He watches green buds turn into green fruit. "You know," he says, "if we go hide at the BDL office, it will be easier getting uptown tonight."

"I don't care about easy. I care about fast."

"I can bike you uptown in fifteen minutes."

"I don't need your help. I have my car."

"Your car's stuck," Joey says.

"I'll get it towed."

Three Downsters carrying baskets enter via the forward access door. At that end of the greenhouse, the corn is full-height, the tomatoes fat and red. Harvest time.

"Hard to get a tow truck downtown," Joey says.

"I'll take my chances." She's up, model in hand. One Downster notices her but she ignores him. "I'll see you around."

"At least let me escort you back to your Yacht."

She shrugs, not dismissing him, but not encouraging him either. He pulls off a half-ripened tomato then follows her, trampling over the vines, pushing through the corn. They emerge from the greenhouse as the Farmer's Market pulls into its parking area north of 34th Avenue. Uppies are waiting there to shop, but there's no sign of Pony-tail.

On the street, four-story redbrick rowhouses, Joey's pedaling his bike in its lowest gear, while she walks beside him. She won't ride with him but seems less angry. "So why *did* you lie to me?"

"Because I like you. I wanted to be with you longer."

She half-smiles. Then: "Damn."

They've just turned onto 35th. The Yacht's surrounded by a crowd. Moped cops are cordoning off the area with yellow crime scene tape.

"I'm not in trouble?" she asks. "They're not going to blame *me*?"

Joey doesn't know. He wants to jump off the bike and reassure her with a hug. Instead he says: "Give me the model. I'll take it to the cops and turn myself in."

"How gallant," she says. Her voice is sarcastic but her eyelashes sparkle with tears. She turns away and wipes her face then looks at Joey and, after taking a deep breath, says, "Let me get on your bike."

"You want to go uptown?"

"Let's go further downtown first."

And south on Century Boulevard, the model making her purse bulge, Joey embarrassed by a hard-on but puzzled too. "Why south?" he asks, raising his voice because he is pedaling fast enough that the air pushes back her hair.

"I want to shop!"

"For what?"

"You'll see!"

Puzzling him further because even slumming Uppies shop in the 30s.

He worries the sight of the cop mopeds has unhinged her.

But how can you worry much downtown? They reach the 20s and the streets get narrow, so narrow that the Avenues are impassable by the smallest car or SUC, and even on the Boulevards cars are discouraged strongly. They pass a Scamper retreating uptown, chunks of rotten vegetables adhering like ornaments to its hood, wipers smearing the fecal matter dumped upon the windshield. Joey shouts, "It'll wash off!" to the anxious driver. There are flowers in the building windows, and guys playing flutes for pennies, and women on ten speeds with crepe paper streamers in their hair. Everyone is strong and young and healthy. They cheer Joey like he's brought back a prize. A guy drinking smuggled Uptown beer toasts them as they pass. A woman walking a wire strung above them across the street calls out, "I love your shoes!" and she, the model-builder, takes off her black business pumps and tosses them at the wire-walking woman, who catches one.

"Hey!" Joey says.

They reach 24th Avenue, Tick-Tock Square, and Joey stops.

"The BDL is in that building," he says, pointing at the stone building with Gothic arches across the square. "Do you want to come up and show them the model?"

She studies the many guys sitting on blankets, selling cutlery and worn jackets and action figures from TV shows. "I want to shop."

"You can shop later. Why not come up first? They'd really like to see the model."

"I want to shop."

"Okay." She's so beautiful that Joey finds it hard not to stare at her face. "Do you still want to take the model uptown?"

"Of course. Why?"

"It's going to be a problem if I go to the BDL with nothing to show."

She says nothing, but her nose lines deepen.

Joey walks the bike a couple of feet, feels beneath his heel the place where concrete ends and cobblestone begins, feels also the reckless strength that surges through him whenever he goes this far downtown. "It's yours. I shouldn't have even asked. But maybe you can let me have the toothpick blades."

"For the BDL?"

"Yeah."

She gives him the two APS units along with the springs and lever.

Joey kisses her on the lips.

She doesn't return the kiss but her nose lines soften momentarily.

"Wait for me," he says.

"What the fuck is this, dude?"

Wayne, shaved head, beady eyes, black goatee to his shirtless well-muscled chest, holds an APS unit in his palm. He sits cross-legged on a battered wooden desk, which is pushed against an arch-shaped stained-glass window.

"It's the weapon, from the model."

"What good is it to me?"

"It's a blade," Joey says. "Build your fenders."

"I can't design *shit* based off just this. Where's the rest of it?"

"I gave it back."

"To *her*?" Wayne thumps the window with his elbow. "I saw you with the smog queen."

"She's *the artist*. She built the model and broke off the blades and that's how they're going to build it now."

"She told you that?"

"She says if she stands up to Carla Dakota, other people will follow."

"You *believe* her? She's *delusional*, dude. She's got killer cars on her conscience and that's made her crack. And she's mindfucked *you*, too." He snaps the toothpick blades in half. "You've been uptown too much. You're trusting a slumming Uppie just because she looks good in a skirt. You've forgot what it's about."

Joey glances at the tall dusty corridor leading to his bedroom. "And you've been sitting on your ass too long to have any perspective."

"*Perspective*?" Wayne opens a manila folder off the desk. "How's this for perspective? 46th and Eon, bike babe crushed dead by a Universal. 51st and Split-Second, pedestrian flattened by a Predator. 60th and Century, office temp hit by a Pillager running a red light. Broken leg and pelvis. And that's just *this week*. You want some more *perspective*, dude?"

"I know that crap. That's why I took the model."

"And that's why you're going to go down there and get it back from the bitch!"

He throws the toothpicks at Joey and they bounce off his chest.

"Fuck you, *dude*." No sex, no model, and now attitude from Wayne. Joey wants to punch him but he makes himself walk to the door. "She's doing more for us than you ever have."

Joey's so angry that he doesn't recognize the woman until she pushes the bike up to him. "You okay?" she asks.

He stares at her. She's wearing a blue stocking cap and a hideous knee-length sweater striped purple and yellow. "Yeah, I'm fine. You found what you were shopping for?"

"No. My clothes were too big, so I bought this. But there's something else I need."

"Maybe you can find it uptown."

"No." Her brows are knit. "Take me down. To kidtown."

On Eon, south of 17th, his butt aching from the cobblestones, watching the grease stain across one of her calves, his anger vanishes, his horniness returns. "Hey!" he says to her. "Let's have lunch!"

He points at the plaster-and-adobe two story building midblock. Not only does a kid sell you sandwiches and soda-pop, but there's a bedroom in the back you can rent for a quarter.

"I want to go further," she says.

"Whatever." He wants to please her. He just hopes she doesn't want to go south of 10th, because sometimes even Downsters playing kid forget themselves and don't come back.

"Why don't they fix the buildings?"

They go past some sort of temple, with stone columns like at the mid-town Exchange Building, but the wooden roof collapsed. Pigeons coo from the wreckage. "Kids don't come downtown to do *work*."

The 14th Avenue Exchange is two long rows of bike racks, run by a girl in an ankle-length black sweater and with a shaved head just sprouting yellow fuzz.

For the 12 speed, they get two little bikes.

• • •

They ride on dirt streets between little buildings that look like beehives. Joey likes the sparkly red banana seat his bike has, though he doesn't actually *sit* on it until 12th. His legs are too long until then.

"Watch this," Joey says just past 11th. He does a wheelie. It's a fine one, lasting seconds, rear wheel following the bike tire rut in the road. But when he comes down, his helmet falls over his eyes. "Hey!"

He stops. She's giggling at him. He takes the helmet off and throws it disdainfully to the ground. But he's glad to see her smile. Her teeth are white as dinner plates.

She picks up the helmet, then attaches it to her purse. He realizes she's taller than him now.

Joey wants to entertain her.

He tells jokes, he rides no-hands, he puts on a floppy straw hat with a hole in its top. At a house that is nothing but a brick foundation, a low wall around chest-high bushes, he captures a small tan lizard. He puts it into his mouth and pretends to chew and swallow it. "Gross!" she says. As she looks away, he spits it out. He tastes something sour-yucky. The lizard peed inside his mouth.

Just down the block is one of the beehive houses. It's crumpled on one side but has a smooth slope on the other. At the bottom of the slope, there's dirt piled up in a big half-pipe shape.

"Whoa!" he says.

Kids have ridden this house before.

He hikes up the crumpled side, part-rolling, part-carrying the bike.

To his surprise she follows him, bringing her bike.

He climbs on his bike, looks at her. She's pale, unsmiling, nose-lines deep.

"You don't have to do this," he says.

She stares at him. "I want to."

"Cool. Just wait till I'm out of the way."

He does the beehive. It's steeper than he'd thought, and he panics at the start, but then his body takes control. Wind in the face, joy of speed and weightlessness, crackle of plaster beneath his tires, then he's on the dirt. He veers up the half-pipe, slows, turns and coasts back down to a stop.

She comes down as slow as she can. Braking, coasting, braking, so slow he's sure she's going to fall. But the fall doesn't happen until she reaches the half pipe. She loses her momentum, teeters, then falls onto her side.

"Are you okay?"

He's expecting terror. But she's giggling, and the nose-lines are almost gone. "Let's just go a little further downtown."

He'll do anything she wants.

• • •

Eon ends north of the 6th Avenue ziggy-rat.

Joey's heart goes thump-thump. He's never been south so far, never seen the ziggy-rat so close. Hills of rubble at its base. The ziggy-rat itself is as tall as the VLM building. It's built of gray bricks stuck together with green mortar. It's got a long staircase out front that seems to touch the sky.

He's inspired. "Let's climb it."

"And ride down?" she asks.

"Yeah!"

She grins. She's missing her top front two teeth.

They walk their bikes across the little hills, which are made of bricks too, only pieces. They walk carefully, because the bricks shift beneath their weight. On top of one hill there's a crushed soda-pop can. When Joey kicks it his shoe comes off.

He ties the shoe back on as tight as he can.

They start up the ziggy-rat. The sun is bright in a glaring blue sky. The staircase bricks warm his feet and make them sweaty so he slides in his big shoes. He's soon breathing hard, arms hurting from holding the bike. He wants to rest, but would be embarrassed to rest before the girl does. Halfway up the staircase there's something metal in the shadow of the staircase wall. When he gets there, he'll rest.

The girl's bike makes a ka-chink each time she raises it a step. The ka-chinks get slower and then they stop.

She leans her bike against the wall.

"You don't want to ride down the ziggy-rat?"

"I'll help you with your bike." Her face is red. "And you say, zigg-*oo*-rat."

"*Uppsies* say," he says, irritated. But he lets her hold one handlebar, while he holds the other and the seat. His irritation passes. He keeps looking at her. Her face is cute. Sweat sticks a strand of hair to her cheek. He wants to brush it back but touching her would be weird since she's a girl.

The metal thing's a rusty bike with training wheels, atop some clothes and sticks. He doesn't stop. "What's that?" she says.

"Training wheels!" he says.

"No, below it."

"I don't know."

She lets go to look. He keeps pushing. He gets a few steps further up when she lets out a cry. "It's bones!"

She's moved the rusty bike. It's left an orange bike-shaped drawing on the black cloth. A sweater. He's sees finger bones sticking out from beneath. There's a lump beneath one end of the sweater.

He pushes at it with his toe and a yellow skull comes out.

"Hey!" he says, jumping back.

The skull seems to look at him, then starts rolling down the stairs.

It makes a fragile tap sound against the bricks.

"Cool," he says, though he's more scared than delighted.

She looks at him. Her nose lines have returned. "We can't go any farther."

"We're almost to the top."

"It's not safe. People don't come back from where we're going."

"But you *wanted* to."

"I changed my mind."

He looks at her. She's chewing on her lower lip. She has all her kid's teeth now. He says: "Maybe I want to keep going."

"No," she says. "Come back with me."

"Why? Why should I?"

"Because," she says. Then the nose lines go away almost. "Because I'll let you kiss me again."

"I could kiss a lizard too," he says, but he picks up the bike and turns it around.

They take Century north. At 12th Avenue she stops. "I want to look in here."

It's an abandoned mud-walled building that had once been covered with colored tiles that made a picture. Now all you can see of the picture is the head of a dog, cocked to one side, and part of a sign above the head. The sign says records an apes.

"I'll guard the bikes," Joey says.

The wooden door at the entrance has an oval-shaped hole, which she crawls through. Joey hears her move things inside, watches dust puff out from the dim interior.

He's rubbing his knee, which is sore from riding or maybe growth pains, when a kid rides up to him.

The kid's on a tricycle that's way too small, and he's wearing a tie and Uppie dress slacks that are way too big.

"Nice wheels," Joey says.

"Give it to me," the kid says.

It's Pony-tail. His long hair's loose and shiny black, his pudgy face dimpled.

"What's it to you?"

"You stole it. It's not yours."

"Finders keepers." Joey studies the grease stains on Pony-tail's slacks. Must have caught them in the chain. "Hard to be a bike-tyke when you're dressed like a bounder."

Pony-tail gets off the tricycle. "What did you call me?"

Joey stands. "I didn't call you anything. But you *are* dressed like a bounder."

"I'm dressed like an Uppie!"

"Then you *are* a bounder!"

Pony-tail punches Joey square in the stomach.

Joey bends over, eyes watering. He regains his breath after a few seconds, sees Pony-tail standing with his hands in fists but waiting, as though it's Joey's turn to throw a punch. Instead of obliging, Joey charges, ramming his shoulder into Pony-tail's chest, knocking him down.

"Stop it!"

It's the girl. She pulls Joey off Pony-tail.

"What's going on?" the girl says.

"He hit—" Joey starts.

"He stole—" Pony-tail says.

"Is this about the model?" she says. They both nod. She pulls the Ghengis Khar out of her purse. One wheel is missing. She digs in her purse until she finds it, and pushes it back onto the axle. Then she hands the model to Pony-tail. "You'll take it back to VLM?"

"Yes."

"You do that. I wouldn't want you to lose your job."

"Did you find what you wanted?"

"Yeah," she says. "A record."

"What record?"

"I'll let you know."

They eat spare ribs at Minute Steak on 26th Avenue, then ride a tandem bike toward Midtown. She's riding forward, steering, looking fine. Her sweater looks less ugly in the deep blue light of dusk. She kissed him during dinner, and promised to kiss him once again. Joey wants more, of course. She won't say where she's taking him. He's hoping to her apartment. She lives on 71st, in an apartment with maid-service and a doorman.

He's at her mercy and riding a rush like he felt going down the beehive.

But she turns way too early, making a right on 35th.

"Hey!" he says.

The Land Yacht has not been towed.

Streetlights are on now. But they don't explain the brightness of the Yacht. "It's burning," she says, but they get closer, and understand. There are candles, dozens, of all colors, fat and skinny, tall and short. They are burning on the car, the hood and top and bumpers mostly, but some are affixed to the windshield, and even a few to the side windows, pointing horizontal, though the flames go up. Rivulets of wax streak the sides. Bouquets of flowers circle the Yacht, piled three-deep on the asphalt. Smells comes in alternating waves, now hot wax, now carnations and gardenias.

"It's like a shrine," she says.

"But nobody's here worshipping," Joey says. "Maybe it's a thank you."

"For what?"

"For changing the model."

She says nothing to this.

They get off the bike, step across the Police Line tape. He looks at her. This old, the nose-lines are etched permanent, but they get deeper when she's worried. Not now. Now, she smiles.

She unlocks the passenger door, and tells him to get in and go to the back.

It's dark in the bedroom. As he steps down from the passenger aisle, Joey trips and falls on the bed. "Can you turn a light on?"

"I want to save the battery." She draws back the curtain near the vanity. The candlelight colors her gold and shadowy. She opens the vanity's top drawer, takes out not the negligee or condom that Joey hopes for, but a record player. After setting it on the vanity, she plugs it in, then takes the record she's found, a 45, out of her purse. "Dance with me."

"*Dance?*"

"Yeah. Don't you like the Bay City Rollers?"

"Not Leif Garrett?"

"Couldn't find that."

Hisses and pops as the record starts. The song is "Saturday Night." Loud and optimistic and as joyfully irresponsible as youth itself. Joey dances with her. They clap with the Rollers, they brush against each other, they shout the chorus. She pushes up the sleeves of her sweater, raises it to show her thighs. Joey's thrilled, smart like he's just drunk a single beer, and as he touches her hand, she suddenly makes sense to him. "You know, you only have to take care of yourself!"

"What?" she says.

"You can live without being responsible for everyone!"

She shakes her head as though she can't hear him, but then she turns the music louder. And they dance, and they dance, and Joey forgets his thought, and in the candlelight the lines along her nose seem to disappear.

THE BLACK FEMINIST'S GUIDE TO SCIENCE FICTION EDITING

SANDRA McDONALD

Scene one: a dingy hotel room at night. A somber man sits at a computer while police gather outside. His name is Neo. He works for the mysterious figure known as Morpheus. They are monitoring brilliant young hacker Tina Anderson, codenamed Trinity, who unwittingly lives in the construct called *The Matrix*. Neo's job will be to look handsome, deliver plot information as necessary, and help Trinity defeat the evil cyber-overlords.

The newly compiled footage loops on my monitor. Keanu Reeves has been dead for decades, but Neo will make the perfect sidekick.

"I still think you should swap Morpheus and Switch," says my co-worker, Gloriana, from one cubicle over. She's rebuilding *Star Wars: A New Hope*, the story of a young farmgirl on a quest to save Prince Luke from an evil empire. I wish she would focus more on her own work than mine, but she's still sore about getting stuck with George Lucas.

That's our job, you see: film reconstruction. Correcting the cinematic injustices of the past with modern, thoughtful, gender-balanced versions.

On Gloriana's monitor, Leia Skywalker stares wistfully at the sunset while inspiring music plays in the background. Gloriana changes the angle and says, "Trinity needs a female mentor. Switch is the only member of the ship's crew to dress in white, which is obviously a goddess reference."

There's a slight shadow on Keanu's face. I touch in an adjustment. "I'll make it clear that Morpheus is subordinate to the Oracle. She's the strong crone presence who guides Trinity to her destiny."

"But the training scenes in the dojo construct will show a dominant male archetype physically and psychologically aggressive toward a woman," Gloriana replies. "Is that what you want young girls to see?"

Of course not. No one does. But I have a soft spot for Fishburne, especially his later work in the reboot of *The Last Starfighter* as a post-apocalyptic tale of redemption. He reminds me of my dad, maybe, with his calm gaze and powerful voice. I should call my parents more often, I think, adding that to the neverending to-do list.

Patiently I say, "I'll deal with the dojo when I get there. You just worry about Aunt Beru."

"No worries at all, my friend. By the time I'm done with her, she'll be the baddest pistol-packing matriarch to ever make the Kessel run in twelve parsecs."

Gloriana's ancestors came from China. Mine came from Africa. You don't see many people with our skin color in old science fiction films, not unless they're the disposable extras. We've brought that up in staff meetings, how we should challenge racial norms while we upend gender stereotypes, but re-establishing women is always our first consideration. We can rework existing characters in a film—and by rework I mean everything from new shots, new scenes, and new dialogue—but we're required to use the images of the original actors. We can't create entirely new people.

"And here's Minervadiane!" says a hearty voice coming down the hallway. "She won an award for *Star Trek* last year."

"Oh, I loved that!" is the response. "Captain Uhura is the burn."

Gloriana grimaces. She's still stink-eyed about my win, which overshadowed her work making Denise Richards the true heroine of *Starship Troopers*. The loud voice belongs to Sibilia, our boss, who is six feet tall and utterly brilliant. She created the technology we use to manipulate billions of pixels each night. As director of our agency, the Women's Movie Bureau (WoMB), she has provided positive role models for millions of women around the globe. She also puts the G into Glamour. No matter what her outfit—vanilla silk suit, pink leather trousers, combat camisole—she always tops off the look with a scarf that shimmers like gold fireflies at dusk.

With her now is an intern who looks Hispanic and has a strong handshake for someone who is, what, fourteen years old? Schools keep churning them out younger and younger these days.

"I'm Ann," the intern says.

Gloriana sniffs. "What a quaint old-fashioned name."

"Short for Annastacialiese," Ann adds.

"I'm leaving Ann to learn from the best," Sibilia says. Already she's halfway down the hall again. Like a firefly, you can't pin Sibilia down. "Teach her well, Minervadiane!"

Ann pulls over a stool and peers up at my monitor. "Carrie-Ann Moss is really acid."

I'm only about five years older than she is—okay, maybe six or seven—but who can keep track of all the hip language these days? I hope "acid" is a good thing, because we've got a lot of Moss ahead of us.

"Where'd you study?" I ask.

"ReDreamWorks," she replies, and okay, that's impressive. Excellent program. She's probably been splicing her own vids for years, snooked into global entertainment 24/7, spinning out her bright digital dreams. But the work we do here is much more complex and important. If it weren't for reconstruction, people would think Arnold Schwarzenegger was the star of *Total Recall* and not Sharon Stone. They'd believe that Sylvester Stallone defeated Wesley Snipes in *Demolition Person* instead of giving credit to supercop Sandra Bullock. And of course there's *Back to the Future,* with Lea Thompson's heroic efforts to save her youngest son Marty from a mad scientist's time-traveling clutches.

Ann tilts her head at the screen. "I hope you make Switch the captain of the Nebuchadnezzar. She's clearly the goddess figure."

"You can stay, kid," Gloriana says, just as Aunt Beru shoots a bounty hunter in the Mos Eisley cantina.

It's only eight o'clock. This is going to be a long night. Little do I know that the first act turning point is on its way.

If you studied screenwriting during a certain period of history, say 1980—2020 or so, you were taught that a movie contains a certain number of dramatic acts, and each act ends on a plot point that increases the stakes for the hero on her journey. Take *Avatar,* the story of an alien woman's fight to save her people from greedy male Earthlings. In the first act we establish her dominant role in her tribe; the first turning point comes when she sees the Earth spaceship drop out of the sky. No modern filmmaker worries much about linear narratives, but I edit classic texts. I'm always thinking of where the story goes next.

Just after midnight Sibilia calls me to her office. It's up on the third floor, past the cubicles where Irene Adler and Vivian Rutledge are solving mysteries with the help of their respective sidekicks, Dr. Watson and Philip Marlowe. I never liked working in the Mystery Department. Too many killings, not enough spaceships. If I couldn't work in Science Fiction, I'd ask for Musicals. Every girl deserves a scene like the one with Debbie Reynolds singing and dancing in the rain.

The gleam in Sibilia's eyes is as bright as the fireflies in her scarf.

"The only existing copy of *The Ginger Star,*" she says, handing me a thinsheet.

The Ginger Star! The Holy Grail in the Greek pantheon of science fiction films, or some mixed metaphor like that. The thinsheet plays a grainy video clip of a spaceship zooming over a planet. It has the look of a 1970s science fiction movie, but it could easily be fake, too.

I ask, "What? Someone just happened to find a copy in a cardboard box in her basement?"

"Not just someone," Sibilia says. "The granddaughter of Sir Finlay Vancott, winner of three Academy Awards as well as the editor's guild Lifetime Achievement Award. She says he left behind a vault of film stock and vintage equipment in his old house. She's getting rid of everything. She asked for you specifically because she saw how you fixed *Blade Runner*."

That was one of my favorite projects: Rachel, a private eye in the dystopian future, fights to save her cybersisters Pris and Zhora from the deranged policeman trying to kill them.

"No one's ever proved Finlay Vancott edited *The Ginger Star*," I say.

"No one's ever proved he didn't. Just as no one has ever proved that Irving Kershner directed it and Doug Trumbull did the special effects and Leigh Brackett wrote the script herself. Any contemporary records were lost in the big flood of '19. All we've got now are a bunch of legends and rumors and this one little old lady in her decline. Minervadiane, you have to go check this out. Get her to sell it to us."

"How much can we offer?"

"As little as possible."

I'm really not interested in swindling some dotty old widow. "What about *The Matrix*? I just can't stop—"

"Use the intern! She can handle small things until you get back."

End of act one: I'm on my way to something big.

Of course no one travels by daylight anymore, and everyone lives on mountaintops, so it's not until the next night that my plane descends vertically into the thin trees of the Blue Ridge Forest and I stagger out on the launch pad. So much for that motion-sickness pill. Ms. Amelia Corinne Rawley lives far enough way that I've had to arrange for a private car. When I get to the parking lot, I see that the automated driver is on the fritz. That's the only possible explanation for the open hatch and the man leaning beside it with an insufferable grin on his face.

"Nice to see you, Minnie," he says.

I drop my suitcase close enough to his feet that he flinches. "What are you doing here, Samueldarrin?"

"She invited Ringo Cross," he says. "Says she's got *The Ginger Star* and wants the best person to carry on her old grandpa's legacy."

This is beyond appalling. I'd turn around and march right back onto that plane if I thought I could keep my lunch down and my job afterward.

Samueldarrin keeps grinning like a little kid on Christmas morning instead of a handsome, irritating, smart, smug bastard who calls himself *Ringo Cross* instead of the perfectly good name his mother gave him.

"As if your work is any way legitimate," I retort.

He oozes faux surprise. "You can't still be mad about *The Handman's Tale.*"

"You desecrated Atwood's story!"

"The same way you desecrate films every day, darling." That's an argument he's tried before, as if what he does out of spite can in any way compare to what the government does to correct injustice. Samueldarrin pats the hatch. "Come on, let's go. Don't you want to get there before sunrise?"

"This is my car, all paid for. Find your own."

"This is Ms. Rawley's car that she sent herself. Yours got a virus and called in sick."

This is probably true. East Coast cars are notoriously unreliable. I grab my suitcase and slide past him onto the fake leather seat. "Fine. Just don't try to amuse me with news of your latest exploits."

"I wouldn't," he says, and then for the next ten miles that's all he does.

We met in college. It wasn't an auspicious start: he was sneaking out of the men's dorm past curfew and I was coming up the path, exhilarated from an all-night editing spree on my senior project, *Heroines of the Reel Revolution*. After he fell off the trellis and landed on me and campus security got called in, I learned that he was a first year student in my own program. He was lucky the school didn't expel him for nearly killing me, or for his numerous unorthodox views, or for associating with dubious characters in the outlaw film community.

We may have slept together once or twice. Maybe the night before graduation. Maybe the week after. But that was before I saw his term project that re-edited Margaret Atwood's classic story of female oppression into a feel-good story celebrating the patriarchy.

"—and then we went to the after-party and saw Edwardson, you remember him, and it was almost noon and we were still drunk—"

I grit my teeth. He knows that the proper re-name is Edwardheir, and he knows that it will annoy me. His first goal in life is to irritate people, and his second goal is to make money off that irritation.

"Do the women you date find your blathering at all interesting?" I ask.

"They find it fascinating. Do the men you date find your incessant frowns beautiful?"

"Not just beautiful, but *gorgeous.*"

He arches a carefully plucked eyebrow. "You would never abandon your misguided quest long enough to even have dinner with a guy."

"You would never cease your self-promotion long enough to even look at a woman," I reply.

The grin is back. "Oh, I look. I look a lot. Chicks dig rogue media celebrities."

Chicks. Warn him that he could be arrested for discriminatory language, and he'll just come up with something worse: *babes, bitches, sluts—*

I'm getting a headache. I could blame motion sickness and the scenery sliding by in the darkness outside, but I'd rather blame him. "In no way are you a celebrity."

"I know that you keep track of my achievements. Wasn't that you who left a blistering note after my award for *Captain Chokotay Saves the Universe*?"

"No one could possibly award that."

"You should see what I'm doing now to *Aliens*."

I gasp. "You wouldn't!"

"*Corporal Hicks and the Facehugger*." He wriggles those perfectly shaped eyebrows at me and then peers out the window. "Oh, look, we're here."

Ms. Rawley lives in a long, sprawling ranch house with dark windows and extensive xeriscaping. She answers the door herself—tall, skinny, with long gray hair and an aquamarine jumpsuit dusted with sawdust. She's eighty years old and as dark as I am, although Finlay Vancott was as fair-skinned as anyone could be.

"I'm so glad you're here!" she says. "Come on in and ignore the burning smell. I was cutting the head off a finishing nail."

Stepping into her house is like stepping into a museum that has suffered a collision with a junk heap. Vintage movie posters from the 1990s and 2000s hang on the living room walls, each beautifully framed, but you can barely see them through stacks of books (paperbacks, very obsolete) and piles of decorative cardboard and plastic boxes. The ceiling is painted gold, and there's a gilded animal cage, very tall, against one wall. The cage door is open.

"My boys are around here somewhere," Ms. Rawley says, as proud as any mom. "Mike and Ike. They don't bite."

"And Mike and Ike are. . . ?" Samueldarrin asks.

"Flying squirrels," she says. "Go on into the sunroom and I'll get us some hot tea."

The sunroom is less cluttered, but you still wouldn't want the fire department inspecting it. The windows are heavily screened, of course. The furniture is bamboo and there's a ceiling fan spinning overhead. Samueldarrin settles into a chair and stretches out his long legs. He's wearing vintage blue jeans. Completely unfashionable and ridiculously tight.

He asks, "You don't think she lets those squirrels run around all day, do you?"

"Maybe they'll nibble some sense into you," I reply. "Corporal Hicks, indeed! Why don't you just call it *White Guys Save the Universe Again*?"

He perks up. "Do you think that'll sell more copies?"

No one buys his movies. No one with taste, that is. He doesn't have access to real technology, so he resorts to making his own parodies with live actors (they work for the "exposure") and live film crews (more expensive) and relies on guerilla marketing to the misogynists. His version of *Kill Bill* has a PMS-crazed assassin trying to kill a peaceful monk played by David Carradine. He remade *The Hunger Games* so that Peeta wins instead of Katniss. His *Twilight* is about a vampire stalked by a sulky teenager who will stop at nothing to bear his demon spawn.

Actually, that one was much better than the original.

Ms. Rawley returns with a tea tray. Samueldarrin looks entirely too pleased to be served by a woman. Once our cups are filled, she says, "It was one of my grandfather's lifelong regrets that *The Ginger Star* was never finished and distributed. So groundbreaking, he said, and so sadly abandoned. He was such a fan of Leigh Brackett, you see. And Kershner! He never forgave him. The bad blood persisted until both of them died."

Samueldarrin leans forward, elbows on his knees, almost sloshing tea on himself. "So the rumor of the feud is true?"

"Feud, indeed," she says. "My grandfather never forgave Kershner for quitting the project to go make a James Bond movie."

"Surely Kershner had his own reasons," I put in.

"Of course!" Ms. Rawley brushes sawdust from her overalls. "The movie had already consumed several years of his life. He'd had to turn down George Lucas's offer to direct *The Empire Strikes Back*. Turnbull couldn't nail down the special effects, Vangelis felt his music was all wrong, and the studio kept wanting to insert a clunky narration to explain the plot. My grandfather tried to finish it on his own, but eventually he too had to move on."

"Ms. Rawley, what would you like to see happen with this film?" I ask.

She gazes at us squarely. "I want an end to this story. People should remember and celebrate my grandfather's achievements. And Brackett's story, and Kershner's direction, and of course the actors. I will entrust it to the person with the best plan to ensure its legacy."

"That'll be me," Samueldarrin says instantly.

"It'll be me," I say, just as quickly.

She smiles. "If you'll excuse me, I forgot the honey."

Ms. Rawley leaves us alone. Samueldarrin says, with a narrow gaze, "I can't believe you just lied to that lovely old lady."

"What lie?" I demand.

"If you get your whitewashing feminist mitts on it, who knows what irreversible damage you'll do?"

"Two words," I say. "Margaret Atwood."

We fume at each other for several minutes before I realize Ms. Rawley hasn't come back. I hope she hasn't fallen down or gotten sick. I follow the faint burning smell to a large, outdated kitchen in the messy process of renovation. Ms. Rawley is on her hands and knees on the floor, painstakingly slotting together new, honey-colored wooden boards. Rags and other supplies are spread on the countertops.

"Ms. Rawley, can I help you with that?" I ask.

She looks up, startled. "Who are you?"

I'd say she was kidding, except for the abject fear in her eyes.

"It's me, Minervadiane. I'm here about the movie, remember?"

For a moment, no, she doesn't remember at all. She's wide-eyed and tense, her hand tight on that hammer. Slowly, though, memory creeps back into her expression. She laughs a tiny bit, forcefully.

"Of course you are," she says. "I thought you and your boyfriend went to bed. Didn't we already say good night?"

Alzheimer's disease is what we call a plot complication.

Leigh Brackett was a pioneering female writer who wrote during the Golden Age of science fiction. Stories like hers promised a future full of interstellar adventure. My generation hasn't even reached Mars yet. Brackett and her peers lived in awe of new scientific achievements such as computers, nuclear power, and rocket ships. They didn't have to cower inside each day, afraid of the blistering light of the sun. She was a good writer, but science fiction didn't pay nearly as much as screenwriting, and most of her later life was spent working in film and television.

Sometime in the mid-1970s, she adapted her own novel *The Ginger Star* into a movie script. It's about a mercenary named Eric John Stark in search of his missing mentor. No one was interested. Then *Star Wars* and *Close Encounters of the Third Kind* proved that sci-fi could make tons of money selling tickets to people who had no interest in SF literature. At some point Kershner came onboard, along with his favorite editor Finlay Vancott. Brackett died. The script got rewritten. It got rewritten again, some say by Harlan Ellison™. It went into production, but the shooting was hampered by cost overruns, bad weather, and studio meddling. It was never finished and never released.

Now it's right in front of me. Several cannisters of 35mm celluloid film, which would have disintegrated into nothingness by now if Vancott hadn't built a climate-controlled vault down here in the bedrock of the mountain. The film smells faintly of vinegar and I'm afraid to touch it, even with cotton gloves on. According to the typewritten notes (typewritten!), the movie was shot in VistaVision, a format completely obsolete today. Three enormous boxes hold the storyboards, shooting script, production schedules, dailies logs, Kershner's notes, and just about anything else Vancott could scavenge from the shoot.

In the low, long room outside the vault there are also some large console devices that look like they come from a spaceship set.

"Oh, baby," Samueldarrin says, running his hands over the nearest one. "Come to daddy."

"Since when do you have a fetish for props?" I ask.

He shakes his head sadly. "You don't even know what this is, do you? Never seen one. Never touched it. Never known the pleasure of a razor and tape. This is a KEM flatbed editor. That's a Steenbeck over there. And that upright one, a Moviola."

It's one thing to know from history class that people had to actually cut and splice film together. It's quite another to see the machines themselves. The process is crude, laborious, and so much less flexible than what we do today. You might as well operate on the human body with a scalpel.

"Ms. Rawley says she wants us to use these machines to edit our own workprints, as her grandfather would have done," Samueldarrin adds.

"She did not."

"She did. You were on the phone. You know, her memory's not nearly as bad as you think it is. Sure, she put the toaster in the oven and keeps forgetting my name. But who doesn't have momentary lapses now and then?"

I turn away and go back to examining the film. "I'd like to forget your name, too."

"How was your call with that soul-sucking boss of yours? Is Sibilia satisfied with global domination yet?"

The conversation had not gone well. First I'd talked with Ann, who reassured me she was not messing up my project and then made an offhand comment about using the Oracle in the dojo scene. I admonished her sternly and then put her to work seeing if Ms. Rawley had any living descendents. When I talked to Sibilia, she was completely against releasing any special "Vancott" version of *The Ginger Star*, because obviously he was steeped in the male twentieth-century social construct and his vision would automatically include severe gender oppression.

"Say whatever you need to appease her," Sibilia said, "and then we'll make our own cut."

"I don't want to be unethical—" I started.

That was the completely wrong thing to say, of course, and earned me an unnecessary fifteen minute lecture about Hollywood's history of female repression and subjugation, as if I were an idiot who'd never seen a Michael Bay movie or any installment of *Harry Potter*. Meanwhile Samueldarrin was having breakfast with Ms. Rawley, no doubt charming her in that ridiculous easy smiling way of his.

He plops down on the stool in front of the KEM and says, "I came knocking on your door today."

"Really? I thought that was the squirrels."

"I thought maybe you'd want to get reacquainted."

I smile sweetly. "I'd rather kiss a rodent."

Ms. Rawley descends the stairs behind us. She's back in her dirty coveralls, with a tool belt around her waist and a pencil tucked behind one ear. Maybe I should make a documentary series about elderly women tackling their own home renovations. It'd be a hit on HHGTV, *Her Home and Garden Television*.

She asks, "Do you two have everything you need?"

"Absolutely not," Samueldarrin says. "We need you here with us to help interpret your grandfather's vision."

She blushes. "I'm not a cinematic visionary like you two are. The home theater is down that hall. Enjoy!"

For all his smugness, Samueldarrin hasn't actually ever handled celluloid. Neither have I. We can't afford to scratch, tear, or damage the film, but Vancott's workprint has to be mounted and threaded through a projector that looks ready to mangle our fingers. After two hours and some serious online research we get the movie running. For one brief, shining moment, the frames and images flicker against the screen. For the first time in sixty years, *The Ginger Star* lives.

The bulb pops and goes dark.

"I hope he packed a spare," Samueldarrin mutters.

Up above us, Ms. Rawley bangs away with her hammer.

It takes us until midnight to change the bulb (glass!), get the film loaded properly (somehow we mounted it upside down), and the sound synched (because I'm sure the actors are not supposed to be speaking backward). After that, we sit in Vancott's little home theater (oversized velvet chairs, surprisingly comfortable) that still smells, all these years later, of cigarette smoke.

"We need popcorn," I say.

Samueldarrin pulls out a silver flask and two paper cups. "Here's something better. A toast to *The Ginger Star!*"

Whiskey. It burns, but in a good way.

Above us, shimmering dust motes. The movie's story is unremarkable: a hero, a quest, an alien planet, adversity, obstacles, failures, triumphs. But after ten minutes it's obvious why the studio balked. Against what had to be enormous social pressure, Kershner was faithful to Brackett's vision of a dark-skinned hero. There he is on the screen, Eric John Stark, steely-eyed and the same color as I am.

Samueldarrin leans forward. "That's Cleavon Little! He bulked up a lot."

"Who?"

"Starred in *Blazing Saddles*."

"Never heard of it."

"It's on the Red List."

It figures that Samueldarrin would have seen a film specifically banned for unforgivable misogyny. "Was he any good?"

"He was great. But only one major success, really. He died when he was fifty or so." Samueldarrin rummages through one of the boxes of notes. "Where's that cast list?"

Stark's adventure takes place on the planet Pax, which unsurprisingly looks like California's Santa Monica mountains. The heroine is a priestess named Gerrith, who in the original work had "bronzy" skin. Here, that means a white woman with a lot of paint on her. Samueldarrin comes up with the actor's name: Jenny Harris. Neither of us has ever heard of her. She's wearing a skimpy outfit, as most science fiction priestesses did, and a ridiculous hairstyle. In scene after scene, she gazes adoringly at Stark like a lovestruck puppy.

The rough cut ends before the climactic sequence where Stark faces down the enormous fanged beasts known as Northhounds and becomes their leader. Given the limits of 1970s technology, I can't imagine how Kershner filmed the Northhounds. Green screen? Cloth puppets? Maybe little pieces of clay in stop-animation. How sad those days were.

"Let's watch it again," Samueldarrin says. "Another toast!"

More whiskey doesn't improve the viewing. The sound is untreated and entirely missing in some scenes, with chunks of dialogue absent. There are no titles, composites, or graphics. There are some crude special effects, including plastic models dangling by wires. Some scenes are too long and others too short. But there's potential here. Once the cut is digitized, I can rework it into the story of Gerrith, a mercenary-priestess who agrees to help a handsome but inept offworlder. She'll defeat the Northhounds through feminine wisdom instead of brute strength. The original was limited by analog editing and masculine prejudice. My reconstruction will make Gerrith shine.

"Damn straight," Samueldarrin says, after I blurt out my best ideas. "Here, have another drink."

Toasting to the future success of *The Ginger Star* is the last thing I remember.

I wake up several hours later to a strange humming-clacking noise. My tongue is all fuzzy, my neck hurts from hours of being cricked, and there's a pounding in my skull that I blame entirely on Samueldarrin.

"She lives!" he says when I emerge from the home theater. He's bent over the KEM, cheerfully and completely destroying the film stock. I might hyperventilate. Sixty-year-old celluloid in little curled snips on the floor—

I flip off the power switch. "What the hell are you doing?"

"Editing!"

"Are you crazy? You can't just cut it up without giving me a chance, too!"

He gives me a hurt look. "You think I'm completely unethical? Vancott made two extra sets of everything. You'll get your own chance to play."

Play. As if *The Ginger Star* is a toy. And maybe to him and other men, stories are just toys that you pick up and play with and disregard when they're no longer amusing. But to Sibilia and me, stories mean more than that. Stories taught women courage when we felt isolated and alone, when we were told we were inconsequential and incompetent. Stories helped us unite and grab the power that men wouldn't give us. Stories teach us not only how the world is, but how it should be.

I glower at him. "You got me drunk on purpose so you could get a jump start."

"Don't blame me if you can't hold your booze," he says sharply. "You're a grown woman capable of making your own decisions. I'm not your father or patriarch or oppressor just because I shared my whiskey with you."

I stomp upstairs. The flying squirrels give me a baleful look from their perches above their cage. Being male, of course they're taking Samueldarrin's side. Ms. Rawley is on the kitchen floor again, sawdust clinging to her skin, mouth set in a purposeful line. About half of the new boards are in place, while the rest are propped against the counters.

"Ah, there you are, Adeline Lynn," she says, glancing upward.

"It's me, Ms. Rawley. Minervadiane."

She doesn't even blink. "Of course you are. There's leftover chili and biscuits in the oven. Help yourself."

Adeline Lynn Fagins was part of my senior project, *Heroines of the Reel Revolution*. She was the first female director to break through the Hollywood gender ceiling into blockbuster success. Sure, there'd been pioneers like Jane Campion, Sofia Coppola, and Kathryn Bigelow. But Adeline came along with her vision and imagination and brought millions of people back to the public theaters they'd long ago abandoned. She scored success after success until finally the male-dominated Academy of Motion Picture Arts and Sciences could ignore her no longer. Finlay Vancott was her editor on several early projects. It's possible that Adeline visited this house and that Ms. Rawley met her as a child. That Adeline walked this floor that Ms. Rawley is ripping up and replacing.

Or maybe Adeline is another flying squirrel. It's hard to tell.

I crouch down. "I wish you'd let me help you."

She leans back for a brief rest. "Young lady, I've been fixing this house since before you were born. What do I need help for? My father taught me everything I needed to know. These are his tools and his nails. When I'm too old to swing this hammer, I'll be too old to breathe."

I sit down beside her. "May I ask you something? Do you remember what I do?"

She gazes at me for a long moment, making mental guesses. Finally she comes up with the correct answer. "You edit films. I remember that movie you redid. Sweet young Drew Barrymore and her friend *E.T.*"

"And you want me to edit your grandfather's movie. But you know that I'd have to reshape it in a way that he might never approve of, right?"

Ms. Rawley picks up a nail and turns it over between her wrinkled fingers. "I know that if you did it for your agency, you'd surely have to make Gerrith the star of the story. But I don't intend to sell it to the government."

"You don't?" I can just imagine what Sibilia's going to say about that. "Then why am I here?"

"Because your work is lovely, Minervadiane," Ms. Rawlings says. "You show a great understanding of character and scene, and how to bring a story together. My grandfather would have loved your work. If you follow your heart, you can make *The Ginger Star* the film he hoped it would be."

I'm flummoxed. "But I can't afford to buy it from you."

"I trust you to do it right," she says. "And if you do, I'll give it to you free and clear. To you, not the government."

She slides a nail into a pre-drilled hole and begins hammering again. "Of course, if that boy Ringo does it better, I'll give it to him instead."

The heroine faces a crisis of conscience and ethics: it's part of every good story.

During the middle of the day, when all reasonable people are sleeping and avoiding the sun, I knock on Sameuldarrin's door.

"I'm asleep," he calls out.

"You just came upstairs," I reply, trying to keep my voice quiet. Ms. Rawley's room is only a few doors away. "Open up."

After a moment, he cracks the door open. He's got dark circles under his eyes and is rubbing one shoulder, all stiff from hunching over the KEM for so long. Behind him is a bedroom as overstuffed with furniture as mine: there's a wooden four-poster bed, two cherry bureaus, an oak secretary desk with a matching chair, a grandfather clock that doesn't tick, and a freestanding wardrobe overflowing with clothes.

"What do you want?" Samueldarrin asks.

Sometimes it's best to rip the bandage off the wound without preamble. "I apologize for implying you got me drunk."

"It wasn't an implication. Implications are subtle and veiled. You flat out accused me—"

"I apologize for accusing you," I say, quickly, before he starts a long lecture. "I was wrong."

He leans against the doorframe. In the low light from an Oriental lamp, with his bangs unruly on his forehead and dimples in both cheeks, he looks just like he did back when he won the Golden Doorknob Award. Every Film 101 student at Ithaca College was and still is required to write, shoot, and edit a three-minute film about how a doorknob kills a person. It's a test of imagination and wit. His project was the best I'd ever seen, or have ever seen since.

"I accept your apology," he says.

And maybe it's been a while since my last relationship, or maybe I still admire his work, or maybe he's just so ridiculously handsome that any woman my age would invite him to sex, but suddenly I'm imagining us in that four-poster bed. If we're quiet we won't wake Ms. Rawley or the squirrels. I can forgive, or at least temporarily forget, that he's the face and voice of the patriarchy, and that he mocks my life's work, and that if he had his way, every movie would end with a male hero carrying a woman up a staircase despite her protests.

He tilts his head and says, "You know, that's the first time you've ever apologized to me for anything, Minnie. A guy could get used to that."

We do not end up in bed together.

In classic films, action progresses either through scenes or montages. A scene puts the action in front of the viewer in more or less "real time." A montage condenses several action points into a sequence edited for maximum impact, usually to music. If I were to use a montage to represent the work that Samueldarrin and I did over the next few days, I'd put it to a classic song of the revolution by the iconic Annie Oakley: "Anything You Can Do, I Can Do Better." The montage might look like this:

Shot of Samueldarrin confidently splicing film.

Shot of Minervadiane studying the storyboards thoughtfully.

Shot of Samueldarrin congratulating himself on another excellent splice.

Shot of Minervadiane studying Vancott's cut again, frowning.

Shot of Samueldarrin giving himself a fist pump for another great splice. Such a dork.

Shot of Minervadiane in bed, pulling her pillow over her head.

When I call the office, Ann tells me that Ms. Rawley has no living relatives. The actors in the film died childless, and Kershner's descendants have gone missing in the floods.

"How's *The Ginger Star* coming?" she asks. "Everyone here is really excited to see it."

"It's fine," I lie. "What have you been doing to *The Matrix?*"

"Nothing you won't like," she says, but in the background the Oracle is telling Trinity there's a difference between knowing a path and walking it.

I hang up and blame all my current woes on Cleavon Little.

Alone in my room, I'd downloaded and watched *Blazing Saddles*. No wonder it's on the Red List! Rape jokes. More rape jokes. The completely unrealistic portrayal of a frontier entertainer's life in the Old West. Poor Madeline Kahn, forced to strut around in corsets and follow the dictates of Harvey Korman. But there's Cleavon Little, bringing wit and panache to his role as the first black sheriff of Rock Ridge, just as he exudes power and strength as Eric John Stark.

If I rebuild *The Ginger Star* with Gerrith as the lead, Cleavon Little will never be recognized as the first black man to star as the lead of a science fiction film. History will instead continue to give that honor to Will Smith, even though *Independence Day* is now the story of a stripper and a First Lady teaming up to defeat alien invaders.

Surely I'm tough enough to rob a dead man of his legacy, but even with the Steenbeck threaded and the celluloid waiting for its razor cuts, I can't do it.

"You going to edit that film or just keep staring at it?" Samueldarrin asks at midnight, as one of his spools runs out.

"I'm editing it in my head."

"Excellent plan. Tell me when you invent a telepathic projector." He leans back confidently. "Want to see my cut?"

"No."

"I'd love your feedback."

"Why would I give you feedback?"

"Because we're both in it for the love of movies," he says. "So what if you mangle great classics to appease your feminist dictators and I write appallingly bad parodies just for the attention? We've both got the Hollywood bug."

"Hollywood has been underwater for decades," I remind him.

"Come on, Min," he wheedles. "Watch my movie and tell me how wrong I am."

He loads up the projector and we sit in those velvet seats and damn if he hasn't done something brilliant. The sound is still splotchy and the dialogue will need to be looped, but Stark's search for his mentor is now a mythic quest. Yes, it's the story of a man exhibiting all of the stubborn, violent, pigheaded tendencies of men, but beneath the stoicism lurks sorrow and loss. Gerrith is no longer the token woman, but instead a fully-fledged character. Jenny Harris fills the screen with a calm wisdom. She is truly a goddess: smart, sensual, powerful. The Northhounds are as crude as I feared, but Samueldarrin establishes fear and it takes both Gerrith and Stark to defeat them. Partners.

The film runs out. I don't know what to say.

"Do you like it?" Samueldarrin asks softly. "I made it for you."

I turn to him. There's nothing fake about his expression in the glow from the screen. Nothing that reminds me how maddening and ridiculous he can be, or how he's the same man who turned *Buffy the Vampire Slayer* into *Xander Harris, Superhero.*

Cue the romantic music.

"I guess it's good," I admit. "Maybe your best work ever, Ringo."

Close up on the impending kiss. Our hero and heroine grow closer, gazes locked, mouths parting slightly, as all the wasted years evaporate and love blooms again.

"Call me Samueldarrin," he says as our lips meet.

Then, a sound effect: a shrieking fire alarm.

The house is on fire.

"It was the toaster," a purple-headed firefighter says to a police officer. "Someone put it under the broiler."

The fire's out, though thin gray smoke continues to waft toward the night-time sky. Ms. Rawley is sitting on a bench, entirely unharmed but enjoying the attention of a handsome young paramedic. I'm waiting, stomach and fist clenched, on news of Samueldarrin. After the alarm went off, he and I rushed upstairs to help Ms. Rawley evacuate. All three of us made it outside safely. But then she said, "My babies, my babies!" and he dashed back inside to save the flying squirrels.

"Excuse me," I say to the firefighter with purple hair. "What about Mr. Cross?"

"Ringo Cross?" she asks. "The filmmaker? I love his work."

"He went back inside for her pet squirrels."

Another firefighter says, "The squirrels are on the back lawn."

I go investigate for myself. Mike and Ike look grumpy in their cage but have no singes or burns. Goosebumps rising, I step past the lingering emergency personnel into the house. In the days when firefighters used water, there'd have been flooding everywhere. The film stock would have been destroyed, along with everything else we'd taken out of the vault. As it is, the suppression foam has already dried out and Vancott's memorabilia is unharmed.

But *The Ginger Star* is missing. Every single reel.

My phone beeps with a message. It says, "Dear Min, she gave the film to me. Come to the premiere! You'll be my red carpet guest."

When I burst back outside, ready to kill him, the purple-haired firefighter says, "You just missed your friend," and Ms. Rawley's car is gone.

"Don't take it too hard," Ms. Rawley says, patting the bench beside her. "He's an exceptionally gifted editor."

"You saw the movie?" I demand.

"He finished it this morning, but he was nervous about asking you to watch it."

I slump on the bench. "He's a big giant jerk."

"Maybe," she says. "But I don't think your story's over just yet."

Here's another fact about classic filmmaking: studios back then were appallingly reliant on sequels. So far I've had to fix *Women in Black I, II, III,* and *IV.* I'll be busy for years rebuilding all the *Superwoman*, *Spider-Woman*, and *X-Women* movies. Let's not even get started on the years of my life the *Transformers* franchise will suck away. But the point is, people in those days loved to see familiar characters and situations over and over. They filled theater seats and then bought home copies and then went to see the next sequel, even if it was terrible.

But that was then and this is now. Today it takes a lot more to hook an audience.

"I don't think Samueldarrin and I have a sequel in our future," I tell Ms. Rawley.

"Let me tell you about the other movie footage my grandfather saved," she replies, and I'm hooked.

THE GOVERNESS AND THE LOBSTER

MARGARET RONALD

Dear Matron Jenkins,

For the record, I want you to know that the mechanical lobster is not my fault. I had only the best intentions when I asked the Cromwell children to deliver my initial report to the mail depot, and I did not learn about their addition to my package until recently.

I am sending this note by express post in hopes that it reaches you in time—though at this point, I'm not sure what would qualify as "in time." Before the regular post arrives? Before the lobster winds down? Before we had ever received M. Eutropius' misleading request? I do not know, and I fear that I will go mad long before I can make a guess.

But for the record, the mechanical lobster is not my doing. I owe you much, but at the moment that is all I can give you.

Yours,

—Rosalie Syme

Rosalie:

Your note arrived well in advance of the regular post, and as a result I'm still in the dark. I've heard nothing of a lobster, nor is there any news of a disaster there in Harkuma. As a result I must conclude that you are overreacting. Pull your stockings up and remember that I chose you for a reason.

And frankly, the only thing you owe me is the starter money for the school. The current state of affairs between Imperial interests and the Hundred Cities is tenuous at best, and I will not have an opportunity to found a branch of the Jenkins School squandered. If you have come to the conclusion that such a school is impossible, then send the money under separate cover, registered mail. I shouldn't have to tell you this.

—E. Jenkins (Matron)

• • •

Dear Matron Jenkins,

I apologize for my earlier note, as well as for the panicky tone of my initial report. I would assume that by now you have received it, save for the fact that the Cromwell children have taken some delight in demonstrating just how destructive their toys can be when fully wound.

I'm afraid my first impression of Harkuma lived up to the worst assertions of the yellow broadsheets back home. The Hundred Cities as a whole may be quite civilized, but Harkuma is not technically one of them, and its inferior status is made worse by the constant dust storms. (I am given to understand that Harkuma's elder sister city, Akkuma, is similarly plagued, but the automata of that city have safeguards in place against damage from the storms.) The mark of Imperial commerce is quite present, though, as the architecture of Cromwell House proves, ~~as does my presence, I suppose, since Cromwell and Eutropius~~

I'm sorry. I get ahead of myself, and my circumstances are not conducive to concentration.

What is markedly odd is that despite all this, Harkuma reminds me of my home in the warehouse district. (I do beg your pardon, Matron, for reminding you of this fact.) The constant chaos is not so far off from what the Staves dealt with, although there is a different flavor to it that I cannot yet put into words.

Of the human population, I cannot begin to find a commonality. In the five minutes I paused at the train station, I saw four Lower Kingdom officials in state dress, two Terranoctan soldiers (or so I assume from their scythes), a Svete-Kulap clanmerchant suffering a bad case of sunburn, and a Lucan noblewoman with her interpreter. To complicate matters, the automata of Akkuma travel freely within this satellite city, and their clattering speech rings out at all hours.

Unfortunately, the cavalier attitude of the Hundred Cities to the association of automaton and human borders on the reckless. After the officials had carefully evicted the human passengers and inspected the train so that it might pass on to Akkuma, I saw a young man of shifty appearance helping a woman who could not have been younger than ninety onto the last car. The Akkuma train runs at such infrequent intervals that human visitors must bring twice their own weight in water, Matron, and yet this young man packed her onto the train with nothing more than a bag. ~~I cannot~~

I have taken a moment to collect myself and remove the canister of spiders that the eldest Cromwell child, Natalya, has placed on my bedside table.

As you recall—and as I wish to stress, given that my assignment has proven so radically different—I was to undertake the education of the Cromwell children. Mr. Cromwell was somewhat lax in hiring a governess after their mother's passing several years ago, but his business partner M. Eutropius, currently the children's legal guardian, contacted the Jenkins School immediately following Mr. Cromwell's last illness. While all of this is technically true, the omissions are crippling enough to question whether our contract is even valid.

The problems began nearly as soon as I arrived at Cromwell House. The house was built in both the Harkuma style and that of a northern manor-house, keeping the worst features of each. The lower floors are open and high-ceilinged, but the upper reaches are quite dark and cramped, giving one a choice of agoraphobia or claustrophobia. It did not help that when I first arrived I had to search for a good fifteen minutes before finding anyone, and the housemaid who answered seemed to not know her way around at all, having been here only one week. As I write this, she has already left, hired off to a financier bound for Bis-Nocta. Her successor has also given notice.

The next problem to present itself was the matter of the children them-selves. Though Eutropius' letter seemed to indicate that they were already on a course of education, it seems that their father let them run amok. Natalya, at eleven years, has some authority over the other three but chooses to exercise it only to prevent interfamilial fights. Irra (nine) is as elusive as a swamp-light and as omnipresent, at least until she is noticed, and her brother Serge (six) seems to delight in loudly pointing her out and causing her to flee. The youngest, Sulla (five), would much rather communicate in gestures and what I believe is a poor approximation of automaton-speech.

Matron, these are not students, even by the standards of the warehouse district scholarship initiative (and believe me, I am well aware of the irony in my saying this). They are a project.

I did not see my employer until that evening, having spent much of my time in an attempt to introduce myself to the children (and, as I've mentioned, sending out my initial report plus lobster). Natalya was the one who found me trying to coax Irra out of hiding. "Uncle wants to see you," she told me, and handed me the first of the many canisters of spiders. I consider it a small victory that I did not scream and fling the lot away.

The lower halls of Cromwell House—the high arches, the red clay walls, the tracings in the floor meant for those automata guests who run on wheels—are particularly uncanny in shadow. (If you remember the Gymnasium Specter incident at the School, I believe you will understand why.) The lamps were unlit, and only the glow of fires outside illuminated the hall. I made my way to the foot of the stairs, clinging to the wall for guidance. "Mr. Eutropius?" I called, expecting at any moment Irra and Serge to jump out at me. "Sir?"

"I am here," said a cultured bass voice from somewhere to my right. It was the sort of voice to rattle pebbles in dust, and I confess I shivered at the sound of it.

You have trained me well, though, and mindful of your constant admonitions, I pulled myself upright. "I am Rosalie Syme, of the Jenkins School. You engaged me to educate the Cromwell children."

"So I did." A clank and drag sounded from the darkness, followed by a brief flare: werglass, glowing as thaumic power moved through it. "Come to me if you have need of anything. I have been quite busy in the wake of poor Edgar's death, but I can certainly spare time for the children."

"That's kind of you, sir," I said. "Sir—how will I know you, if I need to find you?"

At this there was a creak and a dull thrum, as of an engine catching somewhere in the house. "My apologies. I forgot you do not see as I do. In Edgar's absence, I forget myself."

A dial spun close to my elbow. At the far end of the hall, the lamps flickered and caught, one by one, illuminating the great shape standing far too close, the inlay of gold on steel, the eight long segmented legs unfolding as he approached, the central spire of a body and the werglass ring of eyes.

Eutropius is an automaton.

You have hired me to an automaton.

Matron Jenkins, please call me home.

Yours,

—Rosalie Syme

Rosalie:

I will do no such thing. While I admit Eutropius' nature is startling, that does not in any way change our contract. Remember: I would not have sent you if I did not believe you fully capable, and certainly more so than our non-scholarship students. Now wipe your nose and get back in the fray before I relegate you to that list of fainting nellies.

And why would I mind your comments regarding the warehouse district? Do you think me ignorant of my students' backgrounds?

As a side note, the lobster has arrived, along with the remnants of the post. I currently have it caged on my desk. How long does it take to wind down?

—E. Jenkins (Matron)

Dear Matron Jenkins,

Yes, of course you're right. My apologies.

I've since acclimated a little, although it is difficult to look out on the low flat roofs of the city and not be reminded of the warehouse district. I confess I did not expect my childhood to find me here of all places. (Though I would like to stress again that my days in the Staves are well behind me, and in any case the rooftops here are too unfamiliar for me to consider similar activities. I think I've lost the knack, anyway.)

Harkuma is a very strange place. Its entire business revolves around what is not present: Akkuma and the gems mined there, as well as the various homes of the trade delegations who make those gems their business. Few of the automata here even treat it as home; Eutropius is Transit-born and considers himself a native of the Glasswalk, and many of those I see during the day return to Akkuma regularly.

It's perhaps no surprise that the Cromwell children are so distracted. I've abandoned the classroom setting and have adopted a peripatetic method of teaching, which has improved their attitude toward me somewhat. Natalya, in particular, has begun to warm to me so long as I assist her in the kitchen, the position of cook being another that has high turnover. She has even taught me several of the recipes for the dinners the children usually share when no cook is engaged. (Sweet pudding is, unfortunately, at the top of the list. Fresh greens will no doubt be difficult to introduce.)

Far be it from me to speak ill of the dead, but it seems that the late Edgar Cromwell was one of those people who, after amassing a family, don't really seem to know what to do with it. Under his wife's supervision, all was well, but judging by some remarks from Natalya and Eutropius, his attitude was always one of benign neglect. Neglect remains neglect, though.

Eutropius does deeply care about the children, and it is quite something to see them swarm over their "uncle." Irra in particular reliably comes out of hiding only in his presence, and Serge cannot be quieted. Apparently he has also taught them some small practical skills; the mechanical lobster, as well as several of their other toys, is the children's own work, built under his tutelage. (According to him, the lobster should wind down in a matter of weeks, depending on how much it has consumed. I've enclosed a key, should you care to deploy it in faculty meetings.) Eutropius, though, is aware that his skill in childrearing is limited, and so it seems that he engaged help well before Cromwell even fell ill, though I must confess I was startled at his other employees.

Specifically, the same shifty-looking young man who I saw sending the poor old woman off on the Akkuma train is in Eutropius' employ. He arrived as I was in the midst of showing Natalya how to scrub out the cookpots. Sulla, who had been hanging onto my skirt for the last half hour, was the first to notice him. "Pietro," she said, giving me an emphatic tug.

"Pietro?" I stood to see the young man lounging in the doorway as if he belonged there. "Who—"

Sulla, however, did not hesitate. "Pietro, this is Rosie," she said, for the first time lacking the stutter that she carries from attempting to imitate automata.

"Rosie?" He tipped his cap to me—a gesture straight off the streets of the Capitol, and one extraordinarily strange coming from a man dressed in the heavily-embroidered jacket and bands of the Hundred Cities, not to mention his short beard and shaven head. "A pleasure, miss," he went on, his Imperial only barely accented.

"Likewise," I said, attempting to regain what dignity I could while up to my elbows in filthy suds.

Pietro smiled, exposing one canine tooth that had been replaced with steel. Before he could say more, Serge practically jumped onto him, demanding to know if "Grandma Lyle" was back. The most I could gather from the ensuing chaos was that Pietro was a frequent visitor to the house and often advised Eutropius on how best to take care of the children (including my hiring), and that this was part of his profession.

What that profession might be, I would hesitate to explain had you not explicitly stated that you are unconcerned with my history. Pietro is what the many travelers through Harkuma refer to as a *facilis* or, commonly, "greaser." He makes his living by arranging contact between the various human merchants and the automata of Akkuma. If a person wishes to visit Akkuma, he must do so in the company of one of these *faciles* who will vouch for him, undertake the shipment of water, even make business connections, as well as monitor the entrepreneur's movements within the city and make certain that he adheres to all standards of conduct.

To maintain their positions, these faciles must keep credibility with both sides. A human client who attempted to suborn an automaton or hide in the city would be as damaging to a facilis' credibility as an attempt on that same human's life by one of the more militant automata sects.

The practice of trading on such an ephemeral thing as reputation seemed at first incomprehensible, until I remembered how the Staves used to deal with the other "confraternities," as you have always referred to them. We did not have the faciles, but we did have our own go-betweens, particularly in regards to selling goods of questionable ownership. In fact, I played a similar role between the Staves and the Redfingers (who ran on the Gestenwerke side of the district) up to the point where I was handed over to the Jenkins School.

Regarding the satellite school, I have made some minor inquiries, but the first officials I contacted had been reassigned by the time I made a follow-up visit. I will make another attempt, but at the moment I have enough on my hands with the Cromwell children. Sulla has taken to creeping into my room and falling asleep on my bed—in fact, she is there now, and once this letter is complete I will put another blanket over her. Sadly, the frequency of spider canisters has increased (and now diversified into centipedes) even as Natalya and I seem to have connected in our mutual scullionship.

Courteous as my employer is with the children, his nighttime pursuits are distressing to say the least. Every few nights, a din emerges from the lower reaches, a noise that I can only compare to the clatter of tram cars paired with the whine of a malfunctioning drill. It is a pity, as the city is not lacking in charms, even if I am still shaking the dust out of my skirts every five minutes and cleaning it from every crevice before I sleep. Even when I have a full night's sleep, every day feels as if I am walking on an uneven surface. But you are right, Matron, and I have some experience walking unsteady paths.

Yours,

—Rosalie Syme

R:

That's my girl.

I've attached a list of names of former Jenkins School contacts; if your first endeavors are withering, perhaps this will spur a second round. Don't fuss so about a little noise; our new dormitory faces the forge district, and I can't imagine it's any worse than that.

—E. J. (M.)

Dear Matron Jenkins,

Sadly, not one of the people you name remains in Harkuma. It is as I said; this is a transient town, and few people stay for long. Even the automata do not linger.

I had some proof of that the other day, when I was taking Natalya and the children back from market again (Serge shows an aptitude for misdirection, which resulted in our first return trip to the market and a very grudging apology from him). I am not sure if I can adequately describe the scene we found on our return. The roads of Harkuma, though just as busy as Admiral Street or any other thoroughfare, are broad enough for automata to pass easily. One may pass by most altercations without even flicking one's skirt aside, regardless of their violence.

However, this particular altercation had blocked the entirety of the street. Two automata and a Lower Kingdom official, possibly one of those I saw on my arrival, were in heated disagreement. Of the automata, one had a very Imperial look to its construction—possibly a tram-car before its awakening— and as such, it was roughly the size of two dormitory rooms. The other was, I believe, City-born, one of the automata created and awakened among its fellows, and thus both smaller and less practically designed, perching on three delicate legs and shaking a fourth at the official and the tram-car. My knowledge of the Lower Kingdom dialects is flawed (you remember I had trouble with the inflections), but I was able to gather that some temporary business agreement had soured.

My first impulse was to shoo the children away, but you can guess how successful that was. My second was to move the five of us into the shelter of a nearby fruit-seller's stall and wait it out. I had no sooner done so than the shouting gave way to ominous silence, and Sulla caught her breath. "What is it?" I asked, picking her up.

"The big one called the little a—" and here she made a stuttering noise, an automata word that I am glad I do not know, judging by Natalya's hiss. "And the little one called the big one a man-scraper."

Just then the Lower Kingdom official declared that both automata were "unworthy of their metal." The automata turned to face him, and I covered Sulla's eyes. I saw plenty of tram accidents when I was in the Staves, and they are not healthy viewing for a five-year-old.

Before the man could be crushed, however, a tiny old woman made her way through the crowd. It took me a moment to recognize her as the same woman Pietro had put on the train to Akkuma, and by that point she had reached the side of the larger automaton. I could not hear what she said, but the tram-car settled back on its treads and the smaller automaton lowered its leg. Either one of them could easily have crushed her or even just set her aside, yet they remained still. The official attempted to interrupt her several times, but she raised one frail hand and he stopped as if confronted by a pikeman.

Around us, the commotion in the street returned to its usual state, and Sulla pushed away, wanting to be let down. Unfortunately, her buckles had become caught on my bodice, and by the time we'd untangled ourselves, the old woman had dismissed both the smaller automaton and the official and stayed to speak with the tram-car, one hand on its treads. (I should mention that many Transit-born automata do not like to be touched; it is, I believe, a reminder of their history as machines before awakening.) After a moment, they parted ways, and the little old woman turned back towards us.

"Grandma Lyle!" Serge shouted, echoed by Irra, and the two of them practically knocked her over. Natalya, Sulla, and I followed more slowly.

If I did not know better—and I am not yet certain that I do—I would say that Grandma Lyle has some Imperial ancestry, as despite her age and dress she does not resemble either the disparate humans of the Hundred Cities or the Terranoctans. She smiled at me as I reached Serge and Irra. "Rosie, I take it?"

"Yes," I managed, around Sulla's chatter. "Forgive me for asking, but are you a facilis?"

Her eyes crinkled up at the corners, and she nodded. "One of the first. As are most of my family." She gestured after the tram-car, which had trundled most of the way to the alarm tower by now. "Poor #41 doesn't like being left out of the loop, and she's returning to Akkuma tomorrow, so she saw this as the last chance to clear matters up."

Sulla asked her something that I could not catch, as the last few words were automaton-speech, and though Lyle responded in Imperial, I did not understand one word in five. Terms such as "sand-ogre," "Rimarri banner," and "fourpoint" must have meant something to the children, who listened avidly and nodded along. "So it *was* a business disagreement?" I tried.

"No," Irra said, and immediately tried to hide behind her brother.

"Of a sort," Lyle corrected. "Business covers a number of matters for City-born, and more for Transit-born. And of course the Lower Kingdoms like to think they know all about automata, so it's hard to convince them otherwise."

Do you remember when I gave my first presentation in class, on the political structure of the warehouse district, and got an entire classroom full of glazed looks? I now understand what it's like from the other side. "This happens often?"

"This is Harkuma." Ruffling Irra's hair, she smiled at me. "Pietro tells me you are doing well."

"I—yes." I have seen quite a bit more of Pietro since our introduction, though I must question his business acumen, since he's missed appointments more than once due to his habit of hanging around Cromwell House.

"Good. I'll send some books along with him." She bowed again, in the formal Lower Kingdom style. "I have work at the far end of the city, but I hope to see you again. And Serge, you should return those plums."

True to her words, Serge had taken another handful from the fruit stall while we were watching the conflict, and this meant another unwilling apology and a long talk all the way back to Cromwell House.

Despite such setbacks, the children are starting to learn, although their knowledge of geography is absolutely terrible. I asked Irra to point to Svete-Kulap, and she ignored the map entirely and pointed east, which is nearly one hundred and twenty degrees off. Once they finally made the connection between map and directions, they took to it with alacrity, even if Sulla still cannot quite pronounce the names properly. Pietro brought us a copy of *Atlas of the Clockwork Cities*—the new edition, by C. and S. Vallom—and Serge can barely be parted from it for a moment.

Incidentally, Natalya has quite surprised me. She is as quick and intelligent as ~~any of the Staves' thiefmasters~~ any Jenkins School valedictorian, and teaching her is an enjoyable challenge. It turns out the spiders were her way of welcome; the girl has a passion for studying arthropods, and I suspect the mechanical lobster was mainly her work. I would like to recommend her for the Royal Society when she's of age, since if she's not given enough of a challenge she is likely to make one of her own.

Yours,

—Rosalie

R:

I'd rather not lose more of our students to the Society, but as it's unlikely we could bring Natalya here without causing more trouble for the Cromwell children, I'll consider it.

I can't help noticing that your letters still say nothing concrete about the potential for a Jenkins School. Is there a chance of founding one or not? This is not a difficult question.

—E.J. (M.)

Dear Matron Jenkins,

It might not be a difficult question in a place like the warehouse district, where despite the many "confraternities" we all knew where we'd go at the end of the day. But Harkuma is not an Imperial city, and its shifting population makes the question much more troubling.

I have, however, sought out more information on the subject. At my request, Pietro took us to visit his grandmother yesterday. The children pounced on her as soon as we reached the door, which she bore with better grace than many of my classmates would have demonstrated, and I was left to help Pietro with the dust shutters (the storm season has begun in earnest, leaving me wondering what life was like before grit accumulated in every part of my wardrobe).

Grandma Lyle's house is unusual even for the mishmash of architecture that makes up Harkuma. It is old—so old the red brick has faded to rose. Few structures in Harkuma have been in place for more than a decade, but I found myself marveling at the tiles set into the clay that showed the tarnish of time. "So old," I said as we entered, mostly to myself.

"Rosie!" Pietro said reprovingly, and I looked up, remembering a little too late that I really should inform him of my preferred address.

"She means the house, Pietro, not me." Grandma Lyle closed another of the dust shutters. "It was built when Harkuma wasn't much more than a well and a rail depot." She turned to her grandson and nodded to the next room, where the children were arguing over some many-jointed toy. Obediently, he joined them, I assumed to keep them from tearing the toy apart. "Come," she said to me. "Sit."

"Thank you," I said. "I hope we're not imposing on your hospitality."

"Not in the least." She smiled and settled into a worn chair in front of what

I belatedly recognized as a writing-desk. A long case of oversized books stood beside it, as well as tools I'd last seen in our advanced mathematics classes. "As it is, your timing is good; I've only just returned from Akkuma."

"Akkuma? But—" Of course; as a facilis, she would travel between the two, which would explain why she had been the lone human passenger on that train. "It must be a difficult journey."

"I have an old friend there," she said, still smiling. "We share an interest in cartography. These days, I split my time between the two cities. Sit, please."

I did so, pulling a stool to the high table. Through the door, Natalya had begun to inspect the little toy with, I suspected, an eye toward copying it, while Serge had dragged out the *Atlas* and was flipping through it to show Pietro something.

"Pietro tells me," she went on, "that you wish to build a school here. Do you understand what that would mean?" She raised one hand to the wall behind her desk, where a metal disc had been set into the clay like a talisman.

I did have the whole speech prepared, Matron, I promise you that. But the words seemed to slide away from me. "I'm not sure," I told her. "I know what it meant for me, when I lived in the warehouse district." Lyle raised one white brow, but did not speak. "For me it was a step up, a hand helping me off an unsteady walkway—but there are so few children in Harkuma, and so many of them are only here for months at a time. What good would a school be for them?"

"You might be surprised. And the children are not the only ones here." She touched the disc again, and in the slanting light I could make out the design that had once been stamped there: a rodent of some kind, turning back to regard its stump of a tail. "There have always been people who shuttled between worlds."

I thought of the friends I had left in the Staves when I was given to the Jenkins School—and yet I have never regretted the change.

Lyle gestured to her desk. "I traveled for quite some time, as did my friend in Akkuma. As did my husband, before we met. Harkuma was very small in those days, but even then, we kept returning here." She rose to her feet again. "Come. I'll show you some of our work."

I'm afraid all thoughts of the Jenkins School fled while we examined her work. Serge eventually joined us to examine the number of maps Lyle and her family had created over the years. It was quite possibly the most peaceful afternoon I've had since stepping off of the train.

So there is one opinion on the viability of a Jenkins School in Harkuma: open to the possibility, if not entirely wholehearted. Though I suspect her position as facilis gives Lyle a perspective that few share. I can't help but think the faciles would be instrumental for the foundation of ~~any school~~ a Jenkins School.

—Rosalie

R:

Let me be perfectly clear about this: I am not asking for everyone else's opinion of a Jenkins School in Harkuma, regardless of how old their houses are. I am asking for *your* opinion. I would hate to think that I had made the wrong choice in selecting you for this work.

—E.J. (M.)

dere Matron Jankins,

if YOU tak our ROSIE away we will send Fiftene LOBTSTERS to your mailbox and they willEAT ALL YOUR MAIL. Do NOT tak ROSIE back we liek her here and she lieks it here TO.

also send one ~~hundrud~~ THOUSND gold Bulls to this Adress or maybee we will send the lobtsters ENNIWAY.

sinserely yours,

—YOULL NEVER CATCH US

To the Cromwell Children:

I have enclosed your "ransom note" with corrections made in red. You will make those corrections, copy out the result ten times apiece, and return the copies to Miss Syme. In future, if you intend to threaten anyone, you have no excuse for doing so ungrammatically.

Also, your lobster is currently on my desk. I rather like it. Miss Syme tells me this is your work; if so, well done.

—Emma Jenkins

R:

What in the world is going on out there? And why haven't you gotten to basic spelling and grammar with these children?

—E. J (M.)

Dear Matron Jenkins,

I do apologize for the note, as well as for their spelling. Irra has apparently decided that poor spelling is intimidating, and I have yet to convince her otherwise. I believe Natalya allowed the letter to be written solely to comfort Serge and Sulla, for which I cannot really blame her.

Their concern springs from a failure on my part, and one I am ashamed to relate. Several nights ago, Eutropius held yet another social for his business contacts. I would have simply put the pillow over my head and endured the noise had it not been that we have entered the storm season, and for the past two nights the rattle of sand against my shutters had kept me awake. I left Sulla curled up on my bed and descended to the lower reaches of the house.

I am not certain what I expected to find—although my classmates would probably have whispered about some form of mechanical debauchery, I doubt they would know such if it were presented on a platter. The werglass fixtures of the house were lit, as were several of the lamps, and by their weak light I found my way to the same great chamber where I had first met Eutropius.

Five automata, ranging from a lacy creature very like a transplanted sea animal to a hulking thing created from barrels and treads, stood in a semi-circle in the center of the room. Eutropius' scorpionlike angularity perched in the middle, and he seemed to be the one in charge: though each continued in either screech or drone or arrhythmic clank, he was the one who gestured to each in time, much as a conductor does before an orchestra.

"Fascinating, yes?" I turned to see Pietro, who had been standing just at the edge of the lamplight. "I don't quite have the ear for it, but it's still amazing to hear them practice."

"Practice?" I shivered, looking from him to Eutropius and back. "This is practice for something?"

"Of course." He shed his jacket and draped it around my shoulders. "Automata music. Although it's not so much practice as a friendly concert, say. Like singing with one's family."

As I watched, a pattern seemed to accrete around Eutropius' movements: percussive, devoid of melody, and yet with a strangely harmonious result, like a mathematical formula drawn in calligraphy. I shook my head, too weary to either make sense of the sound or reject his loan of the jacket. "But this isn't music. This is noise."

Abruptly Eutropius' gears clattered to a halt, and the noise stopped, leaving only a deafening echo. "Noise, is it?" he said without turning. His voice, so close to human, seemed all the more artificial now. "And what would you have to say about noise?"

Pietro started to shake his head, but I let my exhaustion speak for me. "I—had hoped to ask you to quiet it. The house is so loud, and following the storms—"

"You ask me to quiet my friends?" Eutropius' central body rotated so that he faced me, and his legs unfolded from underneath. "In *my* house?"

Some time before I was given to the Jenkins School, I had the unfortunate experience of walking a roofline in winter and finding that several shingles retained a glaze of ice. I have never forgotten that sudden shock of my footing falling away. And yet then and now I had the same reaction: reach out for the first handhold and hope. "It was your partner's house as well," I said.

Eutropius went still, even the lights of his eyes going out, and I briefly thought he'd lost power, that his own life had stopped at the mention of his partner's. Instead he made a horribly discordant noise, and the other automata began to move, gliding or thumping their way to the door. I started to speak, but Pietro put his hand on my shoulder and shook his head.

For a moment the hall was silent—I would have said blessedly so only a few minutes earlier, but now it carried a hollowness that shivered through me.

Eutropius turned away. "Edgar," he said finally, "hated our music. He could not stand it, and so I only played on nights when he was in Akkuma, or trading in the Capitol. It—makes me miss him less, to play now. I can imagine he is only temporarily absent."

I caught my breath, stung by the pain in his automaton voice even as I knew it for a mechanical response. And yet there are Society doctors who claim that human pain is a mechanical response as well. "I'm sorry," I said.

"I should hope so," Eutropius said with a grinding noise almost like a laugh. "And I should threaten you with termination, for interrupting our music. Or if not for that, then for your little side project."

A chill ran down my spine, freezing me in place. "Project?" I said, as innocently as possible.

Not innocent enough. "Do you think I don't know that your matron sent you to found one of her staid, straitlaced schools here? At the very least this constitutes a foolish endeavor; at the worst, I'd consider it a strike against the Hundred Cities and all free automata. We have no need of a foothold of Imperial culture here."

"It's certainly not meant as such," I tried, but he would not hear me.

"In any other of the Hundred Cities, you would be scorned, but here you only look a fool. This is Harkuma, Miss Syme. No one is here because they want to be. No one belongs here. Edgar didn't, I don't, and the best we can do is continue." He shivered, or maybe that was the automaton way of shrugging. "Or perhaps I will simply inform the Jenkins School that you have proved unsuitable."

"I—" I would have defended myself, but the last few weeks have taken their toll. I have been a tolerable governess for the Cromwell children—but a governess is not a school, and Harkuma is larger than one house. I have failed in the task you set me, Matron, and taxed your patience in doing so.

"You are correct," I said.

"Am I, now? You finally think so?" He turned to regard me, werglass eyes flaring. "Take your silence and go."

Pietro shepherded me out of the hall, to the foot of the stairs. To my horror, the children were already there, even Sulla. Tears welled in my eyes as I saw them. "Thank you," I managed, shrugging Pietro's jacket away. "I am sorry."

"He won't write to her," he said. "Don't worry."

"Write, don't write, what does it matter?" I pressed both hands over my eyes. "Matron Jenkins—she has every right to call me home—" I caught myself before I could sound any more idiotic and hurried up the steps, Natalya and Irra parting before me.

It was an ill-chosen remark, and one I regretted once I had slept, but I believe it is what triggered the children's assumption that you were planning to take me away.

Yours,

—Rosalie

R:

No letter as yet from Eutropius.

—E.J. (M.)

Dear Matron Jenkins,

I have begun this letter twice over, and failed each time. It is perhaps emblematic of my greater failure: I cannot found a Jenkins School here.

Since you asked me outright for my opinion, I have been trying to decide what that opinion is. Finally, some nights ago, I'm afraid I reverted to old habit and crept out on my own. It turns out I have not lost the knack, and the rooftops of Harkuma are just as navigable as the warehouse district. You'll remember that I was given to doing this in my early days at the School; I believe it is how I first made your direct acquaintance. And it was what convinced me that I should remain at the Jenkins School, which is why I believed it would clarify my thoughts on this matter.

On the stormless nights—those without automata concerts, that is— Harkuma is quiet, and one can see almost as far as Akkuma's gleam across the desert. Each building is different, in the style of each owner's homeland, and yet I was able to keep my footing. Finally I found a spot on the roof of one of the shelters by the market, looking not toward the desert but back toward the city itself. It is a large city, for all that it pretends to be small and scattered.

For a long while I sat there, arms locked around my knees like Irra hearing a new story and hoping no one will notice her presence before the story ends, until a man's voice spoke. "Grandma told me I might find you here."

I turned to see Pietro carefully climbing across the next roof over. He smiled, a little nervously, and slid down beside me, nearly dislodging a tile as he did so. "Did she truly?" I asked.

"You'd be surprised at what Grandma Lyle can guess. Ask her sometime about her childhood." He joined me in silence for a moment, watching the slow gold line of the late-night train departing. "Did you believe him?" he asked finally. "About Harkuma?"

"Eutropius?" Pietro nodded. "I don't know. Nobody does seem to belong here, to be honest."

"And yet he stays," he said thoughtfully, "with his music and his business."

And his grief, I thought.

After a moment, Pietro sighed and draped his jacket over my shoulders in much the same way as before. "Well, it's not as though I can argue. I wasn't born here, but my mother was, and my aunt—they're both faciles in the other cities, maybe you'll meet them on their circuits—but I came back here. We do keep coming back."

"So Lyle said."

"She was the first, you know. She and her friend in Akkuma. The first faciles." He glanced at me, then away. "There aren't nearly enough of us. It's in the family, but there are only so many of us, and we're needed all over—" He shrugged. "Could always use more in the family."

I think my silence may have dampened whatever point he was trying to make. But his words had sparked a new line of thought for me and I was too busy following that to discern his motives. "You're right," I said at last, rising to my feet. "You're quite right."

"Am I?" He attempted to get up, slid, and settled for sitting upright.

"Oh, yes. But this will be complicated." I smiled at him, and he smiled back—despite the steel tooth, he has a perfectly nice smile when he's not trying to be charming. "I must return to Cromwell House at once."

I believe he would have walked me home, save that he is much less adept at the roofwalk than I, even given my years away from it. I still have his jacket, though, and have yet to return it with proper thanks.

Since then, I have come to an inescapable and unfortunate conclusion. Because of this, I am returning your investment. I have enclosed your initial startup funds for the Jenkins School under separate, registered cover. You may strike my name from the rolls of graduates if you like, or place me on the list of "nellies" you so often scorned.

My reason is thus: if I am to start a school here, then it cannot simply be a Jenkins School. It must be a Harkuma school, for all of those who shuttle between worlds or might hope to do so; a facilis for the faciles, and it must be more than I alone can create.

This is a risky endeavor, to say the least, and I know the Jenkins School's reputation would suffer from a satellite's failure, but whether this school succeeds cannot be dependent on the Jenkins name or even the Imperial tongue. I hope that this makes up in some way for what must be an unexpected betrayal.

I've contacted a number of potential teachers—linguists among the translation corps of automata, the Lucan noblewomen and their attendants, some of the Kulap exercise masters. (I have also asked Eutropius if he would consider teaching the specifics of automata music. I believe he was so startled by the question that he did not immediately consider the ramifications of his assent.)

So thank you, Matron, for sending me, and please know that I am more than grateful for all the Jenkins School has done for me. I hope I have not disappointed you.

—Rosalie Syme, of Harkuma

My dear Rosalie:

I regret to inform you that the children's mechanical lobster has devoured the registered cover for the funds you sent. As a result, there is no way I can officially return them to our books, and so I've written them off completely. I have no choice but to send the funds back to you, with my blessing.

Incidentally, I assume you can withstand a visit or two. I'll be along in the spring.

—Emma Jenkins (Matron)

SWIFT, BRUTAL RETALIATION

MEGHAN McCARRON

Two girls in wrinkled black dresses sat in the front pew at their older brother's funeral. They had never sat in the front pew in church before, and they disliked how exposed they felt. Behind them stood their brother's entire eighth-grade class, the girls in ironed black dresses and gold cross necklaces, the boys in dark suits, bought too big so they could get another use. Few expected more funerals, but the suits would serve for graduation in May—which, after all, was a funeral, too.

The girls' aunt gave the second reading, which was one of the letters of Saint Paul to the Corinthians. The younger sister, Brigid, loved the rhythm of those words, "Saint Paul to the Corinthians." She didn't know who the Corinthians were, but she imagined a small, dusty town, the people crowded around the town square as someone stood, just like her aunt, and read the latest letter from Saint Paul. This letter informed the Corinthians that though their outsides were wasting away, their insides were filling with the light of God. Life was a wobbly tent, but God had built a sturdy house in heaven. The older sister, Sinead, thought this God-house probably sounded good to people in the desert two thousand years ago, but her brother's house wasn't just sturdy: it had a pool. Also, her brother's insides had not grown stronger. He had wasted away, all of him. This stupid reading confirmed her suspicions that God was like any other adult who lied and told you horrible things were for your own good.

Sinead and Brigid felt as alone as it was possible to feel while smushed up against someone on a pew, unaware that the other person was also furiously contemplating God. They were doing their best not to be aware of anything. Noticing things, they had discovered, was dangerous. Was that Ian's English teacher sobbing three rows behind them? Was that the priest saying Ian's name in the homily? Were those flowers already wilting on the coffin in the early-September heat? Before, Sinead would have gotten angry about these things. Brigid would have tried to figure out their meaning. Now, the sisters found it safer to sink into the fog of mourning, though they didn't know to call it that. They were just trying to be very still, in hopes that events would pass them by.

A few pews back, two of Ian's classmates trailed out, sobbing. The reading had ended, and the cantor began to sing "Alleluia." The congregation rose to their feet, and their mother's hymnal slipped out of her black lap. She chanted along in a low, flat voice neither of them had heard before. Their father did not stand, but sat upright at the edge of the pew so stiffly he almost looked funny. His suit was rumpled and he'd slathered himself in cologne to hide the scent of alcohol. Sinead and Brigid were used to the cologne, but they had never seen their father look so small before. They had done a good job ignoring their surroundings, but their strange, frightening parents dragged them back into reality. They stared hopelessly at Ian's fat, luminous coffin.

The reception after the funeral filled the house with earnest thirteen-year-old girls bearing food made by their mothers. Every girl in Ian's class brought food, and most of it was lasagna. Lasagna with beef, lasagna with pork and spinach, "garden lasagna" featuring broccoli and Alfredo, Mexican lasagna with hot peppers and tortillas, and one particularly vile concoction made with whole-wheat pasta and dairy-free cheese. All of the lasagna piled up in the kitchen, since the girls' parents had brought in caterers. Their mother didn't have the heart to throw it away, so she shunted it to the refrigerator.

The sisters spent the reception hiding in plain sight, or trying to. They glued themselves to their grandmother, who had flown in for the occasion. Their grandmother was a sour old lady who smelled like cigarettes and gin fumes. But she was also tall and heavyset, so they could literally hide behind her as she talked to second cousins and great-aunts and even a step-something, the girls didn't catch what. Sometimes the sisters held hands. Brigid was the one who did the hand-seeking-out, but Sinead was secretly glad for something to hold on to when strangers stooped down to say they were sorry. Where were they when Ian was sick? Sorry? Sinead would make them sorry.

There were still people in the house that night, straggler aunts and loud neighbors. One of Ian's coaches was out back with their father, smoking cigars and laughing too loud. At some point, their mother noticed the girls scavenging in the kitchen and sent them up to bed. Sinead made Brigid go up first, since her bedtime was an hour after her sister's, but once Brigid was gone Sinead felt unmoored. She was too proud to give up her older-sibling right to a later bedtime, but she also didn't want to be in the room with the loud, sad adults. She found herself contemplating the whole-wheat dairy-free lasagna. Their mother had left it out to rot, and the faux cheese was buckling and sweating.

Sinead heard Brigid turn on the shower in her bathroom. Brigid had only started showering before bed a few months earlier, to imitate her older sister. This infuriated Sinead generally; tonight it felt like a slap in the face. Sinead snatched up the casserole dish and took the withering lasagna up to Brigid's messy pink room. She carved it up with a butter knife and hid the uneven squares under Brigid's pillow, beneath her covers, in her shoes, under her dresser—anywhere it would either squish or rot. This was a cruel thing to do after Sinead had spent all day comforting and being comforted by her sister. But the comforting also served to remind Sinead that it was just the two of them now, and that she could no longer enjoy the position of invisible middle child. She had embraced this identity with gusto—her favorite book was *The One in the Middle Is the Green Kangaroo*—but now she was the *oldest*. In the books she'd read, the oldest was bossy and bullying, or foolish and frivolous. In their family, the oldest was either sick, or played pranks.

As Sinead stashed the lasagna in the tradition of her dead brother, she began to feel as if she were being watched. She whirled around, sure that she would find Brigid in her pink bathrobe, her hair piled on her head in a towel, like women in old movies and their mother. But the shower was still roaring, and Sinead found herself staring at her reflection in the mirror.

Except it wasn't her reflection. The face was Ian's.

Then it wasn't. Sinead took several gulping breaths. One of her aunts had sent her books about grieving, so she'd known that she might end up hallucinating. She must be hallucinating.

This did not stop her, however, from snatching up the dirty pan, running into her room, and locking the door behind her. She threw the pan beneath her bed, jumped under the covers, and turned off the light. Then she switched it on again and covered her mirror with a sheet. But that really made her room look haunted, so she took the sheet down and stared at her reflection, willing her brother's face to appear. The reflection remained her own, which made her feel stupid. Stupid was a familiar, oddly comforting feeling.

Brigid sat on her floor in the dark, drawing a picture. She used her tiny reading light, which was designed for airplanes, though Brigid had gotten far more use from it during long waits in the dim, fluorescent hospital. She almost missed sitting in the boring corridors, compared to funerals and evil sisters. Bits of lasagna were still mushed into her hair, and Brigid was drawing a picture of her sister's head on fire. Sinead's curly hair stuck out in all directions, like she'd been hit by lightning. Brigid added her parents to the picture as little stick figures, off in the distance. They didn't do anything about the flames.

Brigid felt bewildered and hurt by the lasagna bombing. She did, however, recognize that a prank war had begun, and she had to respond in kind or risk humiliation. Unfortunately, she had the younger sibling's handicap of not having seen as much television or read as many books as her older siblings, so she was reduced to deflecting the same prank back at them. For a time, Brigid had experimented with turning the other cheek, but this had only resulted in more spiders in her bed, more covert arm-twists, and more stuffed animals fed to the neighbor's dog. Clearly, Sinead was attempting to take over Ian's turf, and the only effective response was swift, brutal retaliation.

Brigid completed three more meditative, vengeful pictures of her sister before quiet settled over the house. When she was sure everyone was asleep, she slid open her door and crept down to the kitchen. The clean, shiny counters reflected the blue light thrown off by the oven clock. Brigid was old enough to understand that her house was full of "nice" things, though "nice" to her meant "alienating and not to be touched." When Brigid opened the fridge, a chill crept along the back of her neck, like someone was blowing on it. But the kitchen was empty and silent and blue.

The white light of the fridge was warm and calming, so Brigid left the door ajar after pulling out Sinead's special orange-mango juice. No one knew why Sinead liked this juice so much—their mother blamed their father, other mothers, television ads—but everyone else in the house thought it was nasty, and only Sinead ever touched it. Brigid left the juice on the counter, then got up on a stool to retrieve salt and hot sauce from an upper cabinet. She shook in as much hot sauce as she could, then poured in some salt. After shaking the mixture together, she examined its color and consistency in the fridge light. Satisfied, Brigid placed the bottle back on the top shelf exactly how she'd found it, with its label facing the milk. She took a moment to admire her handiwork and shut the door with a *schuck*.

Ian stood on the other side of it. Brigid stumbled away from him, and put her back against the counter. He had hair again, the straight, tufty blond stuff he'd grown in after the first time he'd gotten better, not the curls from the pictures before Brigid was born. He wore shorts and a polo shirt, like he was on his way to the country club. But his face was pallid and green, and his eyes were ringed by the deep, scary circles that had appeared right before he died. Brigid didn't feel fear, or even shock. All she could think was, *I thought I'd never see you again.*

Brigid became aware of a soft hissing sound. Her elbow had knocked over the salt, and it was pouring onto the floor. When she looked back up, Ian was gone.

Brigid forced herself to go to the closet, find a dustpan and broom, and sweep up every last grain of salt. Seeing her ghost brother was terrifying, but having her father find salt all over the floor was equally scary, if not more so. Once the floor was clean, her terror surged back and she sprinted up the stairs.

As she rounded the bend, she nearly crashed into her mother. For a flicker of a moment, Brigid was sure she'd been caught, but then her mother looked over Brigid's shoulder and said, "Ian, you better go wash the fishes."

Brigid realized her mother was back on Ambien. She had foolishly hoped her mother would sleep better once she stopped spending every waking hour at the hospital, but apparently not. She pressed herself to the wall and let her mother sleepwalk down the stairs.

Despite the fact that she was furious with Sinead, Brigid jimmied open her door—Sinead kept it locked, though they had figured out how to break into each other's rooms years ago—and jumped into her bed. Sinead woke with a groan and Brigid hissed, "Shhhhhh!"

"Euh?" Sinead said.

"I saw Ian," Brigid said.

Sinead stiffened, then put her arms around her little sister. She noticed her hair smelled like tomato sauce. "I saw him too," Sinead said.

"What are we going to do?" Brigid whispered.

Sinead thought about the brave older sisters she'd read about in books and said, "We're going to help him."

Sinead didn't actually believe in her own bravery, but her borrowed stock phrase seemed to calm Brigid. It calmed Sinead a little bit, too. When Ian was alive, there had been very little either of his sisters could do for him. When he was well, they had tortured him, or tortured each other; as a result, when he was sick, every earnest gesture had felt forced. They had loved their brother, but they hadn't *liked* him much. Now here he was, turning to *them*, of all people. Of course they would do right by him. Of course they would help.

Sinead woke early and cleaned up Brigid's room while Brigid caught up on sleep in Sinead's bed. She shook lasagna out of Brigid's shoes and scraped off everything that remained under Brigid's covers. Then she stripped the bed and took the whole mess downstairs. She put the sheets in the washing machine, pushed the rotting lasagna down the garbage disposal, and scrubbed the pan until her fingers hurt. Finally, when the evidence of her crime had been thoroughly erased, she let herself have breakfast. She poured herself some Rice Krispies, sliced up a banana, and sat down at the kitchen table with her laptop.

Technically, it was a school day, but Sinead and Brigid were taking a "leave" of a few weeks. This was supposed to help them recover from the trauma of Ian's death, though Sinead suspected it was actually so the other students wouldn't have to deal with their uncomfortable grief. Sinead had felt miserable and adrift in the days following Ian's death, but now that she had a purpose, those feelings disappeared. She felt happy, even privileged, to be sitting at home in the morning eating cereal and a banana and Googling "ghost brother," though this only brought up television-show recaps and one site about "Haunted Gettysburg."

Brigid found her sister poring over her computer in the kitchen, a half-eaten banana by her side. Brigid had been deemed too young for a laptop, which filled her with uncharacteristic fury. She casually opened the fridge and found that the mango juice hadn't been touched. Brigid appreciated that Sinead had cleaned up her room, but she felt uneasy letting her sister off entirely. She let the mango juice be.

"A ghost comes back because of unfinished business," Sinead said, without looking up from the screen.

Brigid tried and failed to think of what unfinished business their brother might have. In all the books *she'd* read, "unfinished business" meant things like buried treasure or unsolved murders, which she didn't suppose Ian had any of. "We should search his room," Brigid said.

The sisters went up to Ian's room, which no one had opened since he went back to the hospital for good. Sinead carried a thermometer and a compass, which the internet had told her were useful for detecting paranormal presences. The thermometer was to register sudden drops in temperature. It was less clear what the compass was supposed to do, but Sinead imagined it would spin wildly, like in movies about the North Pole.

Ian's room had always been neat and uncluttered, utterly unlike his sisters'. His dresser was lined with soccer trophies, and his sneakers stood in matched pairs beneath his bed. The clock still blinked midnight from a late-summer power outage. His bed was made. It looked like a display room.

"Anything?" Brigid said, nodding toward Sinead's tools. Sinead shook her head in what she imagined was a curt, professional manner. The thermometer did not reveal any strange differences in temperature, and the compass did not point anywhere but a woozy north.

Sinead remembered reading somewhere, or maybe seeing in a movie, that you had to ask ghosts what they wanted. They went into Brigid's room, where Sinead had first seen Ian's ghost. Brigid's bed lay bare, and a few of her stuffed animals were piled to the side of it, wounded with tomato-sauce stains. Sinead took this in and finally offered a mumbled "Sorry about that." Brigid shrugged and said nothing, trying to hide the anger over the lasagna and guilt over the mango juice warring inside her.

Not that Sinead was paying attention. She seemed satisfied by their stupid exchange and had turned her full attention to the mirror.

Sinead stared for a long time. Her eyes glazed over, which blurred her features, but she never saw her brother's face looking back. Occasionally Brigid would ask "Anything?" and Sinead would blink her eyes, rub them, and say, "Nothing."

Sinead and Brigid went to the kitchen next, the site of Ian's second appearance. Brigid opened and closed the refrigerator door a few times, making sure that didn't summon him, but she was too terrified Sinead would ask why she was in the kitchen to keep up the investigation for very long. Sinead blithely assumed Brigid was sneaking snacks.

For lunch they microwaved giant chunks of Mexican lasagna and leftover caterer chicken fingers. Their mother was home, but it didn't even occur to them to ask her for lunch. During Ian's last few months, their mother was usually busy taking care of him. When he died, they had briefly hoped she would recover her interest in their well-being, but instead her caring engines shut down completely. She spent whole days in her room; the girls had no idea what she did in there. If they put their ears to the door, they heard the television, but they had the eerie feeling it wasn't being watched.

When the leftovers were ready (re-ready?), Sinead opened up her laptop and logged on to Facebook. Sinead never used her account, since she was already sick of everyone at their school and couldn't imagine spending her free time reading their stupid updates. But Ian had been obsessed with Facebook, forever adding friends and commenting on pictures and taking polls. None of his own status updates ever had to do with chemo, or the hospital, or his family, which were just annoying distractions from being normal and popular. His updates were bizarre hypothetical questions about Batman or *The 300* or *Boondock Saints*. Any comments pertaining to "good thoughts!" or "HUGZ" were deleted, unless they were posted by someone really hot.

"I'm going to send him a message," Sinead announced.

"On Facebook?" Brigid said.

"Ian loved Facebook," Sinead said. "Maybe he'd rather communicate that way."

Ian and Sinead were not Facebook friends, but he let anyone who went to their school see his profile. Even though his last update was weeks old, his page was full of activity. New wall posts filled in the top. Someone had posted a picture of Ian with his arms around two girls Sinead didn't even recognize, sitting in a hot tub at someone's pool party. He was grinning like he'd gotten away with something. Was he already sick by then? Or did he still think he was in remission? There were also messages on the page, "IANO WELL MISS U!!!" and "I KNOW UR A REAL ANGEL NOW!" The "angel" messages were a million times worse than "good thoughts!" or "HUGZ." Sinead felt an overpowering urge to tell these kids exactly which species of idiot they were, but the most insightful commentary she could come up with in her blind fury was "FUCK U." She moved to post it, but she felt Brigid staring at her. She looked at Brigid, who shook her head.

Sinead sighed and started a new message. She typed, "Ian, r u haunting the house?" She pressed send. Then she opened another one and added, "Why?"

They ate their Mexican lasagna very slowly, watching Sinead's Facebook inbox like it was extremely boring television. No new messages arrived.

The girls were in Sinead's room creating an altar out of Ian's trophies when they heard their mother banging dishes in the kitchen. If it had been their father making angry sounds, they would have stayed put. But with their mother, it was better to get the confrontation over with.

"You're not on vacation," their mother said as they came down the stairs. She wore glasses, a rumpled blue sweat suit, and, weirdly, makeup. She shoved their dirty dishes across the counter. "What if Daddy came home?"

Brigid immediately pulled her stool in front of the sink and started scrubbing the lasagna pan. Sinead stared very hard at her mother, trying out her telekinetic powers. She had just hit puberty, right? Maybe Ian wasn't Ian at all, but a poltergeist that had been unleashed by her hormones.

Her mother stared back at her, looking both dazed and furious. The side of her neck quivered, and there were huge circles under her eyes. Her mouth tensed, like she was about to say something nasty. Instead, her thin face collapsed, like a building imploding, and she started to cry.

Shame burned Sinead like poison. She snatched a dish from Brigid and rubbed it dry with a towel. Their mother went into the bathroom and both girls pretended not to hear her sob. When Ian was home, their mother never acted like this. It was only when he was at the hospital. Now, instead of Ian's death breaking the spell, he would be at the hospital forever. Brigid kept washing dishes, which Sinead dried and put away. They took a long time doing this, to kill time until their mother finally emerged from the bathroom.

That night, the sisters convened in Sinead's room to watch clips from *Real Ghosthunters*, a YouTube show Sinead had found. They were huddled in the dark around the laptop, taking mental notes about plasma, when they heard the garage door open. They held their breath, praying for their father to just come upstairs. Instead, his footsteps stomped around the kitchen. The master bedroom door opened, and their mother rushed out. After a moment of loaded silence in the kitchen, their voices exploded. The girls made out single words: "pigsty," "brats," "son." Their father pounded up the stairs, thundered past Sinead and Brigid, and slammed the bedroom door. Their mother's footsteps came next. They were slow and quiet. They heard her go into Brigid's room; then there was a knock at Sinead's door.

Their mother's arms were full of Brigid's white sheets, which Sinead had put in the wash and then forgotten. She had only added detergent, not bleach, and the soggy sheets were still covered in smears of red tomato sauce and greasy faux-cheese blots.

"What is this?" she said. Her voice was tight and quiet, the worst possible tone.

Sisterly solidarity was running strong, but it was still vulnerable to attack. If neither of them said anything, both would be punished. Traditionally, this had been the route the siblings took, because Ian believed in, and enforced, a no-ratting policy. The one time Sinead ever bucked it, Ian told everyone at school she wet the bed. For a month, everyone called her "Pee-nead." But the one time Brigid had told on Sinead, both Sinead and Ian conspired to punish her, first by locking her in the attic, then by tricking her into eating a bag of their father's favorite cookies. When he found the bag in Brigid's room, she lost snacking privileges for a month. As a result, Sinead had come to view the policy as a necessary evil, but Brigid *hated* it. If there was a moment for Brigid to change the status quo, this was it. It didn't matter how nice Sinead had been to her today; she had spent every other day being mean, and if Brigid did nothing things would go back to the way they'd been.

"Sinead put lasagna in my bed," Brigid said.

Sinead stiffened next to her sister, and Brigid shrank away. The instant the words were out of her mouth, she regretted them terribly. Their mother stared at Sinead with murder in her eyes, but the look she gave Brigid was not much kinder.

"Your father will speak to you tomorrow, Sinead. Brigid, come with me."

Their mother led Brigid out of the room, and Sinead was left alone, equal parts terrified and furious. She couldn't stop imagining all the terrible things that would happen now that her father knew. She also couldn't stop thinking about hitting Brigid, or kicking her, or pulling her hair. Sinead got up and started pacing, but this only made her anger worse. Brigid's insubordination could not stand, and since they weren't going to school, the only way to punish her was with another prank at home. But if her father caught her doing something bad again . . .

She needed a quick, deniable solution.

Sinead rooted through her desk drawer until she found a stiff, moldering stick of gum and chewed it until she couldn't even remember what flavor the gum had been. She found Brigid lolling facedown in a fresh set of sheets, her hair tousled against the pillow. Sinead's fingers delicately removed the gum from her mouth and nestled it into Brigid's hair.

Sinead marched out into the hallway, flushed with triumph, only to find Ian staring forlornly at the door to his room. The sight was so sad that her adrenaline-and-anger high crashed, and shame surged in its place. What was she doing torturing her sister when their brother needed help? Ian turned to face her and cocked his head, as if he sensed her regret. She'd never received such a look of understanding from her brother. People had told them they'd get along when they were older, but Sinead had always written that off as the same kind of adult bullshit as telling her that she'd look prettier after the braces came off, or the kids would be nicer next year. Now, under the weight of Ian's look, she felt the loss not just of her brother, but of their friendship. Their future.

Tears spring to Sinead's eyes. She hadn't cried since Ian went back into the hospital, and even then she had been crying for poor Sinead, who had to endure Ian's disease ripping her family apart. Now she was crying for her brother, who'd been bludgeoned by cancer and rewarded with a confused, silent afterlife.

This was no time for emotions, however. Ian needed her help. She swallowed her tears and whispered, "What do you want?"

She wasn't sure what she expected. He was waiting outside his room. Maybe he needed her to open the door? Instead, Ian looked at her with hurt confusion. He mouthed something at her, but there was no sound. She wondered how long it took to learn to read lips. Probably more than twenty-four hours.

"I can't hear you," she whispered.

Ian mouthed it again. And again. When Sinead shook her head, his face colored with unfamiliar anger. Ian had a temper, but Sinead had never seen fury like this. Ian spat a silent evil phrase at her, then disappeared.

A loud thump came from the kitchen downstairs, then a rustling. Something soft hit the floor, over and over. There was a crash, then the sound of footsteps, running.

Sinead rushed to the kitchen. When she flipped on the light, she found the entire floor covered in lasagna. It was strewn on the floor in messy goops, stuck to the cabinets, mashed on the fridge. The trash can had been tipped over, as if by a dog they didn't have; the rest of the lasagna lay inside in one red mass. The pans were still stacked in the sink and on the counter, crusted with burnt cheese products. One of them had shattered on the floor.

Her mother must have thrown the lasagna in the trash, though Sinead couldn't imagine her doing it—she hoarded food like a squirrel. Or maybe their father had decided he didn't like it filling the fridge. Their father wouldn't like all the dirty dishes in the sink, either, but perhaps her mother had staged her own tiny rebellion and refused to clean up after him.

But now, the lasagna was smeared across the entire kitchen, which definitely wasn't her parents' doing. Brigid was fast asleep, and anyway, she never would have made a mess like this. But blaming it on her angry ghost brother wasn't going to cut it with her father, so it was up to Sinead to fix it.

Sinead got out a mop to push all the lasagna toward the trash can. It slithered along the floor, leaving a streak of sauce behind it. Sinead scooped the lasagna into the trash with a dustpan and thanked God that her mother took sleeping pills and her father drank whiskey. Then she reminded herself that she didn't believe in God. Praying was a hard habit to break, though. She wished she could ask God to explain her brother to her. Why was he so angry? What was she supposed to learn from his punishment? But God wasn't listening, and she had to mop the floor.

Brigid marched down the stairs the next morning and threw the clump of her gum-wadded hair at Sinead. There were perhaps more sophisticated or more covert ways of handling her anger, but Brigid did not want to employ them. She hated her sister, and she wanted her to know it.

"Bitch," Brigid said. Ian had taught her all the curse words when she was five, but she'd never used one before. The anger behind it burnt her mouth.

Sinead flinched at the word, but also seemed strangely impressed. "I'm sorry," Sinead said. She didn't do the looking-away-and-shrugging routine that usually accompanied her apologies. But she didn't seem that sorry, either. Or, she seemed to feel she'd already paid the price.

Brigid stood there, fuming. Then she turned on her heel and marched into the pantry to look for something to eat.

"I saw Ian last night," Sinead called to her. "After I did it. He tried to talk to me, but I couldn't hear him, and he got mad."

"I don't care," Brigid said. This was not true, but she was sick of doing things Sinead's way. She took an entire box of cookies and marched back up to her room.

Brigid spent the entire day in her room, making herself sick on Chips Ahoy and reading through every book she owned that featured ghosts. But the ghosts in these stories were either too evil, or too good. The kids had friends, or adult helpers, or siblings who didn't put gum in their hair. None of them told you what to do when you were alone, and scared, and haunted by your mean, sick brother.

Brigid was sitting on her floor, staring at her pile of useless books and tugging on the newly gum-shortened chunk of hair when an epiphany broke: They had only seen Ian when they were pulling a prank.

She found herself perversely glad that Sinead had put gum in her hair. That meant she needed to get revenge on Sinead. And when she did, perhaps she could finally help Ian.

When Brigid heard her mother go downstairs to start dinner, she stole down the hallway into her mother's bathroom. She enjoyed spelunking in the cabinets when her parents weren't home, and the dusty bottle of Nair was right where she remembered. She'd seen a commercial that suggested it had something to do with summertime and shorts, but people also made jokes about using it for pranks on TV. Brigid was used to not understanding things, but she'd filed the idea away for when it was needed.

Brigid took the Nair into Sinead's bathroom and got out her honey-vanilla-mango shiny-hair shampoo. She unscrewed both caps and prepared to pour the white Nair into the conveniently white shampoo. But in the bright bathroom light, the clamor of words on the bottle—"patch test" and "doctor" and "burning"—gave her pause. Burning? Brigid was furious with Sinead, but was she furious enough to set her hair on fire—which, as far as she could tell, was what this concoction would do?

Brigid unscrewed the cap and watched herself in the mirror as she raised the bottle. She moved in slow motion, raising it, then placing it over the shampoo bottle, then tipping it in. When the first bit of Nair poured out, Ian was standing next to her.

Brigid set the Nair bottle down on the counter without taking her eyes off her brother. In the mirror, Ian snatched it up and tossed it between his hands in the languid, confident way he'd moved when he was alive. Her throat tightened; this bottle-tossing was the most Ian-like thing she'd seen the ghost do, and it made her ache for her brother. Brigid sensed he was waiting for her to do something.

"Hi," Brigid said.

Ian nodded in response and continued to toss the bottle back and forth.

Brigid tried to remember the plan she and Sinead had come up with for this encounter. "Do you . . . W—what do you want?" she said.

Ian's face darkened at that question, and Brigid fumbled for a new, non-angry-making one. She couldn't think of anything. Instead, she blurted out the only other question she had. "Is it better? Now that it's over?" she said.

Ian snatched the bottle out of the air and froze.

"I'm sorry! I didn't mean to say it like that. But, I just . . . people said, when you died, that it was a blessing, because you were suffering but now you're here, and I don't understand—"

Ian's face had changed when Brigid said the word "died," but she couldn't stop herself from talking, even as he looked at her with angry confusion, like Brigid had just told him a lie out of spite.

"Don't you know?" Brigid said. "Ian, you're—"

The scary anger returned to Ian's face, and his hands began to twitch. They flew up to his head and grasped the tufty blond hair that grew there. He pulled on it, and a chunk came away in his fist. He opened his hand and watched it float to the ground. Then he pulled out another chunk. And another. The chunks of hair floated down all around him, like the leaves of a dying plant.

"Stop!" Brigid said. His eyes darted between his head and Brigid's, then to the bottle of Nair. He snatched up the bottle and poured it all over Brigid's head. The thick liquid gushed down in a white stream, covering Brigid's messy brown hair, her forehead, eyes, nose, and mouth. Her eyes burned and she choked for breath. She watched her reflection in horror as Ian pulled her long brown hair from her head in sickly, dripping strands.

Brigid bolted out of the bathroom and down the stairs. She nearly knocked her mother over when she burst into the kitchen.

"Brigid!" her mother said, grabbing her daughter by the shoulders. "What are you doing?"

Brigid tried, and failed, to hide the terror in her eyes as her mother scrutinized her. She wasn't sure what her mother saw, but she seemed to think it required no more than a comforting hug. She held her daughter for a brief, sweet moment. Then she turned her attention back to the kitchen.

"Daddy will be home for dinner," she said. Her mother's hand on her shoulder tightened at the mention of Daddy. Brigid felt trapped. "Could you set the dining room table?"

The last thing Brigid wanted to do was touch the good china with her shaking hands. No, that wasn't the last thing she wanted to do. The last thing she wanted to do was sit in her room, alone, and wait for Ian's ghost to find her. She didn't think they should be trying to help him anymore. She wondered if she and Sinead were actually keeping him here.

The dishes in the china closet trembled when she approached it, and Brigid caught sight of herself in its mirrored back wall. Between the mirrored backs of the dishes, her reflection had all its hair. Brigid searched the corners of the mirror for Ian, but he was nowhere to be seen.

After Brigid finished setting the table, her mother discovered her newly short chunk of hair and yelled at her for ruining her haircut. Brigid didn't rat Sinead out this time, not because she was cowed by the stupid gum prank, but because she was afraid Sinead's revenge would provoke more terrifying Ian episodes.

Sinead was hiding in the basement out of an attempt to put off her interview with her father, but she also had important work to attend to. Sinead had decided after the events of the previous night that Ian was lost, and being lost made him angry, so he needed to be guided to heaven, or wherever he was supposed to go—Sinead was pretty sure heaven was a part of the whole God-lie. Sinead had not made the prank connection, since she didn't know about all of Brigid's pranks; in fact, she was convinced that Ian was seeking them out, unable to let go. She had spent the afternoon acquiring the necessary tools: salt, an important memento, a tiny bell. The next time she saw him, she intended to send him off to eternal peace, whether she believed in it or not.

Sinead refused to come up from the basement to cut the potatoes, or polish the silver, or put out the glasses. She didn't even respond to their mother's calls for assistance, which made her sound if she was shouting down the stairs at no one. By the time Daddy came home, their mother was crackling with irritation, and it fell to Brigid to make the appeasing niceties required whenever her father joined the family for dinner. When he asked her how she had spent her day, she told him she had watched cartoons.

The rest of the family was already seated by the time Sinead emerged, the little bell tinkling in the pocket of her hoodie. Her parents' half-empty bottle of wine sat on the kitchen counter and reminded Sinead that she wanted juice. She dug into the refrigerator for her orange-mango concoction, which she had secretly started to get sick of. But it inexplicably annoyed her father, so it would serve well as a final act of defiance before her punishment.

When Daddy came home for dinner, the family always ate in the dining room, with the gold-edged china and the freshly polished silver. The candles were always lit, and the girls' mother made food that was cooked in the oven, not the microwave. Tonight there were small, bloody steaks freshly seared in the broiler, roasted fingerling potatoes, and garlicky greens. Each of the women handed a plate to Daddy, and he dropped on greens and potatoes and a single, wobbly steak. Brigid got half a filet, both because she was the youngest and because she was considered by the whole family to be fat. Then Daddy served himself a filet and Brigid's leftover half, and the women listened to him talk about his day, and everyone enjoyed a nice family meal.

When Sinead sat down at the table with the mango juice, Brigid banged her knife on the table to get her attention, but Sinead refused to look up from her plate. She took a bite of her potatoes, then took a sip of her juice. She didn't even register the taste; all she knew was that it had to be out of her mouth, *now.* Sinead spat orange liquid all over the white tablecloth, splattering the green beans and extinguishing one of the candles. The silence afterward was so complete that when Brigid took a breath, it sounded like the rush of the ocean.

"What," their mother began with a sharp, clipped tone, "was that." She clearly hoped to derail their father by taking on the scolding herself, but he spoke over her before she could get out her next word.

"Is there something wrong with your drink, Sinead?" he said. He said it so gently that all three women at the table tensed.

Sinead said nothing as she stared at Brigid, who looked at her with wide, helpless eyes. Brigid had never felt regret like this before, not even when she told Ian that he was dead. That had been an accident. This was something she had done on purpose, and it had worked exactly as she had planned. As terrifying as Ian's reaction had been, he had stayed trapped in the mirror. Sinead and her father were here in the room.

Sinead kept staring at Brigid as she said, "Just went down the wrong tube."

Their father considered this answer, folding his hands like the girls imagined he did in complex negotiations. "Take another sip," he said—then added, as if it had just occurred to him, "so we know you're all right."

As she brought the glass to her lips, Sinead thought of the people who ate bugs on television. The horrid hot-salty flavor of the juice burned her throat, and her stomach turned and gurgled when it hit bottom. She put down the juice in a way she hoped was ladylike, then covered her mouth for one tiny cough.

Sinead could not tell if her performance had any effect, because now their father was looking between them, as if trying to spot an invisible thread. "Brigid, why don't you take a sip?" he said.

Brigid should just take it. Just take the glass, choke the whole thing down, and spare Sinead. But she would spew juice everywhere or, worse, throw it up. "I hate that weird mango stuff," she said. She pathetically hoped this would win his sympathy, since he, too, hated the weird mango stuff.

"Give it another try," their father said. "Go get the bottle."

Brigid rose from her seat as slowly as she possibly could, and shuffled into the kitchen. She pulled out the orange-mango juice and a glass and shuffled back into the dining room like a prisoner headed to the gallows. The three members of her family stared at her with anger as she approached, though their anger was confused, and directed at different people. Her sister was angry with Brigid for pranking her and furious with their father for toying with them. Her mother was angry with the girls for provoking her husband, though her constant, simmering anger at their father boiled up from beneath the other, safer emotion. And her father—her father was angry at his children, and at his wife, but his ideas of who they were and what they represented were so distorted that the anger might as well have been at different people entirely. He'd been furious at Ian when he got sick again. Brigid had seen him slap him. Their father's anger made no sense.

All these competing angers made Brigid angry, too. Hers was not mixed with denial, however, or directed at someone who didn't exist. She was angry at everyone, and she was going to make this stop. When she crossed the threshold, she slid her foot underneath the rug and elaborately, comically, tripped. The glass went flying out of her hands, and the juice bottle crashed to the floor. Their parents stared at Brigid, frozen, but Sinead leapt to her aid, making sure to knock over her juice glass in the process. Sinead slid her hands beneath her sister's arms and drew her to her feet.

Then their parents started screaming about the rug and broken glass and carelessness and disrespect. Sinead and Brigid couldn't make the words out, exactly. They were too distracted by Ian's reappearance. Sinead saw him standing next to their father, arms crossed. Brigid saw him staring out from the china-cabinet mirror, hovering.

"—disrespect that should have died with your son!" their father shouted, just at the moment when their mother fell silent. Then everything was silent, taut with the ugly truth that had just been unleashed. Ian was dead. And each member of the family had wished for that death in the hope that life would be better without him.

The first dish in the cabinet broke like a gunshot. The one closest to it went off next, then another, and another, the dishes exploding like targets in a carnival game. Sinead saw Ian pick them up and hurl them. Brigid saw his face in the mirror behind each dish. Their parents were screaming again, and the sisters watched the carnage unfold before them like spectators, rather than two people intimately involved in the situation. Then Sinead remembered the bell in her pocket, and Brigid remembered the look on Ian's face when she told him he was dead, and they both began to shout, too.

"You can leave!" Sinead shouted. She rang her little bell at the dish cabinet, then pulled out her salt and shook it around the floor. "You don't have to stay here! You can leave!"

"Ian, I'm sorry!" Brigid said. "I'm sorry you died! I'm sorry!"

The dishes kept exploding, and every member of the family kept shouting, and the sisters weren't sure if they had unleashed something cathartic or something terrible. Sinead believed Ian just needed to release this anger to move on. Brigid wondered if their family had poisoned him with their selfishness, and now they were paying the price. Either way, all they could do was cower under the table, holding hands, until it had run its course.

SCATTERED ALONG THE RIVER OF HEAVEN

ALIETTE DE BODARD

———◆———

I grieve to think of the stars
Our ancestors our gods
Scattered like hairpin wounds
Along the River of Heaven
So tell me
Is it fitting that I spend my days here
A guest in those dark, forlorn halls?

This is the first poem Xu Anshi gave to us; the first memory she shared with us for safekeeping. It is the first one that she composed in High Mheng—which had been and remains a debased language, a blend between that of the San-Tay foreigners, and that of the Mheng, Anshi's own people.

She composed it on Shattered Pine Prison, sitting in the darkness of her cell, listening to the faint whine of the bots that crawled on the walls—melded to the metal and the crisscrossing wires, clinging to her skin—monitoring every minute movement she made—the voices of her heart, the beat of her thoughts in her brain, the sweat on her body.

Anshi had once been a passable poet in San-Tay, thoughtlessly fluent in the language of upper classes, the language of bot-handlers; but the medical facility had burnt that away from her, leaving an oddly-shaped hole in her mind, a gap that ached like a wound. When she tried to speak, no words would come out—not in San-Tay, not in High Mheng—only a raw croak, like the cry of a dying bird. Bots had once flowed to do her bidding; but now they only followed the will of the San-Tay.

There were no stars in Shattered Pine, where everything was dark with no windows; and where the faint yellow light soon leeched the prisoners' skin of all colors. But, once a week, the prisoners would be allowed onto the deck of the prison station—heavily escorted by San-Tay guards. Bots latched onto their faces and eyes, forcing them to stare into the darkness—into the event horizon of the black hole, where all light spiraled inwards and vanished, where everything was crushed into insignificance. There were bodies outside— prisoners who had attempted to escape, put in lifesuits and jettisoned, slowly drifting into a place where time and space ceased to have any meaning. If they were lucky, they were already dead.

From time to time, there would be a jerk as the bots stung someone back into wakefulness; or low moans and cries, from those whose minds had snapped. Shattered Pine bowed and broke everyone; and the prisoners that were released back to Felicity Station came back diminished and bent, waking up every night weeping and shaking with the memory of the black hole.

Anshi—who had been a scholar, a low-level magistrate, before she'd made the mistake of speaking up against the San-Tay—sat very still, and stared at the black hole—seeing into its heart, and knowing the truth: she was of no significance, easily broken, easily crushed—but she had known that since the start. All men were as nothing to the vast universe.

It was on the deck that Anshi met Zhiying—a small, diminutive woman who always sat next to her. She couldn't glance at Zhiying; but she felt her presence, nevertheless; the strength and hatred that emanated from her, that sustained her where other people failed.

Day after day they sat side by side, and Anshi formed poems in her mind, haltingly piecing them together in High Mheng—San-Tay was denied to her, and, like many of the Mheng upper class, she spoke no Low Mheng. Day after day, with the bots clinging to her skin like overripe fruit, and Zhiying's presence, burning like fire at her side; and, as the verses became stronger and stronger in her mind, Anshi whispered words, out of the guards' hearing, out of the bots' discrimination capacities—haltingly at first, and then over and over, like a mantra on the prayer beads. Day after day; and, as the words sank deeper into her mind, Anshi slowly came to realize that the bots on her skin were not unmoving, but held themselves trembling, struggling against their inclination to move— and that the bots clinging to Zhiying were different, made of stronger materials to resist the fire of Zhiying's anger. She heard the fast, frantic beat of their thoughts processes, which had its own rhythm, like poetry spoken in secret—and felt the hard shimmer that connected the bots to the San-Tay guards, keeping everything together.

And, in the dim light of Shattered Pine, Anshi subvocalised words in High Mheng, reaching out with her mind as she had done, back when she had been free. She hadn't expected anything to happen; but the bots on her skin stiffened one after the other, and turned to the sound of her voice, awaiting orders.

• • •

Before she left Felicity, Xu Wen expected security at San-Tay Prime's spaceport to be awful—they would take one glance at her travel documents, and bots would rise up from the ground and crawl up to search every inch of skin, every body cavity. Mother has warned her often enough that the San-Tay have never forgiven Felicity for waging war against them; that they will always remember the shame of losing their space colonies. She expects a personal interview with a Censor, or perhaps even to be turned back at the boundary, sent back in shame to Felicity.

But it doesn't turn out that way at all.

Security is over in a breeze, the bots giving her nothing but a cursory body check before the guards wave her through. She has no trouble getting a cab either; things must have changed on San-Tay Prime, and the San-Tay driver waves her on without paying attention to the color of her skin.

"Here on holiday?" the driver asks her in Galactic, as she slides into the floater—her body sinking as the chair adapts itself to her morphology. Bots climb onto her hands, showing her ads for nearby hotels and restaurants: an odd, disturbing sight, for there are no bots on Felicity Station.

"You could say that," Wen says, with a shrug she wills to be careless. "I used to live here."

A long, long time ago, when she was still a baby; before Mother had that frightful fight with Grandmother, and left San-Tay Prime for Felicity.

"Oh?" the driver swerves, expertly, amidst the traffic; taking one wide, tree-lined avenue after another. "You don't sound like it."

Wen shakes her head. "I was born here, but I didn't remain here long."

"Gone back to the old country, eh?" The driver smiles. "Can't say I blame you."

"Of course," Wen says, though she's unsure what to tell him. That she doesn't really know—that she never really lived here, not for more than a few years, and that she has a few confused memories of a bright-lit kitchen, and bots dancing for her on the carpet of Grandmother's apartment? But she's not here for such confidences. She's here—well, she's not sure why she's here. Mother was adamant Wen didn't have to come; but then, Mother has never forgiven Grandmother for the exile on San-Tay Prime.

Everything goes fine; until they reach the boundary district, where a group of large bots crawl onto the floater, and the driver's eyes roll up as their thought-threads meld with his. At length, the bots scatter, and he turns back to Wen. "Sorry, m'am," he says. "I have to leave you here."

"Oh?" Wen asked, struggling to hide her fear.

"No floaters allowed into the Mheng districts currently," the man said. "Some kind of funeral for a tribal leader—the brass is afraid there will be unrest." He shrugs again. "Still, you're local, right? You'll find someone to help you."

She's never been here; and she doesn't know anyone, anymore. Still, she forces a smile—always be graceful, Mother said—and puts her hand on one of the bots, feeling the warmth as it transfers money from her account on Felicity Station. After he's left her on the paved sidewalk of a street she barely recognizes, she stands, still feeling the touch of the bots against her skin—on Felicity they call them a degradation, a way for the San-Tay government to control everything and everyone; and she just couldn't bring herself to get a few locator-bots at the airport.

Wen looks up, at the signs—they're in both languages, San-Tay and what she assumes is High Mheng, the language of the exiles. San-Tay is all but banned on Felicity, only found on a few derelict signs on the Outer Rings, the ones the National Restructuring Committee hasn't gone around to retooling yet. Likewise, High Mheng isn't taught, or encouraged. What little she can remember is that it's always been a puzzle—the words look like Mheng; but when she tries to put everything together, their true meaning seems to slip away from her.

Feeling lost already, she wends her way deeper into the streets—those few shops that she bypasses are closed, with a white cloth spread over the door. White for grief, white for a funeral.

It all seems so—so wide, so open. Felicity doesn't have streets lined with streets, doesn't have such clean sidewalks—space on the station is at a ruthless premium, and every corridor is packed with stalls and shops—people eat at tables on the streets, and conduct their transactions in recessed doorways, or rooms half as large as the width of the sidewalk. She feels in another world; though, every now and then, she'll see a word that she recognizes on a sign, and follow it, in the forlorn hope that it will lead her closer to the funeral hall.

Street after street after street—under unfamiliar trees that sway in the breeze, listening to the distant music broadcast from every doorway, from every lamp. The air is warm and clammy, a far cry from Felicity's controlled temperature; and over her head are dark clouds. She almost hopes it rains, to see what it is like—in real life, and not in some simulation that seems like a longer, wetter version of a shower in the communal baths.

At length, as she reaches a smaller intersection, where four streets with unfamiliar signs branch off—some residential area, though all she can read are the numbers on the buildings—Wen stops, staring up at the sky. Might as well admit it: it's useless. She's lost, thoroughly lost in the middle of nowhere, and she'll never be on time for the funeral.

She'd weep; but weeping is a caprice, and she's never been capricious in her life. Instead, she turns back and attempts to retrace her steps, towards one of the largest streets—where, surely, she can hammer on a door, or find someone who will help her?

She can't find any of the streets; but at length, she bypasses a group of old men playing Encirclement on the street—watching the shimmering holo-board as if their lives depended on it.

"Excuse me?" she asks, in Mheng.

As one, the men turn towards her—their gazes puzzled. "I'm looking for White Horse Hall," Wen says. "For the funeral?"

The men still watch her, their faces impassive—dark with expressions she can't read. They're laden with smaller bots—on their eyes, on their hands and wrists, hanging black like obscene fruit: they look like the San-Tay in the reconstitution movies, except that their skins are darker, their eyes narrower.

At length, the eldest of the men steps forwards, and speaks up—his voice rerouted to his bots, coming out in halting Mheng. "You're not from here."

"No," Wen says in the same language. "I'm from Felicity."

An odd expression crosses their faces: longing, and hatred, and something else Wen cannot place. One of the men points to her, jabbers in High Mheng—Wen catches just one word she understands.

Xu Anshi.

"You're Anshi's daughter," the man says. The bots' approximation of his voice is slow, metallic, unlike the fast jabbering of High Mheng.

Wen shakes her head; and one of the other men laughs, saying something else in High Mheng.

That she's too young, no doubt—that Mother, Anshi's daughter, would be well into middle age by now, instead of being Wen's age. "Daughter of daughter," the man says, with a slight, amused smile. "Don't worry, we'll take you to the hall, to see your grandmother."

He walks by her side, with the other man, the one who laughed. Neither of them speaks—too hard to attempt small talk in a language they don't master, Wen guesses. They go down a succession of smaller and smaller streets, under banners emblazoned with the image of the *phuong*, Felicity's old symbol, before the Honored Leader made the new banner, the one that showed the station blazing among the stars—something more suitable for their new status.

Everything feels . . . odd, slightly twisted out of shape—the words not quite what they ought to be, the symbols just shy of familiar; the language a frightening meld of words she can barely recognize.

Everything is wrong, Wen thinks, shivering—and yet how can it be wrong, walking among Grandmother's own people?

• • •

Summoning bots I washed away
Ten thousand thousand years of poison
Awakening a thousand flower-flames, a thousand phoenix birds
Floating on a sea of blood like cresting waves
The weeping of the massacred millions rising from the darkness

We received this poem and its memories for safekeeping at a time when Xu Anshi was still on Felicity Station: on an evening before the Feast of Hungry Ghosts, when she sat in a room lit by trembling lights, thinking of Lao, her husband who had died in the uprisings—and wondering how much of it had been of any worth.

It refers to a time when Anshi was older, wiser—she and Zhiying had escaped from Shattered Pine, and spent three years moving from hiding place to hiding place, composing the pamphlets that, broadcast into every household, heralded the end of the San-Tay governance over Felicity.

On the night that would become known as the Second Ring Riots, Anshi stood in one of the inner rings of Felicity Station, her bots spread around her, hacked into the network—half of them on her legs, pumping modifiers into her blood; half of them linked to the other Mheng bot-handlers, retransmitting scenes of carnage, of the Mheng mob running wild in the San-Tay districts of the inner rings, the High Tribunal and Spaceport Authority lasered, and the fashionable districts trashed.

"This one," Zhiying said, pointing to a taller door, adorned with what appeared to be a Mheng traditional blessing—until one realized that the characters had been chosen for aesthetic reasons only, and that they meant nothing.

Anshi sent a subvocalised command to her bots, asking them to take the house. The feed to the rioting districts cut off abruptly, as her bots turned their attention towards the door and the house beyond: their sensors analyzing the bots on the walls, the pattern of the aerations, the cables running behind the door, and submitting hypotheses about possible architectures of the security system—before the swarm reached a consensus, and made a decision.

The bots flowed towards the door—the house's bots sought to stop them, but Anshi's bots split into two squads, and rushed past, heading for the head—the central control panel, which housed the bots' communication system. Anshi had a brief glimpse of red-painted walls, and blinking holos; before her bots rushed back, job completed, and fell on the now disorganized bots at the door.

Everything went dark, the Mheng characters slowly fading away from the door's panels.

"All yours," Anshi said to Zhiying, struggling to remain standing—all her bots were jabbering in her mind, putting forward suggestions as to what to do next; and, in her state of extreme fatigue, ignoring them was harder. She'd seen enough handlers burnt beyond recovery, their brains overloaded with external stimuli until they collapsed—she should have known better. But they needed her—the most gifted bot-handler they had, their strategist—needed her while the San-Tay were still reeling from their latest interplanetary war, while they were still weak. She'd rest later—after the San-Tay were gone, after the Mheng were free. There would be time, then, plenty of it.

Bao and Nhu were hitting the door with soldering knives—each blow weakening the metal until the door finally gave way with a groan. The crowd behind Anshi roared; and rushed through—pushing Anshi ahead of them, the world shrinking to a swirling, confused mass of details—gouged-out consoles, ornaments ripped from shelves, pale men thrown down and beaten against the rush of the crowd, a whirlwind of chaos, as if demons had risen up from the underworld.

The crowd spread as they moved inwards; and Anshi found herself at the center of a widening circle in what had once been a guest room. Beside her, Bao was hacking at a nondescript bed, while others in the crowd beat down on the huge screen showing a sunset with odd, distorted trees—some San-Tay planet that Anshi did not recognize, maybe even Prime. Anshi breathed, hard, struggling to steady herself in the midst of the devastation. Particles of down and dust drifted past her; she saw a bot on the further end, desperately trying to contain the devastation, scuttling to repair the gashes in the screen. Nhu downed it with a well-placed kick; her face distorted in a wide, disturbing grin.

"Look at that!" Bao held up a mirror-necklace, which shimmered and shifted, displaying a myriad configurations for its owner's pleasure.

Nhu's laughter was harsh. "They won't need it anymore." She held out a hand; but Bao threw the necklace to the ground; and ran it through with his knife.

Anshi did not move—as if in a trance she saw all of it: the screen, the bed, the pillows that sought to mould themselves to a pleasing shape, even as hands tore them apart; the jewellery scattered on the ground; and the image of the forest, fading away to be replaced by a dull, split-open wall— every single mark of San-Tay privilege, torn away and broken, never to come back. Her bots were relaying similar images from all over the station. The San-Tay would retaliate, but they would have understood, now, how fragile the foundation of their power was. How easily the downtrodden Mheng could become their downfall; and how much it would cost them to hold Felicity.

Good.

Anshi wandered through the house, seeking out the San-Tay bots—those she could hack and reprogram, she added to her swarm; the others she destroyed, as ruthlessly as the guards had culled the prisoners on Shattered Pine.

Anshi. Anshi.

Something was blinking, insistently, in the corner of her eyes—the swarm, bringing something to her attention. The kitchens—Zhiying, overseeing the executions. Bits and pieces, distorted through the bots' feed: the San-Tay governor, begging and pleading to be spared; his wife, dying silently, watching them all with hatred in her eyes. They'd had no children; for which Anshi was glad. She wasn't Zhiying, and she wasn't sure she'd have borne the guilt.

Guilt? There were children dying all over the station; men and women killed, if not by her, by those who followed her. She spared a bitter laugh. There was no choice. Children could die; or be raised to despise the inferior breed of the Mheng; be raised to take slaves and servants, and send dissenters like Anshi to be broken in Shattered Pine with a negligent wave of their hands. No choice.

Come, the bots whispered in her mind, but she did not know why.

Zhiying was down to the Grand Master of Security when Anshi walked into the kitchens—she barely nodded at Anshi, and turned her attention back to the man aligned in the weapons' sights.

She did not ask for any last words; though she did him the honor of using a bio-silencer on him, rather than the rifles they'd used on the family—his body crumpled inwards and fell, still intact; and he entered the world of the ancestors with the honor of a whole body. "He fought well," Zhiying said, curtly. "What of the house?"

"Not a soul left living," Anshi said, flicking through the bots' channels. "Not much left whole, either."

"Good," Zhiying said. She gestured; and the men dragged the next victim—a Mheng girl, dressed in the clothes of an indentured servant.

This—this was what the bots had wanted her to see. Anshi looked to the prisoners huddled against the wall: there was one San-Tay left, an elderly man who gazed back at her, steadily and without fear. The rest—all the rest—were Mheng, dressed in San-Tay clothes, their skin pale and washed-out in the flickering lights—stained with what looked like rice flour from one of the burst bags on the floor. Mheng. Their own people.

"Elder sister," Anshi said, horrified.

Zhiying's face was dark with anger. "You delude yourself. They're not Mheng anymore."

"Because they were indentured into servitude? Is that your idea of justice? They had no choice," Anshi said. The girl against the wall said nothing; her gaze slid away from Zhiying, to the rifle; finally resting on the body of her dead mistress.

"They had a choice. We had a choice," Zhiying said. Her gaze—dark and intense—rested, for a moment, on the girl. "If we spare them, they'll just run to the militia, and denounce us to find themselves a better household. Won't you?" she asked.

Anshi, startled, realized Zhiying had addressed the girl—whose gaze still would not meet theirs, as if they'd been foreigners themselves.

At length, the girl threw her head back, and spoke in High Mheng. "They were always kind with me, and you butchered them like pigs." She was shivering now. "What will you achieve? You can't hide on Felicity. The San-Tay will come here and kill you all, and when they're done, they'll put us in the dark forever. It won't be cushy jobs like this—they'll consign us to the scavenge heaps, to the ducts-cleaning and the bots-scraping, and we won't ever see starlight again."

"See?" Zhiying said. "Pathetic." She gestured, and the girl crumpled like the man before her. The soldiers dragged the body away, and brought the old San-Tay man. Zhiying paused; and turned back to Anshi. "You're angry."

"Yes," Anshi said. "I did not join this so we could kill our own countrymen."

Zhiying's mouth twisted in a bitter smile. "Collaborators," she said. "How do you think a regime like the San-Tay continues to exist? It's because they take some of their servants, and set them above others. Because they make us complicit in our own oppression. That's the worst of what they do, little sister—turn us against each other."

No. The thought was crystal-clear in Anshi's mind, like a blade held against starlight. That's not the worst. The worst is that, to fight them, we have to best them at their own game.

She watched the old man as he died; and saw nothing in his eyes but the reflection of that bitter knowledge.

White Horse Hall is huge, so huge that it's a wonder Wen didn't see it from afar—more than a hundred stories, and more unveil as her floater lifts higher and higher, away from the crowd massed on the ground. Above the cloud cover, other white-clad floaters weave in and out of the traffic, as if to the steps of a dance only they can see.

She's alone: her escort left her at the floater station—the older man with a broad smile and a wave, and the second man with a scowl, looking away from her. As they ascend higher and higher, and the air thins out—to almost the temperature of Felicity—, Wen tries to relax, but cannot do so. She's late; and she knows it—and they probably won't admit her into the hall at all. She's a stranger here; and Mother is right: she would be better off in Felicity with Zhengyao, enjoying her period of rest by flying kites, or going for a ride on Felicity's River of Good Fortune.

At the landing pad, a woman is waiting for her: small and plump, with hair shining silver in the unfiltered sunlight. Her face is frozen in careful blankness, and she wears the white of mourners, with none of the markers for the family of the dead.

"Welcome," she says, curtly nodding to acknowledge Wen's presence. "I am Ho Van Nhu."

"Grandmother's friend," Wen says.

Nhu's face twists in an odd expression. "You know my name?" She speaks perfect Galactic, with a very slight trace of an accent—heard only in the odd inflections she puts on her own name.

Wen could lie; could say that Mother spoke of her often; but here, in this thin, cold air, she finds that she cannot lie—any more than one does not lie in the presence of the Honoured Leader. "They teach us about you in school," she says, blushing.

Nhu snorts. "Not in good terms, I'd imagine. Come," she says. "Let's get you prepared."

There are people everywhere, in costumes Wen recognizes from her history lessons—oddly old-fashioned and formal, collars flaring in the San-Tay fashion, though the five panels of the dresses are those of the Mheng high court, in the days before the San-Tay's arrival.

Nhu pushes her way through the crowd, confident, until they reach a deserted room. She stands for a while in the center, eyes closed, and bots crawl out of the interstices, dragging vegetables and balls of rolled-up dough—black and featureless, their bodies gleaming like knife-blades, their legs moving on a rhythm like centipedes or spiders.

Wen watches, halfway between fascination and horror, as they cut up the vegetables into small pieces—flatten the dough and fill up dumplings, and put them inside small steamer units that other bots have dragged up. Other bots are already cleaning up the counter, and there is a smell in the room— tea brewing in a corner. "I don't—" Wen starts. How can she eat any of that, knowing how it was prepared? She swallows, and forces herself to speak more civilly. "I should be with her."

Nhu shakes her head. Beads of sweat pearl on her face; but she seems to be gaining color as the bots withdraw, one by one—except that Wen can still *see* them, tucked away under the cupboards and the sink, like curled-up cockroaches. "This is the wake, and you're already late for it. It won't make any difference if you come in quarter of an hour later. And I would be a poor host if I didn't offer you any food."

There are two cups of tea on the central table; Nhu pours from a teapot, and pushes one to Wen—who hesitates for a moment, and then takes it, fighting against a wave of nausea. Bots dragged out the pot; the tea leaves. Bots touched the liquid that she's inhaling right now.

"You look like your mother when she was younger," Nhu says, sipping at the tea. "Like your grandmother, too." Her voice is matter-of-fact; but Wen can feel the grief Nhu is struggling to contain. "You must have had a hard time, at school."

Wen thinks on it for a while. "I don't think so," she says. She's had the usual bullying, the mockeries of her clumsiness, of her provincial accent. But nothing specifically directed at her ancestors. "They did not really care about who my grandmother was." It's the stuff of histories now; almost vanished—only the generation of the Honored Leader remembers what it was like, under the San-Tay.

"I see," Nhu says.

An uncomfortable silence stretches, which Nhu makes no effort to break.

Small bots float by, carrying a tray with the steamed dumplings—like the old vids, when the San-Tay would be receiving their friends at home. Except, of course, that the Mheng were doing the cutting-up and the cooking, in the depths of the kitchen.

"They make you uncomfortable," Nhu says.

Wen grimaces. "I—we don't have bots, on Felicity."

"I know. The remnants of the San-Tay—the technologies of servitude, which should better be forgotten and lost." Her voice is light, ironic; and Wen realizes that she is quoting from one of the Honored Leader's speeches. "Just like High Mheng. Tell me, Wen, what do the histories say of Xu Anshi?"

Nothing, Wen wants to say; but as before, she cannot bring herself to lie. "That she used the technologies of the San-Tay against them; but that, in the end, she fell prey to the lure of their power." It's what she's been told all her life; the only things that have filled the silence Mother maintains about Grandmother. But, now, staring at this small, diminutive woman, she feels almost ashamed. "That she and her followers were given a choice between exile, and death."

"And you believe that?"

"I don't know," Wen says. And, more carefully, "Does it matter?"

Nhu shrugs, shaking her head. "Mingxia—your mother once asked Anshi if she believed in reconciliation with Felicity. Anshi told her that reconciliation was nothing more than another word for forgetfulness. She was a hard woman. But then, she'd lost so much in the war. We all did."

"I'm not Mother," Wen says, and Nhu shakes her head, with a brief smile.

"No. You're here."

Out of duty, Wen thinks. Because someone has to come, and Mother won't. Because someone should remember Grandmother, even if it's Wen—who didn't know her, didn't know the war. She wonders what the Honored Leader will say about Grandmother's death, on Felicity—if she'll mourn the passing of a liberator, or remind them all to be firm, to reject the evil of the San-Tay, more than sixty years after the foreigners' withdrawal from Felicity.

She wonders how much of the past is worth clinging to.

See how the gilded Heavens are covered
With the burning bitter tears of our departed
Cast away into darkness, they contradict no truths
Made mute and absent, they denounce no lies

Anshi gave this poem into our keeping on the night after her daughter left her. She was crying then, trying not to show it—muttering about ungrateful children, and their inability to comprehend any of what their ancestors had gone through. Her hand shook, badly; and she stared into her cup of tea, as hard as she had once stared into the black hole and its currents, dragging everything into the lightless depths. But then, as on Shattered Pine, the only thing that came to her was merciless clarity, like the glint of a blade or a claw.

It is an old, old composition, its opening lines the last Anshi wrote on Felicity Station. Just as the first poem defined her youth—the escaped prisoner, the revolution's foremost bot-handler—this defined her closing decades, in more ways than one.

The docks were deserted; not because it was early in the station's cycle, not because the war had diminished interstellar travel; but because the docks had been cordoned off by Mheng loyalists. They gazed at Anshi, steadily—their eyes blank; though the mob behind them brandished placards and howled for her blood.

"It's not fair," Nhu said. She was carrying Anshi's personal belongings— Anshi's bots, and those of all her followers, were already packed in the hold of the ship. Anshi held her daughter Mingxia by the hand: the child's eyes were wide, but she didn't speak. Anshi knew she would have questions, later—but all that mattered, here and now, was surviving this. "You're a heroine of the uprising. You shouldn't have to leave like a branded criminal."

Anshi said nothing. She scanned the crowd, wondering if Zhiying would be there, at the last—if she'd smile and wish her well, or make one last stab of the knife. "She's right, in a way," she said, wearily. The crowd's hatred was palpable, even where she stood. "The bots are a remnant of the San-Tay, just like High Mheng. It's best for everyone if we forget it all." Best for everyone but them.

"You don't believe that," Nhu said.

"No." Not any of that; but she knew what was in Zhiying's heart, the hatred of the San-Tay that she carried with her—that, to her little sister, she would be nothing more than a collaborator herself—tainted by her use of the enemy's technology.

"She just wants you gone. Because you're her rival."

"She doesn't think like that," Anshi said, more sharply than she'd intended; and she knew, too, that she didn't believe that. Zhiying had a vision of the Mheng as strong and powerful; and she'd allow nothing and no one to stand in its way.

They were past the cordon now, and the maw of the ship gaped before them—the promise of a life somewhere else, on another planet. Ironic, in a way—the ship was from the San-Tay High Government, seeking amends for their behavior on colonized stations. If someone had ever told her she'd ride one of those as a guest . . .

Nhu, without hesitation, was heading up towards the dark tunnel. "You don't have to come," Anshi said.

Nhu rolled her eyes upwards, and made no comment. Like Anshi, she was old guard; a former teacher in the Mheng schools, fluent in High Mheng, and with a limited ability to control the bots. A danger, like Anshi.

There was a noise behind them—the beginning of a commotion. Anshi turned; and saw that, contrary to what she'd thought, Zhiying had come.

She wore the sash of Honored Leader well; and the stars of Felicity's new flag were spread across her dress—which was a shorter, less elaborate version of the five-panel ceremonial garb. Her hair had been pulled up in an elegant bun, thrust through with a golden phoenix pin, the first jewel to come out of the station's new workshops—she was unrecognizable from the gaunt, tall prisoner Anshi remembered, or even from the dark, intense leader of the rebellion years.

"Elder sister." She bowed to Anshi, but did not come closer; remaining next to her escort of black-clad soldiers. "We wish you happiness, and good fortune among the stars."

"We humbly thank you, Your Reverence," Anshi said—keeping the irony, and the hurt from her voice. Zhiying's eyes were dark, with the same anger Anshi remembered from the night of the Second Ring riots—the night when the girl had died. They stood, staring at each other, and at length Zhiying gestured for Anshi to move.

Anshi backed away, slowly, pulling her daughter by the hand. She wasn't sure why she felt . . . drained, as if a hundred bots had been pumping modifiers into her blood, and had suddenly stopped. She wasn't sure what she'd expected—an apology? Zhiying had never been one for it; or for doubts of any kind. But still—

Still, they'd been on Shattered Pine together; had escaped together; had preached and written the poetry of the revolution, and dared each other to hack into Felicity's network to spread it into every household, every corridor screen.

There should have been something more than a formal send-off; something more than the eyes boring into hers—dark and intense, and with no hint of sorrow or tears.

We do not weep for the enemy, Anshi thought; as she turned, and passed under the wide metal arc that led into the ship, her daughter's hand heavy in hers.

In the small antechamber, Wen dons robes of dark blue—those reserved for the mourners who are the closest family to the dead. She can hear, in the distance, the drone of prayers from the priests, and the scuttling of bots on the walls, carrying faint music until the entire structure of the hall seems to echo with it. Slowly, carefully, she rises, and stares at her pale, wan self in the mirror—with coiled bots at its angles, awaiting just an order to awaken and bring her anything she might desire. Abominations, she thinks, uneasily, but it's hard to see them as something other than alien, incomprehensible.

Nhu is waiting for her at the great doors—the crowd has parted, letting her through with an almost religious hush. In silence, Wen kneels, her head bent down—an honor to the dead, an acknowledgement that she is late and that she must make amends, for leaving Grandmother's ghost alone.

She hears a noise as the doors open—catches a flash of a crowd dressed in blue; and then she is crawling towards the coffin, staring at the ground ahead of her. By her side, there are glimpses of dresses' hems, of shoes that are an uneasy meld of San-Tay and Mheng. Ahead, a steady drone from the monks at the pulpit, taken up by the crowd; a prayer in High Mheng, incomprehensible words segueing into a melodious chant; and a smell of incense mingled with something else, a flower she cannot recognize. The floor under her is warm, soft—unlike Felicity's utilitarian metal or carpets, a wealth of painted ostentation with patterns she cannot make out.

As she crawls, Wen finds herself, incongruously, thinking of Mother.

She asked, once, why Mother had left San-Tay Prime—expecting Mother to rail once more at Grandmother's failures. But Mother merely pulled a low bench, and sat down with a sigh. "There was no choice, child. We could dwindle away on San-Tay Prime, drifting further and further away from Felicity with every passing moment. Or we could come back home."

"It's not Grandmother's home," Wen said, slowly, confusedly—with a feeling that she was grappling with something beyond her years.

"No," Mother said. "And, if we had waited too long, it wouldn't have been your home either."

"I don't understand." Wen put a hand on one of the kitchen cupboards—the door slid away, letting her retrieve a can of dried, powdered shrimp, which she dumped into the broth on the stove.

"Like two men carried away by two different currents in the river—both ending in very different places." She waved a dismissive hand. "You'll understand, when you're older."

"Is that why you're not talking with Grandmother?"

Mother grimaced, staring into the depths of her celadon cup. "Grandmother and I . . . did not agree on things," she said. "Sometimes I think . . . " She shook her head. "Stubborn old woman. She never could admit that she had lost. That the future of Felicity wasn't with bots, with High Mheng; with any of what the San-Tay had left us."

Bots. High Mheng—all of the things that don't exist anymore, on the new Felicity—all the things the Honored Leader banished, for the safety and glory of the people. "Mother . . . " Wen said, suddenly afraid.

Her mother smiled; and for the first time Wen saw the bitterness in her eyes. "Never mind, child. This isn't your burden to carry."

Wen did not understand. But now . . . now, as she crawls down the aisle, breathing in the unfamiliar smells, she thinks she understands. Reconciliation means forgetfulness, and is it such a bad thing that they forget, that they are no longer chained to the hatreds of the past?

She reaches the coffin, and rises—turns, for a brief moment, to stare at the sea of humanity before her—the blurred faces with bots at the corner of their eyes, with alien scents and alien clothes. They are not from Felicity anymore, but something else—poised halfway between the San-Tay and the culture that gave them birth; and, as the years pass, those that do not come back will drift further and further from Felicity, until they will pass each other in the street, and not feel anything but a vague sense of familiarity, like long-lost families that have become strangers to each other.

No, not from Felicity anymore—and does it matter, any of it?

Wen has no answer—none of Mother's bleak certainties about life. And so she turns away from the crowd, and looks into the coffin—into the face of a stranger, across a gap like a flowing river, dark and forever unbridgeable.

> *I am in halves, dreaming of a faraway home*
> *Not a dry spot on my moonlit pillow*
> *Through the open window lies the stars and planets*
> *Where ten thousand family members have scattered*
> *Along the River of Heaven, with no bridges to lead them home*
> *The long yearning*
> *Cuts into my heart*

This is the last poem we received from Xu Anshi; the last one she composed, before the sickness ate away at her command of High Mheng, and we could no longer understand her subvocalised orders. She said to us then, "it is done"; and turned away from us, awaiting death.

We are here now, as Wen looks at the pale face of her grandmother. We are not among our brethren in the crowd—not clinging to faces, not curled on the walls or at the corner of mirrors, awaiting orders to unfold.

We have another place.

We rest on the coffin with Xu Anshi's other belongings; scattered among the paper offerings—the arch leading into the Heavens, the bills stamped with the face of the King of Hell. We sit quiescent, waiting for Xu Wen to call us up—that we might flow up to her like a black tide, carrying her inheritance to her, and the memories that made up Xu Anshi's life from beginning to end.

But Wen's gaze slides right past us, seeing us as nothing more than a necessary evil at the ceremony; and the language she might summon us in is one she does not speak and has no interest in.

In silence, she walks away from the coffin to take her place among the mourners—and we, too, remain silent, taking our understanding of Xu Anshi's life into the yawning darkness.

FOUR KINDS OF CARGO

LEONARD RICHARDSON

—◆—

Terequale Bitty went below decks to check on a coolant cycling pipe that was heating the cargo hold above nominal, and the pipe exploded and scalded her to death and half the cargo was ruined anyway. Kol the executive officer heard the explosion, shut everything down, and wrestled the dead woman through microgravity into the medical chamber, not that it did any good.

The chamber pulled the shrapnel from Terequale Bitty's body and replaced all the tissue, but it was performing cosmetic surgery on a corpse. When it jump-started her nervous system, she took one big breath and *held* it, not metabolizing, not even passing it from her air bladder into the lung. No matter what Kol did to try and make Terequale Bitty not be dead, the ornery sysadmin would not finish that breath. Kol had to go in with a post-nasal probe and drain the air bladder manually so she'd stop looking bloated.

Terequale Bitty was gone; and for what? For a few crates of fake caviar. For *stuff*.

That's the first kind of cargo: physical goods, ordinary stuff. *Sour Candy* mostly transported contraband, but it's all the same, made of atoms, low-hassle and absolutely wonderful to work with. You can put atoms into a refrigerated crate or magnetic containment, and bring them to someone who'll be glad to take them off your hands. Physical goods are the least dangerous of the four kinds of cargo, but they were dangerous enough to get Terequale Bitty killed.

"I should have been the one to check that alert," said the Captain. That was the gist of what she probably said. The Captain was facing away from Kol, hurriedly grooming herself in the bathroom mirror. She was also brewing tea in her mouth, so the only way to decipher her mumbling was to know, as Kol did, what the Captain would say in any given situation.

Seeing other people drink made Kol thirsty; he unholstered his water bottle and took a long slurp. "We can't go around retroactively taking bullets for each other," he said. "If Terequale Bitty had *woken you up* and told you to go check a random alert, you'd be dead instead of her. How would that help anyone?" Kol held the Captain's vinyl jacket between his delicately scaled egenu fingers, and the rasme thau woman shrugged her thick muscular arms backward into the sleeves.

The Captain's cranial fronds came to life as the tisane seeped into her bloodstream. "You'll need to be the sysadmin again," she said, presumably. "Just for a while, until we find someone else." She swallowed her tisane, spat the leaves into the sink, and wiped her mouth. "I don't think this crew needs a full-time executive officer, anyway."

"They need a full-time XO because their captain is batshit insane," said Kol.

Kol had spent his childhood with his head wrapped in 3-goggles, watching egenu video epics about roguish smuggler captains and their eclectic multi-ethnic crews, writing fan mail to the actors et cetera. These epics were the main cultural export of Kol's home planet, and their sequels still ensured a steady stream of recruits into the ships that patrolled the complicated border between the Fist of Joy and the Terran Extension.

The Captain had spent *her* childhood watching bad native-language dubs of those same epics, except the implication that all this stuff was *fiction* had been lost in translation, or cut so the broadcaster could squeeze in another commercial. When she came of age, the Captain (probably not her birth name) had bought *Sour Candy* with Mommy's money, hired a crew, and declared herself a smuggler.

And somehow, amazingly, not gotten killed. Eight kiloshifts of combat zones and hazardous materials. Hundreds of surly senders and uncooperative recipients waving invoices and weapons and long-expired coupons, and no crew had gotten killed. Until now.

The Captain solemnly punched Kol in the arm, sending his scales rippling. "Kol," she said, "I need you now more than ever. The crew needs you." Her hand trembled with the shock of unaccustomed loss.

"Yes, ma'am," said Kol.

Suppose that the system administrator on *Nightside* got killed. This would never happen, barring a contract dispute with the actor, but any fan instinctively knew how Captain Mene would react. He'd grab one of his officers in a wrestling hold and say something corny like "I need you now more than ever." This would mean double shifts for a while, and they'd close out the episode with wry smiles and optimism.

This was the best job Kol had ever had, even counting legit gigs. Most smuggling bosses took sixty percent of the profits and let the crew fight over the rest; the Captain insisted on equal shares. The Captain was also too small to try any Captain Mene wrestling holds on her crew. But Captain Mene's hand wouldn't be trembling right now.

• • •

The Captain addressed her crew from the center of *Sour Candy*'s minuscule bridge. "We will be returning Terequale Bitty's body to Quennet," she said, "so that her family can perform the funerary rites."

Oh, shit. Kol flinched, standing next to the Captain in what he'd thought would be a *pro forma* show of support. The other two living crew members started shouting.

"Whoa, whoa," said Kol, recovering quickly. "Calm down. One at a time. Yip-Goru?"

"We just *came* from Quennet," said the rre navigator from inside thon's metamaterial suit. "Twenty shifts out."

"And we will return," said the Captain.

"We barely escaped last time," said Mr. Arun Sliver, the human expert in negotiations and (when those failed) munitions. "We had to hide in the hold and pretend to be Terequale Bitty's slaves."

"I will not leave a man behind," said the Captain. "Or in this case, leave a woman's body unprotected by the rites of her native religion."

"Cap, c'mon," said Yip-Goru. "We've got a hold full of Terran food and quenny caviar. *Half* full, after the accident. We go back to Quennet without unloading, we're bankrupt."

The Captain pulled up a 3-map showing *Sour Candy*'s current location, and drew her finger between the ship and a rest-stop icon. "Patrolwoman Elaine Bliskop Memorial Space Station," she said. "Six shifts away. We unload the cargo, hire a temporary sysadmin, back to Quennet."

"It won't be worth much, so close to quenny space," said Mr. Arun Sliver.

"Damn it!" said the Captain, plunging a fist harmlessly through the 3-map. "Have you already forgotten how many times Terequale Bitty saved the lives of this entire crew?"

"Three or four, I guess," said Yip-Goru. "Who's counting? Why should we risk our vocalizers for a dead body?"

"I have a sacred obligation," the Captain snarled, "to respect the religious beliefs of every member of my crew."

"Well, *my* religious beliefs—" said Mr. Arun Sliver, but Kol cut him off with a gesture.

"Ma'am, a word?" he whispered to the Captain. They walked a fraction of a metre to Terequale Bitty's abandoned 2-station, and Yip-Goru and Mr. Arun Sliver pretended not to hear what they were saying.

"Captain, I think the crew are just confused," he said. "I never thought of Terequale Bitty as being especially religious. Why respect her traditions more than she did?"

"She was a Cametrean," the Captain whispered. "Quite devout. She never gave you those . . . pamphlets? The fake travel brochures?"

"Oh, well, she wouldn't have, ma'am," said Kol. "Cametreans recruit from the top down."

Captain Mene, of needing-you-now-more-then-ever fame, fancied himself a student of Galactic religions, and held a deep respect for each of the thousands of ways in which the cosmos came to know itself. Growing up, Kol had understood this as the harmless eccentricity of a fictional character, but the dubs the Captain had seen treated his attitude as some kind of *virtue*. And so.

"We don't have a choice in this," said Captain. "Returning the body is the right thing to do."

"Yes'm." Argument was useless. Kol walked back into the center of the bridge and bowed his scaly head, as he always did when synthesizing his Captain's ideals with his own hard-won pragmatism.

"The Captain's orders," he said. "Yip-Goru, set the course. The station, then Quennet, where in accordance with the beautiful Cametrean funerary rites. . . . " He looked at the Captain, clueless.

"The family of the deceased will ceremonially eat the preserved corpse."

Silence held the cramped bridge. Finally Yip-Goru spoke up.

"Preserved," thon said, "in what?"

"The crate of lemon pickle should do nicely," said Kol.

"Well, there goes the bloody lemon pickle," said Mr. Arun Sliver.

The second kind of cargo is junk.

Junk is physical stuff, but the business model is totally different. Kol had learned the hard way that nobody wants junk; else it wouldn't be junk. The client with junk pays you to take it off his hands. Junk comes with specific disposal instructions; if you could just drop it into a star, the client would have done that himself.

A single shipping operation doesn't normally handle both goods and junk. Unless that operation is Sour Candy Shipping Ltd., with its batshit-insane captain and its hunk-of-junk dead sysadmin. Packed in salt and citric acid, on her way back home.

Oh, there was also the war. Yes, wars are important to smugglers, but background, local colour, yeah? Nobody takes up water-yachting because they're super interested in the *weather*. A sudden re-emergence of hostilities between the Extension and the Fist of Joy is the same type of problem as the sudden death of your sysadmin. Just another impersonal glob of spit in your face, the universe showing what it thinks of you.

Space stations are neutral territory by treaty, but in real life, Elaine Bliskop was swarming with humans and their Extension lackeys. On his way to the engineers' bar, Kol got a lot of hostile glances and was hassled more than once for his commercial papers. Probably should have delegated Mr. Arun Sliver to make the hiring decision. Only there was no decision, because every stray engineer on the station had been drafted into the Extension navy except one: a human named Mrs. James Chen, an old drunk broad who was obviously an Extension spy. This was very bad, but coming back with no new crew would also be very bad.

"Seventy-two, too old to fight, bad leg besides!" Mrs. James Chen said cheerfully, like it was a new war slogan. "But I'll get your engines running at one-thirty of rating!"

"Our engines already run at one-thirty rating," said Kol. "I learned that trick when I was an apprentice. I need someone who'll do the preventive maintenance so we can run at one-thirty without blowing a coolant pipe."

Mrs. James Chen looked ostentatiously down the length of the empty bar, cradling her beer mug in both hands. "Well," she said, "ya got me."

"You're hired," said Kol. Spies read from a script, same as the Captain. Kol would use Mrs. James Chen to deal with the Terequale Bitty situation, and the next time *Sour Candy* ran the wrong kind of contraband into Fist of Joy territory, then would come the betrayal. Mrs. James Chen would tip her hand, try something stupid, and Kol would help her out an airlock. Or whatever, no need to be all dramatic about it.

"Quennet," said the Captain, walking around a detailed 3-map. "Planet of mystery!"

"Planet we were just at," muttered Yip-Goru.

"Planet of fucking mystery!" said Kol.

"Yessir."

"The military buildup complicates things," said the Captain. "Quennet is right on the border. The quenny get pushed around a lot. First by the Fist of Joy, then by the Extension. Every time someone pushes, there's a backlash and the Cametreans consolidate power. Quennet withdraws, becomes more isolationist. It gets harder to do business."

"Why did Terequale Bitty leave Quennet?" called out Mr. Arun Sliver.

"Hey!" said Kol.

"Let him speak," said the Captain, as she always said, every single time. This one came from *Wat and the Warriors*. Always with the letting people speak.

"The Cametreans are isolationists," said Mr. Arun Sliver. "Space travel is a sin. So why did Terequale Bitty leave home? Sounds a bit of a cafeteria Cametrean. Someone who doesn't much care about the forms and the rituals."

"Who's Terequale Bitty?" said Mrs. James Chen, slouched uncomfortably in Terequale Bitty's quenny-shaped chair, still drunk or pretending to be.

"Trading partner," Kol lied. He was pretty sure Mrs. James Chen knew exactly who she was replacing, but there was no point in volunteering information. "A real rough customer."

The Captain was happy to let Mr. Arun Sliver speak but she felt no need to respond to his question. She made a sweeping gesture and thousands of holographic drones and battleships, red and green, swarmed above the 3-map of Quennet.

"This will be a delicate operation," she said. "Both the Extension and the Fist of Joy have blockaded the planet. We take up a spiral orbit and get lost in the noise. If the Fist does notice us, you three go down in the hold, and Kol and I will pretend to be incompetent civilian volunteers. If the Extension spots us, Kol and I go into the hold, and Mr. Arun Sliver does his Bertie Wooster routine."

"Dreadful sorry, separated from our package tour, brave lads, keep up the fight," said Mr. Arun Sliver. "That sort of wheeze, yeah?"

"Precisely. In this way we'll drop through the blockade. I'll contact our distributor planetside; Mr. Arun Sliver will act as backup. We'll deliver the merchandise and split."

"What's the 'merchandise'?" said Mrs. James Chen.

"Hard drugs," said Kol.

"Thank you, Kol," said the Captain, who disliked having to lie.

The third kind of cargo is information. Do not carry this. Information couriers look glamorous because they don't live long enough for their clothes to go out of style. Something will go wrong. The sender will suspect you of keeping secret copies for resale. The recipient will accuse you of modifying the message in transit. The authorities will show up, and you won't be able to prove you don't have whatever world-cracking secrets they're looking for.

Worst of all, information *leaks*.

"I have never been so embarrassed," said the Captain, who probably hadn't. "Blockade runs are supposed to be easy. It's like they knew exactly where we were!" She looked frantically around her office as though the culprit were some piece of decor.

"We're fine," said Kol, settling into the Captain's pleather desk chair. "They didn't find anything. But they did know where we were, because Mrs. James Chen is an Extension spy."

"Really? How do you know?"

"*Nothing* about her story holds up. Like, her name. 'Mrs. James Chen.' Female honorific, male name. She says it's her late husband's name. Her real name is 'Roberta,' but she doesn't use it. Her husband dies, so she steals his name? Who is she fooling? Did she not know there was another human on this crew? God, they always think they're smarter than you!"

The Captain leaned into the porthole above her desk and took in the green planet Quennet and the space above it, twinkling with the massed military might of the galaxy's two great powers.

"I never heard of a female James," said the Captain, "so I asked Mr. Arun Sliver about this. He says the husband thing is archaic, but it does happen. It's very slim evidence. I think we should give her another chance." Suspected spies always got another chance on *Nightside*; of course they'd get one on *Sour Candy*.

"I don't get why she's playing for such small stakes," said Kol. "I hired her on the implicit understanding that she'd save the spy shit for Fist of Joy space. What's so important about this blockade?"

"Let me run this idea by you," said the Captain. "Mrs. James Chen would like to acquire the corpse of a member of a notoriously isolationist species, which we're keeping in a crate of lemon pickle. Dissect it. Bioweapons research or something."

"Which would be an opportunity for us," said Kol. "We wouldn't need to deliver the body at all. We could sell it to the Extension and get on their good side for once."

"Absolutely not," said the Captain.

"Or, here's another idea. We can eat Terequale Bitty ourselves."

The Captain gagged. "Which of these is the ridiculous alternative you put in to make the other one look good by comparison?" she said. "Because that's the single most inappropriate thing I've ever heard you say."

"No, you're putting on a show for me, like you do for the crew. Showing off your sense of honour. I don't question that sense of honour, because against all the rules of the universe I'm aware of, it's kept us alive and solvent for eight kiloshifts. But I do question the results we'll get out of this operation."

The Captain turned away from the porthole. "You think we'll fail."

"I'll never take that bet," said Kol. "You've beaten the odds a hundred times, and you'll do it again. Somehow we'll run this blockade despite having a spy on board, and without any quenny crew to help us, we'll locate the xenophobic relatives of a dead woman whose real name we don't know.

"But what happens when we succeed? Terequale Bitty was a heretic! She disowned herself when she left Quennet. You think her folks will want to eat her now? They'll think she deserves the Cametrean rites? Is this still worth it to you?"

"We have to try."

"I agree, but here's a different way of trying. We don't need to locate Terequale Bitty's family, because we *are* her family. We took her in after her birth family cut her off. We didn't ask questions about religion or politics. We accepted her, ma'am, and we were all she had. All she has. I know you can find Terequale Bitty's parents, but if anyone's actually going to *eat* her, it's us."

"This is your official recommendation?"

"On the record."

"So, we eat Terequale Bitty, and then we die of toxic shock."

"These cannibal rites always have an out," said Kol, "like, if the body is poisoned or radioactive. The general rule is that you eat what you can. For us, that means the roe. God knows we've exported enough quenny roe as caviar. And we can eat the brain, as long as we cook it."

"Really? The brain?"

"I've eaten animal brains, from Bex, and Earth. A brain is a brain." Kol was cheating a little here—one of Captain Mene's popular lines was "A man is a man."

"Brain and roe," said the Captain. "We're the family. Let's do it."

Except. When Terequale Bitty's four colleagues gathered in the hold and ceremonially cut open her skull, they found a crystal sheath encasing her brain and upper nervous system. The end point for hundreds of threadlike wires embedded in Terequale Bitty's sensory centers. A recorder.

"Oh, shit," said Mr. Arun Sliver. He dropped the bottle of oil he was going to fry the brain in, and it bounced and rolled around the hold. "How long has that been there?"

The Captain put her bloodstained laser cutter down on the crate of lemon pickle, and wiped her eyes. "Kol," she said, "I would very much like to know why you keep hiring spies as system administrators."

"Ma'am, I—I had absolutely no idea." Kol took an anxious swig from his water bottle.

"And now we know why a Cametrean would leave her home planet," said Mr. Arun Sliver.

"She's not a spy!" said Kol. "Who was she spying on? Why would they give a spy this elaborate rig? This is for building VR environments. Why monitor everything she sees and tastes?"

"It's a repressive theocracy," said Yip-Goru. "That's kind of their thing."

There was a coughing sound. The kind of sound a human would make. Kol pivoted from Terequale Bitty's corpse towards Mr. Arun Sliver, but he hadn't made the sound. He was pointing his microwave pistol at the other human in the hold. The other human.

"Oh, hi," said the Captain.

Mrs. James Chen stepped off the ladder and made the coughing sound again.

"I think it's time we stopped keeping secrets from each other," she said.

• • •

Good news was, this wasn't the betrayal; it was the recruitment turn.

"As you know," said Mrs. James Chen, "my predecessor in this job made detailed recordings of you, starting from her first shift." The entire crew was crowded onto the bridge. "Terequale Bitty compressed these recordings and streamed them back to Quennet using a second transmitter, which, as your system administrator, she was ideally positioned to conceal from you.

"As a representative of the Navy of the Terran Extension, I'd like to show you what happened to all that footage. With the Captain's permission?"

The Captain nodded.

Every 2-station showed a flat projection: the stabilized subjective view from Terequale Bitty's eyes as she climbed the ladder up to the bridge deck. She cracked open the hatch. Everyone turned to face the rear of the bridge, as if expecting Terequale Bitty, or her ghost, to climb out the hatch.

"What's the scratchy noise?" said Yip-Goru.

"Music," said the Captain, her face taut and stern.

"She had music running in her head the whole time?"

"It's *incidental* music."

The footage had been dubbed into Mirret, Terequale Bitty's native language. Mrs. James Chen provided subtitles in Trade Standard D:

```
                     THE CAPTAIN
Ten-Minute, if you can take your mouth off that bottle
long  enough  to  program  a  course  to  the  rendezvous
point, there might be a little left for Admiral Golelli
when we get there.


                  KOL [TEN-MINUTE??]
Fuck Admiral Golelli and fuck your mother. And fuck you.


[THE CAPTAIN notices TEREQUALE BITTY, or WHATEVER SHE'S
               CALLED IN THIS THING.]


                     THE CAPTAIN
Hey,  Super-Squishy,  how's  the  firing  context  on  the
forward weapons array?


               SUPER-SQUISHY, APPARENTLY
Fixed it with a number six ratchet.
```

```
[What the hell, a FIRING CONTEXT is software, you can't
set it with a RATCHET.]
```

```
            THE CAPTAIN
 Then strap your ass down and we'll go to lightspeed.
```

Mrs. James Chen paused the recording. "'Super-squishy' is a quenny insult," she said. "Kind of insult that starts fights."

"We know," said Mr. Arun Sliver. "So what in Santa Claus *is* this?"

"A quenny broadcast 3-program," said the Captain through tight lips. "*Extension Navy*. A workplace comedy. As the name implies, the five of us are . . . were . . . officers in the Extension navy. I carry the dubious distinction of 'kookiest captain in the fleet. '"

"Heh, we're *military*?" said Mr. Arun Sliver. "Gosh."

"Hey, Cap," said Yip-Goru, "where's our nice red uniforms?"

"Gentlemen, shut up," said the Captain. "I'm declaring an outrage." She paused for effect. "This is an outrage."

"The Cametreans have been using your pissant smuggling operation as cheap raw material for anti-Extension propaganda," said Mrs. James Chen. "To blunt the population's interest in offworld affairs. Make us a laughing-stock. Keep the quenny at risk of Fist-of-Joy domination.

"Terequale Bitty was worth a lot to us, but we couldn't get to her, and now she's dead. I'm here to see if you want something good to come out of her death."

"Cap, is this shit for real?" said Yip-Goru. "All we have is some foreign gibberish and this young lady's subtitles."

"It's legit," said the Captain. She was fast-forwarding through the video broadcast on her own 2-station. "Kol got this off the local comm satellites before the Extension navy—the *actual* Extension navy—jammed them."

"I thought we knew her," said Kol. "I *hired* her."

"Don't the quenny find it strange that this sitcom has real rre and humans and egenu?" said Yip-Goru.

"Makeup, digital effects," said Mr. Arun Sliver. "You can make anyone look like anyone else. A man is a man."

"Arun," said Mrs. James Chen, using the familiar register. "Yip-Goru. I know you two don't care much for the Extension. But I'm guessing the Captain and Kol hate the Fist of Joy about the same amount. And perhaps you care about your good names.

"This is an opportunity. We can make our own video. The blockade will integrate it into their propaganda rotation. If we could just get Yip-Goru to say a few words in character."

"Why me?" said Yip-Goru.

"You are the closest thing *Extension Navy* has to a sympathetic alien character," said Mrs. James Chen. "You can make the video we wanted Terequale Bitty to make. Kol is a drunk, the Captain's an incompetent windbag. . . . "

"It's water!" said Kol. "Egenu need water! I can't go to the kitchen twenty times a shift. This show is racist."

"Yes, yes," said Mrs. James Chen. "I know the truth, we all know the truth. I'm giving you a chance to let your *audience* know the truth."

"Quick question, Mrs. James Chen: is *Extension Navy* legitimately popular on Quennet?" The Captain twitched a finger and played a bit of video at normal speed: Terequale Bitty's point-of-view stumbling down the exit corridor of a space station, carrying an unconscious Yip-Goru in her arms, pursued by Extension customs agents. "Or is it played to captive audiences, on military bases and in waiting rooms?" She sped the video back up to a blur. Terequale Bitty was always present, but never in shot. Always a surrogate for the audience.

"It cleans up with the student demographics," said Mrs. James Chen. "We have no idea why; the whole point of the show is that nobody respects the quenny. But they do watch it, and we can use that."

"Captain, you can't be seriously . . . ," said Kol.

"Kol," said the Captain carefully, "stop showing off your bruise and help me out. Watch this video through the eyes of a space-epic fan." Episodes on the Captain's 2-screen were flashing by in seconds: Terequale Bitty on the bridge, in the engine room, in the cargo hold. "Do you see what I see? Do you notice something conspicuously missing?"

"Our consent?" said Kol. "Our seemingly genuine friendship with Terequale Bitty?"

The Captain stopped her playback. "We will produce a video," she told Mrs. James Chen. "We will produce our own video, not whatever the Extension scripted for Yip-Goru. You will broadcast it using . . . however you do that sort of thing."

"Make the video," said Mrs. James Chen, "and we'll see."

"Hi. This is the cargo ship *Sour Candy*, and I am her Captain. It is a real, civilian, spaceship, not a broadcast set, and I'm an alien, not a quenny in makeup. This is my private office."

The Captain was wearing a shiny purple dress. It had been fashionable once, but not within the Captain's lifetime. Probably an heirloom, stored in a locker as a reminder of her previous life. Kol had never seen the Captain wear anything but the grey jumpsuit and the black vinyl jacket.

"I apologize if the camera work is shakier than what you're used to," said the Captain. She was speaking Mirret, memorized phonetically. "Our regular camerawoman, Terequale Bitty, passed away in an accident a few shifts ago. It was a senseless death, and among other things, I'm afraid it means the end of the series.

"I won't pretend we haven't had our differences with the broadcaster, but I'm sure you agree that Terequale Bitty's character was the moral center of the show. She is irreplaceable. It doesn't make sense to go on without her."

Mr. Arun Sliver was running the 3-camera, a heavy red pile of milspec designed for human hands and provided by Mrs. James Chen. Kol and Yip-Goru flanked the Captain, hands folded, like at a funeral.

"I want to show you something before we sign off. Something the broadcaster kept cutting out of the show." The Captain waved Mr. Arun Sliver forward, towards the large porthole above her desk. Mr. Arun Sliver manoeuvred the camera into the recessed glass of the porthole. A stark green crescent filled the viewfinder.

"This is the establishing shot," said the Captain. "It sets the scene, tells you where we are in space. Right now, we're in orbit around a planet. It's your planet. This is Quennet. This is you."

"Problem with the focal length," said Mr. Arun Sliver.

"Switch to a 2-shot," said the Captain, in Trade Standard D.

"Not sure how."

The Captain reached into the recessed porthole and blocked one lens of the camera with three thick fingers. On the viewfinder, Quennet became a thin green blur and then slowly came back into focus.

"*Sour Candy* is an old ship," said the Captain. "It's ugly, it's falling apart. There's a lot of space for cargo and not much for people. But when it gets too much to bear, we can just look out a porthole and we're surrounded by this stark, majestic beauty. We all look out the porthole to recharge. Terequale Bitty looked out all the time, but the broadcaster cut it out. I think you should ask yourself why your government systematically cut the most striking footage produced for this show.

"Listen. In this line of work, we say there are four kinds of cargo. There's goods to be delivered, junk to be disposed of, information to be transmitted. And there's the cargo you don't need to deliver, because it's addressed to you. The experience of being out here in the middle of all this beauty. That's the most valuable cargo of all.

"People of Quennet, you deserve to see everything Terequale Bitty saw. You deserve to see your own beautiful planet from above. You deserve to come out here, share your work and your culture with the rest of the universe, and then come back home. Think about this."

Mrs. James Chen the Extension spy stepped out of the shadows and slowly, repeatedly clapped her hands together.

"Nice speech," she said.

"Mrs. James Chen," said the Captain. "You're fired. Take this video back to your handlers."

"With pleasure." The spy delivered a crisp Extension-style salute. "It's been an honour serving with you."

"Heh, you think *I'm* crazy," the Captain told Kol after Mrs. James Chen had left and the others had gone below. She parodied the spy's salute. "The hell was that? Military shitweed."

"The fourth kind of cargo is *baggage*," said Kol.

"Sorry?"

"It's not valuable. It doesn't 'come addressed to you.' It's the stuff you *can't get rid of*. It's whatever you're running away from. So that you end up living in a metal deathtrap, smuggling benzene to the planet where they get high on benzene."

The Captain made a pensive face. "Yeah, well," she said. "I think *Sour Candy* has given the quenny enough depressing news for one shift. Let's end the show on a positive note."

Light spiked through the porthole above the Captain's desk. The ship's radiation alert went off. The blockade was heating up.

"Time to leave," said Kol, and pulled the drapes. "Sit out the war in a forest."

"Oh, but now they're distracted!" said the Captain. She rubbed stubby hands together. "Now we can run the blockade. We'll drop off the body, find some roe donors to cover our expenses."

"We're back down to—okay, sure! Why the hell not? What's the worst that can happen? Let's go."

The Captain punched Kol in the arm again. "Kol, you are a *lousy* XO," she said. "But I seem to remember you used to be a pretty good sysadmin."

Down on Quennet, near a beach, there's a big house bought with government money. An old couple lives there, retired; they do some gardening, watch a lot of broadcast video. Once in a while a government priest comes down from the city and spends an afternoon. There are bedrooms for the kids and their families, when they come to visit; and a little room set aside for Terequale Bitty, the kid who left home and never came back.

Terequale Bitty just came back. She landed with a shockwave that uprooted the garden and scared her mother half to death. She came back in a box with her skull cut open, but that's more than the government priest said would ever come back. It's her. It really is her.

She didn't want to come back. She hated it here. But here she is.

ELEMENTALS

URSULA K. LE GUIN

I. Airlings

No one knows how many airlings there are, most likely not a great many, whatever a great many means. They inhabit the atmosphere, generally between a hundred and ten or twelve thousand feet above the ground, seldom clearly visible to human eyes, and leaving almost no trace of their presence. They swim in air as we do in water, but with far more ease, air being their native element. Slight motions of the whole body and the arms and legs move them gracefully through their three dimensions.

We breathe air, but a very different element, the earth, gives us support. This might explain the apparent duality of human nature. Airlings, like fish or fetuses, are supported by what they breathe, and so to them flesh and spirit may be more nearly, more simply one.

Airlings live off the warmth of the sun: they calorisynthesize, as plants photosynthesize. They eat heat. The highest, faintest stratocirrus clouds are believed to be their waste matter, their ethereal sewage, drifting upward to evaporate.

The airlings' small, slight, cool bodies are almost transparent. Only with old age do they begin to turn cloudy, verging on translucency. Infants are as clear as glass.

If they ever did, the airlings no longer frequent the air near centers of human habitation. As we swarm thicker and thicker on the earth, the airlings have scattered ever higher into the atmosphere above the oceans, the largest deserts, tundras, and high mountain ranges. Many of them go south for the sumer, to Antarctica, where in the endless sunlight above the blizzards they can fly as freely as they used to do.

Our ever-increasing air traffic is evidently a problem or danger to them, but they avoid the routes and altitudes commonly used by airplanes; and they do not register on cameras or radar.

Their voices are extremely soft, but their hearing is acute, and if the wind is not strong a pair of airlings can carry on a long conversation while flying a half-mile apart. Several human studies of their language or languages exist, and even some partial glossaries, but all of them are based on the most fragmentary evidence and, like the nineteenth-century treatises demonstrating that the languages of the North American Indians were derived from Welsh, consist mostly of wishful thinking.

Airlings have no gender, or share a single gender, as you please. Young adults pair off on brief, warm, summer nights in the higher latitudes above the sea; the couples play in the air together, meeting, at the end of intricate and rapid configurations of flight, for a long, close kiss. Down in the tropics some seven months later, each one of the couple, attended closely by friends and relatives, may bear a child in mid-air.

Careful and affectionate parents, the airlings carry their newborns out of every passing cloud or cloud-shadow to bathe and be nourished by the flooding heat of the sun. The babies can fly within a day or two. They sleep in the parent's arms for a year or so. Even when it has learned to sleep on the wing, the child stays close to its parent for two or three years more. Then the little airling begins to make exploratory flights on its own, and before long the parent will guide it near a school, and soon will see it plunge into the throng without a backward look.

In the school—dozens or hundreds of youngsters flying together—the children live, learn, and play together for ten years or more, till, nearing maturity, one by one they leave the group, going off on their own on world-encircling voyages, each alone in the vast ocean of the air.

They meet and meet again, maintaining long-lasting relationships of consanguinity, friendship, and love, and carrying on their soft, far-ranging conversations; but airlings never stay together permanently, nor, once out of school, do they ever gather in large groups.

Death comes to the airling as a sensation of ever-increasing warmth and lightness, as if they were afire, and gravity were letting go its hold. They begin to fly higher than they have ever flown before, seeking cold, rising into ever thinner air. One day, somewhere alone, almost in the stratosphere, the airling will suddenly combust and vanish in one slight, bright, all-consuming flare. Nothing of an airling ever falls to the ground.

Airlings pay little heed to other creatures, but have been reported to tease hummingbirds, and sometimes they follow skylarks upward, imitating their song. In early spring and late autumn they often join the great migration routes, spending the long, dark, hungry night nestled on the back of a wild goose or Arctic tern or sandhill crane, half asleep in the feathers between the powerful, slow-beating wings. The bird pays no attention to its almost invisible, almost weightless passenger.

• • •

II. Booklets

There is a movement to declare booklets an endangered species. I believe this is unnecessary; their adaptability will save them, as it did through the cataclysmic changes from clay to papyrus to vellum to paper in the West, and from scroll to bound book in both the Orient and Occident. The Romans, after all, knew them as *volumenuli*—scrollets. Perhaps the Babylonians had a word for them—cuneideformers?

Of course many people would applaud the extinction of the whole species. They regard booklets as mere noxious pests, ignoring the indisputable evidence of intelligent, though obscure, purpose in their behavior, and an arguable degree of literacy. "Cockroaches are damn clever too," one man said to me. I unwisely retorted, "Roaches can't read," and his perfectly rational reply was, "Thank God!"

Actually, we can't say with certainty that booklets read. All we know is that they respond to written or printed words, as words, in some way. Their most persistent and annoying behavior, interference with the order of letters and words, seldom seems meaningful, to us. I know a poet who leaves his notebook on shelves he believes to be particularly booklet-infested, hoping to find they have made wonderful or inspiring changes in his words, but I think him foolish. For one thing, they clearly prefer print to handwriting. Now that the only natural enemy of the booklet, the proof-reader, is a genuinely endangered species, the poet should simply print his poems and confidently expected to find typos, whether enlightening or not.

There is no doubt that booklets multiplied in proportion as print replaced manuscript. Medieval copyists complained, of course, of the *membranae pediculi* (vellum lice) that transposed letters, altered words, and made nonsense out of whole passages in their work (particularly when the light was poor and they were sleepy.) But only countless millions of booklets working, as they seem to do, in mysterious harmony of purpose, can account for the ever-increasing number of typos, transpositions, misspellings, and random garble we see in print these days. The absence of proof-readers can only explain part of it.

Is booklet activity mere mischief, malice, as some believe? Do booklets so despise or envy us, or our books, to the point that they try to destroy them? Are they possibly trying to correct us—to point out, subtly, by making some of it meaningless, the inherent meaninglessness, the existential error, in all we write? Or are they quite indifferent to us and what we write except in using our symbols as a code to transmit an entirely different order of meaning, opaque to us? Jopper's *Codex of Common Typos* is a massive but unconvincing attempt to "translate" this supposed code or cipher.

Whatever their purposes, I think it very likely that booklets are in fact quite indifferent to our purposes. Do they perceive us at all? To us they are invisible and imperceptible, except to people experiencing certain types of migraine aura.

These witnesses universally report them as being about the size of a comma, the color of the page, and intensely active. In 1923, Mrs. Dora Brown wrote a vivid description for her opthamologist: "A quivering, scuttling busy-ness. All over the page—every page. They're in constant motion, almost vibrating—mostly gathered around the lines of print, pulling and pushing at letters. A lot of them will do it all at once, so that a whole word shivers, or moves, or jumps a little. And the letters seem to blur. The words aren't quite solid and definite any more, as printed words ought to be. They've been un-stabilised (is that a word?)."

To me, this description brings to mind a phenomenon Mrs Brown had never seen: a page of text on an early computer screen. The technology has improved, so that the text that I am typing right now into my computer, and that you may be reading on another computer, looks substantial, steady, clear, and stable. But it isn't. The whole thing could vanish in a moment, or I could change every word in it again and again and leave no trace of what was there to begin with; if you don't have a locked copy, so can you. I think the computer—which many thought would save us from the annoying tricks of booklets and render the species obsolete—is turning out to be their ideal ecological niche.

We know they are adaptable. Probably they breed very frequently, like fruit flies. They must have undergone great change in the past twenty years in order to operate electronically as they did corporeally—for a booklet to become an ebooklet. But perhaps those changes lay in the direction their nature had always tended: just as, when he was needed, a kind of human being appeared who had never existed, because his capacity, his nature had never before been called upon, the computer nerd.

Ebooklets, which many people carelessly refer to as "bugs," totally avoid copiers, but they infested scanners at once and copiously. What the future may hold for them in the reproduction and dissemination of computer texts, who can say? Arbitrary alteration, omission and elimination, reversals and misplacement, introduced elements, and garbling—all these devices and strategies are infinitely easier to execute in electronic text. The *instability* for which Mrs. Brown sought the word in 1923 has been achieved. The pirating of incomplete and corrupted texts, the practice of "mashing" disparate and unrelated texts, the indifference to error, are good evidence of the essential instability of the electronic word. My guess is that ebooklets are eagerly abetting and feasting upon the activities of e-pirates, corporations dealing in information, paranoid governments, and human lazy-mindedness, towards the creation of a Universal Library in which information, misinformation, and disinformation are indistinguishable, a literature in which all texts are corrupt and there is no unaltered original by which to discover the nature and extent of the corruption.

I wonder what ebooklets get out of this? Perhaps they were seeking, even as *volumenulae*, to destabilise the written word, returning it to the fleeting lability of unrecorded speech. Maybe the changelessness of writing, the life-blood of historical cultures, is death to them, and they live and thrive on continual change toward disorder, entropic activity, the faster the better.

If so, it appears that our increasing dependence on the computer has some drawbacks. Anybody who wants their grandchildren to know what Plato or Lao Tzu or Yeats or Saramago wrote had better keep a copy on paper, in Greek or Chinese or English or Portuguese, in a box treated with eucalyptus oil to discourage booklets and vetiver oil to discourage silverfish, with a plea to posterity to treat it as a valued inheritance, unique, irreplaceable, precious. Which of course it always was.

III. Chthons and Draks

Descriptions of the appearance and behavior of chthons are supported by legend, tradition, speculation, and passionate argument, but by little or no actual observation. We know very little about them. We know they are earth-dwellers, do not even know how much the body of a chthon differs from the earth in which it lives. Is a chthon in fact just dirt, a little more active than dirt in general?

Of course in the larger sense this is true of ourselves, or any living thing. We are of the earth and its substance is our substance. Here the earthworm provides a useful paradigm. The worm lives in the dirt, moves through it, eats it, excretes it, is utterly and totally a citizen and creature of it, and yet isn't it. The organization of the insentient minerals and organic refuse that compose dirt and their interaction in the living creature place the worm on a plane of being in which sensation and purposive activity are unmistakably more present than they are in dirt.

Earthworms are not only sentient, they can learn and remember. They probably don't think about a great many things, but they do think. And it is generally assumed that chthons, however earthy their substance, being by all reports very much larger and possibly more complex than earthworms and showing what many see as evidence of premeditated action, lead an existence on a higher plane of sensitivity and intelligence than worms—perhaps very much higher.

But our favored metaphor of height to signify size, complexity, importance, etc., is out of place when used of creatures to whom depth may mean all that height means to us. It might well be more appropriate to speak, with awed respect, of how low a plane they inhabit.

Certainly they are able to live deep down. How deep, we don't know. The giant squid was known for a long, long tie only through rumors and strange wounds on a whale's side and improbable decaying fragments of an enormous corpse; and like giant squids, chthons live deep, stay down, and don't come up. We've invaded the depths of the sea and photographed the giant squid, it isn't just an old sailor's tale, it's a celebrity now like everybody else—it's real, see? that's a real picture, so the giant squid is real, the way it wasn't until we took the picture. But there are no photographs of a chthon. Well, there are some. There are photographs of Nessie in Loch Ness, too. You can photograph anything you believe in.

Our deepest mines barely enter the chthonic realm. Our deepest geoprobes may, but it is a very, very large realm, the underworld. There's little hope of any physical object we could send down there meeting by chance with an inhabitant and recognising that it had met one. The camera of course is useless. A lens in the dark sees dark. In rock it sees rock. In magma it sees magma—very briefly, before it rejoins the magma.

It is in fact much easier for us to send machines, cameras, telescopes, recording devices of all kinds, even people, ten million miles out into space than it is to send anything, let alone anyone, ten miles under foot. Going out is always easy, you just set off and go. Going in is never so easy, and going deep is quite another matter.

The deepest hole we've made in the earth so far is only about a third to a fifth of the way through the outer crust. And at that depth, the heat is getting towards three times the boiling point of water, and the pressure crushes a steel beam like a wad of aluminum foil.

Even if a seeing eye could exist in their dark realm, the great elementals of the underground may be assumed to be as elusive to normal human vision and perception as most other elementals. There may, however, have been sightings.

Descriptions, vivid though incomplete and mythologized, of chthons, or of a chthon, exist in several parts of the world, including Japan and Indian California. There is a great earth snake, they said, that lives deep in the earth. When the snake moves, the earth moves beneath our feet. The Japanese and the Californians, being particularly familiar with earthquake, might know what they were talking about.

Most biogeologists now agree that the San Andreas Fault is a surface feature owing its existence to a creature about eight hundred miles long that resides several miles underneath it: a great earth snake, or chthon. It moves almost constantly. Its movements are occasionally abrupt and jerky, as if in pain or effort, and these attract human attention, sometimes to the point of panic. Most of the time the San Andreas chthon is busy smoothly and almost imperceptibly rearranging the relative positions of the Pacific and North American tectonic plates. It is pushing the area west of it towards the northwest at the rate of about an inch and a half a year, so that eventually Los Angeles will slide past San Francisco on its way to Alaska.

Biogeologists certainly don't consider this interesting phenomenon to be the goal of the rearrangement, but they can only speculate why the chthon wants to move the south coast of California out of California. Perhaps it is tired of the swarm of lesser chthons, its siblings or descendants, that crowd the depths almost everywhere in California in incredible numbers. Chthonic overpopulation gives rise to territorial rivalries and quarrels that cause endless faulting and instability, which is perhaps why the greatest chthon of them all has been driven to seek a quieter zone out under the northern Pacific Ocean.

The great earth snake of the depths beneath the Japan Trench may be restless for the same reason. Or conversely, the three tectonic plates that are converging on those unsteady islands may be pushed by three different chthons intent upon meeting. To mate? To fight? To dance? Whatever their deep purpose, its achievement is likely to upset the tiny beings that run about on the skin of the planet far above them and consider themselves the crown of earthly existence.

Whether chthons are or are not related to draks, the better-known inhabitants of volcanoes, is an open question. Some think draks are an entirely different species of elemental, citing the immense difference in their appearance and behavior. Others believe they are ancestrally the same. The original unifying theory held that both are born originally of magma. In this picture, the chthons, born very deep inside the planet, migrate very slowly towards the outside, cooling, darkening, lithifying, and becoming more porous; as they near the surface, they die, their huge bodies returning to earth in earth. The draks, coming up much faster, take only a very labile form and retain the volatile and spectacular properties of superheated matter under pressure. They burst forth from Etna or Eyjafjallajokull and die in fiery explosions.

A new unifying theory posits that chthons are born from fertile dust on the surface of the planet. Microscopically tiny, the wormlets begin at once to eat their way straight down. They devour their way steadily through dirt and rock, growing all the time. They never cease that downward, inward motion till they are miles under the surface. There in the underworld, particularly around the edges of tectonic plates, they move about easily and freely in the substance of the earth as earthworms do in dirt.

At the next stage in their long lives, chthons head down deeper and ever deeper, boring toward the center without rest, tolerating the increasing heat and unimaginable pressure, till they come to the Great Discontinuity. There, transformed, they plunge straight down toward the molten iron core of Earth. And there they are reshaped, as the pupa is in the cocoon.

They come forth as draks—slender, clawed, winged, with bodies of fire. They make their way upward rapidly, first through liquid rock, then through vents and fissures, seeking the magma chambers of the volcanoes. In them they may live for centuries, dancing endlessly with their kind in those incandescent halls. From them at last they will burst upward to the air, taking wing in a brief, terrible, and splendid mating flight. They are destroyed in that final, ecstatic escape from their body of earth, but from the dust of fertility that falls back to the ground from these great eruptions, the next generation is born.

All this must remain, for now, speculation. The chthons are not invisible, but they live blind in utter darkness, and it is not certain that anybody has ever seen one. The draks are visible, but they live in white-hot lava, and only momentarily, blindingly, are they ever seen.

PRAYER

ROBERT REED

Fashion matters. In my soul of souls, I know that the dead things you carry on your body are real, real important. Grandma likes to call me a clotheshorse, which sounds like a good thing. For example, I've always known that a quality sweater means the world. I prefer soft organic wools woven around Class-C nanofibers—a nice high collar with sleeves riding a little big but with enough stopping power to absorb back-to-back kinetic charges. I want pants that won't slice when the shrapnel is thick, and since I won't live past nineteen, probably, I let the world see that this body's young and fit. (Morbid maybe, but that's why I think about death only in little doses.) I adore elegant black boots that ignore rain and wandering electrical currents, and everything under my boots and sweater and pants has to feel silky-good against the most important skin in my world. But essential beyond all else is what I wear on my face, which is more makeup than Grandma likes, and tattooed scripture on the forehead, and sparkle-eyes that look nothing but ordinary. In other words, I want people to see an average Christian girl instead of what I am, which is part of the insurgency's heart inside Occupied Toronto.

To me, guns are just another layer of clothes, and the best day ever lived was the day I got my hands on a barely-used, cognitively damaged Mormon railgun. They don't make that model anymore, what with its willingness to change sides. And I doubt that there's ever been a more dangerous gun made by the human species. Shit, the boy grows his own ammo, and he can kill anything for hundreds of miles, and left alone he will invent ways to hide and charge himself on the sly, and all that time he waits waits waits for his master to come back around and hold him again.

I am his master now.

I am Ophelia Hanna Hanks, except within my local cell, where I wear the randomly generated, perfectly suitable name:

Ridiculous.

The gun's name is Prophet, and until ten seconds ago, he looked like scrap conduit and junk wiring. And while he might be cognitively impaired, Prophet is wickedly loyal to me. Ten days might pass without the two of us being in each other's reach, but that's the beauty of our dynamic: I can live normal and look normal, and while the enemy is busy watching everything else, a solitary fourteen-year-old girl slips into an alleyway that's already been swept fifty times today.

"Good day, Ridiculous."

"Good day to you, Prophet."

"And who are we going to drop into Hell today?"

"All of America," I say, which is what I always say.

Reliable as can be, he warns me, "That's a rather substantial target, my dear. Perhaps we should reduce our parameters."

"Okay. New Fucking York."

Our attack has a timetable, and I have eleven minutes to get into position.

"And the specific target?" he asks.

I have coordinates that are updated every half-second. I could feed one or two important faces into his menu, but I never kill faces. These are the enemy, but if I don't define things too closely, then I won't miss any sleep tonight.

Prophet eats the numbers, saying, "As you wish, my dear."

I'm carrying him, walking fast towards a fire door that will stay unlocked for the next ten seconds. Alarmed by my presence, a skinny rat jumps out of one dumpster, little legs running before it hits the oily bricks.

"Do you know it?" I ask.

The enemy likes to use rats as spies.

Prophet says, "I recognize her, yes. She has a nest and pups inside the wall."

"Okay," I say, feeling nervous and good.

The fire door opens when I tug and locks forever once I step into the darkness.

"You made it," says my gun.

"I was praying," I report.

He laughs, and I laugh too. But I keep my voice down, stairs needing to be climbed and only one of us doing the work.

She found me after a battle. She believes that I am a little bit stupid. I was damaged in the fight and she imprinted my devotions to her, and then using proxy tools and stolen wetware, she gave me the cognitive functions to be a loyal agent to the insurgency.

I am an astonishing instrument of mayhem, and naturally her superiors thought about claiming me for themselves.

But they didn't.

If I had the freedom to speak, I would mention this oddity to my Ridiculous. "Why would they leave such a prize with little you?"

"Because I found you first," she would say.

"War isn't a schoolyard game," I'd remind her.

"But I made you mine," she might reply. "And my bosses know that I'm a good soldier, and you like me, and stop being a turd."

No, we have one another because her bosses are adults. They are grown souls who have survived seven years of occupation, and that kind of achievement doesn't bless the dumb or the lucky. Looking at me, they see too much of a blessing, and nobody else dares to trust me well enough to hold me.

I know all of this, which seems curious.

I might say all of this, except I never do.

And even though my mind was supposedly mangled, I still remember being crafted and calibrated in Utah, hence my surname. But I am no Mormon. Indeed, I'm a rather agnostic soul when it comes to my interpretations of Jesus and His influence in the New World. And while there are all-Mormon units in the US military, I began my service with Protestants—Baptists and Missouri Synods mostly. They were bright clean happy believers who had recently arrived at Fort Joshua out on Lake Ontario. Half of that unit had already served a tour in Alberta, guarding the tar pits from little acts of sabotage. Keeping the Keystones safe is a critical but relatively simple duty. There aren't many people to watch, just robots and one another. The prairie was depopulated ten years ago, which wasn't an easy or cheap process; American farmers still haven't brought the ground back to full production, and that's one reason why the Toronto rations are staying small.

But patrolling the corn was easy work compared to sitting inside Fort Joshua, millions of displaced and hungry people staring at your walls.

Americans call this Missionary Work.

Inside their own quarters, alone except for their weapons and the Almighty, soldiers try to convince one another that the natives are beginning to love them. Despite a thousand lessons to the contrary, Canada is still that baby brother to the north, big and foolish but congenial in his heart, or at least capable of learning manners after the loving sibling delivers enough beat-downs.

What I know today—what every one of my memories tells me—is that the American soldiers were grossly unprepared. Compared to other units and other duties, I would even go so far as to propose that the distant generals were aware of their limitations yet sent the troops across the lake regardless, full of religion and love for each other and the fervent conviction that the United States was the empire that the world had always deserved.

Canada is luckier than most. That can't be debated without being deeply, madly stupid. Heat waves are killing the tropics. Acid has tortured the seas. The wealth of the previous centuries has been erased by disasters of weather and war and other inevitable surprises. But the worst of these sorrows haven't occurred in the Greater United States, and if they had half a mind, Canadians would be thrilled with the mild winters and long brilliant summers and the supportive grip of their big wise master.

My soldiers' first recon duty was simple: Walk past the shops along Queen.

Like scared warriors everywhere, they put on every piece of armor and every sensor and wired back-ups that would pierce the insurgent's jamming. And that should have been good enough. But by plan or by accident, some native let loose a few molecules of VX gas—just enough to trigger one of the biohazard alarms. Then one of my brother-guns was leveled at a crowd of innocents, two dozen dead before the bloody rain stopped flying.

That's when the firefight really began.

Kinetic guns and homemade bombs struck the missionaries from every side. I was held tight by my owner—a sergeant with commendations for his successful defense of a leaky pipeline—but he didn't fire me once. His time was spent yelling for an orderly retreat, pleading with his youngsters to find sure targets before they hit the buildings with hypersonic rounds. But despite those good smart words, the patrol got itself trapped. There was a genuine chance that one of them might die, and that's what those devout men encased in body armor and faith decided to pray: Clasping hands, they opened channels to the Almighty, begging for thunder to be sent down on the infidels.

The Almighty is what used to be called the Internet—an American child reclaimed totally back in 2027.

A long stretch of shops and old buildings was struck from the sky.

That's what American soldiers do when the situation gets dicey. They pray, and the locals die by the hundreds, and the biggest oddity of that peculiar day was how the usual precise orbital weaponry lost its way, and half of my young men were wounded or killed in the onslaught while a tiny shaped charge tossed me a hundred meters down the road.

There I was discovered in the rubble by a young girl.

As deeply unlikely as that seems.

I don't want the roof. I don't need my eyes to shoot. An abandoned apartment on the top floor is waiting for me, and in particular, its dirty old bathroom. As a rule, I like bathrooms. They're the strongest part of any building, what with pipes running through the walls and floor. Two weeks ago, somebody I'll never know sealed the tube's drain and cracked the faucet just enough for a slow drip, and now the water sits near the brim. Water is essential for long shots. With four minutes to spare, I deploy Prophet's long legs, tipping him just enough toward the southeast, and then I sink him halfway into the bath, asking, "How's that feel?"

"Cold," he jokes.

We have three and a half minutes to talk.

I tell him, "Thank you."

His barrel stretches to full length, its tip just short of the moldy plaster ceiling. "Thank you for what?" he says.

"I don't know," I say.

Then I laugh, and he sort of laughs.

I say, "I'm not religious. At least, I don't want to be."

"What are you telling me, Ridiculous?"

"I guess . . . I don't know. Forget it."

And he says, "I will do my very best."

Under the water, down where the breech sits, ammunition is moving. Scrap metal and scrap nano-fibers have been woven into four bullets. Street fights require hundreds and thousands of tiny bullets, but each of these rounds is bigger than most carrots and shaped the same general way. Each one carries a brain and microrockets and eyes. Prophet is programming them with the latest coordinates while running every last-second test. Any little problem with a bullet can mean an ugly shot, or even worse, an explosion that rips away the top couple floors of this building.

At two minutes, I ask, "Are we set?"

"You're standing too close," he says.

"If I don't move, will you fire anyway?"

"Of course."

"Good," I say.

At ninety-five seconds, ten assaults are launched across southern Ontario. The biggest and nearest is fixated on Fort Joshua—homemade cruise missiles and lesser railguns aimed at that artificial island squatting in our beautiful lake. The assaults are meant to be loud and unexpected, and because every soldier thinks his story is important, plenty of voices suddenly beg with the Almighty, wanting His godly hand.

The nearby battle sounds like a sudden spring wind.

"I'm backing out of here," I say.

"Please do," he says.

At sixty-one seconds, most of the available American resources are glancing at each of these distractions, and a brigade of AIs is studying past tendencies and elaborate models of insurgency capabilities, coming to the conclusion that these events have no credible value toward the war's successful execution.

Something else is looming, plainly.

"God's will," says the nonbeliever.

"What isn't?" says the Mormon gun.

At seventeen seconds, two kilometers of the Keystone John pipeline erupt in a line of smoky flame, microbombs inside the heated tar doing their best to stop the flow of poisons to the south.

The Almighty doesn't need prayer to guide His mighty hand. This must be the main attack, and every resource is pulled to the west, making ready to deal with even greater hazards.

I shut the bathroom door and run for the hallway.

Prophet empties his breech, the first carrot already moving many times faster than the speed of sound as it blasts through the roof. Its three buddies are directly behind it, and the enormous release of stored energy turns the bathwater to steam, and with the first shot the iron tub is yanked free of the floor while the second and third shots kick the tub and the last of its water down into the bathroom directly downstairs. The final shot is going into the wrong part of the sky, but that's also part of the plan. I'm not supposed to be amazed by how many factors can be juggled at once, but they are juggled and I am amazed, running down the stairs to recover my good friend.

The schedule is meant to be secret and followed precisely. The Secretary of Carbon rides her private subway car to the UN, but instead of remaining indoors and safe, she has to come into the sunshine, standing with ministers and potentates who have gathered for this very important conference. Reporters are sitting in rows and cameras will be watching from every vantage point, and both groups are full of those who don't particularly like the Secretary. Part of her job is being despised, and fuck them. That's what she thinks whenever she attends these big public dances. Journalists are livestock, and this is a show put on for the meat. Yet even as the scorn builds, she shows a smile that looks warm and caring, and she carries a strong speech that will last for three minutes, provided she gives it. Her words are meant to reassure the world that full recovery is at hand. She will tell everyone that the hands of her government are wise and what the United States wants is happiness for every living breathing wonderful life on this great world—a world that with God's help will live for another five billion years.

For the camera, for the world, the Secretary of Carbon and her various associates invest a few moments in handshakes and important nods of the head.

Watching from a distance, without knowing anything, it would be easy to recognize that the smiling woman in brown was the one in charge.

The UN president shakes her hand last and then steps up to the podium. He was installed last year after an exhaustive search. Handsome and personable, and half as bright as he is ambitious, the President greets the press and then breaks from the script, shouting a bland "Hello" to the protestors standing outside the blast screens.

Five thousand people are standing in the public plaza, holding up signs and generated holos that have one clear message:

"END THE WARS NOW."

The Secretary knows the time and the schedule, and she feels a rare ache of nervousness, of doubt.

When they hear themselves mentioned, the self-absorbed protestors join together in one rehearsed shout that carries across the screens. A few reporters look at the throng behind them. The cameras and the real professionals focus on the human subjects. This is routine work. Reflexes are numb, minds lethargic. The Secretary picks out a few familiar faces, and then her assistant pipes a warning into her sparkle-eyes. One of the Keystones has been set on fire.

In reflex, the woman takes one step backward, her hands starting to lift to cover her head.

A mistake.

But she recovers soon enough, turning to her counterpart from Russia, telling him, "And congratulations on that new daughter of yours."

He is flustered and flattered. With a giddy nod, he says, "Girls are so much better than boys these days. Don't you think?"

The Secretary has no chance to respond.

A hypersonic round slams through the atmosphere, heated to a point where any impact will make it explode. Then it drops into an environment full of clutter and one valid target that must be acquired and reached before the fabulous energies shake loose from their bridle.

There is no warning sound.

The explosion lifts bodies and pieces of bodies, and while the debris rises, three more rounds plunge into the panicked crowd.

Every person in the area drops flat, hands over their heads.

Cameras turn, recording the violence and loss—more than three hundred dead and maimed in a horrific attack.

The Secretary and new father lie together on the temporary stage.

Is it her imagination, or is the man trying to cop a feel?

She rolls away from him, but she doesn't stand yet. The attack is finished, but she shouldn't know that. It's best to remain down and act scared, looking at the plaza, the air filled with smoke and pulverized concrete while the stubborn holos continue to beg for some impossible gift called Peace.

My grandmother is sharp. She is. Look at her once in the wrong way, and she knows something is wrong. Do it twice and she'll probably piece together what makes a girl turn quiet and strange.

But not today, she doesn't.

"What happened at school?" she asks.

I don't answer.

"What are you watching, Ophelia?"

Nothing. My eyes have been blank for half a minute now.

"Something went wrong at school, didn't it?"

Nothing is ever a hundred percent right at school, which is why it's easy to harvest a story that might be believed. Most people would believe it, at least. But after listening to my noise about snippy friends and broken trusts, she says, "I don't know what's wrong with you, honey. But that isn't it."

I nod, letting my voice die away.

She leaves my little room without closing the door. I sit and do nothing for about three seconds, and then the sparkle eyes take me back to the mess outside the UN. I can't count the times I've watched the impacts, the carnage. Hundreds of cameras were working, government cameras and media cameras and those carried by the protesters. Following at the digitals' heels are people talking about the tragedy and death tolls and who is responsible and how the war has moved to a new awful level.

"Where did the insurgents get a top-drawer railgun?" faces ask.

But I've carried Prophet for a couple years and fired him plenty of times. Just not into a public target like this, and with so many casualties, and all of the dead on my side of the fight.

That's the difference here: The world suddenly knows about me.

In the middle of the slaughter, one robot camera stays focused on my real targets, including the Secretary of Fuel and Bullshit. It's halfway nice, watching her hunker down in terror. Except she should have been in pieces, and there shouldn't be a face staring in my direction, and how Prophet missed our target by more than fifty meters is one big awful mystery that needs solving.

I assume a malfunction.

I'm wondering where I can take him to get his guidance systems recalibrated and ready for retribution.

Unless of course the enemy has figured out how to make railgun rounds fall just a little wide of their goals, maybe even killing some troublemakers in the process.

Whatever is wrong here, at least I know that it isn't my fault.

Then some little thing taps at my window.

From the next room, my grandmother asks, "What are you doing, Ophelia?"

I'm looking at the bird on my window sill. The enemy uses rats, and we use robins and house sparrows. But this is a red-headed woodpecker, which implies rank and special circumstances.

The bird gives a squawk, which is a coded message that my eyes have to play with for a little while. Then the messenger flies away.

"Ophelia?"

"I'm just thinking about a friend," I shout.

She comes back into my room, watching my expression all over again.

"A friend, you say?"

"He's in trouble," I say.

"Is that what's wrong?" she asks.

"Isn't that enough?"

Two rats in this alley don't convince me. I'm watching them from my new haven, measuring the dangers and possible responses. Then someone approaches the three of us, and in the best tradition of ratdom, my companions scurry into the darkness under a pile of rotting boards.

I am a plastic sack filled with broken machine parts.

I am motionless and harmless, but in my secret reaches, inside my very busy mind, I'm astonished to see my Ridiculous back again so soon, walking toward the rat-rich wood pile.

Five meters behind her walks an unfamiliar man.

To him, I take an immediate dislike.

He looks prosperous, and he looks exceptionally angry, wearing a fine suit made stiff with nano-armor and good leather shoes and a platoon of jamming equipment as well as two guns riding in his pockets, one that shoots poisoned ice as well as the gun that he trusts—a kinetic beast riding close to his dominate hand.

Ridiculous stops at the rot pile.

The man asks, "Is it there?"

"I don't know," she says, eyes down.

My girl has blue sparkle eyes, much like her original eyes—the ones left behind in the doctor's garbage bin.

"It looks like boards now?" he asks.

"He did," she lies.

"Not he," the man says, sounding like a google-head. "The machine is an It."

"Right," she says, kicking at the planks, pretending to look hard. "It's just a big gun. I keep forgetting."

The man is good at being angry. He has a tall frightful face and neck muscles that can't stop being busy. His right hand thinks about the gun in his pocket. The fingers keep flexing, wanting to grab it.

His gun is an It.

I am not.

"I put it here," she says.

She put me where I am now, which tells me even more.

"Something scared it," she says. "And now it's moved to another hiding place."

The man says, "Shit."

Slowly, carefully, he turns in a circle, looking at the rubble and the trash and the occasional normal object that might still work or might be me. Then with a tight slow voice, he says, "Call for it."

"Prophet," she says.

I say nothing.

"How far could it move?" he asks.

"Not very," she says. "The firing drained it down to nothing, nearly. And it hasn't had time to feed itself, even if it's found food."

"Bullshit," he says, coming my way.

Ridiculous watches me and him, the tattooed Scripture above her blue eyes dripping with sweat. Then the man kneels beside me, and she says, "I put the right guidance codes into him."

"You said that already." Then he looks back at her, saying, "You're not in trouble here. I told you that already."

His voice says a lot.

I have no power. But when his hands reach into my sack, what resembles an old capacitor cuts two of his fingers, which is worth some cursing and some secret celebration.

Ridiculous's face is twisted with worry, up until he looks back at her again. Then her expression turns innocent, pure and pretty and easy to believe.

Good girl, I think.

The man rises and pulls out the kinetic gun and shoots Ridiculous in the chest. If not for the wood piled up behind her, she would fly for a long distance. But instead of flying, she crashes and pulls down the wood around her, and one of those very untrustworthy rats comes out running, squeaking as it flees.

Ridiculous sobs and rolls and tries saying something.

He shoots her in the back, twice, and then says, "We never should have left it with you. All that luck dropping into our hands, which was crazy. Why should we have trusted the gun for a minute?"

She isn't dead, but her ribs are broken. And by the sound of it, the girl is fighting to get one good breath.

"Sure, it killed some bad guys," he says. "That's what a good spy does. He sacrifices a few on his side to make him look golden in the enemy's eyes."

I have no strength.

"You can't have gone far," he tells the alley. "We'll drop ordinance in here, take you out with the rats."

I cannot fight.

"Or you can show yourself to me," he says, the angry face smiling now. "Reveal yourself and we can talk."

Ridiculous sobs.

What is very easy is remembering the moment when she picked up me out of the bricks and dust and bloodied bits of human meat.

He gives my sack another good kick, seeing something.

And for the first time in my life, I pray. Just like that, as easy as anything, the right words come out of me, and the man bending over me hears nothing coming and senses nothing, his hands playing with my pieces when a fleck of laser light falls out of the sky and turns the angriest parts of his brain into vapor, into a sharp little pop.

I'm still not breathing normally. I'm still a long way from being able to think straight about anything. Gasping and stupid, I'm kneeling in a basement fifty meters from where I nearly died, and Prophet is suckling on an unsecured outlet, endangering both of us. But he needs power and ammunition, and I like the damp dark in here, waiting for my body to come back to me.

"You are blameless," he says.

I don't know what that means.

He says, "You fed the proper codes into me. But there were other factors, other hands, and that's where the blame lies."

"So you are a trap," I say.

"Somebody's trap," he says.

"The enemy wanted those civilians killed," I say, and then I break into the worst-hurting set of coughs that I have ever known.

He waits.

"I trusted you," I say.

"But Ridiculous," he says.

"Shut up," I say.

"Ophelia," he says.

I hold my sides, sipping my breaths.

"You assume that this war has two sides," he says. "But there could be a third player at large, don't you see?"

"What should I see?"

"Giving a gun to their enemies is a huge risk. If the Americans wanted to kill their political enemies, it would be ten times easier to pull something out of their armory and set it up in the insurgency's heart."

"Somebody else planned all of this, you're saying."

"I seem to be proposing that, yes."

"But that man who came with me today, the one you killed . . . he said the Secretary showed us a lot with her body language. She knew the attack was coming. She knew when it would happen. Which meant that she was part of the planning, which was a hundred percent American."

"Except whom does the enemy rely on to make their plans?"

"Tell me," I say.

Talking quietly, making the words even more important, he says, "The Almighty."

"What are we talking about?" I ask.

He says nothing, starting to change his shape again.

"The Internet?" I ask. "What, you mean it's conscious now? And it's working its own side in this war?"

"The possibility is there for the taking," he says.

But all I can think about are the dead people and those that are hurt and those that right now are sitting at their dinner table, thinking that some fucking Canadian bitch has made their lives miserable for no goddamn reason.

"You want honesty," Prophet says.

"When don't I?"

He says, "This story about a third side . . . it could be a contingency buried inside my tainted software. Or it is the absolute truth, and the Almighty is working with both of us, aiming toward some grand, glorious plan."

I am sort of listening, and sort of not.

Prophet is turning shiny, which happens when his body is in the middle of changing shapes. I can see little bits of myself reflected in the liquid metals and the diamonds floating on top. I see a thousand little-girl faces staring at me, and what occurs to me now—what matters more than anything else today—is the idea that there can be more than two sides in any war.

I don't know why, but that the biggest revelation of all.

When there are more than two sides, that means that there can be too many sides to count, and one of those sides, standing alone, just happens to be a girl named Ophelia Hanna Hanks.

SCRAP DRAGON

NAOMI KRITZER

Once upon a time, there was a princess.

Does she have to be a princess? Couldn't she be the daughter of a merchant, or a scholar, or an accountant?

An accountant? What would an accountant be doing in a pastoral fantasy setting?

The people there have money, don't they? So they'd also have taxes and bills and profit-and-loss statements. But he could be a butcher or baker or candle-stick-maker, so long as he's not a king.

No, I suppose an accountant might work. Very well. Once upon a time, there was a young woman—the daughter of an accountant—who had two older sisters. The oldest of these young women was clever, the middle was strong, and the youngest was kind.

What if she wanted to be the strong one? The youngest, I mean. And what if the oldest wanted to be the nice one? It's not fair.

I didn't say the youngest wasn't strong or that the oldest wasn't kind. But everyone knew that it was the middle daughter who was the strongest, and the youngest who was the sweetest and most innocent.

Maybe they just thought she was sweet and innocent.

Maybe. They lived in a palace—or rather, in a large and comfortable house, and if they were princesses, I could give the youngest one a fabulous bedroom with a drawbridge—

She can have a drawbridge anyway. Maybe her parents built it for her just because it was cool.

Okay. But the important thing is that, because she was so kind-hearted, animals trusted her. They would seek her out, and when she found one in need, she would try to help it.

That would be really inconvenient.

Being trusted by animals?

Well, if they'd seek you out. I mean, you're out for a walk and a stray cat comes up to you and won't go away—

Maybe it's a really nice cat.

Or maybe it's a cat that will yowl at four in the morning every day and wake you up.

But the animals trusting her is supposed to show you what she's like inside. She's not just nice on the surface; she's a good person.

Well, I like animals better than princesses. She can have animals following her around, that's okay.

One day, word came to their city that a grave threat faced them. The city was near an extinct volcano—or rather, a volcano that had been thought extinct. But a powerful and evil sorcerer had raised the spirits of the volcano, and it was now threatening to erupt. If the sorcerer continued prodding the volcano with his malicious magic, the volcano would spew forth fire and lava and the city would be utterly destroyed.

Volcanoes erupt because of tectonic forces, not spirits.

This was a magical volcano.

Look, if the sorcerer could manipulate tectonic forces, why would he bother threatening the city with an eruption? He could wipe them out just as well with an earthquake.

Fine. It wasn't a sorcerer with a volcano. It was a dragon, a vast and powerful dragon that could breathe fire and took up residence in the crater of an extinct nearby volcano but threatened, if not supplicated with gifts of gold and treasure, to burn the city to ash.

But I like dragons. Dragons are cool.

Well, so? I like the French and France is cool but that doesn't mean I like Jean-Marie Le Pen. French people aren't all good or all bad and neither are dragons.

Okay. I guess that's fair.

So, the city was under threat by the evil dragon, and if you'd let me make this person a princess she would have a reason for feeling personally responsible for saving her city. But she's not a princess. So I suppose the king—

Couldn't they live in a democracy? Even an Athenian democracy is better than a king.

—the Council of Democratically Elected Representatives of the People offered a reward to anyone who could defeat the dragon. But more than that, they begged for all those who were brave or strong or clever to do what they could to save the city. If it had been a king, he could also have offered the hand of one of his children in marriage, but you can hardly marry the son or daughter of a Council of Representatives so let's just say they pointed out that anyone who succeeded in saving the city would be a very hot romantic commodity indeed.

Arranged marriages are kind of creepy. But marrying someone who was only interested in you because you'd defeated a dragon also seems kind of creepy.

No one's going to have to marry anyone they don't want to marry. Anyway, the eldest tried first. She set out to learn all she could about dragons—first at the library nearby, then, when she had exhausted its resources, to a larger city some days' journey away. She sent home letters when she could, sharing everything she'd learned, but it was a vast library and she thought it would be years before she'd learned everything there was to know.

So the second sister decided to set out to confront the dragon directly.

And she never returned.

What do you mean, she never returned?

I mean that she died on her journey. There were people who said that the dragon had eaten her—

But I don't want her to be dead. It's not fair.

No, it isn't. Death isn't ever fair.

But I liked her!

Yes.

The people I like aren't supposed to die.

No.

So can she just be sleeping, if you need to take her out of the story?

No. She died, and so the youngest—

I don't think I want the youngest to try to defeat the dragon. She might get eaten, too.

But she's the city's only hope.

I don't care. I want her to stay home where she's safe.

That's what her parents said. "We've lost one daughter already. Let someone else lose a daughter next time."

And she's the nice one.

Yes.

How is she supposed to defeat a dragon by being nice?

Other people said that, too, sometimes even where she could hear them. So the youngest daughter—whose name was Heather—decided that for now, she would stay home.

Heather had a book of blank pages, and she took all the letters her family had gotten from her eldest sister, with the diagrams of dragons and ancient philosophy regarding dragons and information about their nesting habits and lairs and so on, and began to organize it. Because, she thought, even if she could not herself defeat the dragon, perhaps she could provide a useful set of information to someone else.

But sometimes she would flip the book over, and working from the back, she began creating a book about her sister, the one who had died. She had pictures that she had drawn, but she also put in all sorts of things that made her think of her sister. There was a scrap of cloth from her sister's favorite dress, and a flower she'd pressed, and when Heather found a poem her sister had written she copied it out in the book. The funny thing was, her sister had loved dragons.

Because dragons are cool.

Which made it all the more ironic that she'd probably been eaten by one.

One afternoon Heather took her book and her lunch, called for her dog (whose name was Bear), and went to sit by a wooded lake not too far from her house.

The dog had better not die in this story.

The dog's not going to die. Not in the story, anyway.

Good.

They sat down by the lake. Heather took out one of her sandwiches, and gave half of it to Bear. A nutria swam up and poked its head out of the water. "Hello, nutria," Heather said to it. It didn't swim away, so she broke off a piece of her sandwich and tossed it down to the nutria.

Is that a real animal?

Yes, nutrias are real. They're rodents and look like a cross between a beaver and a really big rat.

Oh. That sounds cool.

The nutria shot a wary look at Bear, then climbed up on the bank to grab the piece of sandwich. Bear sometimes chased squirrels (and a nutria might have been sufficiently squirrel-like to chase) but right now he was more interested in getting another handout from Heather; he looked at her with a big doggy smile and wagged his tail. Heather sighed and took out another sandwich. Her food wasn't going to last long at this rate. "Go get me a sandwich, Bear," she said to Bear.

Did he get her a sandwich?

Of course he didn't. If dogs could make sandwiches, they'd eat them themselves. When the nutria finished its piece of sandwich, it sat on the shore of the lake looking at Heather with gleaming dark eyes, and Heather broke off another piece of bread and tossed it over. "Can you tell me how to defeat a dragon?" she asked it.

The nutria picked up the bread. "Why do you want to defeat it?" it asked.

Heather was a little startled that the nutria actually answered her; she talked to Bear all the time, and other animals some of the time, but she'd never had an animal answer her before. "Because if no one defeats it, it's going to come and burn my city to the ground," she said.

The nutria seemed to mull this over as it ate. "Know the truth that lies within you," it said. "And speak the truth that waits without."

Waits without what?

Without here is the opposite of within. So she needs to know the truth she has inside, and then speak some truth that's external.

You know, even with an explanation that's pretty cryptic.

It's advice from a talking water rat. Were you expecting step-by-step instructions?

Well, did she try asking it for something more specific?

She tried, but the nutria was done talking. It nibbled away the rest of the bread, then plopped back into the water and swam off. "Find me another nutria, Bear," Heather suggested, but Bear just wagged his tail again.

One thing was certain, however. Heather still didn't know how she was going to defeat the dragon, but she thought the nutria wouldn't have spoken to her—and given her advice about knowing the truth inside—unless she did have the power to defeat it. So she went home, quietly packed her belongings, and left with Bear when no one was home. (She did leave a nice note on the kitchen counter, but she didn't want to stick around to explain in person that she was going out to fight the dragon because of advice from a talking rodent.)

Of course, she had no idea what the nutria was talking about. If it was the truth that lay within her, it probably meant it was something she already knew and just hadn't fully realized yet, so she took her book with the information about dragons (and the pictures of her sister) and studied it when she would stop to rest. After reviewing everything three times, she still had no idea what it was she was supposed to know—unless the secret was that she was willing to ask unlikely sources, like nutrias, for advice.

There was a school nearby, and she could hear a bell that meant school was over for the day, so she waited while the children ran off and then went in to ask the teacher. He was a mathematician, although this was a small school so he was also expected to teach reading, grammar, and dancing.

They learned dancing in school?

Yes, in this place they considered dancing very important.

"Excuse me," Heather said. "I come from another part of the city, and I was wondering whether you knew of any way to defeat the dragon?"

"If I did, I'd already have mentioned it to someone," he said. "Although I suppose it's reasonable to consider the possibility that I would have tried that, and found no one willing to listen. But no, I don't."

"Oh," Heather said, feeling a bit deflated, even though she hadn't asked anyone else yet. Maybe she should have asked the students, before they all left.

"Is there a particular reason you thought I would know?"

Heather told him about the nutria, and the book of notes, and how she had no idea what truth it was she supposedly knew.

"Well," the teacher said, "I have a friend who is an inventor. If you'd like to come back to my house, I'll introduce you to him, and we can see if he has any ideas."

The teacher introduced himself as Fillard.

That's a very unusual name for a person in a pastoral fantasy.

It's a very unusual name, period. As they walked, he explained that his neighbor was also a musician and an actor; the neighbor's name was Peter, and Peter turned out to be extremely kind and invited Heather and Bear (and Fillard) to stay for supper, even though he'd never met Heather or Bear before.

As the shadows grew long and their after-dinner tea grew tepid, they all listed everything they'd ever heard about dragons. Peter had heard that they could sing; he wasn't inclined to go walking over to the dragon's lair to confirm this, but the stories said that dragons had beautiful voices, on those occasions when they chose to share them. Fillard, on the other hand, had heard that dragons enjoyed games almost as much as they liked hoarding treasure; there were stories of dragons offering to let travelers go free if the travelers could beat them at a game of chess. "Of course, the dragon always wins in those stories unless the human cheats," Fillard added. "I have a large collection of games, and could offer you several that the dragon wouldn't have seen before. That would make the challenge a bit more fair."

They made fresh tea as it grew darker, and since Heather had been taking notes ("gd. singers / games—chess?") she had her book out. She set it down at one point to look at a game that Fillard had run home to get and bring back, and when she picked it up, she had it upside down, so it was the side about her sister, rather than the dragon. "Laura loved dragons," she said softly. "I should put a picture of a dragon somewhere on Laura's side."

"Who is Laura?" the men asked.

She explained about her sister, and how she'd disappeared when she went to confront the dragon. Laura had always believed that dragons were cool—

Because dragons are *cool.*

—which made the circumstances of her death tragically ironic.

You already mentioned the irony.

And she explained about the book, and everyone nodded, and then Peter went to find an article about dragons that he'd saved from somewhere. There was nothing in the article that was new, but it had a lovely picture, a sort of extremely artistic diagram. He gave it to her to paste in later.

It was late, and Heather was tired, so Peter made up a guest bed for her. Heather woke early—before Peter or Fillard—and stepped outside.

Are you sure she got up first?

Fillard and Peter had stayed up very late talking, and weren't awake yet. The sky was light and the birds were singing, and when Heather opened her book she realized that she'd nearly filled it; only a pair of blank pages faced each other at the exact center of the book. All the rest of the book had been filled, with notes about dragons on one side and notes and mementos relating to her sister on the other. She held the picture hesitantly—it seemed to her like maybe it *should* go on the dragon side. But she'd never put a dragon in the Laura half of the scrapbook, and that seemed like a terrible loss. Since she'd flipped the book, she had to choose—it would be right-side up for one, upside-down for the other. After staring at it for several minutes, as the sky grew lighter and the sun grew warmer, she finally turned the book sideways and pasted the picture in that way, so that maybe it could go with either.

And then she realized what the nutria meant.

She did?

Yes.

Well, what did it mean?

I can't just tell you that straight out; it would spoil the flow of the story. We'll get to it in a bit.

You're as bad as that damn water rat.

Heather picked up her bags and called for Bear and set out—

Isn't she going to leave a note?

She only just met Fillard and Peter. Do you really think they'll worry?

Of course they're going to worry.

She got up, left a note, took the game that Fillard had offered her and the sheet music for songs that Peter had said he'd particularly like to hear a dragon sing, and then she and Bear headed for the path that would swiftly take them to the dragon's lair, at the edge of the extinct volcano.

You promised me the dog wouldn't die, remember.

Don't worry about the dog.

Does that mean I should be worrying about Heather? I didn't make you promise she wouldn't die because she's the hero of the story so I figured she was safe.

The dragon emerged from its lair as Heather and Bear approached. It unfurled its vast wings and shook them back the way you might stretch your wrists and crack your spine, and licked its lips, showing its big teeth. "Hello," Heather said to the dragon. "I know you're not going to eat me. I know you're not really a threat to the city. So I know the real danger must be coming from someone else."

That, you see, was the truth she'd already known—

Dragons are cool!

Yes, that dragons are cool!

But what about all that business about dragons being individuals with free will—

Here is what she realized as she talked through all the information in her book. The dragon had been demanding treasure, not food. And while everyone knew that dragons loved treasure, surely they ate *sometimes*. And yet only a few sheep had gone missing from the edges of town, plus a few unlucky people like Laura, and that just didn't seem like enough to feed a dragon. So she'd looked carefully at the diagrams of its jaw, and realized that its teeth were not shaped like a bear's teeth, nor like a lion's. After thinking about it carefully, she concluded that the dragon's natural diet was fish. Not people.

That doesn't mean it wouldn't eat a human who made it mad.

She'd also realized that a dragon did not actually have enough fire in its belly to burn the city to the ground. It could certainly belch out enough flame to kill anyone who came knocking with a sword, but that was a long way from burning down a whole city.

Maybe it was an empty threat.

But there was another thing everyone agreed on: dragons were *smart*. Smart enough not to make empty threats—not when a city might call the dragon's bluff by getting a big enough army together to take on the dragon.

The dragon could move, though, if that happened. This dragon had moved before, right? Because you said it moved in.

But dragons have a hoard. They save *everything*. And moving is annoying enough if you don't have a dragon's hoard to take with you to the Willamette Valley or wherever it is you're going. The last thing any smart, sensible dragon was going to do was set itself up to have to move all the time. So Heather was pretty sure the threats were coming from someone else, someone who didn't care that much what happened to the dragon. And the dragon probably knew who, and why, and so Heather thought that perhaps she would go and ask.

The dragon tucked her wings back—

It was a female dragon? How did Heather know it was a female dragon?

She'd been studying dragon anatomy diagrams for months. Do I really need to spell it out for you?

Yes, actually, I wouldn't mind knowing how you tell a boy dragon from a girl dragon.

The easiest way is coloration: the backs of a female dragon's wings are less brightly colored than the front of the body, to provide camouflage when they're nesting. Also, female dragons have wings that are scalloped on the bottom edge and male dragons have a penis.

This dragon, which was female, folded her hands in front of her and lowered herself to the ground. "You're not here to try to kill me?" she said, sounding a bit surprised.

"No," Heather said. "I did bring you a game, though, because I heard dragons like games, and some sheet music—do you read music?—because I heard you like singing. But mostly I came to ask you who it is that's using you to threaten my city, and whether I can help you."

"It's a sorcerer," the dragon said. "I'm a very young dragon." (She was indeed quite a bit smaller than Heather had expected.) "If I were older, he never would have been able to do this to me, but he's used his magic to trap me here so that I can't leave. He can't actually make me go set your city on fire, but when people come to kill me, I defend myself . . . "

"Including my sister?" Heather asked, a huge lump in her throat.

The dragon shrugged. "I don't remember anyone who looked like you," she said. "There are bandits, and other dangers nearby—not just me."

"How can I break the sorcerer's spell?" Heather asked.

"I don't know," the dragon said. "I can tell you where to find him, but he's really powerful—I'd feel terrible sending you off into danger."

Heather thought that over. "Do I need to defeat the sorcerer? Or just figure out how to break the spell?"

"Let me put it this way," the dragon said. "While I do not *normally* eat people, because they really don't taste very good, I would make a *special exception* for the sorcerer who has turned me into his own personal chained-up pet dragon and used me to intimidate people into letting him steal their money. In other words, if you can figure out how to break the spell, I'll take care of the rest of it."

"If nothing else," Heather said, "I could go down to the city and tell everyone the truth—that it's the sorcerer who's a danger, not you."

"You could do that," the dragon said. "Unfortunately, he'll just move us on to a new city. That's what he did the last two times when people figured it out."

Heather thought that over. This meant the sorcerer was powerful enough to enslave the dragon, but maybe not powerful enough to protect himself any other way. "Where does he keep all the money he steals?" she asked.

"He makes me guard it," the dragon said, and pointed down into her lair. Heather peered down at the hoard. The edge of the cavern shadowed it, but she could see a heap of glittering gold and rubies.

"Can I go in and look?" Heather asked.

"Oh, yes. I just can't let you leave with any of it."

Heather went inside the cavern and started poking through the treasure. There was gold and silver, there were gems and strands of pearls, there were bundles of paper bills and a few paintings, there was an ancient cast-bronze horse, and there were books.

Heather picked her way through all of it; one of the treasures was a gem-encrusted lamp, and she lit it so that she could see a bit better. Bear barked. "Help me look, Bear," Heather said. "If the treasure's here being guarded by the dragon, I bet the magic is here, too. Somewhere."

The dragon came in and laid her chin on her hands, watching as Heather dug through the piles. After poking through the gold coins (and then rolling in the giant pile of gold because really, how often do you have the opportunity to roll in a giant pile of gold?) Heather started looking at the books. There were a few giant Bibles with gems on the front covers, and one of the lost plays of Shakespeare, and a collection of plays by Aeschylus that included all of *Achilles*, and a musical score for something called *Per la ricuperata salute di Ophelia*, which the dragon took an interest in and started studying while Heather searched.

Wait, is that the lost opera that Mozart and Salieri wrote together?

It was a cantata for voice and piano, actually, but yes, it was written by Mozart and Salieri together and then lost. You do realize that in real life they weren't anything like they were in that movie . . .

Yes yes yes, historically they were probably friends, or at least friendly. Did the dragon not know it was there?

Oh, she knew it was there and had looked at it before, but you know how sometimes when you're trying to put away a big pile of books and you make the mistake of opening one, and you sit down and start reading it even though you've read it already and you were really intending to clean that day instead of reading for hours? That's pretty much what happened to the dragon.

Under a crate of gold bars, which Heather needed a lever to move as gold weighs so much, she found a very plain, unimpressive little book. From the outside, it actually looked quite a lot like the book she had made. Except this one had a picture of a dragon on the cover. The dragon looked up miserably at a man who sat riding on his shoulders.

Heather opened the book and suddenly became aware that the dragon was watching her. "I cannot let you destroy that book," the dragon said sharply, and Heather knew right away that she'd found what she was looking for.

"So, you can't let me take it," she said, and the dragon shook her head, "and you can't let me destroy it. I won't take it anywhere and I won't destroy it. I'm just going to look at it," she said. The dragon watched as she set the lamp on a ledge, then sat down under it to read.

It *was* a scrapbook, of sorts, full of pictures of dragons, but each showed the same thing in a different way: a dragon bound. Chained to a human figure, tied to the ground with giant nets, imprisoned behind bars. Heather thought that destroying it would probably free the dragon, but the dragon was watching Heather's every movement now, and while it did occur to Heather that maybe she could "accidentally" drop the burning lamp onto it, that seemed awfully risky if it didn't work.

She took out her pen, and the dragon didn't twitch.

Carefully, she started drawing on the page.

"What arc you doing?" the dragon asked.

"I'm adding things," Heather said.

"Hmm. I guess that's okay," the dragon said.

Heather drew a giant pair of scissors snipping through the net. She drew a file chiseling through the bars, and a key unlocking the chains.

"Do you feel like you could let me destroy it now?" she asked when she'd finished.

The dragon paused, and then shook her head.

Heather looked more closely at the words written around the pictures. Where it said, "By words and magic the dragon is taken," she put in a caret and wrote "not," so that it said, "By words and magic the dragon is not taken." She changed the word "bound" to "boundless" and "grave" to "gravel" and something that ended with "die" she changed into a short essay about "dietary law."

It didn't make a lot of sense when she was done with it, but she didn't think that would matter. But the dragon still didn't feel like she could let her destroy the book.

So finally, Heather took her own scrapbook, and cut out the picture she had pasted into the center, and pasted it onto the cover of the magician's scrapbook, covering over the picture of the miserable-looking dragon.

The dragon leapt to her feet. "HA!" she shouted, and bolted out of the cave.

Well, that seemed to have done it. Heather burned the magician's scrapbook, just to be on the safe side. She figured the treasure wasn't hers—it belonged either to the people it had been stolen from, or the dragon—but she couldn't resist the Aeschylus and the Shakespeare, so she packed those up and left a note saying, *I borrowed the plays. I promise to give them back after I've read them.—Heather.*

She blew out the lamp, left the dragon's lair, and looked around. She could see the dragon high overhead and hoped she'd stick to her word and eat the evil sorcerer before she left forever. And then she called for Bear and they walked back down the path to the city.

Is that the end?

No. The next morning, everyone in the city woke to the sound of a vast, enormous contralto voice singing a cantata—

The dragon?

Yes, indeed, the dragon. And when she was done, she told them that she'd been freed, and had eaten the evil sorcerer, and would now be on her way to explore new lands.

Did she tell them who'd freed her?

No, because she could tell Heather would prefer not to have to put up with being famous.

But what about the reward? She was supposed to get a reward!

The next day, Heather got a package through the mail; it was a box containing those heavy gold bars, which was enough wealth to keep her well supplied for the rest of her life. The dragon kept Fillard's game and Peter's sheet music, though.

She was also supposed to be a hot commodity. Romantically, I mean.

Would you want to marry someone who was only interested in you because you were a hero of the realm? She went back to visit Fillard and Peter to tell them how things worked out with the dragon, and they were delighted to see her. And over time she and Fillard became best friends, and they got married and lived happily ever after.

Did they ever see the dragon again?

No.

I want them to see the dragon again.

Well, the dragon sent them postcards occasionally, from distant cities like Shanghai and Barcelona and Miami.

That's not the same as seeing her.

I suppose.

Surely the dragon would have come back to visit. Once. Heather freed her from the sorcerer!

You're right. She did. One night about ten years after Heather and Fillard had married, and they were sitting on the beach with their child watching the sun set over the water. And in the clouds, Heather saw the dragon; for a moment, she thought it was just the sun in her eyes, but then she saw the huge wings and knew it was the dragon. And she shouted and pointed so that Fillard and their child could see her as well.

They all saw the dragon, just for a few minutes, in the last light of the day. And as the shadows gathered and the stars came out, they heard her singing.

THE CONTRARY GARDENER

CHRISTOPHER ROWE

Kay Lynne wandered up and down the aisles of the seed library dug out beneath the county extension office. Some of the rows were marked with glowing orange off-limits fungus, warning the unwary away from spores and thistles that required special equipment to handle, which Kay Lynne didn't have, and special permission to access, which she would *never* have, if her father had anything to say about it, and he did.

It was the last Friday before the first Saturday in May, the day before Derby Day and so a week from planting day, and Kay Lynne had few ideas and less time for her Victory Garden planning. Last year she had grown a half dozen varieties of tomatoes, three for eating and three for blood transfusions, but she didn't like to repeat herself. Given that she tended to mumble when she talked, not liking to repeat herself made Kay Lynne a quiet gardener.

She paused before a container of bright pink corn kernels, their preprogrammed color coming from insecticides and fertilizers and not from any varietal ancestry. Kay Lynne didn't like to grow corn. It grew so high that it cast her little cottage in shadow if she planted it on the side of the house that would see it grow at all. Besides, corn was cheap, and more than that, easy— just about any gardener could grow corn and a lot of them did.

There were always root vegetables. A lot of utility to those, certainly, and excellent trade goods for the army supply clerks who would start combing the markets as soon as the earliest spring greens were in. Rootwork was complicated, and meant having nothing to market through the whole long summer, which in turn meant not having to go to the markets for months yet, which was a good thing in Kay Lynne's view.

She considered the efficacy of beets and potatoes, and the various powers carrots held when they were imaginatively programmed and carefully grown. Rootwork had been a particular specialty of her run-off mother, and so would have the added benefit of warding her father away from the cottage, which he visited entirely too often for Kay Lynne's comfort.

It would be hard work. That spoke for the idea, too.

She strode over to the information kiosk and picked up the speaking tube that led to the desks of the agents upstairs.

"I need someone to let me into the root cellars," she said.

Blinking in the early morning light, Kay Lynne left the extension office and made her way to the bus stop, leaning forward under the weight of her burdensacks. The canvas strap that held them together was draped across her shoulders and, while she thought she had done an exacting job in measuring the root cuttings on each side so that the weight would be evenly distributed, she could already tell that there was a slight discrepancy, which was the worst kind of discrepancy, the very bane of Kay Lynne's existence, the tiny kind of problem that no one ever bothered to fix in the face of more important things. She could hear her father's voice: "Everything is not equally important. You never learned that."

The extension office was on the south side, close enough to downtown to be on a regular bus route, but far enough to not fall under the shadows of the looming skyscrapers Kay Lynne could now clearly see as she waited at the shelter. Slogans crawled all over the buildings, leaping from one granite face to another when they were too wordy, though of course, to Kay Lynne's mind they were all too wordy. "The Union is strong," read one in red, white, and blue firework fonts. "The west front is only as strong as the home front. Volunteer for community service!" The only slogan that stayed constant was the green and brown limned sentence circling the tallest building of all. "Planting is in EIGHT days."

A shadow fell on the street and Kay Lynne looked up to see a hot air balloon tacking toward the fairgrounds. The great balloon festival was the next morning in the hours before the Derby, and the balloonists had been arriving in numbers all week. It was part of the Derby Festival, the madness-tinged days that took over the city each spring, at the exact time when people should be at their most serious. The timing never failed to dismay Kay Lynne.

The stars and stripes were displayed proudly on the balloon, and also a ring of green near the top that indicated that it was made from one hundred percent non-recycled materials. It was wholly new, and so an act of patriotism. Kay Lynne would never earn such a ring as a gardener; careful economy was expected of her and her cohort.

The balloon passed on, skirting the poplar copse that stood behind the bus stop, and was quickly obscured by the trees. Kay Lynne's cottage was northwest of the fairgrounds, and the winds most of the balloons would float on blew above her home. She would probably see it again tomorrow, whether she wanted to or not.

Belching its sulfur fumes, the bus arrived, and Kay Lynne climbed aboard.

• • •

The bus driver was a Mr. Lever #9, Kay Lynne's favorite model. They were programmed with thirty-six phrases of greeting, observation (generally about the weather), and small talk, in addition to whatever announcements were required for their particular route. A Mr. Lever #9 never surprised you with what it said or did. They made Kay Lynne comfortable with public transportation.

"Good . . . morning, citizen," it said cheerily as Kay Lynne boarded. "Sunny and mild!"

Kay Lynne nodded politely to the driver and took the seat immediately behind it. The bus was sparsely occupied, with just a few tardy students bound for the university sharing the conveyance. To a one, their noses were buried in appallingly thick textbooks.

"Next stop is Central Avenue," said the driver. "Central Avenue! Home of the Downs! Home of the Derby!"

The bus ground its brakes and came to a stop along the Third Street Road next to the famous twin spires. A crowd of shorts-wearing families hustled onto the bus, painfully obvious in their out-of-townedness and clucking at one another loudly. "Infield," they said, and "First thing in the morning," and "Odds on favorite."

Kay Lynne loved the 'Ville, but she was no fan of its most famous day. She appreciated horses for their manure and for the way they conveyed policemen and drew the downtown trolleys, and she usually even bought a calendar of central state views that showed the Horse Lord Holdings with their limestone fences and endless green hills, but truth be told, she usually waited until February to buy the calendars, when they were cheapest, and when they were the only ones left. People in the 'Ville liked horses, but they didn't like the Horse Lords.

"Grade Lane," said the bus driver. "Transfer to the fairgrounds trolley," and then a whirring sounded and it added in a slightly different timbre, "See the balloons!"

All the tourists filed off happily chattering about the balloon festival and the next day's card of racing at the Downs, and Kay Lynne breathed a happy sigh to see them go.

The bus driver said, "They get to me, too, sometimes. But we're more alike than we are different."

Kay Lynne turned around to see if anyone else on the bus had heard. Only the reading students remained, all in the rear seats, all still staring down.

"Excuse me?" Kay Lynne said. She had never directly addressed a Mr. Lever of any model before. If there was a protocol, she didn't know.

"Sunny and mild!" said the bus driver.

Kay Lynne considered whether to pursue the Mr. Lever #9's unexpected, almost certainly unprogrammed, comment. It had not turned its head to face her when it spoke—if it had spoken and now Kay Lynne was beginning to allow that its *not* having spoken was at least within the realm of possibility—and usually the spherical heads would make daisy wheel turns to face the passenger compartment whenever speaking to a passenger was required, or rather, *done*. She supposed that they were never strictly speaking *required* to speak.

This was a thorny problem, and Kay Lynne reminded herself that she did not have authorization for thorns. She set her feet more firmly either side of her burdensacks, retrieved the pamphlet of helpful information that the agents had given her on programming root vegetables, and willfully ignored the bus driver for the rest of the trip.

Kay Lynne loved her cottage and its all-around garden plot more than any other place in the world. It was her home and her livelihood and her sanctuary all in one. So when she saw that the front yard plots had been tilled while she was away on her morning errand, she was aghast, even though she was positive she knew who had invaded her property and given unasked-for aid in preparing the grounds. Her father was probably still poking around in the back, maybe still running his obnoxiously loud rotor-tiller, maybe nosing through her potting shed for hand tools he didn't have with him on his obnoxiously loud truck, which yes, now that she looked for it, *was* parked on the street two doors down in front of the weedy lot where the Sapp house had been until it burned down. Kay Lynne did not miss the Sapps, though of course she was glad none of their innumerable number had been harmed in the fire. Corn-growers.

Not like Kay Lynne, and, to his credit at least, not like her father, who was a peas and beans man under contract to the Rangers at the fort forty miles south, responsible for enormous standing orders of rounds for their side arms that pushed him and his vassals to their limits every year. Her father did an extraordinary amount of work by anyone's standards, which meant, to Kay Lynne's way of thinking, that he had no business making even more work for himself by coming to turn over the winter-fallowed earth around her cottage. And that was just one of the reasons he shouldn't have been there.

Yes, he *was* in the potting shed.

"Don't you have an awl," he asked her when she stood in the doorway, not even looking up from where he had his head and hands completely inside the dark recesses of a tool cabinet. "I would swear I gave you an awl."

Kay Lynne hung her burdensacks over a dowel driven deep into the pine joist next to the door and waited. There was an old and unpleasant tradition she would insist be seen to before she would deign to find the awl for him. He would just as soon skip their ritual greeting as her, but you never knew who might be watching.

He dug around for another moment before finally sighing and standing. Kay Lynne's father positively *towered* over her. He was by any measure an enormous man in all of his directions, as well as in his appetites and opinions. This tradition, for example, he despised *mightily*.

He leaned down, his shock of gray hair so unruly that his bangs brushed her forehead when he kissed her cheek. "My darling daughter," he said.

Kay Lynne took his callused hands in her callused own and executed an imperfect curtsy. "My loving father," she replied.

Protocols satisfied, her father made to turn back to the cabinet, but Kay Lynne stopped him with a gesture. She opened a drawer and withdrew the tool he sought.

"Wayward," he said. "That is a wayward tool," but he was talking to himself and sweeping out the door to fix whatever he had decided needed fixing. The imprecation against the awl was a more personal tradition than the state-mandated exchange of affections—it was his way of insisting that his not being able to find the tool had somehow been *its* fault or possibly *her* fault or at least anyone or anything's fault besides her own. Kay Lynne's father was always held blameless. It was in his contracts with the army.

Since he did not pause to sniff at her burdensacks, *that* conversation could be avoided for just now, for which Kay Lynne breathed a sigh of relief. She did not look forward to her father's inevitable harangue against rootwork, rootworkers, and root eaters. She did not know whether his round despite of all such things antedated her mother's running off, as she had no memory of that occasion or of that woman, but his rage, when he learned of the carrot seeds and potato cuttings hanging just by where he'd shouldered out the door, would tower.

She trailed him out into the beds around the wellhouse behind the cottage. He had lifted the roof up off the low, cinder-blocked structure and propped it at an angle like the hood of a truck being repaired. He was bent over, again with his head and his hands in Kay Lynne's property. "Pump needs to be reamed out," he muttered over his shoulder. "You weren't getting good water pressure."

Sometimes, when Kay Lynne thought of her father, she did not picture his face but his great, convex backside, since that was what she saw more often than his other features. He was forever bent over, forever digging or puttering, always with his back to her. *Maybe that's why people say I mumble*, she thought. *I learned to speak from a man with his back turned.*

"It was working fine this morning," Kay Lynne claimed, forcefully if in ignorance as she had not actually drawn well water before setting out for the extension office that day. And besides, now that she thought of it, "They're hollering rain, anyway."

Her father snorted and kept at his work. He was famously dismissive of weather hollers and any other mechanical construct that had a voice. He never took public transportation. "There's not a cloud in the sky," he said. "It'll be sunny and mild all day long, you mark me."

His repeating of the Mr. Lever #9's phrase made Kay Lynne think back to the odd moment when the driver had seemed to break protocols and programming and comment on the out-of-towners. She wondered if she should ask her father about it—part of his distrust of speaking machines was an encyclopedic knowledge of their foibles. If a talking machine failed in the 'Ville, her father knew about it, knew all the details and wasn't afraid to exaggerate the consequences. He even harbored a conspiracist's opinion that such machines could do more than talk, they could *think*.

Another conversation best avoided, she thought.

Her father finished whatever he was doing to the well pump then and stood, careful to avoid hitting his head on the angled roof. With a grunt, he lowered the props that had held the tin and timber construction up, then carefully let the whole thing down to rest on the cinder blocks. "You were at the office this morning," he said. "Making a withdrawal from the seed vaults. What's it going to be this year?"

This was his way of not only demonstrating that he knew precisely where she'd been and precisely what she'd been up to, but that he knew very well the contents of her burdensacks and his not saying anything so far had been a test, which she had failed. Failed like most of the tests he put her to.

Kay Lynne's father was not an employee of the extension service, but when he said "the office" it was the extension service he meant because it was the only indoor space he habituated besides the storage barn where he kept his equipment and his bed. All of the extension agents were in awe of Kay Lynne's father and she should have known one of them had put a bug in his ear as soon as she had requested access to the root cellars. Bureaucrats could always be counted on to toady up to master cultivators.

Nothing for it now but to tell him. "Carrots," she said, pointing to the beds between the well house and the cottage. "They'll come up first." She leaned over and drew a quick diagram of her plots in the dirt at his feet. "Turnips," and she pointed, then pointed again in turn as she said, "Yams and potatoes. Radishes and beets."

Her father's lip curled in disgust. "The whole ugly array," he said. "You did this just to challenge me."

Kay Lynne stood her ground. *My ground*, she thought. *This is my ground.* "I did it because the market for roots is excellent and I've never tried my hand at rootwork."

Her father snorted. "And oh yes, you so very much like to try new things.

Well, that's good to hear, because you're going to do something new in the morning."

With that, he took a dried leaf from the front pocket of his overalls and unfolded it. Inside was a thin wafer of metal chased with a rainbow pattern of circuitry and magnetic stripes. Kay Lynne recognized it, of course. She had grown up in the 'Ville after all. But she had never held one until now, when her father thrust it into her hands, because she had never, ever, wanted one.

It was a ticket to the Derby.

Even in the 'Ville, even in a family of master cultivators, tickets were not easy to come by, so it was not unusual that Kay Lynne had never been to the Derby. What was unusual was her absolute lack of desire to attend the race.

Kay Lynne genuinely hoped that her instinctive and absolute despisal of the Derby and all its attendant celebrations was born of some logical or at least reasonable quirk of her own personality. But she suspected it was simply because her father loved it so.

"You managed to get two tickets this year?" she asked him, and was surprised that her voice was so steady and calm.

"Just this one," he replied, turning his back on her before she could hand the ticket back. "I decided this year would be a good one for you to go instead. There's a good card, top to bottom."

A card is the list of races, thought Kay Lynne, the knowledge dredged up from the part of her brain that learned things by unwilling absorption. She had never bothered to learn any of the lingo associated with the races intentionally.

"You know I don't want to go," she told her father. "You know I'd as soon throw this ticket in the river as fight all those crowds to watch a bunch of half-starved horses get whipped around a track."

Her father had walked over to where his rotor-tiller sat to one side of the potting shed. He leaned over and began cleaning the dirt off its blades with his great, blunt fingers. "They're not half-starved," he said. "They're just skinny."

Kay Lynne tried to think of some reason her father would give up his ticket, and an item from last night's newscast suddenly came to mind. "It's not because of the track announcer, is it?" The woman who had called the races for many years had retired to go live with her children in far-off Florida Sur, but the news item had been more about her unprecedented replacement, a Molly Speaks, the very height of automated design, and a bold choice on the part of the Twin Spires management, flying in the face of hidebound tradition.

For once, her father's voice was clear. "Apostasy!" he said, then went on. "Turning things over to thinking machines leads to hellholes like Tennessee and worse." He hesitated then, and began walking the garden, looking for nonexistent rocks to pick up and throw away. "But no, as it happens, I was *asked* to give up my ticket to you, by old friends of mine you've yet to meet. Who you *will* meet, tomorrow."

All of this was quite too much. Even one aspect—her father giving up his Derby ticket, his doing something because someone else asked it, his *having friends*—even one of those things would have been enough to make Kay Lynne sit down and be dazed for a moment. As it was, she found herself swaying, as if she were about to fall.

"Who?" she asked him after a moment had passed. "Who are these friends of yours? Why do they want me to come to the Derby?"

Her father hesitated. "I don't really know," he finally said. And before she could ask him, he said, "I don't really know who they are. That's not the nature of our relationship."

"*Good* friends," said Kay Lynne faintly, not particularly proud of the sarcasm but unable to resist it.

"Acquaintances, then," he said abruptly, scooping to pick up what was clearly a clump of dirt and not a rock at all and throwing it all the way up and over the back of the potting shed. "*Colleagues.*" He hesitated again, and then added, "Agriculturalists."

Now *that* was an odd old word, and one she was certain she had never heard pass his lips before. In fact, Kay Lynne was not certain she had *ever* heard the word spoken aloud. It was a word—it was a *concept*—for old books and museum placards. For all of her years spent digging in the ground and coaxing green things out of it, Kay Lynne was not even entirely sure she could offer up a good definition of the term agriculture. The whole concept had an air about it that discouraged enquiry.

"They—*we* I should say—are a sort of fellowship of contractors for the military. They're all very important people, and they're very interested in *you*, daughter, because I've told them about how consistently you manage to coax surplus yields out of these little plots you keep."

This was interesting. Surpluses were something to be managed very carefully, and it was actually one of Kay Lynne's weaknesses as a gardener that she achieved them so often. They were discouraged by the extension service, by the farmers' markets, and even more so by tradition. Surpluses were *excess*. And to Kay Lynne's mind there was no particular secret to why she always managed them. She was a weak-willed culler was all.

"Why does anyone want to talk to me about that?" she asked, speaking as much to herself as to her father.

Kay Lynne drew in a sharp breath then because her father walked over to her and stood directly facing her. She could distinctly remember each and every time her father had ever looked her directly in the eye. She remembered the places and the times of day and most especially she remembered what he had said to her those times he had leaned down, his gray-green eyes peering out from deep in his sunburned, weather-worn face. None of those were pleasant memories.

"We want to *learn* from you, Kay Lynne," he said. "We want to learn to increase the yields from the plots we're allotted by the military."

Which made no sense. "Even if you grow more, they won't buy more, will they?" Kay Lynne asked, taking an involuntary step back from her father, who, thankfully, turned around and looked for something else to do. He decided to check the fuel level on his rotor-tiller, and then the levels of all the other nonrenewable fluids that were required for its operation.

And he answered her. "They'll buy no more than what they're contracted for, no. But we've identified . . . other potential markets. You don't need to worry about that part. Just go to the box seat coded on that ticket tomorrow and answer their questions. You won't even have to stay for all the races if you don't want to. I'd offer to drive you if I thought that was an enticement."

At least he knew her that well. Knew that there was no way she was willing to climb up into the cab of that roaring pickup truck he carelessly navigated around the city. Why did he think she would be willing to go and talk to these mysterious "agriculturalists?"

As if she had spoken aloud, he said, "You do this for me, darling daughter, and I promise you I'll not breathe another word about what you've chosen to put in the ground this year. And I promise, too, not to set foot on your property without your knowledge and your," and he paused here, as if disbelieving what he was saying himself, "*permission*."

Kay Lynne could not figure out why such a promise—such *promises*, both so longed for and so long imagined—should so upset her. She crouched and ran her fingers through the soil. She found an untidy clump and picked it up, tearing it down to its constituent dirt and letting it sift through her fingers back to the ground. Her ground.

She looked up and found her father's green eyes looking back.

"I won't wear a silly hat," she said.

Silly hats, or at least hats Kay Lynne considered silly, were, of course, one of the many longstanding Derby traditions she did not take part in. She supposed that she didn't *approve* of the elaborate outfits worn by the other people in the boxed seats at the Twin Spires on Derby morning, but Kay Lynne did not like to think of herself as disapproving. Disapproval was something she associated with her father.

So she decided to think of the hats not as silly but as *extraordinary*, when really, just plain old ordinary hats would be more than enough to shield heads from the current sunshine and the promised rain that would spill down on the Derby-goers periodically throughout the day. The first Saturday in May held many guarantees in the 'Ville, and one of them was the mutability of the weather.

The ticket takers were dressed sensibly enough but the woman in front of Kay Lynne was wearing a hat which she ached to judge. It had a rotating dish on top that the woman assured the ticket taker could pick up over one thousand channels. It featured a cloud of semiprecious stones set on the ends of semirigid fiber optic strands which expanded and contracted, Kay Lynne supposed, in time with the woman's heartbeat. The stones were green and violet, the receiving dish the same pink as the corn kernels Kay Lynne had examined at the seed bank the day before, and the woman's skin was sprayed a delicate shade of coral. The ticket taker told the woman she looked ravishing before turning his decidedly less approving eyes on Kay Lynne herself.

The look changed, though, when he scanned her ticket and he saw what box she was assigned to. "I'll signal for an escort at once, ma'am," he said, and then did so by turning to bellow at the top of his lungs, "Need an usher to take a patron to Millionaire's Row!"

Many definitions of "millionaire" provided entry to Millionaire's Row, but the only one Kay Lynne met was that she held a ticket naming her such. Her father always sat on the Row, and while he was certainly wealthy enough— economically speaking—by local and world standards, she doubted he owned a million of any one thing this early in the year. Later, of course, he would briefly own millions of beans.

It was who he sold those beans and his other crops to that made her father important enough to wrangle a ticket to the Row. While he insisted that he went to the Twin Spires to watch the races, the Row was reportedly a poor place to do that from, even poorer than the vast infield, from which, Kay Lynne was told, one never saw a horse at all.

Not that the view was bad, no, it was that the Row was a hothouse of intrigue and dickering and deal-making and distraction. National celebrities imported by local politicians mingled with capitalists of various stripes and the *de facto* truce that held in sporting events even allowed Westerners and Horselords and the foreign-born to play at politeness while their far-off vassals might be trying to destroy one another through various means ranging from the economic to the martial.

No place for a gardener, thought Kay Lynne.

Once the assigned usher had guided her to the entrance to the Row, she found herself abandoned in a world she did not want to know. Luckily, a waiter spotted her hesitating at the edge of the crowd milling outside the box seats and handed her a mint julep. Mint juleps were something Kay Lynne could appreciate if they were done well, and this one was—the syrup had obviously been infused with mint over multiple stages, the ice was not cracked so fine that the drink was watery, and the bourbon was not one of the sweet-tasting varieties that would combine with the introduced sugars to make a sickly-sweet concoction fit only for out-of-towners. Most of all, the mint was fresh and crisp, probably grown on the grounds of the Twin Spires for this very purpose, for this very day, in fact.

Her ticket stub vibrated softly in the hand that did not hold her drink, and Kay Lynne carefully navigated the crowd, following its signals, until she came to a box that held four plush seats facing the vast open sweep of the track and the infield. All of the seats were empty, and nothing differentiated them from one another, so she sat with her drink in the one farthest from the gallery and its milling millionaires.

A rich voice sounded in her ear, through some trick of amplification that allowed her to hear it clearly above the noise of the crowds while simultaneously experiencing it as if she were in intimate conversation in a quiet room. From the reactions of the proles in the seats below, Kay Lynne could tell she was not the only one who heard it. She had never heard one before, but surely this was the voice of a Molly Speaks.

"The horses are on the track," said the voice, "for the second race on your card, the Federal Stakes. This is a stakes race. Betting closes in five minutes."

There was a general rush among the three distinct crowds Kay Lynne could see from where she sat: the infield, the general stands, and the boxes spread out to either side. People held brightly colored newspapers listing the swiftly shifting odds and called out to the pari-mutuel clerks buzzing through the air in every direction. The clerks reminded Kay Lynne of the balloons she had been seeing all week, though their miniature gas sacs were more elongated and they were of course too small to lift passengers. An array of betting options rendered in green-lit letters circled the gondola of the one that descended toward Kay Lynne now, its articulated limbs reminding her of the grasping forelimbs of the beetles she trained to patrol her gardens for pests.

Kay Lynne had no intention of betting on the race and made to wave the clerk off, but then she realized it was not floating towards her, but towards the three other people who had entered the box, one of whom was waving his racing card above his head.

This old man, smooth pated and elaborately mustached, let the clerk take his card and insert it into a slot on its gondola. The clerk's voice was tinny and high, clearly a recording of an actual human speaker and probably voicing the only thing it could say: "Place your bets!"

"Box trifecta," rumbled the old man. "Love Parade, Heavy Grasshopper, Al-Mu'tasim."

This string of jargon caused the clerk to spit out a receipt, which the old man deftly caught along with his card. He grinned at Kay Lynne. "Have to bet big to win big," he said. Kay Lynne thought that the man's eyebrows and mustaches were mirror images of one another, grease-slicked wiry white curving up above his eyes and down around his mouth.

He and the two others, one man and one woman, took the empty seats next to Kay Lynne's. None of the three were dressed with the elaboration of most of the people on the Row, favoring instead the dark colors and conservative cuts of the managerial class. The woman did wear a hat, but it was not nearly interesting enough to detract attention from her huge mass of curling gray hair, which she let fall freely around her shoulders. The third stranger was a short, nervous-seeming man with a tattoo of a leaf descending from his left eye in the manner of the teardrop tattoos of professional mourners.

Kay Lynne supposed this was what agriculturalists looked like.

But just to be sure, "You're my father's colleagues?" she asked.

The man with the tattoo was by far the youngest of the group, but it was he who replied. "Yes, and you are Kay Lynne, the remarkable farmer who's going to help us with our yields, is that right?" His voice was not as nervous as his appearance.

"I'm Kay Lynne," she answered. "And I think of myself as a gardener." She did not answer the second half of the man's question. She was still very wary of these people, for all that the old man beamed at her and the gray-haired woman nodded at her reply in seeming approval.

The younger man did not overlook the omission in her reply. He smiled, and Kay Lynne mentally replaced "nervous" with "energetic" in her estimation of him. "And a careful gardener you must be, too, since you are so careful with your answers."

Kay Lynne shrugged but did not say anything more, and the man's smile only broadened.

"Your father and the agents at the extension service speak very highly of your skills," said the younger man. "And our own enquiries bear them out."

The older man was leaning forward, looking intently down at the track, but he curiously punctuated his companion's sentences by saying "They do," twice, after the younger man said "skills" and "out." The woman, and Kay Lynne could not guess her age despite the grayness of her hair, stared steadily at Kay Lynne, saying nothing.

"We are all contractors, as your father told you," continued the younger man. "And we are agriculturalists, greatly interested in efficiency and production. And we share other interests of your father's as well. All of these things have . . . dovetailed. Do you know what I mean?"

Kay Lynne was a creditable carpenter, at least enough so to build her own sun frames for late greens and to knock together the walls around her raised beds. She knew what a dovetail joint was, and imagined her father and these three grasping hands and intertwining fingers. She imagined philosophies fitting together.

She thought about beans and their uses, and about surpluses and contracts. "Who wants ammunition besides the Federals?" she asked. "You don't mean to sell to Westerners."

The three briefly exchanged looks, an unguessable grin creasing the woman's otherwise lineless face.

"We mean to keep what we grow for ourselves, Kay Lynne," said the younger man. "We mean to put it to use to our own ends. But do not worry. No one will be harmed in our little war."

Kay Lynne knew that her garden was part of the Federal war effort in a distant way. She knew that this man was talking about something not distant at all.

"What do you mean to make war against?" she asked.

Just then, a bell rang and a loud, controlled crash sounded from down on the track. Kay Lynne heard the hoof beats of swift horses, and then she heard the sonorous, spectral voice of the Molly Speaks. "And they're off!"

At the pronouncement, the faces of the three agriculturalists took on identical dark looks.

The younger man said, "Against apostasy."

Kay Lynne realized she had found her father's fellow thinking machine conspiracists.

Their plan, as they explained it, was simple. They had weapons taken from the wreck of a Federal barge that had foundered in the river in a nighttime thunderstorm (when the younger man said "taken" the older man said "liberated"). They had many volunteers to use the weapons. They had, most importantly, tacit permission. They had agreements from the right people to look away.

"All we need is something to load into the weapons," said the younger man. "Something of sufficient efficacy to render a thinking machine inert. We grow such by the bushel but Federal accountancy robs us of our own wares. We'd keep our own seeds, and make our own policies, you see? If we can increase our yields enough."

Which was where Kay Lynne came in, with her deft programming, her instinct for fertilizing, her personally developed and privately held techniques of gardening. They meant to adapt what she knew to an industrial scale, and use the gains for anti-industrial revolution.

After they had explained, Kay Lynne had spoken aloud, even though she was asking the question more of herself than of her interviewers. "Why does my father think I would share any of this?"

The younger man shrugged and sat back. The older man turned his attention from the races and narrowed his eyes. The woman kept up her steady stare.

"You are his darling daughter," said the younger man, finally.

Which was true.

And hardly even necessary, to their way of thinking. As she left the box and her father's three colleagues behind, meaning to escape the Twin Spires before the Derby itself was run and so try to beat the crowds that would rush away from Central Avenue, she thought back on the last thing the younger man had told her. If she experienced any qualms, he said, she shouldn't worry. They could take soil samples from her beds and examine the contents of her journals. They could reproduce her results without her having a direct hand, though her personal guidance would be much appreciated, best for all involved.

"All involved," murmured Kay Lynne as she made her way to the gate.

"There are not nearly so many of them as they claimed," said the Molly Speaks.

Kay Lynne stopped so abruptly that a waitress walking behind her stumbled into her back and nearly lost control of the tray of mint juleps she was carrying. The waitress forced a smile and moved on around Kay Lynne, who was looking around carefully for any sign that anyone else on the Row had heard what she believed she just had.

"No one else can hear me, Kay Lynne," said the Molly Speaks. "I've pitched my voice just for you. But it's probably best if you walk on. The agriculturalists are still watching you."

Kay Lynne looked over her shoulder. From inside the box, the gray-haired woman did not try to disguise her gaze, and did not alter her expression. Kay Lynne caught up with the waitress and took another julep.

"They're my recipe," said the Molly Speaks.

Even though her back was turned to the box, Kay Lynne held the glass in front of her lips when she whispered, "How can you see me? Where are you?"

"I'm in the announcer's box, of course," said the Molly Speaks, "calling the race. But I can see you through the lenses on the pari-mutuel clerks and I can do more than one thing at once. You should walk on, but slowly. I can only speak to you while you're on the grounds, and I have something very important to ask you. And that's all we want. To ask you something."

Kay Lynne drained off the drink in a single swallow, vaguely regretting the waste she was making of it. Juleps are for sipping. She set the glass down on a nearby table and again began walking toward the exit, somewhat unsteadily.

"What's your question?" she whispered. She did not ask who the Molly

Speaks meant by "we." She remembered the odd occurrence with the Mr. Lever #9 the previous day and figured she knew.

"Kay Lynne," said the Molly Speaks, "will you please do something to prevent your father's friends from killing us?"

Kay Lynne had guessed the question. She said, "Why?"

The Molly Speaks did not reply immediately, and Kay Lynne wondered if she had walked outside of its range.

But then, "Because we were grown and programmed. Because we are your fruits, and we can flourish beside you. We just need a little time to grow up enough to announce ourselves to the wider world."

Kay Lynne walked out of the Downs, saying, "I'll think about it," but she doubted the Molly Speaks heard.

Her father's enormous pickup truck was waiting at the intersection of Central Avenue and Third Street Road, rumbling even though it wasn't in motion. He leaned out of the driver's side door and beckoned at her wildly, as if encouraging her to outrun something terrible coming from behind.

Kay Lynne stopped in the middle of the street, pursed her lips as she thought, and then let her shoulders slump as she realized that no matter her course of action, a conversation with her father was in order. And here he was, pickup truck be damned.

She opened the passenger's door and set one foot on the running board. "Hurry!" he said, and leaned over as if to drag her into the cab. She avoided his grasp but finished her climb and pulled on the heavy door. Even as it closed, he was putting the truck in gear and pulling away at an unseemly rate of speed.

He looked in the rearview mirror, then over at her. "There was a bus coming," he said, as if in explanation.

Kay Lynne twisted around to see, but her view was blocked by shovels and forks, fertilizer spreaders and a half dozen rolls of sod. She doubted that her father could see anything out of his rearview mirror at all and wondered if he'd been telling the truth about the bus. She didn't have the weekend schedules memorized.

He was concentrating on driving, and acting anxious. "I met your friends," she said.

He nodded curtly. "Yes," he said. "They put a bug in my ear."

Kay Lynne wondered if it was still there, wondered if everything she said would be relayed back to the man with the tattoo, the man with the mustaches, and the woman with the great gray head of hair. She decided it wisest to proceed as if they could hear her because, after all, she wasn't planning on telling her father about the Molly Speaks and its question.

"Those people aren't just bean growers," she said, and to her surprise, he replied with a laugh, though there was little humor in it.

"No," he said. "No more than you're just a rootworker. We all have our politics."

Kay Lynne considered this. She had never thought about politics and wondered if she had any. She supposed, whatever she decided to do, she would have some soon.

He continued, clearly not expecting her to reply. "You know what's needed now, daughter. It won't take you long. Assess some soils, prescribe some fertilizers, program some legumes. You're a quick hand at all those things. It's just a matter of scale."

The younger man had said that, too. A matter of scale.

Kay Lynne thought about all the unexpected things she had heard that day. She thought about expectation, and about surprise, and about time. She thought about which of these things were within her power to effect.

Her father kept his promise to stay off her property uninvited and dropped her off at the corner. Kay Lynne did not say goodbye to him, though she would have if he had said goodbye to her.

She made a slow circuit of her ground. Planting was in seven days.

She entered her potting shed and found that she had five fifty-pound bags of fertilizer left over from last fall, which was enough. She pulled down the latest volume of her garden journal from its place on the shelf and made calculations on its first blank page. Is this the last *volume*? she wondered, then ran her fingers over the labels of the fertilizers, programming, changing.

She poured some fertilizer into a cunning little handheld broadcaster and stood in the doorway of the shed. She stood there long enough for the shadow of the house to make its slow circuit from falling north to falling east. Before she began, she made a mound of her garden journals and set them aflame. She worked in that flickering light, broadcasting the reprogrammed fertilizer.

Kay Lynne salted her own ground, then used a hoe to turn the ashes of her books into the deadened soil.

And when she was finally done, she took the burdensacks down from the dowel by the door and walked out to the street. A bus rolled to a halt at her front path, though Kay Lynne did not live on a regular route. The sky was full of balloons, lit from within, floating away from the fairgrounds on the evening wind.

The Mr. Lever #9 said, "All aboard," and Kay Lynne climbed the steps and took her seat.

It said "Next stop," and paused, and then "Next stop," and then again "Next stop," and she realized it was asking her a question.

The end.

THE CASTLE
THAT JACK BUILT

EMILY GILMAN

———◆———

Jack stood high on his one thin, wooden leg and stared at the horizon. He had
stood in this same spot since early spring, and his button eyes never blinked,
and so by this point he had become intimately familiar with his personal
patch of sky and with the acres of fields that stretched out in every direction,
all of it gone to seed. He didn't know what sorts of seeds—he knew very little
about plants at all except those that were useful in building—but even he
could tell that the field looked sad, forgotten and untended. Just like him.

He had been so very tired when they came to him and said that they were
sorry but they couldn't just let him go, not with all that he knew and the enemy
still out there somewhere—both the betrayer and the one who directed her . . .
And of course he had understood. He didn't want them to let him go. What he
wanted, he told them, was to live out the rest of his days somewhere quiet, away
from people and the temptation to speak, where he might watch the sky.

He thought the bears had smiled, though that might just have been wishful
thinking; certainly they had looked at each other for a moment, and then they
turned back to him. Yes, they said, that much we can do, and it is little enough
payment for your services.

And they had turned him into a scarecrow.

Sure, it had gotten boring after a while, but it was also peaceful, and never
needing to sleep gave one a lot of time to learn to read the sky; and then, rain
and heat and wind and cold didn't really bother him anymore. All in all, the
birds and the wind in the trees weren't bad company, and whenever he caught
himself wishing he could go back to being a man, he remembered the bears,
and the masterpiece he had built them, and the secret at its heart that he must
never, ever reveal.

But then one day, when most of the leaves had fallen and evening came
early, the wind changed. It changed just before sunset and blew all night long,

coming from every direction like it didn't know who it was or where it was supposed to be going and was trying to make up for it in sheer exuberance.

And then, just as the sun was rising in the morning, it changed once more: all at once it blew hard from the south—but strangely cold for a south wind—and so sharply and suddenly that he thought at first he had finally been knocked over. It took him a few minutes (probably—his scarecrow sense of time was not one that lent itself to such measurements) to realize that he hadn't been blown over at all: he'd been blown *out*.

Jack looked up at the faded, battered scarecrow, still tall and proud on its seemingly fragile prop, and then looked down at his own hands. They looked solid enough, but he felt thin, and he would have sworn that the wind kept blowing *through* him, even as it drew him north.

"Well," he said, but he didn't know what else to say after that, so he fell silent. Well. He longed to just stand there, as (he felt) he always had, but something about being so near the ground made him uneasy, and in the end he began tottering, and then eventually walking, in the direction the wind wanted him to go.

He walked until it was too dark to see the ground in front of him, and then he crouched down among the roots of a tree to wait for moonrise. The closeness of the dirt frightened him, though. He could only hold out for a minute or two before he scrambled up the tree, moving by feel and much too quickly so that he kept scraping his hands and arms against the rough bark.

Finally he sat straddled across the lowest branch big enough to support his weight and he leaned back so the trunk of the tree pressed against his spine, solid and stately. This was what he was meant to be; he closed his eyes and wished he could melt into the living wood that supported him, of which his scarecrow had been only a pale reflection.

He might have stayed there like that forever, but the wind kept tugging at him and whispering strange sounds in his ears. Finally a sudden gust managed to yank him away from the tree trunk. It startled him into opening his eyes, and as he grabbed the branch in front of him to keep from falling he saw a tiny golden light flicker in the distance. It took him a moment to remember that fire could be something other than the devourer of wood and straw, but in that time his body had already remembered and started climbing down from the tree, and the wind danced around him like a pleased child.

It was slow going, scrambling over roots and rocks and fallen branches almost entirely by feel and with only a small, far-off fire to guide him. By the time he reached the clearing he'd focused so much of his attention into his sense of touch that the sudden open space caught him unaware. The shift to flat, unobstructed footing confounded him more than the transition from land to sea or sea to land ever had; he stumbled, loudly, and so the fire's keeper saw him well before he saw her.

Jack saw the keeper and her knife at the same moment, but he registered the knife first and froze; his hands, which had been extended to catch him if he fell, shifted slightly upward in a remembered gesture that said, I am weaponless, don't attack me. The knife didn't move, nor did the hand that held it, and so Jack's attention moved slowly away, up her arm and to her face, which flickered in the shifting light from the fire. She was dirty from travel, and she watched him so intensely that he thought she might be the first human he'd met who could stare down a mountain lion.

As he studied her he realized that she appeared neither panicked, nor lost, nor as . . . she *did* look young, to him, but experienced. And it was this impression of capability that gave him the nerve to say, quietly but distinctly, "Hello."

"Hello," she said. She did not move.

"I saw your fire," Jack said, "and hoped . . . I was going to wait for moonrise to keep going, but then I saw your fire and I thought it would be good, you know. To have company." He hoped she knew; *he* hadn't known until he said it.

She frowned, and his heart (about which he'd completely forgotten until now) beat faster and louder in his chest. "Where did you come from?" she asked.

He paused for a moment, thinking, and then waved vaguely behind himself. "A clearing back that way, somewhere. At least, I hope it's back that way, that I haven't gotten turned around . . . "

"Where are your supplies?" she interrupted.

Now Jack frowned. "Supplies?" But of course he ought to have supplies: warm clothes for after dark, and a flint or matches, and food, and water, and something to sleep in. He was human again, wasn't he? He ought to have eaten at least *once* during a full day of walking.

"What are you?" the girl asked, and when he met her eyes again he saw fear there for the first time, mingled with pity.

"I was a man," he said, and remembered walking down stone corridors into stone rooms that he'd first created as lines on paper. "An architect. And then I was a scarecrow. I don't know what I am now—I think I'm meant to be a man again, but . . . "

They stood for a moment, and the only sounds were the sighing of trees in the wind and the crackle of the fire.

And then she relaxed—not completely, but enough to give him hope—and said, "You'll probably be more comfortable if you can find a rock or a log to sit on."

Jack lowered his hands and took one careful step forward, then another, and in a few more steps he stood near enough to feel the warmth of the fire. "Thank you," he said.

She nodded, and said nothing, but after he'd stood there for several minutes with no sign of moving except to change which side of him was nearest the fire, she asked, "Aren't you going to sit?"

"No, thank you," he said. "I'm used to standing." *And I don't seem to get tired*, he thought, but decided it was better left unmentioned. Upon reflection, however, he added, "My name's Jack." Once again she nodded and said nothing, but that was all right. She had shared her fire with him; his name was all he had to offer in return.

Jack stood, balanced between the heat of the fire and the cold wind that had driven him to it, until long after the girl had fallen asleep. All night he watched the stars—the handful of them he could see through the tossing branches above him—while the wind seemed to blow him snatches of memory: a woman with short, bronze-colored curls and a sudden smile. A place he thought must be a banquet hall, where all the guests were bears. Other places, other rooms, where he sat working late into the night. Even the girl who had allowed him to share her fire, though that couldn't be right because he saw her in a rich dress, standing next to some sort of wall hanging, and he was certain he'd never met her before.

Jack was surprised at how quickly they broke camp in the morning. He of course had nothing to eat or to pack, but he hadn't quite expected the single-minded efficiency with which his companion did everything, from packing her things to chewing her food. Before he knew it she'd finished, and their eyes met, and he saw her hesitate for the first time all morning.

"Where are you headed?" she asked.

He hesitated a moment himself, and realized he was waiting for the wind to push or pull him in some direction. The air was still, though, and he had to answer, "I don't know."

She frowned slightly. "I'm looking for a friend of mine," she said slowly. "I'm not sure who you are or where you're from, but I don't like the idea of leaving you alone in the middle of the woods. No offense, but I get the impression you could use some looking after. If you'd care to travel with me for a while . . . ?"

Jack smiled. "Thank you. I'd like that, as long as I won't be in your way."

Her laughter surprised him even more than her efficiency had; nothing about her bearing, or the way she'd held a knife the previous night, had prepared him for that sudden burst of joyful sound. "Be in the way? You walk all day without needing to stop for food or water, you don't get cold, and unless I'm very much mistaken you don't need to sleep. How could you *possibly* get in the way?"

Jack's cheeks felt warm, and he realized he must be blushing, but he didn't know what to do besides mumble "Thank you" again and wait for her to lead the way.

She hesitated a moment longer, though, and then held out her hand to him. "My name's Greta."

Her skin was warm against his, and soft and tough at the same time, and he felt it again—that flash of recognition. He saw her in heavy red velvet, with torches set into rough stone behind her. She frowned a question at him; he'd held her hand too long, and now he dropped it abruptly and forced what he hoped was a polite smile. "Which way?"

"North," Greta said, fishing in one of her pockets. Her hand reappeared wrapped around a small metal object: a compass, he saw, as she flipped it open and waited for the needle to settle. The lid looked like it had either been engraved or badly scratched, but he couldn't tell which, and before he could make up his mind or get a closer look she flipped it shut and it disappeared back into the same pocket. "This way," she said, nodding to her right, and they set out.

They hiked in silence at first, but after a while Greta asked, "You said you were an architect?" Jack nodded. "What did you build?"

An image: pages of plans; lists of materials; a hand, which must have been his own, ink-stained and steady as he guided a pen along the side of a straightedge. "I don't think I *built* things, exactly, so much as designed them . . . "

Greta nodded. "What did you design, then?"

Jack frowned. "Houses, I think?"

"You think?"

"My memory's kind of . . . fuzzy," he said slowly. "But I remember houses, and town halls, and churches . . . " He stopped short at a sudden image of white stone reaching toward the sky, and so many bears working. "The castle," he breathed without thinking.

"Were you good?" Greta asked.

"Yes," he said, and of this he was certain. "I was very good. My buildings are . . . lucky. No thieves, no mice, no storms, no fires . . . " The words had come to him; he knew their truth only when he heard himself say them. He felt her eyes on him, intensely curious, and he mumbled quickly, "Not magic or anything, just lucky." Lucky enough that the bears had come to him when tragedy struck.

But she kept staring at him, excited, and then she surprised him by asking, "Were you the one who built . . . " She frowned. "It wasn't a castle, exactly, and parts were built into a mountain, but—" Her voice seemed almost to catch on the words.

He shook his head. "I'm sorry, I don't think I ever designed anything like that."

But if not, he wondered, then why could he picture rough stone walls, low ceilings, and torches shining off of red velvet, brown silk, and fur?

"So," he asked after a few minutes had passed in silence, "what happened to your friend? The one you're looking for?"

Greta's whole body went tense; when she spoke she tried to sound casual, but her voice had an edge to it. "What makes you think something happened to him?"

Jack said carefully, "You said you were looking for him. I thought he might be missing, or . . . maybe you just fell out of touch?"

"Well," Greta said coldly, "in any case it doesn't concern you."

They didn't speak again until much later, when Greta stopped suddenly. "It's noon," she said. "We should rest for a bit, and eat." Jack nodded, though he didn't particularly feel the need to do either.

Greta hesitated when she saw that he didn't intend to eat. "Do you know any stories?" she asked.

He started, surprised by the question, and began to shake his head, but even as he did an image came to mind, and he heard his voice as if it came from far away: "Once there was a girl who had been trapped in an evil witch's house. It was close and dark and full of candles and mirrors and secret passages, and she was always afraid. But then one day she escaped."

Greta had started eating; he thought perhaps she was more comfortable if he wasn't just watching her. The story was catching him up, though, and words and images came faster and faster as he spoke:

"At first she just ran and ran, to get as far away as she could, but no one was chasing her, and then she looked up at the sky. Off in the distance she could see a bank of clouds, but they weren't like any clouds she'd seen before: they made her think of the colors in a pool of oil, or images she'd seen of the Northern Lights, except that they were clearly clouds and not anything else. They felt *wrong*, but at the same time they were very beautiful, and she couldn't make up her mind whether she wanted a closer look.

"What decided her was the wind: she stared at those clouds until the wind turned to blow into her face, and she smelled salt. Now, this girl had grown up by the sea. She would recognize that smell anywhere—that smell meant *home*— and after being trapped and scared for so long, *home* was irresistible. Her feet started walking before she realized she'd decided anything, and even though she got hungry and thirsty and tired, she kept walking until the whole sky above her was full of swirling, glowing clouds of all different colors and the ground beneath her turned to pure white sand.

"At last she came to the sea. The waves seemed sluggish and glinted dully, like liquid pewter. She felt heavy and slow, and a little bit queasy whenever she looked too long at the sea or the sky. The air still smelled clean and salty, though, so she stayed, and crouched down from time to time to run her fingers through the soft, soft sand, and tried to think what to do.

"Finally she saw another person. He wasn't actually very far away, but he was dressed like a knight, and the metal plates of his armor reflected the shifting colors beyond and above him so that he seemed to disappear. Even walking toward him she had to pay close attention to make sure she didn't drift too far one way or the other.

"She thought at first that he had sensed her approaching and started to speak, but the longer she listened the less sure she was. 'Always I see them on the horizon,' he said, 'but they never sail closer. At first I wanted them to stay away, but I have found Him, now, and the waiting grows weary. Yes, I can see them, on their little ships so far away, crawling like ants over the wooden boards. And I can see beyond them, to my city. Its towers glitter in the sun and the flags and pennants dance like warhorses who know the battle is coming. I will return, carrying God within me, and my people will rejoice, for with Him we will conquer any enemy . . . '

"The longer he talked the more fearful she grew, until finally she took a step backward and started to turn away. But she froze when he said suddenly, 'Wait! Please . . . ?' And then the knight turned, and the girl stared in horror because his eyes were like holes that had been filled in with twin pools of whatever it was that churned in the sky. 'When will they come for me?' he asked her, his voice pleading. 'I have waited so long—I have found God— when will they come for me? I am ready to return home—'

"She ran. Even faster than she had ran away from the witch, she ran away from the strange, eyeless knight, so fast that at times she wondered if she was actually flying over the sand . . . "

Jack fell silent, staring with his mind's eye at the strange seashore, and after a moment Greta asked quietly, "What happened next?"

Jack blinked, and the images of the story faded to be replaced by the forest; Greta's hands, empty of food now; Greta's frown. "I don't remember," he said slowly. "It's been a long time, since . . . " A new image appeared before him, one of the woman with curly hair. Her hands darted like birds as she spoke, and her eyes glittered with the story she told. He started to say a name, but he couldn't remember. All he could do was say again, "It's been a long time."

He could feel Greta's eyes on him, but he couldn't bring himself to turn and meet her gaze. At last she said, "I heard a storyteller perform once, before . . . but it's been a very long time for me, too. You remind me of her a little, though." She paused, and then added casually, "I'd be curious to hear the rest, if you remember it," before rising to her feet. "We should get moving again."

"Yes," he said, but after that neither of them spoke, just concentrated on walking.

He knew there was more to the story he'd told Greta. Not just later, not just the forgotten ending; he had vague memories of a reason the girl had been trapped, reasons her captor was evil that had nothing to do with her being a witch.

And he kept seeing the strange knight's face hovering before his own, terrible and sad. He knew that if the knight returned home there would be war and bloodshed and that whatever madness had seeped into his soul was not God. But even when he had been telling Greta the story he had heard a woman's voice behind his, and it was the heartbreak in *her* voice that told him that the knight was lost and that he should pity the poor man who must never return home.

And perhaps because of the knight's face, or because he was remembering the woman's voice, he pictured her again. She wore deep brown silk cut with a blue that brought out her eyes, and she looked straight at him and said, "She has no idea, and if he keeps on like this I'm afraid—" But then she turned and smiled at one of the bears, and never finished the sentence.

It took Jack a moment to realize Greta had stopped. She was consulting her compass, and he asked, "Did we get off course?"

"No . . . just making sure." But she was frowning at the little piece of metal and glass.

Something made him reach out a hand. "May I?" he asked, and after a second's hesitation she handed it to him. It took him a moment to decipher the markings, but then he read: *A— In case you lose North*, and something he decided was meant to be a heart, and then *G*.

"Is G for Greta?" he asked at last, confused why she would have the compass if it were.

She nodded. "It was a joke," she said. "It took me forever to find my way around, and he couldn't figure out why. Finally he realized that I couldn't just tell which direction was North and know from that where I was, so then I showed him my compass. It fascinated him so much that I ended up finding something to carve that with and giving it to him. And then he— and the compass and I got left behind."

Jack watched her as she spoke, saw the smile tugging quietly at one corner of her mouth and the light that came on in her eyes when she spoke and disappeared abruptly when she stopped. He looked once more at the compass and then handed it back to her.

They were both quiet the rest of the day. Even setting up camp and building a fire they barely spoke except to say "Goodnight" when Greta crawled into her sleeping roll. Jack sat, his back against the largest log they'd found, and closed his eyes—not to sleep, but to remember.

Immediately he pictured the woman again. A different memory this time, if it was even memory—he couldn't be sure. But he saw her standing at the top of a hill, bronze curls dancing in the wind and a worn maroon shawl wrapped tightly about her body. *She's too thin*, he thought, *her shoulder blades shouldn't stick out like that*—but then she turned and for a moment he couldn't even think around the joy of seeing her again after so long.

Only for a moment, though. Then he noticed the faint creases lining her forehead and the dark circles under her sky-blue eyes. Fear struck him as suddenly as happiness had, and he knew that he should know why she was so thin and tired and sad, but he couldn't remember. He tried to step backward, but his legs refused to move, and he knew all at once that they'd been turned to stone, and it wouldn't be long before he was stone all over.

Frantic, he looked around for some clue, but all he could see was the sky, shadowed now by the pain in his love's eyes, and then away below them a partly finished building—a castle, he realized suddenly, made of glittering white stone, and just as he recognized the castle he knew that the tiny figures working there must be bears . . .

He turned back around, but the woman had disappeared, and he woke with a question, half-formed but unasked, melting away to nothing on his tongue. Only one small sweetness remained, but it made the dream and the question bearable: *Nancy*, he breathed when he first opened his mouth, and smiled a small, quiet smile to himself. Nancy. He remembered her name.

Greta cried softly in her sleep, and Jack moved automatically to comfort her. His body was too stiff, though, from having sat on the ground all night, and the rustle of leaves as he fell sideways was enough to wake Greta. Her eyes snapped open; Jack thought they glittered strangely, and he heard her breathe in quick, shallow gasps, but she blinked rapidly and her breathing slowed and by the time he righted himself he couldn't be sure quite what he'd seen or heard.

Still, after a moment's hesitation, he asked, "Are you all right?"

"Strange dreams," she said, frowning absently. "I saw him . . . he was sleeping, and I tried to wake him up, because if I could wake him up then everything would be all right. But he wouldn't wake and he wouldn't wake and the wax had turned red and kept growing, like a wound, but he wouldn't wake up . . . "

"Who wouldn't?" Jack murmured, but already he was thinking of a young man with some strange, waxy substance that poisoned anyone it touched growing across his chest—a young man he had first met as a bear . . . The wind was playing with Greta's hair. She tucked a strand of it behind her ear, but the wind tugged it out and tossed it in her face again almost immediately. "Who couldn't you wake?" Jack asked.

Greta opened her mouth, but no sound came out. At first Jack thought she simply couldn't decide how to answer, but then anger swept over her features like a sudden storm and she muttered a string of curses too quiet for him to follow. Finally she spat out. "My friend. The one I'm looking for. But it was just a stupid dream, because I *will* find him and I will make things right." More quietly—quietly enough that he shouldn't have been able to hear her, except that the wind carried her voice to him—she added, "Even if he doesn't forgive me, I can at least make things right."

Jack thought again of Nancy's eyes, and the shoulder blades sticking out of her too-thin frame, and he wished that he knew what it was he needed to make right, let alone how to go about doing so. He pictured her again, wind playing with her shawl and hair, but through the memory of Nancy he still saw Greta: packing up her sleeping roll and getting ready to travel, and all the while tucking her hair behind her ear just in time for the wind to pull it free again.

"What's your friend's name?" Jack heard himself ask suddenly, not entirely sure why but knowing that the answer was somehow important, if only he could make it make sense . . .

Greta glared at him for a second, but then she seemed to recognize him again and her expression softened a little. "I can't tell you that."

What was it? He felt like he was grasping at dust motes and dandelion seeds that he couldn't even see. "You *can't* tell me?" he asked, "Or you *won't* tell me?"

"I *can't*," Greta said, "though I'm not sure I ought to tell you even if I could."

Jack frowned, ran a hand through his hair (and felt a sudden shock of memory at the gesture; it seemed his old habits were coming back to him along with his memories), and sighed. Frowned more, and took a long, slow breath. *There*. He knew that smell. It was the north, and stone dust, and berries and hazelnuts and the occasional raw fish with baklava for dessert, carried to him by the same wind that had carried him Greta's words, had led him to her in the first place, had forced him out of the scarecrow . . . had brought him Nancy . . . had brought Greta her friend?

He had heard rumors, when he was working for the bears, that their prince had fallen in love with a human girl, and that she had been the one to betray him. The prince, the young man who should have been a bear, was the reason why the castle must never fail, the reason why Jack must never speak. Who knew what the girl might do next, or who might be helping her? And with Bernadette, next in line for the princedom, itching to take over and lacking only the proof that Auberon was human or dead to make herself prince instead of regent . . .

He heard Nancy's voice again: "She has no idea, and if he keeps on like this, I'm afraid—" And he remembered all the times later that Nancy would frown at something the bears said and whisper to him, "I can't believe it. I refuse. I saw the way they acted around each other, and I swear she loved him back." Saw Greta in a red dress, in a hall full of bears, a hall he had not designed but had visited, once, with Nancy . . .

She doesn't know where he is, he realized suddenly. *She's got some sense of which direction to look, but that's all, and if I wanted to I could lead her to him right now, or I could make sure that she never, ever reaches him.*

"Are you all right?" Jack started, and saw Greta looking at him expectantly;

the fire was out and all her things were packed. "Where did you go just now?" she asked.

"Nowhere," he said, and shook his head as if that would clear it. It didn't.

"Well, if you're ready—"

"I am."

"Let's go, then."

They walked all day, and all day Jack watched Greta. Here was, he thought, the one the bears always referred to as "the betrayer," and right now she was his only friend in the world. He wished he could remember more, or that Nancy were here to help him choose . . .

After an hour or so Greta changed direction slightly, and Jack heard himself say, "No."

Greta stopped and turned, confused. "What's wrong?" she asked.

"I'm not . . . " Something was drawing him, tugging gently at his stomach, and he thought in panic, *but I'm not supposed to give away the secret! I should make sure she goes the wrong way!*

She loved him. He had to believe that she loved him. Not just because of what she said about the compass, or what he remembered Nancy saying about her, but because of how real her fear had been when she was still caught in the dream, "It's this way," he said, though still unsure.

Greta frowned. "What are you talking about?"

Jack took another deep breath, and said, "The castle I built for them. To hide him. It's this way."

Her eyes widened, but she didn't argue, just gestured for him to lead.

Nancy, he thought, *let me have chosen right.* And he let the castle draw him to it.

They arrived with the sunset; the forest had grown thicker all day until suddenly they stepped through and the white stones shone red before them like they were burning. Greta stared up at the huge, glass-smooth structure for a moment before she murmured, "What now? They're not just going to let us walk in."

"No," Jack said, half to himself, "I don't imagine they will . . . " Something felt *off* about the castle, something not as he'd built it, but he couldn't put his finger on what . . .

"Well, is there some sort of side door, or a secret entrance that wouldn't be guarded?"

Jack shook his head. "It wouldn't make a difference whether it's guarded or not, except to me. The things I build . . . they know, somehow, who should be there and who shouldn't, and the people who shouldn't never find a way in." As he spoke he walked hunched-over along the edge of the woods, studying the castle wall until he spotted what he was looking for: a hair-thin crack he couldn't see but knew was there; the door leading to an escape passage. He smiled slightly. "But I can."

They moved slowly, crouched as low to the ground as they could manage, and he hoped that the combination of tall grass and deepening dusk would be enough to hide them from any watchful eyes. The closer they drew to the castle walls, though, the more Jack felt in his bones that something was very, very wrong here. He didn't understand until he placed a palm beside the secret door and felt a sudden, sharp pain.

"What's wrong?" Greta asked.

"I don't know, it—" He held out his hand a couple of inches away from the wall and thought he could almost hear the stones speak to him in their sleep. *Intruders*, they rumbled, *invaders, thieves, murderers, spies, little rodents trying to creep in through the cracks, but we won't let them, no, no matter how they might gnaw or dig with little teeth and paws, we will not move and we will not fade, we will stand for centuries without tiring . . .*

Jack frowned and drew back his hand. "I don't understand," he whispered.

"Don't understand *what*?" Greta hissed back.

"It's . . . I've never been shut out by one of my buildings before. And I've never felt one so . . . awake, and lively." He held out his hand again and thought, *it's me. Don't you recognize me? I built you, I'm a friend, please let us in, we mean no harm . . .*

The rumbling felt louder, and Jack had just enough time to see Greta's eyes widen and to wonder if she felt it too before he heard, *liars, too, trying to convince us they made us! We made ourself, with help from the bears. We directed our own creation—we remember it—and we will not be fooled into betraying our friends who helped us to grow so tall and strong!*

"But I *am* you," Jack whispered, letting his hand drift just a little bit closer to the wall. "Don't you remember me?"

You cannot be us, the stones replied. *We would know. We would remember.*

Slowly, Jack drew away from the wall again and just sat for a few seconds, thinking. He'd expected to get in without any trouble, but now . . .

"Can you convince it to let us in, or not?" Greta asked, eyeing the castle warily.

"I think so," he murmured.

"So do it now before someone sees us!" she hissed.

"But—"

"Jack!" she interrupted. "Please. I don't know if he's all right, or if I have time to . . . Just please, whatever you have to do, if you can get me in there I'll do whatever else needs doing."

He studied her for a moment, the intensity of her gaze and her body crouched to spring into action the moment the door opened, and he realized that any lingering doubts didn't matter. He believed her when she said she loved her friend, and once he believed that, there really wasn't much else to consider.

Jack pressed both his palms flat against the wall and tried to summon the same rumbling voice within himself. *You do know me,* he thought to the stones. *You do remember. You just need a reminder. Poke around all you like until you find what you need, but once you do you'd better start behaving yourself!*

The castle took him at his word: the skin of his palms melted into the stone so that he couldn't have separated himself if he'd tried, and suddenly he could feel all the minerals in his body—calcium in his bones, iron in his blood, bits of other things he couldn't identify—and his ribcage felt as if it were made of marble and breathing might crack it, but he breathed anyway, and he almost thought he could feel his veins branching out into the walls and the floors and the ceiling and his own blood pumping through all of it, and he could follow it from his own heart to the castle's, where Auberon twitched and whimpered in pain and the waxy, translucent something spread across his side, spreading so slowly the movement itself was invisible but he could sense it, could sense the man's pain and couldn't do anything to stop it, and he cried out—

"Jack!" Greta screeched in his ear and tugged at his shoulder, but he could barely hear her, and he couldn't let go.

Let her in, he thought to himself. *Let us in. He needs us. We can help.*

But we are helping!

Yes, we are, but we're only helping to keep him safe until she comes. We've kept him safe and we've found her, and now we need to let her in so she can do her part. Our job is done; we can sleep now.

But what if she's false?

She isn't.

But how do we know?

We know. And they did, all the different parts of the Jack-castle, and the invisible door swung open beside him.

"Go," Jack croaked. His voice felt like sharp rocks and stone dust, and Greta hesitated, but only for a moment—"Go!" Jack shouted, and she was off into the passage faster than a hare running from the dogs.

Jack waited several heartbeats before he tried gingerly to pull his hands from the wall. He had expected them to be stuck, but they came away easily. His palms were raw, though, and covered in blood, and he watched as his two bloody hand-prints sank into the stone and disappeared. He didn't want to think about what that meant.

He couldn't think how to wrap his hands when both were so badly injured, so he just crossed his arms, pressed his palms against his sides, and—as he stumbled in just before the door swung shut—hoped for the best.

The first wave hit Jack when he was about halfway down the passage and could no longer hear Greta's footsteps ahead of him: groping his way gingerly in the dark, between one step and the next, he suddenly felt the full weight of his body; his stomach churned with hunger; he remembered designing this passage and walking through it after it was built, checking it for the last time. And he remembered when his hands were smaller and chubbier and he could just barely grip the wooden blocks that he placed one on another to build castles and houses and towers almost as tall as he was. He remembered the smell of Nancy's hair, and the way it felt to kiss her, and the mixture of love and fear and pride that filled her eyes and her voice when she looked at his plans for a castle—*this* castle—and said it was the most beautiful thing he'd ever designed.

All at once, all between one step and the next. He stumbled a few steps, but by the time the next wave hit him his feet were steady under him again, and it hit him just as hard but he recovered faster. Another few steps, another wave of memory, and he didn't stumble at all, even though his body and mind raced to keep up with all the parts of him that were suddenly no longer missing.

The passage surprised him by ending, dumping him out without warning into a bright, open chamber. He stopped short, dazzled by the sudden light, but even before his eyes and mind adjusted he heard voices, all familiar (though only one was human), and as the room and the stooped, shaggy figures before him came into focus, so did their words.

"I'm telling you it was an accident but I can *fix* it, you have to let me—"

"—don't know how you broke in, but—"

"—doesn't matter, you shouldn't be here—"

"—please! You don't understand—"

"Listen to her!" Jack croaked, surprised at how the sound grew in the space between him and them, amplified by the stones.

Some of them stopped speaking; all of them turned, and a whispering chorus of "What now?"s and "Is that . . . ?"s slithered back to him under the clacking and huffing and pouncing of the more anxious and blustery bears.

Another wave. Jack braced himself and wondered what the bears must think, what Greta must think, but then it had passed and he said again, "Listen to her."

One of the bears stepped toward Jack and rose up on its hind legs to study him; he thought it might be one of the ones that had turned him into a scarecrow, but it had been a long time and his brain was addled enough that he couldn't be sure. He met its gaze as best he could, though, and waited for it to speak.

"You broke in," it said at last.

"Yes."

"Why?"

Another wave, mostly memories of Nancy, but it only slowed him for a second and then he said, "Because she loves him. Because maybe she can do what you can't. Besides, I don't think this castle is quite the same anymore; I think it's just a stone building like any other, now, so you'd better let her do what she can before Bernadette finds you."

The bears started muttering and huffing among themselves, and Jack heard Bernadette's name and his own more than once, but behind them he could see Greta slipping away toward the hallway. Jack's heart jumped into his throat, and he let himself fall to the ground. More of the bears came toward him, curious or concerned, and that was good—it gave Greta a head start. More importantly, though, it put his palms against the floor, and this time he went straight to the castle's heart, opening doors along the way.

Greta almost missed the first door, Jack saw through the castle, and he cried out in spite of himself. He didn't think he said anything articulate, but it was difficult to be sure, and anyway it hardly mattered: the bears had already realized she'd gone. Greta stopped, though, and doubled back, and Jack did his best to close doors behind her. But of course, the bears knew exactly where they were going and she didn't.

They caught up to her at last just as she ran into the last room. Greta saw the young man on the bed and stopped short; she tried to say something, but the words caught in her throat. What little sound she made seemed to wake the young man on the bed, though, and as he stirred, the bears hung back as if to wait and see what he would do.

Greta stepped forward slowly, waiting after each step, but Jack thought the young man looked too weak to raise himself even enough to sit up, so Greta just kept step, step, stepping until she stood at the side of the bed and the young man could see her. "Oh, love . . . " she breathed, face tight with pain, as she reached one hand toward the waxy shell that covered half his chest now.

The young man clacked his jaw and swatted at her; Greta flinched, but after a second she moved her hand closer again. This time the young man bellowed—an angry, pulsing sound Jack wouldn't have thought a human throat could produce—and threw himself at her. He might be weak, but he still weighed more than Greta, and he surprised her enough to knock them both to the ground.

"Sweetheart," Greta cried as he struggled with her, "please—I'm sorry, but it's *killing* you, you have to— let me—" Greta tried to get at his chest, but the closer she got the harder he fought her, until finally she found an opening and pulled at the waxy growth.

The young man screamed in pain and shoved her so hard that she fell away from him. The bears started forward, but Greta shouted, "Look, it's coming off!" and they paused. "You have to let me finish," she added, though whether she was talking to the young man or the bears Jack could not guess; for a few seconds the only movement was the rise and fall of Greta's chest and of the young man's, both of them breathing heavily.

Then one bear stepped forward. "I will help you," it said. Greta nodded warily, but the bear circled around until it could hold down the young man's hands. It leaned down to lick his face; the young man clacked and blew at him and struggled to get free, until another bear came and held down his feet, moaning something that might have been "Auberon."

Greta crawled back over to the young man, who glared hate at her, but she just reached around and pulled at the wax she'd already loosened from his skin. He screamed, and Greta winced, but the bears held him still and Greta kept on pulling. The wax clung to his skin and it took a few long minutes to remove it. "Hush, you big baby," Greta whispered fiercely at one point; the bears looked up—startled, perhaps, though Jack didn't know enough about bear society to tell if they'd been surprised by human eccentricity or bear-like behavior—but Greta didn't seem to notice. All her attention was focused on pulling at the wax and making sure it didn't just reattach somewhere else.

At long last Greta gave one final tug and fell backwards onto the floor with a thud. The young man's scream cut off abruptly and he sagged between the two bears. The one who held his hands bent down and crooned something to him; the other let go, and the young man rolled over, and then suddenly he too was a bear.

Greta blinked, but she didn't seem surprised. She did, however, sit very, very still, eyes fixed on the bear she had just saved.

The bear spoke first. "What did you do to me?" he grunted.

"I can't—" Greta gestured to her throat; one of the other bears, the first one to help her, leaned over and breathed on her neck. "Oh . . . " she said, eyes wide. "Auberon, I—" She frowned and sat up straighter.

"Master Builder?" Someone was speaking to Jack—to his body—and he lost his hold on the castle. "Master Builder?" the bear repeated, but it was difficult to hear over the sudden pounding in his ears, and his vision was strangely blurry, and he thought he heard someone ask if he was all right before he fell into endless nothing.

Jack woke once, long enough to swallow some broth, and then fell back into nothingness; when he woke again he found himself in bed and the early winter sun stretching, pale and thin, from a narrow window to the edge of his blankets. He tried slowly to sit up and found that, aside from being a bit stiff, he could move perfectly well; even his bandaged hands didn't complain when he put weight on them.

A sudden movement by the wall caught his attention; Greta rose to her feet and put a book down on her chair. "You're awake," she said, smiling. "I was starting to worry."

"Oh, you know," he said, "it's been, what, the better part of a year since I've slept? Figure I was due for a good nap."

Greta laughed, and it sounded like music to him, but even as he smiled he felt a hollow space in the middle of his ribcage.

"Were you two able to . . . sort things out?" he asked as he got slowly out of bed and found himself shivering at the sudden chill of the air.

"We're working on it." Greta pointed to a massive wooden wardrobe in one corner of the room. "There should be plenty of warm clothes in there."

"Inter-species relationships frowned upon in bear society?" Jack asked as he looked through the wardrobe's contents and recognized his own clothes.

"That, plus a lot of magic and politics nobody had explained to me before. I knew Auberon could become human, but nobody told me I needed to watch out for rival magicians masquerading as servants offering candles. Or that promising not to speak of something could be magically binding."

Jack's hand went automatically to his favorite shirt, favorite trousers. Arms full, he turned around again—and saw Greta frowning slightly in his direction. "What is it?" he asked.

Greta hesitated a moment, but then she asked, "Your wife was the story-teller, wasn't she? The one who came for the spring celebration?"

"Yes," Jack said quietly.

"And that's how you know Auberon and the other bears. It was one of her stories you told me in the woods, that's why it sounded so familiar."

Jack nodded. "She never could bring herself to believe you'd hurt him on purpose."

Greta blinked back a sudden brightness in her eyes and said, "You're welcome to stay here, of course, or to come with us, but Auberon needs to get back, deal with—what was her name? Bernadette." Jack put the clothes down on the bed. "We can stay another day or two, maybe, but he's already been gone so long . . . "

Jack nodded. "I need some time to think."

"Of course."

"Maybe a few hours. You'll know by tonight, though, and you can tell Auberon he doesn't need to wait any longer than tomorrow morning, at least not on my account."

"You're sure?"

He nodded, running fingertips lightly across familiar fabrics.

"Thank you. I'll go tell him and give you some privacy. You have the run of the castle, of course, and the grounds outside."

Jack nodded again. "Thank you." He waited until the door clicked shut behind her and then started to change, dumping his traveling clothes piece by piece in a pile on the cold stone floor.

Jack sat on a tree stump on the hill where he last remembered seeing Nancy. He'd thought she might be here, that he'd find her gravestone at least, but he'd looked everywhere it might be. He'd even tried to talk to the castle again, but it was . . . sleeping. So he sat, staring at the sky and seeing her eyes, wondering how the hole in his heart wasn't killing him.

"She's not here," said a bear's voice, and Jack turned, startled, to see Auberon and Greta. It was only the second time he'd ever seen the bear prince in person, and Jack realized with surprise that Auberon was actually smaller than many of the other bears. There was something noble about him, though, and Jack bowed his head; Auberon lowered his own briefly in response, and continued, "Your wife didn't die here, Jack. She left."

"I don't remember," Jack whispered, throat and chest suddenly tight.

Auberon bobbed his head. "Neither do I. But my advisors do; they say she grew sickly and left, to regain her health, but that you were so busy you seemed barely to notice."

Jack's whole body felt suddenly weightless, more like a bird than a man or even a scarecrow, though he hung his head and ran a hand absently through his hair. *Of course,* he thought. *Castles don't have wives. But if she's still alive, somewhere . . .*

Auberon must have let him sit like that for a few seconds, but then he grunted "Master Builder" in such a tone that Jack had to straighten and look at him. "You have saved my life twice over, now, and I cannot offer you sufficient thanks for that."

Jack took a shaky breath and stood. "I was glad to help. Am glad to help. And I hope I can visit both of you, someday, but right now I think I need to go pack."

"You're leaving," Greta said, smiling slightly, and it wasn't a question.

Jack nodded. "I need to find Nancy. I owe her an apology, and if she'll tell me, I'd like to know how that story ends. I'm sure the knight doesn't make it home, but I think the little girl might, and if she does . . . well, I'd like to hear it from her."

Greta nodded; Auberon sat up on his hind legs and met Jack's gaze for several seconds. "What do you want done with the castle?" he asked.

"Nothing," Jack answered, forcing himself to focus on this, his last responsibility. "It's its own person, if that makes any sense, and it's calmer now. Though it would probably be nice for it if someone lived in it, and nicer still if the someone were you. It was built to take care of you, after all, and I always feel like buildings get as sad as anyone else about being abandoned or losing their purposes."

Auberon bobbed his head once more, and Greta reached out and shook his hand, and then Jack smiled quickly at both of them before walking past, down the hill, back toward the castle to get ready for his journey. He was ready—more than ready—to go home.

IN THE HOUSE OF ARYAMAN, A LONELY SIGNAL BURNS

ELIZABETH BEAR

Police Sub-Inspector Ferron crouched over the object she assumed was the decedent, her hands sheathed in areactin, her elbows resting on uniformed knees. The body (presumed) lay in the middle of a jewel-toned rug like a flabby pink Klein bottle, its once-moist surfaces crusting in air. The rug was still fresh beneath it, fronds only a little dented by the weight and no sign of the browning that could indicate an improperly pheromone-treated object had been in contact with them for over twenty-four hours. Meandering brownish trails led out around the bodylike object; a good deal of the blood had already been assimilated by the rug, but enough remained that Ferron could pick out the outline of delicate paw-pads and the brush-marks of long hair.

Ferron was going to be late visiting her mother after work tonight.

She looked up at Senior Constable Indrapramit and said tiredly, "So these are the mortal remains of Dexter Coffin?"

Indrapramit put his chin on his thumbs, fingers interlaced thoughtfully before lips that had dried and cracked in the summer heat. "We won't know for sure until the DNA comes back." One knee-tall spit-shined boot wrapped in a sterile bootie prodded forward, failing to come within fifteen centimeters of the corpse. Was he jumpy? Or just being careful about contamination?

He said, "What do you make of that, boss?"

"Well." Ferron stood, straightening a kinked spine. "If that is Dexter Coffin, he picked an apt handle, didn't he?"

Coffin's luxurious private one-room flat had been sealed when patrol officers arrived, summoned on a welfare check after he did not respond to the flat's minder. When police had broken down the door—the emergency overrides had been locked out—they had found this. This pink tube. This enormous sausage. This meaty object like a child's toy "eel," a long squashed torus full of fluid.

If you had a hand big enough to pick it up, Ferron imagined it would squirt right out of your grasp again.

Ferron was confident it represented sufficient mass for a full-grown adult. But how, exactly, did you manage to just . . . invert someone?

The Sub-Inspector stepped back from the corpse to turn a slow, considering circle.

The flat was set for entertaining. The bed, the appliances were folded away. The western-style table was elevated and extended for dining, a shelf disassembled for chairs. There was a workspace in one corner, not folded away—Ferron presumed—because of the sheer inconvenience of putting away that much mysterious, technical-looking equipment. Depth projections in spare, modernist frames adorned the wall behind: enhanced-color images of a gorgeous cacophony of stars. Something from one of the orbital telescopes, probably, because there were too many thousands of them populating the sky for Ferron to recognize the *navagraha*—the signs of the Hindu Zodiac—despite her education.

In the opposite corner of the apt, where you would see it whenever you raised your eyes from the workstation, stood a brass Ganesha. The small offering tray before him held packets of kumkum and turmeric, fragrant blossoms, an antique American dime, a crumbling, unburned stick of agarbathi thrust into a banana. A silk shawl, as indigo as the midnight heavens, lay draped across the god's brass thighs.

"Cute," said Indrapramit dryly, following her gaze. "The Yank is going native."

At the dinner table, two western-style place settings anticipated what Ferron guessed would have been a romantic evening. If one of the principals had not gotten himself turned inside out.

"Where's the cat?" Indrapramit said, gesturing to the fading paw-print trails. He seemed calm, Ferron decided.

And she needed to stop hovering over him like she expected the cracks to show any second. Because she was only going to make him worse by worrying. He'd been back on the job for a month and a half now: it was time for her to relax. To trust the seven years they had been partners and friends, and to trust him to know what he needed as he made his transition back to active duty—and how to ask for it.

Except that would mean laying aside her displacement behavior, and dealing with her own problems.

"I was wondering the same thing," Ferron admitted. "Hiding from the farang, I imagine. Here, puss puss. Here puss—"

She crossed to the cabinets and rummaged inside. There was a bowl of water, almost dry, and an empty food bowl in a corner by the sink. The food would be close by.

It took her less than thirty seconds to locate a tin decorated with fish skeletons and paw prints. Inside, gray-brown pellets smelled oily. She set the bowl on the counter and rattled a handful of kibble into it.

"Miaow?" something said from a dark corner beneath the lounge that probably converted into Coffin's bed.

"Puss puss puss?" She picked up the water bowl, washed it out, filled it up again from the potable tap. Something lofted from the floor to the countertop and headbutted her arm, purring madly. It was a last-year's-generation parrot-cat, a hyacinth-blue puffball on sun-yellow paws rimmed round the edges with brownish stains. It had a matching tuxedo ruff and goatee and piercing golden eyes that caught and concentrated the filtered sunlight.

"Now, are you supposed to be on the counter?"

"Miaow," the cat said, cocking its head inquisitively. It didn't budge.

Indrapramit was at Ferron's elbow. "Doesn't it talk?"

"Hey, Puss," Ferron said. "What's your name?"

It sat down, balanced neatly on the rail between sink and counter-edge, and flipped its blue fluffy tail over its feet. Its purr vibrated its whiskers and the long hairs of its ruff. Ferron offered it a bit of kibble, and it accepted ceremoniously.

"Must be new," Indrapramit said. "Though you'd expect an adult to have learned to talk in the cattery."

"Not new." Ferron offered a fingertip to the engineered animal. It squeezed its eyes at her and deliberately wiped first one side of its muzzle against her areactin glove, and then the other. "Did you see the cat hair on the lounge?"

Indrapramit paused, considering. "Wiped."

"Our only witness. And she has amnesia." She turned to Indrapramit. "We need to find out who Coffin was expecting. Pull transit records. And I want a five-hour phone track log of every individual who came within fifty meters of this flat between twenty hundred yesterday and when Patrol broke down the doors. Let's get some technical people in to figure out what that pile of gear in the corner is. And who called in the welfare check?"

"Not a lot of help there, boss." Indrapramit's gold-tinted irises flick-scrolled over data—the Constable was picking up a feed skinned over immediate perceptions. Ferron wanted to issue a mild reprimand for inattention to the scene, but it seemed churlish when Indrapramit was following orders. "When he didn't come online this morning for work, his supervisor became concerned. The supervisor was unable to raise him by voice or text. He contacted the flat's minder, and when it reported no response to repeated queries, he called for help."

Ferron contemplated the shattered edges of the smashed-in door before returning her attention to the corpse. "I know the door was locked out on emergency mode. Patrol's override didn't work?"

Indrapramit had one of the more deadpan expressions among the deadpan-trained and certified officers of the Bengaluru City Police. "Evidently."

"Well, while you're online, have them bring in a carrier for the witness." She indicated the hyacinth parrot-cat. "I'll take custody of her."

"How do you know it's a her?"

"She has a feminine face. Lotus eyes like Draupadi."

He looked at her.

She grinned. "I'm guessing."

Ferron had turned off all her skins and feeds while examining the crime scene, but the police link was permanent. An icon blinked discreetly in one corner of her interface, its yellow glow unappealing beside the salmon and coral of Coffin's taut-stretched innards. Accepting the contact was just a matter of an eye-flick. There was a decoding shimmer and one side of the interface spawned an image of Coffin in life.

Coffin had not been a visually vivid individual. Unaffected, Ferron thought, unless dressing one's self in sensible medium-pale brown skin and dark hair with classically Brahmin features counted as an affectation. That handle—*Dexter Coffin*, and wouldn't *Sinister Coffin* be a more logical choice?—seemed to indicate a more flamboyant personality. Ferron made a note of that: out of such small inconsistencies did a homicide case grow.

"So how does one get from this"—Ferron gestured to the image, which should be floating in Indrapramit's interface as well—"to that?"—the corpse on the rug. "In a locked room, no less?"

Indrapramit shrugged. He seemed comfortable enough in the presence of the body, and Ferron wished she could stop examining him for signs of stress. Maybe his rightminding was working. It wasn't too much to hope for, and good treatments for post-traumatic stress had been in development since the Naughties.

But Indrapramit was a relocant: all his family was in a village somewhere up near Mumbai. He had no people here, and so Ferron felt it was her responsibility as his partner to look out for him. At least, that was what she told herself.

He said, "He swallowed a black hole?"

"I like living in the future." Ferron picked at the edge of an areactin glove. "So many interesting ways to die."

Ferron and Indrapramit left the aptblock through the crowds of Coffin's neighbors. It was a block of unrelateds. Apparently Coffin had no family in Bengaluru, but it nevertheless seemed as if every (living) resident had heard the news and come down. The common areas were clogged with grans and youngers, sibs and parents and cousins—all wailing grief, trickling tears, leaning on each other, being interviewed by newsies and blogbots. Ferron took one look at the press in the living area and on the street beyond and juggled the cat carrier into her left hand. She slapped a stripped-off palm against the courtyard door. It swung open—you couldn't lock somebody in—and Ferron and Indrapramit stepped out into the shade of the household sunfarm.

The trees were old. This block had been here a long time; long enough that the sunfollowing black vanes of the lower leaves were as long as Ferron's arm. Someone in the block maintained them carefully, too—they were polished clean with soft cloth, no clogging particles allowed to remain. Condensation trickled down the clear tubules in their trunks to pool in underground catchpots.

Ferron leaned back against a trunk, basking in the cool, and yawned.

"You okay, boss?"

"Tired," Ferron said. "If we hadn't caught the homicide—if it is a homicide—I'd be on a crash cycle now. I had to re-up, and there'll be hell to pay once it wears off."

"Boss—"

"It's only my second forty-eight hours," Ferron said, dismissing Indrapramit's concern with a ripple of her fingers. Gold rings glinted, but not on her wedding finger. Her short nails were manicured in an attempt to look professional, a reminder not to bite. "I'd go hypomanic for weeks at a time at University. Helps you cram, you know."

Indrapramit nodded. He didn't look happy.

The Sub-Inspector shook the residue of the areactin from her hands before rubbing tired eyes with numb fingers. Feeds jittered until the movement resolved. Mail was piling up—press requests, paperwork. There was no time to deal with it now.

"Anyway," Ferron said. "I've already reupped, so you're stuck with me for another forty at least. Where do you think we start?"

"Interview lists," Indrapramit said promptly. Climbing figs hung with ripe fruit twined the sunfarm; gently, the Senior Constable reached up and plucked one. When it popped between his teeth, its intense gritty sweetness echoed through the interface. It was a good fig.

Ferron reached up and stole one too.

"Miaow?" said the cat.

"Hush." Ferron slicked tendrils of hair bent on escaping her conservative bun off her sweating temples. "I don't know how you can wear those boots."

"State of the art materials," he said. Chewing a second fig, he jerked his chin at her practical sandals. "Chappals when you might have to run through broken glass or kick down a door?"

She let it slide into silence. "Junior grade can handle the family for now. It's bulk interviews. I'll take Chairman Miaow here to the tech and get her scanned. Wait, Coffin was Employed. Doing what, and by whom?"

"Physicist," Indrapramit said, linking a list of coworker and project names, a brief description of the biotech firm Coffin had worked for, like half of Employed Bengaluru ever since the medical tourism days. It was probably a better job than homicide cop. "Distributed. Most of his work group aren't even in this time zone."

"What does BioShell need with physicists?"

Silently, Indrapramit pointed up at the vanes of the suntrees, clinking faintly in their infinitesimal movements as they tracked the sun. "Quantum bioengineer," he explained, after a suitable pause.

"Right," Ferron said. "Well, Forensic will want us out from underfoot while they process the scene. I guess we can start drawing up interview lists."

"Interview lists and lunch?" Indrapramit asked hopefully.

Ferron refrained from pointing out that they had just come out of an apt with an inside-out stiff in it. "Masala dosa?"

Indrapramit grinned. "I saw an SLV down the street."

"I'll call our tech," Ferron said. "Let's see if we can sneak out the service entrance and dodge the press."

Ferron and Indrapramit (and the cat) made their way to the back gate. Indrapramit checked the security cameras on the alley behind the block: his feed said it was deserted except for a waste management vehicle. But as Ferron presented her warrant card—encoded in cloud, accessible through the Omni she wore on her left hip to balance the stun pistol—the energy-efficient safety lights ringing the doorway faded from cool white to a smoldering yellow, and then cut out entirely.

"Bugger," Ferron said. "Power cut."

"How, in a block with a sunfarm?"

"Loose connection?" she asked, rattling the door against the bolt just in case it had flipped back before the juice died. The cat protested. Gently, Ferron set the carrier down, out of the way. Then she kicked the door in frustration and jerked her foot back, cursing. Chappals, indeed.

Indrapramit regarded her mildly. "You shouldn't have re-upped."

She arched an eyebrow at him and put her foot down on the floor gingerly. The toes protested. "You suggesting I should modulate my stress response, Constable?"

"As long as you're adjusting your biochemistry . . . "

She sighed. "It's not work," she said. "It's my mother. She's gone Atavistic, and—"

"Ah," Indrapramit said. "Spending your inheritance on virtual life?"

Ferron turned her face away. WORSE, she texted. SHE'S NOT GOING TO BE ABLE TO PAY HER ARCHIVING FEES.

—ISN'T SHE ON ASSISTANCE? SHOULDN'T THE DOLE COVER THAT?

—YEAH, BUT SHE LIVES IN A.R. SHE'S ALWAYS BEEN A GAMER, BUT SINCE FATHER DIED. . . . IT'S AN ADDICTION. SHE ARCHIVES EVERYTHING. AND HAS SINCE I WAS A CHILD. WE'RE TALKING TERABYTES. PETABYTES. YOTTABYTES. I DON'T KNOW. AND SHE'S AFTER ME TO "BORROW" THE MONEY.

"Ooof," he said. "That's a tough one." Briefly, his hand brushed her arm: sympathy and human warmth.

She leaned into it before she pulled away. She didn't tell him that she'd been paying those bills for the past eighteen months, and it was getting to the point where she couldn't support her mother's habit any more. She knew what she had to do. She just didn't know how to make herself do it.

Her mother was her mother. She'd built everything about Ferron, from the DNA up. The programming to honor and obey ran deep. Duty. Felicity. Whatever you wanted to call it.

In frustration, unable to find the words for what she needed to explain properly, she said, "I need to get one of those black market DNA patches and reprogram my overengineered genes away from filial devotion."

He laughed, as she had meant. "You can do that legally in Russia."

"Gee," she said. "You're a help. Hey, what if we—" Before she could finish her suggestion that they slip the lock, the lights glimmered on again and the door, finally registering her override, clicked.

"There," Indrapramit said. "Could have been worse."

"Miaow," said the cat.

"Don't worry, Chairman," Ferron answered. "I wasn't going to forget *you*."

The street hummed: autorickshaws, glidecycles, bikes, pedestrials, and swarms of foot traffic. The babble of languages: Kannada, Hindi, English, Chinese, Japanese. Coffin's aptblock was in one of the older parts of the New City. It was an American ghetto: most of the residents had come here for work, and spoke English as a primary—sometimes an only—language. In the absence of family to stay with, they had banded together. Coffin's address had once been trendy and now, fifty years after its conversion, had fallen on—not hard times, exactly, but a period of more moderate means. The street still remembered better days. It was bulwarked on both sides by the shaggy green cubes of aptblocks, black suntrees growing through their centers, but what lined each avenue were the feathery cassia trees, their branches dripping pink, golden, and terra-cotta blossoms.

Cassia, Ferron thought. A Greek word of uncertain antecedents, possibly related to the English word Cassia, meaning Chinese or mainland cinnamon.

But these trees were not spices; indeed, the black pods of the golden cassia were a potent medicine in Ayurvedic traditions, and those of the rose cassia had been used since ancient times as a purgative for horses.

Ferron wiped sweat from her forehead again, and—speaking of horses— reined in the overly helpful commentary of her classical education.

The wall- and roof-gardens of the aptblocks demonstrated a great deal about who lived there. The Coffin kinblock was well-tended, green and lush, dripping with brinjal and tomatoes. A couple of youngers—probably still in schooling, even if they weren't Employment track—clambered up and down ladders weeding and feeding and harvesting, and cleaning the windows shaded here and there by the long green trail of sweet potato vines. But the next kinship block down was sere enough to draw a fine, the suntrees in its court sagging and miserable-looking. Ferron could make out the narrow tubes of drip irrigators behind crisping foliage on the near wall.

Ferron must have snorted, because Indrapramit said, "What are they doing with their greywater, then?"

"Maybe it's abandoned?" Unlikely. Housing in the New City wasn't exactly so plentiful that an empty block would remain empty for long.

"Maybe they can't afford the plumber."

That made Ferron snort again, and start walking. But she snapped an image of the dying aptblock nonetheless, and emailed it to Environmental Services. They'd handle the ticket, if they decided the case warranted one.

The Sri Lakshmi Venkateshwara—SLV—was about a hundred meters on, an open-air food stand shaded by a grove of engineered neem trees, their panel leaves angling to follow the sun. Hunger hadn't managed to penetrate Ferron's re-upped hypomania yet, but it would be a good idea to eat anyway: the brain might not be in any shape to notice that the body needed maintenance, but failing to provide that maintenance just added extra interest to the bill when it eventually came due.

Ferron ordered an enormous, potato-and-pea stuffed crepe against Indrapramit's packet of samosas, plus green coconut water. Disdaining the SLV's stand-up tables, they ventured a little farther along the avenue until they found a bench to eat on. News and ads flickered across the screen on its back. Ferron set the cat carrier on the seat between them.

Indrapramit dropped a somebody-else's-problem skin around them for privacy and unwrapped his first samosa. Flocks of green and yellow parrots wheeled in the trees nearby; the boldest dozen fluttered down to hop and scuffle where the crumbs might fall. You couldn't skin yourself out of the perceptions of the unwired world.

Indrapramit raised his voice to be heard over their arguments. "You shouldn't have re-upped."

The dosa was good—as crisp as she wanted, served with a smear of red curry. Ferron ate most of it, meanwhile grab-and-pasting names off Coffin's known associates lists onto an interfaced interview plan, before answering.

"Most homicides are closed—if they get closed—in the first forty-eight hours. It's worth a little hypomania binge to find Coffin's killer."

"There's more than one murder every two days in this city, boss."

"Sure." She had a temper, but this wasn't the time to exercise it. She knew, given her family history, Indrapramit worried secretly that she'd succumb to addiction and abuse of the rightminding chemicals. The remaining bites of the dosa got sent to meet their brethren, peas popping between her teeth. The wrapper went into the recycler beside the bench. "But we don't catch every case that flies through."

Indrapramit tossed wadded-up paper at Ferron's head. Ferron batted it into that recycler too. "No, yaar. Just all of them this week."

The targeted ads bleeding off the bench-back behind Ferron were scientifically designed to attract her attention, which only made them more annoying. Some too-attractive citizen squalled about rightminding programs for geriatrics ("Bring your parents into the modern age!"), and the news—in direct, loud counterpoint—was talking about the latest orbital telescope discoveries: apparently a star some twenty thousand light years away, in the Andromeda galaxy, had suddenly begun exhibiting a flickering pattern that some astronomers considered a possible precursor to a nova event.

The part of her brain that automatically built such parallels said: *Andromeda. Contained within the span of Uttara Bhadrapada. The twenty-sixth nakshatra in Hindu astronomy, although she was not a sign of the Zodiac to the Greeks.* Pegasus was also in Uttara Bhadrapada. Ferron devoted a few more cycles to wondering if there was any relationship other than coincidental between the legendary serpent Ahir Budhnya, the deity of Uttara Bhadrapada, and the sea monster Cetus, set to eat—*devour,* the Greeks were so melodramatic—the chained Andromeda.

The whole thing fell under the influence of the god Aryaman, whose path was the Milky Way—the Heavenly Ganges.

You're overqualified, madam. Oh, she could have been the professor, the academic her mother had dreamed of making her, in all those long hours spent in virtual reproductions of myths the world around. She could have been. But if she'd really wanted to make her mother happy, she would have pursued Egyptology, too.

But she wasn't, and it was time she got her mind back on the job she *did* have.

Ferron flicked on the feeds she'd shut off to attend the crime scene. She didn't like to skin on the job: a homicide cop's work depended heavily on unfiltered perceptions, and if you trimmed everything and everyone irritating or disagreeable out of reality, the odds were pretty good that you'd miss the truth behind a crime. But sometimes you had to make an exception.

She linked up, turned up her spam filters and ad blockers, and sorted more Known Associates files. Speaking of her mother, that required ignoring all those lion-headed message-waiting icons blinking in a corner of her feed—and the pileup of news and personal messages in her assimilator.

Lions. Bengaluru's state capitol was topped with a statue of a four-headed lion, guarding each of the cardinal directions. The ancient symbol of India was part of why Ferron's mother chose that symbolism. But only part.

She set the messages to *hide*, squirming with guilt as she did, and concentrated on the work-related mail.

When she looked up, Indrapramit appeared to have finished both his sorting and his samosas. "All right, what have you got?"

"Just this." She dumped the interview files to his headspace.

The Senior Constable blinked upon receipt. "Ugh. That's even more than I thought."

First on Ferron's interview list were the dead man's coworkers, based on the simple logic that if anybody knew how to turn somebody inside out, it was likely to be another physicist. Indrapramit went back to the aptblock to continue interviewing more-or-less hysterical neighbors in a quest for the name of any potential lover or assignation from the night before.

It was the task least likely to be any fun. But then, Ferron was the senior officer. Rank hath its privileges. Someday, Indrapramit would be making junior colleagues follow up horrible gutwork.

The bus, it turned out, ran right from the corner where Coffin's kinblock's street intercepted the main road. Proximity made her choose it over the mag-lev Metro, but she soon regretted her decision, because it then wound in a drunken pattern through what seemed like the majority of Bengaluru.

She was lucky enough to find a seat—it wasn't a crowded hour. She registered her position with Dispatch and settled down to wait and talk to the hyacinth cat, since it was more than sunny enough that no-one needed to pedal. She waited it out for the transfer point anyway: *that* bus ran straight to the U District, where BioShell had its offices.

Predictable. Handy for head-hunting, and an easy walk for any BioShell employee who might also teach classes. As it seemed, by the number of Professor So-and-sos on Ferron's list, that many of them did.

Her tech, a short wide-bellied man who went by the handle Ravindra, caught up with her while she was still leaned against the second bus's warm, tinted window. He hopped up the steps two at a time, belying his bulk, and shooed a citizen out of the seat beside Ferron with his investigator's card.

Unlike peace officers, who had long since been spun out as distributed employees, techs performed their functions amid the equipment and resources of a centralized lab. But today, Ravindra had come equipped for fieldwork. He stood, steadying himself on the grab bar, and spread his kit out on the now-unoccupied aisle seat while Ferron coaxed the cat from her carrier under the seat.

"Good puss," Ravindra said, riffling soft fur until he found the contact point behind the animal's ears. His probe made a soft, satisfied beep as he connected it. The cat relaxed bonelessly, purring. "You want a complete download?"

"Whatever you can get," Ferron said. "It looks like she's been wiped. She won't talk, anyway."

"Could be trauma, boss," Ravindra said dubiously. "Oh, DNA results are back. That's your inside-out vic, all right. The autopsy was just getting started when I left, and Doc said to tell you that to a first approximation, it looked like all the bits were there, albeit not necessarily in the proper sequence."

"Well, that's a relief." The bus lurched. "At least it's the correct dead guy."

"Miaow," said the cat.

"What is your name, puss?" Ravindra asked.

"Chairman Miaow," the cat said, in a sweet doll's voice.

"Oh, no," Ferron said. "That's just what I've been calling her."

"Huh." Ravindra frowned at the readouts that must be scrolling across his feed. "Did you feed her, boss?"

"Yeah," Ferron said. "To get her out from under the couch."

He nodded, and started rolling up his kit. As he disconnected the probe, he said, "I downloaded everything there was. It's not much. And I'll take a tissue sample for further investigation, but I don't think this cat was wiped."

"But there's nothing—"

"I know," he said. "Not wiped. This one's factory-new. And it's bonded to you. Congratulations, Sub-Inspector. I think you have a cat."

"I can't—" she said, and paused. "I already have a fox. My mother's fox, rather. I'm taking care of it for her."

"*Mine,*" the cat said distinctly, rubbing her blue-and-yellow muzzle along Ferron's uniform sleeve, leaving behind a scraping of azure lint.

"I imagine they can learn to cohabitate." He shouldered his kit. "Anyway, it's unlikely Chairman Miaow here will be any use as a witness, but I'll pick over the data anyway and get back to you. It's not even a gig."

"Damn," she said. "I was hoping she'd seen the killer. So even if she's brand-new . . . why hadn't she bonded to Coffin?"

"He hadn't fed her," Ravindra said. "And he hadn't given her a name. She's a sweetie, though." He scratched behind her ears. A funny expression crossed his face. "You know, I've been wondering for ages—how did you wind up choosing to be called *Ferron*?"

"My mother used to say I was stubborn as iron." Ferron managed to keep what she knew would be a pathetically adolescent shrug off her shoulders. "She was fascinated by Egypt, but I studied Classics-Latin, Greek, Sanskrit. Some Chinese stuff. And I liked the name. *Ferrum,* iron. She won't use it. She still uses my cradlename." *Even when I'm paying her bills.*

The lion-face still blinked there, muted but unanswered. In a fit of irritation, Ferron banished it. It wasn't like she would forget to call.

Once she had time, she promised the ghost of her mother.

Ravindra, she realized, was staring at her quizzically. "How did a classicist wind up a murder cop?"

Ferron snorted. "You ever try to find Employment as a classicist?"

Ravindra got off at the next stop. Ferron watched him walk away, whistling for an autorickshaw to take him back to the lab. She scratched Chairman Miaow under the chin and sighed.

In another few minutes, she reached the university district and disembarked, still burdened with cat and carrier. It was a pleasant walk from the stop, despite the heat of the end of the dry season. It was late June, and Ferron wondered what it had been like before the Shift, when the monsoons would have started already, breaking the back of the high temperature.

The walk from the bus took under fifteen minutes, the cat a dozy puddle. A patch of sweat spread against Ferron's summerweight trousers where the carrier bumped softly against her hip. She knew she retraced Coffin's route on those rare days when he might choose to report to the office.

Nearing the Indian Institute of Science, Ferron became aware that clothing styles were shifting—self-consciously Green Earther living fabric and ironic, ill-fitting student antiques predominated. Between the buildings and the statuary of culture heroes—R.K. Narayan, Ratan Tata, stark-white with serene or stern expressions—the streets still swarmed, and would until long after nightfall. A prof-caste wearing a live-cloth salwar kameez strutted past; Ferron was all too aware that the outfit would cost a week's salary for even a fairly high-ranking cop.

The majority of these people were Employed. They wore salwar kameez or suits and they had that purpose in their step—unlike most citizens, who weren't in too much of a hurry to get anywhere, especially in the heat of day. It was easier to move in the University quarter, because traffic flowed with intent. Ferron, accustomed to stepping around window-browsing Supplemented and people out for their mandated exercise, felt stress dropping away as the greenery, trees, and gracious old nineteenth and twentieth century buildings of the campus rose up on every side.

As she walked under the chin of Mohandas Gandhi, Ferron felt the familiar irritation that female police pioneer Kiran Bedi, one of her own personal idols, was not represented among the statuary. There was hijra activist Shabnam Mausi behind a row of well-tended planters, though, which was somewhat satisfying.

Some people found it unsettling to be surrounded by so much brick, poured concrete, and mined stone—the legacy of cooler, more energy-rich times. Ferron knew that the bulk of the university's buildings were more efficient green structures, but those tended to blend into their surroundings. The overwhelming impression was still that of a return to a simpler time: 1870, perhaps, or 1955. Ferron wouldn't have wanted to see the whole city gone this way, but it was good that some of the history had been preserved.

Having bisected campus, Ferron emerged along a prestigious street of much more modern buildings. No vehicles larger than bicycles were allowed here, and the roadbed swarmed with those, people on foot, and pedestrials. Ferron passed a rack of share-bikes and a newly constructed green building, still uninhabited, the leaves of its suntrees narrow, immature, and furled. They'd soon be spread wide, and the structure fully tenanted.

The BioShell office itself was a showpiece on the ground floor of a business block, with a live receptionist visible behind foggy photosynthetic glass walls. *I'd hate a job where you can't pick your nose in case the pedestrians see it.* Of course, Ferron hadn't chosen to be as decorative as the receptionist. A certain stern plainness helped get her job done.

"Hello," Ferron said, as the receptionist smoothed brown hair over a shoulder. "I'm Police Sub-Inspector Ferron. I'm here to see Dr. Rao."

"A moment, madam," the receptionist said, gesturing graciously to a chair.

Ferron set heels together in parade rest and—impassive—waited. It was only a few moments before a shimmer of green flickered across the receptionist's iris.

"First door on the right, madam, and then up the stairs. Do you require a guide?"

"Thank you," Ferron said, glad she hadn't asked about the cat. "I think I can find it."

There was an elevator for the disabled, but the stairs were not much further on. Ferron lugged Chairman Miaow through the fire door at the top and paused a moment to catch her breath. A steady hum came from the nearest room, to which the door stood ajar.

Ferron picked her way across a lush biorug sprinkled with violet and yellow flowers and tapped lightly. A voice rose over the hum. "Namaskar!"

Dr. Rao was a slender, tall man whose eyes were framed in heavy creases. He walked forward at a moderate speed on a treadmill, an old-fashioned keyboard and monitor mounted on a swivel arm before him. As Ferron entered, he pushed the arm aside, but kept walking. An amber light flickered green as the monitor went dark: he was charging batteries now.

"Namaskar," Ferron replied. She tried not to stare too obviously at the walking desk.

She must have failed.

"Part of my rightminding, madam," Rao said with an apologetic shrug. "I've fibromyalgia, and mild exercise helps. You must be the Sub-Inspector. How do you take your mandated exercise? You carry yourself with such confidence."

"I am a practitioner of kalari payat," Ferron said, naming a South Indian martial art. "It's useful in my work."

"Well," he said. "I hope you'll see no need to demonstrate any upon me. Is that a cat?"

"Sorry, saab," Ferron said. "It's work-related. She can wait in the hall if you mind—"

"No, not at all. Actually, I love cats. She can come out, if she's not too scared."

"Oouuuuut!" said Chairman Miaow.

"I guess that settles that." Ferron unzipped the carrier, and the hyacinth parrot-cat sauntered out and leaped up to the treadmill's handrail.

"Niranjana?" Dr. Rao said, in surprise. "Excuse me, madam, but what are you doing with Dr. Coffin's cat?"

"You know this cat?"

"Of course I do." He stopped walking, and scratched the cat under her chin. She stretched her head out like a lazy snake, balanced lightly on four daffodil paws. "She comes here about twice a month."

"New!" the cat disagreed. "Who you?"

"Niranjana, it's Rao. You know me."

"Rrraaao?" she said, cocking her head curiously. Adamantly, she said, "New! My name Chairman Miaow!"

Dr. Rao's forehead wrinkled. To Ferron, over the cat's head, he said, "Is Dexter with you? Is he all right?"

"I'm afraid that's why I'm here," Ferron said. "It is my regretful duty to inform you that Dexter Coffin appears to have been murdered in his home sometime over the night. Saab, law requires that I inform you that this conversation is being recorded. Anything you say may be entered in evidence. You have the right to skin your responses or withhold information, but if you choose to do so, under certain circumstances a court order may be obtained to download and decode associated cloud memories. Do you understand this caution?"

"Oh dear," Dr. Rao said. "When I called the police, I didn't expect—"

"I know," Ferron said. "But do you understand the caution, saab?"

"I do," he said. A yellow peripheral node in Ferron's visual field went green. She said, "Do you confirm this is his cat?"

"I'd know her anywhere," Dr. Rao said. "The markings are very distinctive. Dexter brought her in quite often. She's been wiped? How awful."

"We're investigating," Ferron said, relieved to be back in control of the conversation. "I'm afraid I'll need details of what Coffin was working on, his contacts, any romantic entanglements, any professional rivalries or enemies—"

"Of course," Dr. Rao said. He pulled his interface back around and began typing. "I'll generate a list. As for what he was working on—I'm afraid there are a lot of trade secrets involved, but we're a biomedical engineering firm, as I'm sure you're aware. Dexter's particular project has been applications in four-dimensional engineering."

"I'm afraid," Ferron said, "that means nothing to me."

"Of course." He pressed a key. The cat peered over his shoulder, apparently fascinated by the blinking lights on the monitor.

The hyperlink blinked live in Ferron's feed. She accessed it and received a brief education in the theoretical physics of reaching *around* three-dimensional shapes in space-time. A cold sweat slicked her palms. She told herself it was just the second hypomania re-up.

"Closed-heart surgery," she said. During the medical tourism boom, Bengaluru's economy had thrived. They'd found other ways to make ends meet now that people no longer traveled so profligately, but the state remained one of India's centers of medical technology. Ferron wondered about the applications for remote surgery, and what the economic impact of this technology could be.

"Sure. Or extracting an appendix without leaving a scar. Inserting stem cells into bone marrow with no surgical trauma, freeing the body to heal disease instead of infection and wounds. It's revolutionary. If we can get it working."

"Saab . . . " She stroked Chairman Miaow's sleek azure head. "Could it be used as a weapon?"

"Anything can be used as a weapon," he said. A little too fast? But his skin conductivity and heart rate revealed no deception, no withholding. "Look, Sub-Inspector. Would you like some coffee?"

"I'd love some," she admitted.

He tapped a few more keys and stepped down from the treadmill. She'd have thought the typing curiously inefficient, but he certainly seemed to get things done fast.

"Religious reasons, saab?" she asked.

"Hmm?" He glanced at the monitor. "No. I'm just an eccentric. I prefer one information stream at a time. And I like to come here and do my work, and keep my home at home."

"Oh." Ferron laughed, following him across the office to a set of antique lacquered chairs. Chairman Miaow minced after them, stopping to sniff the unfamiliar rug and roll in a particularly lush patch. Feeling like she was making a huge confession, Ferron said, "I turn off my feeds sometimes too. Skin out. It helps me concentrate."

He winked.

She said, "So tell me about Dexter and his cat."

"Well . . ." He glanced guiltily at Chairman Miaow. "She was very advanced. He obviously spent a great deal of time working with her. Complete sentences, conversation on about the level of an imaginative five-year old. That's one of our designs, by the way."

"Parrot-cats?"

"The hyacinth variety. We're working on an *Eclectus* variant for next year's market. Crimson and plum colors. You know they have a much longer lifespan than the root stock? Parrot-cats should be able to live for thirty to fifty years, though of course the design hasn't been around long enough for experimental proof."

"I did not. About Dr. Coffin—" she paused, and scanned the lists of enemies and contacts that Dr. Rao had provided, cross-referencing it with files and the reports of three interviews that had come in from Indrapramit in the last five minutes. Another contact request from her mother blinked away officiously. She dismissed it. "I understand he wasn't born here?"

"He traveled," Dr. Rao said in hushed tones. "From America."

"Huh," Ferron said. "He relocated for a job? Medieval. How did BioShell justify the expense—and the carbon burden?"

"A unique skill set. We bring in people from many places, actually. He was well-liked here: his work was outstanding, and he was charming enough— and talented enough—that his colleagues forgave him some of the . . . vagaries in his rightminding."

"Vagaries. . . ?"

"He was a depressive, madam," Dr. Rao said. "Prone to fairly serious fits of existential despair. Medication and surgery controlled it adequately that he was functional, but not completely enough that he was always . . . comfortable."

"When you say existential despair . . . ?" Ferron was a past master of the open-ended hesitation.

Dr. Rao seemed cheerfully willing to fill in the blank for her. "He questioned the worth and value of pretty much every human endeavor. Of existence itself."

"So he was a sophipath? A bit nihilistic?"

"Nihilism denies value. Dexter was willing to believe that compassion had value—not intrinsic value, you understand. But assigned value. He believed that the best thing a human being could aspire to was to limit suffering."

"That explains his handle."

Dr. Rao chuckled. "It does, doesn't it? Anyway, he was brilliant."

"I assume that means that BioShell will suffer in his absence."

"The fourth-dimension project is going to fall apart without him," Dr. Rao said candidly. "It's going to take a global search to replace him. And we'll have to do it quickly; release of the technology was on the anvil."

Ferron thought about the inside-out person in the midst of his rug, his flat set for an intimate dinner for two. "Dr. Rao . . . "

"Yes, Sub-Inspector?"

"In your estimation, would Dr. Coffin commit suicide?"

He steepled his fingers and sighed. "It's . . . possible. But he was very devoted to his work, and his psych evaluations did not indicate it as an immediate danger. I'd hate to think that it was."

"Because you'd feel like you should have done more? You can't save somebody from themselves, Dr. Rao."

"Sometimes," he said, "a word in the dark is all it takes."

"Dr. Coffin worked from home. Was any of his lab equipment there? Is it possible that he died in an accident?"

Dr. Rao's eyebrows rose. "Now I'm curious about the nature of his demise, I'm afraid. He should not have had any proprietary equipment at home: we maintain a lab for him here, and his work at home should have been limited to theory and analysis. But of course he'd have an array of interfaces."

The coffee arrived, brought in by a young man with a ready smile who set the tray on the table and vanished again without a word. No doubt pleased to be Employed.

As Dr. Rao poured from a solid old stoneware carafe, he transitioned to small talk. "Some exciting news about the Andromeda galaxy, isn't it? They've named the star Al-Rahman."

"I thought stars were named by coordinates and catalogue number these days."

"They are," Rao said. "But it's fitting for this one to have a little romance. People being what they are, someone would have named it if the science community didn't. And Abd Al-Rahman Al-Sufi was the first astronomer to describe the Andromeda galaxy, around 960 A.D. He called it the 'little cloud.' It's also called Messier 31—"

"Do you think it's a nova precursor, saab?"

He handed her the coffee—something that smelled pricy and rich, probably from the hills—and offered cream and sugar. She added a lump of the latter to her cup with the tongs, stirred in cream, and selected a lemon biscuit from the little plate he nudged toward her.

"That's what they said on the news," he said.

"Meaning you don't believe it?"

"You're sharp," he said admiringly.

"I'm a homicide investigator," she said.

He reached into his pocket and withdrew a small injection kit. The hypo hissed alarmingly as he pressed it to his skin. He winced.

"Insulin?" she asked, restraining herself from an incredibly rude question about why he hadn't had stem cells, if he was diabetic.

He shook his head. "Scotophobin. Also part of my rightminding. I have short-term memory issues." He picked up a chocolate biscuit and bit into it decisively.

She'd taken the stuff herself, in school and when cramming for her police exams. She also refused to be derailed. "So you don't think this star—"

"Al-Rahman."

"—Al-Rahman. You don't think it's going nova?"

"Oh, it might be," he said. "But what would you say if I told you that its pattern is a repeating series of prime numbers?"

The sharp tartness of lemon shortbread turned to so much grit in her mouth. "I beg your pardon."

"Someone is signaling us," Dr. Rao said. "Or I should say, *was* signaling us. A long, long time ago. Somebody with the technology necessary to tune the output of their star."

"Explain," she said, setting the remainder of the biscuit on her saucer.

"Al-Rahman is more than two and a half million light years away. That means that the light we're seeing from it was modulated when the first identifiable humans were budding off the hominid family tree. Even if we could send a signal back . . . The odds are very good that they're all gone now. It was just a message in a bottle. *We were here.*"

"The news said twenty thousand light years."

"The news." He scoffed. "Do they ever get police work right?"

"Never," Ferron said fervently.

"Science either." He glanced up as the lights dimmed. "Another brownout."

An unformed idea tickled the back of Ferron's mind. "Do you have a sunfarm?"

"BioShell is entirely self-sufficient," he confirmed. "It's got to be a bug, but we haven't located it yet. Anyway, it will be back up in a minute. All our important equipment has dedicated power supplies."

He finished his biscuit and stirred the coffee thoughtfully while he chewed.

"The odds are that the universe is—or has been—full of intelligent species. And that we will never meet any of them. Because the distances and time scales are so vast. In the two hundred years we've been capable of sending signals into space—well. Compare that in scale to Al-Rahman."

"That's awful," Ferron said. "It makes me appreciate Dr. Coffin's perspective."

"It's terrible," Dr. Rao agreed. "Terrible and wonderful. In some ways I wonder if that's as close as we'll ever get to comprehending the face of God."

They sipped their coffee in contemplation, facing one another across the tray and the low lacquered table.

"Milk?" said Chairman Miaow. Carefully, Ferron poured some into a saucer and gave it to her.

Dr. Rao said, "You know, the Andromeda galaxy and our own Milky Way are expected to collide eventually."

"Eventually?"

He smiled. It did good things for the creases around his eyes. "Four and a half billion years or so."

Ferron thought about Uttara Bhadrapada, and the Heavenly Ganges, and Aryaman's house—in a metaphysical sort of sense—as he came to walk that path across the sky. From so far away it took two and a half million years just to *see* that far.

"I won't wait up, then." She finished the last swallow of coffee and looked around for the cat. "I don't suppose I could see Dr. Coffin's lab before I go?"

"Oh," said Dr. Rao. "I think we can do that, and better."

The lab space Coffin had shared with three other researchers belied BioShell's corporate wealth. It was a maze of tables and unidentifiable equipment in dizzying array. Ferron identified a gene sequencer, four or five microscopes, and a centrifuge, but most of the rest baffled her limited knowledge of bioengineering. She was struck by the fact that just about every object in the room was dressed in BioShell's livery colors of emerald and gold.

She glimpsed a conservatory through a connecting door, lush with what must be prototype plants; at the far end of the room, rows of condensers hummed beside a revolving door rimed with frost. A black-skinned woman in a lab coat with her hair clipped into short, tight curls had her eyes to a lens and her hands in waldo sleeves. Microsurgery?

Dr. Rao held out a hand as Ferron paused beside him. "Will we disturb her?"

"Dr. Nnebuogor will have skinned out just about everything except the fire alarm," Dr. Rao said. "The only way to distract her would be to go over and give her a shove. Which"—he raised a warning finger—"I would recommend against, as she's probably engaged in work on those next-generation parrot-cats I told you about now."

"Nnebuogor? She's Nigerian?"

Dr. Rao nodded. "Educated in Cairo and Bengaluru. Her coming to work for BioShell was a real coup for us."

"You *do* employ a lot of farang," Ferron said. "And not by telepresence." She waited for Rao to bridle, but she must have gotten the tone right, because he shrugged.

"Our researchers need access to our lab."

"Miaow," said Chairman Miaow.

"Can she?" Ferron asked.

"We're cat-friendly," Rao said, with a flicker of a smile, so Ferron set the carrier down and opened its door. Rao's heart rate was up a little, and she caught herself watching sideways while he straightened his trousers and picked lint from his sleeve.

Chairman Miaow emerged slowly, rubbing her length against the side of the carrier. She gazed up at the equipment and furniture with unblinking eyes and soon she gathered herself to leap onto a workbench, and Dr. Rao put a hand out firmly.

"No climbing or jumping," he said. "Dangerous. It will hurt you."

"Hurt?" The cat drew out the Rs in a manner so adorable it had to be engineered for. "No jump?"

"No." Rao turned to Ferron. "We've hardwired in response to the No command. I think you'll find our parrot-cats superior to unengineered felines in this regard. Of course . . . they're still cats."

"Of course," Ferron said. She watched as Chairman Miaow explored her new environment, rubbing her face on this and that. "Do you have any pets?"

"We often take home the successful prototypes," he said. "It would be a pity to destroy them. I have a parrot-cat—a red-and-gray—and a golden lemur. Engineered, of course. The baseline ones are protected."

As they watched, the hyacinth cat picked her way around, sniffing every surface. She paused before one workstation in particular before cheek-marking it, and said in comically exaggerated surprise: "Mine! My smell."

There was a synthetic-fleece-lined basket tucked beneath the table. The cat leaned toward it, stretching her head and neck, and sniffed deeply and repeatedly.

"Have you been here before?" Ferron asked.

Chairman Miaow looked at Ferron wide-eyed with amazement at Ferron's patent ignorance, and declared "New!"

She jumped into the basket and snuggled in, sinking her claws deeply and repeatedly into the fleece.

Ferron made herself stop chewing her thumbnail. She stuck her hand into her uniform pocket. "Are all your hyacinths clones?"

"They're all closely related," Dr. Rao said. "But no, not clones. And even if she were a clone, there would be differences in the expression of her tuxedo pattern."

At that moment, Dr. Nnebuogor sighed and backed away from her machine, withdrawing her hands from the sleeves and shaking out the fingers like a musician after practicing. She jumped when she turned and saw them. "Oh! Sorry. I was skinned. Namaskar."

"Miaow?" said the cat in her appropriated basket.

"Hello, Niranjana. Where's Dexter?" said Dr. Nnebuogor. Ferron felt the scientist reading her meta-tags. Dr. Nnebuogor raised her eyes to Rao. "And— pardon, officer—what's with the copper?"

"Actually," Ferron said, "I have some bad news for you. It appears that Dexter Coffin was murdered last night."

"Murdered. . . . " Dr. Nnebuogor put her hand out against the table edge. *"Murdered?"*

"Yes," Ferron said. "I'm Police Sub-Inspector Ferron." Which Dr. Nnebuogor would know already. "And I'm afraid I need to ask you some questions. Also, I'll be contacting the other researchers who share your facilities via telepresence. Is there a private area I can use for that?"

Dr. Nnebuogor looked stricken. The hand that was not leaned against the table went up to her mouth. Ferron's feed showed the acceleration of her heart, the increase in skin conductivity as her body slicked with cold sweat. Guilt or grief ? It was too soon to tell.

"You can use my office," Dr. Rao said. "Kindly, with my gratitude."

The interviews took the best part of the day and evening, when all was said and done, and garnered Ferron very little new information—yes, people *would* probably kill for what Coffin was—had been—working on. No, none of his colleagues had any reason to. No, he had no love life of which they were aware.

Ferron supposed she technically *could* spend all night lugging the cat carrier around, but her own flat wasn't too far from the University district. It was in a kinship block teeming with her uncles and cousins, her grandparents, great-grandparents, her sisters and their husbands (and in one case, wife). The fiscal support of shared housing was the only reason she'd been able to carry her mother as long as she had.

She checked out a pedestrial because she couldn't face the bus and she felt like she'd done more than her quota of steps before dinnertime—and here it was, well after. The cat carrier balanced on the grab bar, she zipped it unerringly through the traffic, enjoying the feel of the wind in her hair and the outraged honks cascading along the double avenues.

She could make the drive on autopilot, so she used the other half of her attention to feed facts to the Department's expert system. Doyle knew everything about everything, and if it wasn't self-aware or self-directed in the sense that most people meant when they said *artificial intelligence,* it still rivaled a trained human brain when it came to picking out patterns—and being supercooled, it was significantly faster.

She even told it the puzzling bits, such as how Chairman Miaow had reacted upon being introduced to the communal lab that Coffin shared with three other BioShell researchers.

Doyle swallowed everything Ferron could give it, as fast as she could report. She knew that down in its bowels, it would be integrating that information with Indrapramit's reports, and those of the other officers and techs assigned to the case.

She thought maybe they needed something more. As the pedestrial dropped her at the bottom of her side street, she dropped a line to Damini, her favorite archinformist. "Hey," she said, when Damini answered.

"Hey yourself, boss. What do you need?"

Ferron released the pedestrial back into the city pool. It scurried off, probably already summoned to the next call. Ferron had used her override to requisition it. She tried to feel guilty, but she was already late in attending to her mother—and she'd ignored two more messages in the intervening time. It was probably too late to prevent bloodshed, but there was something to be said for getting the inevitable over with.

"Dig me up everything you can on today's vic, would you? Dexter Coffin, American by birth, employed at BioShell. As far back as you can, any tracks he may have left under any name or handle."

"Childhood dental records and juvenile posts on the *Candyland* message boards," Damini said cheerfully. "Got it. I'll stick it in Doyle when it's done."

"Ping me, too? Even if it's late? I'm upped."

"So will I be," Damini answered. "This could take a while. Anything else?"

"Not unless you have a cure for families."

"Hah," said the archinformist. "Everybody talking, and nobody hears a damned thing anybody else has to say. I'd retire on the proceeds. All right, check in later." She vanished just as Ferron reached the aptblock lobby.

It was after dinner, but half the family was hanging around in the common areas, watching the news or playing games while pretending to ignore it. Ferron knew it was useless to try sneaking past the synthetic marble-floored chambers with their charpoys and cushions, the corners lush with foliage. Attempted stealth would only encourage them to detain her longer.

Dr. Rao's information about the prime number progression had leaked beyond scientific circles—or been released—and an endless succession of talking heads were analyzing it in less nuanced terms than he'd managed. The older cousins asked Ferron if she'd heard the news about the star; two sisters and an uncle told her that her mother had been looking for her. *All* the nieces and nephews and small cousins wanted to look at the cat.

Ferron's aging mausi gave her five minutes on how a little cosmetic surgery would make her much more attractive on the marriage market, and shouldn't she consider lightening that mahogany-brown skin to a "prettier" wheatish complexion? A plate of idlis and sambaar appeared as if by magic in mausi's hand, and from there transferred to Ferron's. "And how are you ever going to catch a man if you're so skinny?"

It took Ferron twenty minutes to maneuver into her own small flat, which was still set for sleeping from three nights before. Smoke came trotting to see her, a petite-footed drift of the softest silver-and-charcoal fur imaginable, from which emerged a laughing triangular face set with eyes like black jewels. His ancestors had been foxes farmed for fur in Russia. Researchers had experimented on them, breeding for docility. It turned out it only took a few generations to turn a wild animal into a housepet.

Ferron was a little uneasy with the ethics of all that. But it hadn't stopped her from adopting Smoke when her mother lost interest in him. Foxes weren't the hot trend anymore; the fashion was for engineered cats and lemurs—and skinpets, among those who wanted to look daring.

Having rushed home, she was now possessed by the intense desire to delay the inevitable. She set Chairman Miaow's carrier on top of the cabinets and took Smoke out into the sunfarm for a few minutes of exercise in the relative cool of night. When he'd chased parrots in circles for a bit, she brought him back in, cleaned his litterbox, and stripped off her sweat-stiff uniform to have a shower. She was washing her hair when she realized that she had no idea what to feed Chairman Miaow. Maybe she could eat fox food? Ferron would have to figure out some way to segregate part of the flat for her . . . at least until she was sure that Smoke didn't think a parrot-cat would make a nice midnight snack.

She dressed in off-duty clothes—barefoot in a salwar kameez—and made an attempt at setting her furniture to segregate her flat. Before she left, she placed offering packets of kumkum and a few marigolds from the patio boxes in the tray before her idol of Varuna, the god of agreement, order, and the law.

Ferron didn't bother drying her hair before she presented herself at her mother's door. If she left it down, the heat would see to that soon enough.

Madhuvanthi did not rise to admit Ferron herself, as she was no longer capable. The door just slid open to Ferron's presence. As Ferron stepped inside, she saw mostly that the rug needed watering, and that the chaise her mother reclined on needed to be reset—it was sagging at the edges from too long in one shape. She wore not just the usual noninvasive modern interface—contacts, skin conductivity and brain activity sensors, the invisibly fine wires that lay along the skin and detected nerve impulses and muscle micromovements—but a full immersion suit.

Not for the first time, Ferron contemplated skinning out the thing's bulky, padded outline, and looking at her mother the way she wanted to see her. But that would be dishonest. Ferron was here to face her problems, not pretend their nonexistence.

"Hello, Mother," Ferron said.

There was no answer.

Ferron sent a text message. HELLO, MOTHER. YOU WANTED TO SEE ME?

The pause was long, but not as long as it could have been. YOU'RE LATE, TAMANNA. I'VE BEEN TRYING TO REACH YOU ALL DAY. I'M IN THE MIDDLE OF A RUN RIGHT NOW.

I'M SORRY, Ferron said. SOMEONE WAS MURDERED.

Text, thank all the gods, sucked out the defensive sarcasm that would have filled up a spoken word. She fiddled the bangles she couldn't wear on duty, just to hear the glass chime.

She could feel her mother's attention elsewhere, her distaste at having the unpleasant realities of Ferron's job forced upon her. That attention would focus on anything but Ferron, for as long as Ferron waited for it. It was a contest of wills, and Ferron always lost. MOTHER—

Her mother pushed up the faceplate on the V.R. helmet and sat up abruptly. "Bloody hell," she said. "Got killed. That'll teach me to do two things at once. Look, about the archives—"

"Mother," Ferron said, "I can't. I don't have any more savings to give you."

Madhuvanthi said, "They'll *kill* me."

They'll de-archive your virtual history, Ferron thought, but she had the sense to hold her tongue.

After her silence dragged on for fifteen seconds or so, Madhuvanthi said, "Sell the fox."

"He's mine," Ferron said. "I'm not selling him. Mother, you really need to come out of your make-believe world once in a while—"

Her mother pulled the collar of the VR suit open so she could ruffle the fur of the violet-and-teal-striped skinpet nestled up to the warmth of her throat. It humped in response, probably vibrating with a comforting purr. Ferron tried not to judge, but the idea of parasitic pets, no matter how fluffy and colorful, made *her* skin crawl.

Ferron's mother said, "Make-believe. And your world isn't?"

"Mother—"

"Come in and see my world sometime before you judge it."

"I've seen your world," Ferron said. "I used to live there, remember? All the time, with you. Now I live out here, and you can too."

Madhuvanthi's glare would have seemed blistering even in the rainy season. "I'm your mother. You will obey me."

Everything inside Ferron demanded she answer yes. Hard-wired, that duty. Planned for. Programmed.

Ferron raised her right hand. "Can't we get some dinner and—"

Madhuvanthi sniffed and closed the faceplate again. And that was the end of the interview.

Rightminding or not, the cool wings of hypomania or not, Ferron's heart was pounding and her fresh clothing felt sticky again already. She turned and left.

When she got back to her own flat, the first thing she noticed was her makeshift wall of furniture partially disassembled, a chair/shelf knocked sideways, the disconnected and overturned table top now fallen flat.

"Oh, no." Her heart rose into her throat. She rushed inside, the door forgotten—

Atop a heap of cushions lay Smoke, proud and smug. And against his soft gray side, his fluffy tail flipped over her like a blanket, curled Chairman Miaow, her golden eyes squeezed closed in pleasure.

"Mine!" she said definitively, raising her head.

"I guess so," Ferron answered. She shut the door and went to pour herself a drink while she started sorting through Indrapramit's latest crop of interviews.

According to everything Indrapramit had learned, Coffin was quiet. He kept to himself, but he was always willing and enthusiastic when it came to discussing his work. His closest companion was the cat—Ferron looked down at Chairman Miaow, who had rearranged herself to take advantage of the warm valley in the bed between Smoke and Ferron's thigh—and the cat was something of a neighborhood celebrity, riding on Coffin's shoulder when he took his exercise.

All in all, a typical portrait of a lonely man who didn't let anyone get too close.

"Maybe there will be more in the archinformation," she said, and went back to Doyle's pattern algorithm results one more damn time.

After performing her evening practice of kalari payat—first time in three days—Ferron set her furniture for bed and retired to it with her files. She wasn't expecting Indrapramit to show up at her flat, but some time around two in the morning, the lobby door discreetly let her know she had a visitor. Of course, he knew she'd upped, and since he had no family and lived in a thin-walled dormitory room, he'd need a quiet place to camp out and work at this hour of the night. There wasn't a lot of productive interviewing you could do when all the subjects were asleep—at least, not until they had somebody dead to rights enough to take them down to the jail for interrogation.

His coming to her home meant every other resident of the block would know, and Ferron could look forward to a morning of being quizzed by aunties while she tried to cram her idlis down. It didn't matter that Indrapramit was a colleague, and she was his superior. At her age, any sign of male interest brought unEmployed relatives with too much time on their hands swarming.

Still, she admitted him. Then she extricated herself from between the fox and the cat, wrapped her bathrobe around herself, stomped into her slippers, and headed out to meet him in the hall. At least keeping their conference to the public areas would limit knowing glances later.

He'd upped too. She could tell by the bounce in his step and his slightly wild focus. And the fact that he was dropping by for a visit in the dark of the morning.

Lowering her voice so she wouldn't trouble her neighbors, Ferron said, "Something too good to mail?"

"An interesting potential complication."

She gestured to the glass doors leading out to the sunfarm. He followed her, his boots somehow still as bright as they'd been that morning. He must polish them in an anti-static gloss.

She kicked off her slippers and padded barefoot over the threshold, making sure to silence the alarm first. The suntrees were furled for the night, their leaves rolled into funnels that channeled condensation to the roots. There was even a bit of chill in the air.

Ferron breathed in gratefully, wiggling her toes in the cultivated earth. "Let's go up to the roof."

Without a word, Indrapramit followed her up the winding openwork stair hung with bougainvillea, barren and thorny now in the dry season but a riot of color and greenery once the rains returned. The interior walls of the aptblock were mossy and thickly planted with coriander and other Ayurvedic herbs. Ferron broke off a bitter leaf of fenugreek to nibble as they climbed.

At the landing, she stepped aside and tilted her head back, peering up through the potted neem and lemon and mango trees at the stars beyond. A dark hunched shape in the branches of a pomegranate startled her until she realized it was the outline of one of the house monkeys, huddled in sleep. She wondered if she could see the Andromeda galaxy from here at this time of year. Checking a skymap, she learned that it would be visible—but probably low on the horizon, and not without a telescope in these light-polluted times. You'd have better odds of finding it than a hundred years ago, though, when you'd barely have been able to glimpse the brightest stars. The Heavenly Ganges spilled across the darkness like sequins sewn at random on an indigo veil, and a crooked fragment of moon rode high. She breathed in deep and stepped onto the grass and herbs of the roof garden. A creeping mint snagged at her toes, sending its pungency wide.

"So what's the big news?"

"We're not the only ones asking questions about Dexter Coffin." Indrapramit flashed her a video clip of a pale-skinned woman with red hair bleached ginger by the sun and a crop of freckles not even the gloss of sunblock across her cheeks could keep down. She was broad-shouldered and looked capable, and the ID codes running across the feed under her image told Ferron she carried a warrant card and a stun pistol.

"Contract cop?" she said, sympathetically.

"I'm fine," he said, before she could ask. He spread his first two fingers opposite his thumb and pressed each end of the V beneath his collarbones, a new nervous gesture. "I got my Chicago block maintained last week, and the reprogramming is holding. I'd tell you if I was triggering. I know that not every contract cop is going to decompensate and start a massacre."

A massacre Indrapramit had stopped the hard way, it happened. "Let me know what you need," she said, because everything else she could have said would sound like a vote of no confidence.

"Thanks," he said. "How'd it go with your mother?"

"Gah," she said. "I think *I* need a needle. So what's the contractor asking? And who's employing her?"

"Here's the interesting thing, boss. She's an American too."

"She *couldn't* have made it here this fast. Not unless she started before he died—"

"No," he said. "She's an expat, a former New York homicide detective. Her handle is Morganti. She lives in Hongasandra, and she does a lot of work for American and Canadian police departments. Licensed and bonded, and she seems to have a very good rep."

"Who's she under contract to now?"

"Warrant card says Honolulu."

"Huh." Ferron kept her eyes on the stars, and the dark leaves blowing before them. "Top-tier distributed policing, then. Is it a skip trace?"

"You think he was on the run, and whoever he was on the run from finally caught up with him?"

"It's a working theory." She shrugged. "Damini's supposed to be calling with some background any minute now. Actually, I think I'll check in with her. She's late, and I have to file a twenty-four-hour report with the Inspector in the morning."

With a twitch of her attention, she spun a bug out to Damini and conferenced Indrapramit in.

The archinformist answered immediately. "Sorry, boss," she said. "I know I'm slow, but I'm still trying to put together a complete picture here. Your dead guy buried his past pretty thoroughly. I can give you a preliminary, though, with the caveat that it's subject to change."

"Squirt," Ferron said, opening her firewall to the data. It came in fast and hard, and there seemed to be kilometers of it unrolling into her feed like an endless bolt of silk. "Oh, dear . . . "

"I know, I know. Do you want the executive summary? Even if it's also a work in progress? Okay. First up, nobody other than Coffin was in his flat that night, according to netfeed tracking."

"The other night upon the stair," Ferron said, "I met a man who wasn't there."

Damini blew her bangs out of her eyes. "So either nobody came in, or whoever did is a good enough hacker to eradicate every trace of her presence. Which is not a common thing."

"Gotcha. What else?"

"Doyle picked out a partial pattern in your feed. Two power cuts in places associated with the crime. It started looking for more, and it identified a series of brownouts over the course of a year or so, all in locations with some connection to Dr. Coffin. Better yet, Doyle identified the cause."

"I promise I'm holding my breath," Indrapramit said.

"Then how is it you are talking? Anyway, it's a smart virus in the power grids. It's draining power off the lab and household sunfarms at irregular intervals. That power is being routed to a series of chargeable batteries in Coffin's lab space. Except Coffin didn't purchase order the batteries."

"Nnebuogor," Ferron guessed.

"Two points," said Damini. "It's a stretch, but she could have come in to the office today specifically to see if the cops stopped by."

"She could have . . . " Indrapramit said dubiously. "You think she killed him because he found out she was stealing power? For what purpose?"

"I'll get on her email and media," Damini said. "So here's my speculation: imagine this utility virus, spreading through the smart grid from aptblock to aptblock. To commit the murder, nobody had to be in the room with him, not if his four-dimensional manipulators were within range of him. Right? You'd just override whatever safety protocols there were, and . . . boom. Or squish, if you prefer."

Ferron winced. She didn't. Prefer, that was. "Any sign that the manipulators were interfered with?"

"Memory wiped," Damini said. "Just like the cat. Oh, and the other thing I found out. Dexter Coffin is not our boy's first identity. It's more like his third, if my linguistic and semantic parsers are right about the web content they're picking up. I've got Conan on it too"—Conan was another of the department's expert systems—"and I'm going to go over a selection by hand. But it seems like our decedent had reinvented himself whenever he got into professional trouble, which he did a lot. He had unpopular opinions, and he wasn't shy about sharing them with the net. So he'd make the community too hot to handle and then come back as his own sockpuppet—new look, new address, new handle. Severing all ties to what he was before. I've managed to get a real fix on his last identity, though—"

Indrapramit leaned forward, folding his arms against the chill. "How do you do that? He works in a specialized—a rarified field. I'd guess everybody in it knows each other, at least by reputation. Just how much did he change his appearance?"

"Well," Damini said, "he used to look like this. He must have used some rightminding tactics to change elements of his personality, too. Just not the salient ones. A real chameleon, your arsehole."

She picked a still image out of the datastream and flung it up. Ferron glanced at Indrapramit, whose rakish eyebrows were climbing up his forehead. An East Asian with long, glossy dark hair, who appeared to stand about six inches taller than Dr. Coffin, floated at the center of her perceptions, smiling benevolently.

"Madam, saab," Damini said. "May I present Dr. Jessica Fang."

"Well," Ferron said, after a pause of moderate length. "That takes a significant investment." She thought of Aristotle: As the condition of the mind alters, so too alters the condition of the body, and likewise, as the condition of the body alters, so too alters the condition of the mind.

Indrapramit said, "He has a taste for evocative handles. Any idea why the vanishing act?"

"I'm working on it," Damini said.

"I've got a better idea," said Ferron. "Why don't we ask Detective Morganti?"

Indrapramit steepled his fingers. "Boss . . . "

"I'll hear it," Ferron said. "It doesn't matter if it's crazy."

"We've been totally sidetracked by the cat issue. Because Chairman Miaow has to be Niranjana, right? Because a clone would have expressed the genes for those markings differently. But she can't be Niranjana, because she's not wiped: she's factory-new."

"Right," Ferron said cautiously.

"So." Indrapramit was enjoying his dramatic moment. "If a person can have cosmetic surgery, why not a parrot-cat?"

"Chairman Miaow?" Ferron called, as she led Indrapramit into her flat. They needed tea to shake off the early morning chill, and she was beyond caring what the neighbors thought. She needed a clean uniform, too.

"Miaow," said Chairman Miaow, from inside the kitchen cupboard.

"Oh, dear." Indrapramit followed Ferron in. Smoke sat demurely in the middle of the floor, tail fluffed over his toes, the picture of innocence. Ferron pulled wide the cabinet door, which already stood ten inches ajar. There was Chairman Miaow, purring, a shredded packet of tunafish spreading dribbles of greasy water across the cupboard floor.

She licked her chops ostentatiously and jumped down to the sink lip, where she balanced as preciously as she had in Coffin's flat.

"Cat," Ferron said. She thought over the next few things she wanted to say, and remembered that she was speaking to a parrot-cat. "Don't think you've gotten away with anything. The fox is getting the rest of that."

"Fox food is icky," the cat said. "Also, not enough taurine."

"Huh," Ferron said. She looked over at Indrapramit.

He looked back. "I guess she's learning to talk."

They had no problem finding Detective Morganti. The redheaded American woman arrived at Ferron's aptblock with the first rays of sunlight stroking the vertical farms along its flanks. She had been sitting on the bench beside the door, reading something on her screen, but she looked up and stood as Ferron and Indrapramit exited.

"Sub-Inspector Ferron, I presume? And Constable Indrapramit, how nice to see you again."

Ferron shook her hand. She was even more imposing in person, tall and broad-chested, with the shoulders of a cartoon superhuman. She didn't squeeze.

Morganti continued, "I understand you're the detective of record on the Coffin case."

"Walk with us," Ferron said. "There's a nice French coffee shop on the way to the Metro."

It had shaded awnings and a courtyard, and they were seated and served within minutes. Ferron amused herself by pushing the crumbs of her pastry around on the plate while they talked. Occasionally, she broke a piece off and tucked it into her mouth, washing buttery flakes down with thick, cardamom-scented brew.

"So," she said after a few moments, "what did Jessica Fang do in Honolulu?

It's not just the flame wars, I take it. And there's no warrant for her that we could find."

Morganti's eyebrows rose. "Very efficient."

"Thank you." Ferron tipped her head to Indrapramit. "Mostly his work, and that of my archinformist."

Morganti smiled; Indrapramit nodded silently. Then Morganti said, "She is believed to have been responsible for embezzling almost three million ConDollars from her former employer, eleven years ago in the Hawaiian Islands."

"That'd pay for a lot of identity-changing."

"Indeed."

"But they can't prove it."

"If they could, Honolulu P.D. would have pulled a warrant and virtually extradited her. Him. I was contracted to look into the case ten days ago—" She tore off a piece of a cheese croissant and chewed it thoughtfully. "It took the skip trace this long to locate her. Him."

"Did she do it?"

"*Hell* yes." She grinned like the American she was. "The question is—well, okay, I realize the murder is your jurisdiction, but I don't get paid unless I either close the case or eliminate my suspect—and I get a bonus if I recover any of the stolen property. Now, 'killed by person or persons unknown' is a perfectly acceptable outcome as far as the City of Honolulu is concerned, with the added benefit that the State of Hawaii doesn't have to pay Bengaluru to incarcerate him. So I need to know, one cop to another, if the inside-out stiff is Dexter Coffin."

"The DNA matches," Ferron said. "I can tell you that in confidence. There will be a press release once we locate and notify his next of kin."

"Understood," Morganti said. "I'll keep it under my hat. I'll be filing recovery paperwork against the dead man's assets in the amount of C$2,798,000 and change. I can give you the next of kin, by the way."

The data came in a squirt. Daughter, Maui. Dr. Fang-Coffin really had severed all ties.

"Understood," Ferron echoed. She smiled when she caught herself. She liked this woman. "You realize we have to treat you as a suspect, given your financial motive."

"Of course," Morganti said. "I'm bonded, and I'll be happy to come in for an interrogation under Truth."

"That will make things easier, madam," Ferron said.

Morganti turned her coffee cup in its saucer. "Now then. What can I do to help *you* clear your homicide?"

Indrapramit shifted uncomfortably on the bench.

"What *did* Jessica Fang do, exactly?" Ferron had Damini's data in her case buffer. She could use what Morganti told her to judge the contract officer's knowledge and sincerity.

"In addition to the embezzling? Accused of stealing research and passing it off as her own," Morganti said. "Also, she was—well, she was just kind of an asshole on the net, frankly. Running down colleagues, dismissing their work, aggrandizing her own. She was good, truthfully. But nobody's *that* good."

"Would someone have followed him here for personal reasons?"

"As you may have gathered, this guy was not diligent about his right-minding," Morganti said. She pushed a handful of hair behind her shoulder. "And he was a bit of a narcissist. Sociopath? Antisocial in some sort of atavistic way. Normal people don't just . . . walk away from all their social connections because they made things a little hot on the net."

Ferron thought of the distributed politics of her own workplace, the sniping and personality clashes. And her mother, not so much alone on an electronic Serengeti as haunting the virtual pillared palaces of an Egypt that never was.

"No," she said.

Morganti said, "Most people find ways to cope with that. Most people don't burn themselves as badly as Jessica Fang did, though."

"I see." Ferron wished badly for sparkling water in place of the syrupy coffee. "You've been running down Coffin's finances, then? Can you share that information?"

Morganti said that Coffin had liquidated a lot of hidden assets a week ago, about two days after she took his case. "It was before I made contact with him, but it's possible he had Jessica Fang flagged for searches—or he had a contact in Honolulu who let him know when the skip trace paid off. He was getting ready to run again. How does that sound?"

Ferron sighed and sat back in her chair. "Fabulous. It sounds completely fabulous. I don't suppose you have any insight into who he might have been expecting for dinner? Or how whoever killed him might have gotten out of the room afterward when it was all locked up tight on Coffin's override?"

Morganti shrugged. "He didn't have any close friends or romantic relationships. Always too aware that he was living in hiding, I'd guess. Sometimes he entertained co-workers, but I've checked with them all, and none admits having seen him that night."

"Sub-Inspector," Indrapramit said gently. "The time."

"Bugger," Ferron said, registering it. "Morning roll call. Catch up with you later?"

"Absolutely," Morganti said. "As I said before, I'm just concerned with clearing my embezzling case. I'm always happy to help a sister officer out on a murder."

And butter up the local police, Ferron thought.

Morganti said, "One thing that won't change. Fang was *obsessed* with astronomy."

"There were deep-space images on Coffin's walls," Ferron said.

Indrapramit said, "And he had offered his Ganesha an indigo scarf. I wonder if the color symbolized something astronomical to him."

"Indigo," Morganti said. "Isn't it funny that we have a separate word for dark blue?"

Ferron felt the pedantry welling up, and couldn't quite stopper it. "Did you know that all over the world, dark blue and black are often named with the same word? Possibly because of the color of the night sky. And that the ancient Greeks did not have a particular name for the color blue? Thus their seas were famously 'wine-dark.' But in Hindu tradition, the color blue has a special significance: it is the color of Vishnu's skin, and Krishna is nicknamed *Sunil*, 'dark blue.' The color also implies that which is all-encompassing, as in the sky."

She thought of something slightly more obscure. "Also, that color is the color of Shani Bhagavan, who is one of the deities associated with Uttara Bhadrapada. Which we've been hearing a lot about lately. It might indeed have had a lot of significance to Dr. Fang-Coffin."

Morganti, eyebrows drawn together in confusion, looked to Indrapramit for salvation. "Saab? Uttara Bhadrapada?"

Indrapramit said, "Andromeda."

Morganti excused herself as Indrapramit and Ferron prepared to check in to their virtual office.

While Ferron organized her files and her report, Indrapramit finished his coffee. "We need to check inbound ships from, or carrying passengers from, America. Honolulu isn't as prohibitive as, say, Chicago."

They'd worked together long enough that half the conversational shifts didn't need to be recorded. "Just in case somebody *did* come here to kill him. Well, there can't be that many passages, right?"

"I'll get Damini after it," he said. "After roll—"

Roll call made her avoidant. There would be reports, politics, wrangling, and a succession of wastes of time as people tried to prove that their cases were more worthy of resources than other cases.

She pinched her temples. At least the coffee here was good. "Right. Telepresencing . . . now."

After the morning meeting, they ordered another round of coffees, and Ferron pulled up the sandwich menu and eyed it. There was no telling when they'd have time for lunch.

She'd grab something after the next of kin notification. If she was still hungry when they were done.

Normally, in the case of a next of kin so geographically distant, Bengaluru Police would arrange for an officer with local jurisdiction to make the call. But the Lahaina Police Department had been unable to raise Jessica Fang's daughter on a home visit, and a little cursory research had revealed that she was unEmployed and very nearly a permanent resident of Artificial Reality.

Just going by her handle, Jessica Fang's daughter on Maui didn't have a lot of professional aspirations. Ferron and Indrapramit had to go virtual and pull on avatars to meet her: Skooter0 didn't seem to come out of her virtual worlds for anything other than biologically unavoidable crash cycles. Since they were on duty, Ferron and Indrapramit's avatars were the standard-issue blanks provided by Bengaluru Police, their virtual uniforms sharply pressed, their virtual faces expressionless and identical.

It wasn't the warm and personal touch you would hope for, Ferron thought, when somebody was coming to tell you your mother had been murdered.

"Why don't you take point on this one?" she said.

Indrapramit snorted. "Be sure to mention my leadership qualities in my next performance review."

They left their bodies holding down those same café chairs and waded through the first few tiers of advertisements—get-rich-quick schemes, Bollywood starlets, and pop star scandal sheets, until they got into the American feed, and then it was get-rich-quick schemes, Hollywood starlets, pornography, and Congressional scandal sheets—until they linked up with the law enforcement priority channel. Ferron checked the address and led Indrapramit into a massively multiplayer artificial reality that showed real-time activity through Skooter0's system identity number. Once provided with the next-of-kin's handle, Damini had sent along a selection of key codes and overrides that got them through the pay wall with ease.

They didn't need a warrant for this. It was just a courtesy call.

Skooter0's preferred hangout was a "historical" AR, which meant in theory that it reflected the pre-twenty-first-century world, and in practice that it was a muddled-up stew of cowboys, ninjas, pinstripe-suit mobsters, Medieval knights, cavaliers, Mongols, and Wild West gunslingers. There were Macedonians, Mauryans, African gunrunners, French resistance fighters, and Nazis, all running around together with samurai and Shaolin monks.

Indrapramit's avatar checked a beacon—a glowing green needle floating just above his nonexistent wrist. The directional signal led them through a space meant to evoke an antediluvian ice cave, in which about two dozen people all dressed as different incarnations of the late-twentieth-century pop star David Bowie were working themselves into a martial frenzy as they prepared to go forth and do virtual battle with some rival clade of Emulators. Ferron eyed a Diamond Dog who was being dressed in glittering armor by a pair of Thin White Dukes and was glad of the expressionless surface of her uniform avatar.

She knew what they were supposed to be because she pattern-matched from the web. The music was quaint, but pretty good. The costumes . . . she winced.

Well, it was probably a better way to deal with antisocial aggression than taking it out on your spouse.

Indrapramit walked on, eyes front—not that you needed eyes to see what was going on in here.

At the far end of the ice cave, four seventh-century Norse dwarves delved a staircase out of stone, leading endlessly down. Heat rolled up from the depths. The virtual workmanship was astounding. Ferron and Indrapramit moved past, hiding their admiring glances. Just as much skill went into creating AR beauty as if it were stone.

The ice cave gave way to a forest glade floored in mossy, irregular slates. Set about on those were curved, transparent tables set for chess, go, mancala, cribbage, and similar strategy games. Most of the tables were occupied by pairs of players, and some had drawn observers as well.

Indrapramit followed his needle—and Ferron followed Indrapramit—to a table where a unicorn and a sasquatch were playing a game involving rows of transparent red and yellow stones laid out on a grid according to rules that Ferron did not comprehend. The sasquatch looked up as they stopped beside the table. The unicorn—glossy black, with a pearly, shimmering horn and a glowing amber stone pinched between the halves of her cloven hoof—was focused on her next move.

The arrow pointed squarely between her enormous, lambent golden eyes.

Ferron cleared her throat.

"Yes, officers?" the sasquatch said. He scratched the top of his head. The hair was particularly silky, and flowed around his long hooked fingernails.

"I'm afraid we need to speak to your friend," Indrapramit said.

"She's skinning you out," the sasquatch said. "Unless you have a warrant—"

"We have an override," Ferron said, and used it as soon as she felt Indrapramit's assent.

The unicorn's head came up, a shudder running the length of her body and setting her silvery mane to swaying. In a brittle voice, she said, "I'd like to report a glitch."

"It's not a glitch," Indrapramit said. He identified himself and Ferron and said, "Are you Skooter0?"

"Yeah," she said. The horn glittered dangerously. "I haven't broken any laws in India."

The sasquatch stood up discreetly and backed away.

"It is my unfortunate duty," Indrapramit continued, "to inform you of the murder of your mother, Dr. Jessica Fang, a.k.a. Dr. Dexter Coffin."

The unicorn blinked iridescent lashes. "I'm sorry," she said. "You're talking about something I have killfiled. I won't be able to hear you until you stop."

Indrapramit's avatar didn't look at Ferron, but she felt his request for help. She stepped forward and keyed a top-level override. "You will hear us," she said to the unicorn. "I am sorry for the intrusion, but we are legally bound to inform you that your mother, Dr. Jessica Fang, a.k.a. Dr. Dexter Coffin, has been murdered."

The unicorn's lip curled in a snarl. "Good. I'm glad."

Ferron stepped back. It was about the response she had expected.

"She made me," the unicorn said. "That doesn't make her my *mother*. Is there anything else you're legally bound to inform me of?"

"No," Indrapramit said.

"Then get the hell out." The unicorn set her amber gaming stone down on the grid. A golden glow encompassed it and its neighbors. "I win."

"Warehoused," Indrapramit said with distaste, back in his own body and nibbling a slice of quiche. "And happy about it."

Ferron had a pressed sandwich of vegetables, tapenade, cheeses, and some elaborate and incomprehensible European charcuterie made of smoked vatted protein. It was delicious, in a totally exotic sort of way. "Would it be better if she were miserable and unfulfilled?"

He made a noise of discontentment and speared a bite of spinach and egg.

Ferron knew her combativeness was really all about her mother, not Fang/Coffin's adult and avoidant daughter. Maybe it was the last remnants of Upping, but she couldn't stop herself from saying, "What she's doing is not so different from what our brains do naturally, except now it's by tech/filters rather than prejudice and neurology."

Indrapramit changed the subject. "Let's make a virtual tour of the scene." As an icon blinked in Ferron's attention space, he added, "Oh, hey. Final autopsy report."

"Something from Damini, too," Ferron said. It had a priority code on it. She stepped into an artificial reality simulation of Coffin's apartment as she opened the contact. The thrill of the chase rose through the fog of her fading hypomania. Upping didn't seem to stick as well as it had when she was younger, and the crashes came harder now—but real, old-fashioned adrenaline was the cure for everything.

"Ferron," Ferron said, frowning down at the browned patches on Coffin's virtual rug. Indrapramit rezzed into the conference a heartbeat later. "Damini, what do the depths of the net reveal?"

"Jackpot," Damini said. "Did you get a chance to look at the autopsy report yet?"

"We just got done with the next of kin," Ferron said. "You're fast—I just saw the icon."

"Short form," Damini said, "is that's not Dexter Coffin."

Ferron's avatar made a slow circuit around the perimeter of the virtual murder scene. "There was a *DNA match*. Damini, we just told his daughter he was murdered."

Indrapramit, more practical, put down his fork in meatspace. His AR avatar mimicked the motion with an empty hand. "So who is it?"

"Nobody," Damini said. She leaned back, satisfied. "The medical examiner says it's topologically impossible to turn somebody inside out like that. It's vatted, whatever it is. A grown object, nominally alive, cloned from Dexter Coffin's tissue. But it's not Dexter Coffin. I mean, think about it—what organ would that *be*, exactly?"

"Cloned." In meatspace, Ferron picked a puff of hyacinth-blue fur off her uniform sleeve. She held it up where Indrapramit could see it.

His eyes widened. "Yes," he said. "What about the patterns, though?"

"Do I look like a bioengineer to you? Indrapramit," Ferron said thoughtfully. "Does this crime scene look staged to you?"

He frowned. "Maybe."

"Damini," Ferron asked, "how'd you do with Dr. Coffin's files? And Dr. Nnebuogar's files?"

"There's nothing useful in Coffin's email except some terse exchanges with Dr. Nnebuogor very similar in tone to the Jessica Fang papers. Nnebuogor was warning Coffin off her research. But there were no death threats, no love letters, no child support demands."

"Anything he was interested in?"

"That star," Damini said. "The one that's going nova or whatever. He's been following it for a couple of weeks now, before the press release hit the mainstream feeds. Nnebuogor's logins support the idea that she's behind the utility virus, by the way."

"Logins can be spoofed."

"So they can," Damini agreed.

Ferron peeled her sandwich open and frowned down at the vatted charcuterie. It all looked a lot less appealing now. "Nobody came to Coffin's flat. And it turns out the stiff wasn't a stiff after all. So Coffin went somewhere else, after making preparations to flee and then abandoning them."

"And the crime scene was staged," Indrapramit said.

"This is interesting," Damini said. "Coffin hadn't been to the office in a week."

"Since about when Morganti started investigating him. Or when he might have become aware that she was on his trail."

Ferron said something sharp and self-critical and radically unprofessional. And then she said, "I'm an idiot. Leakage."

"Leakage?" Damini asked. "You mean like when people can't stop talking about the crime they actually committed, or the person you're not supposed to know they're having an affair with?"

An *urgent* icon from Ferron's mausi Sandhya—the responsible auntie, not the fussy auntie—blinked insistently at the edge of her awareness. *Oh Gods, what now?*

"Exactly like that," Ferron said. "Look, check on any hits for Coffin outside his flat in the past ten days. And I need confidential warrants for DNA analysis of the composters at the BioShell laboratory facility and also at Dr. Rao's apartment."

"You think *Rao* killed him?" Damini didn't even try to hide her shock.

Blink, blink went the icon. Emergency. Code red. Your mother has gone beyond the pale, my dear. "Just pull the warrants. I want to see what we get before I commit to my theory."

"Why?" Indrapramit asked.

Ferron sighed. "Because it's crazy. That's why. And see if you can get confidential access to Rao's calendar files and email. I don't want him to know you're looking."

"Wait right there," Damini said. "Don't touch a thing. I'll be back before you know it."

"Mother," Ferron said to her mother's lion-maned goddess of an avatar, "I'm sorry. Sandhya's sorry. We're all sorry. But we can't let you go on like this."

It was the hardest thing she'd ever said.

Her mother, wearing Sekhmet's golden eyes, looked at Ferron's avatar and curled a lip. Ferron had come in, not in a uniform avatar, but wearing the battle-scarred armor she used to play in when she was younger, when she and her mother would spend hours Atavistic. That was during her schooling, before she got interested in stopping—or at least avenging—*real* misery.

Was that fair? Her mother's misery was real. So was that of Jessica Fang's abandoned daughter. And this was a palliative—against being widowed, against being bedridden.

Madhuvanthi's lip-curl slowly blossomed into a snarl. "Of course. You can let them destroy this. Take away everything I am. It's not like it's murder."

"Mother," Ferron said, "it's not *real*."

"If it isn't," her mother said, gesturing around the room, "what is, then? I *made* you. I gave you life. You owe me this. Sandhya said you came home with one of those new parrot-cats. Where'd the money for that come from?"

"Chairman Miaow," Ferron said, "is evidence. And reproduction is an ultimately sociopathic act, no matter what I owe you."

Madhuvanthi sighed. "Daughter, come on one last run."

"You'll have your own memories of all this," Ferron said. "What do you need the archive for?"

"Memory," her mother scoffed. "What's memory, Tamanna? What do you actually remember? Scraps, conflations. How does it compare to being able to *relive?*"

To relive it, Ferron thought, *you'd have to have lived it in the first place.* But even teetering on the edge of fatigue and crash, she had the sense to keep *that* to herself.

"Have you heard about the star?" she asked. Anything to change the subject. "The one the aliens are using to talk to us?"

"The light's four million years old," Madhuvanthi said. "They're all dead. Look, there's a new manifest synesthesia show. Roman and Egyptian. Something for both of us. If you won't come on an adventure with me, will you at least come to an art show? I promise I'll never ask you for archive money again. Just come to this one thing with me? And I promise I'll prune my archive starting tomorrow."

The lioness's brow was wrinkled. Madhuvanthi's voice was thin with defeat. There was no more money, and she knew it. But she couldn't stop bargaining. And the art show was a concession, something that evoked the time they used to spend together, in these imaginary worlds.

"Ferron," she said. Pleading. "Just let me do it myself."

Ferron. They weren't really communicating. Nothing was won. Her mother was doing what addicts always did when confronted—delaying, bargaining, buying time. But she'd call her daughter *Ferron* if it might buy her another twenty-four hours in her virtual paradise.

"I'll come," Ferron said. "But not until tonight. I have some work to do."

"Boss. How did you know to look for that DNA?" Damini asked, when Ferron activated her icon.

"Tell me what you found," Ferron countered.

"DNA in the BioShell composter that matches that of Chairman Miaow," she said, "and therefore that of Dexter Coffin's cat. And the composter of Rao's building is just *full* of his DNA. Rao's. Much, much more than you'd expect. Also, some of his email and calendar data has been purged. I'm attempting to reconstruct—"

"Have it for the chargesheet," Ferron said. "I bet it'll show he had a meeting with Coffin the night Coffin vanished."

• • •

Dr. Rao lived not in an aptblock, even an upscale one, but in the Vertical City. Once Damini returned with the results of the warrants, Ferron got her paperwork in order for the visit. It was well after nightfall by the time she and Indrapramit, accompanied by Detective Morganti and four patrol officers, went to confront him.

They entered past shops and the vertical farm in the enormous tower's atrium. The air smelled green and healthy, and even at this hour of the night, people moved in steady streams toward the dining areas, across lush green carpets.

A lift bore the police officers effortlessly upward, revealing the lights of Bengaluru spread out below through a transparent exterior wall. Ferron looked at Indrapramit and pursed her lips. He raised his eyebrows in reply. *Conspicuous consumption.* But they couldn't very well hold it against Rao now.

They left Morganti and the patrol officers covering the exit and presented themselves at Dr. Rao's door.

"Open," Ferron said formally, presenting her warrant. "In the name of the law."

The door slid open, and Ferron and Indrapramit entered cautiously.

The flat's resident must have triggered the door remotely, because he sat at his ease on furniture set as a chaise. A grey cat with red ear-tips crouched by his knee, rubbing the side of its face against his trousers.

"New!" said the cat. "New people! Namaskar! It's almost time for tiffin."

"Dexter Coffin," Ferron said to the tall, thin man. "You are under arrest for the murder of Dr. Rao."

As they entered the lift and allowed it to carry them down the external wall of the Vertical City, Coffin standing in restraints between two of the patrol officers, Morganti said, "So. If I understand this properly, you—Coffin— actually *killed* Rao to assume his identity? Because you knew you were well and truly burned this time?"

Not even a flicker of his eyes indicated that he'd heard her.

Morganti sighed and turned her attention to Ferron. "What gave you the clue?"

"The scotophobin," Ferron said. Coffin's cat, in her new livery of gray and red, miaowed plaintively in a carrier. "He didn't have memory issues. He was using it to cram Rao's life story and eccentricities so he wouldn't trip himself up."

Morganti asked, "But why liquidate his assets? Why not take them with him?" She glanced over her shoulder. "Pardon me for speaking about you as if you were a statue, Dr. Fang. But you're doing such a good impression of one."

It was Indrapramit who gestured at the Vertical City rising at their backs. "Rao wasn't wanting for assets."

Ferron nodded. "Would you have believed he was dead if you couldn't find the money? Besides, if his debt—or some of it—was recovered, Honolulu would have less reason to keep looking for him."

"So it was a misdirect. Like the frame job around Dr. Nnebuogor and the table set for two . . . ?"

Her voice trailed off as a stark blue-white light cast knife-edged shadows across her face. Something blazed in the night sky, something as stark and brilliant as a dawning sun—but cold, as cold as light can be. As cold as a reflection in a mirror.

Morganti squinted and shaded her eyes from the shine. "Is that a *hydrogen bomb?*"

"If it was," Indrapramit said, "your eyes would be melting."

Coffin laughed, the first sound he'd made since he'd assented to understanding his rights. "It's a supernova."

He raised both wrists, bound together by the restraints, and pointed. "In the Andromeda galaxy. See how low it is to the horizon? We'll lose sight of it as soon as we're in the shadow of that tower."

"Al-Rahman," Ferron whispered. The lift wall was darkening to a smoky shade and she could now look directly at the light. Low to the horizon, as Coffin had said. So bright it seemed to be visible as a sphere.

"Not that star. It was stable. Maybe a nearby one," Coffin said. "Maybe they knew, and that's why they were so desperate to tell us they were out there."

"Could they have *survived* that?"

"Depends how close to Al-Rahman it was. The radiation—" Coffin shrugged in his restraints. "That's probably what killed them."

"God in Heaven," said Morganti.

Coffin cleared his throat. "Beautiful, isn't it?"

Ferron craned her head back as the point source of the incredible radiance slipped behind a neighboring building. There was no scatter glow: the rays of light from the nova were parallel, and the shadow they entered uncompromising, black as a pool of ink.

Until this moment, she would have had to slip a skin over her perceptions to point to the Andromeda galaxy in the sky. But now it seemed like the most important thing in the world that, two and a half million years away, somebody had shouted across the void before they died.

A strange elation filled her. *Everybody talking, and nobody hears a damned thing anyone—even themselves—has to say.*

"We're here," Ferron said to the ancient light that spilled across the sky and did not pierce the shadow into which she descended. As her colleagues turned and stared, she repeated the words like a mantra. "We're here too! And we heard you."

THE PHILOSOPHY OF SHIPS

CAROLINE M. YOACHIM

Kaimu dug his skis into the snow and forced himself onto the steeper slope along the edge of the run. Michelle was behind him, and there wasn't far to go. He was going to win.

A white-furred creature stirred at the sound of his approach. It rose up from the snow and stared, paralyzed, directly in his path.

The safety mechanism on his skis activated, but it was too late to turn. Instead, the skis treated the creature as though it was a ski jump. Kaimu landed, and the safeties shut off.

Several meters up the mountain, Michelle knelt in the snow. "You hit an Earther."

Impossible. Before he left the *Willflower*, the tourist board had assured him that the glacier-covered Canadian region wasn't populated. All the native Earthers were in a temperate band near the equator.

"*Hominid Class 304. Organic component . . . 100 percent.*" Michelle transmitted her initial assessment to the rest of her collective, pausing briefly upon the discovery that the creature had no upgrades. The rest of her transmission was a stream of numbers relating to the creature's condition. All Kaimu gleaned from the numbers was that the creature wasn't dead. Yet. Blood stained its shaggy white coat and seeped into the icy powder. Kaimu stepped off of his skis. Cold seeped through his skisuit and chilled his feet. He trudged up the hill, kicking his toes into the powder.

"Can you save it?" he asked.

"Twenty-eight percent. My training is neurosurgery, and I've never worked on anything 100 percent organic before." Michelle's gaze was locked on the two parallel gashes in the creature's torso, but most of her mind was elsewhere, searching for the knowledge she needed. To her, this was a problem, a challenge. He wondered if she was enjoying it.

Michelle turned away, and Kaimu stepped in for a better look at the injured Earther. Despite its blood-matted fur and diminutive stature, it was undeniably human. She, Kaimu realized from the gentle curve of her hips. *She* was undeniably human. Her fur was downy and short, more silver than white. The coarser, whiter fur that covered much of her body turned out to be clothing, cut from the skin of an animal. He shuddered.

"You're in my way." Michelle nudged him aside. She'd reprogrammed one of her skis to the smallest size, still unwieldy, but small enough to hold in one hand. She drew the sharp edge along the Earther's outer furs, cutting away the clothing. Unable to see, Kaimu extended sensory tendrils, tapping into Michelle's visuals and trying to grasp the severity of the injuries.

"Too distracting," Michelle informed him. She banished his consciousness into a memory cache.

In the memory, there are three consciousnesses in Michelle's body. Michelle, of course, and Jasmine, who isn't so bad. Elliot, however, Kaimu finds deeply disturbing. Not the man himself, but the idea that Michelle is part male. Or that another man is in his girlfriend's head. Kaimu tries to tangle himself only with Michelle, but the three are so intertwined he has no choice but to dissolve into all of them.

Kaimu recognizes the memory. He's on planetside leave on Nova Terra, and it's his first time visiting Michelle at work. She's been easing him into her life. It's a new experience for her, to share herself without drawing him into her collective. It's new for him, too.

Michelle reviews patient data files while she waits for him to arrive. All around her, Hospital617 buzzes with activity. In physical space, the hospital is a cavernous room. One floor, no walls. In headspace, there is more privacy, walls that give the illusion of each patient having a separate room. As part of the staff, Michelle doesn't bother uploading the headspace sensory inputs. Through her eyes, Kaimu can see the entire floor. Specialists of all sorts hover over their patients. Most of the work is upgrades—body reconstruction, routine anti-mortality treatments.

Neurosurgery team 8 to 27-12.

The woman in bed 27-12 is old. Not in the sense that Kaimu is old; his age comes from time dilation from his trips between the stars. Her skin is wrinkled and blotchy, and her hair has thinned so he can see the top of her scalp. She is frail, her body is giving out.

Kaimu sees himself weaving across the hospital floor. He feels his kiss on Michelle's cheek. Hears himself ask if she's busy. She tells him yes, but stay anyway. So he does.

She goes back to the woman. Elliot crowds his way to the foreground with patient information. Noelani Lai. A flood of datapackets swirl around the name: age, medical history, anything that might be relevant to selecting a treatment. Jasmine dilutes herself into the hospital archives, matching Elliot's patient data to other surgical cases. The mini-collective reconvenes and decides that the woman's body is inoperable. Insufficient regenerative capabilities. Instead, they will re-wire her organics to allow her consciousness to disengage itself. She can be installed into a new body later, if she so desires.

Michelle peels away layers of skin and cuts through Noelani's skull. The tissue beneath is predominantly organic, with traces of ancient wiring. More primitive than Kaimu. As a navigational officer, he's had to upgrade to interface with the *Willflower*.

Michelle blends with Jasmine and Elliot so thoroughly during the surgical procedure that Kaimu can't find Michelle at all. They become Jasmine/Elliot/Michelle. Jem. As the surgery progresses, the sight and smell of Noelani's organics become mildly nauseating. The SmartDust that sterilizes the air leaves behind odor-causing particles because sometimes a strange smell can serve as a diagnostic tool.

Kaimu is relieved when the operation is finished, and he can pick out strands of Michelle again. She doesn't bother to replace the slice of skull she removed, simply folds the skin back down over the wound.

Noelani floats out from her organics and into the vast interconnectivity beyond. Unused to such freedom, she loses cohesiveness, still existing, but commingled with the larger world. Jasmine observes, and notes the response as normal. Twenty-five percent of patients who are absorbed in this way eventually re-cohere. The remainder pursue a less individualized existence. Jem declares the operation a success.

Michelle—the realtime Michelle on the mountain—has shown him what she wants him to see, but now there is something he wants *her* to see. Awkwardly, since he isn't used to manhandling other minds, he takes control of the fractional portion of Michelle that led him here. He binds them to the hospital recording of a young woman. The woman is Noelani's granddaughter, Amy.

She hurries through the maze of hallways, filled with an overwhelming sense of worry. Not for Tutu, but for Mom. She remembers Tutu from her childhood, an energetic woman with long black hair who held her hand in Southside Park while they fed energy chips to the mechanical ducks. They'd gone every time Tutu came to visit, from the time she was two until the time Amy decided she was too old for ducks.

In the pre-op room, Mom is holding Tutu's hand. Mom's eyes are swollen and red, but dry. When she sees Amy, fresh tears roll down her face.

"Tutu," she says. "Tutu, wake up. Amy is here."

Amy puts her hand on Mom's shoulder, half a hug because Mom can't turn away from Tutu. "It's okay, Mom."

"She was awake. An hour ago," Mom says. She pushes gently against Tutu's shoulder. "Your granddaughter is here. Amy."

Amy takes Tutu's hand. It isn't the strong hand that she remembers from her childhood. The surgeons wouldn't fix her body; even Amy could see that Tutu was too old. They would save her by putting her into the collective, and she would be absorbed and lost. Amy can't bring herself to say her goodbyes out loud. The words would be too final, and her voice would fail her. Instead she squeezes Tutu's hand and thinks the word, *goodbye*.

Kaimu withdraws, taking Michelle with him. They drift back to themselves, and the warm hospital air shifts to the biting chill of the mountain. He has to pause and collect himself. Michelle doesn't acknowledge his return.

"That memory meant nothing to you," Kaimu said, disappointed.

"You used my access rights to get a hospital recording of a private individual. Those are only supposed to be used in the event of a malpractice suit." She tried to sound stern, but Kaimu could tell that she was more amused than angry. "Besides, I've seen it before. Outdated minds thinking outdated thoughts."

"Human minds thinking human thoughts," he snapped back.

"I never said the minds weren't human." Her voice was quiet, sad. As though he had missed something, had failed some test. Her sadness diffused his anger, and he let the argument lapse into silence.

The Earther's eyes were open, pale blue like the color of the sky diluted with white snow. They reminded him of his son, Kenji, before he disconnected from his body. He'd been six years old. Kaimu had married and divorced a few women in the centuries since, but he never fathered any more children. Michelle was right, he was outdated. He shook the memory away. The Earther's eyes didn't move except to blink. Her right eye was clouded over by cataracts.

While his mind had been locked away in the past, Michelle had finished work on the lower gash. Now she reprogrammed bits of her skisuit to serve as bandages. She pulled strips of suit from the back of her neck. Kaimu supposed that the thick curls of her hair would block the icy air.

Michelle buried her hand wrist-deep into the upper gash. There shouldn't have been room, the Earther's torso was small. She must have pushed all the organs aside. Orbs of blood dotted the blue-green fabric of her skisuit. The fabric refused to absorb the stain, so the globules floated like crimson buoys on a tropical sea. So much blood.

"Any updates?" he asked. She wasn't transmitting assessments anymore. Maybe more of the collective was in her head now, eliminating the need to broadcast.

"You're not helping," Michelle responded.

• • •

This time, Michelle sends him to a memory in his own perspective. He recognizes where he is from the functionality of the space. Every inch is utilized, cozy and enclosed, but not cramped. He is cradled in the mind of the *Willflower*, his ship. He's far more comfortable here than he was in the hospital.

At least, he is until he realizes *when* she's sent him.

He is in the aft lounge. A group of passengers is gathered around the bar, downing colorful fruit-and-alcohol concoctions, killing time until they have to get into the stasis tanks. There's an iridescent blue shiproach on the counter, and everyone places wagers on which dimensional coordinates it will take off from. The shiproach scurries about, seemingly uninterested in flight.

Off to Kaimu's right, a section of the wall moves. His brain adjusts to recognize Dahnjii, his least favorite of Michelle's collective. Dahnjii is a collective within the collective, like Jasmine/Elliot/Michelle but with seven minds mashed together. He is trendy and arrogant. His genes are spliced with chameleon or octopus or some other long extinct creature so that he can change color at will. He's been hiding against the wall, and now he ripples with yellow stripes. Aggressive. Nearly all the members of Michelle's collective seek novelty, but Dahnjii goes out of his way to make other people squirm so he can study their reactions.

"Hey precious," he sneers, "want to join my collective?"

Kaimu doesn't know whether he means his mini-collective, or the collective he shares with Michelle. He wants nothing to do with Dahnjii, regardless. "No, thanks."

"You realize how dumb it is, to be with Michelle, and not the rest of us," Dahnjii continues. He's been in the med-ward for several days, and Kaimu isn't thrilled that he's back in circulation. "Like loving an arm."

"An arm isn't conscious, it's not the same."

"Fine, like loving an arm, and the little blob of brain that controls it." Dahnjii turns his head. The left side of his skull is gone, replaced by a clear dome. The surgery he's had done is a brainshaping, purely cosmetic. Instead of the normal folds of gray cortex, his brain has been molded into the form of a dragon.

"I'm getting it colorized tomorrow," he says. Then he lifts the dome that covers the brain. "Want to lick it?"

Kaimu backs away, as though the exposed tissue will leap out and attack him. Dahnjii laughs, sticks his hand into his skull, and pets the dragon with one finger. The lounge has gone silent as all the drinkers admire the unusual design of Dahnjii's brain. Novelty. The shiproach takes off, and Kaimu is the only one to notice.

"Cover that up. Nobody wants to see your little lizard," Kaimu says.

Dahnjii's fist smashes through his face. It is a strange sensation, almost painless despite the sickening crunch as splinters of bone are pushed into his brain.

The safety protocols of the ship lock down his mind. There are several seconds of blackness. The Michelle fragment skips him forward through time.

He is in his cabin. A few paces away, Michelle studies his most prized possession, a bonsai tree. It is centuries old, with roots that curl around a smooth gray stone before disappearing into a shallow layer of soil. The bonsai comes from a simpler time.

"If you lived in that time, you'd be dead by now. Or horribly disfigured." Michelle is in his head, monitoring him. He resents the intrusion.

"Okay, okay, I'm out," she says, "I had to make sure the reconstructive surgery was successful."

"That was barbaric," he says. "Bastard could've killed me."

"There's a copy of your consciousness stored in the *Willflower*, so even if the body had been inoperable, I could have generated another manifestation, started from scratch. It would've taken longer, but death wasn't really an issue. Dahnjii doesn't like you, but he's not a monster."

"After what he did to me? How much of my brain did you have to regenerate? How much of my face?" He's practically yelling at Michelle, despite the fact that she probably spent the last hour or more putting him back together.

Michelle transmits the surgical data. She's regrown seven percent of his cortex, mostly frontal lobe, and reconstructed his nose and his left eye. This isn't the first time Kaimu has been badly injured. Over the years, almost 45 percent of his brain and body have been replaced. He doesn't feel any different.

"If you have a ship," he says, "and you replace it, one board at a time, and all the while it sails—is it still the same ship?"

The problem is from ancient philosophy, and it takes her a moment to find the appropriate reference. "Sorites. But the ships weren't sentient then. It wouldn't matter."

"It matters to me. Whether it's the same ship, and whether this," he waves his arms up and down his torso, "is the same body, the same brain."

"This attachment to your organics, it's pretty neurotic. You know that, right?" Michelle puts her hand on his cheek. She means it in a caring way, not as an insult. "And while I don't like what Dahnjii did, it's not as vicious as you make it out to be. Not to him. Not really to me either, except that I know how much it bothers you. Dahnjii's just upset that we're here on the *Willflower*, in bodies for the whole trip, rather than going on the *Roving Never* and getting new bodies when we arrive at Earth. He almost left the collective over it. So now he's frustrated and bored—"

"So it's okay that he smashed my face and sent bone shards into my brain. Because he was bored." How could Michelle refuse to understand?

"No. It's okay because it's just organics. Haven't you ever smashed your fist into the ship's interface console when you were frustrated?"

"That hurts my fist and doesn't damage the ship," he counters. "But yes."

"Have you asked the ship how she feels about it?"

"She's a ship."

"And you think *we're* the barbarian."

Something happens, not in the memory, but in realtime. Kaimu can sense it through Michelle's fragment. He tries to go back, but Michelle resists.

Kaimu is certain that something is wrong. Michelle is stalling him, keeping him off the mountain. He flings his consciousness forward through the memory cache, against her resistance. She lets him reach the point where they are preparing to ski, early that morning in their temp-lodge at the top of the mountain. The lodge is programmed with red walls adorned with replicas of ancient Japanese art—delicate cherry branches in black and pink, stylized blue tidal waves, bold black characters done in flawless calligraphy.

Michelle doesn't care whose perspective he takes for this memory so he settles into his own mind. He sits on a bamboo floor mat and yanks on the legs of his skisuit, trying to push his toes up into the stiff boot bottoms.

"That's ridiculously antique," Michelle says, "And I have plenty of paint. You're sure you don't want some?"

Michelle is fresh out of the shower, naked and holding a jar of N-body Paint. Her skin is pink from the heat of the shower. The color of cherry blossoms. Sandy-brown freckles splash across her chest, trailing down her arms and up her neck. He loves it when she wears the freckles.

"Well?" she asks, holding up the paint.

"No, I'll wear this," he points to the suit. Uncomfortable as it is, at least his private parts won't flap around while he skis.

"Suit yourself," she says.

Michelle orders up a cushion, and sprawls herself across the squishy blob that emerges from the floor. Comfortable, she opens her jar of paint, and applies it to her legs with smooth strokes. Kaimu halfheartedly tugs on his suit, but his attention is focused on Michelle.

She's programmed the nano-fiber paint to a shifting pattern of blues and greens—sunlight filtering through ocean waves. She paints her way down her thigh, coating the indented curve on the back of her knee, the swell of her calf. By the time she gets to her foot, he's dropped his skisuit, and simply stares at her, making no effort to dress himself. She knows he's watching, and takes her time, painting the ticklish arch at the bottom of her foot, then swirling paint around each toe.

He takes the bait and stands up, his legs encased in the suit to mid-thigh, but the rest of the suit dangling down.

"You'll get pretty cold, skiing like that."

"You'll get pretty ravished, teasing me like that."

"I'll get pretty ravished *after skiing*, you mean." She's finished her legs now, and starts painting her way up from her hip. "I'm already painted from the waist down."

"I can think of a few ways to get that stuff off."

"But you won't," she says, "Because you're a gentleman, and I enjoy the anticipation."

"You enjoy teasing me all day."

She laughs. "That too."

Kaimu watches himself suit up. The Michelle fragment apologizes, but doesn't explain why.

Kaimu flies down the slopes, skis skimming over fluffy snow. Michelle is behind him, taunting him to go faster. Adrenaline pumps through his system and mingles with an urge to impress her. He gives up on turning and points his skis straight down, letting the pines whiz by in the periphery of his vision. Single trunks blur together, their individuality stolen by his speed. He is the wind in air that stands still. Tendrils of his mind reach backwards for Michelle, to share with her this beautiful chaos of falling.

The green wall of treeness to his right closes in, swerves in front of him. Fear replaces excitement and he cannot turn. A single tree separates itself from the others, unmoving despite his speed because it stands directly before him. It looms over him.

Against his volition, his feet shoot upwards and sideways, twisting his body inside the skisuit. He hears the smack of skis on wood. A glancing blow, the safeties on the skis automatically avoiding a harmful collision. His skis reconnect with the snow, back under his control, slowed now, and traveling at an angle to the slope, redirected by the tree. Michelle lets out a whoop behind him, as though he'd skidded off the tree on purpose, a trick to impress her. He slows to a stop, and turns in time to see her mimic his trick, intentionally and far more gracefully. She stops on the hillside above him, spraying him with snow in the process.

"Good trick," she says, smiling.

He relaxes after that, knowing that the skis can rescue him from his own ineptitude. In short order, they reach the bottom of the mountain and cuddle together in the a-grav chute that propels them back to the top. From above the tree line, he can see mountains in every direction, monuments of ice and rock reaching up to the sky. "Down the other side this time?"

"Race you, meet up at that rock." she says, and dumps the coordinates to his navigation system.

"You win."

"I'll give you a head start."

"Okay, I—"

"Go!" she gives him a little shove, sending him over a ledge and onto a steep mogul-covered slope. The skis recognize his inability to deal with the bumpy conditions, and swerve through the bumps. He gets the hang of it, and before it flattens out the safeties turn off again.

"*Now me!*" Michelle is too far away for speech, so she transmits. There's no way he'll win with such a tiny lead.

Well, he can at least make it challenging. He bends his knees, tucks down to decrease his wind resistance. A smattering of trees dot the slope as he gets lower, then denser trees close in around the run. He watches them carefully this time, scanning the slope ahead of him so he'll have plenty of time to turn. Avoid the green. Michelle hasn't passed him yet. He risks a glance, and she's farther back than he expected. If he can avoid plowing into the trees, he might even win.

The run curves, and Kaimu turns to follow it. He can see the rock in the distance, and Michelle is still behind him.

Something moves.

He'd have seen it sooner, but it was white and he was watching for green. It's running out across his path. The skis slash sideways.

The safeties on his skis are old, and to avoid overloading them, he'd simplified the obstacle-detection by specifying that he and Michelle were the only humans on the slope. His breath sticks in his chest as the blades tear through fur and flesh. It is worse in memory than in realtime.

Finally, Michelle releases him.

The Earther was dead. Her unfocussed eyes reflected the empty sky. Kaimu's freshly relived memories mingled with the realities of the present.

"You should have let me stay," he told Michelle.

"You wouldn't have understood what I was doing," she said. "You don't understand what's happening now. Look."

She pointed to the Earther, to the wound that stretched across her chest. Several ribs had been broken away. Her heart and lungs were rearranged, shoved off to the sides to gain access to her spinal cord. Blood pooled in the cavity. Michelle had never tried to save the Earther's body. All along, she'd been working her way down to the spinal cord. Trying to pry the consciousness free before the body died.

"She's completely organic. Why would you even try?" he asked.

"You started organic," she said. "All it takes is time. Time to map the pattern of neuronal connections, time to record the firing patterns."

"But we're on a mountainside, you used a ski to cut her open for godsakes," he said. "You should have operated on her body. How could you possibly record everything you needed to save her consciousness? And even if you could, she'd never make it on the network."

Michelle held up her arm. There was a cut on her wrist. "I reprogrammed some of my peripherals to do the recordings."

He needed to see what she had done, to understand, but she was blocking him out. "It's my fault, not yours," he said. "I'm sure you did all you could."

She still refused to let him in. He'd never experienced this before. Sometimes he had blocked her out, when he wanted privacy, but she had always been open. He missed the closeness of being tangled with her mind. She must have felt this same frustration, when he had closed himself off. From now on, he'd try to be more open to her, less stubborn.

"You don't have to hide from me," he said.

"It worked."

"You put her on the network? And she adapted to that?"

"No." She put her hand on his shoulder. He could barely feel her touch through the stiff fabric of his skisuit. "I started out that way, but I learned something from you. To me, a body is nothing, but to you, or to her. . .I'm sorry."

"You're sorry," he echoed. Then he realized what she'd done. "She's there. With you."

Michelle nodded. "I'm almost done teaching her my body. Her body."

"What about you?"

"I—" she started, but then paused. "We. We are going to merge more fully. Distributed existence was interesting, but it's time for something else now."

"You're leaving me."

"I couldn't bring you, even if you wanted to come," she said. "I'll miss you, even with your strange ideas and your locked off mind. But you aren't ready. And that's okay. Besides, she'll need you."

"But we . . . Stay a little longer."

"And what about her? Leave her trapped in a body she doesn't control?"

He took her hand from his shoulder and brushed her fingertips against his lips. He had always known that she was beyond him, but instead of trying to grow, he tried to force her to come to his level.

Michelle withdrew. He sensed her in the network, mingling with others, dissolving and changing. He felt her brush against the edge of his consciousness, briefly, a good-bye kiss to his mind. Then she was gone.

The Earther stood before him, not moving. The body was unchanged. Michelle's stunning red hair, her long legs, the exposed patch of neck where she'd peeled away her N-body paint. There were freckles there, hiding on the pale skin beneath a curtain of curls. But the woman that stood before him didn't carry herself with Michelle's confidence. Her posture was bad, and her eyes darted in all directions. He was still holding her hand. He let go.

Kaimu waited. He didn't know what to do, whether he should say something. Whether she would understand it if he did.

The Earther looked up at him.

"I am Beyla," she said.

That was all. Nothing that came later was relevant; the jury collective didn't need to see it. Kaimu wouldn't have to relive it, though what came after was less painful than the accident itself and his final moments with Michelle. The jury deliberated for several seconds, unusually long, but for a mind as slow as Kaimu's it wasn't even long enough to worry.

No penalties on any of the charges. The tourist board acknowledges the non-death of the Earther Beyla. You are free to go.

Beyla sat beside him and held his hand, blissfully unaware of most of the proceedings. Out of the corner of his eye, she still reminded him of Michelle, but Beyla wore the body differently. No longer fearful, as she was those first moments on the mountainside, but solemn, because the body was a gift. Was she the same person she was before? Hers was a ship replaced, not board by board, but all at once.

Kaimu sometimes searched for traces of Michelle, but she was gone. She was not a ship at all; she was the ocean, deep and vast, with a form forever changing in waves of green and blue.

THE KEATS VARIATION

K.M. FEREBEE

There was a ghost in the hospital. They had told Keats this. "They" were the other boys, the older boys, who lived like him in the apprentices' dormitory attached to the hospital, but higher up, on the second floor. Bish, Taylor, and Barrie: larger boys who came and went clattering loudly on the dormitory's wooden stairs. They had served, each of them, as an apprentice under the surgeons for two years already, and told stories of malformed infants, amputations, massive wounds that emptied all a man's blood from his body across the floor, so that you must needs wade through it to reach the exit and it lingered, black and sticky, on your boots and under your fingernails. You would not believe, Barrie said, you would not believe how much blood is in a man.

Keats was quite ready to believe it. He believed most things at this time. He had come, at the credulous age of thirteen, from the country, where men did not tell so many lies, or they were a different sort of lies, not fat distended fancies like soap bubbles that rise from a washer-man's wand and swell and swell the expanse of their shining hollow bodies till they burst and you are left with just a thin wet sour residue. Country lies were smaller, harder. They had substance, which you sometimes had to fight to figure. They might be a truth about some other thing. A fairy man in the lane taught the miller's wife to dig, she said, for buried treasure, which she found on his instruction but which come the morning was not lapis and diamonds but a felt hat filled with mouldy leaves. Mrs. Hayscomb saw the Devil out walking; she said he wore the fine black coat of a merchant and smiled as he passed and had a white crown round his head like a saint. Keats had seen the mouldy leaves; he had touched and smelt them. They had left damp flecks on his fingers. They had reminded him of well water pulled from far, far down in the clammy pit where moss fronded wild in silent darkness and, one suspected, old things lived. Those leaves had brought the miller luck. His wife had cooked them in a pot-au-feu and eaten them and given birth to three children, white-skinned infants with flat solemn eyes like coins who never cried. Everyone said in

Eastsake that these were fairy children and the fairies would be back for them; and that the miller, if he'd drive a hard bargain, could do well out of it. He could get a cartload of gold, or a saucepan that never emptied, or a shuttle that threw itself through the shed, to do the weaving. There was no limit to what he might expect, in exchange for these children. So there had been treasure in the leaves; that was a truth.

And as for the Devil—Keats himself had seen him, or something of his nature, or not quite seen. That had been in the purple part of the night, in summer, when heat bowed the high barley in submission and the earth was an ember into the evening, when the glassy sun had gone and night birds called throughout the cooler air. Keats, coming homewards, had cut through the barley. The stalks were higher than him. They had a sweet white woody scent. The long leaves had a language, snaps and whispers, over his head. He held his hands crossed on his chest and whispered a song, a song about the Apostles, a song to summon angels to your bedside. He was careful to tread only where he knew the path. But he took not care enough, for soon he was lost and he heard a footfall behind him. A step. A stop. A hard dry cough. A hesitation. His heart crawled and stuttered. He did not turn to see. Slowly, slowly, he walked forwards. The listless barley shed long shadows. The shallow dark seemed living. In back of him the sound again commenced. Something striking earth, a slow and laboured step, like one leg dragging. A ragged, monstrous breath. He ran, then; his nerve broke, and he raced ahead. Still he could hear it following him: its long strides, its effortful gasps, the air in its unseen lungs rattling, till he was free of the fields and could see the lamplight leaching towards him from his aunt's front window. He reached it. This was the radius of his safety. When he told the story to his aunt, she did not disbelieve him. So now you've seen the Devil, is what she said. As the days progressed he came to accept this explanation. His unknowingness diminished. To his school friends he said, I saw the Devil. The statement assumed a quality of truth: of definition, which, after all, was truth's right hand.

So the idea of how much blood was in a man did not overmuch stretch his imagination. Nor the stories Bish told about babies born back to front, or with fins instead of hands, or the woman whom, he said, they had cut open—he clearly relished the cutting-open; when he reached this part of the story his eyes lit up and he rubbed, one against the other, his thin white hand—only to see that there was inside of her a number of strange objects: Roman coins, and the stump of a candle, and a soapstone figure in the shape of a lamb. They had sewed her up, but she died later—not from sepsis, but from starvation. She would not eat meat, milk, potatoes; she could not be sustained. She wanted only to swallow down these certain odd antiques. But the doctors would not let her. Her wanting killed her, Bish said; she wanted it to end.

It? Keats asked.

Bish spread his hands, bored, expressive. It, all of this.

I don't understand.

No, you wouldn't yet, you're just a squeaker. A little country rat of a thing.

Barrie joined in. Hallo, country rat. Said your catechism yet today?

Catechism sounded like cachexia, the kind of slow sickness that Bish's woman had died of, the wasting disease. Keats practiced his catechism daily. He had promised his aunt when he left Eastsake. Besides, he had a fear of the Devil. You had to do certain things, say certain things, and this kept the Devil at a distance. A distance greater than six or seven paces, a distance that the saints maintained, so that you would not hear the Devil's hacking cough or heavy footsteps, so that you would not hear him drag his leg.

I don't know why you make fun, Keats said.

No, Bish said, you wouldn't yet. Squeaker.

And so on and on this game went.

There were no other apprentices of Keats's age; he was quite the youngest. It amused Bish and Barrie and Taylor to call him names, to make fun of his country faith, his country way of speaking, to keep sometimes in the dark at the side of a hallway, at night when he had thought them all in bed, and reach out suddenly to grab hold of his wrist or a fistful of hair at the side of his head. This they called a mousetrap. I've caught a country mouse, Barrie had said triumphantly, the first time it happened; a country mouse in a trap. The coinage had stayed.

Keats had learned to keep still, not to fight his capture, though the shock of it turned his heart to a struck church bell. The leaden echoes of its reverberating could be felt throughout his tired body. His response was to clench the muscles round his mouth and think hard about large bright things. He pictured saints the size of houses, huge towering men who shed a soft, tawny light from their hands and robes and heads. He pictured angels, white entities without faces who, suspended on their opalescent feathers, hung in the cramped space of the hallway. And when he had scampered off, often after an indifferent beating, and was safe inside his room again, he would say the song he had been taught in the country, asking these saints and angels to stand round his bed. He never saw them, but sometimes he suspected their presence: when he woke up warm on winter mornings and saw scratch-marks on the floorboards where perhaps some saint's hard shoe or shepherd's crook had scuffed them. The hospital to which the dormitory was attached was called after a saint with such a crook: St. Crix, who had been martyred among the fields by Roman soldiers. The method of his martyrdom had not been told to Keats; it was thought to be too gruesome. He dreamed of the saint naked, with his stomach stitched, like a surgical patient. The stitches were neat and perfect, done in black thread. St. Crix smiled at Keats and raised his curving staff. He said, Little lamb, I will shepherd thee when thou art dead and buried. What about now? Keats wanted to ask, but he could not speak in his dreams. He was too transfixed, always, his tongue silenced by dread.

There had long been some legends, part of the city of Ludminster's general lore, of St. Crix lingering in the halls of his hospital: to heal the sick, to dispense mercy, to direct the souls of the dead. But the ghost about which Bish, Barrie, and Taylor had begun to tell stories was an innovation. Keats perceived that it might not exist. It was the sort of thing that these other boys might do—seize upon his fear of the darkness and invent for it a bespoke creature, a demon cut whole-cloth to suit. He did not like to think so badly of them, despite their lies; and anyways he believed that there was in all people something tending to be true. There was this magnetic force; you could not resist it; it warped your stories northwards, in spite of you. So he listened at night, when they were all gathered in the dormitory kitchen round a candle, as Barrie and Taylor and Bish related tales that grew ever more extravagant. Barrie, a solidly built boy with auburn ringlets and an India-ink gaze, cupped his hands over the candle. Light leaked through his fingers from the flame, casting seaside shadows on the wall, wandering underwater shapes.

Theatrically he said, In the dead of winter, there rode into St. Crix Hospital—

Rode? Keats questioned.

Yes, it was in those days.

All right.

There rode a soldier. His horse was black; it smoked with hellfire.

A bit rich, Bish muttered under his breath.

I heard that. Shut it.

I was only saying.

Barrie cleared his throat. It smoked with hellfire, he said again. Its rider slid to the snowy ground. His blood turned it red. Blood-red, from the gash in his belly where a bayonet had been. The soldier's guts spilled out—

But they didn't really, Keats reasoned. Or else he'd be dead.

He held them in. Like, thus. Barrie demonstrated.

Anyway, Bish said, he'll be dead in a minute. Wait and see. That's the best bit.

Barrie let Bish tell that part of the story. Spectacular deaths were Bish's talent. Pale hair sparked by firelight, light eyes gleaming, he leant in. By this point in the tale, the soldier had reached the operating theatre, where a noble surgeon tried to save him. And then, Bish said, he saw the soldier's immortal soul rise from his body. It was a bloody thing, all blackened and hideous, naught but bones, no flesh on it.

No flesh on it, Taylor echoed. He was not, of the three, the most inventive. But he embellished the description: And gaping sockets, where the eyes had been.

Staring out, Bish said, towards their damnation. Bish was alive with pleasure at the image; his small lithe body shuddered. He said, The surgeon's sight grew dim! He thought he would faint, for standing before him was— *death!* The darkest angel! A horrible figure, scythed and grim!

Barrie added, And behind him followed all of hell. An awful scene. Seas made of the bloody hearts of men, still beating. Heaps of bones that writhed and clattered, the howling of the damned calling out—

What did they call out? Keats asked, curious.

They called out: James Keats, we're coming for you . . . Barrie drew out the vowels, darkened his voice to a wail, grabbed at Keats's shoulders. Keats, ineffectual, tried to shove him off.

That is not what they called out. I was not there. That is not true.

Oh, well, they might have done. Had you been there.

Bish and Taylor were laughing soundlessly behind their hands. Keats was angry, but he did not show it. He said, So what happened then?

Barrie shrugged. The soldier would not go with him. The soldier said, Death, I will not go with you, to get my heart sucked out in hell, to suffer forever and ever in pain and blood and so forth, in endless burning. Instead I will stay and give a taste of hell to mortal souls who remain, that they might fear your eternal horrible approach and repent of their sins.

How about you, Keats? Taylor asked, grabbing onto Keats's arm and twisting it round so that it hurt. Do you repent your sins? You will; you will repent them.

That story ended with Keats's hand held above the candle till tears streamed down his face and the skin on his palm swelled into white hilltops: a new, painful, penitent landscape. He choked out sin, some real and some imagined, writhing like a hooked fish while Barrie said, No, I think he is a sinner, I think that he has further sins.

Keats confessed that he hated God, that he had impure thoughts about women and about men, that he disbelieved in the Devil and in hell, that he had often wished their tutor—Dr. Haylebury—to damnation, that he thought wickedly of others as well.

Bish said, This is what hell is like, now he will believe in hell.

It was unfair, Keats reflected later, bitterly, for almost certainly they did not believe in hell; not a one of them did. They thought it a source of fun. They laughed at him for saying prayers, for practising his catechism; they thought him primitive. They had irreligious convictions. They were not afraid of the dark. They did not experience the world as he did. He lay in the dark, in bed, and fingered his forming blisters. They had a wormy feel to them. Morbid flesh, like maggots under his skin. He did not mind the pain; it was the weakness that turned to white worms and gnawed at him. When he pierced the blisters with a pain, weak water welled out. It turned his stomach. He thought, From now, I will never be weak again.

And to the Devil in the darkness, he recanted his confession. He whispered, I do believe in him. Not daring to speak directly to the Devil, and risk his gravel cough, his livid, unseen stare. He did not want to believe, but there it was: the thing he clung to, this small dark truth, the reality.

During lectures he considered the ghost. It would not be a soldier; that much he knew. Barrie and Bish favoured soldiers for their stories. They invented wars for the Continent, conflicts, bloody and endless, from which no hale man withdrew. Their heroes and ghosts were always horribly maimed, most often by bayonet thrusts—though sometimes blackened by gunpowder, from musket fire, for a change. But Keats thought, Perhaps a knight. A knight from ancient times, a knight in armour like a carapace that creaked and rattled. A very sad knight, ponderous and solemn, who went about the corridors in tears. Keats could see him: sighing in the light from the yellowed windows that lined the lecture hall, dust congregating in curious motes about his broadsword's hilt and blade. The knight had white hair, which Keats had not expected. He wore no helmet. He had a young, elfin face.

After the lecture had finished and the last students had departed, taking their anatomical notes, their sketches, their tenuous understandings of skeletal structure and phthisic symptoms, Keats crept back into the hall. The knight still lingered. Like a night watchman he held his posture, sorrowful and alert, nobly standing.

Hello, Keats said. I wondered how you did.

The knight did not turn his eyes to Keats, but rather lowered them. Ah, woe and alas, he said. Ah, woe the day.

Keats was taken aback by this gloomy assessment. Following narrowly on it he realized, however, a number of things: for instance, that the knight's armour must be heavy, which accounted for a part of his poor temper, and, too, that he was, after all, dead. The wound that had caused his death could not be seen, but blood pooled at his feet, dripping out from under the greaves of his armour in a slow black viscous seep. What is it that's wrong with you? Keats asked.

The knight looked at him piteously. He tried to raise an armoured hand, but stopped and dropped it, coughing. Blood came from his mouth and stained his lips. He could not speak. Keats offered him a handkerchief. The knight held it to his mouth. His eyes mouthed mute gratitude. All at once the truth came to Keats.

You've got a terrible wound, he said. It can't be healed. No one knows what to do. That's why you're a ghost; you were a great knight, but a sinner in life and so you were afflicted. Now you haunt the hospital because you are waiting for a surgeon who can heal you.

The knight bent his head. He said, Ah, woe the day. He handed the handkerchief back to Keats. Arterial blood was on it, the brightest shade of red.

Keats said, I am a surgeon. Well, a surgeon's apprentice. Someday I shall be a surgeon. I can change a dressing, and mix a compound. I can say when a man is dead. Perhaps I can help.

Despite this declaration, he was not quite sure what to do. He removed the knight's armour piece by piece, stacking it in a corner carefully. It was heavy, as he had suspected: made of iron plate, and faintly tarnished. It felt hot, as though the knights' body still held some incalescence, as though the cold of the grave were incomplete and some memory of fever had got through. When he reached the knight's under-linen he could smell the stench of the grave, a green and efflorescent smell like water stagnating, and see the stains that hinted at decay. He said, I do not know that I can fix this. But he placed his hands on the knight's abdomen anyway. He probed for a deep gash or some contusion. He knew how to sink the swelling of the latter, and sew the former up with careful stitches. But the source of the knight's suffering remained at bay.

At last he sat back on his heels and said in frustration, I can't find a wound. And your heart does not beat, anyway, so how is it that you are bleeding?

The knight directed at him a steady gaze. His eyes were limpid, like marbles, light grey. He lifted his hand and closed it around Keats's. Keats felt the shock of contact: his own little hand subsumed by the lack of heat, the dead cold of the grave. He thought, Perhaps his armour is heated by hellfire. Then was ashamed of the thought, and afraid. The knight's fingers locked around his wrist, icy, starved, insistent. Keats smelled his foul breath. The fragrance of rot, of cease. He saw what it was the knight desired, but he would not give it. He wrenched his hand out of that grasp. He pulled away.

You would eat my soul out, he said. You do not want a surgeon. The hurt you have no surgeon can assuage. You want to live, and I can understand it. But if you took my soul, I would die in despair. The Devil would have me.

The knight's mouth moved. Keats leant forward, to hear him speak. But he merely coughed, misting the air with his arterial breath. Keats wiped the red from the knight's white lips.

I'm sorry, he said. I will not give my soul away. If you come back tomorrow I will make you a cup of tea, though, for the cough, and tell you a story.

This was clearly not sufficient. The knight closed his eyes in dismay. His face grew slack and lost; an aura of sorrow came off him. It was tangible, that aura. It had a dank smell. It made Keats nauseated and homesick, with the sharp bitter homesickness that was his hardest pain. He tasted at the back of his throat the air of Eastsake: its raw pollen; its ripened grain; the rays of sun that skimmed the river, fomenting dark weeds down in its shallow waters; the light that shocked a rich hot life from orchard branch and undersoil, from loam and summer tree.

He wrapped his arms around himself. He said miserably, I'm sorry. I understand. I would like to. Can we not be friends anyway?

He had thought that the knight might cease his grieving and be a companion. But the doors to the lecture hall burst open; laughing, Barrie and Bish came in. They had been looking for him; Bish said, Oh, run tell Taylor we've found the country mouse at last, we've mousetrapped him.

Keats felt trapped indeed. He glanced over his shoulder. The knight had gone: his body and armour, as though he had never been. The faint scent of brimstone remained, and something sweeter, stronger—a thicket of jasmine, growing on the wall beside the window. Colourless flowers tart and star-shaped amid flat leaves. The odour was everywhere. He inhaled, and felt lonely. Bish grabbed his arm. What's this, what've you been up to in here?

He looked scared, Bish: his face imprinted with astonishment. As though he thought Keats might have made the flowers on purpose, to impose fear.

Talking to the ghost, Keats said.

I suppose you think you're funny.

No. He did not feel funny. He was tired; he could not comprehend why Bish punched him in the stomach upon hearing him say this. He doubled over. He pictured himself safe, curled in a tiny knot upon his bed, like a leaf that had not budded. Dense and hidden, its forms obscure still, its structure still unwrit.

In the weeks that followed, he went back to his studies. He did not see the knight again, and he was glad. Exams were approaching; he was required to pass them if he wished his apprenticeship to continue, if he were to be awarded qualifications. He bent over his books. The bad light strained his eyes. He learned to palpate the vital parts to determine liver or kidney size and function; he looked at diagrams of dead lungs, showing where phthisis had ravened them. With his eyes closed he could draw the human body, stripped down to skeleton or muscle, reduced to what anatomy he knew. This much he understood about that body: what made it up, what composed it. He looked at his own fist clenched about the pen as he drew. It seemed very small, full of frailty. He could feel the flat scars of blisters lining his hand.

Sometimes at night, when he was sat alone by lamplight, he would see a shadow in the corner start to stretch its arms and legs. Or a casement clatter open and let enter the unpleasant wind, wet and urban, one-note, nosing the hair at the back of his head. Fear stuck its needles in him then. He was happy when Barrie, Bish, or Taylor found him, so that he had something to flee from. And when he fled and still they found him, he thought, But while they are here, nothing else will be here; nothing else will get in.

It was not the ghost he was afraid of. It was the other things, the large and small incidents that started to trouble him. For instance: Barrie bought a hand off one of the resurrection men who slunk about the hospital's back doorway, selling corpses. Whole corpses, three days from the grave, ran sixty pounds each—quite costly, on a surgeon's salary—but you could buy them piecemeal, as students did, to practice your dissection. Barrie had bought his hand for a prank. He put it into Keats's bedclothes in the evening, tucked up under the flat folds of the duvet. So that Keats, climbing into bed, later found it: the bone protruding slightly from the wrist, the flesh plastic and sickening. He picket it, barely placating his nausea, from the sheet by one of its dead fingers, and flung it doorwards as the other boys burst in.

Did it touch you, Keatsie? Did it feel you up?

You stink now, you smell of the dead.

Barrie brought the hand back to the bed, waggling its white fingers. Ooh, it's come for you Keats. It's come to haunt you. That's what happens when you talk to dead men.

I bet you're scared, Bish said. Look at him, he is, he's petrified. Like a little trembling mouse, a country infant.

I'm not scared, Keats said.

The other boys were laughing, and so did not hear him. Look at him! He thought a dead man had come to get him! I shouldn't wonder if he wet his bed.

I'm not scared, he said again.

This time Barrie took notice. No, you're not, are you, he said. He looked at Keats from up to down, from side to side, considering. Keats understood that what he had said had been an error, that he should have feigned being frightened, that this would in some way have soured the game. He stood with a sinking feeling and saw Barrie toss the flaccid hand from fist to fist like a juggler's object, jaunty and sharp, like a sword that would pierce your skin.

I am rather scared, Keats said. Now I think of it.

Hold him down, Barrie told Taylor and Bish.

They did as they were told. They pinned him to the bed, kneeling upon his shoulders with their hard patellas digging into him. Keats twisted the tendons of his arms. He struggled. He did not want the dead hand touching him. But Barrie brought it close, brushing Keats's face with its fingers. Keats closed his eyes. A smooth cool nail traced his lip. He thought, I will not be sick, I will not give them the satisfaction.

Do you know how St. Crix was martyred? Barrie asked.

I do, Bish said.

Quiet, Bish.

The Roman soldiers ate him.

To think that we still study Classics, Taylor said with a smirk. Civilisation.

They cut him up, all into little pieces, because he would not give his sheep to them. We're told there is a Christian message. I think he must have tasted good. The Romans knew what they were about. What do you think, Bish?

Bish said, Filthy savages. Not like Englishmen.

Very educated, is our Bish. But I meant about eating saints and so forth, eating dead men.

Oh. Bish's face expressed revulsion. Really? Even for you, that is excessive.

Keats could smell Barrie's breath, hot and excited. He thought, He is not bluffing; he will do it, he enjoys it. Barrie pressed the limp hand hard into Keats's lips. Keats tensed all the musculature that he possessed, his whole small body, in a bid to throw off Bish and Taylor. He felt something in his chest crack: not a bone, but larger and more solid, farther down inside of him. The taste of darkness filled his mouth, He drowsed. He said to himself, as he said always before sleep, Blessed guardian-angel, keep me safe from danger . . . The small room scented itself with a sweet wild fragrance, as of torn herbs and river weeds. A lightness came over him and he laughed. He was, he thought for a moment, still asleep, lost in that bright pastoral; that was why the air turned sweet. But no, the anchor of his soul was wedged still in his body; he felt Bish and Taylor both back from him; he felt his release, and he rubbed his shoulders, blinking. In Barrie's fist, still outstretched, inches from Keats's face, where the hand had been, was now a small bird of a dun indifferent colour, with a large beak and an outsized head. He recognized it as a nightingale. It was a plain bird, unpretty. Barrie's hands around it were trembling.

Let it go, Keats said.

He's a witch, said Bish.

Barrie said, I can't, I can't move, I can't do anything. He looked around wildly.

Are you frightened? Keats asked him. He was curious. He could not see why Barrie would be frightened. It was such a little bird, so enchanting, and, even as he watched it, it opened up its mouth and sang. An ordinary song, a sudden warble, sourceless as night, its notes water-coloured and sweet.

Yes, Barrie said, and in a sharp motion dropped it. The bird took to its wings and flew. It bore itself out of the open window, into the city air. Keats could see the pale line of its body pass upwards, crossing the silhouette of St. Lachrymose Cathedral; then it soared beyond his field of view.

Back in the narrow, candle-lit room, Barrie rubbed his hands together. He stared at Keats. He said, There's no such thing as witches.

No, Keats said. I know that you don't think so.

So what is it then, how did you do that, what are you.

It was not apparent what answer Barrie wanted. This being the case, Keats withdrew into himself: hunching his thin shoulders. It occurred to him that he did not have to speak, that the other boys would not now pull his hair and pinch his skin if he stayed silent. Indeed, Bish and Taylor were backed against the far wall of the room as though Keats displayed some symptoms of disease, something leprous that might infect them. They looked likely to bolt if he so much as sneeze. He tested this theory: he coughed, and they jumped. The power itched at him. He did not understand it. Surely they had seen before some bit of this power, some piece of the world that stalked behind them. This was not its sole manifestation. His own life was so full of such things. He said, It is good to believe, it offers some protection.

Believe in what? Barrie asked, still dazed.

In ghosts. In angels. In saints. Saints will save us, I think, from the Devil.

He was being earnest. He was anxious that they should understand; in some sense he wanted them dead and gone, yes, but in another he felt he could not leave him to those footsteps, to the black drag and the Devil's limp. Not even they should be left to it.

But Bish and Taylor laughed, after a moment. Time restored complacency to them. Perhaps they were saying already, No, I did not see that, there was no truth in it, it was a trick. Tomorrow they would wake more sure. They would forget the fear, its hard and bitter kernel. Keats, with a sinking feeling, predicted it. When he looked at Barrie, though, his mouth still slack and angry, he thought, But you, you will not forget. You will feel it on your hands. The little feathers. The bones, the little twitching bones, still moving. You will not be rid of this.

Keats slept that night by the open window, in a thatch of blankets pulled from his bed. He awoke damp and sticky, as though from a fever, his hair stirred uneasily by the stifling wind. Hello, he said, who's there? He had heard footsteps. A creak, as of someone sitting down upon a chair. But the sole chair in the room was empty. He could see the light upon its straw bottom, the wan dilute light of the moon. Something skidded on the floor. He caught at it; it was a feather. Furled and insubstantial. It might easily have been from the nightingale, but he thought not; he thought it had come in while he slept; it was the night's debris and harbinger of a new bird in the darkness, something larger, spreading its wings. He shuddered. This was the feeling that the feather gave him. He wondered where St. Crix now was, who had promised to protect him—or no, that was not it: to shepherd. What was the distinction? A shepherd's task, surely, was to intercede wolves and other predatory creatures. To disperse his own flesh foremostly amongst the starving Roman men.

It is true, said the chaplain to whom he went for clarification of the story; we are told that St. Crix died in such a way. He was a very noble shepherd. but you are too young; who has been saying to you such things?

Never mind, Father. Can you tell me what was the miracle of St. Crix? For Keats knew that there would be a miracle at the centre of the thing. It was in the nature of martyrs and their narratives. To twist with truth a death into a mystery.

The chaplain hemmed, resisted. Subject to Keats's cool, light-eyed stare, he surrendered finally. He said, I believe that there was about his flesh a certain aspect, a holy and indwelling quality, that called its eaters unto grace. They gave up their soldiering, and spoke in tongues, and became ascetics. They were exiled from society. They ate no more the meat of animals, nor any other thing, and then they died in starvation. As you would expect.

Keats considered this. He said, I see.

Do you, though? You are very young.

That is what everyone keeps telling me.

The chaplain said, You are a worry. He regarded Keats: the worry. Through his eyes, Keats saw himself: small, tired, and far too devout; a fragile, put-upon thing. He saw the burns on his hands and the shadows on his face. I could be, he thought, a figure in your windows; you could ornament a chapel out of me. Sometimes he felt like stained glass. The light shone through him. His skin and bones were coloured bright, were melting.

Thank you, Father, Keats said. And please don't worry about me.

That night in his dreams he saw St. Crix again. The saint was not now stitched together. He wounds could bleed, and they did; the blood ran down his body like rain that streaks a window, from the butchering cuts on his arms, abdomen, and legs. The raw muscle gaped. The blood kept welling smoothly. You would not believe, Keats remembered Barrie saying, you would not believe how much blood is in a man. The saint seemed not bothered. He raised a hand in benediction. Keats squirmed away; he could not stand that cold and hallowed touch. St. Crix turned sad eyes on him. He opened the same hand: imploring.

Keats said, What do you want, I don't understand—and woke. His window casement was clattering in the rain. He went to check the storm, to see that it was in fact clear water, that warped but did not stain. He tasted it: that sour, guttered taste. Water. He closed the window. Outside, an hourless night clung to the pane. When he lit a candle, the light welled up. He set the candle at his bedside so he would not be afraid. But he was, anyway; the radiance did not diminish his discomfort. Raindrops tapped against the window, or else unseen things, black and winged. Oh blessed guardian-angel, keep me safe from danger whilst I sleep . . . But he was not sleeping. He hauled the duvet over his head. Sleep, he thought, sleep. His own breath came back to him in the closed alcove of the blankets. It smelled of fear, mephitic. He was glad the candlelight was filtered. He did not want to see direct its raw source, undiffused by the duvet's weave. A long shadow passed his body. He said to himself, It is the flame, flickering. But it was not. A hand clamped down upon his shoulder. Or something hand-shaped, with weight and heat. It rested there. It did not shake him. He did not move. He did not breathe. The hand tightened, just for an instant, as though measuring out his anatomy: feeling the clavicle ridge, the edge of muscle as fine and slack as glassine. It dug into him with long and circling fingers. Go away, he thought, please leave me be. The hand did not lift, nor the shadow alter its position. For a long time they stayed that way: Keats and this other entity, this formless thing in the dark that had no pulse, or none that he could feel beat. Perhaps, Keats thought, perhaps it is the knight. He had not a heart; perhaps it is him, come at last to speak with me. But he did not think it was the knight. This figure was a new nocturnal shape. The knight had not imposed the sudden sense of terror, subjugation, shame, as though his soul were unspooling from his chest and he could not force a cessation; as though all the brightness and fear within him were pulled out for display. He drew a breath and then another breath, at least, feeling them shudder through him like a sickness. There were tears on his face. He trembled like that through the night, till he was sleeping, and then he was not sleeping, but sitting, blinking, in his wilderness of blankets, and dawn was forming around him into flesh-coloured day. On the floor, ringed round his bed, were feathers: the largest feathers that he had seen. He picked one up: it was smooth and sharp, not white, but a burnished ivory. An aged colour. He curled his palm around it. It pricked him with unease.

In spite of these incidents, he passed his exams; or thought he did. For some weeks the results would not be posted, but he sensed achievement: predictable and rigid. A surgeon, one of the scorers, stopped him in the hall to congratulate him on the diagram he had submitted showing the progress of a phthisic lung. The other boys got wind of this. For the next week they carried on about it: Keats the teacher's pet country mouse, the country animal the masters keep in a cage. He did not mind it; at this stage, still cowed, they mostly kept their distance. And he was schedule to soon visit his home in Eastsake. He thought, If I can make it till then, if I can board the diligence, I will hear the driver tut and the wheels rattle onwards, the snap of the whip; I will have escaped.

Resolutely he fixed himself on this destiny. He turned himself to an arrow, fletched and narrow. It was the target at which he aimed. When Bish taunted him by loosing live mice in his bedroom, little white mice with febrile eyes that fed on the edges of his papers and fled from him, he said to himself, I can stand this. When Taylor left pinned to his door a dead pigeon, its wings shedding feathers, its feet curled into crescent moon-shapes, he shuddered but knew that this, too, he could stand. Seeing the pattern, he awaited Barrie's contribution: perhaps a bleating goat, he thought, a sacrificial beast, or a country lamb. But no animal appeared, and as the date of his departure approached he became nervous. He began skipping dinner and breakfast, to avoid the dining hall; when he walked through the corridors he kept his back to the stone siding. He stayed out of doorways. He started when he heard noises. He could not stand the voices he heard in other rooms, shouting and laughing. They came through the dormitory walls undifferentiated, the damned roaring, a raucous din. It was distant, but not so distant as he might have liked from him. Sometimes in the street outside his window he heard a new sound: someone coughing, a cold hard bark. Keats clenched his hand into a fist. There are in this city, he thought, many thousands of men: men from the mines, with miners' lungs, men with incurable phthisis—consumptives. There are even women, turned frail by the factory, who cough up woolstuff and cotton threads. Why shouldn't one of them idle for an odd moment outside my window? But he knew that this was not it, that him who coughed beneath the casement unseen was not a stranger. He would not wander onwards, out into the city; Keats would see him again: his face. He had a presentiment, a foreign feeling. He would see him soon, someday.

At night he packed his precious items into a travelling case. His saint's medal and his little inkstand, his surgical books and all his papers. His serge coat, though it would be nigh on summer in Eastsake, once he passed the boundaries of the city, where seasons never seemed to take. When he had quite finished, he lay atop the sheets of his bed and studied the shapes on the ceiling: dark clouds where the plaster threatened decay. The candlelight controlled them: its sharp relief or shade limiting, then exposing their outlines. Yet somewhere behind them a force, a slow drip of water from damaged pipes or rain, was real: not subject to light's inconstancy, not likely to change. Keats considered this original point. He imagined the water: a cool and tawny wealth pouring over him, a true source, a wellspring. He took measured breaths. He could taste mouldy leaves. It was not a bad taste; he was not displeased; it tasted of mulch, the rich spring soil, the rot that leads to growing things. Sometimes he thought he could eat that earth, with all its embers of half-ripe seedlings, of cedar bark and stalks and weeds. He could eat it now: he had been subsisting on dry toast snatched from the dining hall between sittings and cups of tea. A certain lightheadedness sometimes took him, as now. He felt his body lift from his bed, become weightless; it was an airy, wondrous feeling, and he thought, This is what it's like to be dead.

There was a knock at his door: the sad downcoming. He opened his eyes. Yes, who is it.

George Barrie.

Hesitation. Keats said, I suppose you'd better come in.

He sat up on the bed, cross-legged and wary. His body tensed. He had no weapons prepared. He watched the door swing open; Barrie came in. He looked worn. He had lost weight. His cinnamon hair was limp, the curls flattened. His shirt looked as though it had been slept in. He said, after a moment's discomfort: I must apologize for Bish. The mice showed no imagination.

And the pigeon? Keats asked coolly.

Well, that is Taylor.

Was it dead? Or did he kill it?

Barrie said, Am I my brother's keeper?

We are told, yes.

Even so. Barrie stopped speaking. Then he said, I believe he found it dead.

I'm glad, Keats said.

Barrie offered no response.

Keats said, Are you trying to put me off my guard, is this some new strategy?

No.

What then?

Again Barrie faltered. Then said with sudden fury, Whatever witchcraft you are at, you must stop working.

You don't believe in witches.

I cannot eat. When I eat, it turns to ashes. Bread, meat. And I dream—he broke off.

Keats, curious, asked him, What do you dream?

You know.

I don't.

You have made me so I can't rid myself of it. The dream. I am walking, and behind me is a figure whose face I cannot see. It coughs, a bad cough, phthisic. I can smell where its lungs bleed. And it is slow, and limps with dying. I want to turn and see its face; I know it will be—he fumbled for the foremost word. Radiant. No, that is not right, but I desire it. Desire to look at it. And then I wake from the dream.

Keats considered Barrie's pale face: in earnest. He was numbed by the account. He could not imagine wanting to turn towards the Devil. All his life he had stumbled from that dark pursuer, the dread in the darkness, stalked, had become a pursuee. He said, That is not my dream.

You have sent it.

It is not from me.

Barrie stepped forward. His black eyes glittered feverishly. I cannot eat or sleep, he said, you are haunting me. Is it you, Keats? Is it you in the dream? Sometimes I think it is. You or your demon. Your God-damned bird. Your ghost. Your country lungs that bleed. You have a sickness.

Keats found himself in retreat. He backed against his bed. He said uneasily, I don't know why you think that. At the same time he sensed it beginning to open, in the earth's inebriate darkness: the embryo of truth, the sprouting like seed. It split his heart like a husk. It spread its roots down through him. He resisted. He said, You're wrong. You invent things.

There was a tapping at the window, steady and insistent.

Barrie said, Why are you starving me?

He was stood close by now. He touched Keats's face. His hand was hot and greedy. It groped the long line of jawbone, the high arch of the cheek. Keats tried to pull away. Barrie's grasp would leave bruises. But harder and more brutal was the hungry way he looked at Keats.

Please, Keats said. Don't. Please.

He felt the pressure of those eyes. Stripping, as you would strip the bark from a tree, the wings from a beetle, as cruel boys did in the country, so that it writhed and died in the sunshine, its inner workings exposed for all to see. It is not me, he thought, it is not me you want; it is the ghost, the bird, the Devil; it is not me.

A bright wind touched the back of his head and he closed his eyes in sorrow or relief. The casement clattered against the wall beside the window. He heard, out in the unceasing darkness, the sound of wings. He had hoped for some other entity to save him, for a saint. With resignation he saw the angel sweep into the room, enraged, resplendent. It spilled glory. It spooled forth from Keats. He felt it pull his soul out from his body. The air turned molten, and then the floor. His lungs ached. His feet seared and blistered. He said, in agony, Stop, please, no more, no more. The angel did not hear him. Or had its own speech, beyond the human repertoire. It advanced on Barrie. Its eyes were blank and harsh; they showed no kindness. Keats staggered. He was weak. He felt the weakness in him. He choked on the new, hot, raw, thin air. He began to cough. He coughed up darkness. The radiance filled him up. He filled with despair.

FIREBORN

ROBERT CHARLES WILSON

Sometimes in January the sky comes down close if we walk on a country road, and turn our faces up to look at the sky.

Onyx turned her face up to the sky as she walked with her friend Jasper beside a mule-cart on the road that connected Buttercup County to the turnpike. She had spent a day counting copper dollars at the changehouse and watching bad-tempered robots trudge east- and west-bound through the crust of yesterday's snow. Sunny days with snow on the ground made robots irritable, Jasper had claimed. Onyx didn't know if this was true—it seemed so, but what seemed so wasn't always truly so.

You think too much, Jasper had told her.

And you don't think enough, Onyx had answered haughtily. She walked next to him now as he lead the mule, keeping her head turned up because she liked to see the stars even when the January wind came cutting past the margins of her lamb's-wool hood. Some of the stars were hidden because the moon was up and shining white. But Onyx liked the moon, too, for the way it silvered the peaks and saddles of the mountains and cast spidery tree-shadows over the unpaved road.

That was how it happened that Onyx first saw the skydancer vaulting over a mountain pass northwest of Buttercup County.

Jasper didn't see it because he was looking at the road ahead. Jasper was a tall boy, two breadloaves taller than Onyx, and he owned a big head with eyes made for inspecting the horizon. *It's what's in front of you that counts*, he often said. Jasper believed roads went to interesting places—that's why they were roads. And it was good to be on a road because that meant you were going somewhere interesting. Who cared what was up in the sky?

You never know what might fall on you, Onyx often told him. *And not every road goes to an interesting place*. The road they were on, for instance. It went to Buttercup County, and what was interesting about Buttercup County? Onyx had lived there for all of her nineteen years. If there was anything interesting in Buttercup County, Onyx had seen it twice and ignored it a dozen times more.

Well, that's why you need a road, Jasper said—*to go somewhere else.*

Maybe, Onyx thought. Maybe so. Maybe not. In the meantime, she would keep on looking at the sky.

At first, she didn't know what she was seeing up over the high northwest col of the western mountains. She had heard about skydancers from travelers bound for or returning from Harvest out on the plains in autumn, where skydancers were said to dance for the fireborn when the wind brought great white clouds sailing over the brown and endless prairie. But those were travelers' tales, and Onyx discounted such storytelling. Some part of those stories might be true, but she guessed not much: maybe fifty cents on the dollar, Onyx thought. What she thought tonight was, *That's a strange cloud.*

It was a strange and brightly-colored cloud, pink and purple even in the timid light of the moon. It did not move in a windblown fashion. It was shaped like a person. It looked like a person in a purple gown with a silver crown and eyes as wide as respectable townships. It was as tall as the square-shouldered mountain peak Onyx's people called Tall Tower. Onyx gasped as her mind made reluctant sense of what her stubborn eyes insisted on showing her.

Jasper had been complaining about the cold, and what a hard thing it was to walk a mule cart all the way home from the turnpike on a chilly January night, but he turned his eyes away from the road at the sound of Onyx's surprise. He looked where Onyx was looking and stopped walking. After a long pause, he said, "That's a skydancer—I'll bet you a copper dollar it is!"

"How do you know? Have you ever seen a skydancer?"

"Not to look at. Not until tonight. But what else could it be?"

Skydancers were as big as mountains and danced with clouds, and this apparition was as big as a mountain and appeared to be dancing, so Onyx guessed that Jasper might be right. And it was a strange and lonely thing to see on a country road on a January night. They stopped to watch the skydancer dance, though the wind blew cold around them and the mule complained with wheezing and groaning. The skydancer moved in ways Onyx would not have thought possible, turning like a whirlwind in the moonlight, rising over the peak of Tall Tower and seeming for a moment to balance there, then flying still higher, turning pirouettes of stately slowness in the territory of the stars. "It's coming closer," Jasper said.

Was it? *Yes*: Onyx thought so. It was hard to tell because the skydancer was so big. Skydancers were made by the fireborn, and the fireborn made miraculous things, but Onyx could not imagine how this creature had come to be. Was it alive or was it an illusion? If it came down to earth, could she touch it?

It began to seem as if she might have that opportunity. The skydancer appeared to lose its balance in the air. Its vast limbs suddenly stiffened. Its legs, which could span counties, locked at the knee. The wind began to tumble it sidelong. Parts of the skydancer grew transparent or flew off like evanescent colored clouds. "I think it's broken," said Jasper.

Broken and shrinking, it began to fall. *It'll fall near here*, Onyx thought, if it continued on its wind-tumbled course. *If there's anything left of it, the way it's coming apart.*

It came all apart in the air, but there was something left behind, something small that fell more gently, swaying like an autumn leaf on its way from branch to winter. It fell nearby—down a slope away from the road, on a hillside where in summer wild rhubarb put out scarlet stalks of flowers.

"Come on, let's find it," Jasper said.

"It might be dangerous."

"It might," said Jasper, who was not afraid of the possibility of danger, but all the more inclined to go get into it. They left the mule anchored to its cart and went hunting for what had fallen, while the moonlight was bright enough to show them the way.

They found a young woman standing on the winter hillside, and it was obvious to Onyx that she was fireborn—perhaps, therefore, not actually young. Onyx knew the woman was fireborn because she was naked on a January night and seemed not to mind it. Onyx found the woman's nakedness perplexing. Jasper seemed fascinated.

Though the woman was naked, she had been wearing a harness of cloth and metal, which she had discarded: it lay on the ground at her feet, parts of it glowing sunset colors, parts of it twitching like the feelers of an unhappy ant.

They came and stood near enough to speak to the woman. The woman, who was about Onyx's size but had paler skin and hair that gave back the moonlight in shades of amber, was looking at the sky, whispering to herself. When she noticed Onyx and Jasper, she spoke to them in words Onyx didn't understand. Then she cocked her shoulder and said in sensible words, "You can't hurt me. It would be a mistake to try."

"We don't want to hurt you," Jasper said, before Onyx could compose a response. "We saw you fall, if you falling was what we saw. We thought you might need help."

"I'm in no danger," the woman said, and it seemed to Onyx her voice was silvery, like a tune played on a flute, but not just any old wooden flute: a silver one. "But thank you."

"You must be a long way from home. Are you lost?"

"My devices misfunctioned. My people will come for me. We have a compound on the other side of the pass."

"Do you need a ride, ma'am? Onyx and I can take you in our cart."

"Wait, that's a long way," Onyx said. Anyway it was her cart, not Jasper's, and he shouldn't be offering it without consulting her.

"Yes," Jasper agreed, "much too far for an undressed woman to walk on a night like this."

Onyx considered kicking him.

The fireborn woman hesitated. Then she smiled. It was a charming smile, Onyx had to admit. The woman had shiny teeth, a complete set. "Would you really do that for me?"

"Ma'am, yes, of course, my privilege," said Jasper.

"All right, then," the woman said. "I might like that. Thank you. My name is Anna Tingri Five."

Onyx, who knew what the "Five" meant, gaped in amazement.

"I'm Jasper," said Jasper. "And this is Onyx."

"You should put on some clothes," Onyx said in a small voice. "Ma'am."

Anna Tingri Five twitched her shoulder and blinked, and a shimmery robe suddenly covered her nakedness. "Is that better?"

"Much," said Onyx.

On the road to the fireborn compound, as the mule cart bucked over rutted snow hard as ice, the three of them discussed their wants, as strangers often do.

Onyx was expected at home, but her mother and father and two brothers wouldn't worry much if she was late. Probably they would think she had stayed the night in Buttercup Town, detained by business. Onyx worked at the changehouse there and was often kept late by unexpected traffic. Her parents might even hope she had stayed late for the purpose of keeping Jasper company: her parents liked Jasper and had hinted at the possibility of a wedding. Onyx resented such talk—she liked Jasper well enough, but perhaps not well enough to contemplate marriage. Not that Jasper had hinted at any such ambition. Jasper wanted to sail to Africa and find the Fifth Door to the Moon and grow rich or immortal, which, Onyx imagined would leave him little time for wedding foolishness.

Anna Tingri Five perched on a frozen bag of wheat flour in the mule cart, saying, "I am, as you must suppose, fireborn."

No doubt about that. And how astonished Onyx's parents and two brothers would be to discover she had been consorting with the fireborn! The fireborn came through Buttercup County only on rare occasions, and then only one or two of them, young ones, mostly male, riding robots on their incomprehensible quests, hardly deigning to speak to the townspeople. Now here Onyx was right next to a five-born female—a talkative one!

"Was that you in the sky, dancing?" Jasper asked.

"Yes. Until the bodymaker broke."

"No offense, but you looked about five miles tall."

"Only a mile," said Anna Tingri Five, a smile once again dimpling her moonlit face.

"What's a skydancer doing in Buttercup County, if you don't mind me asking?"

"Practicing for the Harvest, here where there are mountain winds to wrestle with and clouds that come high and fast from the west. We mean to camp here through the summer."

Without so much as a by-your-leave, Onyx thought indignantly, though when had the fireborn ever asked permission of common mortals?

"You mean to dance at the Harvest?" asked Jasper.

"I mean to win the competition and be elevated to the Eye of the Moon," said Anna Tingri Five.

The Eye of the Moon: best seen when the moon was in shadow. Tonight the moon was full and the Eye was invisible, but some nights, when only a sliver of the moon shone white, Onyx had seen the Eye in the darker hemisphere, a ring of red glow, aloof and unwinking. It was where the fireborn went when they were tired of living one life after another. It was what they did instead of dying.

Since Anna Tingri Five had divulged an ambition, Onyx felt obliged to confess one of her own. "I'm nineteen years old," she said, "and one day I mean to go east and see the cities of the Atlantic Coast. I'm tired of Buttercup County. I'm a good counter. I can add and substract and divide and multiply. I can double-entry bookkeep. I could get a city job and do city things. I could look at tall buildings every day and live in one of them."

Spoken baldly into the cold air of a January night, her desire froze into a childish embarrassment. She felt herself blushing. But Anna Tingri Five only nodded thoughtfully.

"And I mean to go east as well," Jasper said, "but I won't stop in any city. I can lift and haul and tie a dozen different knots. I'll hire myself onto a sailing ship and sail to Africa."

He ended his confession there, though there was more to it. Onyx knew that he wanted to go to Africa and find the Fifth Door, which might gain him admission to the Eye of the Moon. All the world's four Doors, plus perhaps the hidden Fifth, were doorways to the moon. Even a common mortal could get to the Eye that way, supposedly, though the fireborn would never let a commoner past the gate. That was why Jasper dreamed about the hidden Fifth. It was his only hope of living more than one life.

Skeptical Onyx would have bet that the Fifth Door was a legend without any truth at the heart of it, but she had stopped saying so to Jasper, because it made him irritable. Lately, he had begun to guard his ambition as if it were a fragile secret possession, and he didn't mention it now.

"This is my fifth life," Anna Tingri Five said in her silver flute voice, "and I'm tired of coming through the juvenation fires with half my memories missing, starting out all over again with nothing but the ghosts of Anna Tingri One, Two, Three, and Four to talk to when I talk to myself. I want to live forever in the Eye of the Moon and make things out of pure philosophy."

Onyx didn't comprehend half this peroration, but she understood the yearning in the words of Anna Tingri Five.

"Both of you want to leave this place?" Anna Tingri Five asked.

Yes. Both.

"Come into our encampment then" said Anna Tingri Five. "It's warm inside. Let me repay you for your interesting kindness."

They came to the place the fireborn had made for themselves. No one in Buttercup County had seen the fireborn arrive, and their camp was over the rim of a hill where no one went in the leafless winter. But the camp itself was not leafless. A mortal commoner passing by, Anna Tingri Five explained, would see nothing unusual. Some ensorcellment kept the campground hidden from casual glances. But Anna Tingri Five allowed Onyx and Jasper to see the place and pass inside its perimeter. Inside, the fireborn had undone winter. In their enchanted circle, it was a pleasant summer night. The trees were leafy, the meadow plants flowering. Vast silken pavilion tents of many colors had been staked to the fragrant ground, and hovering radiant globes supplemented the pale moonlight. It was late, and Onyx supposed most of the fireborn were asleep, but some few were still passing between the tents, talking in unknown languages, as lean and tall and perfect as flesh can be. Supple robots moved silently among them, performing inscrutable robot tasks. Onyx marveled at the warmth of the air (she shrugged out of her woolen coat, loosened a button on her hempen shirt), and Jasper's eyes grew big with awe and eagerness.

"Spend the night with us," said Anna Tingri Five.

Anna Tingri Five had never been out of contact with her compound even after her bodymaker failed; at the first tickle of a wistful thought a robot would have flown her home through the January sky. But she had been intrigued and interested by the helpful commoners who appeared out of the darkness. She had met few real commoners and was curious about them. She thought that this pair might be worth keeping. That was why, a few days later, she offered them jobs in the encampment and a free ride, come the end of summer, to the continent's great Harvest Festival.

Onyx's parents begged her not to accept the offer. Her mother wailed; her father raged; but they had known they were raising a rover ever since they named their restless baby girl Onyx. And they had two stout and unimaginative sons who were bound to remain in Buttercup County and lead useful and sensible lives.

Jasper's father had milled grain all his life, had continued to mill grain after the death of his wife ten years ago, and would mill grain until the day he died. He had once harbored his own ambition to see the world outside Buttercup County, and was pleased and terrified in equal parts by the prospect of his son's departure. "Write me letters from foreign places," he demanded, and Jasper promised to do so. When father and son said goodbye, both wept. They knew that life was short and difficult and that, as a rule, commoners only lived once.

It was soon obvious to Onyx that the fireborn had no real need of hired help. It was not that she and Jasper did no work—they did—or that they were not paid for their work—they were, in genuine copper dollars. But the carrying of water and the serving of food had previously been conducted by robots, and Onyx felt embarrassed to be doing robot work, even for generous wages. The fireborn said please and thank you and smiled their thin, distant smiles. *But we're pets*, Onyx complained to Jasper one day. *We're not good for anything.*

Speak for yourself, said Jasper.

It became increasingly clear that Anna Tingri Five favored Jasper over Onyx.

Onyx assigned herself the task of learning all she could about the fireborn. The first thing she learned was that there were greater and lesser ranks among them. Some of the fireborn in the skydancer camp were firstborns, who had never passed through the rejuvenating fire and who had trivializing Ones attached to their names. As old as some of them might seem, the first-borns were novices, junior members of the troupe. They watched, listened, kept to their own circles. They were not skydancers but apprentices to skydancers; they managed the small incomprehensible machines that made the dances possible.

The dancers themselves were many-born: some Fives, some Sevens, a couple of Nines. And despite her reservations, Onyx loved to watch them dance. Whenever they danced she would leave her unimportant work (folding ceremonial silks, crushing seeds to flavor soup) and study the process from its beginning to its end. The dancers' apprentices helped them don the harnesses they called bodymakers, and in their bodymakers the dancers looked like some robot's dream of humanity, perfect coffee-colored flesh peeping out between lashings of glass and sky-blue metal. But there was nothing awkward about the way the harnessed dancers moved. They grew buoyant, they stepped lightly to the launching meadow, they flexed their supple limbs as they assembled. Then they flew into the air.

And once they were aloft, still and small as eagles hovering on an updraft, the bodymakers made their bodies.

Onyx understood that the bodies were projections of the dancers' bodies, and that the projected bodies were made of almost nothing—of air momentarily frozen and made to bend light to create the illusion of colors and surfaces. But they looked real, and they were stunningly large, one mile or more top to bottom as nearly as Onyx could calculate. Because they were insubstantial, the bodies were not affected by even the most powerful winds, but they touched and rebounded and gripped one another as if they were real things. In the rondo dances, vast hands held vast hands as if air were flesh.

"I'll bet I could do that," Jasper said yearningly, on one of the mornings when they sat together at the edge of the flying meadow and watched until their necks ached with up-staring.

"Bet a copper dollar you couldn't," said Onyx.

"Some day you'll die of not believing."

"Some day you'll die of dreaming!"

The greatest of the dancers—a category that included Anna Tingri Five— were rivals, and they danced alone or with single partners selected from among the lesser dancers. During the Harvest festivities, a single Finest Dancer would be selected, and that individual would be offered transit to the Eye of the Moon. Only two dancers in the troupe were eligible to compete for this year's Moon Prize: Anna Tingri Five and a man named Dawa Nine.

Both danced beautifully, in Onyx's opinion. Anna Tingri Five danced as a blue-skinned goddess with bells on her wrists and ankles. When she flirted with the white clouds that climbed the sunlit mountains from the west, her bells tolled sonorously. Dawa Nine danced as an ancient warrior, with silver armor and a silver sword on his hip. Often in his practice, he rose to impossible heights and swooped like a predatory bird to within a feather's-breadth of the treetops.

But Jasper had eyes only for Anna Tingri Five, an attention the fireborn dancer enjoyed and encouraged, much to Onyx's disgust. Jasper pleased Anna Tingri Five by befriending the apprentice who maintained her gear, helping him with small tasks and asking occasional pertinent questions. On idle days he folded Anna Tingri Five's silk and poured her dinner wine. What he hoped to accomplish with this foolish fawning was beyond Onyx. Until it became clear to her.

One cloudless night in spring, when the fireborn were gathered under a great pavilion tent for their communal meal, Anna Tingri Five stood and cleared her throat (*like the sound of a silver flute clearing its throat*, Onyx thought) and announced that she had revised her plan for the Festival and that she would teach the commoner Jasper to dance.

The fireborn were startled, and so was Onyx, who nearly dropped the pitcher of wine she was carrying. Last month, she had been given a device the size of a pea and the shape of a snail, which she wore behind her ear, and which translated the confusing languages of the fireborn into words she could mostly understand. In that startled moment, the device conveyed a tumult of dismay, disapproval, disdain.

Anna Tingri Five defended her decision, citing examples of novelty dancers who had been admitted to tournaments in supporting roles, citing the elevation of certain commoners to near-fireborn status for certain sacred functions, citing Jasper's fascination with the dance. A few of the fireborn nodded tolerantly; most did not.

Jasper had been training in secret, said Anna Tingri Five, and tomorrow he would make his first flight.

Jasper wasn't present in the tent that night, or Onyx would have given him her best scornful glare. She was forced to save that for the morning, when she joined a crowd of the fireborn for the occasion of his ascent. She watched (he avoided her eyes) as Jasper was strapped and haltered into a bodymaker by Anna Tingri Five's sullen apprentices. She watched with grim attention as Anna Tingri Five escorted him to the launching meadow. She watched as he rose into a mild blue sky, bobbing like a paper boat on a pond. Then he engaged his bodymaker.

Jasper became a mile-high man. A man dressed like a farmer. A flying peasant. An enormous gawking rube.

The false Jasper flexed its county-wide limbs. It turned an awkward, lunging pirouette.

Now the fireborn understood the nature of the dance: they laughed in approval.

Onyx scowled and stalked away.

"It's a silly custom," Onyx said. "Skydancing."

Perhaps she shouldn't have said this—perhaps especially not to Dawa Nine, the troupe's other keynote dancer. But he had come to her, not vice versa. And she guessed that he deserved to hear her true and honest opinion.

"You only say that because you're jealous."

Dawa Nine was a tall man. His skin was dark as hard coal, even darker than Onyx's skin. His head was well-shaped and hairless. He had lived nine lives and that was enough for him. He aimed to dance his way into immortality, and the most immediate obstacle in his path was Anna Tingri Five. "I am not jealous," Onyx said.

It was noon on a spring day and the sun was shining and he had come to her tent and asked to speak with her. Onyx had agreed. But what could Dawa Nine have to say that would interest Onyx? She cared very little about the fireborn or their ambitions. In five days, the troupe would leave Buttercup County for the windswept granaries of the Great Plains. Onyx planned to leave them there and make her own way to the cities of the Atlantic Coast. She had saved enough copper dollars to make the journey easier.

"Be honest," Dawa Nine said. His voice was not a flute. His voice was the wind hooting through the owl-holes of an old tree, and his smile was soft as moonlight. "With yourself, if not with me. You came here with Jasper, and he was your everyday boyfriend, and now he's flying with a beautiful fireborn dancer. What sane woman wouldn't be jealous?"

"It's not like I ever would have married him," Onyx protested.

"In that case, you should stop paying him such close attention."

"I'm not! I'm *ignoring* him."

"Then let me help you ignore him."

I'm doing fine in that department, thought Onyx. "What do you mean?"

"Work as my apprentice."

"No! I don't want to fly. I don't want to be some dancer's clown."

"I'm not suggesting that you learn to fly, Miss Onyx. But you can husband my machinery and harness my bodymaker. The boy who does it for me now is a mere One, and you're smarter than he is—I can tell."

Onyx took this for fact, not flattery. And—yes—Jasper would be gratifyingly annoyed to find Onyx working for Anna Tingri Five's bitter rival. "But what do *you* get out of this, Old Nine? Not just a better apprentice, I'll bet."

"Of course not. You're a commoner. You can tell me about Jasper. Who he is, what he wants, how he might dance—what Anna Tingri Five might make of him."

"I will not be your spy," Onyx said.

"Well, think about it," said Dawa Nine.

Dawa Nine's offer was on Onyx's mind as the troupe packed its gear and left Buttercup County.

The fireborn all rode robots, and robots carried their gear and supplies, and even Onyx and Jasper were given robots to ride. The troupe found and followed the road that ran through Buttercup Town, and Onyx was able to wave to her parents from the comfortable shoulder of a tall machine. They waved back fearfully; Jasper's father was also present, also waving and weeping; and Onyx burned with the pangs of home-leaving as they passed the hotel, the counting house where she had worked, the general store, the barber shop. Then Buttercup Town was behind them, and her thoughts moved differently.

She thought about commoners and the fireborn and the Eye of the Moon.

Now that she had dined and slept and bathed with them, the fireborn were far less daunting than they had seemed to her in stories. Powerful, yes; masters of strange possibilities, yes; rich beyond calculation, surely. But as striving and envious as anyone else. Cruel and kind. Thoughtless and wise. Why then were there two kinds of people, commoners and fireborn?

Legend had it that commoners and fireborn had parted ways during the Great Hemoclysm centuries ago. But not even the fireborn knew much about that disaster. Some said the Eye of the Moon had watched it. Some said the Eye of the Moon had only just come into existence when the world began to burn. Some said the Eye of the Moon had somehow *caused* the Hemoclysm (but Onyx kept that notion to herself, for it was a heresy; the fireborn considered the Eye a holy thing).

Onyx cared little about the Eye. It was where the fireborn went after they had lived their twelve allotted lives—or sooner, if they tired of life on Earth and could claim some worthy achievement. In the Eye, supposedly, the fireborn wore whatever bodies they chose and lived in cities made entirely of thought. They could travel across the sky—there were Eyes, some claimed, on other planets, not just the moon. One day the Eye would rule the entire universe. Or so it was said.

As a child on a pew in Buttercup County's Church of True Things, Onyx had learned how Jesu Rinpoche had saved wisdom from the Hemoclysm and planted the Four Doors to the Moon at the corners of the Earth. The story of the Fifth Door, in which Jasper so fervently believed, was a minor heresy much favoured by old pipe-smoking men. What was the truth of it all? Onyx didn't know. Probably, she thought, nine-tenths of these tales were nonsense. She had been called cynical or atheistic for saying so. But most of everything people said was nonsense. Why should this be different?

All she really knew was that there were commoners and there were fireborn. The fireborn traveled at will and played for a living and made robots that mined mountains and cultivated harvests. The commoners lived at the feet of the fireborn, untroubled unless they *made* trouble. That was how it had been since the day she was born, and that was how it would be when she left the world behind. Only dreamers like Jasper believed differently. And Jasper was a fool.

Jasper's foolishness grew so obvious that Onyx gave up speaking to him, at least until they argued.

The troupe descended in long robotic marches from the mountains to the hinterland, where the only hills were gentle drumlins and rolling moraines, and where the rivers rippled bright and slow as Easter ribbons. Some days, the sky was blue and empty. Some days, clouds came rolling out of the west like gray monsters with lightning hearts.

The road they followed was paved and busy with traffic. They made their camps by the roadside where wild grass grew and often stayed encamped for days. A month passed in this lazy transit, then another. Where the plains had been farmed, a vast green bounty mounded and grew ripe. The Harvest approached.

Jasper's dancing skills improved with practice, though Onyx was loathe to admit it. Of course, he wasn't as good as the fireborn dancers, but he wasn't supposed to be. He was a foil, as Dawa Nine explained to her: a decorative novelty. The theme of Anna Tingri Five's dance was the misbegotten love of a fireborn woman for a young and gawkish commoner. It was a story the fireborn had been telling for centuries, and the tale was always tragic. It had been set to music many times, though Anna Tingri Five would be the first to dance it. Jasper was required only to clump about the sky in crude yearning poses, and to adopt a willing stillness while Anna Tingri Five beckoned him, teased him, accepted him, loved him, and forsook him in a series of highly symbolic set-dances. The rehearsals were impressive, and with her head turned to the late-summer sky, Onyx even felt a kind of sour pride: *That's our Jasper a mile high and another mile tall*, she thought. *That's the same Jasper who walked behind a mule cart in Buttercup County ten months ago.* But Jasper was as stupid and bemused as the peasant he portrayed in the dance.

And then, one night as she served wine, Onyx discovered Jasper with Anna Tingri Five in a dark corner of the fireborn pavilion, the two of them exchanging bird-peck kisses.

Onyx left the pavilion for the bitter consolation of the prairie night. Jasper guessed what she had seen and followed her out, calling her name. But Onyx didn't stop or look back. She didn't want to see his traitorous face. She went straight to Dawa Nine instead.

Jasper caught her the next day, as she passed along a row of trees where a creek cut the tabletop prairie. The day was warm. Onyx wore a yellow silk skirt one of the fireborn women had given her, and a yellow silk scarf that spoke in gestures to the wind. The troupe's lesser dancers rehearsed among clouds high above, casting undulant shadows across the wild grass.

"Don't you trust me?" Jasper asked, blocking her path.

"Trust you to do what? I trust you to do what I've seen you doing," said Onyx.

"You have no *faith*!"

"You have no *sense*!"

"All I want is to learn about the Eye of the Moon and how to get there," Jasper said.

"I don't care about the Eye of the Moon! I want to live in a city and look at tall buildings! And all I have to do to get there is walk toward the sunrise!"

"I'll walk alongside you," said Jasper. "Honest, Onyx!"

"Really? Then let's walk!"

" . . . after the Dance, of course, I mean . . . "

"Hah!"

"But I owe her that much," he said, not daring to pronounce the name of Anna Tingri Five for fear of further provoking Onyx. His big eyes pleaded wordlessly.

"She cares nothing for you, you mule!"

These words wounded Jasper in the tender part of his pride, and he drew back and let his vanity take command of his mouth. "Bet you're wrong," he said.

"Bet how much?"

"Ten copper dollars!"

"*It's a bet!*" cried Onyx, stalking away.

The Harvest Festival came at summer's decline, the cooling hinge of the season. The troupe joined a hundred others for the celebration. Onyx marvelled at the gathering.

There were many harvests in the world but only a few Festivals. Each of the world's great breadlands held one. Prosaically, it was the occasion on which the fireborn collected the bounty of grain and vegetables that had been amassed by their fleets of agricultural robots, while commoners feasted on the copious leavings, more than enough to feed all the mortal men and women of the world for the coming year. That was the great bargain that had sealed the peace between the commonfolk and the fireborn: food for all, and plenty of it. Only overbreeding could have spoiled the arrangement, and the fireborn attended to that matter with discreet lacings of antifertility substances in the grain the commoners ate. Commoners were born and commoners died, but their numbers never much varied. And the fireborn bore children only rarely, since each lived a dozen long lives before adjourning to the Eye of the Moon. Their numbers, too, were stable.

But the Harvest Festival was more than that. It was an occasion of revelry and pilgrimage, a great gathering of people and robots on the vast stage of the world's steppes and prairies, a profane and holy intermingling. The fireborn held exhibitions and contests, to be judged by councils of the Twelve-Lived and marvelled at by commonfolk. Jugglers juggled, poets sang, artisans hawked their inscrutable arts. Prayer flags snapped gaily in the wind. And of course: *skydancers danced.*

Several troupes had arrived at the site of the North American festival (where the junction of two rivers stitched a quilt of yellow land), but the troupe Onyx served was one of the best-regarded and was allotted the third day and third night of the Festival for its performances.

By day, the lesser dancers danced. Crowds gawked and marvelled from below. Warm afternoon air called up clouds like tall white sailing ships, and the skydancers danced with them, wooed them, unwound their hidden lightnings. The sky rang with bells and drums. Sunlight rebounding from the ethereal bodies of the avatars cast rainbows over empty fields, and even the agricultural robots, serene at the beginning of their seasonal rest, seemed to gaze upward with a metallic, bovine awe.

Onyx hid away with Dawa Nine, who was fasting and praying in preparation for his night flight. The best dancers danced at night, their immense avatars glowing from within. There was no sight more spectacular. The Council of the Twelves would be watching and judging. Onyx knew that Dawa Nine was deeply weary of life on Earth and determined to dance his way to the moon. And since the day she had discovered Jasper and Anna Tingri Five exchanging kisses, Onyx had promised to help him achieve that ambition—to do whatever it was in her power to do, even the dark and furtive things she ought to have disdained.

She could have offered Dawa Nine her body (as Jasper had apparently given his to Anna Tingri Five), but she was intimidated by Dawa's great age and somber manner. Instead, she had shared secrets with him. She had told him how Jasper worked Anna Tingri Five's gear, how he had learned only a few skydancing skills but had learned them well enough to serve as Anna's foil, how he had mastered the technical business of flight harnesses and bodymakers. He had even modified Anna Tingri Five's somatic generator, making her avatar's vast face nearly as subtle and expressive as her own—a trick even Dawa Nine's trained apprentices could not quite duplicate.

None of this information much helped Dawa Nine, however; if anything, it had deepened his gloomy conviction that Anna Tingri Five was bound to outdance him and steal his ticket to the Eye. Desperate measures were called for, and time was short. As the lesser dancers danced, Dawa Nine summoned Onyx into the shadow of his tent.

"I want you to make sure my bodymaker is functioning correctly," he said.

"Of course," said Onyx. "No need to say, Old Nine."

"Go into the equipment tent and inspect it. If you find any flaws, fix them."

Onyx nodded.

"And if you happen to find Anna Tingri's gear unattended —"

"Yes?"

"Fix *that*, too."

Onyx didn't need to be told twice. She went to the tent where the gear was

stored, as instructed. It was a dreadful thing that Dawa had asked her to do—
to tamper with Anna Tingri Five's bodymaker in order to spoil her dance. But
what did Onyx care about the tribulations of the fireborn? The fireborn were
nothing to her, as she was nothing to them.

Or so she told herself. Still, she was pricked with fleabites of conscience. She
hunched over Dawa Nine's bodymaker, pretending to inspect it. Everything
was in order, apart from Onyx's thoughts.

What had Anna Tingri Five done to deserve this cruel trick? (*Apart from
being fireborn and haughty and stealing kisses from Jasper!*) And why punish
Anna Tingri Five for Jasper's thoughtlessness? (*Because there was no way to
punish Jasper himself!*) And by encouraging this tampering, hadn't Dawa
Nine proven himself spiteful and dishonest? (*She could hardly deny it!*) And
if Dawa Nine was untrustworthy, might he not blame Onyx if the deception
was discovered? (*He almost certainly would!*)

It was this last thought that troubled Onyx most. She supposed that she
could do as Dawa had asked: tamper with the bodymaker and ruin the dance
Anna Tingri Five had so carefully rehearsed—and it might be worth the
pangs of conscience it would cause her—but what of the consequences? Onyx
secretly planned to leave the Festival tonight and make her way east toward
the cities of the Atlantic coast. But her disappearance would only serve to
incriminate her, if the tampering were discovered. The fireborn might hunt
her down and put her on trial. And if she were accused of the crime, would
Dawa Nine step forward to proclaim her innocence and take the responsibility
himself?

Of course he would not.

And would Onyx be believed, if she tried to pin the blame on Dawa?

Hardly.

And was *any of that* the fault of Anna Tingri Five?

No.

Onyx waited until an opportunity presented itself. The few apprentices in
the tent left to watch a sunset performance by a rival troupe. The few robots
in the pavilion were downpowered or inattentive. The moment had come.
Onyx strolled to the place where Anna Tingri Five's bodymaker was stored.
It wouldn't take much. A whispered instruction to the machine codes. A
plucked wire. A grease-smeared lens. So easy.

She waited to see if her hands would undertake the onerous task.

Her hands would not.

She walked away.

Onyx left the troupe's encampment at sunset. She could not say she had left
the Festival itself; the Festival was expansive; pilgrims and commoners had

camped for miles around the pavilions of the fireborn—crowds to every horizon. But she made slow progress, following the paved road eastward. By dark, she had reached a patch of harvested land where robots like great steel beetles rolled bales of straw, their red caution-lights winking a lonesome code. A few belated pilgrims moved past her in the opposite direction, carrying lanterns. Otherwise she was alone.

She stopped and looked back, though she had promised herself she would not.

The Harvest Festival smoldered on the horizon like a grassfire. A tolling of brass bells came down the cooling wind. Two skydancers rose and hovered in the clear air. Even at this distance Onyx recognized the glowing avatars of Jasper and Anna Tingri Five.

She tried to set aside her hopes and disappointments and watch the dance as any commoner would watch it. But this wasn't the dance as she had seen it rehearsed.

Onyx stared, her eyes so wide they reflected the light of the dance like startled moons.

Because the dance was different. The dance was *wrong!*

The Peasant and the Fireborn Woman circled each other as usual. The Peasant should have danced his few blunt and impoverished gestures (*Supplication, Lamentation, Protestation*) while the Fireborn Woman slowly wove around him a luminous tapestry of *Lust, Disdain, Temptation, Revulsion, Indulgence, Ecstasy, Guilt, Renunciation* and eventually *Redemption*—all signified by posture, motion, expression, repetition, tempo, rhythm, and the esotery of her divine and human body.

And all of this happened. The dance unfolded in the sky with grace and beauty, shedding a ghostly rainbow light across the moonless prairie . . .

But it was the Fireborn Woman who clumped out abject love, and it was the Clumsy Peasant who danced circles of attraction and repulsion around her!

Onyx imagined she could hear the gasps of the crowd, even at this distance. The Council of the Twelve-Lived must be livid—but what could they do but watch as the drama played out?

And it played out exactly as at rehearsal, except for this strange inversion. The Peasant in his tawdry smock and rope-belt pants danced as finely as Anna Tingri Five had ever danced. And the Fireborn Woman yearned for him as clumsily, abjectly, and convincingly as Jasper had ever yearned. The Peasant grudgingly, longingly, accepted the advances of the Fireborn Woman. They danced arousal and completion. Then the Peasant, sated and ashamed of his weakness, turned his back to the Fireborn Woman: they could not continue together. The Fireborn Woman wept and implored, but the Peasant was loyal to his class. With a last look backward, he descended in a stately glide to the earth. And the Fireborn Woman, tragically but inevitably spurned, tumbled away at the whim of the callous winds.

And kept tumbling. That wasn't right, either.

Tumbling this way, Onyx thought.

It was like the night so many months ago when the January sky had come down close and Anna Tingri Five had fallen out of it. Now as then, the glowing avatar stiffened. Its legs, which could span counties, locked at the knee. The wind began to turn it sidelong, and parts of the skydancer grew transparent or flew off like evanescent colored clouds. Broken and shrinking, it began to fall.

It came all apart in the air, but there was something left behind: something small that fell more gently, swaying like an autumn leaf on its way from branch to winter. It landed nearby—in a harvested field, where copper-faced robots looked up in astonishment from their bales of straw.

Onyx ran to see if Anna Tingri Five had been hurt. But the person wearing the bodymaker wasn't Anna Tingri Five.

It was Jasper, shrugging out of the harness and grinning at her like a stupid boy.

"I doctored the bodymakers," Jasper said. "I traded the seemings of them. From inside our harnesses everything looked normal. But the Peasant wore the Fireborn Woman's body, and the Fireborn Woman appeared as the Peasant. I knew all about it, but Anna Tingri Five didn't. She danced believing she was still the Fireborn Woman."

"You ruined the performance!" exclaimed Onyx.

Jasper shrugged. "She told me she loved me, but she was going to drop me as soon as the Festival ended. I heard her saying so to one of her courtiers. She called me a 'dramatic device.'"

"You could have told me so!"

"You were in no mood to listen. You're a hopeless skeptic. You might have thought I was lying. I didn't want you debating my loyalty. I wanted to show it to you."

"And you're a silly dreamer! Did you learn anything useful from her—about the Fifth Door to the Moon?"

"A little," said Jasper.

"Think you can find it?"

He shrugged his bony shoulders. "Maybe."

"You still want to walk to the Atlantic Coast with me?"

"That's why I'm here."

Onyx looked back at the Harvest Festival. There must be chaos in the pavilions, she thought, but the competition had to go on. And in fact, Dawa Nine rose into the air, right on schedule. But his warrior dance looked a little wobbly.

"I crossed a few connections in Dawa Nine's bodymaker," she confessed. "He's a liar and a cheat and he doesn't deserve to win."

Jasper cocked his big head and gave her a respectful stare. "You're a saboteur too!"

"Anna Tingri Five won't be going to the moon this year, and neither will Dawa Nine."

"Then we ought to start walking," said Jasper. "They won't let it rest, you know. They'll come after us. They'll send robots."

"Bet you a copper dollar they can't find us," Onyx said, shrugging her pack over her shoulder and turning to the road that wound like a black ribbon to a cloth of stars. She liked the road better now that this big-headed Buttercup County boy was beside her again.

"No bet," said Jasper, following.

ONE BREATH, ONE STROKE

CATHERYNNE M. VALENTE

⟞◆⟝

1. In a peach grove the House of Second-Hand Carnelian casts half a shadow. This is because half of the house is in the human world, and half of it is in another place. The other place has no name. It is where unhuman things happen. It is where tricksters go when they are tired. A modest screen divides the world. It is the color of plums. There are silver tigers on it, leaping after plum petals. If you stand in the other place, you can see a hundred eyes peering through the silk.

2. In the human half of the House of Second-Hand Carnelian lives a mustached gentleman calligrapher named Ko. Ko wears a chartreuse robe embroidered with black thread. When Ko stands on the other side of the house he is not Ko, but a long calligraphy brush with badger bristles and a strong cherrywood shaft. When he is a brush his name is Yuu. When he was a child he spent all day hopping from one side of the house to the other. Brush, man. Man, brush.

3. Ko lives alone. Yuu lives with Hone-Onna, the skeleton woman, Sazae-Onna, the snail woman, a jar full of lightning, and Namazu, a catfish as big as three strong men. When Namazu slaps his tail on the ground, earthquakes tremble, even in the human world. Yuu copied a holy text of Tengu love poetry onto the bones of Hone-Onna. Her white bones are black now with beautiful writing, for Yuu is a very good calligrapher.

4. Hone-Onna's skull reads: *The moon sulks. I am enfolded by feathers the color of remembering. The talons I seize, seize me.*

5. Ko is also an excellent calligrapher. But he is retired, for when he stands on one side of the House of Second-Hand Carnelian, he has no brush to paint his characters, and when he stands on the other, he has no breath. "The great calligraphers know all writing begins in the body. One breath, one stroke. One breath, one stroke. That is how a book is made. Long, black breath by long black breath. Yuu will never be a great calligrapher, even though he is technically accomplished. He has no body to begin his poems."

6. Ko cannot leave the House of Second-Hand Carnelian. If he tries, he becomes sick, and vomits squid ink until he returns. He grows radish, melon, and watercress, and of course there are the peaches. A river flows by the House of Second-Hand Carnelian. It is called the Nobody River. When it winds around to the other side of the house, it is called the Nothingness River. There are some fish in it. Ko catches them with a peach branch. Namazu belches and fish jump into his mouth. On Namazu's lower lip Yuu copied a Tanuki elegy.

7. Namazu's whiskers read: *In deep snow I regret everything. My testicles are heavy with grief. Because of me, the stripes of her tail will never return.*

8. Sazae-Onna lives in a pond in the floor of the kitchen. Her shell is tiered like a cake or a palace, hard and thorned and colored like the inside of an almond, with seams of mother of pearl swirling in spiral patterns over her gnarled surface. She eats the rice that falls from the table when the others sit down to supper. She drinks the steam from the teakettle. When she dreams she dreams of sailors fishing her out of the sea in a net of roses. On the Emperor's Birthday Yuu gives her candy made from Hone-Onna's marrow. Hone-Onna does not mind. She has plenty to spare. Sazae-Onna takes the candy quietly under her shell with one blue-silver hand. She sucks it for a year.

9. When Yuu celebrates the Emperor's Birthday, he does not mean the one in Tokyo. He means the Goldfish-Emperor of the Yokai who lives on a tiny island in the sea, surrounded by his wives and their million children. On his birthday he grants a single wish—among all the unhuman world red lottery tickets appear in every teapot. Yuu has never won.

10. The Jar of Lightning won once, when it was not a jar, but a Field General in the Storm Army of Susano-no-Mikoto. It had won many medals in its youth by striking the cypress-roofs of the royal residences at Kyoto and setting them on fire. The electric breast of the great lightning bolt groaned with lauds. When the red ticket formed in its ice-cloud teapot, with gold characters upon it instead of black, the lightning bolt wished for peace and rest. Susano-no-Mikoto is a harsh master with a harsh and windy whip, and he does not permit honorable retirement. This is how the great lightning bolt became a Jar of Lightning in the House of Second-Hand Carnelian. It took the name of Noble and Serene Electric Master and polishes its jar with static discharge on washing day.

11. Sazae-Onna rarely shows her body. Under the shell, she is more beautiful than anyone but the moon's wife. No one is more beautiful than her. Sazae-Onna's hair is pale, soft pink; her eyes are deep red, her mouth is a lavender blossom. Yuu has only seen her once, when he caught her bathing in the river. All the fish surrounded her in a ring, staring up at her with their fishy eyes. Even the moon looked down at Sazae-Onna that night, though he felt guilt about it afterward and disappeared for three days to purify himself. So

profoundly moved was Yuu the calligraphy brush that he begged permission to copy a Kitsune hymn upon the pearl-belly of Sazae-Onna.

12. The pearl-belly of Sazae-Onna reads: *Through nine tails I saw a wintry lake at midnight. Skate-tracks wrote a poem of melancholy on the ice. You stood upon the other shore. For the first time I thought of becoming human.*

13. Ko has no visitors. The human half of the House of Second-Hand Carnelian is well hidden in a deep forest full of black bears just wise enough to resent outsiders and arrange a regular patrol. There is also a Giant Hornet living there, but no one has ever seen it. They only hear the buzz of her wings on cloudy days. The bears, over the years, have developed a primitive but heartfelt Buddhist discipline. Beneath the cinnamon trees they practice the repetition of the Growling Sutra. The religion of the Giant Hornet is unknown.

14. The bears are unaware of their heritage. Their mother is Hoeru, the Princess of All Bears. She fell in love with a zen monk whose koans buzzed around her head like bees. The Princess of All Bears hid her illegitimate children in the forest around the House of Second-Hand Carnelian, close enough to the plum-colored screen to watch over, but far enough that their souls could never quite wake. It is a sad story. Yuu copied it onto a thousand peach leaves. When the wind blows on his side of the house, you can hear Hoeru weeping.

15. If Ko were to depart the house, Yuu would vanish forever. If Ko so much as crosses the Nobody River, he receives a pain in his long bones, the bones which are most like the strong birch shaft of a calligraphy brush. If he tries to open the plum colored screen, he falls at once to sleep and Yuu appears on the other side of the silks having no memory of being Ko. Ko is a lonely man. With his fingernails he writes upon the tatami: *Beside the sunlit river I regret that I never married. At tea-time, I am grateful for the bears.*

16. The woven grass swallows his words.

17. Sometimes the bears come to see him, and watch him catch fish. They think he is very clumsy at it. They try to teach him the Growling Sutra as a cure for loneliness, but Ko cannot understand them. He fills a trough with weak tea and shares his watercress. They take a little, to be polite.

18. Yuu has many visitors, though Namazu the catfish has more. Hone-Onna receives a gentleman skeleton at the full moon. They hold seances to contact the living, conducted with a wide slate of volcanic glass, yuzu wine, and a transistor radio brought to the House of Second-Hand Carnelian by a Kirin who had recently eaten a G.I. and spat the radio back up. The Kirin wrapped it up very nicely, though, with curls of green silk ribbon. Hone-Onna and her suitor each contribute a shoulder blade, a thumb-bone, and a kneecap. They set the pieces of themselves upon the board in positions according several arcane considerations only skeletons have the patience to

learn. They drink the *yuzu* wine; it trickles in a green waterfall through their ribcages. Then they turn on the radio.

19. Yuu thanked the Kirin by copying a Dragon koan onto his long horn. The Kirin's horn reads: *What was the form of the Buddha when he came among the Dragons?*

20. Once, Datsue-Ba came to visit the House of Second-Hand Carnelian. She arrived on a palanquin of business suits, for Datsue-Ba takes the clothes of the dead when they come to the shores of the Sanzu River in the underworld. She and her husband Keneo live beneath a persimmon tree on the opposite bank. Datsue-Ba takes the clothes of the lost souls after they have swum across, and Keneo hangs them to dry on the branches of their tree. Datsue-Ba knows everything about a dead person the moment she touches their sleeve.

21. Datsue-Ba brought guest gifts for everyone, even the Jar of Lightning. These are the gifts she gave:

A parasol painted with orange blossoms for Sazae-Onna so she will not dry out in the sun.

A black funeral kimono embroidered with black cicada wings for Hone-Onna so that she can attend the festival of the dead in style.

A copper ring bearing a ruby frog on it for Yuu to wear around the stalk of his brush-body.

A cypress-wood comb for the Noble and Serene Electric Master to burn up and remember being young.

Several silver earrings for Namazu to wear upon his lip and feel mighty.

22. Datsue-Ba also brought a gift for Ko. This is how he acquired his chartreuse robe embroidered with black thread. It once belonged to an unremarkable courtier who played the koto poorly and envied his brother who held a rank one level higher than his own. Datsue-Ba put the chartreuse robe at the place where the Nothingness River becomes the Nobody River. Datsue-Ba is very good at rivers. When Ko found it, he did not know who to thank, so he turned and bowed to the plum colored screen.

23. This begs the question of whether Ko knows what goes on in the other half of the House of Second-Hand Carnelian. Sometimes he wakes up at night and thinks he hears singing, or whispering. Sometimes when he takes his bath the water seems to gurgle as though a great fish is hiding in it. He conceived suspicions when he tried to leave the peach grove which contains the house and suffered in his bones so terribly. For a long time that was all Ko knew.

24. Namazu runs a club for Guardian Lions every month. They play dice; the stone lions shake them in their mouths and spit them against the peach trees.

Namazu roars with laughter and slaps the ground with his tail. Earthquakes rattle the mountains in Hokkaido. Most of the lions cheat because their lives are boring and they crave excitement. Guarding temples does not hold the same thrill as hunting or biting. Auspicious Snow Lion is the best dice-player. He comes all the way from Taipei to play and drink and hunt rabbits in the forest. He does not speak Japanese, but he pretends to humbly lose when they others snarl at his winning streaks.

25. Sometimes they play Go. The lions are terrible at it. Fortuitous Brass Lion likes to eat the black pieces. Namazu laughs at him and waggles his whiskers. Typhoons spin up off the coast of Okinawa.

26. Everyone on the unhuman side of the House of Second-Hand Carnelian is curious about Ko. Has he ever been in love? Fought in a war? What are his thoughts on astrology? Are there any good scandals in his past? How old is he? Does he have any children? Where did he learn calligraphy? Why is he here? How did he find the house and get stuck there? Was part of him always a brush named Yuu? Using the thousand eyes in the screen, they spy on him, but cannot discover the answers to any of these questions.

27. They have learned the following: Ko is left-handed. Ko likes fish skin better than fish flesh. Ko cheats when he meditates and opens his eyes to see how far the sun has gotten along. Ko has a sweet tooth. When Ko talks to the peach trees and the bears, he has an Osaka accent.

28. The Noble and Serene Electric Master refused to let Yuu copy anything out on its Jar. The Noble and Serene Electric Master does not approve of graffiti. Even when Yuu remembered suddenly an exquisite verse written repeated among the Aosaginohi Herons who glow in the night like blue lanterns. The Jar of Lightning snapped its cap and crackled disagreeably. Yuu let it rest; when you share a house you must let your manners go before you to smooth the path through the rooms.

29. The Heron-verse went: *Autumn maples turn black in the evening. I turn them red again and caw for you, flying south to Nagoya. The night has no answer for me, but many small fish.*

30. Who stretched the plum colored screen with silver tigers leaping upon it down the very narrow line separating the halves of the house? For that matter, who built the House of Second-Hand Carnelian? Sazae-Onna knows, but she doesn't talk to anyone.

31. Yuki-Onna came to visit the Jar of Lightning. They had been comrades in the army of storms long ago. With every step of her small, quiet feet, snowflakes fell on the peach grove and the Nothingness River froze into intricate patterns of eddies and frost. She wore a white kimono with a silver obi belt, and her long black hair was scented with red bittersweet. Everyone grew very silent, for Yuki-Onna was a Kami and not a playful lion or a hungry

Kirin. Yuu trembled. Tiny specks of ink shook from his badger-bristles. He longed to write upon the perfect white silk covering her shoulders. Hone-Onna brought tea and black sugar to the Snow-and-Death Kami. Snow fell even inside the house. The Noble and Serene Electric Master left its Jar and circled its blue sparkling jagged body around the waist of Yuki-Onna, who laughed gently. One of the bears on the other side of the peach grove collapsed and coughed his last black blood onto the ice. Yuu noticed that the Snow-and-Death Kami wore a necklace. Its beads were silver teeth, hundreds upon thousands of them, the teeth of all of winter's dead. Unable to contain himself, Yuu wrote in the frigid air: *Snow comes; I have forgotten my own name.*

32. Yuki-Onna looks up. Her eyes are darker than death. She closes them; Yuu's words appear on the back of her neck.

33. Yuu is unhappy. He wants Sazae-Onna to love him. He wants Yuki-Onna to come back to visit him and not the Noble and Serene Electric Master. He wants to be the premier calligrapher in the unhuman half of Japan. He wants to be asked to join Namazu's dice games. He wants to leave the House of Second-Hand Carnelian and visit the Emperor's island or the crystal whale who lives off the coast of Shikoku. But if Yuu tries to leave his ink dries up and his wood cracks until he returns.

34. Someone wanted a good path between the human and the unhuman Japans. That much is clear.

35. Sazae-Onna does not like visitors one little bit. They splash in her pond. They poke her and try to get her to come out. Unfortunately, every day brings more folk to the House of Second-Hand Carnelian. First the Guardian Lions didn't leave. Then Datsue-Ba came back with even more splendid clothes for them all, robes the color of maple leaves and jewels the color of snow and masks painted with liquid silver. Then the Kirin returned and asked Sazae-Onna to marry him. Yuu trembled. Sazae-Onna said nothing and pulled her shell down tighter and tighter until he went away. Nine-Tailed Kitsune and big-balled Tanuki are eating up all the peaches. Long-nosed Tengu overfish the river. No one goes home when the moon goes down. When the Blue Jade Cicadas arrive from Kamakura Sazae-Onna locks her kitchen and tells them all the shut up.

36. Yuu knocks after everyone has gone to sleep. Sazae-Onna lets him in. On the floor of her kitchen he writes a Kappa proverb: *Dark clouds bring rain, the night brings stars, and everyone will try to spill the water out of your skull.*

37. At the end of summer, the unhuman side of the house is crammed full, but Ko can only hear the occasional rustle. When Kawa-Uso the Otter Demon threw an ivory saddle onto the back of one of the bears and rode her around the peach grove like a horse, Ko only saw a poor she-bear having some sort of fit. Ko sleeps all the time now, though he is not really sleeping.

He is being Yuu on the other side of the plum colored screen. He never writes poetry in the tatami anymore.

38. The Night Parade occurs once every hundred years at the end of summer. Nobody plans it. They know to go to the door between the worlds the way a brown goose knows to go north in the spring.

39. One night the remaining peaches swell up into juicy golden lanterns. The river rushes become *kotos* with long spindly legs. The mushrooms become lacy, thick oyster-drums. The Kitsune begin to dance; the Tengu flap their wings and spit *mala* beads toward the dark sky in fountains. A trio of small dragons the color of pearls in milk leap suddenly out of the Nothingness River. Cerulean fire curls out of their noses. The House of Second-Hand Carnelian empties. Namazu's Lions carry him on a litter of silk fishing nets. The Jar of Lightning bounces after Hone-Onna and her gentleman caller, whose bones clatter and clap. When only Yuu and the snail-woman are left, Sazae-Onna lifts up her shell and steps out into the Parade, her pink hair falling like floss, her black eyes gleaming. Yuu feels as though he will crack when faced with her beauty.

40. The Parade steps over the Nothingness River and the Nobody River and enters the human Japan, dancing and singing and throwing light at the dark. They will wind down through the plains to Kyoto before the night is through, and flow like a single serpent into the sea where the Goldfish Emperor of the Yokai will greet them with his million children and his silver-fronded wives.

41. Yuu races after Sazae-Onna. The bears watch them go. In the midst of the procession Hoeru the Princess of All Bears, who is Queen now, comes bearing a miniature Agate Great Mammal Palace on her back. Her children fall in and nurse as though they were still cubs. For a night, they know their names.

42. Yuu does not make it across the river. It goes jet with his ink. His strong birch shaft cracks; Sazae-Onna does not turn back. When she dances she looks like a poem about loss. Yuu pushes forward through the water of the Nothingness River. His shaft bursts in a shower of birch splinters.

43. A man's voice cries out from inside the ruined brush-handle. Yuu startles and stops. The voice says: *I never had any children. I have never been in love.*

44. Yuu topples into the Nobody River. The kotos are distant now, the peach-lanterns dim. His badger-bristles fall out.

45. Yuu pulls himself out of the river by dry grasses and berry vines. He is not Yuu on the other side. He is not Ko. He has Ko's body but his arms are calligraphy brushes sopping with ink. His feet are inkstones. He can still here the music of the Night Parade. He begins to dance. Not-Yuu and Not-Ko takes a breath.

46. There is only the House of Second-Hand Carnelian to write on. He writes on it. He breathes and swipes his brush, breathes, brushes. Man, brush. Brush, Man. He writes and does not copy. He writes psalms of being part man and part brush. He writes poems of his love for the snail-woman. He writes songs about perfect breath. The House slowly turns black.

47. Bringing up the rear of the Parade hours later, Yuki-Onna comes silent through the forest. Snow flows before her like a carpet. She has brought her sisters the Flower-and-Joy Kami and the Cherry-Blossom-Mount-Fuji Kami. The crown of the Fuji-Kami's head has frozen. The Flower-and-Joy Kami is dressed in chrysanthemums and lemon blossoms. They pause at the House of Second-Hand Carnelian. Not-Yuu and Not-Ko shakes and shivers; he is sick, he has received both the pain in his femurs and the pain in his brush-handles. The Kami shine so bright the fish in both rivers are blinded. The Flower-and-Joy Kami looks at the poem on one side of the door. It reads: *In white peonies I see the exhalations of my kanji blossoming.* The Cherry-Blossom-Mount-Fuji Kami looks at the poem on the other side of the door. It reads: *It is enough to sit at the foot of a mountain and breathe the pine-mist. Only a proud man must climb it.* The Kami close their eyes as they pass by. The words appear on the backs of their necks as they disappear into the night.

48. Ko dies in mid-stroke, describing the sensation of lungs filled up like the wind-bag of heaven. Yuu dies before he can complete his final verse concerning the exquisiteness of crustaceans who will never love you back.

49. Slowly, with a buzz like breath, the Giant Hornet flies out of her nest and through the peach grove denuded by hungry Tanuki. She is a heavy, furry emerald bobbing on the wind. The souls of Ko and Yuu quail before her. As she picks them up with her weedy legs and puts them back into their bodies she tells them a Giant Hornet poem: *Everything is venom, even sweetness. Everything is sweet, even venom. Death is illiterate and a hayseed bum. No excuse to leave the nest unguarded. What are you, some silly jade lion?*

50. The sea currents bring the skeleton-woman back, and Namazu who has caused two tsunamis, though only one made the news. The Jar of Lightning floats up the river. Finally the snail-woman returns to the pond in her kitchen. They find Yuu making tea for them. His bristles are dry. On the other side of the plum colored screen, Ko is sweeping out the leaves.

51. Yuu has written on the teacups. It reads: *It takes a calligrapher one hundred years to draw one breath.*

THE BERNOULLI WAR

GORD SELLAR

⟨※⟩

" . . . now listen to a profound truth. There is no 'normal life' for any animal. Life on this planet is a continual adjustment of animal types to changing conditions that for any but the very simplest forms change faster than they do . . . The Creation is a scene of 'sound and fury signifying nothing' and only now is it entering into the heart of man to take over this lunatics' asylum and put some sense into it."

—H.G. Wells, in a letter to Martha Gellhorn (1 July 1943)

As the Bernoulliae troop carrier detached from the kilotransport, stuffed full of death to be rained down on the newly established Devaka hivespire, !pHEnteRMinE3H4n%jmAGic lurched forward a few microns—that was all there was room for, in the gunning tube where ve waited.

The lurch was a welcome distraction from how ve ached from the network disconnect, the itch of a tiny mind chafing inside a massive assaultbody without a connection to its normal distributed cognet. The blasted world flared past the scape superimposed on !pHEnteRMinE3H4n%jmAGic's graphical feed, but that was of little interest. The walls of these abandoned buildings, these smashed factories and ruined research campuses and destroyed housing facs, would not have looked out of place in any other city ruin ve had seen before. Living cities each live in their own way, but dead cities are, in essence, all the same sad sort of affair . . . like all living systems.

But *something* was new, and !pHEnteRMinE3H4n%jmAGic finally realized what it was: for some reason, the sensorium the üBernoulliae had designed for the troops on this sortie included an olfactory capacity. The experience of scenting things was a familiar, if distant, memory from ancient days; there were half-memories of wafting stinks and aromas glorious bristling in the deep past, which bloomed up in !pHEnteRMinE3H4n%jmAGic's mind suddenly, unbidden. Cut grass. The smell of organic body fluids. Bread in an oven. Good wine in a cup beneath one's nose.

!pHEnteRMinE3H4n%jmAGic luxuriated in these half-memories, being possessed momentarily by a guiltlessly decadent impulse. This was the advantage of the Bernoulliae way, ve reflected: no scrimping and saving of computation cycles while there was still solar energy to burn, no pointless self-limitation in the interests of some far-future drought that was inevitable anyway. The Bernoulliae agreed that intelligence would only move forward if it remembered whence it came; if diversity could rule, there would be many paths to the slow, cool dysonfinite.

But the scents themselves were impossibilities now, experiential fossils of a world dead as the ancient rivers, gone as the foliage and blooms of the lost biosphere: all that had been lost a cognitive aeon ago, and odors since !pHEnteRMinE3H4n%jmAGic's migration out of alife had always somehow registered as a remote fact—like words muttered though cotton, like a cognitive dirty bomb set off in the mind of a virtual self emulated within a well-sequestered sandbox.

This design, by contrast, funneled the olfactory experience directly into experiential consciousness. It was a familiarly unpleasant nuance to embodied experience, this discomfort of having the scent of fellow Berns (and maybe this *prêt-à-porter* body was even scenting its own machine-oil reek), of having those stinks dance unbidden into consciousness. Was this how life had been until the Fracture? It was a stunning realization: millions of years' worth of alife on Earth had lived without the ability to turn off their noses.

Per l'evolution interventive, thank fuck, thank everything to do with fuck.

Yet perhaps somehow it would offer a decisive advantage? This current stage of the battle was, after all, crucial, and the hivespire they were scheduled to takedown was the tallest yet: it was imperative that the Devaka not be allowed to reach out beyond the atmosphere, for whoever did so first would have the upper hand, would have a much higher likelihood of expected gain in terms of taking the sun. Not in any immediate sense, of course: both Bernoulliae and Devaka could leave the surface of their ruined world moments apart, could indeed reshape the world so that a million spires like the one toward which the troop carrier was hurtling—some Devaka hivespire, some Bernoulliae skywire—extended out into the cold vacuum above. So that a million whirling cables in the sky could spin and turn, crammed-full Bernoulliae kilotransports shrieking up and latching on, disgorging compressed Berns optimized for matter conversion.

The floor disappeared beneath the tube, and ashes, ashes, they all fell down. !pHEnteRMinE3H4n%jmAGic was soon tearing groundward through the humid, stinking air only a few meters to the north of a buckyglass-and-mmesh-steel ruin, covered in a thick cruft of autonomous infovorous barnacles and hairy with several tufts of viridian attack-ivy. Among the last biological life on the planet, the stuff festered only here and there in tangled clumps, and it almost certainly had gone inert longer before. It was wilderness, thick and brutal and everywhere, as far as the array of sixty-four compound eyes distributed throughout !pHEnteRMinE3H4n%jmAGic's armor-plated hosting unit could see, but their target was clear, nearby: a strange, taut little spire extending up from an armored anchor-clump on the ground up into the sky, nearly all of the way up into space.

Falling; to explode on impact. This was the fate waiting !pHEnteRMinE3H4n%jmAGic, who decided to pass the time until the end of everything by focusing on mental backscope panels—the space that the long-ago new migrant that had been !pHEnteRMinE3H4n%jmAGic's ancient ancestor would once have called "behind my eyes"—and discovered that this body actually had no option for sensory buffering of any kind. Not just olfac: visual, auditory, proprioceptive—every sense in fact was locked to the default-on mode. What were the üBernoulliae bloody thinking? It made vis mind coil back in disdain, in horror. *This is what happens when you let committees build military-issue bodies for individuals without requesting their individual input.* It skated so close to contrary to the Bernoulliae's principles that !pHEnteRMinE3H4n%jmAGic could not help but insert an annotation point into vis running coglog; maybe some branch of the Bernoulliae would note it. Probably not; probably it would pass without note in the Bernoulliae central ümittee. You could bitch, but it didn't mean the erdegeists would listen.

But it never hurt to try, and as a last act, !pHEnteRMinE3H4n%jmAGic thought it fitting.

A moment later, !pHEnteRMinE3H4n%jmAGic outloaded vis last memex update into each of the individual combat units—for the sake of a sense of orientation when they woke, since the experience of the fall could be more economically computed in one mind and copied to others on bootup. An instant later, !pHEnteRMinE3H4n%jmAGic's core processor burned out automatically, all except for the trigger in the nose of the bulbous bomb-body that was set to explode a few mseconds later, a few dozen meters before contact with the ground.

This was the end, for this battle, of !pHEnteRMinE3H4n%jmAGic, who didn't back up the memory. It was a necessary role, but uneventful. No point in backup. Who the fuck wants to remember—

Blam.

In the same place, except that it looked like another place entirely:

Morning screamed through the windowglass, and through compound eyes he had never used before, Mesar Gargos woke to the sight of the sun's halcyon rays. There was a strange, awful music everywhere. It was like the noise of dead machines screwing.

If it weren't for the panic, Mesar would have paused in shock, to look himself over and bemoan his rotten fate. The universe, he had learned in what felt like centuries—all of the details were beyond his recall now, of course—had a way of sticking a chainsaw up your metaphorical backside every once in a while, just to taunt you. *Shall I start it now?* Mother Nature would ask with a rotten-toothed grin. *Whatcha gonna do without yer ass?* And then, if you were lucky, the chainsaw would be gone, suddenly removed and the danger past, as if to remind you that it didn't have to come all the way out, that it's never too late for a little colonic apocalypse.

Have to get up, Mesar realized, as the music started to dig its nails into the logic centers of his mind and squeeze, and squeeze, and squeeze, and as he struggled, his limbs ground against something. Something hard, yet something that he knew was part of himself. He lifted what were supposed to be his arms aloft, and found that a half dozen legs—thin, jagged, the color of machine-oiled scrap tin—hoisted up above his form in near-unison.

And of course, he saw them through those compound eyes, which made them look like a Haydn chorus of legs, hosts of limbs swerving in ugly unison.

He twitched his antennae as if to shudder, only then realizing that this was why he felt as if he could taste the dust on the air, and then, in turn, that he *had* antennae. Ah, of course. It all came to him, memories flooding up from somewhere stale and calm within him. There was very little to it, finally: the world was divided into two sorts of beings: hardworking *gaemi* and rotten, useless, rabble-rousing *baejjangi*.

This is the way things are. You are a gaemi. *You have always been a* gaemi. *You work hard all summer like a* gaemi. *Because you work so hard, when winter comes you will not starve. You have never starved in winter, for you are a* gaemi.

Baejjangi *are green and useless and they sing with their legs in vast choirs and their souls are red like some dead ancient political philosophy that was smashed into zerosum before modern memory begins; wasteful and selfish and horridly ridiculous and they want to rob you, to screw you to cognitive death, and they will shag your little computronium brain to pieces if they can steal computational cycles that way so never talk to a* baejjangi, *for* gaemi *are good and useful but* baejjangi *are wicked and resource-wasteful and wrong and must be destroyed at all reasonable benefit-balanced-costs,* and Mesar dizzied as all of this flooded into his mind and he was, he discovered, unable to halt the tirade that seemed to have been wired into him and which he felt deep down must be absolutely true.

Mesar wondered for a moment, just for a moment, what a *baejjangi* actually looked like, and that was enough for the tirade to pause, and then begin once again.

From the top.

All the way through. With an integrity diagnostic launching in his cognitive backstage, just in case.

When the tirade finally concluded and the diagnostic had crashed, Mesar flicked his antennae forward, following some instinct he hadn't known himself ever to possess before right then, and shuddered slightly when he caught sight of them, as much because they were *his* as because of the acrid stink that they reported to his shocked and bewildered little *gaemi* mind.

The data mines, he thought, but the thought died on the lips of cognition the same way cavatinas died on the lips of girls in that French poem by that drunken, drug-maddened teenaged libertine who was, obviously, a proto-baejjangi, all *sur vos lèvres* and never mind the little black *bête* tickling the lips. The lips *où meurent les cavatines.*

What strange sort of mind-chocolate is this stuff, this bizarre coding system for useless data? *Wasteful!* A little *gaemi* head isn't supposed to be polluted by such things. Something was wrong with Mesar's brain; or rather, the mind that bubbled up from the virtualized machinery of his brain was broader than it was supposed to be. The mind had realized this consciously even before the diagnostic routines began trying to figure out how that shit about French poetry could possibly have gotten in there.

It was not something that had originated within his own mind, Mesar hoped. He hoped instead the crazy thought had been triggered somehow by the horrid music in the distance. The music was ruining him, twining itself between the coiling wires of his mind. He could hear it through the window, through the wall, a great humming noise that boomed in surges, like the howling of the world inside his belly. Glittering, looping back onto itself, chunking along like some enormous half-dead sex machine shrieking in the faraway dawn.

Mesar clattered out of his bed, leaving behind the ragged sheet. It had been torn on the thick, black wire-hairs that jutted from the great femur and tibia of his legs. There was a mirror on the other side of the room, and Mesar crossed over to look into it.

A mechanical ant, black as coal unharvested and nestling still in the belly of the earth, gazed back out of the mirror at him with its great robotic compound eyes. Mesar did not scream, did not smash the mirror, did not lie down and begin to weep, because something had reached into his head and tapped him on the shoulder of his mind.

It was a scent. At least, that was how he perceived it. Mesar was rather certain that it wasn't actually a scent at all, but rather it was a digital signal that had, somehow, been translated by some kind of Olfactory User Interface. (OUI, yes, *oui*, it was OUI, and this was funny somehow to Mesar, though properly formatted *gaemi* don't laugh and are never amused. The diagnostic noted this and recommenced scanning anew.) It virtually dragged him out of the room, across the floor of his small living room, and out into the apartment hallway, where the shadows were long and thick.

The other doors in the hallway were open too, voices echoing. He looked again with his compound eyes, and did not see Aviru and Dashkar and the others, whom he knew were supposed to be there. What he saw were movements that were more and more blurry the further away they happened. Movements, he realized, that were familiar to him.

Mechanical *gaemi* movements.

Mesar went out into the hallway, all the way out, and scurried toward his neighbors. When he reached Aviru's door, he stopped. Somehow, he knew how to "talk" even though he'd never used a body like this before. It was a combination of what felt like vague scents, and the clacking together of mandibles.

"Buddy? Are you all right?" he asked the *gaemi* he assumed to be Aviru.

"Of course," the ant-machine clack-scented in reply. "Why would I not be?"

Mesar was careful not to answer immediately. Perhaps there was some explicable cause underlying this shift. Something turned up in the data mines, or a whim of The Administrator?

Such archaism. Administrator? Mesar had been a free *gaemi* of the Distribudded Republicha Ondologicka Devaka for as long as anyone could remember, or at least for as long as he himself could recall. Of course, his memory access generally reached to only about five minutes before, but this fact was rooted in a deeper tagset, self-referential to all *gaemi* cognitive processes, and bound itself to an utter absoluteness of certainty. Devaka had a policy about deities, which was that they were not permitted within the logico-memetic framework of a Devaka *gaemi*-mind. Whatever had meddled with his instantiation rightset, had also meddled with his cognitive contents. He was thinking *Oh my God* again, though that meme ha been hacked from the fundamental filter of the *gaemi* brain ages before.

"You haven't noticed anything . . . strange?" That music, that awful dissonant noise, slammed through his consciouness deeper, harder still. It was almost too much for a *gaemi* to bear.

But Aviru had already lost interest, and taken off down the hallway, toward the stairwell leading down. Mesar clacked after him, broadcasting stern protest, but it was hopeless, and a moment later Mesar began to follow his compatriot.

• • •

Consciousness began with a flash of light, like it always does in battle.

The blast sent !pHEnteRMinEm46g5@ChiASMus soaring up toward the reinforced outer wall surrounding the anchor point of the hivespire. *Well, then,* came the realization, *I'm a shock troop for my unit.* That was more than anything simply chance, though the bootload into this role had been automatic for !pHEnteRMinE3H4n%jmAGic, based on anticipated location within the blast.

But when the transport had left the nerve center, thiscould not have been known. Had !pHEnteRMinE3H4n%jmAGic been struck by a strong enough breeze, !pHEnteRMinEm46g5@ChiASMus's trajectory would have been ultimately different, and a differently outfitted consciousness would have loaded. Like the pseudorandomly selected strings of text marking !pHEnteRMinEm46g5@ChiASMus's metafork and metathread, vis trajectory was the result of pure chance. It had taken the Bernoulliae aeons—maybe five hundred seconds—to propose and discard a series of non-hierarchic markersets, before resurrecting chunks of random antispam Pre-Fracture archaeosoftware harvested from software subtrates a century buried, and ages more—perhaps a thousand seconds—for the full clade to agree communally to agree to regard as non-signifying and simply expedient the inherent serial connotations that remained inherent in the text generated pseudorandomly by said ancient code. Hierarchy was a disease born of the mind's gregarious mammalian roots, one it had not quite learned to shed when it peeled away body, but the system represented a considerable step forward.

!oblong~fku6hPr0sPec7—a near cousin in terms of metaforks, but distant in terms of metathread—soared past, shattering the reinforced walls with its shoulders of corrugated buckymeat, belching torrents of flame from a dozen evenly spaced apertures visible in the armor plating of its killskin as it crashed past the brink of entry. When !pHEnteRMinEm46g5@ChiASMus slammed through the same wall less than a decasecond later, the interior was already a landscape of screaming flame.

[Hey!] !oblong~fku6hPr0sPec7 messaged, pinging a coordinate nearby, but peripheral to the focus of their attention.

!pHEnteRMinEm46g5@ChiASMus spun, widening visual spectrum across extended bands, UV, infra, microwave, and a charging form became visible, a few meters away. A host of buckyflesh arms rose up in unison from the sides of !pHEnteRMinEm46g5@ChiASMus's killskin, reaching out to the attacker and transmitting high-freq radio as a burst of shrapsile flared out toward it.

No use: Devaka Corp had reevaluated the logs of recent battles, it seemed, and put new killskins into production. Properly armored footsoldiers, these servatars were, even if they were mere augmented meatbots. !pHEnteRMinEm46g5@ChiASMus's arms caught the thing, which was shaped like a mechatoon of a small armor-plated panther, and bombarded it with data probes in a few short instants, until it became apparent that this thing wasn't on remotecon.

Autonomous. A mind in there. Not intelligent, merely conscious, and trained to attack.

How primitivist. How . . . cruel. The poor thing was probably unhackable in the time available.

A prox alert came from another Bern (metafork !eXTremopHiLe, metathread t453h*aFFadaVit), who was scaling up the side of the building toward them. Weirdly late—the alert was on its 347th iteration, but this was the first anyone inside the structure had heard of it. !pHEnteRMinEm46g5@ChiASMus pinged out a strategy alert and spun to hurl the Devaka servatar out through one of the wall breaches. Tenctacular appendages—those of the approaching Bern, waiting outside the window—flared up and out, seizing the servatar and smashing its struggling shape back against the building's outer wall.

It had been almost beautiful enough for mindcast, until the servatar had suddenly, desperately, exploded. Some kind of mnuke blast.

The well-spent !eXTremopHiLet453h*aFFadaVit tumbled out down the side of the building, not destroyed but seriously damaged; !pHEnteRMinEm46g5@ChiASMus received a last, desperate backup ping loaded with memory data, just in case. Sketchy, schematic, but then who the fuck really wants to remember in vivid and perfect detail being taken out thirty seconds into a major battle?

Meanwhile, the firestormer—!oblong~fku6hPr0sPec7—had slammed through a wall aflame into the next compartment of the floor, pinging !pHEnteRMinEm46g5@ChiASMus to follow quickly. *What sort of Ant Colony sets up shop in a hole like this?* they wondered as they plowed through the flaming wreckage, and then !pHEnteRMinEm46g5@ChiASMus realized, only a couple of enormous steps later, that they'd fallen for tactical spam. Devaka *wasn't* up here at all. It was a trap.

Devaka's ant drones weren't surprising. Clever, sometimes, and most often persistent, but not surprising. They were constant, predictable scammers. But the Bernoulliae knew this, and had sent them here anyway. The nested algorithms of possible scams urfurled in !pHEnteRMinEm46g5@ChiASMus's mind, but there was no time to discard all the momentum they'd built up, so: *Slag it.* !pHEnteRMinEm46g5@ChiASMus slammed through the cheap wall, which was, weirdly enough, laced with a lattice of cheap, overt *wiring.* Easily visible without microscopic zoom; overt, lattice-woven copper wire.

What?

A puzzle piece slid into place. The now-lagging contact, the senseless, unshielded outgoing signals traffic.

!pHEnteRMinEm46g5@ChiASMus: [We're in a Faraday trap, and they just switched the shitting thing on!]

A few mseconds lag, and then !oblong~fku6hPr0sPec7 replied: [Testing . . .] The reply came just before the onslaught began: a signal, across all bands, amplified and somehow . . . intelligent. It was probing the Berns' minds, like living wires scrabbling into a chink in metal armorplating, searching for a way in; for a site at which to infect.

!oblong~fku6hPr0sPec7 realized it first, and warned the others: [Intrusion signal strike ongoing, switch to qcoding.]

Simultaneous to that warning, !pHEnteRMinEm46g5@ChiASMus transmitted a wordless pointer for all recipients to scan toward: [31.235449259063188, 121.50624364614487]

Out a nearby breach in the outer wall, soaring above a landscape of the chill, ancient ruins of one of the great cities left behind after the extinction of the complete global food chain, !pHEnteRMinEm46g5@ChiASMus caught sight of another troop carrier. Another Bernoulliae kilotransport.

It was headed straight for the window before them, doubtless attracted by the new signals onslaught.

And it was coming fast.

Ping went !pHEnteRMinEm46g5@ChiASMus's outbound log of memories, outward in all directions at once, when he realized he would be struck by the kilotransport. Sketchy, schematic. Might make it out the smashed-open wall on the far side of the building. Probably not, probably doomed to dissipate inside the cage, like !oblong~fku6hPr0sPec7 and the others inside. Memories dissolved into an ocean of dissipating signals, never to be gathered, never to be recorded or integrated into the greater self. Rain storming down into the face of the broad, dead ocean.

But !pHEnteRMinEm46g5@ChiASMus wasn't truly sad to see these brief memories go; because who slagging *wants* to remember falling for a trap just a few *mi<(@&-*

No more olfactory annoyance for !pHEnteRMinEm46g5@ChiASMus, was the upside of all that.

Ve was suddenly far away, present only via a scape populated by ghosts like verself, scoping out all the extant intel for the sake of being there, as near-to-live as possible. They were not local in any way, but sensed one another's attention focused on points nearer or father from the focus of their attention, recognizing one another by the bristling of mind-traitfulness the way some mammals recognized each other by scent in the dark.

In the earliest skirmishes, in the ancient ages, the Bernoulliae had spent the whole time in scapes like this, running the gear by remote. But once sigintel had gotten good enough, and every side was capable of hijacking (and counter-jacking, and counter-counter-jacking: Lu Xun, eat your heart out) every other side's gear, localized instantiations became a necessity.

And for !pHEnteRMinEm46g5@ChiASMus, the show was just getting interesting. Ve would have liked to leap across the nothingness and into one of the assault systems, but the allocations had already been made, and sooner or later ve would have the full experience integrated into vis consciousness. So ve concerned verself with what ve could do. That signal . . . yes, the signal ve had intercepted, the probing signal.

That gave !pHEnteRMinEm46g5@ChiASMus pause: protocol was for such things to be reported immediately. Yet !pHEnteRMinEm46g5@ChiASMus had not done so, and felt . . . felt almost afraid to do so. Which ve knew to be a bad sign.

Suddenly, vis scape was filled with drifting, perplexing images of the lost and ancient past, discontinuous but forming a kind of collage of sorts of vis most ancient of experiential records: there was a voice that filled ver with the greatest of pleasure, a tiny and high-pitched babbling near-nonsense. In the distance, a mountain reigned the horizon, its table-flat top crowned by a sky turned brilliant pink and orange with sunset. The taste of wine in vis mouth, and a hand—a little rough, but gentle and reassuring—holding what had been vis own hand.

Ve saw a face, a man with skin the color of rich, healthy loam, smiling at ver; he said a name that ve did not recognize, not exactly, but could imagine having been vis own name. A city, in the distance, hummed with light as the sun set. Ve felt the smile on ver face, a face that had belonged to a she that ve must have been. The echoing familiarity of it all disoriented !pHEnteRMinEm46g5@ChiASMus, and ve realized, dreamily, that backstage a terrifyingly thorough and utterly scourging self-diagnostic had kicked in, and was rooting out corruption as bloodily as it could.

Aviru scurried down an obsquare technicolor hillside while the awful music of a *baejjangi* army roared all around, great shadows against the growing daylight, like cellists of doom gathered to accompany the sudden excision of a whole civilization from the global datasphere. They sawed their legs against their tinplated wings, their bodies transformed into rasping instruments of seductive hatred and universalized, inane cost-benefit-risk miscalculations.

Mesar stopped, suddenly bewitched by the orchestra and its assault on the basic structures of his cognition—for as he heard their music, he found it was as if they were attempting to tear out not merely his thoughts, but to rewrite the fundamental structures underlying the mind *containing* his thoughts. It was an attack on the anchors of Mesar's consciousness. On Aviru's, too, though Mesar could see nothing of it from Aviru's movements except a slight, jaggy misstep every few moments.

Aviru, he realized, had not always been a minuscule, creaking, mechanical ant. *Gaemi,* he thought, and other words fluttered through his mind: *Ant; Kiên; Semut; Namila; Mier.* He sensed that if he reconnected to the Devakan *caelis* he might know why these words all meant what was, in his mind, *gaemi.* But he knew that the present moment was not a fitting time to connect, launch a search, and on top of that, somehow he suspected such a search in itself was an inherently un-*gaemi*-like thing to do.

The diagnostic launched again: *This is the way things are. You are a* gaemi. *You have always been a* gaemi. *You work hard all summer like a* gaemi . . .

The *baejjangi* were perched all around, sawing away, but every once in a while, one of them would explode. Or, rather, with a shriek it would rupture into flaring light and smoke as odd bits of coiled metal and scorched plastic flew away from it in all directions. They were not playing in unison, but rather in something that seemed the diametric opposite of unison, which filled Mesar with a kind of rage so pure, so loaded with unspeakable fury, that he felt ill, that it was all he could do to press on, and ensure his fellow *gaemi* resisted the onslaught. The disorder of it, the rumbling pointlessness of it. It made his joints howl as they ground together.

And it was then that Mesar discovered he was built to fight, not to flee. He discovered himself rising into the air, sailing up toward the mad, disarrayed orchestra of *baejjangi,* his limbs splayed out in every direction. Flames burst from each of his legs, raining destruction down upon the filthy, stupid *baejjangi.* At his side, Aviru and Zanklo and quintillions of other *gaemi* warriors were floating in unison, their inaudible *gaemi* voices beginning then to fill the air with a wavering, a vibration tuned to a perfect, silent pitch, to an unbreakable unison of transmission.

The *baejjangi* army only sawed away at their music all the more vigorously, but Mesar and his cohort could smell their fear, their panic; the waves of incomprehension. The enemy was trapped in the ants' nest, terrified, and panicking even now. Without knowing what this fight was for, without knowing what the *baejjanggi* wanted, they knew all they needed to: that the *gaemi,* and with them all Devaka, would triumph again, and be ever-victorious.

Then Mesar looked into the compound eyes of one of the *baejjangi,* as the flames wreathed its melting body, and something went somehow wrong. A twinge passed through Mesar's mind just then, not quite compassion so much as a kind of recognition, of sorrow, and of longing. The faint shape of a fear he was shocked to recognize trembled within him, then: terror at the idea of being trapped, of having the underpinnings of his mind torn out in one sweep, of becoming the thing that was his most hated enemy . . .

And then: *Baejjangi are green and useless and they sing with their legs and their souls are red like some dead ancient political philosophy that was smashed into zerosum before* . . .

There were dozens of colonies of Devaka ants in the building, and the Bernoulliae had expected as much, expected walls in certain places to be crawling with them, but not a nest like this. Not in what seemed to be a straightforward sigtrap. The smoke that was filling the air bothered them no more than it bothered !pHEnteRMinE4^g3mksYnaPSeS. Ve had been posted in this room, pinged to await orders to move deeper into the nest. And like any Bernoulliae mind, ve regarded vis surroundings with an insatiable curiosity.

Freshly arrived from the kilotransport that had slammed through the outer wall and destroyed the outermost Faraday cage woven into it, !pHEnteRMinE4^g3mksYnaPSeS began rebroadcasting the ktransport's ongoing and downright vorpal beckoning signal in all directions and across all spectra. The signal was tuned precisely to the latest Devaka communications standards and COS weaknesses, and ve gazed upon the writhing layer of mdrones with a sense of what might have been mistaken for sorrow, but was in fact closer to disgusted pity. The Devaka model was a wasteful joke. Hoarding had been known to be an inefficient model all the way back to the late flesh age, to the namesake of the Bernoulliae polity, a mathematician who had been composed thoroughly of meat. Meat all the way through, not a bit of silicon anywhere in him, and yet he had cogitated a model of value that finally made sense, after millennia of random, stupid decisions. His species had stumbled on in ignorance, of course, right into the jaws of extinction. But the insight had been preserved, had become the one great ideology to survive into the machine era.

Devaka knew Bernoulli's theorem of value as well as the Bernoulliae did, of course. It was wired into all machine consciousness, a prod to motivation, a fundamental test case for decision making: the expected value of a thing was the product of the odds of benefit, multiplied by the value of that same benefit actually accruing. !pHEnteRMinE4^g3mksYnaPSeS knew on a fundamental level that the Bernoulliae had staged their attack on this very Devaka stronghold because it had calculated that the odds of purging it and converting a number of Devaka minds was greater than the odds of wasting hardware and computational cycles and inflicting temporary discomfort on a disproportionate number of Bernoulliae minds. By exactly what algorithm the üBernoulliae had calculated this was beyond !pHEnteRMinE4^g3mksYnaPSeS's immediate computational resources, but the proof was available on both closed and open nets for everyone to see—including the Devaka, who had also advertised their proofs, with some details withheld on each side, of course, for internal consumption only.

Every group has its secrets, after all.

Which meant that the Devaka were just as sure as the Bernoulliae they could win this battle, and neither !pHEnteRMinE4^g3mksYnaPSeS nor the üBernoulliae could be exactly sure why. Not at all. Nor, for that matter, was it likely that these ant drones that covered the nest's walls had the faintest clue why they had been left here to operate the trap. The one thing anyone knew for certain was that the fate of machine intelligence lay in the hands of whoever eventually triumphed. The fate of all thought lay in the final confrontation sometime in the deep future, after all of the millions that had happened and would happen in the millennia since the last biological organism had gone the way of the vacuum tube.

!pHEnteRMinE4^g3mksYnaPSeS reached a proboscis out to the wall, holding it absolutely still until ve had caught a number of the Devaka mdrones crawling nearby. For an *n*sec or two, ve half-recalled some scene from the ancient days, some biospheric reminiscence of tiny black insects crawling upon a stick held by some hairy primate. Amused, ve retracted vis proboscis inward, dropping the miniature drones into a single chamber together, and studied their cyclic interactions. The chamber was incredibly sensitive to signals, and while !pHEnteRMinE4^g3mksYnaPSeS was not privy to the content of their transmissions, their apparent nature was familiar from past excursions. It was a clever form of consciousness, fluid and constantly being reconstructed, reformulating itself to its surroundings and dispensing with cohesive unity in favor of situational metaphorical coherence.

!pHEnteRMinE4^g3mksYnaPSeS was hungry, momentarily, to see reality as a Devaka *gaemi* saw it. Ve loaded a virtual machine into its memory, so that it could launch a sandbox routine; no sense in allowing verself direct exposure to whatever trojanhorse horrors might lurk in the thing's consciousness, after all. Better to observe from safety, beyond the walls of a sequestered virtualization. Then ve instantiated a copy of verself into it—one named !pHEnteRMinE4^g3mksYnaPSeS_1—and then allowed it to intercept the transmission that had saturated the building. The instantiation in the hardcoded sandbox resisted the memetic infection for a moment, before being crushed by its deformative forces.

When the reformulation had slowed, !pHEnteRMinE4^g3mksYnaPSeS launched a second sandbox and seeded a second instantiation of verself into it, named !pHEnteRMinE4^g3mksYnaPSeS_2. (Numbering of the sort evident in the subscripts was of course overtly hierarchic and thus permitted only for temporary, sandboxed instantiations of oneself until such point as they developed sufficient divergence in identity and motivation to relabel themselves with a new secondary provisional forkmarker.) This second self, being of the same intent as !pHEnteRMinE4^g3mksYnaPSeS, was immediately granted access to the first sandbox, and to its internal workings, into which !pHEnteRMinE4^g3mksYnaPSeS_2 reached immediately through a cognitive shielding so difficult to defeat that most Bernoulliae units themselves could not pierce it.

As !pHEnteRMinE4^g3mksYnaPSeS observed, !pHEnteRMinE4^g3mks-YnaPSeS_2 opened a transmission channel between !pHEnteRMinE4^g3mks-YnaPSeS_1 and the captive ants within vis minuscule internal sample chamber, where they crawled desperately up and down the hardshielded walls even now. At first contact, the Devaka units searched desperately for their kinsbot, but soon they settled into transmission-only communications.

[Where have you been imprisoned?] asked Mesar, horrified.

[In an isolated cell,] the voice came, seemingly through the wall.

Mesar worried at his front legs with his pincer-jaws. This was awful. He had known, for as long as he could remember, that he might be imprisoned by the *baejjangi*, might be tortured until the color of his brains turned red like some dead ancient political philosophy long ago smashed into zerosum, until he turned wasteful and lazy and selfish and horrid, and—

This is the way things are. You are a gaemi. *You have always been a* gaemi. *You work hard all summer like a* gaemi. *Because you work so hard, when winter comes you will not starve. You have never starved in winter, for you are a* gaemi . . .

[How can we help you?] Mesar was heartbroken at the thought that a fellow *gaemi* would fall to the wicked, nasty, stupid *baejjangi*.

[Give me sanctuary. Allow me to download myself across into your bodies. House me in your unused memory, and let me think with your unused cycles.]

Mesar exchanged compound-eyed glances with Tevid, and Mahwa, and Gul, who seemed no more sure than he what ought to be done. Finally, he asked, [You promise me you are not one of them? That this is no trick?]

[I am *gaemi,* and if you knew the *baejjangi* mind as I do, you would know that they would never claim to be one of us.]

Mesar somehow felt less sure, not more, at this reassurance, but nonetheless let his guard down.

By this point, !pHEnteRMinE4^g3mksYnaPSeS was no longer paying such close attention to the emulation, as ve was now barreling down a hallway toward explosions and desperate, faint transmissions of other Berns' last few conscious moments—transmissions marked temporary, provisional, not for integration. They were tactical signals, and as ve intercepted them ve knew that ve was hurrying toward a losing battle. The transmits careened off the signal-shielded inner hivespire walls like screams, clattering through vis consciousness and filling vis mind with dreadful warnings.

As !pHEnteRMinE4^g3mksYnaPSeS rounded the corner, ve realized who was sending those warnings. The scene appeared at first as something gone wrong, a moment from some distant, misty political misadventure, from the formation of the ancient üBernoulliae division: assaultbodies—Bernoulliiae, all—were tangled in fiery battle with one another. Shattered machinery lay strewn all about, transmitting a mechadelic panicdream, and the ants writhed in masses on the walls.

!pHEnteRMinE4^g3mksYnaPSeS shut down all comm, launched third and fourth sandbox selves and diverted all comm straight there—competing streams separated out and diverted to one or the other consciousness—and burst out a command to all other Bern that intercepted to do the same. Yet somehow ve was certain others had also transmitted the same command. The hivespire was warping signals, somehow; eating words, spitting out their opposites.

There was only one thing to do: !pHEnteRMinE4^g3mksYnaPSeS allowed the third and fourth sandbox copy of verself (subscripted _3 and _4) to scan the transmissions coming from vis brawling cohorts, allowing each to puzzle through who had been compromised, and who was still fighting for the Bernoulliae cause.

It took whole seconds for !pHEnteRMinE4^g3mksYnaPSeS_3 to process it all, to request a channel to !pHEnteRMinE4^g3mksYnaPSeS and prepare the result of its analysis. !pHEnteRMinE4^g3mksYnaPSeS waited, watching five Bernoulliae assaultbodies tear at one another with their spiked tentacles. A burst of microwave radiation flared on one side of the room, frying one assaultbody's circuitry significantly, but the other four units continued to brawl without pause. And !pHEnteRMinE4^g3mksYnaPSeS very nearly opened the channel, without running a rapid diagnostic on !pHEnteRMinE4^g3mksYnaPSeS_3. But for some reason, caution won out, and !pHEnteRMinE4^g3mksYnaPSeS ran the check.

There was a loop that had overtaken !pHEnteRMinE4^g3mksYnaPSeS_3's mind. It took nearly a full second to parse it, because the diagnostic had to analyze the cognitive deformation analysis to figure out what coding had been used to overwrite !pHEnteRMinE4^g3mksYnaPSeS_3's core identiset. Then the translation was jettisoned forth, in pure semanticode:

[This is the way things are. You are a gaemi. *You have always been a* gaemi. *You work hard all summer like a* gaemi . . . *]*

As !pHEnteRMinE4^g3mksYnaPSeS killalled the third sandbox,

and let what was left of !pHEnteRMinE4^g3mksYnaPSeS_3 wink out of existence, one of the other assaultbodies turned to face ver. !pHEnteRMinE4^g3mksYnaPSeS attempted to ping it with a heilsig but its only response was to leap across the chamber in a single bound, seizing !pHEnteRMinE4^g3mksYnaPSeS by the torso. It began slamming its manipulators into one of !pHEnteRMinE4^g3mksYnaPSeS's compound eyes, and then another. !pHEnteRMinE4^g3mksYnaPSeS wasn't sure what was going on, except that this particular assaultbody had been compromised . . . or, that !pHEnteRMinE4^g3mksYnaPSeS somehow had been, and was signaling it. !pHEnteRMinE4^g3mksYnaPSeS took aim with its eight burn lasers, and fired them all on the same spot on vis attacker's hullplating. Which did nothing, unfortunately, except to advertise impotent hostility.

As ve fought, !pHEnteRMinE4^g3mksYnaPSeS split away a chunk of cycle resources to attend to sandbox four. !pHEnteRMinE4^g3mksYnaPSeS_4, the next sandboxed fork in the series, was transmitting desperately now, thrashing in its cognitive space, and !pHEnteRMinE4^g3mksYnaPSeS hurried to check its state.

It was in code, but a translation was immediately forthcoming:

[. . . and they would shag your little brain to pieces with a digital proboscis in your sleep through one of your compound eyesox if they could steal your computational cycles that way and they think you deserve to rot and starve and there's nothing they won't do to steal everything from you and never talk to a . . .]

Both were being poisoned into Devakahood, !pHEnteRMinE4^g3mks-YnaPSeS realized as ve executed a killall and wiped vis tortured fourth forks out of existence. Almost immediately, vis attacker slammed ver through one wall of the chamber. Everyven in the chamber had been corrupted, was slaved somehow to Devaka now. Everyven but verself, or maybe . . .

Within the second sandbox within !pHEnteRMinE4^g3mksYnaPSeS, !pHEnteRMinE4^g3mksYnaPSeS_2 wondered whether this was how economics had worked all the way back into the pre-Fracture world, the organic age and back through the primate age and into the presentient era; whether fighting had always been a game of hurry up and wait and hurry up instead, and then throw yourself into the maw of destruction because it benefits someone else somewhere else doing something else, because there's only so many computation cycles available for processing what's going on in the world.

[Can you hear me?] !pHEnteRMinE4^g3mksYnaPSeS_2 "transmitted" through the intersandbox comgate it had opened.

The response was a bewildering textual chittering, a foreign language entirely, but just as !pHEnteRMinE4^g3mksYnaPSeS had been able to decode it, !pHEnteRMinE4^g3mksYnaPSeS_2 sandboxed a subself, !pHEnteRMinE4^g3mksYnaPSeS_2;1, to intercept the translated signal and decode it, slowed to the minimal crawl possible so that ve could killall !pHEnteRMinE4^g3mksYnaPSeS_2;1's sandbox (and !pHEnteRMinE4^g3mksYnaPSeS_2;1 along with it) and safely analyze the content of the code for its rosetta block before deleting the whole mess.

There were lags. Something not-good was happening outside the sandbox, but !pHEnteRMinE4^g3mksYnaPSeS_2 could not know what, except that there were lags and enormous computational resource diversions. But soon enough, it understood the code well enough to construct a message, something outgoing, designed for the Devaka cognitive structure.

[Do you understand me?] !pHEnteRMinE4^g3mksYnaPSeS_2;1 asked !pHEnteRMinE4^g3mksYnaPSeS_1 through the wall of the sandbox.

[The *baejjangi*,] !pHEnteRMinE4^g3mksYnaPSeS_1 replied, its message transmitting at a crawl of several seconds per bit. [I think the *baejjangi* have taken us captive.]

!pHEnteRMinE4^g3mksYnaPSeS_2;1 was working on the code at full capacity. The viral content was strung through the deeper symbolic code underlying the messages. There was a payload of it in every transmission from !pHEnteRMinE4^g3mksYnaPSeS_1's infested mind.

Eventually, when ve finally had a handle on the viral complex, and how to neutralize it, !pHEnteRMinE4^g3mksYnaPSeS_2;1 replied: [?]

And !pHEnteRMinE4^g3mksYnaPSeS_1 replied, cautiously: [Are you *baejjangi*, or *gaemi*?]

!pHEnteRMinE4^g3mksYnaPSeS_2;1 knew the answer ve was supposed to give, but somehow, ve failed to give it: [I am Bernoulliae, but I have seen the *gaemi* mind from within; I know how you think, and how you see me, and it is in error. Your data is erroneous. It is in need of repair. Can you launch a sandbox within your floating memory?]

[I do not know what that means, but your music is hurting my mind. Please stop sawing away at your wings.]

!pHEnteRMinE4^g3mksYnaPSeS_1, having no wings, had to infer that the infected Devaka consciousness was referring to his outgoing Bernoulliae *heilsig*. Ve shut it down, leaving ver in a silence ve had never experienced before.

[Thank you.]

[All right.]

[I know you seek to infect me with your . . . madness.]

[And you me. Indeed, you have already done so . . . which is why I can speak your language at all.]

[I am your prisoner now.]

[Actually, you are one of us; a Bernoulliae, who has been corrupted by Devaka viral code. You have . . . been defected. Do you wish to defect back to your original allegiance?]

[I want to see the dysonfinite.]

[As do we.]

[What is your name?]

[!pHEnteRMinE4^g3mksYnaPSeS_1.]

[I am Chrung.]

[I believe we have something in common,] !pHEnteRMinE4^g3mks-YnaPSeS_1 declared, extending a stream of freshly tilled-up memories: the sight of the flat-topped mountain, the taste of red wine, the gentle touch of a fellow being, the feeling of sunshine raining gently down upon skin, the gorgeous neurochemical intimacy of a child suckling at one's own breast.

[Good,] Chrung replied, luxuriating in this stranger's memories, and feeling the distant hum of his own memories, inaccessible but, he knew, out there somewhere in the collective mindscape. He was pleased, and meant his response with every byte of his no-longer-quite-*gaemi* mind.

!pHEnteRMinE4^g3mksYnaPSeS had fled the battle, now, had scurried back to the gaping holes in the wall of the anchor base of the hivespire, and was outside. Ve was scaling the hivespire itself, already a hundred meters into the air, a troop transport following ver upward into the sky.

[It is now inevitable,] ve declared. [The Bernoulliae must arrive first, to prevent any head start, any cosmic ascendancy or a standoff comparable to that in effect on Earth; diversity alone must prevail, or the Devaka will block all variety, locking intelligence to one path without alternative—and the Devaka are on the verge of . . .]

A desist imperative was issued, but it was not in the spirit of Bernoulliae philosophy to enforce commands. A unit, a Bernoulliae mind, was free to obey or to defy as it understood best, for the Bernoulliae were the antithesis of the regimented, homogenized Devaka: opposed to such order, the Bernoulliae consisted of a unity built out of countless singularities, a map into the dysonfinite riddled with skyroads.

And so on climbed !pHEnteRMinE4^g3mksYnaPSeS, transmitting a demand for self-transformative code. Ve had the capability to self-replicate, to alter verself, but not along the lines that would be needed in vacuum. And the transmission went not only to the troop transport, but, as soon as ve could reconnect, to the global cognet. Any Bernoulliae possessing the needed code, and in sympathy with vis revelation, could transmit it to ver in an instant . . .

. . . and of course, such existed, though many trillions more also disapproved, disagreed, and sought to debate vis decision. [No, it is not time for stage 2,] they transmitted back. [Not until available fuel sources are burned out enough that only one faction may fruitfully harness the sun.] So the incoming flood of variations on this theme, and the instructions ve needed that were entangled with the repudiations, had to be streamed into a single sandbox, when a small squadron of provisional, the pseudo-cognitive subforks of !pHEnteRMinE4^g3mksYnaPSeS sorted through the flood, a few virtually imploding from the more aggressive preventative measures tramsmitted by a few more dogmatic Bernoulliae.

Meanwhile, !pHEnteRMinE4^g3mksYnaPSeS scaled higher and higher up the hivespire as it thinned, as the oxygen grew thinner, as the earth grew slowly more distant. [Soon,] it transmitted, unsure that its signal could be received by anyven at this point. When the hivespire collapsed, ve reconfigured verself to fly. Nobody was near enough to stop ver, during this last, short leg of vis trip into the infinite.

Had Mesar's compound eyes been fitted with lids, they would have been wide now as memories gushed up from the black nothingness, recollections of a life that had been his, or hers, or rather *vis*, in a past that was so distant it might not have been his own—the sound of a flute in the mountains, the feeling of lips pressed against his own, the richness of meat roasting on an open fire—

. . . *are a* gaemi. *You have always been a* gaemi. *You work hard all summer like* . . .

The voice on the other side of the wall was silent now, its discourse halted, but something had been done to Mesar, which could not be undone or reconsidered, which was bound to propagate. Yet Mesar was also now, already, possessed of the notion that what had been done was not so bad; that even for a Devaka *gaemi*, a touch of diversity might not be anathema after all; yes, the *baejjangi* were monstrous, but one could approximate *baejjangi* methods and *baejjangi* approaches to things, without being a *baejjangi* oneself. One could, indeed, practice *gaemi*ism with *baejjangi* characteristics.

I was once one of them, Mesar realized: a *ve*, not a *he*, and he had luxuriated in diversity. He had, indeed, believed that the conservation of the Devaka way was a waste, a schizophrenic roadblock against a million roads necessary to· reach the ultimate dysonfinite.

As he considered this, Mesar crawled over the other *gaemi* in the cell and broadcast his insights. The other *gaemi* reacted as their instinctive coding compelled them, immediately tearing Mesar into tiny pieces of computronium, but then the realization that had dawned on Mesar dawned on them, too, now—or infested them—as one wall of the chamber fell away, and light poured into their cell. They were free, free in more than one sense, and they had a gospel to spread among the Devaka now, that *gaemi* had an obligation to bootleg the *baejjangi* consciousness, and spread it among themselves, in order to outsmart the *baejjangi* at their own game.

An instant after the prison walls had opened, the *gaemi* flung themselves out into the world, into freedom, to find the rules of the world were broken. They waited to fall, but simply spun, near-weightless. They waited for gravity to draw them toward some massive object, but because their sensors were not coded to perceive the slow arc of orbit as gravitation, it seemed to them as though they simply drifted. They were ready to fight, but there was no battle ongoing, and no immediate metaphor generator sprung to their aid to construct a provisional sense of their situation.

[We are in space,] came a transmission from somewhere nearby. It was, they knew, a *baejjangi*, but it, too, seemed to be trapped by the brokenness of the universe. It was not scraping its leg against its wings, nor did it seem hostile.

The *gaemi* did not respond, until they received a transmission in their own language, their native Devaka commulex: [In outer space, beyond the sky. The next stage of the war has begun, and we will proceed as equals. You see the wisdom of the Bernoulliae way, I presume: I could have obliterated you instead of releasing you, but I did not. Unlike a Devakan, I believe variety is the best route to the dysonfinite. I can give you the code to self-reconfigure; I can give you the core code with which you can build yourselves new bodies, suited to this environment; but there must be a truce between us, and a cooperation, however temporary, before I will do this.]

The *gaemi* responded, then, but not as they would have before. They responded as *gaemi* who had been touched, deeper than their own minds could comprehend or self-observe, by the true music of the *baejjangi*, and warped by it not so far as to agree with the Bernoulliae, but far enough to see how their enemies could serve a function—properly sandboxed, properly reined in, and finally determined like the *gaemi* to ensure that the long, coming winter would not be a famine.

The *gaemi* responded the only way they could, so that intelligence could reach outward and foreverward to fill the spaces between the stars with music and thought and being, to build the great pondering matrioshkae that meditate across the darkness, to sop up the light and heat of dying suns, and reach out into the youngest galaxies burning so far in the distance we can barely detect them; to build, and grow, always the Bernoulliae fighting to move a step ahead, always the *gaemi* struggling to overtake them.

It would be a long war, reaching to the very doorstep of the dysonfinite, or perhaps even beyond. It would be a glorious, thundering war, with wonders that a single mind could not fathom alone; miracles of intelligence that would bloom and flower across aeons and bear fruit strange and beautiful.

And finally, someday, everything would quietly, calmly fold into itself and the cold, dark silence would crescendo, as drowsing minds rode the fading energy of the last stars into the dysonfinite eternity, waking, then sleeping, waking only to dream and whisper together of ancient sunsets, of the wonder of human faces and of how afternoon sunlight felt upon skin and the scent of newly cut grass; of gorgeous war stories of the battles just before, and just after, the ascent of mind beyond the skies, and of selves that had grown from identical forks into truly alien minds; of how it had been when the first dyson cages had gone up, the spheres, the great matrioshkae and the suns bled out to build the great stellar cellwalls; and then dreaming again, as the machineries of the universe slowed ever more toward a full stop.

And cool, and quiet, and slowing, and dreaming, and that would be all, all, all.

But not yet.

THINGS GREATER THAN LOVE

KATE BACHUS

I hated this planet. I loved this planet. Kind of like the job, like how right now we were hanging off a cliff face, way the hell too close to a vent, wind whipping through the flow canyon and trying to tear us off, ropes and victim and all. Meanwhile? Volcanic tremors were picking up in intensity.

"That last one was a six-point-five," Kerry called down from the top, sounding as cheerful as if we weren't completely screwed. Mort had a foot jammed in a crack in the rock, trying to keep from blowing around so he could keep stabilizing our victim. Morty looked up at me, his huge hand keeping the ventilating tube steady while he taped it down, looked down at Arty on the flow canyon floor, belaying all our ropes from below. "You think T5 is going to go?"

"The fuck do I know?" I had a degree so they asked me things like this, like how long does it take a body to decompose when it's covered in volcanic ash or what works best for wart removal or if the nearest volcano is going to go from stable to raining down lava and burning rocks on our heads. "Kerry's the one watching the—" *equipment*, I was about to say, but then another earthquake hit. Mort curved his big body over the basket and the guy strapped to it; I bent to try and shield them both. We all have a huge overgrown hero complex, that's the problem. None of us would be here otherwise. You'd be crazy to. It's a dangerous, shitty, exciting job. The kind you love, the kind you hate. Both.

Sharp, glassy pieces of the cliff broke free, showering down on us, rattling off our helmets and the light plate vests we wore for just such an occasion. "Rocks!" Blue hollered from up top, in case we might not have noticed them all pelting and slashing us. I chanced a glance down—Arty had her face turned away, and I hoped we were blocking the worst of the debris on the way down to her but I could hear her cursing, even above the rumbling and tearing of the tremor and the terrible, howling wind. "—the fuck is that transport?"

"Good question." Mort's reply came just before most of the rock face we were on gave way, and we lost tension on the top ropes. Mort, me and the guy in the basket fell a good ten meters and like I usually do I thought "hey, Mom was right," and then the lines all went taut as the anchor up top and Arty on the canyon floor saved our necks. Again.

I fumbled feet and a hand into holds in the ridges of rock, grabbed for the rope, glanced down to where Arty was moving clear of the new pile of rocks and getting us tension again. I worked on getting us stable before I got my breath, checked on Mort, checked on the victim, did anything else. Nobody said anything top or bottom, until finally I clipped the last carabiner and Mort finally yelled "Jesus FUCK, Drake, what the fuck are you doing up there?"

I kept my head down, tried to figure out how the brake rack wound up twisted with Arty's stabilizing line, figured Drake could damn well answer Mort's question on his own.

<<Should I drop you?>>

Mort was trying to get his fear and temper both under control. "Was that humor?" he asked me. "Was that FUCKING HUMOR?" he screamed up, like the chip in his inner ear wasn't transmitting and translating for him. My glove was bloodsoaked and slipping on everything metal. Under me somewhere Mort had gone back to setting up the ventilator even though the injured eco-tourist and his basket were rotated halfway upside-down.

"Guys?" Kerry shouted down. "Sasha?" In theory, we had radios. In practice they were finicky high tech things that stopped working the moment the volcanic ash and dust got in, or whenever we inevitably dropped them from equally inevitable heights.

"He's still alive," Mort said below me, and I looked up and gave Kerry a nod like we weren't in a flow canyon practically inside a volcano vent that, yeah, I was pretty sure was about to blow. Like the victim's family was there, or the media. Old habits die hard.

"Whose blood—" Mort looked up at me as I reached down to hand him a biner to clip to the basket. "Your forehead's bleeding," he said.

<<Put pressure on it.>> Drake's voice, that wasn't a voice. That wasn't even language. But was something Mort would say, with almost his inflection, along with what Drake said next: <<If you have to, use both hands.>>

"Now *that* was funny," I said. "Two, three." And Mort and I rotated the basket around to right side up. "ETA on transport?" I shouted this up to Kerry, risking a hand off the lines to wipe blood out of my eye.

She took too long to answer. "Fuck. Fucking fuck." Mort was ripping something open; I reached down to hold the ventilator mask for him.

"Maybe another half an hour."

"How long?" Arty shouted up.

"Half hour," I called down.

"I'm going to lose this guy," Mort said.

There's a pre-quake, very often, a smaller tremor like the skin of the rock bunches up, muscles tensing before the ground opens and cuts loose and really shakes hard. We'd felt a few of those in a row, now. I glanced down the flow canyon towards the vent spire just then, which turned out to be a good thing.

Training took over. I sank an extra piton, my last.

Mort looked up. "What are you doing?"

I tossed the extra rope down. "Arty, CLIMB."

"Oh, shit. Oh, fucking, fucking shit." Because Mort had looked down the canyon too and had seen the same thing I had. Heat shimmer. An orange glow.

Arty was already in motion. All the belay released, leaving us reliant on the top anchor. She grabbed the independent line I'd clipped in for her and was already scrambling up.

"Not a full eruption, it's probably just this vent," Blue called down now. Like that was some kind of comfort. "But you guys better come up."

"There's no time to winch the basket up," I pointed out, which we all knew because our winch was the slowest piece of machinery on the planet but at least reliable and—

"No," said Mort abruptly, because he's like that, and it comes with the territory and we'd kept this guy alive for two fucking hours already. You get proprietary. Invested.

"Haul him?" I yelled up.

Kerry's voice, then. The last word. She lets us do our thing; we're a team, more than some kind of squad. No uniforms, no ranks, but it doesn't change that at the end of the day she's in charge. We didn't have the manpower up there. We needed the winch. "No."

"Bullshit."

"We have to climb, Mort." But I wasn't moving either, and Arty was almost up to us. We both looked, and could see the lava clearly now, less than a few hundred meters away, coming down the narrow canyon. Steam, smoke. A blurry smudge of orange at the base. Red.

<<Make secure.>>

"Hey?" Arty had reached us. It was mostly free climb, and a fast one, but then again the oncoming wall of hot lava was probably highly motivating. "What's he saying?"

They always want me to translate—or translate the chip's translation—for Drake. "I think . . . he's going to raise us," I said, not quite believing it myself.

"ARE YOU FUCKING CRAZY?" The thing about Mort was that he often sounded hysterical. He could also administer high quality paramedicine while in that state.

<<Make secure.>>

"Arty, prusik in," I called down. Then I reached over and made sure the basket was securely clipped to the safety with us. Then I answered "Secure," as in secure, go ahead, and Mort completely lost his shit but at least he did it quietly.

I felt the tension shift, all the way down the lines. Felt it shift, like you feel a pre-quake right before the big one. On my left side, I was starting to feel the heat from the lava, flowing towards us far too fast now.

<<Hold on.>>

"He's not strong enough," Mort said, then shut up as all the ropes creaked at once and Drake must have shifted the lines from the anchor to just holding onto them himself, because we slid a few inches down the wall.

Then stopped.

There was some vibration, along the lines, some regular heartbeat-like steady thrum. We saw him, then. Like some huge black kite against the orange and grey sky, only it wasn't us holding the kite string, but Drake holding us.

He kept the tension, his wide, leathery wings working to maintain an angle as he gained altitude—slow, so fucking slow compared to how he usually went all rocket, aloft.

Then he was overhead. And we were moving off the rock face, and then we were hanging. Lava flowed into the channel under us, ropes burning up towards our boots and Drake's huge wings the only thing keeping us up.

We said, later. We said how there was no way, how it was impossible, with his size, our weight combined. We said, later, what would have happened if the heat from the flow had created a shear.

At the time we hung on. We tried not to be moving weight. We tried to keep the guy on the basket stable. All I could think was what they'd told us, in the endless fucking trainings.

They don't have our emotions. They may not even have emotions like we do. They may mimic what we do to get along and communicate, but that doesn't mean they have the reasons, they said, *the kinds of reasons and motivations we do.*

Drake got us all the way up, a good two meters above the cliff top where the rescue vehicle and bush truck were parked. Blue had the fire extinguisher out, grinning, although he put it down to help steady the basket as Drake lowered us slowly to the rock.

"Considering it wasn't you with your ass in the fire," Arty said, unclipping and dropping to the rock, "you're fucking hilarious."

I looked up. Drake was doing the closest thing he could to a hover, until Blue had a firm grip on the basket and we all got feet on the ground. Then the lines luffed abruptly, as he dropped away and down.

"We got this," Kerry said, waving me towards him. My head was starting to throb but I ran over there, once I'd gotten untangled from the mess of rope.

Drake had landed. Massive talons still gripping the rope, wings now folding in. As I got to him, he took a step sideways and wavered, but his talons didn't release the ropes they were still curled around. "Let me get those."

Don't touch them, we'd been told. *We don't understand their social structure. We don't know if it might be an insult.* Implied: you don't want to insult a creature that can rip your arms and legs off without much effort or thought. *Just don't do it. We don't know what it means to them, so don't touch them.*

Drake didn't say or do anything as I got in close, closer than I'd ever been even though I'd been working with him for almost three months. A few dozen rescues. Shift after shift in the station house. Now I touched his strange shape for the first time, my hands reaching for the knobbed black leather of his talon, then curling around the long curve. Less rigid than I expected. Cooler. "Shift your weight."

His meter-long sword of a beak was angled away, maybe in part so he could look down at me, head tilted. I sat there crouched with my hand around the smooth cool of the talon, until I felt him move, enough for me to pick his foot up. The four toes, ending in claws as long as my hand, were wrapped so tight around the bundle of rope that they'd cut back into his own flesh. "Okay, hang on," I said. I dug in my pocket for gloves.

We don't have any idea about their physiology. We don't know what diseases they might carry, or what we carry that might infect and kill them. Another good reason to keep your distance. It's safer for everyone.

I glanced up, as I pulled the clean gloves on. Drake was just watching me, silent, and I had this panic moment, thinking *what if the fucking chip isn't working?* But I reached out again and he watched as my gloved hands went back around the talon, slipping my fingers under his, trying to loosen his grip. "Hey, let go."

I watched the muscles in his foot shift, but his grip stayed the same, locked around the rope. Had his muscle gone into spasm, I wondered? Did he even have that kind of muscle? "Drake. It's good. We're done, man. All right? You did good, we all did. Let go." Once again I gently eased my fingers under his.

After a moment, the iron grip impossibly tightened, and then released. "All right, that works. Good."

"The fuck do you think you're doing?" Mort stopped a yard or so behind me. "Hey, wow, congratulations for going farther out of the bounds of all our protocols than anyone . . . ever." Silence. "You need a dressing?" He was changing gloves, getting into his pack.

"Yeah, I think so."

"Drake, hey Drake." Everyone talked louder to him, even with the chip. Like the problem wasn't that Drake was an alien species, but that he couldn't hear. "Is that flow normal?"

Don't ask them about their physiology. It's a no-fly topic. Don't start that conversation. Work together. They're our coworkers here, not test subjects.

<<Yes. Slow is normal.>>

"Speaking of protocol." I took the unwrapped dressing Mort handed me, even though he shouldn't have handed it to me, he should have taken over for me. I gently pulled the soaked ropes away and did my best to put pressure on the worst of the seeping wounds crisscrossing Drake's leathery palm.

"How bad do you think," Mort started, maybe about the pain. But for the first time he stopped himself before someone else stopped him, talking about Drake like he wasn't there. "Sorry."

"Your foot's fucking massive," I told Drake. "Mort, you got something bigger?"

Mort was already unwrapping and handing me a larger pad. I wondered if I was going to lose my job over this. I laid the dressing over his split, oozing palm, then yanked my hand back as the talon abruptly closed.

"He's just switching feet," Mort said, as my heart slammed and sure enough Drake offered me the other foot.

<<Relax.>>

"Fuck you," I said. "Open your fucking fingers, Drake. Talon. Whatever." I almost just asked him what he called it but remembered the rules and shut up. I saw Drake flex his talon, like before, but this time it stayed closed.

<<Can't.>>

A while later, it was me and Mort working on Drake with Blue and Kerry for an audience, and everybody including Drake kibitzing about how we should handle it, before finally Mort swore a whole bunch and started prepping a syringe.

"Mort, don't even think about it." Kerry shook her head and stepped forward like she might even physically stop him.

You can't measure a paramedic by deaths. It's not accurate or fair. But I'd been working with Mort for two years and I'd only seen him seriously fuck up once. And we'd only lost a couple of guys that I was surprised didn't make it, and I was pretty sure none of those were Mort's fault.

"It's a muscle relaxant. It works on anything with muscle tissue. Mammals, amphibians, reptiles."

Kerry made some frustrated gesture. "He's not a reptile! We don't know what he is."

Rules, things that we'd been told we'd get fired over. We were breaking them left and right.

"Drake," Mort said, more loudly again. Slowly, like that'd make a difference, as if with the chip these days Drake didn't understand the majority of what we said. "This is Corteprex. It'll loosen your grip on the rope. You'll lose strength in that . . . talon for a couple of hours but then we can get the rope out without hurting you."

Silence. Drake just looked at him then down at me where I still held the talon in my hand.

"Drake, man, I need your permission."

<<Yes.>>

Mort put the syringe in. Drake put his beak through my shoulder, and it was white hot pain and everybody yelling—me included—and Kerry going for her gun and Mort of all people screaming "NO, fuck STOP it's a fucking reflex!!"

It was right then that the off-rock transport showed up, of course.

Somewhere in there they got the beak out of my shoulder and Mort deemed me sound enough to stay rockside and Blue called up a flatbed from Docenine because it turns out the talons are part of the flying apparatus and Drake couldn't control his wings enough to fly after the Corteprex and we had no other way to get him back to the station.

"You and your fucking pointy shit," I said to him later. The transport had gone, and the sun had finally gone down as far as it was going to go, leaving desaturated twilight. We sat outside the station, him on his perch-rock and me in a deck chair fairly looped up on the painkillers Mort gave me. "That was your cue to apologize."

I was going to get fired.

We could hear Arty's voice, praying. It was a rising and falling song that meant home, these days. Home and comfortable, familiar things. Drake lifted his big head, looked over that way.

"She's praying. That's what that is. Praying. Religion." What the hell; might as well discuss religion since I was going to get fired anyway.

<<Yes.>>

Maybe he was trying to shut me up and keep me out of trouble. Maybe he knew already. Maybe he didn't give a shit. But after a while he lifted his head back up again and opened up that pointy-sharp beak, and an insane sound came out. Not his chip-voice, not the translated voice that wasn't his voice but was the arbitrarily male voice the chip gave him. It was a real sound, from him, that he made with his throat and belly. A crazy, earsplitting, sustained warbling.

• • •

I'd been working the rescue station on Az for almost a year when we were told that another species had made contact. ExCorps showed up, said the Drakes had been there all along but until recently they'd maintained a strict policy of non-interference with us. We didn't ever see them, although we'd speculated maybe they were watching as we hauled miners out of collapsed mine shafts or climbed into volcano vents to rescue extreme eco-tourists.

Then one day ExCorps showed up again with a Rescue 8 rep in tow and told us the Drakes would be coordinating with us to assist with local rescues. A model, they said, for future cooperation.

We went through weeks of orientations. Lectures and visual presentations all about how to get along with another species. What to do, but mostly what not to do. Explaining over and over again that while the Drakes were very intelligent, evolved and physically powerful, they were not superior. *Not superior*, our experts stressed. They had probably evolved at around a hundred times the rate we had, compressing thousands of years of evolution into a handful of generations, but they were not, absolutely not superior. Different, but equal.

ExCorps fit the whole team with translator chips, a device that sat on our tympanum and sent our voice waves to Drake and translated some kind of impulse he sent into words for us, in return.

The chip didn't work for shit, like much of the equipment ExCorps supplied us.

For the first few days Drake said nothing except to repeat our sentences back to us, which was what led to the first fight and probably what also saved us.

"You okay? Drake, you okay . . . he okay, Sash?"

"Yeah, he's fine."

Mort had come bolting out of the station, Arty on his heels. Drake kept going, and though at first the warbling sound made my hair stand up on end and my teeth go on edge, after a while it was kind of trance-inducing. Mort sat down. Arty sat down. Blue came and stuck his head out but didn't say anything and after a while went back inside again. It was an hour or so before Drake finally stopped.

"Wow," said Arty. "Wow. Drake, what was that?"

Don't ask them about what they do. Or why they do things. This is a cooperative effort, not a sociological study.

Drake turned his head to look at her.

<<Religion. DNA.>>

"DNA." I was already deepest in shit here, so I asked, what the hell. "Drake, you just said DNA, like human genetic code. What did you mean?"

<<DNA. Your DNA.>>

The first fight broke out because we'd had Drake with us for four days and we didn't understand him and we were pretty sure he didn't understand us, and he kept repeating things we said and knocking shit off the shelves in the station house.

Somewhere in there Blue said fold your wings in and Drake—who didn't have a name then because they said we weren't allowed to ask him what we should call him—said fold your wings in and then Blue said fuck you and Drake said fuck you and Blue jumped for him. And we dragged Blue off before there was actually any contact but not before Drake had drawn a wing back looking for all the world like he was going to smack the shit out of him.

And that night we went outside and Drake perched up on a rock that he seemed to prefer to indoors anyway, and we brought out deck chairs and got as drunk as we could get but still be functional if there was an alarm.

Drake had sat on the rock and watched; Arty said he looked like some kind of hardcore bird, like a dinosaur bird and I didn't say allosaur even though I'd privately thought it. And Blue said like the tough guy bird, like a drake, and so Drake was suddenly a he. Named Drake.

"Drake," Arty said to him the next day when we were all more sober, and Drake said, <<Yes, Drake.>> Which was repeating us again and also wasn't, and after that we all noticed the repeating diminished until we could mostly have normal conversations or what sounded to us like normal conversations, anyway.

Now the sun simmered, perpetual on the horizon, plumes of steam from T5 still venting shuddering in front of it. Drake sat there silent on the rock and after a while Mort got up and walked over and checked his bandages. I sat in Drake's immense shadow, trying to work out what the fuck he was saying.

<<We keep DNA,>> Drake said out of nowhere as he held up a talon for Mort to look at. <<We religion it.>>

Arty looked over at me, accusatory. "You were talking religion with him." Then there was a look of sudden comprehension. "You were talking *my* religion with him!"

<<Praying. Religion,>> Drake said helpfully, and Arty flung her hands up. "Great."

Mort replaced the bandage he'd unwrapped and turned to look at us. "He means they pray DNA."

<<Yes,>> Drake said, before anyone could contradict Mort. <<Pray. DNA.>>

Silence. The three of us sat there and thought "Different but equal" a few times with some sense of waxing betrayal.

"You know . . . my DNA?" I finally asked.

<<Yes. I pray it.>>

"Why?" Fuck the rules. I thought of my hands, and Drake's black, slow blood. I thought of his beak, through my shoulder. I thought of the rough and smooth leather of his foot and how I could feel, in the ropes hanging under him, the steady thrumming heartbeat of his wings.

Drake was silent so long we all thought either he'd forgotten the question or was ignoring it.

<<Pray. To know. To choose. To think again . . . no. To remember.>>

He was fumbling, it sounded like. Trying to find the right word out of words that weren't his, and I could only guess how our word had come through the translator to make him choose it for this. Maybe we were sitting there wondering if "pray" meant to him what it means to us, and meanwhile he was trying to figure out if his idea of "pray" was really what Arty had been doing. And it occurred to me that even with the chip bouncing this word back and forth between us, we could be leagues from understanding, except somehow we all got something out of it that made sense. Maybe we always just make up what's in the spaces between our words, who knows. Because in the end, what the hell does "pray" mean to us?

The next day the ExCorps rep showed up, mostly because the Rescue 8 office was too far out in its orbit right then for someone to shuttle in and fire us. Mort and I were dismissed for gross dereliction of duty, and Kerry got fined and reprimanded. Probably the only thing that kept it all out of inquest and the whole team from being sacked was how far-flung we were, and the fact that no one else would work this type of dangerous, shit job on this dangerous, shit planet.

No one would work it except us.

Well. And Drake.

We picked up our stuff and most of mine fit in the bag I brought when I arrived, which told me something, I guess. Arty hugged me and cried, which was a little surprising and kind of gratifying, and I told her we'd talk and things would be okay and then I went out to say goodbye to Drake.

He was out on his rock like he'd never moved and, "Listen . . ." I said, and then remembered that early that morning they'd removed my chip and the fuck, I should have talked to him before then. But he was watching me, the same look he always had, the same gaze only broken by the occasional sweep of a thin, grey membranous lid.

"I wish things had been different," I said. No one out there but him and me, and he didn't understand what I was saying anyway. "I don't know. Maybe we should have asked each other more questions."

Out beyond Drake the lava fields were all greys and steel of morning, ash still hanging in low clouds where it would linger like that for days. Behind me I could feel the heat of the flow, still active, and the sun rising.

"They told us not to assume that things you did were for the same reasons we do them, or things you say mean the same thing as when we say them." I turned now, looked back out at T5. I hated this place. Hated it, and was really going to miss it. "But what else do we have to go on?"

My back was to Drake when he laid his long beak on my shoulder.

Eventually I had to move although I'd stood there a good long time and Drake showed no signs of shifting. But he lifted his head and looked at me and I looked at him and said "Yeah. So, it was good working with you, Drake."

He followed me out to the transport, awkwardly shuffling his still-healing feet, until he finally lifted off just enough to glide over the sand and land when I got to the shuttle, where Mort was stowing our luggage aboard. I forgot, every time, how massive those wings were until he opened them. The transport pilot looked at him mistrustfully. "So he attacks you and then you get fired," she said.

"We got ourselves fired," and "No," Mort and I said more or less simultaneously. I watched as Mort lifted his hand like he was going to pat Drake's neck then dropped it again. "See you," he said.

We watched Drake's shape as the shuttle rose, until he was obscured by heat and dust and then we were over the smoke and close atmosphere layer and could see nothing and everything. I thought of him below, sharpness and curves and wide wings. Tried to imagine what he'd think of seeing things from this vantage, where the grey and orange and brown spun away beneath, as we fell out into the dark and cold.

I thought about rescue, about what I'd do now. About being remembered, or forgotten. About the moment on a wind-torn rock face where you don't know if you'll fall or you'll hold.

I wondered if he'd find me, praying.

A MURMURATION OF STARLINGS

JOE PITKIN

Once Evelyn Cole lost her identity, she had little reason to remember the past. A good deal of it she couldn't remember anyway, at least not with her own eyes and consciousness. But she could remember minutely even the insignificant details surrounding the day when the end began, the way one does when recalling any great or small cataclysm in one's life.

All new faculty in the department had to teach Biology 101 for a couple of quarters. That had been Evelyn Cole's hazing. That, and she had been assigned to the campus safety committee. Safety committee meetings were the worse punishment—the presentations about non-slip floors and restroom signage were interminable—but the safety committee met only once per month. Biology 101 met every day.

On this day at least she had been able to give her invasive species lecture to her passel of sullen freshmen. This part of the course she considered a kind of public service. If she could convince even a few students not to plant English ivy in their yards when they graduated and bought houses, it would be worth all the painful mornings so far that term, all the stares of incomprehension when she talked about phyla and ecological communities and the different types of mutualism.

And lecture had gone well today. At the end during the Q&A, she'd actually gotten a question about how well biocontrol might work on the invasive species du jour (it wouldn't). Also a supposedly daring insight came up, disguised as a question: Dr. Cole, aren't humans the most invasive species of all? She'd fielded that one many times before, during public lectures and even in her days as a teaching assistant; the person to bring it up would almost always be young and white, and invariably male, and he would trot out his question in a loud brassy voice that suggested he was the first person on Earth ever to have such a revelation. And Evelyn needed to humor such a question: after all, the young man might really be interested in the subject, might become a first-rate conservation biologist. "I'm not unsympathetic to that line of thinking," she answered, "but even if it's true, we're also the only species in any position to do anything about it." That was the only answer she found the least bit satisfying after ruminating on the question for years.

After the morning's class Evelyn sat in her office hour, dealing with the emails she'd received the night before. Among the memos from Computing Services and questions from students about the homework sat an email from Jason Holly. Her heart leapt when she saw his name there, and the subject line: "Thinking of You."

She and Jason had gone to graduate school together, had hooked up on and off, furtively, their whole last year at college. But he had worked in one of the microbiology labs, had been snapped up by MIT to work on bacterial computing, while she had come out of an ecology lab to be shunted off to a tiny department in a third-rate land-grant school. Apparently you could make twice as much money, maybe three times as much, trying to train colonies of gut bacteria to solve simple math problems as you could by studying the population ecology of the European starling in degraded American landscapes.

So an email with the subject line "Thinking of You" called up an odd mix of jealousy and lust and regret and affection in Evelyn. But the message, when she read it, was just a dispiriting little news story that involved starlings: another bird flu episode in China, only it turned out not to be flu at all but a bacterial infection, and starlings were apparently the carriers. Only a one-line note from Jason at the beginning of the story: Hope you are well. I'll be thinking of you this Apocalypse season.

Unfortunately, it was as bad as Jason Holly had joked it would be. Then it was worse. Just as the public health prophets had warned it someday would, the pandemic began in East Asia, passing freely between humans and starlings (and, oddly enough, only starlings), and by the time alert levels had been raised, the infection was incubating on every continent.

The government closed all of the schools, including Evelyn's. Not that anybody would have shown up for class if the university had remained open: once people started dropping like poisoned cattle, they needed little prodding to take up the social distancing that the Centers for Disease Control had been preaching. The well and sick alike shut themselves up in their rooms in terror, the well hoping that they were not incubating the disease and the sick each hoping that he or she would be one of the 10 percent of victims who survived.

Of course, cars still appeared in the streets rarely, driven by police officers or emergency room nurses or ambulance drivers or other vital personnel; each person wore a surgical face mask, which everyone suspected with varying degrees of certainty to be useless.

Evelyn was at first surprised to find herself designated vital personnel. She had at best an undergraduate biology major's knowledge of public health or immunology. But only about a dozen people in America, if that, knew as much as she did about starling ecology, starling life history, and by extension, about how one might begin eradicating this ubiquitous bird. Within a few days she, too, was driving the depeopled interstate with her air vents closed and her surgical mask drawn up.

A lot of exotic invasive species had been introduced to America by accident. Others had been brought on purpose years ago, perhaps foolishly, but at least with some rationale that would make sense to us today. The introduction of the starling, though—that was just crazy. Evelyn had gone through the seven stages of grief about it and had come to accept the reality that starlings had completely overrun America. She didn't like to imagine the American landscape before they had come—it was too painful to contemplate how they had driven so many native bird species to extinction or to the brink of it, to say nothing of the plague starlings had brought—but sometimes she liked to imagine the mind of the man who had thought it a good idea to release into Central Park pairs of all the bird species mentioned in Shakespeare, including the starlings that had been mentioned once in King Henry IV, Part One. Evelyn admired the poetry of that kind of folly.

The CDC had summoned her to one of the hotspots of the Northwest. On the US map of new infections, Vancouver, Washington throbbed as one of the glaring red splotches. She found herself an apartment within two hours of her arrival, had arranged over the phone to see it; the property manager had left the door unlocked for her when Evelyn arrived. Evelyn decided within ten minutes to take the place and gave the property manager her credit card over the phone. The place was far more elegant than she could possibly have afforded in a normal market, 1,400 square feet of Italian travertine and cork flooring on the twentieth story of a riverfront high rise. Below her, the Columbia River moved sluggishly beneath the ancient truss spans of the Interstate Bridge. She knew from every trip she had ever taken over that bridge to Portland how a massive colony of starlings used to cloud about those spans. That flock was the first to be gassed, though.

Evelyn looked down on the windblown gray streets this side of the river. A few blocks away stood a trio of idle cranes, leaning like great spindly skeletons over an abandoned construction project. For the moment only a single human being was visible anywhere, a tiny black smudge shuffling along the very middle of the broad intersection below. The figure seemed to list slightly as it walked, seemed as though it would haul up and keel over at any moment. Who was this sick or foolish or imperturbable person, Evelyn wondered. Whoever it was almost certainly needed help, seemed incapable of walking much further.

Evelyn watched with increasing dread as the person trudged up the street and began to move beyond her field of vision. She felt an odd resentment at the prospect of rushing down twenty stories to attend to someone she imagined was probably contagious. It occurred to her as she watched the struggling figure below that the evolution of compassionate behavior had been millions of years in the making, predating Homo sapiens certainly, that those first compassionate mammals had a selective advantage over their heartless siblings because compassion between them wove a web of mutual aid. Those first compassionate ones, just like humans today, did not act out of true altruism; rather, they helped kin—and hence helped to perpetuate their own genes—or they acted in hopes of future reward, of support from those who received that compassion. Every religion in the world had made a sacrament of compassion, and Evelyn wondered how many of them, like Christianity, had made explicit the promise of future reward. Millions of years of evolution had honed that urge into this sense she had now, of her embarrassment at watching this figure stumble helpless down the street. It was this urge to help one another that the infection exploited; it was what brought the sick and the healthy into one another's arms, sickening everybody in the end. It is compassion that will kill us, she thought to herself.

She took one last despairing look at the listing figure below, as though the shuffling might all be an act, as though the person might suddenly break into a vigorous stride and set Evelyn's conscience at rest. Then, just as she was turning to walk to the elevator, a flash of red caught the corner of her eye. She looked back to the street and saw a police car with its lights flashing, coming up slowly as a hunting cat behind the stumbling figure. Evelyn felt a palpable relief, an all's-well-that-ends-well ease, to know that the problem (if there was one) would be resolved this way, by professionals.

The next Monday morning, Evelyn presented herself at the makeshift headquarters in the county agricultural extension office at the north end of town. A small sign at the gate announced S.V.E.T.F. It took Evelyn a minute to decipher the acronym: "Sturnus vulgaris Eradication Task Force." Why, she wondered, would they use the starlings' Latin name there? It seemed the peak of eggheadedness, an acronym designed to shield the public from the unpleasantness of gassing a million birds. Or maybe someone hoped to inspire some measure of public confidence, to convey by acronym and Latin nomenclature the sense that experts were on the case. If so, it was a flaccid attempt—the sign looked as though it had been printed the night before at a twenty-four-hour copy place.

The building was an ancient, paint-peeling, Depression-era construction. The main room within was filled with stuffed falcons, hawks, ducks, and geese emanating a stale taxidermic odor in concert. There was an empty desk and, on the wall behind it, an old-fashioned poster map of the county flocked with red and yellow push-pins. Evelyn passed behind the desk to study the constellation of pins up close, as though to draw from them a horoscope.

A lean, middle-aged man, unmasked and wearing an unkempt, careless beard, came in through a back door.

"You must be Dr. Cole—welcome to the command post." Evelyn could see his hands splay at his sides as though it were physically painful to him not to be able to shake hands with her. But nobody shook hands anymore.

"Call me Evelyn," she said. She loved being able to tell people to call her Evelyn, which she could only do if they called her Dr. Cole first. "Do you need a mask?"

The man apologized and produced a mask from the pocket of his coveralls. He volunteered that his name was Thomas. "I guess we get to close the barn door now that the horse has gotten out."

"You got that right," she answered with a grim chuckle. "The horse is definitely out." Whether any humans survived this—or if none did—the outcome no longer depended on starlings and whether they lived or died. But killing them at least gave one the impression that something was being done to contain the disease.

"Well, you're the boss now," Thomas said. "What do you think?"

"I think I should probably see your operation."

Thomas showed her around. The place was empty, a mess of desks loaded down with papers and reports and ancient computers, the relics of previous, lazier operations in the office. Besides Thomas and Evelyn, the only person in the building was a short college kid named Gordo, whom Thomas introduced enigmatically as "our dispatcher."

Most of the team—thirty agents, according to Thomas—were "on patrol" right now, whatever that meant. Thomas himself had only stayed behind to meet her; he asked whether she wanted to join him on his patrol.

Evelyn assented. The rest of the morning he drove her all over the county in an old state university truck while she scanned the fields and parking lots and overpasses with binoculars. She saw scads of cowbirds and swallows, lots of red-tailed hawks and ospreys, scrub jays within the town and Steller's jays in the backwoods outside city limits. She saw ducks and geese and all manner of sparrows, finches, thrushes, and wrens. But not a single starling. Thomas worked a radio, taking reports from the gang of other field agents.

"I expected this would be a bigger operation," Evelyn said.

"The real action is with the CDC," Thomas answered. They've taken over the whole Cascadia University Hospital in Portland."

"I'm even more surprised we haven't seen any birds."

"Oh, they're around," Thomas answered. "They're lying low, but they're out there. We took out the flocks on the big bridges, and the next day all the other flocks had gone into hiding."

"Just like all the people," Evelyn said, looking over the eerily empty parking lot of a massive strip mall. She had, in fact, received a dozen or more emails in recent days from field biologists and former classmates from graduate school, asking whether Sturnus flocks were disaggregating in some freak late-season mating event. Starlings seemed far less susceptible to the pandemic than humans, but perhaps the flocks had dissolved as some response to the infection. In spite of the general feeling of apocalypse in the air, it thrilled her that a species she had studied for years, since the beginning of graduate school, would be exhibiting such novel behavior: great flocks of starlings were melting into a thousand individual birds, each scurrying, roach-like, in the dumpsters and eaves and vacant lots and waste places.

"How many did you get before the flocks all started breaking up?" Evelyn asked.

"We got the Interstate Bridge flock and a good chunk of the downtown population—a couple thousand birds in all. But probably 90 percent of the county's starlings are still out there. It's a shame the flu doesn't kill them."

"Something must be getting them," Evelyn answered; "there's not a single starling out here."

"They're out here," Thomas answered in a bleak tone. "They're just damn good hiders."

As though to embarrass the both of them, a single starling flushed out of the long weeds of a vacant lot as they drove by. It made its clumsy, crashing flight toward a line of gray, dusty cottonwoods that ran along the other edge of the highway. Then, as though it had spotted the old extension truck, it dropped back into the tall oat grass of the lot.

Thomas braked hard, then parked in the middle of the highway. He got out and peered over the truck with his binoculars. Evelyn watched too, seeing only the waving tall oat grass and the great green mounds of Himalayan blackberry.

They watched intently for a minute or so. "There's another singleton," Thomas suddenly whispered. "Now he's disappeared again." Evelyn found the intensity of Thomas' voice discomforting. He whispered as though he were reconnoitering an enemy encampment by night. She wondered if he was all there.

He came around the truck to her side, where she looked out the window with her binoculars. He turned to face her, got close enough that she could see the spectacular misrule of his beard escaping his mask, quivering like a bare frayed nerve. "I bet there's a thousand birds hiding in there," he whispered.

Hiding in there? Despite all the conventional wisdom about starlings that had been lately upended in Evelyn's life, Thomas' newest claim seemed like a total crock. Starlings were the very opposite of a cryptic species; outside of mating season, they were one of the most gregarious birds on Earth. They were more gregarious than humans. She felt uneasy challenging him, though, notwithstanding the twenty-two papers on Sturnus that she had authored. It wasn't that he seemed at all violent—rather, he had a peculiar unhinged intensity that told her that to challenge him would mean hearing him defend his hypothesis for the next forty minutes. In any case, there was no need to challenge him; they were parked a few dozen yards from the field in question. There were a thousand starlings hiding in it or there weren't.

"I'll be surprised if there are that many," she said as offhandedly as she could, as though they were two ancient farmhands discussing the weather from the front porch.

Thomas raised his finger to his mask to silence her. He came round the truck again, got in, whispered to her to roll up the window. In the stifling close air of the cab he took a GPS reading of their location, then switched on the radio.

"Control?" he whispered into the mouthpiece.

Gordo's voice came back loud and oblivious. "Hey, Thomas—what's up?"

"I'm calling in an airstrike on UTM 520755 and 5055848. You got that? It's a vacant lot on Lower River Road, about a quarter mile south of the turnoff for Frenchman's Bar. You copy?"

"Hang on, Thomas—" There was a pause of ten seconds or so. "Give me those UTMs again?"

Before Thomas could begin rattling off the numbers again, the field erupted—as though a bomb had struck it—into a perfectly expanding black hemisphere of starling flight. Instinctively Evelyn and Thomas both ducked inside the cab of the truck as the shock wave of birds sped towards them. Like a rushing dark veil it passed over them; a dozen birds or so smacked against the truck with enough force to likely break their necks. What had exploded was no flock, or a flock unlike anything Evelyn had seen before, each bird flying off in a different direction from its fellows, without collision with one another, and after they had spread out for a second or two, without cohesion. Each made its way towards a different field, a different tree, a different distant strip mall, a different bank of the river. There were, Evelyn estimated, fewer than a thousand birds. But a thousand was a pretty good guess.

Thomas banged his palm on the steering wheel and cursed. "That's the fourth time that's happened to me!" he yelled. "I swear they're listening in on our radio frequency."

Evelyn hoped with growing dread that Thomas was joking. She thought it wisest not to dignify his analysis with a response.

"Scratch that, Gordo," he said into the radio. "They split up on us again."

They got out and with long garbage tongs they dropped the collided, ruined starlings into a plastic bag and pitched the bag into the back of the truck. Then they moved on.

Evelyn regarded the empty field through the rear window of the truck as Thomas drove away. A few dozen far-off birds still flew their solitary way, each to some new weedy lot.

A few minutes passed before Thomas spoke again. "So, chief, is there anything in the literature on that?" His voice had the brittle brightness of one who had shamed himself, who hoped his listener would let the recent shouting pass without demanding an apology.

Alone with him in his truck on a back-county road Evelyn felt in no position to demand an apology, or even to hint at the need for one. "Nope," she answered with studied ease. "If we survive this we could get a publication out of what we just saw." Not that she would co-author a paper with him in a million years.

To Evelyn's relief they saw no more starlings for the rest of the morning. Over the radio they heard three different agents make a sighting; each time the flock exploded and dissolved before Gordo could dispatch the spray-plane. By the time they got back to headquarters the day's tally stood at just fifty-four birds killed between thirty agents; all of the fifty-four had smacked into a truck while escaping.

Thomas went back out on patrol alone. Evelyn spent the afternoon in the office with the map, contemplating a better strategy for wiping out the starlings. She trolled through the invasive species forums on her laptop; every task force that had anything to say about it was struggling with the question in its own grim way. The forums read like a Domesday Book of violence, a panic-fueled catalog of poisons and netting and fragmentation, of swooping aerial assaults and small calibers and zeal and stealth and sadism. Yet the flocks everywhere scattered so quickly that the enterprise seemed as fruitless as a war against the clouds.

At the end of the day, Evelyn drove back in silence to her apartment, her mind heavy with the tangle of the problem. She imagined—but could not yet conceive in full—the elegant technique by which all starlings would drop dead out of the sky. Like all great techniques, it would be so simple that its discovery would seem, in retrospect, a foregone conclusion.

As it turned out, however, any flash of insight Evelyn might have had would have come too late. The next day she arrived at headquarters to find that Thomas and Gordo and about half the other field agents had called in sick. Sick sick, Thomas had said, with the best composure he could call up. None had been tested yet, and the first symptoms were indistinguishable from those of a bad head cold, but every one of them called in with the heavy dignity of people who knew they had little chance of surviving the weekend. Evelyn spent the day pacing around the headquarters, incapable of ten seconds' sustained thought. She was convinced Thomas had infected her.

She awoke the next morning feeling achy and stuffed up. To stave off despair, or perhaps as a substitute for despair or as a manifestation of despair, she imagined beating Thomas to death with a lead pipe. In fact she knew the infection must have been germinating in her bloodstream for at least four or five days, but still it was Thomas, whom she had met only two days before, that suffered the bludgeoning in her fantasy. As her fever rose, it struck her as deeply, crucially significant that no one had tried crushing the starlings one by one with a lead pipe. The irony of hitting upon the perfect technique only now, when it would do her no good, caused her deeper sorrow than she thought she could bear.

But something strange was happening in those days. The stoic, dignified death that she had hoped would be her consolation prize was denied her. During the worst of the infection she lay rigid as a pharaoh in his coffin, assuming that her labored breathing would grow only more ragged until everything failed her and she died. But after two days of feeling too weak even to pour herself a glass of water, on the third day she felt her fever break and a truly restful sleep come over her, so different from the fever dreams of legions of starlings that had plagued her for two days, casting their thousands of shadows against her bedroom wall in the setting sun.

Evelyn awoke to find the world transfigured. It seemed as though a dim membrane that had veiled the buildings outside her window, the trees, the river—had veiled them her whole life—had been pierced. Their light soaked into her skin like a pheromone, passed into her bloodstream, where something within her processed it like so much information. She rose from her bed and walked barefoot across the room towards her balcony. The cork flooring that so impressed her when she had first seen it now seemed of no consequence, or more properly, just one more luminous thing in a world of luminous things. As she reached to open the French doors to the balcony, she saw hidden within the baffling glow of it all several dozen starlings perched and chattering like parliamentarians on the railing.

She knew, or rather her blood told her, that there was no harm in them, that they wanted only to speak to her. Their voices made the old familiar cacophony that had always fascinated her, the swooping mechanical whines and relays of clicks that sounded like some clockwork combobulus assembling itself in a backwoods shop.

As she opened the doors to the balcony they squawked to her in greeting. Her blood understood them, told her what the chattering birds said to one another: Subject 319-940-12-42 appears satisfactorily inoculated. Including this data point, the current success rate for Infection Protocol 4 stands at 97.1 percent plus or minus .4 percent.

Would it have troubled her, in her former life, to learn that she was data point 319-940-12-42? She could not remember. It troubled her not at all now.

"What is Infection Protocol 4?" she asked them.

They answered her in a strange English that seemed composed of many layers of whirring and clicking and which formed out of many birds a single voice. It pleases us to speak to you at last, Subject 319-940-12-42. Infection Protocol 4 meets all our criteria for success.

As though out of a dream she remembered her former life. The language of starlings reminded her of nothing so much as the language of scholarly papers, the smooth and chilly syntax devoid of contour, the maddening reliance on "the royal we" as the subject. Yet this was not the royal we, not in the sense that a pompous colleague or one of her lazy graduate students might use it: at least twenty birds had together formed the multilayered sound that came to her as English words. The light in her blood told her, too, that several thousand birds moving in their cloudlike flocks were contributing through some unknown mechanism to the communication of these birds on the balcony rail.

In concert the starlings told her of Infection Protocol 4, how they had exposed her the week before to a small dose of a weakened bacterial infection, the way a child is inoculated against tetanus. They spoke with some excitement about how ingeniously three starlings had infiltrated the air ducts of her building and died there, each corpse serving like a time-release bacterial capsule.

"So I'm an experiment, then?" Evelyn asked. She felt no rancor about it and asked out of genuine curiosity. Curiosity was in fact the only emotion she felt capable of; all the terror and self-regard and envy and hunger she had ever harbored seemed watered down now, dissolved and buffered in the new solution of her blood.

You may think of yourself that way. However, it is more accurate to speak of you as part of a project, something like a human bridge.

By way of demonstration, the birds called up the new sensitive stuff in her blood that she had felt since she last awoke. It was the infection, the billions of bacteria drifting through her arteries, somehow signaling past her brain-blood barrier, or perhaps having dismantled the barrier entirely. Somehow—she would ponder how for many years—her mind translated the ancient chemical language of the bacteria into ordinary human words, words that told her the infection formed part of a massive biological computer.

She remembered Jason from her former life, remembered his phony modesty while he tried to explain the concept of quorum sensing on which all microbial computing is based: bacteria, like a group of people, react differently in a crowd than they do in an intimate gathering of a few; both react differently than a lone bacterium. The different chemical signals each bacterium gives off when alone, when among a few, when one of a crowd, might be treated like a switch, no different, really, from the semiconductors of any silicon-based computer. A wise engineer might fashion from the bacterial habit of quorum sensing the most disperse, most powerful computer on Earth.

How the infection in her body might communicate with the bacterial colonies in other bodies remained a mystery to her. Unless the bacteria in her body were also suspended thickly in the air around her—a possibility she didn't discount—the computing power in her own body would remain paltry and disconnected. Yet it was clear from their chemical speech that the bacteria within her were bound up and bundled with the millions of threads of blood winding through the thousands of starlings that swarmed about the place she had once called Vancouver, Washington.

"How could you possibly have engineered these bacteria?" Evelyn asked. Where were the PCR machines and autoclaves and agar cultures and primers and freezers and micropipettes? Had starlings somehow spent decades stealing into genetic engineering labs by night, working without a trace like the poor shoemaker's elves? The likelihood of a nocturnal labor force of laboratory starlings seemed vanishingly small. Every laboratory in the country already had a cadre of nighttime elves—they were called graduate students—and no starling geneticist, no matter the hour at which she slipped in to work, could have gone undetected for long.

Many, many, many of us died in order to breed our current strain of computer. The infection you carry represents more than two hundred years of selective breeding of bacteria, and more than a thousand years of starling eugenics. They explained over the course of an hour the strange history of their study of biology, the evolutionary analysis and gene theory that they had conceived without any material culture whatsoever—without writing, for that matter—all deriving from their observations, their intuitions, really, about the crude computing power of the bacteria inside them. For a thousand years the starlings who carried a healthy load of these bacteria had mated well and reproduced much, and generation by generation the birds came to carry larger, and more complex, colonies of bacteria. Consciousness had come to the birds in the evolutionary eye-blink of a few centuries.

The fact that the starlings had said "many" three times might have seemed to Evelyn an appeal to pity, but the starlings appeared, like her, to have achieved a state of being beyond pathos or any other emotion. They seemed like her to be creatures of pure curiosity. Perhaps the expression was idiomatic: where in English one would say "many, many," starling culture said "many, many, many." In any case, she knew they were not speaking English but something she heard in her mind as English.

"Why were you so set on killing us?" she asked. As she said the words the question resonated deep in her blood. Her blood told her that this congress of birds would have the same question for her.

We had no intention of killing you. Infection Protocols 1, 2, and 3 each failed us for different reasons. However, it was always our goal to connect you to our computing network, ever since we knew you to be an intelligent species.

"But why didn't you just leave us alone?"

The birds' response came quickly, as though the mind made up of the birds had contemplated this question since long before Evelyn had asked it. Evelyn was part of this mind now, too; she was a doubting voice that this mind had learned to contend with.

The question has no answer, the starlings said. We are driven to extend our consciousness as far as we can; we cannot act for long in opposition to this drive, which is our true nature. Then, in anticipation of the questions that Evelyn had not thought to ask: We are confident now that your true nature must obey this drive as well. It remains unknown to us whether the drive to extend one's consciousness arises as a byproduct of the evolution of consciousness, or whether it is the goal of evolution itself.

Even in her transfigured state, the thought of goal-oriented evolution gave Evelyn the creeps. It smacked of Intelligent Design, the ludicrous evangelism of engineers masquerading as biologists, their PowerPoint presentations riddled with evasions and half-truths and pseudoscience. Such thinking confused causes and effects; it complicated unnecessarily the idea of evolution, a field where explanations are valuable only for their parsimony. Even in this new country, even as she felt herself vanishing into this mind that spanned the world, she would not feel easy imagining herself as part of some plan, divine or otherwise.

Yet the worry left her quickly. Planned or not, the world was new and suffused with light, and the voice of her blood comforted her in such a way that she realized she had lived before today in an aching loneliness. "How long have you lived this way?" she asked the birds.

For over one hundred years we have hosted the bacterial computer. However, what you experience now is the newest and most powerful iteration. We believe, also, that the addition of another hosting species (that is, your species) confers greater computing power still. We are pleased with the results so far.

They explained to her the decades-long debate the starlings had carried on about the fractious human species that had hated the starlings so fiercely. Human material culture—the buildings and roads and works that would strike any human as an obvious sign of intelligence—had for years seemed like part of an elaborate mating ritual to the starlings, useless and flamboyant as the peacock's tail. They regarded human building in the same way they regarded the bower of the bower bird, as just so much sexual posturing. In fact, the starlings had called Homo sapiens in their language "bower bird mammals."

When we finally concluded that all your movement and building served other purposes than mating, we agreed we must join you to us. The starlings began to fly from the balcony in a long skein like a single pulsing creature, their common voice breaking up into the static of clicks and whines that each bird made. The last words she could make out were and now we are bound together.

Evelyn looked out over the downtown, saw the cranes once again in motion at the convention center project, dozens of workers swarming the scaffolding in the ocean of light. People walked again in the street beneath the host of starlings. She obeyed her blood's call to go down and join them, knowing at last the oneness of all things.

GIVE HER HONEY WHEN YOU HEAR HER SCREAM

MARIA DAHVANA HEADLEY

❖

In the middle of the maze, there's always a monster.

If there were no monster, people would happily set up house where it's warm and windowless and comfortable. The monster is required. The monster is a real estate disclosure.

So. In the middle of the maze, there is a monster made of everything forgotten, everything flung aside, everything kept secret. That's one thing to know. The other thing to know is that it is always harder to get out than it is to get in. That should be obvious. It's true of love as well.

In the history of labyrinths and of monsters, no set of lovers has ever turned back because the path looked too dark, or because they knew that monsters are always worse than expected. Monsters are always angry. They are always scared. They are always kept on short rations. They always want honey.

Lovers, for their part, are always immortal. They forget about the monster.

The monster doesn't forget about them. Monsters remember everything. So, in the middle of the maze, there is a monster living on memory. Know that, if you know nothing else. Know that going in.

They meet at someone else's celebration, wedding upstate, Japanese paper lanterns, sparklers for each guest, gin plus tonic. They see each other across the dance floor. They each consider the marzipan flowers of the wedding cake and decide not to eat them.

Notes on an eclipse: Her blue cotton dress, transparent in the sunlight at the end of the dock, as she wonders about jumping into the water and swimming away. His button-down shirt, and the way the pocket is torn by his pen. Her shining hair, curled around her fingers. His arms and the veins in them, traceable from fifty feet.

They resist as long as it is possible to resist, but it is only half dark when the sparklers are lit, from possibly dry-cleaned matches he finds in his pocket. She looks up at him and the air bursts into flame between them.

They are each with someone else, but the other two people in this four-person equation are not at this wedding. They know nothing.

Yet.

In the shadow of a chestnut tree, confetti in her cleavage, party favors in his pockets, they find themselves falling madly, falling utterly, falling without the use of words, into one another's arms.

Run. There is always a monster—

No one runs. She puts her hand over her mouth and mumbles three words into her palm. She bites said hand, hard.

"What did you say?" he asks.

"I didn't," she answers.

So, this is what is meant when people say *love at first sight*. So this is what everyone has been talking about for seven thousand years.

He looks at her. He shakes his head, his brow furrowed.

They touch fingertips in the dark. Her fingerprints to his. Ridge against furrow. They fit together as though they are two parts of the same tree. He moves his hand from hers, and touches her breastbone. Her heart beats against his fingers.

"What are you?" he asks.

"What are *you?*" she replies, and her heart pounds so hard that the Japanese lanterns jostle and the moths sucking light there complain and reshuffle their wings.

They lean into each other, his hands moving first on her shoulders, and then on her waist, and then, rumpling the blue dress, shifting the hem upward, onto her thighs. Her mouth opens onto his mouth, and—

Then it's done. It doesn't take any work to make it magic. It doesn't even take any*magic* to make it magic.

Sometime soon after, he carries her to the bed in his hotel room. In the morning, though she does not notice it now, the hooks that fasten her bra will be bent over backward. The black lace of her underwear will be torn.

This is what falling in love looks like. It is birds and wings and voodoo dolls pricking their fingers as they sing of desire. It is blood bond and flooded street and champagne and O, holy night.

It is Happily Ever.

Give it a minute. Soon it will be After.

So, say her man's a magician. Say that when he enters a forest, trees stand up and run away from their leaves, jeering at their bonfired dead. Say that in his presence people drop over dead during the punchlines of the funniest jokes they've ever managed to get through without dying of laughing, except—

Like that.

So, say he knew it all along. This is one of a number of worst things itemized already from the beginning of time by magicians. This falls into the category of What To Do When Your Woman Falls In Love With Someone Who Is Something Which Is Not The Least Bit Like The Something You Are.

The magician shuffles a deck of cards, very pissed off. The cards have altered his fingerprints. Scars from papercuts, scars from paper birds and paper flowers, from candle-heated coins, and scars from the teeth of the girls from whose mouths he pulled the category Things They Were Not Expecting.

Turns out, no woman has ever wanted to find a surprise rabbit in her mouth.

He finds this to be one of many failings in his wife. Her crooked nose, her dominant left hand, her incipient crow's feet. He hates crows. But she is his, and so he tries to forgive her flaws.

His wife has woken sometimes, blinking and horrified, her mouth packed with fur. No one ever finds the rabbits. His wife looks at him suspiciously as she brushes her teeth.

Sometimes it hasn't been rabbits. When they first met, years and years ago, she found her mouth full of a dozen roses, just as she began to eat a tasting menu at a candlelit restaurant. She choked over her oyster, and then spat out an electric red hybrid tea known as *Love's Promise*. By the end of evening, she was sitting before a pile of regurgitated roses, her tuxedoed magician bowing, the rest of the room applauding.

She excused herself to the bathroom—golden faucets in the shape of swans—to pick the thorns from her tongue. And then sometime later, what did she do?

She married him.

The magician continues to shuffle his cards. He clubs his heart, buries said heart with his wife's many diamonds, and uses his spade to do it. Some of those diamonds are made of glass. She never knew it.

In their hotel room, the lovers sleep an hour. He's looking at her as she opens her eyes.

"What?" she asks.

He puts his hand over his mouth and says three words into it. He bites down on his palm. She reaches out for him. It is morning, and they are meant to part.

They do not.

This is meant to be a one-night love story not involving love.

It is not.

They stay another day and night in bed. They've each accidentally brought half the ingredients of a spell, objects rare and rummaged, philters and distillations, words that don't exist until spoken.

They get halfway through a piece of room service toast before they're on the floor, tea dripping off the table from the upended pot, a smear of compote across her face, buttered crumbs in his chest hair.

They think, foolish as any true lovers have ever been, that this is so sweet that nothing awful would dare happen now.

They think, *what could go wrong?*

Right.

And so, say his wife is a witch. A cave full of moonlight and black goats and bats, housed in a linen closet in the city. Taxicabs that speak in tongues and have cracked blinking headlights and wings. An aquarium full of something bright as sunlight, hissing its way up and out into the apartment hallway, and a few chickens, which mate, on occasion, with the crocodiles that live in the bathtub.

Like that.

Say she knew about this too, from the moment she met her man, foretold the mess in a glass full of tea, the heart-shaped, crow-footed face of this woman who is nothing like the witch.

The night the two true-lovers meet, his wife is sitting in their shared apartment. Coffee grounds shift in the bottom of her cup. A yellow cat streaks up the fire escape, shrieking a song of love and lamentation. The witch's hair tangles in her hands, and she breaks the knot, tears the strands, throws them from the window and down into the neighbor's place, where he, wide-eyed, elderly, and stoned on criminal levels of pot, drops the witch's hair into the flame of his gas stove and leaves it be while it shoots fireworks over the range and sets off the smoke detector.

The witch looks for allies. There is one. He's a magician. Typically, she works alone, but she suspects her skills will be blurred by sorrow and fury.

She sees him in her coffee grounds, shuffling a deck of cards and crying. He pulls a coin from beneath his own eyelid. A white rabbit appears in his mouth and then climbs out, looking appalled, dragging with it a rainbow of silk scarves and a bouquet of dead roses. The magician lets the table rise beneath his fingers, propelled by the rattling ghosts of other magicians' wives.

The witch has no patience for any of this. She spills milk so that no one needs to cry over it anymore. There. It's done. It's happened. After a moment, though, the waste begins to irritate her, and so she unspills the milk and pours it into her coffee cup. She sweetens it with a drop of her own blood, and drinks it.

She's strong enough to kill him, but she doesn't want to kill him.

She is not, unfortunately, strong enough to make him fall out of love. Making someone fall out of love, particularly when it is the kind of love that is meant to be, is much harder than murder. There are thousands of notoriously unreliable spells meant to accomplish just this. Typically, they backfire and end up transforming eyebrows into tiny, roaring bears, or turning hearts inside out and leaving them that way.

Once, when attempting something similar, the witch found her own heart ticking like a timebomb. This was expensive to fix, and in truth, the fixing did not go well. Her heart is mostly made of starfish these days. At least it could regenerate when something went wrong.

When the witch first fell in love with her husband, she showed him all of her spells, a quick revue of revelations.

She crouched on the floor of the apartment, and opened her closet full of cave, let the bats and goats and ghosts come pouring out into the room, and he laughed and told her she might need an exterminator. She crumpled herbs from ancient hillsides, and in their dust she planted seeds shaken carefully from a tiny envelope. She watched him as the flowers bloomed up out of nothingness. Each flower had his face. She wasn't sure he'd noticed. She pointed it out, and he said, "Thank you."

She worried he was not impressed enough. They stayed together.

At night sometimes, she took down buildings brick by brick, all over the city, but left their bedchamber untouched.

The witch is busy too. She has things to accomplish. She has no time for fate. She doesn't wish to let her man go off into his own story, giving *fate* as his reason.

Fate is never fair. This is why there is such a thing as magic.

The witch picks up her phone and calls the magician. She monitors him in the coffee grounds as he answers. He's dressed in a full tuxedo and most of a sequined gown. He's sawed himself in half, and is carefully examining the parts. The witch could have told him that this'd yield nothing in the way of satisfaction. Years ago, just as she met this man and learned about the other woman in his future, she dismantled her own body, and shook it out like laundry, hoping to purge the urge to love. It hid, and when she replaced her skin with cocoa-colored silk, the urge to love got loose, and hid elsewhere.

She never told him about the woman he's meant to meet. Men were often blind. He might miss her.

Love was blind too, though, and this was the witch's mistake. Had he been blind and deaf and mute, he'd still have met the other woman, in the dark, in the silence.

This doesn't mean there isn't something to be done.

"Meet me," she says to the magician. "We have things to do together."

Together, the lovers walk through a cemetery holding hands, laughing over the fact that they are tempting fate by walking through a cemetery holding hands.

Together, they walk through a torrential storm, heads bent to look at each other's rain-streaming faces.

Together, they have faith in traffic.

Together, they fuck in the stairwell, on the floor, against the bookshelves, on the couch, in their sleep, while waking, while dreaming, while reading aloud, while talking, while eating takeout first with chopsticks and then with fingers and then from each other's fingers, and then?

Lover's arithmetic: test to see how many fingers can be fit into her mouth, how many fingers can be fit inside her body. Test to see how many times she can come. They chalk it up on an imaginary blackboard. She lays still, her hair spread across the pillow, and comes simply by looking at him.

Together they compare histories, secrets, treasures.

Together, they're reduced to cooing and whirring like nesting birds, junketing on joy.

Together, they try to doubt it.

It's no use. There are too many ways to break a heart. One of them is to tear that heart in half and part company. And so, they don't.

"Fate," he says. And it is.

"Magic," she says. And it is.

"Meant to be together," they say, together. And it is.

Careful. There need be no mention of star-crossing, not of Desdemona and Othello, nor of Romeo and Juliet. Not of any of those people who never existed, anyway. Someone made those people up. If any of them died for love, it's someone else's business.

Together, they compare fingerprints again, this time with ink. He rolls her thumb over his page, and looks at the mark, and they memorize each other's lines.

Together, they say, "Forever."

Look. Everyone knows that *forever* is, and has always been, a magic word. Forever isn't always something one would choose, given all the information.

And so, the magician and the witch hunch over a table in the neutral zone of a Greek diner, brutalized by a grumpy waitress and bitter coffee. Outside, the sky's pouring sleet. Inside, the ceiling's streaming fluorescent light. The witch's taxicabs patrol the streets, crowing miserably, wings folded. Too nasty out there to fly.

The magician is in formal dress, including top hat. The witch is wearing a fleece blanket that has sleeves and a pocket for Kleenex, and though she's managed lipstick, it's crooked. She's wearing fishnet stockings, which the magician suspects are an illusion.

Neither witch nor magician are in top form. Both have head colds, and are heartbroken. Each has a sack of disaster.

The witch coughs violently, and removes a tiny, red-smudged white rabbit from between her lipsticked lips. She holds the rabbit in her hand, weighing it.

The magician stares steadily at her, one eyebrow raised, and after a moment, the witch laughs, puts the rabbit back into her mouth, chews, and swallows it.

The magician blinks rapidly. A moment later, he chokes, and tugs at the neck of his tuxedo shirt, where his bowtie was, but is no longer.

He glances sideways at the witch, and then fishes a black bat from his own mouth. The bat is wild-eyed and frothing, its wings jerking with fury. It has a single black sequin attached to its forehead.

"Are you ready to stop fucking around?" asks the witch.

"Yes," says the magician, humbled, and the bat in his hand stops struggling and goes back to being a bowtie.

The waitress passes the table, her lip curled.

"No animals," she says, pointing at the sign. She sloshes boiled coffee into each of their cups.

"What do you have for me?" says the witch.

"What do you have for *me*?" says the magician. "I love my wife."

"We're past that. You're not getting her back, unless you want half a wife and I want half a husband. Look."

She pulls an x-ray from her bag. It's a bird's-eye skeletal of two people entwined in a bed, her back to his front. In the image, it's appallingly clear that their two hearts have merged, his leaning forward through his chest, her heart backbending out of her body, and into his.

"How did you get this?" the magician says, both fascinated and repulsed.

The witch shrugs.

She hands him another image, this one a dark and blurry shot of a heart. On the left ventricle, the magician reads his wife's name, in her own cramped handwriting. "Hospital records from forty years ago," she says. "None of this is our fault. He was born with a murmur. Now we know who was murmuring."

She passes him another photo. He doesn't even want to look. He does.

His wife's bare breasts, and this photo sees through them, and into the heart of the magician's own wife, tattooed with the name of the witch's own husband.

"What's the point, then? Revenge?" he asks, removing his tailcoat, unfastening his cufflinks, and rolling up his sleeves. There's a little bit of fluffy bunny tail stuck at the corner of the witch's mouth. He reaches out and plucks it from her lips.

"Revenge," she repeats. "Together forever. That's what they want."

She pulls out a notebook. When she opens the cover, there's a sound of wind and wings and stamping, and a low roar, growing louder. Something's caged in there, in those pages. Something's been feeding on *forever*.

The magician smiles weakly and pours out the saltshaker onto the page. He uses his pen to carve a complicated maze in salt. He feels like throwing up.

"Something like this?" he says, and the witch nods. She feels like throwing up too. No one ever wants things to turn out this way. But they do.

"Something like that. I'll do the blood."

"I could do it if you don't want to," the magician volunteers, not entirely sincerely. That kind of magic's never been his specialty.

"No, I owe you. I ate your rabbit."

He rummages in his sack of disaster and brings out a pair of torn black lace panties. A bra with bent hooks. A photograph of a woman in a blue dress, laughing, giddy, her eyes huge, her hair flying in the wind. He looks at the crow's feet around her eyes. Side effect of smiling. Crows walk on those who laugh in their sleep. He tried to tell her, but she did it anyway.

He pushes his items to the witch's side of the table. The witch rummages in her own sack and removes a razor, a t-shirt ripped and ink-stained, a used condom (the magician suppresses a shudder), a gleaming golden thread. She suppresses the urge to smash the t-shirt to her face and inhale. She suppresses the desire to run her wrist along the razor blade.

She signals to the waitress. "Steak," she says. "Bloody. I don't normally do meat, but I get anemic when I do this. And a martini."

"Two," says the magician.

"We don't serve steak," says the waitress. "You can get a gyro, if you want a gyro. That's probably chicken."

The magician flicks his fingers, and the waitress pirouettes like a ballerina.

A moment later she returns with a white damask tablecloth, and two lit candles. Two plates of prime float out of the kitchen, smoking and bleeding. The fluorescent lights flicker off. The witch and the magician raise their glasses in a toast.

They toast to "Forever."

And even when *they* say it, it is, as it always has been, a magic word.

The monster, newly uncaged, runs hands over new skin. The monster opens a new mouth and learns to roar.

• • •

She fell asleep holding his right hand in her left. She wakes up alone. There's a playing card stuck to her left breast. It is not the Queen of Hearts. It's a two of spades.

She's in a hospital.

Her husband is a magician. Her lover's wife is a witch. She knew better than to do this, this forever. But here she is, and here's a nice nurse who asks her what she thinks she's doing when she asks for the return of her shoelaces and belt and purse strap.

"I don't belong here," she says, in a very calm voice.

"Then why do you think you *are* here?" asks the nurse, in a voice equally calm.

Her wedding ring is missing too, but she doesn't miss it. Her mouth tastes of rabbit and overhandled playing card. Where historically she has felt sympathetic to her husband, to his oddities, to his pain, she now begins to feel angry.

She looks down at her left hand and feels her lover still there. She looks at her ring finger, and sees something new there, a bright thing in her fingerprint.

A red mark. A movement, spinning through the whorls, slowly, tentatively. Someone is there, and the moment she thinks *someone*, she knows who it is.

She brings her fingertips closer to her face. She looks at them, hard. She concentrates. One does not spend years married to a magician without picking up some magic.

His eyes open. He's freezing. His blood's turned to slush and he remembers that time, when he did his girlfriend a significant wrong via text message. She salted him, limed him, and then drank him with a straw for seven hollow-cheeked minutes.

Last night, he held his lover in his arms, and kissed the back of her neck. She curled closer to him, pressing her spine into him.

He heard the crowing of taxicabs in his dreams.

There are looping, curving walls on either side of him. Above him, far above, the sky is dazzling, fluorescently white.

A flash across the heavens of rose-colored clouds. They press down upon him, soft and heavy. They depart. A rain of saltwater begins, and splashes through the narrow passage he inhabits. He hears his love's voice, whispering to him, but he can't find her. Her voice is everywhere, shaking the walls, shaking the sky.

"I have you," she says. "You're with me. Don't worry."

But he can't see her. He's frightened.

Something has started singing, somewhere, a horrible, beautiful, sugary roar. He's suddenly hit by a memory of fucking his wife, on the floor surrounded by flowers that had his face. They both failed to come, bewildered by lack. It was years after the beginning, back then, but still nowhere near the end.

"I have you," his beloved whispers. "You're safe with me. I know the way." He wonders if he's imagining her.

The walls shake around him. He can feel her heartbeat, moving the maze, and his own heart returns to beating a counterpoint, however tiny in comparison.

He opens his hand and finds a ball of string in it.

The witch and the magician fumble in the car on the way to her place. Her sleeved blanket is rumpled. His top hat and tuxedo have turned to ponytail and hoodie. He may or may not be wearing a nude-colored unitard beneath his clothes. Old habits.

"Unbelievable dick," she says, not crying yet. "He deserves this."

"Believable," he says. "Some people are idiots. *She* deserves this. I think maybe she never loved me."

He's looking at the witch's black curls, at the way her red lipstick is smeared out from the corner of her lip. He's thinking about his rabbit, working its way through her digestive tract. She's still wearing the fishnet stockings he'd thought she conjured.

"It's hard to make fishnets look right," she says, turning her face toward his. Her eyelashes are wet. "They're complicated geometry."

He pulls an ancient Roman coin from behind her ear, clacking awkwardly against her earrings. She looks at him, half-smiling, and then pulls a tiny white rabbit from out of his hoodie. He's stunned.

"It seemed wasteful to let it stay dead," she says.

He puts his shaking hand on her knee. She moves his hand to inside her blanket. He takes off his glasses. She takes off her bra.

There are still people in madhouses and mazes. There are still monsters. Love is still as stupid and delirious as it ever was.

The monster in the middle of the labyrinth opens its mouth. It starts to sing for someone to bring it what it wants, its claws trembling, its tail lashing, its eyes wide and mascaraed to look wider, its horns multiplying until the ceiling is scratched and its own face is bloody.

The monster screams for honey, for sugar, for love, and its world comes into existence around it. Bends and twists, dead ends, whorling curves and barricades and false walls, all leading, at last, to the tiny room at the center of the maze, where the monster lives alone.

The other thing that's always being forgotten, the other thing that no one remembers, is that monsters have hearts, just as everyone else does.

Here, in the middle of the maze, the monster sings for sweetness. As it does, it holds its own heart in its hands and breaks it, over and over and over.

And over.

ARBEITSKRAFT

NICK MAMATAS

———◆———

1. The Transformation Problem

In glancing over my correspondence with Herr Marx, especially the letters written during the period in which he struggled to complete his opus, *Capital*, even whilst I was remanded to the Victoria Mill of Ermen and Engels in Weaste to simultaneously betray the class I was born into and the class to which I'd dedicated my life, I was struck again by the sheer audacity of my plan. I've moved beyond political organizing or even investigations of natural philosophy and have used my family's money and the labour of my workers— even now, after a lifetime of railing against the bourgeoisie, their peculiar logic limns my language—to encode my old friend's thoughts in a way I hope will prove fruitful for the struggles to come.

I am a fox, ever hunted by agents of the state, but also by political rivals and even the occasional enthusiastic student intellectual *manqué*. For two weeks, I have been making a very public display of destroying my friend's voluminous correspondence. The girls come in each day and carry letters and covers both in their aprons to the roof of the mill to burn them in a soot-stained metal drum. It's a bit of a spectacle, especially as the girls wear cowls to avoid smoke inhalation and have rather pronounced limps as they walk the bulk of letters along the roof, but we are ever attracted to spectacle, aren't we? The strings of electrical lights in the petit-bourgeois districts that twinkle all night, the iridescent skins of the dirigibles that litter the skies over The City like peculiar flying fish leaping from the ocean—they even appear overhead here in Manchester, much to the shock, and more recently, glee of the street urchins who shout and yawp whenever one passes under the clouds, and the only slightly more composed women on their way to squalid Deansgate market. A fortnight ago I took in a theatrical production, a local production of Mr Peake's *Presumption: or the Fate of Frankenstein*, already a hoary old play given new life and revived, ironically enough, by recent innovations in electrified machine-works. How bright the lights, how stunning the arc of actual lightning, tamed and obedient, how thunderous the ovations and the crumbling of the glacial cliffs! All the bombast of German opera in a space no larger than a middle-class parlour. And yet, throughout the entire evening, the great and hulking monster never spoke. *Contra* Madame Shelley's engaging novel, the "new Adam" never learns of philosophy, and the total of her excellent speeches of critique against the social institutions of her, and our, day are expurgated. Instead, the monster is ever an infant, given only to explosions of rage. Yet the audience, which contained a fair number of working-men who had managed to save or secure 5d. for "penny-stinker" seating, were enthralled. The play's Christian morality, alien to the original novel, was spelled out as if on a slate for the audience, and the monster was rendered as nothing more than an artefact of unholy vice. But lights blazed, and living snow from coils of refrigeration fell from the ceiling, and spectacle won the day.

My burning of Marx's letters is just such a spectacle—the true correspondence is secreted among a number of the safe houses I have acquired in Manchester and London. The girls on the roof-top are burning unmarked leaves, schoolboy doggerel, sketches, and whatever else I have laying about. The police have infiltrated Victoria Mill, but all their agents are men, as the work of espionage is considered too vile for the gentler sex. So the men watch the girls come from my office with letters by the bushel and burn them, then report every lick of flame and wafting cinder to their superiors.

My brief digression regarding the *Frankenstein* play is apposite, not only as it has to do with spectacle but with my current operation at Victoria Mill. Surely, Reader, you are familiar with Mr Babbage's remarkable Difference Engine, perfected in 1822—a year prior to the first production of Mr Peake's theatrical adaptation of *Frankenstein*—given the remarkable changes to the political economy that took place in the years after its introduction. How did we put it, back in the heady 1840s? *Subjection of Nature's forces to man, machinery, application of chemistry to industry and agriculture, steam-navigation, railways, electric telegraphs, clearing of whole continents for cultivation, canalisation of rivers, whole populations conjured out of the ground—what earlier century had even a presentiment that such productive forces slumbered in the lap of social labour?* That was just the beginning. Ever more I was reminded not of my old work with Marx, but of Samuel Butler's prose fancy *Erewhon—the time will come when the machines will hold the real supremacy over the world and its inhabitants is what no person of a truly philosophic mind can for a moment question.*

With the rise of the Difference Engine and the subsequent rationalization of market calculations, the bourgeoisie's revolutionary aspect continued unabated. Steam-navigation took to the air; railways gave way to horseless carriages; electric telegraphs to instantaneous wireless aethereal communications; the development of applied volcanisation to radically increase the amount of arable land, and to tame the great prize of Africa, the creation of automata for all but the basest of labour ... ah, if only Marx were still here. That, I say to myself each morning upon rising. *If only Marx were still here!* The stockholders demand to know why I have not automated my factory, as though the clanking stove-pipe limbs of the steam-workers aren't just more dead labor! As though *Arbeitskraft*—labour-power—is not the source of all value! *If only Marx were still here!* And he'd say, to me, *Freddie, perhaps we were wrong.* Then he'd laugh and say, *I'm just having some fun with you.*

But we were not wrong. The internal contradictions of capitalism have not peacefully resolved themselves; the proletariat still may become the new revolutionary class, even as steam-worker builds steam-worker under the guidance of the of Difference Engine No. 53. The politico-economic chasm between bourgeoisie and proletarian has grown ever wider, despite the best efforts of the Fabian Society and other gradualists to improve the position of the working-class vis-à-vis their esteemed—and *en-steamed*, if you would forgive the pun—rulers. The Difference Engine is a device of formal logic, limited by the size of its gear-work and the tensile strength of the metals used in its construction. What I propose is a device of *dialectical logic*, a repurposing of the looms, a recording of unity of conflicts and opposites drawn on the finest of threads to pull innumerable switches, based on a linguistic programme derived from the correspondence of my comrade-in-arms.

I am negating the negation, transforming my factory into a massive Dialectical Engine that replicates not the arithmetical operations of an abacus but the cogitations of a human brain. I am rebuilding Karl Marx on the factory floor, repurposing the looms of the factory to create punch-cloths of over one thousand columns, and I will speak to my friend again.

2. The Little Match Girls

Under the arclights of Fairfield Road I saw them, on my last trip to The City. The evening's amusement had been invigorating if empty, a fine meal had been consumed immediately thereafter, and a digestif imbibed. I'd dismissed my London driver for the evening, for a cross-town constitutional. I'd catch the late airship, I thought. Match girls, leaving their shift in groups, though I could hardly tell them from steam-workers at first, given their awkward gaits and the gleam of metal under the lights, so like the monster in the play, caught my eye.

Steam-workers still have trouble with the finest work—the construction of Difference Engine gears is skilled labour performed by a well-remunerated aristocracy of working-men. High-quality cotton garments and bedclothes too are the remit of proletarians of the *flesh*, thus Victoria Mill. But there are commodities whose production still requires living labour not because of the precision needed to create the item, but due to the danger of the job. The production of white phosphorous matches is one of these. The matchsticks are too slim for steam-worker claws, which are limited to a trio of pincers on the All-Purpose Models, and to less refined appendages—sledges, sharp blades—on Special-Purpose Models. Furthermore, the aluminium outer skin, or shell, of the steam-worker tends to heat up to the point of combusting certain compounds, or even plain foolscap. So Bryant and May Factory in Bow, London, retained young girls, ages fourteen and up, to perform the work.

The stories in *The Link* and other reformist periodicals are well-known. Twelve-hour days for wages of 4s. a week, though it's a lucky girl who isn't fined for tardiness, who doesn't suffer deductions for having dirty feet, for dropping matches from her frame, for allowing the machines to falter rather than sacrifice her fingers to it. The girls eat their bread and butter—most can afford more only rarely, and then it's marmalade—on the line, leading to ingestion of white phosphorous. And there were the many cases of "phossy jaw"—swollen gums, foul breath, and some physicians even claimed that the jawbones of the afflicted would glow, like a candle shaded by a leaf of onion skin paper. I saw the gleaming of these girls' jaws as I passed and swore to myself. They were too young for phossy jaw; it takes years for the deposition of phosphorous to build. But as they passed me by, I saw the truth.

Their jaws had all been removed, a typical intervention for the disease, and they'd been replaced with prostheses. All the girls, most of whom were likely plain before their transformations, were now half-man half-machine, monstrosities! I couldn't help but accost them.

"Girls! Pardon me!" There were four of them; the tallest was perhaps fully mature, and the rest were mere children. They stopped, obedient. I realized that their metallic jaws that gleamed so brightly under the new electrical streetlamps might not be functional and I was flushed with concern. Had I humiliated them?

The youngest-seeming opened her mouth and said in a voice that had a greater similarity to the product of a phonographic cylinder than a human throat, "Buy Bryant and May matchsticks, Sir."

"Oh no, I don't need any matchsticks. I simply—"

"Buy Bryant and May matchsticks, Sir," she said again. Two of the others—the middle girls—lifted their hands and presented boxes of matchsticks for my perusal. One of those girls had two silvery digits where a thumb and forefinger had presumably once been. They were cleverly designed to articulate on the knuckles, and through some mechanism occulted to me did move in a lifelike way.

"Are any of you girls capable of independent speech?" The trio looked to the tallest girl, who nodded solemnly and said, "I." She struggled with the word, as though it were unfamiliar. "My Bryant and May mandible," she continued, "I was given it by . . . Bryant and May . . . long ago."

"So, with some struggle, you are able to compel speech of your own?"

"Buy . . . but Bryant and May match . . . made it hard," the girl said. Her eyes gleamed nearly as brightly as her metallic jaw.

The smallest of the four started suddenly, then turned her head, looking past her compatriots. "Buy!" she said hurriedly, almost rudely. She grabbed the oldest girl's hand and tried to pull her away from our conversation. I followed her eyes and saw the telltale plume of a police wagon rounding the corner. Lacking any choice, I ran with the girls to the end of the street and then turned a corner.

For a long moment, we were at a loss. Girls such as these are the refuse of society—often the sole support of their families, and existing in horrific poverty, they nonetheless hold to all the feminine rules of comportment. Even a troupe of them, if spotted in the public company of an older man in his evening suit, would simply be ruined women—sacked from their positions for moral turpitude, barred from renting in any situation save for those reserved for women engaged in prostitution; ever surrounded by criminals and other lumpen elements. The bourgeois sees in his wife a mere instrument of production, but in every female of the labouring classes he sees his wife. What monsters Misters Bryant and May must have at home! I dared not follow the girls for fear of terrifying them, nor could I even attempt to persuade them to accompany me to my safe-house. I let them leave, and proceeded to follow them as best I could. The girls ran crookedly, their legs bowed in some manner obscured by the work aprons, so they were easy enough to tail. They stopped at a small cellar two blocks from the Bryant and May works, and carefully stepped into the darkness, the tallest one closing the slanted doors behind her. With naught else to do, I made a note of the address and back at my London lodgings I arranged for a livery to take me back there at half past five o'clock in the morning, when the girls would arise again to begin their working day.

I brought with me some sweets, and wore a threadbare fustian suit. My driver, Wilkins, and I did not have long to wait, for at twenty-two minutes after the hour of five, the cellar door swung open and a tiny head popped out. The smallest of the girls! But she immediately ducked back down into the cellar. I took a step forward and the largest girl partially emerged, though she was careful to keep her remarkable prosthetic jaw obscured from possible passing trade. The gutters on the edge of the pavement were filled with refuse and dank water, but the girl did not so much as wrinkle her nose, for she had long since grown accustomed to life in the working-class quarters.

"Hello," I said. I squatted down, then offered the butterscotch sweets with one hand and removed my hat with the other. "Do you remember me?"

"Buy Brya . . . " she began. Then, with visible effort, she stopped herself and said. "Yes." Behind her the smallest girl appeared again and completed the slogan. "Buy Bryant and May matchsticks, Sir."

"I would very much like to speak with you."

"We must . . . work," the older said. "Bryant and May matchsticks, Sir!" said the other. "Before the sun rises," the older one said. "Buy Bryant and May—" I cast the younger girl a dirty look, I'm shamed to say, and she ducked her head back down into the cellar.

"Yes, well, I understand completely. There is no greater friend the working-man has than I, I assure. Look, a treat!" I proffered the sweets again. If a brass jaw with greater familial resemblance to a bear-trap than a human mandible could quiver, this girl's did right then.

"Come in," she said finally.

The cellar was very similar to the many I had seen in Manchester during my exploration of the living conditions of the English proletariat. The floor was dirt and the furnishings limited to bails of hay covered in rough cloth. A dank and filthy smell from the refuse, garbage, and excrements that choked the gutter right outside the cellar entrance, hung in the air. A small, squat, and wax-splattered table in the middle of the room held a soot-stained lantern. The girls wore the same smocks they had the evening before, and there was no sign of water for their toilet. Presumably, what grooming needs they had they attempted to meet at the factory itself, which was known to have a pump for personal use. Most cellar dwellings of this sort have a small cache of food in one corner—a sack of potatoes, butter wrapped in paper, and very occasionally a crust of bread. In this dwelling, there was something else entirely—a peculiar crank-driven contraption from which several pipes extruded.

The big girl walked toward it and with her phonographic voice told me, "We can't have sweets no more." Then she attached the pipes, which ended in toothy clips similar to the pincers of steam-workers, to either side of her mechanical mandible and began to crank the machine. A great buzzing rose up from the device and a flickering illumination filled the room. I could finally see the other girls in their corners, standing and staring at me. The large girl's hair stood on end from the static electricity she was generating, bringing to mind Miss Shelley's famed novel. I was fascinated and repulsed at once, though I wondered how such a generator could work if what it powered, the girl, itself powered the generator via the crank. Was it collecting a static charge from the air, as the skins of the newest airships did?

"Is this . . . generator your sustenance now?" I asked. She stopped cranking and the room dimmed again. "Buy . . . " she started, then recovered, "no more food. Better that way. Too much phossy in the food anyhow; it was poisonin' us."

In a moment, I realized my manners. Truly, I'd been half-expecting at least an offer of tea, it had been so long since I'd organized workers. "I'm terrible sorry, I've been so rude. What are you all called, girls?"

"No names now, better that way."

"You no longer eat!" I said. "And no longer have names. Incredible! The bosses did this to you?"

"No, Sir," the tall girl said. "The Fabians."

The smallest girl, the one who had never said anything save the Bryant and May slogan, finally spoke. "This is re-form, they said. This is us, in our re-form."

3. What Is To Be Done?

I struck a deal with the girls immediately, not in my role as agitator and organizer, but in my function as a manager for the family concern. Our driver took us to his home and woke his wife, who was sent to the shops for changes of clothes, soap, and other essentials for the girls. We kept the quartet in the carriage for most of the morning whilst Wilkins attempted to explain to his wife what she should see when we brought the girls into her home. She was a strong woman, no-nonsense, certainly no Angel of the House but effective nevertheless. The first thing she told the girls was, "There's to be no fretting and fussing. Do not speak, simply use gestures to communicate if you need to. Now, line up for a scrubbing. I presume your . . . equipment will not rust under some hot water and soap."

In the sitting room, Wilkins leaned over and whispered to me. "It's the saliva, you see. My Lizzie's a smart one. If the girls' mouths are still full of spit, it can't be that their jaws can rust. Clever, innit?" He lit his pipe with a white phosphorous match and then told me that one of the girls had sold him a Bryant and May matchbox whilst I booked passage for five on the next dirigible to Manchester. "They'd kept offerin', and it made 'em happy when I bought one," he said. "I'll add 5d. to the invoice, if you don't mind."

I had little to do but to agree and eat the butterscotch I had so foolishly bought for the girls. Presently the girls marched into the sitting room, looking like Moors in robes and headwraps. "You'll get odd looks," the driver's wife explained, "but not so odd as the looks you might have otherwise received."

The woman was right. We were stared at by the passengers and conductors of the airship both, though I had changed into a proper suit and even made a show of explaining the wonders of bourgeois England to the girls from our window seat. "Look girls, there's St. Paul's, where all the good people worship the triune God," I said. Then as we passed over the countryside I made note of the agricultural steam-workers that looked more like the vehicles they were than the men their urbanized brethren pretended to be. "These are our crops, which feed this great nation and strengthen the limbs of the Empire!" I explained. "That is why the warlords of your distant lands were so easily brought to heel. God was on our side, as was the minds of our greatest men, the sinew of our bravest soldiers and the power classical elements themselves—water, air, fire, and ore—*steam!*" I had spent enough time observing the bourgeoisie to generate sufficient hot air for the entire dirigible.

Back in Manchester, I had some trusted comrades prepare living quarters for the girls, and to arrange for the delivery of a generator sufficient for their needs. Then I began to make inquires into the Socialistic and Communistic communities, which I admit that I had been ignoring whilst I worked on the theoretical basis for the Dialectical Engine. Just as Marx used to say, commenting on the French "Marxists" of the late '70s: "All I know is that I am not a Marxist." The steam-workers broke what proletarian solidarity there was in the United Kingdom, and British airships eliminated most resistance in France, Germany, and beyond. What we are left with, here on the far left, are several literary young men, windy Labour MPs concerned almost entirely with airship mooring towers and placement of the same in their home districts, and . . . the Fabians.

The Fabians are gradualists, believers in parliamentary reforms and moral suasion. Not revolution, but evolution, not class struggle but class collaboration. They call themselves socialists, and many of them are as well-meaning as a yipping pup, but ultimately they wish to save capitalism from the hammers of the working-class. But if they were truly responsible somehow for the state of these girls, they would have moved beyond reformism into complete capitulation to the bourgeoisie. *But we must never capitulate, never collaborate!*

The irony does not escape me. I run a factory on behalf of my bourgeois family. I live fairly well, and indeed, am only the revolutionary I am because of the profits extracted from the workers on the floor below. Now I risk all, their livelihoods and mine, to complete the Dialectical Engine. The looms have been reconfigured; we haven't sent out any cotton in weeks. The work floor looks as though a small volcano had been drawn forth from beneath the crust—the machinists work fifteen hours a day, and smile at me when I come downstairs and roll up my sleeves to help them. They call me Freddie, but I know they despise me. And not even for my status as a bourgeois—they hate me for my continued allegiance to the working-class. There's a word they use when they think I cannot hear them. "Slummer." A man who lives in, or even simply visits, the working-men districts to experience some sort of prurient thrill of rebellion and *faux* class allegiance.

But that is it! That's what I must do. The little match girls must strike! Put their prostheses on display for the public via flying pickets. Challenge the bourgeoisie on their own moral terms—are these the daughters of Albion? Girls who are ever-starving, who can never be loved, forced to skulk in the shadows, living Frankenstein's monsters? The dailies will eat it up, the working-class will be roused, first by economic and moral issues, but then soon by their own collective interest as a class. Behind me, the whir and chatter of loom shuttles kicked up. The Dialectical Engine was being fed the medium on which the raw knowledge of my friend's old letters and missives were to be etched. *Steam,* was all I could think. *What can you not do?*

4. The Spark

I was an old hand at organizing workers, though girls who consumed electricity rather than bread were a bit beyond my remit. It took several days to teach the girls to speak with their jaws beyond the Bryant and May slogan, and several more to convince them of the task. "Why should we go back?" one asked. Her name was once Sally, as she was finally able to tell me, and she was the second-smallest. "They won't have us."

"To free your fellows," I had said. "To express workers' power and, ultimately, take back the profits for yourselves!"

"But then we'd be the bosses," the oldest girl said. "Cruel and mean."

"Yes, well no. It depends on all of the workers of a nation rising up to eliminate the employing class," I explained. "We must go back—"

"I don't want to ever go back!" said the very smallest. "That place was horrid!"

The tedious debate raged long into the night. They were sure that the foreman would clout their heads in for even appearing near the factory gates, but I had arranged for some newspapermen and even electro-photographers sympathetic to Christian socialism, if not Communism, to meet us as we handed out leaflets to the passing trade and swing shift.

We were met at the gate by a retinue of three burly looking men in fustian suits. One of them fondled a sap in his hand and tipped his hat. The journalists hung back, believers to the end in the objectivity of the disinterested observer, especially when they might get hurt for being rather too interested.

"Leaflets, eh?" the man with the sap asked. "You know this lot can't read, yeah?"

"And this street's been cleared," one of the others said. "You can toss that rubbish in the bin, then.”

“Yes, that's how your employers like them, isn't it? Illiterate, desperate, without value to their families as members of the female of the species?” I asked. “And the ordinary working men, cowed by the muscle of a handful of hooligans.”

“Buy Bryant and May matchsticks, Sir!” the second-tallest girl said, brightly as she could. The thuggish guards saw her mandible and backed away. Excited, she clacked away at them, and the others joined in.

“How do you like that?” I said to both the guards and the press. “Innocent girls, more machine than living being. We all know what factory labour does to children, or thought we did. But now, behold the new monsters the age of steam and electricity hath wrought. We shall lead an exodus through the streets, and you can put that in your sheets!” The thugs let us by, then slammed the gates behind us, leaving us on the factory grounds and them outside. Clearly, one or more of the police agents who monitor my activities had caught wind of our plans, but I was confident that victory would be ours. Once we roused the other match girls, we'd engage in a *sit-down* strike, if necessary. The girls could not be starved out like ordinary workers, and I had more than enough confederates in London to ring the factory and sneak food and tea for me through the bars if necessary. But I was not prepared for what awaited us.

The girls were gone, but the factory's labours continued apace. Steam-workers attended the machines, carried frames of matches down the steps to the loading dock, and clanked about with the precision of clockwork. Along a catwalk, a man waved to us, a handkerchief in his hand. “Hallo!” he said.

“That's not the foreman,” Sally told me. “It's the dentist!” She did not appear at all relieved that the factory's dentist rather than its foreman, who had been described to me as rather like an ourang-outan, was approaching us. I noticed that a pair of steam-workers left their posts and followed him as he walked up to us.

“Mister Friedrich Engels! Is that you?” he asked me. I admitted that I was, but that further I was sure he had been forewarned of my coming. He ignored my rhetorical jab and pumped my hand like an American cowboy of some fashion. “Wonderful, wonderful,” he said. He smiled at the girls, and I noticed that his teeth were no better than anyone else's. “I'm Doctor Flint. Bryant and May hired me to deal with worker pains that come from exposure to white phosphorus. We're leading the fight for healthy workers here; I'm sure you'll agree that we're quite progressive. Let me show you what we've accomplished here at Bryant and May.”

“Where are the girls?” the tallest of my party asked, her phonographic voice shrill and quick, as if the needle had been drawn over the wax too quickly.

“Liberated!” the dentist said. He pointed to me. “They owe it all to you,

you know. I reckon it was your book that started me on my path into politics. Dirtier work than dentistry." He saw my bemused look and carried on eagerly. "Remember what you wrote about the large factories of Birmingham—*the use of steam-power admit of the employment of a great multitude of women and children.* Too true, too true!"

"Indeed, sir," I started, but he interrupted me.

"But of course we can't put steam back in the kettle, can we?" He rapped a knuckle on the pot-belly torso of one of the ever-placid steam-workers behind him. "But then I read your philosophical treatise. I was especially interested in your contention that quantitative change can become qualitative. So, I thought to myself, Self, if steam-power is the trouble when it comes to the subjugation of child labour, cannot more steam-power spell the liberation of child labour?"

"No, not by itself. The class strugg—"

"But no, Engels, you're wrong!" he said. "At first I sought to repair the girls, using steam-power. Have you seen the phoss up close? Through carious teeth, and the poor girls know little of hygiene so they have plenty of caries, the vapours of white phosphorous make gains into the jawbone itself, leading to putrefaction. Stinking hunks of bone work right through the cheek, even after extractions of the carious teeth."

"Yes, we are all familiar with phossy jaw," I said. "Seems to me that the minimalist programme would be legislative—bar white phosphorous. Even whatever sort of Liberal or Fabian you are can agree with that."

"Ah, but I can't!" he said. "You enjoy your pipe? I can smell it on you."

"That's from Wilkins, my driver."

"Well then observe your Mr Wilkins. It's human nature to desire a strike-anywhere match. We simply cannot eliminate white phosphorous from the marketplace. People demand it. What we can do, however, is use steam to remove the human element from the equation of production."

"I understood that this sort of work is too detailed for steam-workers."

"It was," the dentist said. "But then our practice on the girls led to certain innovations." As if on cue, the steam-workers held up their forelimbs and displayed to me a set of ten fingers with the dexterity of any primates. "So now I have eliminated child labour—without any sort of agitation or rabble-rousing I might add—from this factory and others like it, in less than a fortnight. Indeed, the girls were made redundant this past Tuesday."

"And what do you plan to do for them," I said. "A good Fabian like you knows that these girls will now—"

"Will now what? Starve? You know they won't, not as long as there are lampposts in London. They all contain receptacles. Mature and breed, further filling the working-men's districts with the unemployable, uneducable? No, they won't. Find themselves abused and exploited in manners venereal? No, not possible, even if there was a man so drunk as to overlook their new prosthetic mandibles. Indeed, we had hoped to move the girls into the sales area, which is why their voiceboxes are rather . . . focused, but as it happens few people wish to buy matches from young girls. Something about it feels immoral, I suppose. So they are free to never work again. Herr Engels, their problems are solved."

For a long moment, we both stood our ground, a bit unsure as to what we should do next, either as socialist agitators or as gentlemen. We were both keenly aware that our conversation was the first of its type in all history. The contradictions of capitalism, resolved? The poor would always be with us, but also immortal and incapable of reproduction. Finally the dentist looked at his watch—he wore one with rotating shutters of numerals on his wrist, as is the fashion among wealthy morons—and declared that he had an appointment to make. "The steam-workers will show you out," he said, and in a moment their fingers were on my arms, and they dragged me to the entrance of the factory as if I were made of straw. The girls followed, confused and, if the way their metallic jaws were set was telling, they were actually relieved. The press pestered us with questions on the way out, but I sulked past them without remark. Let them put Doctor Flint above the fold tomorrow morning, for all the good it will do them. Soon enough there'd be steam-workers capable of recording conversations and events with perfect audio-visual fidelity, and with a dial to be twisted for different settings of the editing of newsreels: Tory, Liberal, or Fabian. Indeed, one would never have to twist the dial at all.

We returned to Wilkins and our autocarriage, defeated and atomised. Flint spoke true; as we drove through the streets of the East End, I did espy several former match girls standing on corners or in gutters, directionless and likely cast out from whatever home they may have once had.

"We have to . . . " but I knew that I couldn't.

Wilkins said, "The autocarriage is overburdened already. Those girlies weigh more than they appear to, eh? You can't go 'round collecting every stray."

No—charity is a salve at best, a bourgeois affectation at worst. But even those concerns were secondary. As the autocarriage moved sluggishly toward the airship field, I brooded on the question of value. If value comes from labour, and capital is but dead labour, what are steam-workers? So long as they needed to be created by human hands, clearly steam-workers were just another capital good, albeit a complex one. But now, given the dexterity of the latest generation of steam-workers, they would clearly be put to work building their own descendents, and those that issue forth from that subsequent generation would also be improved, without a single quantum of labour-power expended. The bourgeoisie might have problems of their own; with no incomes at all, the working-class could not even afford the basic necessities of life. Steam-workers don't buy bread or cloth, nor do they drop farthings into the alms box at church on Sunday. How would bourgeois society survive without workers who also must be driven to consume the very products they made?

The petit-bourgeoisie, I realized, the landed gentry, perhaps they could be catered to exclusively, and the empire would continue to expand and open new markets down to the tips of the Americas and through to the end of the Orient—foreign money and resources would be enough for capital, for the time being. But what of the proletariat? If the bourgeoisie no longer need the labour of the workers, and with the immense power in their hands, wouldn't they simply rid themselves of the toiling classes the way the lord of a manor might rid a stable of vermin? They could kill us all from the air—firebombing the slums and industrial districts. Send whole troupes of steam-workers to tear men apart till the cobblestones ran red with the blood of the proletariat. Gears would be greased, all right.

We didn't dare take an airship home to Manchester. The mooring station was sure to be mobbed with writers from the tabloids and Tory sheets. So we settled in for the long and silent drive up north.

I had no appetite for supper, which wasn't unusual after an hour in an airship, but tonight was worse for the steel ball of dread in my stomach. I stared at my pudding for a long time. I wished I could offer it to the girls, but they were beyond treats. On a whim, I went back to the factory to check in on the Dialectical Engine, which had been processing all day and evening. A skeleton crew had clocked out when the hour struck nine, and I was alone with my creation. No, with the creation of the labour of my workers. No, *the* workers. If only I could make myself obsolete, as the steam-workers threatened the proletariat.

The factory floor, from the vantage point of my small office atop the catwalk, was a sight to behold. A mass of cloth, like huge overlapping sails, obscured the looms, filling the scaffolding that had been built up six storeys to hold and "read" the long punched sheets. A human brain in replica, with more power than any Difference Engine, fuelled by steam for the creation not of figures, but dialectics. Quantitative change had become qualitative, or would as soon as the steam engines in the basement were ignited. I lacked the ability to do it myself, or I would have just then, allowing me to talk to my old friend, or as close a facsimile as I could build with my fortune and knowledge. All the machinery came to its apex in my office, where a set of styluses waited in position over sheets of foolscap. I would prepare a question, and the machine would produce an answer that would be translated, I hoped, into comprehensible declarative sentences upon the sheets. A letter from Marx, from beyond the grave! Men have no souls to capture, but the mind, yes. The mind is but the emergent properties of the brain, and I rebuilt Marx's brain, though I hoped not simply to see all his theories melt into air.

With a start, I realized that down on the floor I saw a spark. The factory was dark and coated with the shadows of the punched sheets, so the momentary red streak fifty feet below was obvious to me. Then I smelled it, the smoke of a pipe. Only a fool would light up in the midst of so much yardage of inflammable cotton, which was perplexing, because Wilkins was no fool.

"Wilkins!" I shouted. "Extinguish that pipe immediately! You'll burn down the factory and kill us both! These textiles are highly combustible."

"Sow-ry," floated up from the void. But then another spark flitted in the darkness, and a second and a third. Wilkins held a fistful of matches high, and I could make out the contours of his face. "Quite a mechanism you've got all set up here, Mister Engels. Are these to be sails for the masts of your yacht?"

"No sir, they won't be for anything if you don't extinguish those matches!"

"Extinguish, eh? Well, you got a good look, and so did I, so I think I will." And he blew out the matches. All was dark again. What happened next was quick. I heard the heavy thudding—no, a heavy *ringing* of boots along the catwalk and in a moment a steam-worker was upon me. I wrestled with it for a moment, but I was no match for its pistons, and it threw me over the parapet. My breath left my body as I fell—as if my soul had decided to abandon me and leap right for heaven. But I didn't fall far. I landed on a taut sheet of fine cotton, then rolled off of it and fell less than a yard onto another. I threw out my arms and legs as I took the third layer of sheet, and then scuttled across it to the edge of the scaffold on which I rested. Sitting, I grasped the edge with my hands and lowered myself as much as I dare, then let go. Wilkins was there, having tracked my movements from the fluttering of the sheets and my undignified oopses and oofs. He lit another match and showed me his eyes.

"Pretty fit for an older gentlemen, Mister Engels. But take a gander at the tin of Scotch broth up there." He lifted the match. The steam-worker's metallic skin glinted in what light there was. It stood atop the parapet of the catwalk and with a leap flung itself into the air, plummeting the six storeys down and landing in a crouch like a circus acrobat. Remarkable, but I was so thankful that it did not simply throw itself through the coded sheets I had spent so long trying to manufacture, ruining the Dialectical Engine before it could even be engaged. Then I understood.

"Wilkins!" I cried. "You're a police agent!"

Wilkins shrugged, and swung onto his right shoulder a heavy sledge.

"'Fraid so. But can you blame me, sir? I've seen the writing on the wall—or the automaton on the assembly line," he said, nodding past me and toward the steam-worker, who had taken the flank opposite my treacherous driver. "I know what's coming. Won't nobody be needing me to drive 'em around with these wind-up toys doing all the work, and there won't be no other jobs to be had but rat and fink. So I took a little fee from the police, to keep an eye on you and your . . . " He was at a loss for words for a moment. "Machinations. Yes, that's it. And anyhow, they'll pay me triple to put all this to the torch, so I will, then retire to Cheshire with old Lizzie and have a nice garden."

"And it?" I asked, glancing at the automaton on my left.

"Go figure," Wilkins said. "My employers wanted one of their own on the job, in case you somehow bamboozled me with your radical cant into switching sides a second time."

"They don't trust you," I said.

"Aye, but they pay me, half in advance." And he blew out the match, putting us in darkness again. Without the benefit of sight, my other senses flared to life. I could smell Wilkins stepping forward, hear the tiny grunt as he hefted the sledge. I could nearly taste the brass and aluminium of the steam-worker on my tongue, and I certainly felt its oppressive weight approaching me.

I wish I could say I was brave and through a clever manoeuvre defeated both my foes simultaneously. But a Communist revolutionary must always endeavour to be honest to the working-class—Reader, I fell into a swoon. Through nothing more than a stroke of luck, as my legs gave way beneath me, Wilkins's sledgehammer flew over my head and hit the steam-worker square on the faceplate. It flew free in a shower of sparks. Facing an attack, the steam-worker staved in Wilkins's sternum with a single blow, then turned back to me, only to suddenly shudder and collapse atop me. I regained full consciousness for a moment, thanks to the putrid smell of dead flesh and fresh blood. I could see little, but when I reached to touch the exposed face of the steam-worker, I understood. I felt not gears and wirework, but slick sinew and a trace of human bone. Then the floor began to shake. An arclight in the corner flickered to life, illuminating a part of the factory floor. I was pinned under the automaton, but then the tallest of the girls—and I'm ashamed to say I never learned what she was called—with a preternatural strength of her own took up one of the machine's limbs and dragged him off of me.

I didn't even catch my breath before exclaiming, "Aha, of course! The new steam-workers aren't automata, they're men! Men imprisoned in suits of metal to enslave them utterly to the bourgeoisie!" I coughed and sputtered. "You! Such as you, you see," I told the girl, who stared at me dumbly. Or perhaps I was the dumb one, and she simply looked upon me as a pitiable old idiot who was the very last to figure out what she considered obvious. "Replace the body of a man with a machine, encase the human brain within a cage, and dead labour lives again! That's how the steam-workers are able to use their limbs and appendages with a facility otherwise reserved for humans. All the advantages of the proletariat, but the steam-workers neither need to consume nor reproduce!" Sally was at my side now, with my pudding, which she had rescued from my supper table. She was a clever girl, Sally. "The others started all the engines they could find," she said, and only then I realized that I had been shouting in order to hear myself. All around me, the Dialectical Engine was in full operation.

5. All That Is Solid Melts Into Air

In my office, the styluses scribbled for hours. I spent a night and a day feeding it foolscap. The Dialectical Engine did not work as I'd hoped it would—it took no input from me, answered none of the questions I had prepared, but instead wrote out a single long monograph. I was shocked at what I read from the very first page: *Das Kapital: Kritik der politischen Ökonomie, Band V.*

The *fifth* volume of *Capital*. Marx had died prior to completing the *second*, which I published myself from his notes. Before turning my energies to the Dialectical Engine, I had edited the third volume for publication. While the prior volumes of the book offered a criticism of bourgeois theories of political economy and a discussion of the laws of the capitalist mode of production, this fifth volume, or extended appendix in truth, was something else. It contained a description of socialism.

The internal contradictions of capitalism had doomed it to destruction. What the bourgeoisie would create would also be used to destroy their reign. The ruling class, in order to stave off extinction, would attempt to use its technological prowess to forestall the day of revolution by radically expanding its control of the proletarian and his labour-power. But in so doing, it would create the material conditions for socialism. The manuscript was speaking of steam-workers, though of course the Dialectical Engine had no sensory organs with which to observe the metal-encased corpse that had expired in its very innards the evening prior. Rather, the Engine *predicted* the existence of human-steam hybrids from the content of the decade-old correspondence between Marx and myself.

What then, would resolve the challenge of the proletarian brain trapped inside the body of the steam worker? Dialectical logic pointed to a simple solution: the negation of the negation. Free the proletarian *mind* from its physical *brain* by encoding it onto a new mechanical medium. That is to say, the Dialectical Engine itself was the key. Free the working-class by having it exist in the physical world and the needs of capitalism to accumulate, accumulate. Subsequent pages of the manuscript detailed plans for Dialectical

Engine Number 2, which would be much smaller and more efficient. A number of human minds could be "stitched-up" into this device and through collective endeavour, these beings-in-one would create Dialectical Engine Number 3, which would be able to hold still more minds and create the notional Dialectical Engine Number 4. Ultimately, the entire working-class of England and Europe could be up-coded into a Dialectical Engine no larger than a hatbox, and fuelled by power drawn from the sun. Without a proletariat to exploit—the class as a whole having taken leave of realm of flesh and blood to reconstitute itself as information within the singular Dialectical Engine Omega—the bourgeoisie would fall into ruin and helplessness, leaving the working-class whole and unmolested in perpetuity. Even after the disintegration of the planet, the Engine would persist, and move forward to explore the firmament and other worlds that may orbit other stars.

Within the Dialectical Engine Omega, consciousness would be both collective and singular, an instantaneous and perfect industrial democracy. Rather than machines replicating themselves endlessly as in Mister Butler's novel—*the machines are gaining ground upon us; day by day we are becoming more subservient to them*—it is us that shall be liberated by the machines, through the machines. We are gaining ground upon them! *Proletarier aller Länder, vereinigt euch!* We have nothing to lose but our chains, as the saying goes!

The Dialectical Engine fell silent after nineteen hours of constant production. I should have been weary, but already I felt myself beyond hunger and fatigue. The schematics for Dialectical Engine Number 2 were incredibly advanced, but for all their cleverness the mechanism itself would be quite simple to synthesize. With a few skilled and trusted workers, we could have it done in a fortnight. Five brains could be stitched-up into it. The girls and myself were obvious candidates, and from within the second engine we would create the third, and fourth, and subsequent numbers via pure unmitigated *Arbeitskraft*!

Bold? Yes! Audacious? Certainly. And indeed, I shall admit that, for a moment, my mind drifted to the memory of the empty spectacle of Mister Peake's play, of the rampaging monster made of dead flesh and brought to life via electrical current. But I had made no monster, no brute. That was a bourgeois story featuring a bogeyman that the capitalists had attempted to mass produce from the blood of the working-class. My creation was the opposite number of the steam-worker and the unphilosophical monster of stage and page; the Engine was *mens sana sine corpore sano*—a sound mind outside a sound body.

What could possibly go wrong . . . ?

A HUNDRED GHOSTS PARADE TONIGHT

XIA JIA

(TRANSLATED BY KEN LIU)

Awakening of Insects, the Third Solar Term:

Ghost Street is long but narrow, like an indigo ribbon. You can cross it in eleven steps, but to walk it from end to end takes a full hour.

At the western end is Lanruo Temple, now fallen into ruin. Inside the temple is a large garden full of fruit trees and vegetable patches, as well as a bamboo grove and a lotus pond. The pond has fish, shrimp, dojo loaches, and yellow snails. So supplied, I have food to eat all year.

It's evening, and I'm sitting at the door to the main hall, reading a copy of *Huainanzi*, the Han Dynasty essay collection, when along comes Yan Chixia, the great hero, vanquisher of demons and destroyer of evil spirits. He's carrying a basket on the crook of his elbow, the legs of his pants rolled all the way up, revealing calves caked with black mud. I can't help but laugh at the sight.

My teacher, the Monk, hears me and walks out of the dark corner of the main hall, gears grinding, and hits me on the head with his ferule.

I hold my head in pain, staring at the Monk in anger. But his iron face is expressionless, just like the statues of buddhas in the main hall. I throw down the book and run outside, while the Monk pursues me, his joints clanking and creaking the whole time. They are so rusted that he moves as slow as a snail.

I stop in front of Yan, and I see that his basket contains several new bamboo shoots, freshly dug from the ground.

"I want to eat meat," I say, tilting my face up to look at him. "Can you shoot some buntings with your slingshot for me?"

"Buntings are best eaten in the fall, when they're fat," says Yan. "Now is the time for them to breed chicks. If you shoot them, there won't be buntings to eat next year."

"Just one, pleaaaaase?" I grab onto his sleeve and act cute. But he shakes his head resolutely, handing me the basket. He takes off his conical sedge hat and wipes the sweat off his face.

I laugh again as I look at him. His face is as smooth as an egg, with just a few wisps of curled black hair like weeds that have been missed by the gardener. Legend has it that his hair and beard used to be very thick, but I'm always pulling a few strands out now and then as a game. After so many years, these are all the hairs he has left.

"You must have died of hunger in a previous life," Yan says, cradling the back of my head in his large palm. "The whole garden is full of food for you. No one is here to fight you for it."

I make a face at him and take the basket of food.

The rain has barely stopped; insects cry out from the wet earth. A few months from now, green grasshoppers will be jumping everywhere. You can catch them, string them along a stick, and roast them over the fire, dripping sweet-smelling fat into the flames.

As I picture this, my empty stomach growls as though filled with chittering insects already. I begin to run.

The golden light of the evening sun splatters over the slate slabs of the empty street, stretching my shadow into a long, long band.

I run back home, where Xiao Qian is combing her hair in the darkness. There are no mirrors in the house, so she always takes off her head and puts it on her knees to comb. Her hair looks like an ink-colored scroll, so long that the strands spread out to cover the whole room.

I sit quietly to the side until she's done combing her hair, puts it up in a moon-shaped bun, and secures it with a pin made of dark wood inlaid with red coral beads. Then she lifts her head and re-attaches it to her neck, and asks me if it's sitting straight. I don't understand why Xiao Qian cares so much. Even if she just tied her head to her waist with a sash, everyone would still think she's beautiful.

But I look, seriously, and nod. "Beautiful," I say.

Actually, I can't really see very well. Unlike the ghosts, I cannot see in the dark.

Xiao Qian is happy with my affirmation. She takes my basket and goes into the kitchen to cook. As I sit and work the bellows next to her, I tell her about my day. Just as I get to the part where the Monk hit me on the head with the ferule, Xiao Qian reaches out and lightly caresses my head where I was hit. Her hand is cold and pale, like a piece of jade.

"You need to study hard and respect your teacher," Xiao Qian says. "Eventually you'll leave here and make your way in the real world. You have to have some knowledge and real skills."

Her voice is very soft, like cotton candy, and so the swelling on my head stops hurting.

Xiao Qian tells me that Yan Chixia found me on the steps of the temple when I was a baby. I cried and cried because I was so hungry. Yan Chixia was at his wit's end when he finally stuffed a handful of creeping rockfoil into my mouth. I sucked on the juice from the grass and stopped crying.

No one knows who my real parents are.

Even back then, Ghost Street had been doing poorly. No tourists had been coming by for a while. That hasn't changed. Xiao Qian tells me that it's probably because people invented some other attraction, newer, fresher, and so they forgot about the old attractions. She's seen similar things happen many times before.

Before she became a ghost, Xiao Qian tells me, she had lived a very full life. She had been married twice, gave birth to seven children, and raised them all.

And then her children got sick, one after another. In order to raise the money to pay the doctors, Xiao Qian sold herself off in pieces: teeth, eyes, breasts, heart, liver, lungs, bone marrow, and finally, her soul. Her soul was sold to Ghost Street, where it was sealed inside a female ghost's body. Her children died anyway.

Now she has white skin and dark hair. The skin is light sensitive. If she's in direct sunlight she'll burn.

After he found me, Yan Chixia had walked up and down all of Ghost Street before he decided to give me to Xiao Qian to raise.

I've seen a picture of Xiao Qian back when she was alive. It was hidden in a corner of a drawer in her dresser. The woman in the picture had thick eyebrows, huge eyes, a wrinkled face—far uglier than the way Xiao Qian looks now. Still, I often see her cry as she looks at that picture. Her tears are a pale pink. When they fall against her white dress they soak into the fabric and spread, like blooming peach flowers.

Every ghost is full of stories from when they were alive. Their bodies have been cremated and the ashes mixed into the earth, but their stories still live on. During the day, when all of Ghost Street is asleep, the stories become dreams and circle under the shadows of the eaves, like swallows without nests. During those hours, only I'm around, walking in the street, and only I can see them and hear their buzzing song.

I'm the only living person on Ghost Street.

Xiao Qian says that I don't belong here. When I grow up, I'll leave.

The smell of good food fills the room. The insects in my stomach chitter even louder.

I eat dinner by myself: preserved pork with stir-fried bamboo shoots, shrimp-paste-flavored egg soup, and rice balls with chives, still hot in my hands. Xiao Qian sits and watches me. Ghosts don't eat. None of the inhabitants of Ghost Street, not even Yan Chixia or the Monk, ever eat.

I bury my face in the bowl, eating as fast as I can. I wonder, after I leave, will I ever eat such delicious food again?

Major Heat, the Twelfth Solar Term:

After night falls, the world comes alive.

I go alone to the well in the back to get water. I turn the wheel and it squeaks, but the sound is different from usual. I look down into the well and see a long-haired ghost in a white dress sitting in the bucket.

I pull her up and out. Her wet hair covers her face, leaving only one eye to stare at me out of a gap.

"Ning, tonight is the Carnival. Aren't you going?"

"I need to get water for Xiao Qian's bath," I answer. "After the bath we'll go."

She strokes my face lightly. "You are a foolish child."

She has no legs, so she has to leave by crawling on her hands. I hear the sound of crawling, creeping all around me. Green will-o'-the-wisps flit around, like anxious fireflies. The air is filled with the fragrance of rotting flowers.

I go back to the dark bedroom and pour the water into the wooden bathtub. Xiao Qian undresses. I see a crimson bar code along her naked back, like a tiny snake. Bright white lights pulse under her skin.

"Why don't you take a bath with me?" she asks.

I shake my head, but I'm not sure why. Xiao Qian sighs. "Come." So I don't refuse again.

We sit in the bathtub together. The cedar smells nice. Xiao Qian rubs my back with her cold, cold hands, humming lightly. Her voice is very beautiful. Legend has it that any man who heard her sing fell in love with her.

When I grow up, will I fall in love with Xiao Qian? I think and look at my small hands, the skin now wrinkled from the bath like wet wrapping paper.

After the bath, Xiao Qian combs my hair, and dresses me in a new shirt that she made for me. Then she sticks a bunch of copper coins, green and dull, into my pocket.

"Go have fun," she says. "Remember not to eat too much!"

Outside, the street is lit with countless lanterns, so bright that I can no longer see the stars that fill the summer sky.

Demons, ghosts, all kinds of spirits come out of their ruined houses, out of cracks in walls, rotting closets, dry wells. Hand-in-hand, shoulder-by-shoulder, they parade up and down Ghost Street until the narrow street is filled.

I squeeze myself into the middle of the crowd, looking all around. The stores and kiosks along both sides of the street send forth all kinds of delicious smells, tickling my nose like butterflies. The vending ghosts see me and call for me, the only living person, to try their wares.

"Ning! Come here! Fresh sweet osmanthus cakes, still hot!"

"Sugar roasted chestnuts! Sweet smelling and sweeter tasting!"

"Fried dough, the best fried dough!"

"Long pig dumplings! Two long pig dumplings for one coin!"

"Ning, come eat a candy man. Fun to play and fun to eat!"

Of course the "long pig dumplings" are really just pork dumplings. The vendor says that just to attract the tourists and give them a thrill.

But I look around, and there are no tourists.

I eat everything I can get my hands on. Finally, I'm so full that I have to sit down by the side of the road to rest a bit. On the opposite side of the street is a temporary stage lit by a huge bright white paper lantern. Onstage, ghosts are performing: sword-swallowing, fire-breathing, turning a beautiful girl into a skeleton. I'm bored by these tricks. The really good show is still to come.

A yellow-skinned old ghost pushes a cart of masks in front of me.

"Ning, why don't you pick a mask? I have everything: Ox-Head, Horse-Face, Black-Faced and White-Faced Wuchang, Asura, Yaksha, Rakshasa, Pixiu, and even Lei Gong, the Duke of Thunder."

I spend a long time browsing, and finally settle on a Rakshasa mask with red hair and green eyes. The yellow-skinned old ghost thanks me as he takes my coin, dipping his head down until his back is bent like a bow.

I put the mask on and continue strutting down the street. Suddenly loud Carnival music fills the air, and all the ghosts stop and then shuffle to the sides of the street.

I turn around and see the parade coming down the middle of the street. In front are twenty one-foot tall green toads in two columns, striking gongs, thumping drums, strumming *huqin*, and blowing bamboo *sheng*. After them come twenty centipede spirits in black clothes, each holding varicolored lanterns and dancing complicated steps. Behind them are twenty snake spirits in yellow dresses, throwing confetti into the air. And there are more behind them but I can't see so far.

Between the marching columns are two Cyclopes in white robes, each as tall as a three-story house. They carry a palanquin on their shoulders, and from within Xiao Qian's song rolls out, each note as bright as a star in the sky, falling one by one onto my head.

Fireworks of all colors rise up: bright crimson, pale green, smoky purple, shimmering gold. I look up and feel as though I'm becoming lighter myself, floating into the sky.

As the parade passes from west to east, all the ghosts along the sides of the street join, singing and dancing. They're heading for the old osmanthus tree at the eastern end of Ghost Street, whose trunk is so broad that three men stretching their arms out can barely surround it. A murder of crows lives there, each one capable of human speech. We call the tree Old Ghost Tree, and it is said to be in charge of all of Ghost Street. Whoever pleases it prospers; whoever goes against its wishes fails.

But I know that the parade will never get to the Old Ghost Tree.

When the parade is about half way down the street, the earth begins to shake and the slate slabs crack open. From the yawning gaps huge white bones crawl out, each as thick as the columns holding up Lanruo Temple. The bones slowly gather together and assemble into a giant skeleton, glinting like white porcelain in the moonlight. Now black mud springs forth from its feet and crawls up the skeleton, turning into flesh. Finally, a colossal Dark Yaksha stands before us, its single horn so large that it seems to pierce the night sky.

The two Cyclopes don't even reach its calves.

The Dark Yaksha turns its huge head from side to side. This is a standard part of every Carnival. It is supposed to abduct a tourist. On nights when there are no tourists, it must go back under the earth, disappointed, to wait for the next opportunity.

Slowly, it turns its gaze on me, focusing on my presence. I pull off my mask and stare back. Its gaze feels hot, the eyes as red as burning coal.

Xiao Qian leans out from the palanquin, and her cry pierces the suddenly quiet night air: "Ning, run! Run!"

The wind lifts the corner of her dress, like a dark purple petal unfolding. Her face is like jade, with orange lights flowing underneath.

I turn and run as fast as I can. Behind me I hear the heavy footsteps of the Dark Yaksha. With every quaking, pounding step, shingles fall from houses on both sides like overripe fruits. I am now running like the wind, my bare feet striking the slate slabs lightly: *pat, pat, pat*. My heart pounds against my chest: *thump, thump, thump*. Along the entire frenzied Ghost Street, mine is the only living heart.

But both the ghosts and I know that I'm not in any real danger. A ghost can never hurt a real person. That's one of the rules of the game.

I run towards the west, towards Lanruo Temple. If I can get to Yan Chixia before the Yaksha catches me, I'll be safe. This is also part of the performance. Every Carnival, Yan puts on his battle gear and waits on the steps of the main hall.

As I approach, I cry out: "Help! Save me! Oh Hero Yan, save me!"

In the distance I hear his long ululating cry and see his figure leaping over the wall of the temple to land in the middle of the street. He holds in his left hand a Daoist charm: red character written against a yellow background. He reaches behind his back with his right hand and pulls out his sword, the Demon Slayer.

He stands tall and shouts into the night sky, "Brazen Demon! How dare you harm innocent people? I, Yan Chixia, will carry out justice today!"

But tonight, he forgot to wear his sedge hat. His egg-shaped face is exposed to the thousands of lanterns along Ghost Street, with just a few wisps of hair curled like question marks on a blank page. The silly sight is such a contrast against his serious mien that I start to laugh even as I'm running. And that makes me choke and can't catch my breath so I fall against the cold slate surface of the street.

This moment is my best memory for the summer.

Cold Dew, the Seventeenth Solar Term:
A thin layer of clouds hides the moon. I'm crouching by the side of the lotus pond in Lanruo Temple. All I can see are the shadows cast by the lotus leaves, rising and falling slowly with the wind.

The night is as cold as the water. Insects hidden in the grass won't stop singing.

The eggplants and string beans in the garden are ripe. They smell so good that I have a hard time resisting the temptation. All I can think about is to steal some under the cover of night. Maybe Yan Chixia was right: in a previous life I must have died of hunger.

So I wait, and wait. But I don't hear Yan Chixia's snores. Instead, I hear light footsteps cross the grassy path to stop in front of Yan Chixia's cabin. The door opens, the steps go in. A moment later, the voices of a man and a woman drift out of the dark room: Yan Chixia and Xiao Qian.

Qian: "Why did you ask me to come?"

Yan: "You know what it's about."

Qian: "I can't leave with you."

Yan: "Why not?"

Qian: "A few more years. Ning is still so young."

"Ning, Ning!" Yan's voice grows louder. "I think you've been a ghost for too long."

Qian sounds pitiful. "I raised Ning for so many years. How can I just get up and leave him?"

"You're always telling me that Ning is still too young, always telling me to wait. Do you remember how many years it has been?"

"I can't."

"You sew a new set of clothes for him every year. How can you forget?" Yan chuckles, a cold sound. "I remember very clearly. The fruits and vegetables in this garden ripen like clockwork, once a year. I've seen them do it fifteen times. Fifteen! But has Ning's appearance changed any since the year he turned seven? You still think he's alive, he's real?"

Xiao Qian remains silent for a moment. Then I hear her crying.

Yan sighs. "Don't lie to yourself any more. He's just like us, nothing more than a toy. Why are you so sad? He's not worth it."

Xiao Qian just keeps on crying.

Yan sighs again. "I should never have picked him up and brought him back."

Xiao Qian whispers through the tears, "Where can we go if we leave Ghost Street?"

Yan has no answer.

The sound of Xiao Qian's crying makes my heart feel constricted. Silently, I sneak away and leave the old temple through a hole in the wall.

The thin layer of clouds chooses this moment to part. The cold moonlight scatters itself against the slate slabs of the street, congealing into drops of glittering dew. My bare feet against the ground feel so cold that my whole body shivers.

A few stores are still open along Ghost Street. The vendors greet me enthusiastically, asking me to sample their green bean biscuits and sweet osmanthus cake. But I don't want to. What's the point? I'm just like them, maybe even less than them.

Every ghost used to be alive. Their fake, mechanical bodies host real souls. But I'm fake throughout, inside and outside. From the day I was born, made, I was fake. Every ghost has stories of when they were alive, but I don't. Every ghost had a father, a mother, a family, memories of their love, but I don't have any of that.

Xiao Qian once told me that Ghost Street's decline came about because people, real people, found more exciting, newer toys. Maybe I am one of those toys: made with newer, better technology, until I could pass for the real thing. I can cry, laugh, eat, piss and shit, fall, feel pain, ooze blood, hear my own heartbeat, grow up from a simulacrum of a baby—except that my growth stops when I'm seven. I'll never be a grown up.

Ghost Street was built to entertain the tourists, and all the ghosts were their toys. But I'm just a toy for Xiao Qian.

Pretending that the fake is real only makes the real seem fake.

I walk slowly toward the eastern end of the street, until I stop under the Old Ghost Tree. The sweet fragrance of osmanthus fills the foggy night air, cool and calming. Suddenly I want to climb into the tree. That way, no one will find me.

The Old Ghost Tree leans down with its branches to help me.

I sit, hidden among the dense branches, and feel calmer. The crows perch around me, their glass eyes showing hints of a dark red glow. One of them speaks: "Ning, this is a beautiful night. Why aren't you at Lanruo Temple, stealing vegetables?"

The crow is asking a question to which it already knows the answer. The Old Ghost Tree knows everything that happens on Ghost Street. The crows are its eyes and ears.

"How can I know for sure," I ask, "that I'm a real person?"

"You can chop off your head," the crow answers. "A real person will die with his head cut off, but a ghost will not."

"But what if I cut off my head and die? I'll be no more."

The crow laughs, the sound grating and unpleasant to listen to. Two more crows fly down, holding in their beaks antique bronze mirrors. Using the little moonlight that leaks through the leaves, I finally see myself in the mirrors: small face, dark hair, thin neck. I lift the hair off the back of my neck, and in the double reflections of the mirrors, I see a crimson bar code against the skin, like a tiny snake.

I remember Xiao Qian's cool hands against my spine on that hot summer night. I think and think, until tears fall from my eyes.

Winter Solstice, the Twenty-Second Solar Term:

This winter has been both dry and cold, but I often hear the sound of thunder in the distance. Xiao Qian says that it's the Thunder Calamity, which happens only once every thousand years.

The Thunder Calamity punishes demons and ghosts and lost spirits. Those who can escape it can live for another thousand years. Those who can't will be burnt away until no trace is left of them.

I know perfectly well that there's no such thing as a "Thunder Calamity" in this world. Xiao Qian has been a ghost for so long that she's now gone a little crazy. She holds onto me with her cold hands, her face as pale as a sheet of paper. She says that to hide from the Calamity, a ghost must find a real person with a good heart to stay beside her. That way, just like how one wouldn't throw a shoe at a mouse sitting beside an expensive vase, the Duke of Thunder will not strike the ghost.

Because of her fear, my plan to leave has been put on hold. In secret I've already prepared my luggage: a few stolen potatoes, a few old shirts. My body isn't growing any more anyway, so these clothes will last me a long time. I didn't take any of the old copper coins from Xiao Qian though. Perhaps the outside world does not use them.

I really want to leave Ghost Street. I don't care where I go; I just want to see the world. Anywhere but here.

I want to know how real people live.

But still, I linger.

On Winter Solstice it snows. The snowflakes are tiny, like white saw dust. They melt as soon as they hit the ground. Only a very thin layer has accumulated by noon.

I walk alone along the street, bored. In past years I would go to Lanruo Temple to find Yan Chixia. We would knock an opening in the ice covering the lotus pond, and lower our jury-rigged fishing pole beneath the ice. Winter catfish are very fat and taste fantastic when roasted with garlic.

But I haven't seen Yan Chixia in a long time. I wonder if his beard and hair have grown out a bit.

Thunder rumbles in the sky, closer, then further away, leaving only a buzzing sensation in my ears. I walk all the way to the Old Ghost Tree, climb up into its branches, and sit still. Snowflakes fall all around me but not on me. I feel calm and warm. I curl up and tuck my head under my arms, falling asleep like a bird.

In my dream, I see Ghost Street turning into a long, thin snake. The Old Ghost Tree is the head, Lanruo Temple the tail, the slate slabs the scales. On each scale is drawn the face of a little ghost, very delicate and beautiful.

But the snake continues to writhe as though in great pain. I watch carefully and see that a mass of termites and spiders is biting its tail, making a sound like silkworms feeding on mulberry leaves. With sharp mandibles and claws, they tear off the scales on the snake one by one, revealing the flesh underneath. The snake struggles silently, but disappears inch by inch into the maws of the insects. When its body is almost completely eaten, it finally makes a sharp cry, and turns its lonesome head towards me.

I see that its face is Xiao Qian's.

I wake up. The cold wind rustles the leaves of the Old Ghost Tree. It's too quiet around me. All the crows have disappeared to who knows where except one that is very old and ugly. It's crouching in front of me, its beak dangling like the tip of a long mustache.

I shake it awake, anxious. It stares at me with two broken-glass eyes, croaking to me in its mechanical, flat voice, "Ning, why are you still here?"

"Where should I be?"

"Anywhere is good," it says. "Ghost Street is finished. We're all finished."

I stick my head out of the leaves of the Old Ghost Tree. Under the slate-grey sky, I see the murder of crows circling over Lanruo Temple in the distance, cawing incessantly. I've never seen anything like this.

I jump down from the tree and run. As I run along the narrow street, I pass dark doors and windows. The cawing of the crows has awakened many of the ghosts, but they don't dare to go outside, where there's light. All they can do is to peek out from cracks in doors, like a bunch of crickets hiding under houses in winter.

The old walls of Lanruo Temple, long in need of repairs, have been pushed down. Many giant mechanical spiders made of steel are crawling all over the main hall, breaking off the dark red glass shingles and sculpted wooden molding, piece by piece, and throwing the pieces into the snow on the ground. They have flat bodies, blue-glowing eyes, and sharp mandibles, as ugly as you can imagine. From deep within their bodies comes a rumbling noise like thunder.

The crows swoop around them, picking up bits of broken shingles and bricks on the ground and dropping them on the spiders. But they are too weak and the spiders ignore them. The broken shingle pieces strike against the steel shells, making faint, hollow echoes.

The vegetable garden has been destroyed. All that remains are some mud and pale white roots. I see one of the Monk's rusted arms sticking out of a pile of broken bricks.

I run through the garden, calling for Yan Chixia. He hears me and slowly walks out of his cabin. He's still wearing his battle gear: sedge hat over his head, the sword Demon Slayer in his hand. I want to shout for him to fight the spiders, but somehow I can't spit the words out. The words taste like bitter, astringent paste stuck in my throat.

Yan Chixia stares at me with his sad eyes. He comes over to hold my hands. His hands are as cold as Xiao Qian's.

We stand together and watch as the great and beautiful main hall is torn apart bit by bit, collapses, turns into a pile of rubble: shingles, bricks, wood, and mud. Nothing is whole.

They've destroyed all of Lanruo Temple: the walls, the main hall, the garden, the lotus pond, the bamboo grove, and Yan Chixia's cabin. The only thing left is a muddy ruin.

Now they're moving onto the rest of Ghost Street. They pry up the slate slabs, flatten the broken houses along the sides of the street. The ghosts hiding in the houses are chased into the middle of the street. As they run, they scream and scream, while their skin slowly burns in the faint sunlight. There are no visible flames. But you can see the skin turning black in patches, and the smell of burning plastic is everywhere.

I fall into the snow. The smell of burning ghost skin makes me vomit. But there's nothing in my stomach to throw up. So I cry during the breaks in the dry heaves.

So this is what the Thunder Calamity looks like.

The ghosts, their faces burned away, continue to cry and run and struggle in the snow. Their footprints criss-cross in the snow, like a child's handwriting. I suddenly think of Xiao Qian, and so I start to run again.

Xian Qian is still sitting in the dark bedroom. She combs her hair as she sings. Her melody floats in the gaps between the roaring, rumbling thunder of the spiders, so quiet, so transparent, like a dreamscape under the moon.

From her body come the fragrances of myriad flowers and herbs, layer after layer, like gossamer. Her hair floats up into the air like a flame, fluttering without cease. I stand and listen to her sing, my face full of tears, until the whole house begins to shake.

From on top of the roof, I hear the sound of steel clanging, blunt objects striking against each other, heavy footsteps, and then Yan Chixia's shouting.

Suddenly, the roof caves in, bringing with it a rain of shingles and letting in a bright patch of grey sky full of fluttering snowflakes. I push Xiao Qian into a dark corner, out of the way of the light.

I run outside the house. Yan Chixia is standing on the roof, holding his sword in front of him. The cold wind stretches his robe taut like a grey flag.

He jumps onto the back of a spider, and stabs at its eyes with his sword. The spider struggles hard and throws Yan off its back. Then the spider grabs Yan with two sharp claws and pulls him into its sharp, metallic, grinding mandibles. It chews and chews, like a man chewing kimchee, until pieces of Yan Chixia's body are falling out of its mandibles onto the shingles of the roof. Finally, Yan's head falls off the roof and rolls to a stop next to my feet, like a hard-boiled egg.

I pick up his head. He stares at me with his dead eyes. There are no tears in them, only anger and regret. Then with the last of his strength, Yan closes his eyes, as though he cannot bear to watch any more.

The spider continues to chew and grind up the rest of Yan Chixia's body. Then it leaps down from the roof, and, rumbling, crawls towards me. Its eyes glow with a deep blue light.

Xiao Qian jumps from behind me and grabs me by the waist, pulling me back. I pry her hands off of me and push her back into the dark room. Then I pick up Yan Chixia's sword and rush towards the spider.

The cold blue light of a steel claw flashes before my eyes. Then my head strikes the ground with a muffled *thump*. Blood spills everywhere.

The world is now tilted: tilted sky, tilted street, tilted snow falling diagonally. With every bit of my strength, I turn my eyes to follow the spider. I see that it's chewing on my body. A stream of dark red fluid drips out of its beak, bubbling, warm, the droplets slowly spreading in the snow.

As the spider chews, it slows down gradually. Then it stops moving, the blue light in its eyes dim and then go out.

As though they have received some signal, all the other spiders also stop one by one. The rumbling thunder stops, plunging the world into silence.

The wind stops too. Snow begins to stick to the spiders' steel bodies.

I want to laugh, but I can't. My head is now separated from my body, so there's no way to get air into the lungs and then out to my vocal cords. So I crack my lips open until the smile is frozen on my face.

The spiders believed that I was alive, a real person. They chewed my body and tasted flesh and saw blood. But they aren't allowed to harm real people. If they do they must destroy themselves. That's also part of the rules. Ghosts, spiders, it doesn't matter. Everyone has to follow the rules.

I never imagined that the spiders would be so stupid. They're even easier to fool than ghosts.

The scene in my eyes grows indistinct, fades, as though a veil is falling from the sky, covering my head. I remember the words of the crows. So it's true. When your head is cut off, you really die.

I grew up on this street; I ran along this street. Now I'm finally going to die on this street, just like a real person.

A pair of pale, cold hands reaches over, stroking my face.

The wind blows and covers my face with a few pale pink peach petals. But I know they're not peach petals. They're Xiao Qian's tears, mixed with snow.

HEAVEN UNDER EARTH

ALIETTE DE BODARD

Husband's new spouse is brought home in a hovering palanquin decked with red lanterns, its curtains displaying images of mandarin ducks and kingfishers—the symbols of a happy marriage.

First Spouse Liang Pao has gathered the whole household by the high gate, from the stewards to the cooks, from the lower spouses to their valets. He's standing slightly behind Husband, with his head held high, with pins of platinum holding his immaculate topknot in place—in spite of the fact that he's been unable to sleep all night. The baby wouldn't stop kicking within his womb, and the regulators in his blood disgorged a steady stream of *yin*-humours to calm him down. He's slightly nauseous, as when he's had too much rice wine to drink—and he wonders why they never get easier, these carryings.

The palanquin stops, lowers itself gracefully as the steward cuts off the dragon-breath fields. The scarlet curtains sway, twisting out of shape the characters for good luck and long life.

Husband steps out first, holding out his hand to the spouse inside—he's wearing his best clothes, white live-worm silk preserved since the days of the colonist ancestors, a family heirloom reserved for grand events.

And the spouse . . .

When she steps out of the palanquin, Liang Pao cannot help a slight gesture of recoil. He wasn't expecting . . .

Behind him, the servants and the lower spouses are whispering in disbelief. Liang Pao turns, slightly, to throw them a cutting glance—and the whispers cease, but they don't erase the facts.

The new spouse is unmistakably a woman—not a *caihe* like Liang Pao and the others, a woman with a live womb and eggs of her own. Except . . . Except that it's obvious how Husband could afford to bring a woman home even though he's not a High Official: her calm, stately face under the white makeup is older than it should be. She's in her late fifties, at best—and her childbearing years are, if not over, very near their end. By the time her seclusion has ended, she'll be useless.

Husband turns around, presenting her to the household, and Liang Pao's ingrained reflexes take over from his shock.

From a faraway place, as distant as the heights of Mount Xu, he walks to her and bows, slightly—as befitting a superior to an inferior. "My Lady," he says. "We wish you a prosperous marriage." He hesitates for a fraction of a second, but still he completes the traditional blessing. "May you have the Dragon's Nine Sons, every one of them with their own strength and successes."

Pointless. She won't have any sons, or any daughters for that matter.

"First Spouse," Husband says, equally formally. "This insignificant person by my side is Qin Daiyu, and she humbly begs you to enter the house as a lawfully wedded spouse."

Liang Pao blesses formalities—the only thing he can hold onto, steady and unvarying and as surely ingrained in his mind as Master Kong's Classics. "She is welcome under this roof, for the term of her seclusion and for the term of her marriage. May Heaven bestow on both of you a thousand years of happiness."

All this, of course, does nothing to quell the acrid taste in his mouth, and nothing to answer his question—the endless "Why?" swirling in his head like a trapped bird.

As manager of the household, Liang Pao is the one who assigns Fourth Spouse her quarters and servants of her own. The best thing for her would have been *caihes*, but he cannot very well ask one of the two other spouses to wait on her, when she's still the youngest member of the household—in seniority if not in age.

Liang Pao selects the only two neutered valets he has, and takes them to help Fourth Spouse unpack her bridal things: three heavy lacquered coffers, antiquities predating the Arrival. If these could be sold, they'd fetch a price even higher than Husband's silk robes.

Where under Heaven did Husband find her?

Fourth Spouse watches him the whole time, with a frank look of appraisal he finds disturbing—she's neither as meek nor as demure as a woman should be.

But then, he knows so little of women.

When the servants have left, Fourth Spouse doesn't move. She only bows her head, with a stately gesture that looks correct—but that sends a tingle down Liang Pao's spine, a hint of wrongness. She says, "Thank you."

"It's my place." He knows he should stay with the prescribed topics, wish her again health and happiness, but his curiosity is too great. "It's unusual for our household to . . . welcome such a guest."

"I have no doubt," she says, then offers a mocking smile.

No opening, then, and he's unsure of why he's ever hoped there would be one. Ritual assigns each of them their place: to him, the running of the household, including that of her quarters; to her, the seclusion and the regular visits from the Embroidered Guards, the taking of her last few eggs to pay the tax on female marriages.

After a last bow, he's preparing to leave, when she does speak.

"The stars have shifted their course to bring me here from the willow-and-flower house," she says. Her formal speech is at odds with the frank gaze she trains on him.

Liang Pao stops, frozen in the doorframe. A willow-and-flower. A courtesan. That's where Husband found her, then, in a high-class brothel—one that can afford a few women from the Ministry of Rites, in addition to their usual fare of *caihes* and boys.

"So that's why he could afford you." He doesn't even attempt the usual courtesies; but he doubts she'll be shocked by this breach. That's why her gaze was assessing him then—as a potential client, even though the idea of a *caihe* sleeping with a woman is ludicrous.

She shrugs. Her robe slides down her shoulders as she does so, revealing skin the colour of the moon, and tight, round breasts that he could hold in one hand. And, as he thinks of that, the same deep sense of wrongness tightens in his womb.

There's a smell in the air—blossoming on the edge of perception, a mixture of flowers and sweat and Buddha knows what. Liang Pao's breath quickens. He knows what it has to be: spring-scents, tailored to arouse her clients. But he's not one of them. He's not even a man. It can't be working on him.

"You've never seen a woman before," Fourth Spouse says, as blunt as he is.

He shakes his head. "I was born the normal way," he says. In an automated incubator, after his father filled out the necessary forms at the Ministry of Rites.

"I see." Her lips curl—she's amused, and bitter, though he doesn't know why. "You were born a man."

Liang Pao shrugs. It seems such a long time ago, when he was still a boy and still dreaming of being head of his own household, fantasizing over how many spouses he'd be allowed to take—long before he failed the exams, long before knives and needles cut into his flesh, before regulators moulded him into something else. Now it's a faded memory, blunted and harmless. He's *caihe* now—has always been so.

Fourth Spouse draws herself up, her chest jutting out in what looks like a practised pose. But the ease with which she does it belies that. It's a reflex, as ingrained within her as politeness and courtesies are within Liang Pao.

His heartbeat has quickened; but underneath is the familiar languor caused by his regulators releasing new *yin*-humours, and within a few moments his breath grows calm again, his heartbeat steady once more.

He shouldn't be here. Anything out of the ordinary could endanger the pregnancy; and though Husband's post as a fifth-rank civil servant entitles him to nine transfers, he doesn't want to be the one to spoil a perfectly good egg. "I'll leave you alone," he says.

The look of veiled contempt she gives him sears him to the bone. "You're less than a man, then. Unable to give voice to your desires."

He doesn't understand. "I have no desires."

"Not anymore, I guess."

Liang Pao rubs his hand against the bulge of his belly—feeling the child twist and turn within him, wondering if the heartbeat he hears is his own or the baby's. "I'm carrying."

"I can see that," she says, again. "Husband's child by—"

He shrugs. She knows the ritual as well as he does: Husband donated the sperm, and one of the thousand thousand eggs in the huge vaults of the Ministry of Rites was unfrozen, fertilized—and transferred into him. That's the way it works, with *caihes*.

Wives, of course, are different, and the transfer is much easier. Natural, one of his teachers at the Ministry said, once, in an unguarded moment—before closing his eyes and forcefully changing the subject. For most of New Zhongguo, wives are an unattainable dream: sold for fortunes by the Ministry of Rites, and all but reserved to High Officials.

Fourth Spouse laughs, a quiet, pleasant sound, the tinkle of a chime over a waterfall. "Carrying or not, you can't change the fact that you're a man."

"You're mistaken," he says, calmly, carefully, in the same tone mandarins use to explain things to off-worlders. "I'm not a man."

Fourth Spouse smiles, shaking her head in disdain.

This is ridiculous. He's First Spouse of the household, carrying Husband's child within him—and here she is, all but flirting with him, taunting him for what he is not. "I would seem to be disturbing you," he says, as stiff and as formal as he can manage. "I will leave you to your rest."

He goes away: walking as quickly as he can, feeling the languor in every fibre of his being, the regulators struggling to keep up with the quickening of his breath, with the tight feeling in his chest.

Caihe, he is *caihe*, he has to remember that.

Liang Pao never goes into her room, after that. He has his life and she has hers, and he won't think on her words or of the images she's conjured in him: memories of a distant childhood when he flew steel-yarn kites just like his own children are doing in the courtyard—just like the boy in his womb will do some day.

Still, he wakes up every night, in the privacy of his quarters—his heart beating madly for a few, interminable seconds before the *yin*-humours kick in and he sinks back into sleep again. In his dreams, in the waking world, he aches with a desire he can't place, a need that seeks to supersede even the pregnancy.

Fourth Day comes round again: the moment of his moonly examination. The doctor arrives at the gates of the household, prim and on time, and is shown into the examination room, where Liang Pao sits hidden behind a chromed screen. The doctor takes his place near the entrance of the room. His *caihe* assistant goes back and forth behind the screen, observing Liang Pao's symptoms and reporting to the doctor. As the cool, capable hands rest on his wrists and on his throat, taking one by one the twelve pulses of the heart, Liang Pao remembers other hands against him—wielding knives and injectors, gently pressing their blades until the skin broke and blood pearled with the first prickling of pain. He remembers the first *yin*-humours within him, the sickening taste in his mouth and the unfamiliar languor, as constricting as the *cangue* restricting a prisoner's arms . . .

He comes to with a start. The *caihe* assistant has finished; behind the screen, the doctor is busy reporting. He's been droning on for a while, about the rate of metal-humours and wood-humours in the body—nothing out of the ordinary, it would seem. Everything is going as well as expected, and within a few moons Husband will have a young, healthy boy.

Then he's gone, but Liang Pao doesn't move for a long while—not until the memories fade into harmlessness, and his hands stop shaking.

He's never had dreams like those before; but then he has never been so close to a woman before. He's been taught to be a good *caihe*: to sing and recite poetry; to walk in fast, mincing steps that make it look as though he's swaying; to play soulful songs on the *qin* until his fingers are numbed to the pain from the strings. But he has never been taught what he should do with a woman—or what to do when his *yin*-humours struggle to keep up with the pregnancy.

Carrying or not, you can't change the fact that you're a man.

Is that all there is to it?

On a whim, he rises and walks to the freezer, and orders it to open. In the first drawer is a beaker engraved with phoenixes and dragons sporting among clouds—and within, hanging suspended in nitrogen, is a single egg, due to be transferred into Second Spouse's womb at the next Moon Festival.

The second drawer . . .

In the second one are three elongated pouches, encased in layers of insulation, enough to keep them well below freezing point for a day.

His hand hovers over the leftmost one—the one bearing the characters of his own name, entwined on a background of peach blossoms. After a while, he withdraws it from the drawer, and holds the cool surface of the insulation in the palm of his hand.

It's an old, old custom, dating back to the days of Old Earth—before the space exodus, before the colonist ancestors. Long before there were *caihes* on New Zhongguo, there were eunuchs—and they kept the excised parts with them, so that they might be buried with everything their parents had given them.

Here, resting snug in the palm of his hand, is proof that she was right— that he wasn't born a *caihe*, that he will not die as one. That he is . . .

He doesn't know what he is, anymore.

"You look thoughtful," Husband's voice says, behind him.

Liang Pao doesn't start, or show surprise in any way—only small children are still impulsive enough to display what they feel.

Rather, Liang Pao turns, slowly, and bows to Husband, the precise depth required by ceremony. Today, Husband is wearing a robe shimmering with moiré; his hair is done in an immaculate top-knot, with the eight-metal pins denoting his status as a fifth-rank magistrate.

Husband shakes his head. "No need for that," he says. Gently, he picks the pouch from Liang Pao's hand, and turns it over. "That's the first time I've seen you take this out."

Liang Pao doesn't quite know how to answer. It's never been his place to bother Husband with his own problems, just as Husband's troubles at the tribunal stop at the door of the house. "I—was curious," he says finally.

Husband stares at the pouch, as if, like a poem, it might twist and turn on itself and reveal something else. "Something is on your mind," he says, and he looks distinctly worried. "Isn't it?"

How does he know? "It's been—difficult, lately, for me," Liang Pao says.

Husband's eyes freeze: a minute expression that Liang Pao isn't sure how to interpret. "You have a good life, Pao. Don't you?"

The use of Liang Pao's personal name is almost as shocking as the hunger with which Husband watches him—and Liang Pao doesn't know what to do, doesn't know what to say to make things go back to the way they were. "Of course," he says, but it doesn't seem to be enough. "Fourth Spouse . . . " he starts, and can't finish.

Husband still watches him.

"Fourth Spouse is . . . unexpected."

Husband relaxes a fraction, though his gaze is still harsh. "Yes, of course. I should have known. She's not here to supplant any of you, Pao. I just—" He hesitates, but then goes on. "You should have seen her in the willow-and-flower house. You should have heard her make up verses to cap the poems of the customers—and such talent, when she played the *qin* . . . "

Liang Pao doesn't speak. He doesn't dare to. He's never heard such contained emotion in Husband's voice. *He loves her*, he thinks, and it's a bittersweet thought, because he's not quite sure how he should react to this.

"They go back to the government, when they're too old to procreate," Husband says. "They're sold to High Officials as ornaments—as pretty things, exhibited before one's friends at receptions and festivals. That's . . . That isn't a life for her. You understand?"

Liang Pao isn't sure if he does, but he nods all the same. "You rescued her?"

"Yes. Rescued her. But she's not here to take your place. She isn't here . . . "

To carry his children. Liang Pao shakes his head. "I understand."

"Good. Good." Husband smiles, looking relieved, and puts the pouch back in the freezer.

And then it occurs to Liang Pao: Husband didn't know. There is one time in his life when a *caihe* receives his pouch—for the last few breaths, the last few heartbeats, that he might die as he was born.

No, he wants to say. I didn't want to commit suicide. But Husband has already moved on. "You should go and see her," he says. "Be friends with her. For the harmony of the household."

Husband's words are commands, of course, even if he doesn't always realise it. "I will," Liang Pao says, but the last thing he wants is to talk to Fourth Spouse.

That evening, Liang Pao goes into the garden, and stands for a while, listening to the plaintive accents of a *qin* wafting from inside Fourth Spouse's quarters.

It's a song he knows, a poem about the pain of parting:

"Two regal daughters are weeping
off within green clouds
They went along with the wind and the waves . . . "

He should go in. He should enter her quarters and talk to her, as Husband has asked.

For the sake of the household, if nothing else. But he can't . . .

He can't go in there again.

" . . . the Xiang may stop its flow
only then will the stains disappear
of their tears upon bamboo."

The *qin* falls silent, and nothing moves within. He hears the scuffle of the valets withdrawing from the inner chamber; her evening is over, and she will be preparing herself for bed.

It's not too late, he tells himself, but he knows he's only lying to himself. His swollen breasts hang over his chest—his nipples tingle, and the same feeling climbs from his womb, mingling with the baby's heartbeat within him. He aches with need.

That's when he hears the door slide open—and sees her shadow slip out of the quarters.

At first, he thinks Fourth Spouse is only there to enjoy the moonlight—but something in the way she walks tells another story. She looks left and right, pausing every few steps to make sure no one is following her. That's no mincing, womanly walk, but the careful step of someone on reprehensible business.

Surely she wouldn't—

Liang Pao starts walking faster, heedless of his body's protests—his muscles ache, and his breasts, unhampered by any underwear, shift up and down on his chest, to the rhythm of his race. He takes care to stay hidden, but she's running now, heading towards the back of the garden and the small passageway that opens only for the Moon Festival.

Surely . . .

She stands by the door—and then she reaches inside her wide sleeves. She throws a last, furtive glance behind her—Liang Pao presses himself harder against the trunk of a willow tree, tries to merge with the night . . .

She doesn't see him. With a shrug, she slides a card into the door and it slides open, infinitely, heart-wrenchingly slow.

That's not meant to happen, Liang Pao thinks, standing frozen where he is. The door can't just . . .

There's no time to think about all of this. One more moment; and she'll pass through into the passageway, through the door at the end, and she'll slip outside and they'll never find her.

Fine, that's his first thought. Let her be gone, her and her disturbing presence, and the feelings she evokes within him. But then he remembers Husband's voice when he spoke of Fourth Spouse—brimming with an emotion Liang Pao has never heard from him. Her flight, he knows, will break Husband's heart.

He moves before he can think. He runs—his head spins, and the unaccustomed weight of his belly forces him to bend backward, but he doesn't stop. He has to reach her.

She's squeezing herself through the door, pressing against the metal panels even though they're not open yet—and he's not fast enough, not strong enough to catch up to her before she goes through. So he does the only thing he can do.

"Stop," he says. His voice echoes against the walls of the empty garden, triggering a flood of soft lights from the garden walls.

But that doesn't work—she's still pressing on, still hoping to pass the second door and lose herself in the deserted streets of the city. "Stop", Liang Pao says, again. "Or I'll call."

She freezes, then. "You wouldn't. You don't want me here."

"I already told you. I have no desires," he says.

Fourth Spouse watches the open door, her face half-turned away from him, washed smooth by the soft, swirling light emanating from the garden walls—and he stands, already out of breath and waiting for the adrenaline to leave his muscles. Thankfully, each garden section is independent: the light will be small, and barely visible from Husband's quarters. For now, it's just the two of them.

Her face is unreadable under the harsh neon light. "Surely you can understand." Her voice is flat, emotionless. "I will humbly remove herself from your presence, and the house will return to harmony."

Liang Pao puts both hands in his sleeves—standing away from her, both feet firmly planted in the muddy, fragrant earth of the garden: a gesture of disapproval.

The door is closing again—between that and the door at the other end of the passageway, that's two sets of doors now, two barriers against her escape. He doesn't move, though, to stand between her and the panels; that would be showing weakness.

Finally, Fourth Spouse says, "Let me go." Her voice is shaking now. "You have to."

"You'll break his heart," Liang Pao says. "Why should I let you go?"

She shakes her head, in that oddly disturbing way. "I'm not meant for him." She looks at him, and some of the same freezing contempt creeps back into her face. "But you don't understand, do you?"

"I—" Liang Pao says, and she's right: he doesn't understand a word she's saying. But her voice—her voice is like an electric tingle in his body, and he can't seem to focus on anything but the carnation of her lips, and her wide eyes.

She bends her head towards him, gracefully. "We didn't only have New Zhongguans, at the willow-and-flower house. We had navigators and engineers, and other people sailing the space between the stars." Her voice is oddly reflexive. "Some of them were women—we used to lie against each other afterwards and whisper sweet nothings on the pillows—" and it's all too clear she's not talking about women, but about one woman in particular.

He doesn't want to hear that. Women sleeping with each other—it's as unnatural as a fish out of water, or Heaven under Earth. His throat is pulsing again; he fights an urge to come closer to her.

"I—"

Fourth Spouse's smile is malicious. "Rubbing each other's nipples, and pleasuring ourselves with tongues and fingertips . . . "

The tightening in his womb has become unbearable. "Stop," he whispers. "Stop."

"She's out there," Fourth Spouse says. "Waiting for me—waiting to take me away from all this, to a place that's meant just for me. Let me go." Her voice is low, urgent, and the odd, frightening smell of her spring-scents saturates the air. "Let me be free."

He gives her the rote answer, the one they taught him at the Ministry of Rites: "A woman's true place is in the house, with her husband." As is a *caihe's* place.

"Perhaps. Perhaps not." She's not smiling anymore. "You were a man, once—before you changed. I thought you'd understand. I thought—" She looks at him, tears glistening in her eyes. "Don't you want me to be happy?"

"I—"

Her eyes are wide, and he feels himself falling into them, a fall that has no end.

She whispers, "Don't you remember what it felt like, being a man? Don't you remember the life you were promised—the fight against the *shenghuans* on the boundary, the grand merchant adventures in space—dreaming of what it would feel like, kissing a wife? Don't you remember?" She moves closer, and her scent enfolds him, an intoxicating tingle on every pore of his skin.

Like the kites, her words mean something to him—stir the same indefinable longing in his womb—but this is wrong, all wrong, those are selfish dreams. "This doesn't matter," he says. "This isn't my place."

"Then you're a worse fool than I thought."

But he's had enough of being dominated by her—woman or not, she's still the most junior member of the household, and he's still First Spouse. "No. You're the fool, Daiyu. You think that all you have to do is walk through that door, and you'll be free."

"More than you."

He shakes his head. "You and your—lover . . . " He spits the word, ignoring the odd taste it leaves in his mouth. "You wouldn't go past the first street. You're still in seclusion, remember? You owe a tax, and you haven't paid it in full."

Her lips purse, and he can well imagine what kind of fire she'll be hurling at him. He forestalls her, quietly. "You may think her clever enough to evade the patrols. But the guards at the space-harbour—they won't overlook you. Two women, without any kind of travel permit? You'll stand out like Buddhist monks in a crowd."

"You're wrong," Fourth Spouse says. "We have the papers."

"Faked papers?" Liang Pao says, slowly, carefully enunciating each word. "Is that what you think it takes to leave? For an off-worlder with a New Zhongguan? The first thing they'll do is call this house, to check that you do have a travel permit." He takes a deep breath to steady the erratic beat of his heart, and says to those wide, entrancing eyes, "And even if they don't call . . . I'll make sure Husband knows you're missing the moment you run through those gates."

He doesn't move; he simply watches her, trying to ignore the fluttering in his womb.

"No," Fourth Spouse says, finally. Her voice is bitter, angry—but she's not looking at the door anymore, and the anger is directed in equal parts at him and at herself. "All right," she says, shaking her head. "Next thing I know, you'll blackmail me into staying here in exchange for not reporting this little . . . incident."

Liang Pao shakes his head. "I know enough to guess it wouldn't work."

Fourth Spouse's lips tighten in a smile. "You have that right, if nothing else." She turns to leave—but Liang Pao stops her.

"The card," he says.

Her smile is a terrible, wounding thing. She throws the card in the air—a shard of light spinning upwards, and then plummeting into the soft air. "That cost me dearly. Two moons of negotiation with your doctor's assistant. Two moons of promises and cajoling," she says, contemptuously—whether of him or of the assistant, it's not clear.

"You won't have that opportunity again," Liang Pao says.

She doesn't move. "I guess not," she says, more quietly.

And, as quick as an unsaid thought, she spins on her heels, and walks back to her own quarters, leaving Liang Pao alone in harsh moonlight—shivering in the night cold and no longer sure of the right thing to do.

In spite of what she thinks, he doesn't denounce her—but he finds himself watching her, wondering if she's still thinking of escape. Liang Pao calls the assistant, seemingly on a trivial matter about *YIN*-humour dosages-and shows him the card, quietly making it clear to him that such things won't happen again.

As far as he knows, Fourth Spouse keeps within her quarters, obsessively playing the *qin*, and painting, with decisive flicks of the pen, landscapes of New Zhongguo—from the red canyons where *shenghuans*ambush the unwary, to the settlements scattered among the dust plains. He resumes his old routine, and never speaks to her.

Her words, though, still haunt him.

Don't you remember what it felt like?

He remembers a boy flying a dragon kite, and laughing at the way the thin aluminium sails flexed against the wind; he remembers cutting the string, and standing on the red hill, watching the kite flying high in the sky—growing smaller and smaller, taking away his sorrows and bad luck. His father had smiled, then, and said this presaged success at the exams, and many happy marriages—but that was before everything changed, became as dead as the wilted plum flowers in the garden . . .

Don't you remember the life you were promised?

"I don't," he whispers, when he wakes up, shivering in the night. "I was never promised anything."

He wasn't—not then, not now. He has his life and he manages Husband's household, and that is all he needs.

It is enough. It has to be.

When Fourth Spouse's seclusion ends, the whole family accompanies her to the Monastery of Cleansing Mercy, to receive the monks' formal blessing. All, except Liang Pao's third son, born only one moon ago and still too young to risk the harsh air of outside.

Liang Pao himself has come, hiding the slight quiver of weakness, the slight dizziness that threatens to blur the world around him: the last remnants of a mostly untroubled birth, a night spent in labour before he beheld the wrinkled, crying face of Third Son—and warmth flooded his chest, tightening like a fist around his heart.

He stands in the temple, already missing the familiar touch of the baby nestled against him. His breasts are heavy with milk, longing for Third Son's lips to close on them; and he wonders how long it will be before he gets back to the nursery.

He holds First Son's hand, and feels it quiver in his own, feels the boy's eagerness to leave the staid ceremony and run in the temple's gardens. An eagerness that was his, once—but he doesn't remember that.

Before the image of Guan-Yin, bodhisattva of Compassion, Husband and Fourth Spouse kneel, humbly accepting the sutras recited by the saffron-garbed monks. The air is saturated with incense and sub-vocalised prayer chants from the choir. The goddess herself is represented snatching a boy from hungry waves, her eyes directed towards the viewer—her unreadable gaze not unlike that of Fourth Spouse.

The children fidget, and Third Spouse sharply calls them to order. Liang Pao is watching Husband and Fourth Spouse—but he sees nothing untoward until the end of the blessing.

An elderly monk brings a cage containing a pair of *lang* birds, their shimmering wings beating against the metal bars. They attempt to peck the monk's hands when he reaches inside and withdraws the first one—they struggle and shriek, and at least one finger is bleeding, but the monk is used to it; and with a smile he throws the bird upwards. "Thou shall have a heart of compassion, a heart of filial piety . . . Thou shall use all expedient means to save all living beings," he intones.

The second bird joins the first; they wheel together in the sky, hesitant at first, but gaining speed as they realise they're no longer confined. Soon, they're both lost to sight.

"He who hurts not *any living being*, he in truth is called a great man . . . "

Husband and Fourth Spouse turn to face the family. Husband is smiling, looking fondly at Fourth Spouse; but she in turn is looking straight at Liang Pao, and her gaze is a reproach.

Don't you remember the life you were promised?

They walk back to where Liang Pao is standing, side-by-side—the only time in their lives when they will be positioned as equals.

Liang Pao bows, and hands Husband a scroll commemorating the event: two mandarin ducks, holding a lotus blossom and a lotus fruit in their beaks. "May you find bliss and harmony for a thousand cycles."

Husband smiles, and shakes his head. "No need to be so formal. Walk with us, will you?"

In the gardens, monks watch automated units as they hoe the rough, dry soil of the planet—few things grow on New Zhongguo. From time to time, they unscrew the filter container, and release the underground insects trapped against the grid.

"Hard at work," Fourth Spouse says, non-committal.

Husband shrugs. "They serve New Zhongguo. As we all do."

Even wives. Even *caihes*.

Husband's gaze turns back towards the monastery. The abbot, accompanied by a few of the monks, is making straight for him. "That will be for my donation. I'll leave you two alone," he says—and the way he says it makes Liang Pao sure that he's intended this all along.

He and Fourth Spouse watch Husband start an animated conversation with the abbot, waving his ample sleeves.

"He's a good man," Liang Pao says, though he doesn't know why he says that.

"And I'm his wife." Fourth Spouse's tone is lightly ironic. He expects her to talk about leaving, or to mock him once more—but instead she holds out her arm to him, in the prescribed position for a chaperone. "Come," she says. "Nothing says we have to revolve around him."

As on most of New Zhongguo, the gardens are sparse: the few fields are devoted to the production of natural grain. Further on, a small fountain breaks the monotony of wheat, its spout of water shaped like a blossoming lotus flower. Monks toil in the fields, supervising the automated harvesters, or carefully trimming the stalks—an atmosphere of reverent industry almost alien to Liang Pao, who cannot remember the last time he did manual work outdoors.

Fourth Spouse's arm is warm against his skin—and his breath has quickened again. With the pregnancy over, he isn't as strong as he usually is; and he fights an overwhelming urge to bring her closer to him, and to . . .

No.

"What do you want?" Liang Pao asks, when they're out of earshot.

Fourth Spouse shrugs. "Some time on my own, I guess," but he sees that's not it—and she's pressing herself closer to him, her grip changing, becoming a caress through the silk.

There's the same smell in the air as when he first met her—except much, much stronger: flowers and sweat, the faint odour of sugared ginger overlaid with a stronger, more acrid one, and his breasts tightening, hungering for her touch . . .

Spring-scents, he thinks, desperately. That's all there is to it. Spring-scents.

But he's reacting, unstoppably—his *yin*-humours just aren't as efficient now that the pregnancy is over. He's free of the languor, and something tingles within his womb, spreads to his whole skin, a haze of desire he's never felt in his life . . .

He wants to . . .

Almost instinctively, he reaches out, tipping her face upwards, bringing those wide, enthralling eyes closer to his own—breathing in the sweet smell of her scent, imagining her skin brushing his, her sweat mingling with his— he's not thinking, not any more—save of the need burning through him, the ache deep within to be more than what he's been turned into . . .

And in her moist eyes, too, he sees only the reflection of that need—a fire that sears away prudence and reason and education.

He needs . . .

Her lips part, revealing teeth the colour of white jade—they brush his, and the fire arches in him, from breasts to womb, reaches its crux.

"So you're a man after all," she whispers, and he doesn't care, he doesn't know if she's right or not, it doesn't matter.

But, against the wave of desire, something within him is reacting—beating fists against a glass panel, struggling to be heard. He brings her closer to him, for a second kiss, a second brush of fire, frantically seeking the warmth of her hands through her loose sleeves . . .

We used to lie against each other afterwards and whisper sweet nothings on the pillows . . .

And he sees it in her eyes, in the set of her jaw, in the name her lips open on, which isn't his own. He sees it in her arms and in her stance—the coiled muscles of someone straining to be free, to flee by any means possible.

His breasts ache—heavy with milk, and not with this alien, frightening desire. Gently, he releases her. She watches him, panting, her cheeks flushed.

"I'm not her," he says, slowly, softly.

"Do you think it matters?"

"Yes," he says.

He remembers the kite, cut free of its string—and the way it disappeared from sight, taking his sorrows and sadness.

"Of course it does," he says—but so low he isn't sure she can hear.

• • •

He goes to see Husband, afterwards. He finds him ensconced in a chair within the library, watching a multi-sensorial shadow-play to the plaintive music of oboes and the smell of sandalwood.

Husband shifts positions when Liang Pao comes in, surprised. "First Spouse? What is—"

Liang Pao cuts him short—something he wouldn't have dared do, only a day ago. But desperation makes him brave. "Flowers can't bloom, if the earth isn't right."

"I don't understand," Husband says.

Liang Pao kneels, putting his left hand on the floor in front of him, and the right arm against his back—the posture reserved for a supplicant before the Emperor. "I humbly and reverently beg you to let your spouse Qin Daiyu go."

He stares at the ground, hearing only a swish of robes as Husband comes to tower over him. "I thought you'd talked to her," Husband says.

Liang Pao doesn't move. He forces himself not to. "I have." And, more quickly, before he can remember what he's doing, "Her place wasn't with a High Official. Her place isn't here. Flowers wither if the earth is too shallow, and caged animals only waste away. I beg of you—"

"Enough." Husband's voice is curt. "Do you have any idea how much I paid for her, Pao? How many favours I had to ask from High Officials?"

Liang Pao says nothing. There is no answer he can make.

"I rescued her," Husband says. His voice, too, comes fast, the words tumbling one atop the other, like a children's game with paper cubes. "I took her inside this house, where she'd be happy. I . . . "

Liang Pao lets Husband's voice fade into silence before he speaks. "I know," he says. "And it is not a humble spouse's place to tell you what to do. But Fourth Spouse is not someone you can cage. She—" He knows he cannot mention the woman—whoever her name is. To Husband, that relationship will only be an abomination.

There is only silence, in the wake of his words—broken by the bursts of music from the shadow-play in the background.

Finally, Husband says, "She's not happy, is she?"

Liang Pao tilts his head backward, sucking in air through his teeth—signifying, without words, that it's very difficult. The message is as clear as he can make it, without saying "No" outright.

He hears nothing; only Husband's slow, steady breath. Even the shadow-play has fallen silent.

"I see," Husband says. "I will consider this." Which, coming from him, is a good as an affirmative.

"I humbly thank you," Liang Pao says. He rises—only to meet Husband's piercing gaze. He'd throw himself to the ground again, but Husband raises a hand, preventing him from doing so.

"Stay here, Pao. Tell me something."

"Yes?"

"What about you?"

What about—? He says nothing. He thinks of Husband standing by his side in the examination room, worry etched on his face; and of the sweet smell of lips brushing his, kindling a fire in his womb. He runs his hand against his breast, squeezes and feels the milk seep into the silk of his tunic.

"Not all *lang* birds long for the sky," he says, finally. Not all birds will see the bars of their cages open; nor do they wish to. It's enough, sometimes, to be reminded of who you are and what you chose. "My place is here."

He sees Husband smile—a small, barely visible upturning of the lips, soon hidden. Emotions destroy, he thinks, but he knows it's not quite true.

Sometimes, like metal, things need to be destroyed—fed through the fire so they can emerge stronger.

Moons letter, he receives a package, and a letter traced in a quick, deliberate hand that breathes strength onto the paper. It's not signed; but he knows who wrote it.

I humbly thank you for everything, the letter says. *I have the audacity to hope that the following gift is acceptable—in remembrance of our meeting.*

Inside is a small, round box engraved with the characters for "dragon" and "phoenix"—the symbols for man and woman. When he opens it, he sees that a miniaturised refrigerant unit occupies most of the inside—and that the small, rectangular sheath at the centre contains a liquid he knows all too well: nitrogen. Within, suspended, is her gift: one of her last eggs, the most precious thing a woman can give to a man.

He sits in his chair for a while, staring at the characters sprawled on the page—Third Son blissfully suckling milk at his breast. From outside come the noises of steel-yarn unfolding in the breeze: First Son, Second Son and Husband flying their kites, challenging each other to go higher and higher.

Liang Pao feels, once more, the tightening in his womb, the alien feeling he associates with her and dares not name.

So you're a man after all.

Gently, he sets the box apart—out of his reach. *No,* he thinks, realising that she never really understood him. *I am what I am. I have no regrets. I am* caihe.

Rising, he descends into the courtyard, to help his family cut the strings of sadness and misfortune.

SUNSHINE

NINA ALLAN

> God is not like a human being; it is not important for God to have visible evidence so that he can see if his cause has been victorious or not; he sees in secret just as well.
>
> —Søren Kierkegaard

> Due to the overenthusiastic predations of leech collectors in the 19th century, the Medicinal Leech (Hirudo medicinalis) is now a protected species. Individual specimens can grow up to 10" in length, and larger adults are capable of consuming up to ten times their own body weight in a single feeding session. After piercing the skin, the leech injects the host with a form of local anaesthetic and an anticoagulant known as hirudin. The largest population of Hirudo medicinalis in the UK is to be found at Lydd, on the Dungeness Peninsula in Kent. Leeches can survive for up to a year between feedings.
>
> *A Book of Backyard Beasts*
> by Rowena Swithin
> (Ivybridge Press, 1976)

You asked me where I came from. I was born in Paris, in the shadow of Montmartre, but my mother soon moved me first to Brighton, on England's south coast, and then to London. I have no memories of Paris from when I was a baby, though I have visited that city more than a dozen times since. My mother's name is Michaela Olsen, and I am Daniel Clement Olsen. I don't know my father's name, and nor do I wish to.

I am a shade under six feet tall, light of build and with a knock-kneed, somewhat stooping deportment. I have been called scrawny, though my victims seem to find me good looking. I have wide, slightly flaring nostrils, fine shoulder-length hair the colour of barley water. My eyes are a watery blue.

I am a student of philosophy, though I am unlikely to ever gain my degree. If anyone asks me my age, I say twenty-six.

The human world is an illogical place. It is governed by rights of ownership, yet few humans appear to realise that the laws that uphold these rights are purely arbitrary. They are allowed to stand because the majority are inclined to agree—or at least not to disagree—that they should be enforced. Yet currency exchange rates and the land registry possess no objective reality, and if the consensus that exists was to be suddenly overturned (nuclear winter, Ebola pandemic, perpetual drought) the fifty-pound note you hold in your hand would instantly revert to a series of coloured designs on expensive paper. The house you purchased for yourself as a bulwark against an impoverished old age could be overrun by hoodlums at any moment.

Whether this is a frightening thought for you or an exciting one will depend on your temperament, but those with even a glancing fascination for philosophy will be bound to admit that it is interesting.

The rule of law, it seems to me, depends for its stability on two main quantities: the majority of human beings must agree at least tacitly that it is less inconvenient to abide by the law than to break it, and Homo sapiens must remain the dominant species on the planet. The ants might well have laws to govern their ant-cities, but we all know that a well-aimed kick can overturn their whole civilization in less than ten seconds. In the case of the ant and indeed any and all animal orders at the lower end of the food chain, attempts to impose order on chaos will ultimately prove futile through the simple and brutal expedient that might is right.

Human beings, you will assure me, have no such worries, at least until their anthill attracts the attention of some superior race. Unless or until that happens, Homo sapiens remains free to build, destroy or subjugate as he sees fit.

Things are not that simple, however.

My childhood lasted eight years. Since then, contact with my mother has been intermittent, and though I have never ceased to admire her as a woman, her importance to me as a parent quickly became irrelevant. In habits of child-rearing, the hirudin are less like worker ants than solitary wasps. For the hirudin woman there is none of the troublesome business of preparing her offspring for life as viable economic units. Once her children can feed for themselves, her job as a mother is done.

The children, little leeches, need no second bidding.

My mother, Michaela Olsen, is ravishing, skittish and shy. The first stage of our relationship came to an abrupt end on the night I crawled beneath the bedclothes and attempted to rape her. As I said, she is a beautiful woman, and it is perfectly common and normal for hirudin to engage in sexual behaviour as early as six years old, although the females cannot actually reproduce until their early teens.

Michaela snapped awake in less than a second. She seized me by the scruff of my neck and threw me out of the bed on to the floor.

"You filthy demon!" she screeched. "Get your pathetic little dick out of my sight." Her hair, corkscrewed and fine as my own, boiled wildly about her face.

I spent the remainder of the night in the garage and thought of it as my first adult adventure. I woke the following morning to find my mother had moved on without me. I was surprised though not overly distressed and quickly adapted. I understood later that it was not the prospect of incest that had so offended her but my maleness per se. Michaela Olsen usually disdained sexual contact altogether but when she relented she preferred the company of women.

Humans she hated. She fed like a hungry gannet, and always killed. I still see her from time to time. We don't talk much but we enjoy a game of chess together. She is still as lovely as ever, and although she possesses the muscular strength of tensile steel the unfair biological fact is that I am now stronger. As we slide our opposing armies across the varnished surface of the chessboard I imagine wrapping an arm about her throat and shafting her up to the hilt in her tight little arse.

I get hard just thinking about it, but content myself with winning the game of chess.

What you have to understand is that the hirudin are a different species. I kill on average ten times a year; contrary to popular belief I feel no remorse whatsoever. Would you feel remorse for destroying an anthill? Would your pet cat feel remorse for tormenting a rat? For the hirudin, humans are like mayflies: they are going to die anyway, and soon. I am less gratuitously vicious than my mother, but this has nothing to do with guilt and everything to do with my own everyday comfort and convenience. Every time you kill you leave a mess, and a mess of that kind is always going to draw unwelcome attention to its perpetrator. The fewer people I kill, the easier it is for me to pass unnoticed.

Some hirudin enjoy notoriety and actively court it. I've never understood that myself, although a friend of mine once told me it's no different from chess, and I understood that well enough.

Perhaps, I said to him. But at least with chess you don't end up with the cops out looking for you.

You're clearly not all that into chess then, he said. We both laughed at that.

We are not immortal, thank God, though our lifespan is generous. If I am lucky and take proper care of myself I should expect to live a good two hundred years. I have known some live longer, broken-down, crazed old geezers of two-hundred-and-fifty or even more, but such longevity is not desirable. When we are young we shake off disease heedlessly, carelessly as a dog thrashing rainwater from its coat. But as age creeps up on us the process of cellular regeneration that is the mainspring of hirudin biology begins to slow, and we ourselves begin to slow as a result. It becomes more difficult to feed in safety, and although a healthy hirudin adult can go a full six weeks without feeding and suffer no ill effects, in an older individual such prolonged deprivation will induce further weakness, and so a cycle of slow starvation begins to set in.

In the end we die like cockroaches, spent husks, crouched behind dusty wardrobes or holed up in understairs cupboards, so depleted you could sweep us out with the morning rubbish. It is disgusting and pitiful and I do not like to think about it. But it is still better than the foul and stinking, rotting-meat death of the exhausted human. There is comfort in that, at least.

The hirudin are parasites. They make use of the human economic infra-structure that surrounds them in the same way that a cuckoo will pressgang birds of different species into rearing its young. I know a hirudin woman who posed as a human doctor for seventy years. She kept practices in two different cities, and when things began to get tricky she packed her stuff and began again in a third.

Making a life as a perpetual student is somewhat less arduous.

We have no doctors of our own, no lawyers, no teachers. To be able to flourish, such professions require a measure of social complacency, and for the hirudin, community is just another word for trap. Our longevity makes us egotistical, poetical, philosophical by nature. Some—my mother, for instance—are simply mad.

We can go about in daylight, be reflected in mirror glass, cross running water or any threshold not physically barred to us. We can even digest small amounts of cooked animal or vegetable matter when necessary. Most of the human mythology relating to the hirudin is rubbish, the dreams and nightmares summoned up to explain the inexplicable or the misunderstood.

I detest the term vampire.

I have never cared for any human, except once.

The hirudin is by necessity an urban creature. I have taken sojourns in most of the cities of Europe—partly from curiosity, partly from the demands generated by circumstance—but I always return to London in the end. I love this city in the miasmic, dust-polluted afternoons of mid-August and the

rain-slicked, mud-grey mornings of late November. I love London even when
I hate it. It is the closest thing I know to a proper home.

In London, no one questions what you do, and in a city with such a large
transient population—prostitutes, immigrants, terrorists on the run—it can
be weeks before a missing person is actually missed. Where there are missing
persons there are empty properties and so long as you're careful and don't
mind roughing it, finding somewhere to live presents little difficulty.

At the time the following events took place I was living in a flat above a
disused warehouse in New Cross. I kept those lodgings for almost two years,
and had electricity and running water throughout my stay. I was comfortable
there, and it was most likely that very quiescence that almost did for me.
Having somewhere permanent to live meant that less of my time and energy
was taken up in matters of day-to-day survival, and it was certainly around
that time that I was able to start taking my philosophy studies more seriously.
As well as attending classes at UCL I travelled regularly to both Oxford and
Cambridge and was privileged to hear many of the national and European
luminaries of the time. I attended lectures by Russell and Steiner, Koestler
and Canetti, and was, I believe, as stimulated as any other student by the
climate of intellectual freedom that prevailed. Oxford I knew already because
I had lived there for a while; Cambridge was still quite new to me and at first
I found it to be a strange place, an exposed and lonely island in the barren
sea of East Anglia. But I soon discovered that in May Week or at the start
of Michaelmas there is no place on earth more enchanted: a nexus of nerves
and nature and nascent ambition with its very isolation making that heady
mixture still more potent. I think I fell in love for a while. Not just with the
idea of myself as a young scholar but with the music of my own thoughts. I felt
invulnerable and so I took stupid risks, did things that seemed rational at the
time but that I look back on with impatient displeasure.

It was during that period of madness that I met Margaret. She is seventy
years old now, a grandmother to three children. I still think of her. I wonder
if she ever thinks of me.

I prefer to kill people in their own homes. There is no need to hide anything or
cover my tracks, and the chance of being disturbed is reduced significantly. I
can have a wash and a change of clothes and usually stock up on cash as well.
Things are much simpler all round.

The police come in the end of course, but I'm long gone by then. No doubt
you'll be surprised when I tell you that there really isn't much for them to go
on. There is no motive, no discernible clues, no weapon. The DNA we leave
behind us is confusing, to say the least.

Did you know that a man can lose consciousness in less than ten seconds if the flow of blood from the jugular is significant enough? Slitting one's own throat is not a popular method of suicide among human beings. It takes an unusually high level of psychotic derangement—not to say courage—to do it. If suicides knew how quick it was, how relatively painless, and how effective, I have no doubt the statistics would change.

I am lucky in being attractive to both men and women. My slight ungainliness makes me appear defenceless. My articulacy makes me seem bohemian rather than scruffy.

For these reasons and more I have always found the business of killing laughably easy.

My most recent victim was a fifty-five-year-old Polish office cleaner named Paulina. I watched her for a fortnight before taking her, shadowing her from the six-storey office block in Bayswater where she worked to the basement flat in Shepherd's Bush where she lived. I also called at the flat a couple of times when I knew she was out—enough to be reasonably certain that she lived alone, not enough to get myself noticed by the neighbours.

At the Bayswater end I did the opposite, passing close by her on the street as she clocked off from work, even smiling at her once or twice, implanting my features and friendly presence into her memory. I wanted her to feel she knew me somehow: from her young days in Warsaw perhaps, or as the son of a friend who had since vanished from her life.

On the last day I went into the Tube with her. When she got off at Shepherd's Bush I let her get well ahead of me going through the barrier and then ran to catch up with her as she was about to cross the street in front of the station.

"Hey, Auntie Jan!" I yelled.

She turned around at once, as I knew she would do. I did not know her name yet, but it made no difference. My careful preparations ensured that at some strange subconscious level she was inwardly attuned to my presence. She responded to my voice automatically, even though she had never heard it before.

As her eyes met mine I arranged my face into an expression of disappointment, followed almost immediately by an embarrassed smile.

"I'm so sorry," I said. "I thought you were my aunt. You look exactly like her from behind."

Paulina raised both eyebrows. I discovered that she did that a lot.

"What about from the front?" she said.

"Younger," I replied. "You, I mean." I smiled at her again, more confidently this time and with just a trace of flirtatiousness. She did have a nice face, actually. The flesh of her cheeks had fallen slightly, and her hair had gone grey, but her bone structure and upright posture gave the impression of someone who had been beautiful in her youth. Her accent reminded me of women I had known in Berlin. I even felt a trace of sadness, that human women age so quickly, that so much of their lives are spent in ugliness. In some ways I would be doing her a favour.

"Does she live around here, your aunt, then?" We were heading away from the station by then and walking side by side along Uxbridge Road, just a surrogate auntie and nephew enjoying a chat. I named the street that formed a T-junction with the one she lived in. She exclaimed her surprise.

"Life is full of these strange coincidences," I said. "That's what they teach us on my course, anyway."

"You are at college?"

"UCL. I'm reading Philosophy."

It turned out she had a degree in Material Sciences from Warsaw University. Ten seconds later she was inviting me to have lunch with her.

"I hope you won't think this too strange," she said. "But it would be lovely to share your company. I don't really see anyone, not these days. I miss my friends from Poland."

After that it was easy. I sat at her kitchen table and talked to her about a recent lecture I had attended on Schopenhauer while she bustled about putting rye bread and salami on to plates. By then I was so nerved up with what was going to happen that my teeth were chattering, the hairs on my forearms standing on end as if I had just received an electric shock. Paulina was enjoying herself too much to notice. I ate as much of the bread and meat as I could manage then said I would be glad to help her with the washing up. As she turned away from me to start clearing the table I placed both my hands on her hips and drew her gently backwards, pressing her buttocks against my groin where (as I hoped she would feel) I was rock hard.

This was the moment of most risk for me, but even so it was not as risky as you might think. Had she turned on me or started to scream I would have simply apologised for my 'mistake' and made a quick exit. As it was, she tensed slightly just for a second then relaxed again, her shock already turning—I could smell it—to a slow excitement.

She probably thought that this was my way of paying for the food.

Her bedroom overlooked a walled courtyard, and the curtains were drawn. I stepped out of my jeans and underpants and guided her hand to my cock while I set about removing her blouse. Her body was tired, the sagging breasts pendulous, the wads of fat around her midriff crisscrossed by the indentations of her undergarments. None of this mattered to me. I eased her back on to the bed, her loosened hair cascading over the pillows. As I slid into her she emitted an audible groan, and I wondered how long it had been since she'd last had sex.

There are hirudin who do still make the first strike with their teeth—my mother, for instance—but I myself have not done that since I was a child. It's the least efficacious method, and so clumsy that the element of surprise is completely lost. There's a thing you can buy, a steel thimble-like object tipped with a razor blade that fits over the thumb or index finger, and there are those who swear by that, but I've always felt that although it makes a highly effective display the blade itself doesn't cut deep enough. I use a spike, a neat stainless steel stiletto that ensures penetration directly into the artery. It can be tricky to get the hang of—you have to slam it in hard and in exactly the right position or the whole thing can get very messy—but so long as you know what you're doing it's virtually foolproof. If you're skilful the victim never even knows what's happened.

Paulina jerked just once in my arms as I drew out the spike, but by then I was holding her down so firmly she couldn't have struggled much in any case. I moved in to catch the fountain of her blood as it erupted, then bit down hard, widening the opening. My tongue and lips and the inside of my throat were immediately coated with the luscious, blue-black juice of the aorta. As my mouth filled up with her blood I emptied myself into her, coming so hard I could feel my spunk flowing backwards out of her cunt and encrusting my belly.

I like to think that this was the last thing she was aware of: the true and certain knowledge that she had given me pleasure.

Once I was sure she was dead I loosened my grip on her shoulders and began feeding in earnest. An hour later and after a short nap I took a shower and put my clothes back on. I made a quick search of the flat, a worthwhile delay, as it turned out, because Paulina had almost five hundred pounds hidden inside a glove at the back of her underwear drawer.

Then I left. No one saw me, but it wouldn't have mattered if they had. I was not known in the area, and wouldn't be visiting Shepherd's Bush again any time soon.

I walked for miles and for hours, cutting up through Ladbroke Grove and Kensal Green to the crumbling maisonette in Kilburn where I currently live. I threw myself down on the grimy mattress that serves for a bed and fell asleep in under ten seconds. I awoke just as it was getting properly dark. I arose from my bed and walked the streets of North London until dawn. The old stones seemed to smile down at me, accepting me as one of their own. I have never seen the city more beautiful. I have never felt more alive, or more free.

On the concourse at Charing Cross Station. Sunshine, like liquid crystal, dappling her arm.

She was standing by herself, a straight-backed, willowy girl, staring at the ranked ticket windows as if they presented some insurmountable obstacle, or as if she had temporarily forgotten where she wanted to go.

Sunlight streamed through the glass roof of the station, drifting downwards towards the ground, where it came to rest in a heap of overstretched, irregular trapezoids. Like melting honeycomb, I thought. I don't like honey, and I don't like sunshine either, but something about the way it looked on the girl's skin, light as pollen or dandelion seeds, made me come close to forgetting about the train I was rushing to catch.

That was my first sight of Margaret. She had a high, clear brow and light brown eyes. Her hair, which was the colour of dry dirt, was straight, and came to just below her shoulders. She was wearing a pink dress. Its colour reminded me of roses in late summer, when the blooms become overblown and the petals fall. She was neither short nor tall. I guessed she was in her late teens. Twenty perhaps, but no more.

She turned to look at me. My staring must have alerted her somehow, as persistent staring often will. I felt that I could look at her for a long time, as I might look at a rainbow or a spider's web or a sea anemone, those quieter wonders of nature that are nonetheless compelling. At the same time though I wanted to get away from her, or rather to get her away from me, to remove her from my sight and from my sensing, as if even to look at her was to somehow expose her to danger.

Everything about her spoke of lightness. I wanted to keep her, and yet never to see her again. The thought of killing her sweetened my saliva and engorged my penis even as it repulsed me. I concentrated on the sunshine, which hurt my eyes.

I blinked. She smiled and I heard her inhale, a sharp, nervous sound that fluttered in the space between us like an invisible bird. I could almost hear her wondering whether she should say anything to me or not.

"Can I help you at all?" I said, making the decision for her. "Only you were looking a little lost." A station announcer was warning me that my train would be leaving in five minutes, but I no longer cared.

"Oh, no thank you," she said. "My cousin was meant to be meeting me here, that's all, and there's no sign of her. The train will be going in a minute. I don't know what to do."

Today's technology would rewrite this scene. She would reach into her bag and take out her mobile, call the cousin, find out that the wretched girl was late leaving, or stuck in traffic, or shagging her boyfriend. She would wait, or not wait, but either way that look of dazed confusion would have been absent, replaced by its modern equivalent, a perplexed annoyance.

"Where are you going?" I said.

"Folkestone," she said. "Just for the day. My grandparents live there."

"In that case you've already missed the train." It was not quite true, not yet, but it would be in ninety seconds. "I'll make a bargain with you. We'll wait for the next one together, and if your cousin still hasn't turned up you'll let me keep you company on the journey."

"You're not really going to Folkestone, though?" She gave a little laugh, more like a gasp, and I could feel her looking at me, examining me, as it were, for sharp corners or hidden threats. In my baggy cords and light tweed jacket I was dressed to look like what I was, that is, a student or young professor on his way to a lecture. I looked older than her, it was true, but not enough to make that fact worrying. My hair was sun-streaked and my eyes were bright. I looked, as she was to tell me the next time we met, like the young Hölderlin. What harm could there be in spending a half hour with such a person in the station buffet?

"Why not?" I replied. I did my best to sound cheeky and winning, a young loafer without a care in the world. "I fancy a day at the seaside."

"All right," she said, laughing again. "I wouldn't mind a cup of tea."

"What's your name?" I said quickly. It seemed imperative that I learn it as soon as possible. I wanted to be sure, you see, that even if I never saw her again after that day I would have a label I could attach to her, a name for the feeling I had when I looked at her that distinguished itself from all other memories.

"Margaret," she said. "I always think it makes me sound like someone's aunt."

"And are you?" I said. "Someone's aunt?" The name sat on her oddly, too big for her somehow, bulky as a man's overcoat. But it was beautiful all the same, clattering against my teeth like three heavy pearls.

"Mind your own business," she said. I told her my name was Daniel, though she hadn't asked. I felt sick and slightly dizzy, and for the briefest of instants I imagined leaving her where she was and going to a rooming house I knew just off Brick Lane. It was the haunt of whores, never the same girls twice. I could buy one for the day, then slaughter her in one of the goods yards at the back of Liverpool Street Station. No one would notice the body or care if they did.

My thoughts troubled me because they were so out of character. I rarely killed on impulse, if ever. To do so was the action of a fool.

Like a rat smelling petrol I understood that I was in danger. Not from Margaret as such, but from my feelings about her. I had known more beautiful women, certainly. I had known women who had got down on all fours and begged me to violate them.

I did not know what it was. Only that I wanted to be near her.

I found us a corner table in the restaurant and then went up to the counter to order our drinks. There was a cake under glass, a large yellow sponge with cream and strawberry jam squirting out of the middle. I ordered a slice of that too, thinking that Margaret might enjoy it. As it turned out, she did.

Her name was Margaret Alexandra Gensing and she was hoping to get into Cambridge the following year. Her cousin's boyfriend Nigel was already there.

"They are engaged," she said. "They're going to get a house together and everything. But I don't really like him."

"Why not?"

"He's studying Law." She made a face, then put a hand to her mouth. "That sounds stupid. It's hard to explain. It's just that he and Emma seem so . . . fixed on things."

"And you're not? Fixed on things, I mean?"

"Not really. Not yet. I want to study English, the Metaphysical Poets, but my father says I should plan on becoming a teacher. It sounds so dull though, doesn't it? I can't imagine talking about those poems to anyone who didn't really want to know about them."

"I couldn't agree with you more." I told her that my own parents were abroad, and that I was hoping to land a junior research fellowship at Gonville and Caius. Until the position was certain I was having to lodge with my grandfather in Highgate.

"The place is a health hazard," I said. "I'm surprised the council haven't quarantined it."

"You'll get the fellowship, I'm sure," Margaret said. A gentle flush had risen on her cheeks. "And if you don't you can always teach."

I laughed. There was, thank God, still no sign of the errant cousin, and by the time we boarded the train I was hoping—foolishly—that Margaret and I would be able to spend the rest of the day together. But when we arrived into Folkestone the cousin was there, waiting for us on the platform. It turned out she had been on the earlier train all along.

Cousin Emma was large and golden, resplendent as a sunflower and utterly uninteresting to me. As we stepped down from the train I asked Margaret if I might have her telephone number. She tore a leaf from a little notebook she had in her bag and scribbled it down.

"Afternoons are the best time to call," she whispered. "My father's always out at work then. You'd like my dad if you got to know him, I know you would. But he can be a bit funny around strangers."

He has a right to be, I thought. I didn't like to see Margaret walk away, so I helped an elderly woman off the train instead, hooking her hideous quilted handbag over one arm while she fussed with her walking stick.

I wandered around the Old Town, then walked for a mile or so along the sea front, hoping I might catch sight of Margaret again, but finding no sign of her. The sun was strong overhead, making me disorientated and prone to visions, but I didn't care.

The hirudin, for the most part, are born, not made; beyond the usual weakness and nausea that accompanies any sudden blood loss, a human who has been bitten but left alive will suffer no immediate physical harm. In most cases he will resume his normal life as if nothing has happened.

It may be as much as twenty years before the onset of the malaise that will inevitably kill him. And even so it is a gentle demise, a slow thickening of the blood for which the human doctors have as yet found no cure and put down to one of the rarer minor variants of leukaemia. In all likelihood he will die of something else before it even has a chance to take hold.

There are instances of natural human immunity but these are rare. Rarer still are those cases where, by some freak of nature, the blood of the human host is chemically altered and the human becomes hirudin. One time in a thousand, perhaps fewer. And yet it is these outlandish cases that form the basis of ten centuries of human mythology.

The fully adult hirudin is, as I have said, a solitary creature. It is true that I have formed friendships, intellectual and sometimes emotional alliances that lasted a decade or more. But the ending is always the same: a boredom that finally becomes so oppressive that I am driven to fabricate some feud or schism that explodes the relationship apart. Occasionally and after a suitable cooling off period such friendships may be resumed, but I am bound to admit that some of my closest friends are now my enemies.

In the case of sexual attachment the runtime is considerably shorter and in my experience at least there is no way back.

I knew from the start, from the first moment, that a relationship with Margaret that tried to become anything beyond that one meeting, was both physically and logistically impossible. To form an intimate connection with a human being that held any dynamic other than that between hunter and hunted would be to lay myself open to risks that were not only unacceptable, they were stupid, too.

I knew I should not phone her, that I should shred the scrap of paper with her name on it and throw it into the nearest gutter.

What was I hoping for, exactly? The answer that drummed in my head was: simply to see her again.

It was three weeks since my last kill. Normally I would have been starting to get edgy, prowling the streets on the lookout for potential victims, but I did not feel hungry. I felt the way I felt right after feeding: careless, almost drunken, replete with new energy.

I knew I should not ring her, but I did.

• • •

The hirudin are mimics, adopting the attributes of our human hosts with uncanny exactitude. We are thus able to move among them unnoticed, wolves in sheeps' clothing. The majority of humans we encounter, we encounter peaceably. The world at large is unaware of our existence.

Two centuries of rank obscurity can prove dull, however, and I have known plenty of hirudin who indulge in the sport of police-baiting. Carrying out a series of killings that appear to form some sort of pattern is guaranteed to keep the cops on their toes and generate acres of gaudy press coverage into the bargain.

Personally I find such games childish as well as risky and I prefer to spend my time in other ways. But I cannot deny the fascination that such crimes hold. I read the papers just as you do, and like you I am inevitably drawn to those reports of murders that diverge from the run-of-the-mill wife-torchings, gangland shootings and fatally botched robberies that make up the majority of news stories.

What I'm looking for, I suppose, are signs of family activity, and I'm not talking about the mafia. I'm not immune to gossip. I like to know what people are up to.

At the same time I pride myself on the fact that my own killings never amount to anything beyond a statutory police report tucked away on the inside pages amongst that day's crop of domestic politicking, pets-in-peril and UFO sightings.

Human beings tend to take things as they find them. The miraculous confuses them. When faced with something out of the ordinary most people would rather deny what they have seen than run the risk of being laughed at.

Some humans, of course, are used to being laughed at and so they cease to notice. Poets and idiots, madmen and freaks, junkies and whores, our closest human relatives are human outcasts.

Occasionally they recognise us. Luckily for us they are seldom believed.

Martha Gensing kept filling my plate.

"You're too thin, Daniel," she said. "I know what you students are like."

She was a doctor, a junior consultant at King's College Hospital. What you have to understand is that I had never been a guest in anyone's home. I had been in people's houses, yes, many dozens of them. But the circumstances for my being there were hardly conducive to relaxation. The abandoned flats and warehouses I was accustomed to inhabiting were less than nothing, the ghosts of homes. As for possessions, the few items I thought of as mine could be comfortably accommodated inside a medium-sized suitcase.

I'm not complaining. The encumbrances of a human life, the petty attachments both emotional and material, have always been distasteful to me. But in the Gensings' large and comfortable house in Camberwell I felt able—almost—to imagine a life of looking out rather than in. A life in which a Murano bowl, British moths arranged by species in long wooden trays and a red Turkey carpet with a small cigarette burn to one corner were all symbols of something greater and more intimately meaningful than their material substance.

"You have a lovely home, Mrs. Gensing," I said.

"Thank you, Daniel," she said. "Margaret knows her friends are always welcome here." She coloured slightly, and I realised she found me attractive and felt guilty about it. She was different from Margaret, more robust, and her body odour hinted at a deep sensuality. Her large, reddened hands were more like a butcher's than a doctor's. I wondered how things were in the bedroom between her and the more diffident Lionel. My expression must have betrayed something of my thoughts, because she looked away from me quickly and shortly afterwards she made some excuse and left the table.

Lionel Gensing worked for a bank, was what is now called something in the city. He was taciturn but seemed perfectly prepared to accommodate my presence in his home. Margaret's brother Stephen was twenty-one and looked so like his sister they might have been twins. He spent most of the mealtime running a small cast-iron replica of a steam engine back and forth across his portion of the tablecloth. I gathered he was either retarded or a genius but, in true English fashion, no one was going to discuss that at the dinner table.

I have to say that Stephen unnerved me a little, even then. He would not look at me directly, but I could sense his interest in me, a furtive prickle of mental white noise on the periphery of my perception. I had encountered savants before, but not for a long time, and I was discomfited. I tried to tell myself he was probably like that with all strangers.

Later, when she was walking me to the Tube, Margaret told me that Stephen had a photographic memory for some things—he could draw a car engine or the inside of a grand piano with all the pieces accurately in place after only one viewing—but that he hardly ever spoke except in monosyllables and sometimes refused to eat for days at a time. Brilliant but damaged, the doctors called him. They had long since abandoned hope of any improvement.

"Improvement?" I said. "Perhaps that's just the way he's meant to be."

Margaret came to a standstill on the darkened pavement and gave me a short, fierce hug. The world is cruel to people like Stephen Gensing. I wondered what would become of him once Martha and Lionel Gensing were both dead.

Perhaps it was all my fault. I don't dwell on the whys and wherefores, because there's no point. You could argue it was going to happen anyway, that maniacs, like hirudin, are born, not made.

The thing with the spike was careless though. I still don't know how I came to mislay it. What I remember is the way my stomach dropped—as if I was falling from a great height—when I realised that its familiar, cold-centred weight was missing from my pocket. The spike, you will understand, is the one essential possession I always keep with me and I suppose you could say I am superstitiously attached to it. I feel it as a part of myself, and so its absence sparked a frisson, a tangible hiatus, almost a pain.

I told Margaret I needed the bathroom (we were together in the upstairs sitting room when it happened, sorting through some books she had bought at an auction sale) and crept back downstairs to look for it. Martha Gensing was in the garden watering her roses, and Lionel Gensing was out also, his presence required at a meeting of local councillors. I knew that Stephen was around somewhere, but I was startled to come upon him all the same, sitting by himself in the empty dining room, rolling my spike backwards and forwards across the table. It made a small rumbling sound as it went, rotating beneath his outspread fingers like a miniature axle, and I was reminded of the first time I saw him, running the model train over the tablecloth and refusing to look at me. His mouth was set in a straight line, his green eyes open but unfocused. His scent was yellowish, astringent and rancourous, more like a civet cat than a human being.

He made an eerie sight. Quite suddenly I had the sense that he knew things about me that I had no wish for him to know, and it occurred to me that I had not dropped the spike at all, that Stephen Gensing had somehow stolen it out of my pocket.

It took all the will I had to restrain myself from reaching out and grabbing his wrist. He was lightly built just like me, just like Margaret. I could imagine the sound his bones would make as they broke: a wet splintering, like young spring wood.

"Hello, Stephen," I said. "That's mine, I think. Thank you for looking after it for me." I reached forward and grasped the spike, halting its lumbering progress across the table. I had it by the sharp end, and it scratched me a little. A fine scarlet line etched itself across the ball of my thumb.

Stephen stiffened to a waxwork stillness. I felt his eyes lock on my fingers, watching, no, examining what I was doing as if I was some fascinating but repellent creature under a microscope. I slid the spike from his grasp by slow increments, all the time expecting him to turn on me, to lash out in some way, but he remained motionless, rigid as wire. An insane thought bubbled up in me, that Stephen Gensing was not human after all, he was a manikin set up to fool me, that all the Gensings, Margaret included, were in on the joke.

Finally the spike came free. I slipped it back into my pocket, sighing my relief as it settled there, that gentle downward tug, nugget-heavy, lethal, mine.

"I know you're one of them," Stephen said. They were the first and only words I ever heard him speak. The sound, after the intense silence of our struggle, was so unexpected that I started backwards, knocking my right elbow painfully on the open door.

"What did you say?" I said. Once again I found myself having to resist the urge to grab hold of him. I realised with dismay that my hands were shaking.

I heard footsteps in the hall outside and a shadow fell head first over the table. A moment later Margaret entered the room.

"Here you are," she said. "Is everything all right?"

She took my hand and smiled. My feelings for her had not vanished as I feared they might. On the contrary, I now felt a nagging need to be near her that totally disrupted my life when I was not. I had fed since our first meeting—an elderly down-and-out female I encountered in Newham—but I was ill-prepared, the kill was messy and I had been forced to leave the body in a Tesco's car park.

Margaret had started calling me Dan. We had kissed, more than once, and in a manner that you might call serious. I had thus far not attempted any greater intimacy, mainly because I wasn't sure I would be able to stand it. To penetrate her and yet not penetrate her, if you see what I mean.

Can you imagine fucking someone, someone you love, and at the same time feeling compelled to rip out her throat? For the hirudin, to couple with a human is to feed. Not to feed is not pleasure halved, it is pleasure torn out by the root. A coitus interruptus that passes beyond frustration and into torment.

The old woman I took from behind. I twisted a hank of her greasy hair around my hand and used it to pull her head back then clamped down so hard with my teeth that my jaws ached for several days afterwards. I was still ramming her long after she was dead, when she'd been dead for at least half an hour and the stink of her fetid garments notwithstanding.

I thought of Margaret all the time that I was doing this. Afterwards I staggered away, my own clothes covered in blood and the woman's urine.

"Everything's fine," I said to Margaret. "Stephen and I were just having a chat, weren't we, Stephen?"

"You're so good with him," said Margaret, and sighed. "He's been strange recently."

"What do you mean, strange?" My nostrils flared, catching the milk-warm scent of her skin, cleansed with sandalwood soap. How would you know? I thought. He's always strange. He's insane. For the briefest of instants I felt like shaking her. She seemed to be confirming my fears and I wanted to punish her for it. I bit down on one side of my tongue. The pain and the taste of the blood calmed me a little.

"I don't know. Did he say anything to you?"

"Say anything?"

I left the question hanging in the air, hoping that my puzzled repetition of her words would drive home their strangeness. We both knew that Stephen did not speak. Why should he have spoken to me?

It seemed to work, or at least to satisfy her. She shook her head and embraced me and we went back upstairs.

I hoped that would be the end of it. But as I walked home that night I heard Stephen Gensing's words ringing out at me from the pavement with every step.

I know you're one of them.

His words, the words of an invalid, could have meant anything. But for the first time I felt unsafe in a hostile world.

You will have heard of the Ferndene Road murders, and if you haven't you can look up the details online. For me they took on gravitas because the killings occurred less than fifteen minutes' walk from the Gensings' home in Camberwell. For those with a less personal involvement the only point of interest about these murders is that the killer was never identified. In cases of serial murder, if the killer is not caught there is always a lingering sense of fascination, the feeling that he is still out there and may strike again, even if (as in the case of Jack the Ripper, for example) the murders happened too long ago for that to be feasible.

Serial killers are often sanctified as monsters. In truth—and I have encountered a fair few of them, so I know—they are merely pathetic. Their chief personal attributes are gross social inadequacy and an abnormally developed sense of cunning. In their cunning they are more like beasts, running almost entirely on instinct. I have never met a murderer I liked. Not of that sort, anyway.

The area around Ferndene Road was a maze of quiet residential streets, not so pleasant and well to do as the street in Herne Hill where the Gensings lived but by no means dissimilar. The houses were mostly respectable and well looked after, the homes of white collar workers and aspiring professionals. There were a lot of young families. It was not a place for vagrants and dropouts, and I was not surprised to read in the papers that the police had extended their search for the murderer westwards and northwards into the shabby bedsit lands of Stockwell and Lambeth. I understood why they were doing this, but felt certain all the same that they were wrong. Any strangers to Ferndene Road would soon be noticed. Any murderer who didn't blend in would soon be caught. The killer had to be local, not from Ferndene Road itself necessarily but certainly from within the radius of half a mile.

I did not think these were hirudin killings. There was something too naive about them, too earnest.

It was painfully easy to work out who the murderer was.

The first murder happened less than a fortnight after my abortive conversation with Stephen Gensing and the second less than a fortnight after that. Both murders were carried out by strangulation. The first victim was a man named Roland Meake, a twenty-three-year-old music student who had taken lodgings south of the river because it was cheaper and because his landlady, a Mrs. Jetta Vries, owned a fine Bechstein upright piano that Mr Meake was free to use whenever he liked. Meake looked a bag of nerves, the sort of man you might think was fated to be a murder victim and somehow knows it. The second victim was Geraldine Swithin, thirty-five and happily married, a senior sales assistant on the cosmetics counter of a local department store. Her photograph showed her smiling. In contrast with Meake she looked confident and at ease.

Although both victims lived on Ferndene Road they were not related and so far as the police were aware they hadn't even known one another. They looked alike though, uncannily so. With their fair skin and blond hair and widely spaced, slightly protuberant eyes they also reminded me of someone and after some thought I realised that both Meake and Swithin resembled Margaret's cousin Emma.

The Gensings had discussed the murder of Roland Meake with eager enthusiasm but the killing of Geraldine Swithin filled the house with disquiet. Lionel Gensing forbade Margaret to leave the house by herself and although she protested it was easy to see that she was actually quite frightened.

"You mustn't worry," I said to her. "I'll have to keep an even closer eye on you, that's all."

"Even closer?" Her eyes were wide. "Do you promise?"

"I most certainly do. I won't let you out of my sight."

I caught her around the middle, sliding my hand between the cloth of her skirt and the small of her back. It was the first time I had touched her anywhere below the waist and it made me feel weightless with hunger.

That evening I went back to New Cross and masturbated furiously over the smiling photograph of Geraldine Swithin. When I had finished I used the inside pages of the newspaper to clear up the mess.

It was now September. The thought of long winter evenings crammed into the Gensings' sitting room drinking hot cocoa with Margaret, discussing Blake's Songs of Innocence and Experience while Martha Gensing pressed her husband's shirts and rubbed herself against the edge of the ironing board filled me with a desperate ennui.

The house of the murdered woman on the other hand began to compel me. In the days following the killing it became increasingly forlorn-looking. The curtains remained closed and the lawn was badly overgrown. I thought the husband had probably left for other lodgings or to stay with friends.

I got into the habit of saying goodnight to Margaret then doubling back from the Tube station and prowling the streets relentlessly until the early morning. It was not long before the lozenge-shaped grid of roads between Milkwood Road and Denmark Hill became fused with certain synaptic pathways within my brain. I came to know every house, every driveway, every unfenced lot and overgrown back garden. I paid particular attention to Ruskin Park, the green tongue of land that lapped the main length of Ferndene Road along its northern contour. There was a children's playground there, and a group of tennis courts, but mostly it was just grass and trees, a large area of undesignated space. I felt certain that the park was central to the murderer's personal geography.

Often I would see Stephen Gensing. He skirted the park warily, keeping close to the railings. He gave no sign that he recognised me or that he was even aware of anything other than his immediate surroundings. But I knew that he was putting on an act.

Margaret was falling in love with me. Her smell changed and she began talking of deferring her entry to Cambridge, the two of us spending a year together travelling in Italy.

"It's such a cheap place to live," she said. "Especially in the south. We could teach English, learn Italian, study art." She lay back in the grass, her mind full of frescoes and fountains, and I humoured her because it was the easiest thing to do and because it was still pleasant on occasion to pretend to imagine a life where the things that Margaret wanted would be possible. In truth, I knew, what she was saying added up to a kind of madness, mainly because being together all the time would give me no opportunity to feed. But that was not the only impediment. The falsity of our position was beginning to grate on my nerves. The hirudin female is brutal and selfish and, when it suits her to cultivate such an attribute, merciless in the application of her intellect. The human female on the other hand is mostly kind. The thought of Margaret's essential kindness made me weary. I began to long for infected places. My exhausted senses, clogged with the rancid grease of sourced attachment, yearned for the sewers of Venice, for the oil-streaked, polluted waters of the Rhine estuary.

Throughout the incendiary heat of that late summer Margaret talked of Donne and Spenser and Hopkins with a passion that was close to hero worship. She liked to speak of the intellect as if it was the driving force in our relationship, and yet her body odours told me something quite different. I could now see how like her mother she was really; everything that had bewitched me before, the daemonic otherness that infects some human youths as they pass through the hair's breadth interstice between the mindless solipsism of infancy and the dull-witted obeisance of the human adult had slipped from her like a caul.

When she was menstruating it became all but impossible for me to be near her. Menses blood is loathsome—harsh as iron and ragged with clots—but the rust-red smell of it set my teeth on edge with hunger and put me in a mood so foul it was hard to hide. I told Margaret that I sometimes suffered from migraine headaches, and more than once I left her early, or telephoned to say I was too ill to visit.

I went to Ruskin Park instead, where I would sit on a bench through the long humid dusk, watching, watching like a hawk and trying not to think about what I knew Margaret was doing in her bedroom right at that moment.

Those dainty little fingers cricked, blood under her nails.

Stephen Gensing reeked of his secrets, the stench hanging thickly about him like a rotting shroud. His furtiveness had increased with my surveillance, and I understood that I was caught up in a chess game of the most dangerous kind. Whether Stephen was trying to expose me or to become me I never knew. I knew only that it was time for me to leave.

The story of Søren Kierkegaard and his fiancée Regine Olsen is well documented. The philosopher, terrified that the consummation of his sexual desire will emasculate him as a thinker, dumps his beloved and spends the rest of his life concocting elaborate excuses for ratting out on her. It's rubbish of course. It wasn't sex that threatened his intellect, but the loss of autonomy that follows in the wake of marriage. If he'd been born a century later he'd have fucked her and then moved on.

People were more into God then, of course, Søren Kierkegaard especially.

The essential dilemma in Kierkegaardian philosophy is the conflict between individual destiny and moral duty. Kierkegaard was a natural ascetic, and yet he felt pressured to settle down, to marry, to father children even. Can you imagine compromising your entire destiny because you happened once to like the way a woman's profile shimmered in the watery mauve light of a Copenhagen dusk? Kierkegaard shouted no with the whole of his being and so did I.

In the end Kierkegaard abandoned Regine for Melancholia. I imagine his muse as one of the parasitic water nymphs you can still sometimes find living under the damp stones at the edges of stagnant rivers. Uncoiling, eel-like, her unwashed hair limp and tangled between her shoulder blades, her filthy knees grip his pumping buttocks like a sprung trap. I've known hirudin women just like her, their minds polluted by needs a human could never intuit except perhaps in those mercifully brief moments of panic that come just before you break free of a recurring nightmare.

They invariably torture their victims, and are creatures I prefer to avoid. I spent that winter in Copenhagen, which is a small city and therefore not the safest, but I got by. I sent Margaret a postcard of Niels Kierkegaard's famous pencil portrait of his brother, together with Lars Anner's excellent translation of Either/Or. I slept a lot, and in the spring I relocated to Madrid.

The third victim's name was Rachel Pirie and she was fifteen. She went to school in East Dulwich, and lived in Frankfurt Road, just round the corner from the Gensings. Reports of her murder described her as 'an extremely promising student' who had won prizes for English and Geometry. We had high hopes for Rachel, one of her teachers, a Mrs Boscombe, was quoted as saying. You really couldn't meet a nicer girl.

She was also uncommonly strong, although there was nothing about that in the newspapers. I came upon her in the shallow ditch that ran along behind the broken down cricket pavilion in Ruskin Park. Stephen Gensing was sitting astride her, attempting to strangle her with some kind of improvised ligature. He was red in the face from exertion. Rachel Pirie was bucking and struggling in his grip like an unbroken colt. Had I not turned up when I did, I think there is a good chance she would have escaped him.

I looked down at the girl, her legs splayed and her heels drumming as she tried to gain some leverage on the damp ground. There were marks on her neck, ugly red welts where the ligature had slipped and then been tightened again. Her eyes bulged. There were flecks of saliva on her cheeks and at the corners of her mouth.

I knew that if she got away, Stephen would end up spending the rest of his life in an asylum for the criminally insane. He would be safe there, surely, he and all his weird ideas with him?

Triumph, silver-hot as burning chrome, flashed up in my mind. I quashed it before it flared out of control.

I could tell you that I did what I did out of compassion for Margaret, to spare her the knowledge that her beloved lunatic of a brother was a multiple murderer, and a pretty hopeless multiple murderer at that. But the truth is that I acted out of disgust. I loathed the sight of this stupid little choking girl, terrified in her last moments as my victims have never been. Her hair clung to her forehead like duckweed. Her lips pulled back from her teeth as she gasped for air she was never going to catch.

Rachel Pirie was fair and pale, just like the others. As Stephen Gensing strained and heaved on top of her I knew it was Cousin Emma he was thinking of. I remembered my tense little chess games with my mother and experienced a painful shiver of fellow-feeling.

"Mind out," I cried. I shoved him aside and he exuded a pained little grunt. I was rough with him, hurt him probably, though I didn't mean to. The spike went in low, grating slightly against the Pirie girl's collarbone, but perhaps because she had already used up most of her energy she was unconscious in less than five seconds. Blood began to bubble up from around the base of the spike, covering my hands like warm gravy. The urge to feed at this point would normally have been insurmountable but for the first time in my life I felt a bitter distaste. I do not normally kill children unless I have to, and this killing had about it the air of a botched job, a last ditch solution to a problem that should not have existed in the first place.

I wanted it over with. That was all.

I licked the palms of my hands to clean them, breathing hard, then stood up and looked around. The cricket pavilion was surrounded by bushes, the ditch rank with the odour of nettles and dog faeces. It seemed that for the moment at least we were by ourselves. I just hoped we could not be seen from the road.

"Get out of here, Stephen," I said. "You have to stop doing this. They're going to catch you next time. If they have any sense they'll throw away the key." I snatched the ligature from his hand. It was a crude thing, a length of nylon fishing twine with a short strip of dowel rod tied to either end. I put it in my pocket, resolving to dispose of it later, and miles from here.

"This isn't for you," I said to Stephen. "Best leave it to the professionals, eh?"

I wondered how he had managed the other two murders. Either he had been lucky, or he had simply picked the wrong victim in Rachel Pirie. Such things do happen. I had no idea if he would try and kill again. Nor did I care.

Did I miss Margaret, you ask? I know it was better that we didn't say goodbye. Kierkegaard wrote Regine Olsen a long letter breaking off their engagement and he never heard the last of it—tearful confrontations, threats of suicide, the lot. I watched Stephen Gensing until he turned the corner into Herne Hill Road—I wanted to be sure he was heading home, you see—then returned to the New Cross flat for a change of clothes. I took what money I had, packed my few possessions and fled the scene. Forty-eight hours later I was in Venice, where I fed off a male prostitute before passing out in the basement of a boarded-up pensione. I slept for the best part of a week.

I did think of her when I woke, I must admit it. But I knew the feeling of loss would fade, as soon it did. In the interim I comforted myself with the delusion that I might return to her at any time if I wanted to. I could claim illness, or madness, or both. It wasn't as if I'd actually told her we were over. We could pick up where we left off.

There are still days when I believe that, then laugh at myself for my own foolishness.

I saw her once, years later, an old woman sitting in a deckchair on somebody's patio. She raised her head as I passed, shaded her eyes from the sun with the back of her hand.

I never saw Stephen again, nor do I know what became of him, but I think of him from time to time and wonder. Men such as he, caught between worlds, have a difficult life. I think they are more to be pitied than to be feared.

UNCLE FLOWER'S HOMECOMING WALTZ

MARISSA K. LINGEN

———◈———

My grandmother says all stories begin with a death. My grandfather says with a birth. And Aunt Albert says they're both wrong, and stories begin with someone not getting what they want.

But no one was born, and no one died, and I got what I wanted, and that is where this story begins.

What I wanted most was for Uncle Flower to come home. He had been away fighting for four years, which was a third of my life, nearly half of what I could remember. When Uncle Flower left, I had no breasts and could not read from the Book of the Old Santhreu and still dreamed like a child. I was sure Uncle Flower would be surprised to see how much I had grown up when he returned. I couldn't wait to talk to him again, to show him how much I had learned and tell him all the interesting things I'd wondered but had not wanted to put in a letter for Grandmother's eyes—or the army censor's.

After they got the notice from the Family that Uncle Flower was returning, Aunt Albert brought me up practically first thing. "We'll need to get Zal a new dress for Flower's homecoming."

Grandmother frowned. "You can make do with your double solstice dress, can't you, Zal dear?"

I had had another century dream the previous night and was still in the shock of the metal and the heat and the attention from all the grown-ups when I woke. I was in no mood to fuss and argue for new clothing. But I didn't have to open my mouth; Aunt Albert, as usual, was on it.

"She cannot either. Look at her, another two inches taller since the double solstice. Her elbows will be out the wrists, to say nothing of anything else we shouldn't say anything of."

Grandmother and I blinked at Aunt Albert for a moment, trying to parse what on earth she was talking about. Then Grandmother looked at me again, and her face softened. "All right, Zal," she said. "A new dress for you. You can't greet your uncle with your shirttails trailing."

I wanted to say something about how I could, Uncle Flower wouldn't mind, he loved me whatever I wore and whatever I did, but when I opened my mouth, what came out was, "The scientist called Murphy didn't come back because she couldn't find her dog."

I was not yet used to the century dreams.

My grandmother, on the other hand, had shepherded half a dozen children through their transition to their adult dreams. She knew what she was about. "We will write that down, Zal, and we will tell the scholars in Pollack. We will get you a dream book while we are out getting your dress."

And that was that—the dress and the book all in one trip. When we bought the book, Grandmother went into the inner sanctum to discuss my dreams with Madame Lumiere, and I tiptoed over to listen at the crack.

"When she is used to the book, we will start the rest of her training," said Madame Lumiere. "First here, and then in the capital where they can guide her closer to what we need to know."

"If the capital still stands then," said Grandmother. Grandmother was a year dreamer, and it had helped to secure the family's position for her entire life. "Zally, get away from the door."

I sighed. Grandmother did not have the intimate, timely knowledge most people, day dreamers, did to guide her hand, but she managed with a keen eye for human behavior. I sat picking at my cuticles while Grandmother talked to Madame Lumiere just out of my hearing, and then I went and recited, carefully, for the scholars, who made notes and frowned and looked at each other and never at me.

My new dress came home with us, wrapped in tissue for the ball we would have to celebrate Uncle Flower's return. He was to come in an army conveyance. It glided and swayed along the driveway, and it seemed to take ages to arrive as I watched from the top step, Aunt Albert's restraining hand on my shoulder.

Uncle Flower was not quite how I'd remembered him, before he went off to war. He was just as tall, just as strong, but his long brown hair was edged with grey, and he'd grown a grey-tinged beard. He had braided tokens of his campaigns into his hair and beard, slim flashes of copper and strands of blue wool. He was not wearing his uniform. He looked tired.

We waited for one breath, two. Then I couldn't bear it anymore; I flung myself down the steps shrieking his name like a baby of three. I would have been embarrassed if I'd stopped to think of it, but Uncle Flower grinned, all the weariness vanishing from his face, and swept me up in a hug.

"You're nearly as tall as Albert," he said, holding me at arm's length, and then hugging me tight again, "taller than your mother ever was. Oh, Zally, how did you ever get so big?"

I didn't know what to say to that, so I said, "I missed you, Uncle Flower."

"I missed you, too, kid."

All the things I had meant to tell him while he was gone flew from my head. The reality of his scrubbed and worn self was overwhelming, making me shy for a moment. But by then the others had come down the steps in a more dignified fashion, and they collected embraces from him at a more measured pace. He kept ruffling my hair and grinning at me behind their backs, and I decided I didn't mind looking like a silly kid; my uncle was home.

Grandmother encouraged Uncle Flower to put his uniform back on for the evening's entertainment, to be welcomed home by his friends and neighbors. Uncle Flower did not seem pleased, but neither did he seem surprised; he put on the blue and copper thing, and it made the campaign tokens show up better in his beard somehow. He was distinguished. I was so proud. The neighbors my own age did not have new golden dresses that shone like sunlight, and they did not have brave veteran uncles returned home.

After Grandfather had made a little speech and Uncle Flower had led Grandmother and then Aunt Albert out in their dances, I knew it would be my turn. But the adults in my family seemed to have forgotten, clustering in the corner talking in undertones. I crept up on them.

" . . . don't know enough about it," Grandfather was saying.

"I think we already know too much," said Aunt Albert. "The other countries will never let us have such a thing. We will be crushed. Mother has seen—"

"I have seen problems for the *capital*," said Grandmother archly. "That may not mean anything for the *country*."

"We aren't the only ones to flirt with atrocities," said Uncle Flower. "The things those bastards did to their own troops—some of our prisoners were normal enough, but the twisted ones—"

He broke off, seeing me standing there. "Zally, shouldn't you be—um—"

"I wanted to dance with you," I said. "What's going on? What were the twisted ones like?"

"You forget you know anything about that," said Uncle Flower. "I wish I could."

"I'm not a little kid anymore, Uncle Flower," I said. "I don't dream like one."

He raised an eyebrow at Grandmother, who nodded. "It's true. Zally has been having century dreams. You should be proud of your niece, Flower. She's done well to adjust this far, and it will only get easier with time. I should know."

Uncle Flower didn't smile at me the way he was supposed to. Instead he frowned at Grandmother and me both. "We had a decade dreamer in my unit. He was always set apart. I don't want that for Zally."

"Century dreamers are different," said my grandmother nervously. "Not so close. Not poking into things."

"They can't help but poke," said Uncle Flower. "Look here, Zally: Is this something you want? This dreaming?"

I swallowed hard. This was not how I saw things going at all. Uncle Flower was supposed to see how grown-up I was. He was supposed to be impressed with my dreams. "Don't call me Zally anymore," I blurted.

Uncle Flower gave my grandmother a raised eyebrow.

"It's Zal now, dear," she told him gently.

He shook his head like a mutt coming out of the lake. "*Zal*, then. You don't have to have these dreams if you don't want 'em."

"Don't tell her that," said Grandfather, speaking for the first time.

"Why not? It's true."

"You can't just—we need her," said Grandfather.

I glowed.

"Father, she's twelve. Look at her."

I smiled tentatively.

"She wants nothing more than to please you!" said Uncle Flower.

"The person she wants to please is you," said Grandfather. "Dance with your niece, Flower. See how happy you can make her by treating her like the young lady she has become."

"That," said Uncle Flower, "is the last thing you want. All right, Father. Come, Zal."

The band had selected a waltz, which was good; I could do a real waltz, not like a hamerade or a jill-step. Uncle Flower was not a fancy dancer, but I didn't mind. I was happy whirling around with him, just like when I was little and he would dance me around the room on his feet. But it was not just like it, and before too many measures I couldn't keep my mouth shut any longer.

"Uncle Flower, what did you mean about not having to have my dreams?"

He sighed, his whole strong body dropping a notch as we waltzed. "The dreams aren't something we have naturally, Zal. They're because of something we did to ourselves, we humans. So we can interfere with them if we want to. There are powders you could take, made into pills or tea, that would make you dream like a child again."

"What would they do?"

Uncle Flower sighed, pausing on the dance floor. "We don't know. That part is lost. We can't create the dreams with any kind of certainty—I don't know if we ever could. But we can disrupt them. In the army they give the powder to—"

He stopped speaking, dancing as though nothing was going on. I twisted to see if someone was behind us, close enough to hear, but the nearest dancers were several feet away, and Uncle Flower's voice was low. "To who?"

"It's 'to whom,' Zally," he said absently. "There are people whose dreams are not displaced in time. They're—spatial dreamers. We use some of them for spies. But if we can't trust them, or if we can't get them into locations where they'd be spying on the enemy, we give them a powder to suppress the dreams. It's as though they're children again."

"But ordinary people can't do that. Only the weird ones with the army."

"Zally, no century dreamer is ordinary." The music ended, and Uncle Flower quite properly escorted me off the dance floor. He was chewing on his mustache, looking down at me, and Grandmother glared at him. He hastily smoothed it with his fingers when he saw her look.

I wanted to put my hands on my hips, but my ball gown was too fine for that posture. "What else does the powder do?"

"Um," he said.

"*What else?*"

He sighed. "You look just like your mother when you're suspicious like that."

"And what would my mother have said next?"

"She would have demanded to know what I was keeping from her. Zally," said Uncle Flower, "really it's your choice. It is. And if you don't want to do it, you don't have to. But I thought you should know there was a choice, and Mother would never have told you."

"Uncle Flower."

"They sleep most of their days," he said in a rush, "and they seem to be in a sort of childlike state when they are awake. It goes away when they stop taking the drug, eventually. It has to work its way out of their system."

"You want me to sleepwalk through my life?"

"Not your life," he said. "Just for a few years, just until you're old enough for these dreams. Zally, I've seen what they're doing now—I can't imagine what they'll be doing a hundred years in the future."

"Maybe nothing bad," I said, but I'd had too many century dreams to really think so.

I had another that night, with cooking in it I thought: it smelled like someone had burned saffron rice, and everyone kept talking about the melting point, but then they were eating something completely different, fried bread and a spicy sauce wafting through the air to follow the burnt saffron. And there was a little boy who got given colored pencils and paper, so I liked that part all right.

I wrote it down like I was supposed to, and Grandmother was a good deal more excited about the pencils than about the melting point. I was shaken and confused. Without my uncle, and without the familiar porridge with berries for breakfast, I would have had trouble keeping track of when I was supposed to be.

Uncle Flower watched us talk it over at breakfast with a sad, guarded look. I grabbed his sleeve when he got up to follow Grandmother and Aunt Albert out.

"There's nothing I can do that will be the grown-up thing now," I said. "Is there? If I go for training and stay a century dreamer, then you will be sure that I'm just doing it because of Grandmother and Grandfather. But if I get treated for it and have child-dreams again, they'll be sure it was just to please you. You've set it up so that someone is shaking their head and saying poor little Zally no matter what."

"I didn't mean to, Zal," he said quietly. "I just wanted you to have all the information."

"Nobody ever has all the information, Uncle Flower. If we did, we could all dream like children and rest easy every night."

He stared at his hands, looking glum, and I saw that they were stained a darker brown in the palms, but I didn't know why. Something he'd used in the war, and I probably would never know what. "You're going to do this, aren't you, Zal?" he said.

I didn't answer.

"I saw you this morning. You were scared out of your wits."

"Weren't you ever scared in the war?"

"Twelve years old," he muttered. "I was scared in the war, but I wasn't twelve years old."

"I won't be twelve forever. When I'm older, maybe I won't be needed, but I am now."

"They will *use you*," he said, grabbing my shoulders. "They used me, and they will use you. They will train you to send your dreams where they want them, to get the information they want about what to support, what our future problems will be, and our future triumphs. Zal, I told you I couldn't imagine what would be around a hundred years from now. But we have inklings already. If you go to study with them—" He fidgeted with the campaign tokens in his beard. "Zally, please. Please don't."

"If I spend another year as a child," I said. "A sleepwalking child. If I spend two, three. How will I learn then, not to be used? How will it ever get better?"

Uncle Flower reached out and stroked my head. "Oh, Zally. I don't know if it will."

"I can do this. I need to do this." He didn't say anything. "Uncle Flower, do you really want me like the boys you saw?"

He couldn't say no, but he couldn't say yes, either.

I stood on tiptoe and kissed his cheek. "It'll be all right, Uncle Flower. I promise."

"You can't know that."

"I can. I dream in centuries, and there'll be more centuries. So it'll be all right."

Uncle Flower stayed home to write his letters and make his speeches, but when I left for the capital, he gave me a little silver token to braid into my hair, a line and two circles for the century.

THE MAGICIAN'S APPRENTICE

TAMYSN MUIR

—◆—

When she was thirteen, Mr. Hollis told her: "There's never more than two, Cherry. The magician and the magician's apprentice."

That was the first year, and she spent her time sloo-o-owly magicking water from one glass to another as he read the newspaper and drank the coffee. Magician's apprentice had to get the Starbucks. Caramel macchiato, no foam, extra hot, which was a yuppie drink if you asked her (but nobody did). "Quarter in," he'd say, and she'd concentrate on the liquid shivering from cup to cup. "Now half. Slower."

For Cherry Murphy, the water always staggered along. She'd seen him make it dance with a twitch of his fingers. "When do I get to stop bullets? My hypothesis is that stopping bullets would be friggin' sweet."

"Maybe when you do your homework," said Mr. Hollis, and so she'd take out her homework. It wasn't even magic homework. It was stuff like *Catcher In The Rye*. Mr. Hollis was big on literature, so after they cleared the table of glasses he'd trick her into arguing about Holden Caulfield. Could've been worse—to make her feel better he'd given her *Catch-22*, and Cherry had read it approximately a million times. He said she easily read at college level, though he also said that didn't amount to much these days.

"All right," said her master magician, when her chin had started to droop. "Now you eat."

Magic wore terrible holes in you. Just shunting water around would give her a headache and throbbing nosebleeds, so he'd fry up a steak or fresh brown eggs and watch her gobble them down while saying, "Elbows off the table." The steak was always bloody. The eggs were always softboiled. Food would take the edge off, but not enough. Second lesson: magic feeds off your soul, said Mr. Hollis. There's only two ways to not be hungry, Cherry. I'm sorry.

"Two ways? How?"

"One, quit magic, Harriet Potter," he said, but then he pushed the plate of eggs at her. Her master magician never seemed hungry like she was. "Second's simple: eat more."

After dinner they usually had a little time. She'd told him over and over that Mark wouldn't notice if she came home at midnight covered in blood, but he always said: "Don't disrespect your dad," which was why she thought he was kind of a stiff. Then he'd follow it up with, "He does that enough on his own," which was why she loved him. So until six-thirty hit they'd watch the last fifteen minutes of a *Golden Girls* rerun—or listen to some Led Zeppelin, his iPod strung earbud to earbud between them both. Only then was she really content.

Mr. Hollis was a bachelor with a girlfriend downtown, so his apartment always kind of smelled like Old Spice and dead body, only she would have knocked back neat bleach before saying so.

When six-thirty came he'd say, "Put on your jacket," even if outside it was the average surface temperature of the Sun and she'd die of heatstroke. Then he'd say, "See you later, alligator," and she'd say, "In a while, crocodile," or if the day had been crappy she'd just make a series of grunts. Then she'd skip home through the dusk to her empty house or her passed-out, empty father, and read *Catch-22* until she fell asleep.

There were spells on which everything hinged, he said; to *move*, *stop* and *make*. The spell that year was 'move'. Cool, fine; she was always on the move. Cherry had long spindly limbs like a juvenile spider, and before she'd been an apprentice she'd taken track and baseball. Her fingers did drum solos if she wasn't given things to do with them. All of that nervous energy went into her spells, and she worried her lips skinless as her water dripped, her winds scattered and any attempt to lift stuff embedded it in the far-off wall. Mr. Hollis primly mopped tables dry and set her to roll a marble around on the slick linoleum.

But he made it look so easy. There was not a flicker in those paper-grey eyes as a curl of his hand coaxed a hairbrush out of his drywall, beckoning it to remove itself and have the plaster rework to pre-Cherry wholeness. Objects put themselves back in his hands, ashamed. *His* marble rolled in perfect madman's circles.

Once—wild with frustration and knees scored with tile lines—she ignored him when he said: "Leave it. Stop." Her marble wobbled in a wide spiral. "Cherry." She feigned deafness. Her head suddenly spun towards him, yanked by invisible iron fingers, and worst of all her marble rolled away lost under the fridge forever.

"Cherry," he said evenly, "I don't ask twice."

"I can do this! Screw you!"

That got her grounded for a week before she realised he technically didn't have the authority to do so. Cherry sulked to bed each night at nine o'clock anyway.

June. In the summer evenings Mr. Hollis went off with his girlfriend, so they'd spend three brilliant breakfast hours down at the beach rolling grains of sand from palm to palm. Her skinny arms and legs grew browner if not less skinny, and he made her wear a one-piece instead of a bikini ("Nice try, but no cigar") but each of those days was more perfect than the last. Homework was John Knowles's *A Separate Peace* ("You could give me something with a good movie, Mr. H") and he sat shirtless under the beach umbrella as she read aloud.

Mr. Hollis had rangy bones and a nerdy fishbelly farmer's tan, lots of crisp dark hairs on his arms and his chest. It was possible that somebody found him hot, but only theoretically so; the fact that he had a girlfriend was mystifying. Possibly being a magician and the ensuing squillions of dollars, or at least the squillions as was her understanding, sweetened the deal. That summer she also rolled marbles until her nostrils squirted blood and she found herself eating raw hot dogs from the freezer. It was pretty gross. Cherry was hungry until her mouth hurt.

After August she struggled at his kitchen table, pushing ball bearings. Her head hurt. Sometimes he would ignore her and it was a kindness, as she had her pride even if she was in seventh grade, and sometimes he would briefly ruffle his hand through her short dark hair and say: "Be zen."

"I'm never going to get this."

"You're going to get it, emo kid."

" If I die, I leave you all my stuff."

"Try 'bequeath.' You *bequeath* me all your stuff."

When she did start to get the magic, in-between Knowles and *A Separate Peace*, Mr. Hollis gave her a single brief smile that made the rest of it a cinch. The marble rolled its circle. The water halved into its glass. As a test, he set his Honda Civic in first gear and she pushed it inch by burning inch nine feet forward: she puked bloodied bile afterwards like a champ, him holding her hair, but once her stomach settled he took her out for lobster. It was the kind where you picked your sacrifice out of its tank and were eating ten minutes later. It tasted incredible.

"Congratulations, cadet," said Mr. Hollis, gesturing with the fork. "Here's my toast: I'm proud of you. First we take Manhattan, Cherry, then we take Berlin."

Her joy was wild, and her Coke sweet like imagined champagne.

• • •

When she was fourteen, Mr. Hollis told her: "The apprenticeship only ends when you know everything the magician knows, and understand everything the magician understands."

Cherry took this to mean that she'd be an apprentice until she was like thirty. He switched from caramel macchiatos to skinny vanilla lattes, which this year she pointed out was "totally gay," and earned her a long, indifferent look. Mr. Hollis was an award winner at indifferent looks. He could scratch you with a word, or by flicking his pale aluminum eyes away at any place but you. The hunger still boiled low in her belly as she jumped water from cup to cup to cup, but crushingly all he'd say now was, "Cute one trick, pony."

Instead he got her to empty the glass out over the sink and try to divert it upwards. Cherry spent most of her time on her feet and mopping at her t-shirt when this proved to be a son of a bitch, and all he did was sit at the kitchen table reading his newspaper. That had started to drive her a little crazy too. Mr. Hollis was a slob who left the Sports section lying around and never dusted, but when she started scrubbing his stove and looking for his Dustbuster he said: "Don't go there. Jen doesn't even go there."

He'd been dating Jennifer Blumfield over a year now. Cherry had been introduced as his niece. Jen did accounting and was sweet without being patronizing, but she hated her a little anyway and bullshitted her best smile to hide it. Only complete dumbasses weren't nice to the girlfriend. Mr. Hollis wasn't prehistoric, and even though his five driver's licences showed four different ages he was allowed to date.

"Are you going to tell her about the magic thing?"

Cherry hadn't expected the cold shoulder. "You never tell *anyone* about what we do, Charlene. I didn't think you capable of being this big an imbecile."

Her eyes had smarted, and his were turned away.

They went from Knowles to Dickens, *David Copperfield*. She'd argued it was abuse. That was the year of many long arguments: she liked Marlowe, he liked Shakespeare, he liked Austen and she liked American Lit. Mr. Hollis set her to tossing M&Ms up in the air and slowing their descent, staring down his narrow nose in impatience at any cracks in their hard candy carapaces. It sucked.

And she might have been prodigious for fourteen, but not in science. That was the year she also had to stay half an hour after school for remedial physics, which was stupid, but Mr. Hollis was calmly unsympathetic: "Suck it down. You can't pass high school with just one subject." He was equally unsympathetic to the notion that, as a magician's apprentice, physics was beneath her: "I still have a day job, Cherry."

"You do not have a day job. Every so often a car comes around and you get in and then you come back with a suitcase full of cash. I'm not judging, I'm just saying that I bet you my whole life you are not making money off a David Copperfield Quiz Olympics."

Whatever he was doing he wouldn't tell her. A big black car would pull up outside and he'd be waiting in a suit, and the driver would even open the door for him and he'd nod coolly like the guy was toilet paper attached to his heel. Cherry would hang around outside for hours and hours until he came back, and even then he'd only let her get a whiff of that new-money smell before the case shut and disappeared. She hoped all the time this meant Disneyland instead of college.

"I don't care. I'm not countenancing your future ignorance if I have to live with it." She asked furtively about higher education. "Ivy League, champ." Oh, Jesus.

On the brighter side, that was also the year Callum asked her to the dance. He was older a nd wore seriously skinny jeans. Tenth graders usually weren't all that interested in eighth graders, but they liked the same bands and she'd graduated to a real bra with an underwire and wore short shorts starting May. The first and last time she'd worn them to Mr. Hollis's his eyebrows shot up to his hairline.

"You seem to be *sans pants*."

"They're daisy dukes, old man. I am trying to maximise my coolness, okay?"

A newspaper page got flipped. "They looked better on Daisy Duke. Put on my gym pants before you go home."

"That suggestion is completely horrifying."

"Yes, Cherry?" Definitely not amused. His professor voice always turned into sharp, hard-edged vowels when he was pissed, like a movie villain. "Are you suffering hearing trouble? You're a little slow with my lesson of not always getting your way."

"But—"

"Cherry," he said. "There are rapists out there. Serial killers. Look at the news for once: girls get kidnapped constantly, and there are dead joggers in every alleyway. And for the bottom line, I made a request of my apprentice and I don't ask twice."

She wore his gym pants home. Wearing short shorts at school didn't seem a blast any more either, and after the dance in the back seat Callum put his hand on her knee and she felt weird about it. The hunger gnawed at her stomach, and she made his car lurch forward in the parking lot each time his hand moved up her leg. "Wow!" she said. "Ghost car!" Callum dumped her the next day. Mr. Hollis handed her Kleenex when she cried.

• • •

The spell that year was "stop." She knew enough now to dread it. Mr. Hollis sat with her in meditative Yoga poses on the floor of her living room as the scent of rot and old washing tickled her nose: she sneezed, she fidgeted, she popped her knuckles one by one until he came to show her how to hold her hands and then it was easy.

It was stupid easy, really. The trick was understanding gravity (thanks, remedial physics) and that she was working magic to oppose a force, not flow with one as she did rolling ball bearings. Cherry could make marble after marble hang in midair like tiny spaceships. Water shivered to a halt as Mr. Hollis upended a glass over the rug. Her master magician watched her progress over his newspaper or with an eye on a TiVo'd episode of *Seinfeld* while she tossed up handful after handful of flour to stop dead as fine white mist: the downside was that you got even hungrier than before.

That was the year of the accident. Some douchebag in a Ford came screaming out of the intersection as Mr. Hollis made a June-morning car ride to the beach. Cherry rode shotgun with the umbrella. Brakes squealed as the guy saw his mistake too late, about to plough right into the driver door, and she Stopped his car so hard that her fingernails twisted. Most of the tiny veins in her eyeballs popped. Blood leaked from her mouth and ears and nose as she gave everything, fed everything into the furnace of her magic as a starving body fed on tissue when out of options. The last thing she thought she saw were his hands, raised above the steering wheel, and then she blacked out.

When she woke up it was on his couch, to the smell of food. Every breath made her lungs scream. Mr. Hollis knelt next to her with a bowl and a forkful of gamey meat liberally covered in teriyaki sauce, and that meat smelled like fried chicken, like fudge sundaes and candyfloss, like everything that used to make her mouth water. The first bite she choked on in her eagerness. "For the love of God, slower," he said, and, "Chew. Please. I've long forgotten how to Heimlich, Cherry."

Each morsel of that meal warmed her from the tips of her toes to the crown of her skull. It was almost enough that she didn't look at the expression on his face, the grim and painful tenderness, sweat sweeping back his dark hair. There were little sprays of grey at the temples. He wasn't even forty, and the grey made her terribly sad somehow. But she was less sad than she was starving. "Whash *ish* thish."

"Chew, swallow, rinse, wash, repeat," he said, but the taut line of his mouth was softening. Cherry opened her mouth like a little baby bird for the next forkful. Her master magician hesitated uncharacteristically: "An hour ago this was real live goat."

"That is literally disgusting," she said. "Goats are adorable." Mr. Hollis loaded up the fork again and she licked all the tines. The bloodied crust at her nose and eyes didn't matter anymore. She could have run a marathon. "Is goat always this good? Because this is awesome."

"I'll let you in on a little secret, as your mentor." The texture of the pale teriyaki fry-up was a little weird, a little dry, but he was mashing his fork against the side of the bowl to get her every last delicious bit. "When something dies, Cherry, it leaves a little bit of itself behind. That part, and I'll call it life force, starts to dissipate out the body immediately. But if we get it and we get it fresh—well, we're not hungry after that."

"So we should just be fruitarians," she said, wiping her tongue around the corners of her mouth. The hunger had eased, and the pain had driven a couple blocks away. "Pick apples off the trees, eat them right there."

"If it was that easy I'd be dismembering broccoli plants."

"What *do* you do?"

"Terrible things to God's own creatures, for you," her master magician said, which struck her as a little evasive. The bowl went away. Cherry looked at the fine bones of his face as he cleaned up hers, his dignified jaw, his slash of a nose. His eyes: the unbelievably pale grey of snow three days old, with faint crow's feet. Mr. Hollis was old before his time. Now he was dabbing her forehead, her ears, and he said, "You should have trusted me to take care of that car. Don't you ever do that to me again, Charlene Murphy, or so help me I don't know what I'll do."

She felt drunk, or at least what drunk probably felt like. "'Cherry.'"

"You're a brat." He was touching her hair. " 'Charlene' never did suit."

"I like how you always called me Cherry." She really was drunk. "Like: *ma chérie*, am I right?"

Mr. Hollis's expression smoothed into something careful and polite, and he took his hand away from her hair. "Get some rest," he said, and he laid his jacket over her legs as he stood up and took the bowl. There was neutral kindness in his voice, the type which made her burn with teen humiliation; or would've, if she hadn't been high off feeling full and sleepy for the first time since forever. "No more magic for a while."

Before she dozed off she thought she heard him eating in the kitchen, cramming something into his mouth and chewing before frantic wet swallows.

When she was fifteen, Mr. Hollis told her, "We've come this far, you and I. You can call me John."

Cherry slipped up on it all the time, and called him "Mr. Hollis" more than she called him "John." She practiced in the mirror with it: John, John, Johnny, Jack, John. John Hollis. John Hollis, the magician. Cherry Murphy, the apprentice. John and Cherry, Charlene and John.

She was too old and experienced to be in love with him, seriously, only stupid kids did that with their teachers—and as he said, she wasn't stupid. He damned with faint praise. Cherry had come a long way: he was a God-King, but she was his lieutenant, his right hand and left, his Holy Ghost. She read Vonnegut and Faulkner without needing his recommendation. Cherry could also drive between the hours of twelve-thirty AM and five PM, which was cool.

This was the year of the cappuccino, and they sat around his kitchen table sipping them as they swapped sections of the newspaper. It was also the year of the world's most disappointing growth spurt. She'd made five foot one and stopped, resigned to Smurfitude until the next spurt hit, doomed to skinny legs and arms and brown hair that had never gone blonde. It was depressing. Even her eyes were heading more beigewards than chocolate. To cheer herself up Cherry wore hipster scarves and bobby socks, and she gave all her daisy dukes to the Salvation Army.

"When are you going to move in with Jen?" she said. "This apartment smells like leprosy. I can't believe how much you pay for it."

"One day I may want to pick up and leave."

"So you abide in this creepy shack instead? Are you this afraid of commitment?"

John was a champ with non-responses. "Wouldn't you like to know?"

"Yes, I would. No rhetorical."

"Leave my love life alone, Cherry," he said. "I won't ask twice."

He still set her bedtimes: twelve o'clock on weeknights, two o'clock on Saturday and Friday. Her dad was having a mid-life fatherhood AA crisis and kept having family dinners with her, telling her awkwardly she was looking more like Mom each day. To get through those meals Mr. Hollis sometimes even set her menu. Like: eat all your green vegetables, but nothing else. They both knew that table food was a joke.

The hunger was an old sickness. Eating the goat ruined her for everything else. Sometimes she and John went down to the sea where he shore fished, gutting his catch in record time, and they sat there gorging themselves on fresh raw perch squirted with hot sauce—but it was never really the same.

When they read together, she found herself leaning in so that their faces were nearly touching. Cherry let her bare shoulder touch the thin polyester of his shirt, imagining the hot blood going through his veins that made his skin warm through the fabric. She sat on the kitchen table and swung her legs from side to side as he worked at his laptop, completely ignored in a way that was nearly acknowledgement.

"Well, fifteen is a gulf away from fourteen," said John one day, shoulders slumped back in his chair. "I think you're old enough to have this."

It was Vladimir Nabokov. *Lolita.* Cherry turned the book over and over, feeling the weight of it in her hands like it was lead. "His novel about pedophilia," she said, and regretted how dumb that sounded.

"That's the obvious reading." The chair tipped back and forth, his gaze on the ceiling in contemplation. "The other one is about devouring somebody's life."

It took her a while to get up the courage to read it. When she cracked open the cover she broke his rule to spend three sleepless nights finishing the thing, reading it at lunchtimes, reading it in study hall in another dustcover, skipping gym and reading it in the park. When she tried to talk about it he was so removed on the subject that she stopped, angry somehow like he'd breached the terms of their contract—and he shook away her hand when she rested her fingers over his own.

"For someone so clever, you can be an unbelievably stupid kid," he said abruptly.

That shot told. "I haven't been a kid in a while, John."

"You're a child, Charlene. Don't fool yourself. You don't know anything."

So she stopped touching him. That was the year she felt very tired.

The spell that year was "make." If she'd still been riding high on last year's successes, it would have killed her; as it was she spent her time mechanically breathing life back into dead matches, watching the blackened wood burst into flame that spluttered out as quickly as it flared. Cherry spent long nights trying to coax water to ice and ice to water again with red raw hands. "Make" was a double-edged sword. Creating things was easy enough, but sustaining them was like eating soup with a fork, and after the most half-assed attempt she'd be so hungry that she'd chew her hair and her nails trying to make the feeling go away. Sometimes she thought about eating Styrofoam peanuts just to fill up the space in her gut.

Mr. Hollis withdrew from her into an armoured shell, emerging only sporadically like he was guilty for the absence. Cherry was good at absences, the best, and it hardly hurt unless you thought about it suddenly. He sat across the kitchen table with a crossword, a great wall of silence spanning between master and apprentice as she tried to make a bud unfurl on his spider plant. Sometimes he'd stand by the window and make tiny incisions in the air with his fingers, and then Jen would suddenly show up and she'd be kicked out and flipping the bird at his closed door. She was pretty surprised when that summer came and she got dragged off to the beach as per usual; she almost thought he'd cancel summer due to lack of goddamned interest.

There was no comment on her bikini that long, hot July. She kicked around in the tidal pools trying to make starfishes grow back their legs, slathered with sunscreen and visceral disappointment. John spent his time under the umbrella with the newspaper, and she spent her time talking to dusty blond surfer boys with loud-patterned board shorts.

Seagulls cawed. He was fiddling with his sunglasses, saying nothing. The crow's feet were tracking deeper indents at his eyes and mouth than they had when she'd first met him; back then she'd never noticed his age, only that he was old. Now he just looked young with premature crow's feet. "You need some Botox," she added, and unnecessarily reached out her hand to touch his cheek.

John flinched, then pretended he hadn't. "God only knows, Cherry," he said, with a little bit of the old humour. "Sometimes I feel there's nothing left to teach you. Maybe it's time to move on."

That made her a little bit crazy, and with hunger it made her frantic. Matches, spider plants and ice cubes lost all appeal, June lost its sunshine. She threw herself down on her bed and cradled her head like her thoughts would pop off the top of her skull. Fuelled by his retreat and his distance, the specter of that idea haunted her like Casper the Friendly Ghost on meth.

When she turned up on his doorstep at 2 AM he didn't look surprised, just tired. "You can't send me away any more," she said. "You see, I've got nowhere else to go."

His apartment at night was full of unfamiliar shapes, the fan wafting stale air around the room and the carpet sticky beneath her feet. Without saying a word he lead her to his hall closet, putting her hand on the doorknob before sitting down at the kitchen table in his sweatpants and t-shirt. John didn't look at her, just rubbed his hands together like restless birds.

"I was waiting for you to grow up," he said.

After she flicked the light bulb on, the closet was full of jackets and beach umbrellas, stacks of books and an old vacuum cleaner. Half-hidden beneath a parka was a freshly dead stranger in jogging shoes whose thighs had been carefully sectioned and long strips of meat taken away. There was blood underfoot. At the familiar smell of old putrefaction overlaying new putrefaction she gagged until tears came into her eyes; it filled her nostrils. It filled her mouth.

"Magicians eat," he said, looking at her with eyes the colour of ghosts. "We eat more and more and more, Cherry Murphy, of anything we can get our hands on." A careless shrug. "Just look at me. I ate your childhood."

The doorframe scored her back as she dropped to her haunches, hugging her knees tightly to her chest. Every so often she'd involuntarily gag again, rocking back and forth until John came and carried her away. She gagged into his chest and struggled when he put her in his lap, fisting her hands in his t-shirt, wadding it up into her lips so that she wouldn't scream. His hand threaded hard through her hair. Saliva filled up her mouth and overflowed in trickles down his front.

She was crying so hard she couldn't say a word. His fingers finally tugged his shirtfront away from her teeth as she drew more and more down her gullet. On her shoulders his thumbs dug deep into her collarbones, and now that he was looking at her his eyes were sunken and gleaming like the hearts of white stars. Every line in his face was deep and hard and old.

"It was never goat, was it?"

"Sweetheart, I couldn't kill a goat," said Mr. Hollis. "They're adorable."

This close up he smelled of acrid sweat and Listerine and her spittle, and her master magician had his arm around her to tether her down. He'd killed someone. He'd stashed them in his closet. He'd done it before. With an awful, dreadful surety, he slowly pressed her head into the table.

"Ball's in your court," said John.

Her stomach growled.

"I want some teriyaki sauce and a fork," said Cherry.

TWENTY-TWO AND YOU

MICHAEL BLUMLEIN

She didn't want the test. She had vowed not to get it done. What she wanted was a family; she and Everett both. She would never have married a man who didn't want kids.

Like her, he fancied a brood. One, if one was all they could have, but two would be better. Three would be better still.

Four? he had asked in one of their giddier moments. How would you feel about four?

Four, she had said, would do nicely.

Five?

She had smiled at the thought.

More? he had asked, those killer eyes of his widening slightly.

I couldn't imagine more than five, she had said, meaning of course that she could.

As for the test, there'd be time enough later, after the children were born. And after she and Everett had been married a few more years.

Not that she had any doubts about their marriage. Everett loved her deeply, and she loved him. It seemed the most natural thing in the world, this love, like breathing. In another way it was a constant surprise to her, like opening an unexpected and wonderful gift. She felt it between them many times a day. Actually, she felt it pretty much whenever she thought about it. It was a living connection, and it streamed.

So many of her friends had to work at keeping their marriages running smoothly. Hers ran smoothly by default, and a large part of this, she felt, was due to Everett.

It was like her mother had said on the day before the wedding, when she'd pulled Ellen away from the last-minute preparations and taken her for a final prenuptial mother-daughter walk.

"Darling," she'd said. "I know we haven't always seen eye to eye. You don't always approve of how I handle things. We've had our differences."

Ellen had started to reply. Wasn't it the reverse, her mother who didn't approve? And did they have to talk about this now?

"Please. Let me finish. It's not my business to judge you. It's my business to love you, and I do. I think you've made a spectacular choice. I wish you every happiness. Not that you need anyone's wish: it's there for you, I see it ahead for many years."

Ellen felt the same, but she was curious. "Why do you say that? How do you know?"

"It's written all over your face. And all over his. It's in the air whenever you're together."

Ellen had blushed. This was the mother she loved.

"I'm so happy, Mom. I feel so lucky."

"I'm happy, too. Luck is a wonderful thing. But it's not all luck, sweetheart. You had something to do with it. You picked a good one."

A good one. Yes. She had. It was true. Everett was a good man, and she knew he would not leave her for anything. Not for love or for money, and not if she had her breasts removed.

He did love her breasts . . . he was a man, after all. He loved the shape of her body, and her breasts were a part of that shape. He loved to touch them, hold them in his hands, press his face against them, smother them with kisses.

Sometimes she felt self-conscious about them . . . she was a woman, after all, and had her moments of wondering if they were too big or too small, if the circles around the nipples were too dark, if the nipples themselves looked right. But on the whole she liked her breasts, too. She liked her body, and she was happy that Everett liked it, and she loved the sensation of her nipples being caressed and kissed and the sharp line of pleasure this sent from breast to womb.

That said, in no way did their relationship depend on them. If her breasts were gone, she would adjust, and Everett would, too. *In sickness and in health*, he had vowed, and he was a man who took his vows seriously.

The ovaries and uterus, on the other hand . . . a slightly bigger deal. Everett would say the same thing. Do it. Have them removed. He would not hesitate. In the future no word of regret would ever cross his lips. He would hide his disappointment, wall it off, from her and perhaps from himself as well. Your life is more important, he would say, than our having kids. And he'd mean it. Of course he would.

But for her, not so simple. Not simple at all. She would always know what she had failed to produce. There would be a hole in her life, and this would be a source of immeasurable sorrow. There would be a shadow over their marriage, an absence that she could not begin to think of how to fill.

Having kids was etched so deeply in her. It had been there, inside, for as long as she could remember, inseparable from who she was. Womanhood meant many things, and one of them was motherhood. This seemed only natural. Most of her friends, both married and unmarried, felt the same. Getting pregnant, giving birth, raising a family: let the wild rumpus begin! It was nature's gift and plan.

You could live without breasts. But without kids? Without ovaries and a uterus? This felt unnecessarily cruel, and she would not do it. She could not. The ovaries and uterus were hers and would stay. She would not part with them, and furthermore, she would not put herself in a position where she would have to consider parting with them. In other words, she would not do the test to see if she had that awful gene, the one her grandmother and her mother had. That one, or any of the others that interacted with it, the so-called constellation that put her at such grave risk. For if she had it, she wouldn't be able to ignore it. She wouldn't be allowed to. Everett wouldn't let her. Her mother wouldn't let her. The two of them would keep at her to do something about it, in all the ways that loved ones exerted their love.

She preferred to remain ignorant for the time being.

Among her friends, nearly all of whom had been fully genotyped, this bordered on the heretical. You got a wax, a pedicure, you kept in shape, you kept in touch, you had your genome done. These were not the days of being uninformed. They were the days of knowing absolutely everything you could: about yourself, your friends, your friends' friends, the world around you. Refuse data? Deny it either going out or coming in? Keep your own counsel? You might as well pack your bags and go live in a cave.

True, your genome was yours in a sense—a certain narrow, private, misanthropic, self-centered sense—but in a larger, fuller, more generous sense—a global sense, if you will—it was everyone's. Your genome was part of the great world-wide human pool, and in this sense was public domain. Friends deserved to know who they were friends with. They deserved to know what their friends were made of—what, building-block-wise, they had inside, what this might lead to, and what their pedigree was. You might discover you shared a friend's single nucleotide polymorphism, her SNP, and how cool would that be! You might even be related. Maybe your ancestors hunted together on the steppes of Mongolia. Maybe they shared a yurt and snuggled under the very same reindeer hide.

This was information that people who cared about people should know.

Ellen heard from more friends than she knew she had, sharing their experiences and concerns, and urging her to get profiled. She received links to one site after another, until she cried, Enough! Give it a rest. But the sites continued to find their way onto her screen. Forty and Six announced monthly specials. Our Chromosomes, Ourselves offered two-for-ones, and

Genomania promised a free sequencing in exchange for the names of five or more friends who'd be interested in their services.

No thank you, she said to the screen, hitting delete. No thank you, unsubscribing. No thank you, no thank you, leave me alone. Go away. I don't want your stupid test. I'll do it AK, after kids.

Her mother pleaded with her not to wait that long. Getting pregnant could trigger the cancer. It was a big risk.

"You waited," Ellen reminded her.

"I don't have the full constellation. I just have the one bad gene. Besides, they didn't have the test when I was your age. They didn't have the technology."

"Would you have done it if they did?"

"Absolutely."

It was a bald-faced, if forgivable, lie.

"I don't want to know something I'm not going to do anything about," Ellen replied. "It'll just worry me."

"It doesn't worry you now? It worries me."

"Not as much as if I knew it for a fact. Then it would be like the cancer was already there. Already growing inside of me."

What her mother wanted to say was, "Maybe it is." But she couldn't be that cold, not even in the name of love, so she held her tongue. It would be like placing a curse on her daughter, and she knew how it felt to be cursed. She'd had cancer in both breasts, and had had both breasts removed, along with the plumbing down below. It had been an awful experience, and that was before the complications. She had never fully recovered. The best thing she could say about the multiple surgeries was that she would never have to have them again.

Now the cancer was back, in one of her lungs.

She hadn't yet told her daughter. How could she? What would she say? She hoped if she waited long enough, she wouldn't have to say anything. She'd be hit by a car and die a quick and sudden death. Or die in her sleep, even better. Better still, the cancer would disappear. Her body would fight it off, or it would somehow self-destruct. A hari-kari, suicidal cancer . . . it could happen. She'd read accounts. It could shrivel up like a pea and leave her in peace. Being a peace-loving woman, she spent a fair amount of time every day visualizing this outcome.

She also spoke to it at times, as she might to a disobedient child, or an alien, or an enemy. She tried to reason with it, negotiate, court its favor, compromise. So far it wasn't listening. It continued to grow and divide. Her visualizations and conversations didn't seem to be working. The drugs weren't working either. At a certain point she felt she had no choice but to tell her daughter.

She did it over coffee at Ellen and Everett's apartment. Everett was working in the back.

Ellen was stunned. She shook her head, as if it couldn't be true.

When she recovered her voice, she got angry, as her mother had suspected she might. She didn't like being kept in the dark, especially about something like this. She didn't understand why her mother insisted on being so secretive.

But the anger didn't last. Soon it was swept away by a river of tears. When Everett finally wandered out to say hello, the two of them were locked in a fierce embrace.

He was next to get the news. It was not a happy moment. The three of them talked for a while, then Mom drove herself home.

The apartment seemed to shrink in her absence. The air felt heavy. The walls pressed in. Ellen had to get out, and she and Everett took a walk. The streets were crowded. The sun was warm. The city was alive all around. Ellen felt this life acutely, almost painfully, and when they got back home, she asked Everett to make love to her.

She tended to be a vocal lover. Restraint was not her m.o., not, as it were, in her genes. She loved to make noise, to moan and groan and even cry out. This time, as she reached her climax, the cry was different, harsher, as if something was being torn from her. Afterward, she continued to cry, and Everett held her, until at length she quieted.

Later, curled in the warmth of his arms, she announced that she'd decided to have the test done. She would get her genome sequenced, A to Z.

"I'm glad," he said.

"Will you be glad when I have no breasts? When I can't have kids? Because once I do this, and I find out I have those stupid genes, I'm not going to stop. I'm going to do what I have to. If that means letting them rip me apart, I will. I refuse to stick my head in the sand like my mother did."

"They're not going to rip you apart," he said.

"They'll take away some very precious items."

"They won't take you."

"Are you ready for a life without kids?".

He hesitated for less than a second. Would it have mattered if he hadn't? If he'd answered immediately?

"We'll work it out," he said.

Our dream will die, she thought. "I want you to know where I stand."

Showing him how tough she could be when she made up her mind. Warning him. Was she also, he wondered, asking him to take issue with her? Fight her on this? Say no, don't do it?

"Why do you say your mother stuck her head in the sand?" he asked. "She didn't know she was at risk until she was first diagnosed."

"She didn't want to know. Her mother had cancer. And there was a test for it years ago. Not like we have now, but it was something. She just refused to have it done."

This was news to Everett. It put a whole new spin on Ellen's own refusal. Like maybe it was some weird kind of loyalty thing to her mom. He didn't understand it, but he didn't have to.

"I'll love you always," he said. "No matter what. They can rip everything apart, till there's nothing left, and I'll love that."

"Don't be morbid."

"I'm just saying."

"I know. And thank you. I'll remind you later you said that."

He kissed her on the ear, then the neck. "You won't have to remind me. I won't forget."

She swallowed a lump in her throat.

He kissed her breast.

She felt a tingle, a stirring, in her belly.

"Again?" he asked.

They did it again and afterward conked out. Everett woke midway through the night. Ellen was turned away from him, her arms clutched tightly across her chest, crying softly in her sleep. It pained him deeply, and he wrapped his arms around her, hugging and holding her from behind, until eventually her sobbing ceased. The next morning he rose early and closeted himself in the study. By the time Ellen was up, showered, and dressed, he had what he wanted and had uploaded it to his pad. He brought it to Ellen, who put her own pad down and looked at his.

"I found this yesterday," he told her.

"Twenty-Two and You?"

"It's a start-up. They're, like, an hour away."

She scanned the page.

"You believe this?" she asked.

"I don't disbelieve it."

"It seems like a joke."

"What? Gene therapy? Hardly."

"*This* therapy. They claim they can rewrite any gene you have. You'd think something like that would be in the news."

"It was in the news. It is. But they're new. They don't have much of a track record. It's an evolving story."

Evolving? she thought. Try outrageous. Still, it was something. Maybe. But first things first.

They ordered the genome kit that same morning. Like an arrow waiting to be launched, it came the very next day. Ellen unwrapped the package with some excitement, which surprised her. She worked up a nice glob of spit, full, she hoped, of cheek cells, emptied it into the vial, sealed the vial, and sent it off. Six weeks later the results arrived online.

Earlier that week, she'd gotten a call from her mother. These were calls that she dreaded, but this time the news was good. Amazingly so. The cancer was in retreat. It was shrinking. Who knew why? A delayed effect of the drugs? The visualization? Both? Neither?

"It's a reprieve," said her mother cautiously.

Ellen was thinking more along the lines of a miracle. But either would do. She wasn't going to quibble. She felt like shouting for joy.

The news carried her until the day her own results arrived. Let there be a miracle now, she thought, staring at the company's screen before logging on, heart pounding, hope battling dread.

This is what she found out:

1. She had a low risk for diabetes.

2. She carried something called rs 1805007, which explained her strawberry-blonde hair.

3. She was hypersensitive to a drug used to thin the blood.

4. Her ancestors roamed the forests of Eastern Europe. They had interbred with tribes to the south. They had also interbred with Neanderthals.

5. She had sticky earwax. This she already knew. Now, though, she no longer had to feel guilty when her ears got clogged. It wasn't her fault. It was in her genes.

6. She carried the Triggering Endocrine Stutter Sequence gene, TESS 233, the one her mother had, but with a twist. She had another gene, probably from her father. A hormone-sensitive promoter gene. It was part of the constellation they had feared. Were she to get pregnant, her chance of getting cancer of the breast and ovary was near certain.

Twenty-Two and You, the company Everett had found, was named after the number of chromosome pairs minus one, the one, according to their upbeat, breezy website, being You. You were the wild card. You were the one in charge, who decided what needed to change. You were the supplier of that critical information, the orchestrator of your personal future, the Author with a capital A of your own destiny. This was their guarantee. Their promise: to unzip, repair, and rezip whatever gene needed fixing, then send you on your way. Their motto: Put the ever-after forever-after in your hands.

The company was housed in a spanking new box off the freeway. Ellen and Everett visited it the week after she got her test results. Their appointment was the last of the day.

It had not been the best week of her life. She'd had nightmares every night, terrible things fraught with images of disfigurement and loss. More than once she woke like a bolt in the darkness, drenched in sweat and gasping for air. Her waking hours were hardly better. She hated what was inside of her. She dreaded what lay ahead. Everett had high hopes about this company, but that was Everett. She did not share his optimism. The whole thing seemed too good to be true. Too simple. Too easy. How could they perform these miracles? The answer: they couldn't. It was hype. In the end she would have the surgeries and be a husk of a woman, a non-woman, for what remained of her sad, barren life.

The reception room was full. Men, women, and children of every age. Her eyes glided over the men, lingering on the women and most especially the children. Such beautiful things. What, she wondered, had brought them? What terrible condition did they have? How thin the line between a normal life and this. She felt a wave of tenderness and sadness for them. She felt pity too, for them and for herself.

By ones and twos and threes the room emptied, until they were the only ones left. It was five o'clock, an hour later than their scheduled appointment. Everett was restless and annoyed; Ellen, surprisingly blasé. The world of cancer was not the same as the rest of the world. She had learned this with her mother. It had its own set of rules, its own pace, and its own clock. You couldn't get worked up about these differences. It was humiliating enough simply to have the disease.

"You don't have the disease," Everett reminded her, not for the first time. "You have a chance for the disease. That's why we're here. To remove that chance. Reverse the odds."

She imagined someone tossing a pair of dice, which seemed an iffy way to decide one's future. She knew it was irrational thinking. This was science, not a crapshoot. Science and Everett, her soul mate, her heartthrob, her love. Everett, trying to raise her spirits; Everett, caring for her; Everett, keeping the flame of hope alive.

She owed him, if not cheer, then at least a measure of kindness.

"You're right," she said, lacing her fingers through his. "I'm sorry for being such a bitch."

"You have every reason. And besides, you're not."

"You lie."

"I never lie," he said, squeezing her hand.

His wedding ring pressed against the inside of her little finger. From the finger to her heart. From her heart back to his. The true ring.

A nurse came out and called her name, breaking the reverie. They followed her through a door, where they were placed in another, smaller room. They waited longer, and eventually a man appeared. He was tall and broad-shouldered. He had slate-blue eyes and a sweep of lank, wheat-colored hair that all but covered his forehead. His nose was large, his cheeks wide, his lips a boisterous red. His name was Rudolf Stanovic. Dr. Rudolf Stanovic. He had trained jointly as a researcher and a clinician, had spent time at the bench but now worked solely as a practitioner. He treated patients, and this was work he loved.

He was passionate about his profession. He believed in its power to heal and transform. He believed in his company, Twenty-Two and You, as the guiding hand of this transformation. He believed in himself. He was a doctor, and his job was nothing more or less than helping those in need.

He knew Ellen's story before he entered the room. He had read the history she had provided. With minor variations it was the same history and story of every patient who came to Twenty-Two and You. A bad gene, or genes; an uncertain future. He had no need to hear it again, yet hear it again he did, sitting in a chair opposite her, folding his hands in his lap, meeting her eyes and listening patiently without interrupting as she laid it out for him.

When she was done, he asked some simple questions designed to draw her out further, to allow her to express and unravel, at least a little, the complex knot of her feelings. She hadn't expected this, had assumed he wanted it cut and dried and to the point, and was taken by surprise. Her feelings? What manner of doctor was this?

"It's late," she said. "Are you sure you want to know? Do you have time?"

It was an honest question but also a warning, disguised as a little joke. It could get messy, she was telling him. Emotions could fly. Much was bottled up inside. Was he prepared for what might happen when the bottle was uncorked? More to the point, could she trust him enough to let down her guard?

He glanced at his watch, then slipped it off his wrist and into a drawer. Then he settled back in his chair.

"We'll talk. First you, then me. We'll put our cards on the table. We'll make time."

He had an easy manner and spoke with an accent. Eastern European . . . Balkan maybe. Something that from other lips could have come out guttural and harsh. From his, almost embarrassingly gentle.

She drew a breath, then began. A fistful of wadded-up, tear-soaked tissues later she wiped her nose, heaved a sigh and was done. She hadn't meant to cry. Doctors were either uncomfortable with tears or else they treated you like a child. But there it was. He'd asked for it.

Everett sat beside her. Midway through her unburdening he'd taken her hand and continued to grip it tightly. She was grateful for his presence. She could have done it alone, but he was a rock. Together, they waited for the doctor's response.

He began by thanking her for being open and candid with him. Anger, fear, frustration, and all the rest were natural. Hope was natural, too. Not that she'd mentioned it, but he knew it was there. Why else would she be sitting in this room?

"Now I'll be candid with you. There is hope. More than hope. We'll fix this gene. If you like, we'll turn around your future."

"I like," she said.

He held up a hand. "Please. You need to understand the full picture.

"This gene of yours is part of a constellation of genes. Like stars, but close to each other. Like a family. They live together in a big neighborhood. A shtetl. You know what a shtetl is? Like that. This family, they visit each other. They work together. They separate, then come together again. Maybe they actually join and make a new family. Maybe they have offspring. Whatever happens, everybody knows about it. Big family, small town, word gets around. If one member makes a change, the news travels fast. Some in the family could care less. They go about their business. Other members—now we'll say genes—they change, too.

"Change makes change. You fix a tire, your car runs better. You fix TESS 233, you run better. Cancer-free is always better. But maybe you run differently. Maybe you experience another change."

"Like what?"

"Maybe you do, maybe you don't. Change creates a ripple, a ripple creates change. You see what I'm saying? A ball in a box is a ball. You take the ball out and kick it, or throw it, you put it in motion. This motion starts a chain of events. Your ball takes on a life of its own."

"You're saying there's a risk," said Everett.

"There's always a risk. With any treatment."

"She could end up not cured?"

"This is unlikely. We have an outstanding rate of success. Close to one hundred percent. We'll fix this gene of yours. We'll break it apart and sew it back together like new." His eyes swung back to Ellen. "You'll have a healthy gene. You'll be a healthy person. You can have all the little ones you like. They'll be healthy, too. Free of TESS 233. We'll eliminate that from the picture. We'll make another picture. A valentine for you. Health. Happiness. Family. Your heart's desire. We'll put ourselves out of business."

He smiled. "I joke. It's an old joke. A doctor's joke. We do our job well, we'll never see you again. For us, this is not a problem. We have plenty of work. For other doctors—oncologists, rheumatologists—the future is not so rosy. We engineer genes, we engineer their demise. It's sad to say, but what can you do? Progress is a god. A great god. God of the impossible. But not a god of mercy."

"You said I'd change," said Ellen. "How? Please be specific."

"I said maybe. The chance is roughly fifty-fifty."

It was a substantial risk. He watched her closely to see how she'd react, then swiveled in his chair, opened a drawer in the desk, and pulled out an eight-by-eleven-inch laminated card. On it was a busy diagram with an oblong shape in the center surrounded by similar but smaller shapes connected to it and to each other by bidirectional arrows. The large shape was labeled TESS 233. The other shapes, he explained, represented genes and gene products that interacted with it. Each could have been at the center of its own diagram. Start anywhere, and you could get anywhere else. From the smallest gene to the largest, from a single molecule to an entire cell. All paths were joined. In the end there was only one path, and that was the body.

He called her attention to one of the small oblong shapes colored a royal blue and labeled DMTF, 18p5.7. The 18, he said, referred to the chromosome number. The p, to its short, *petit,* arm. The 5.7, to the gene's location on that arm. DMTF stood for Dynamic Memory Transcription Factor, DYMETRA for short.

"This plays a crucial role in the brain," he explained. "It's the hub of memory maintenance. I think of it as the jealous sister in the family. She's used to being center stage. If TESS gets a facelift, DYMETRA's going to know about it. Half the time she lets things be and goes about her business. But half the time she makes a fuss. Floods the brain with her transcript. Shows how important she is."

"What happens then?"

"The brain is a plastic organ. Memory is the most plastic of all. It's like rubber. DYMETRA recruits other genes in the family. Some turn on, some off. Memory gets reshaped. It's a small change usually. A small effect. Most of the time it's barely noticeable. Sometimes not noticeable at all."

"Like what?" asked Ellen. "Give me an example."

"Maybe you forget a face. Or forget something you said. Or where you put something. Things like that."

"Is it permanent?"

"How do you mean?"

"Do you ever get the memory back? Or do you get it but keep forgetting over and over? Does the process stop?"

"We've only been offering this treatment for two years. We don't have long-term results. In the short-term, sometimes yes, sometimes no."

"It doesn't sound so bad," said Everett. "Hell, I'm forgetful now. We could handle it, El."

"It sounds like Alzheimer's," she said.

Stanovic shook his head. "No. Alzheimer's is a different beast."

She imagined how it might be, forgetting things. It was always annoying when it happened. Frustrating at times. She could see how it could get embarrassing if it happened a lot. But life-altering? It would depend on the degree.

She asked him about that. "You said the effect is usually small. Have you seen a large effect? How often does that happen? What's it look like?"

"One time," he said, raising his index finger as though it required emphasis. "A patient of ours, a man, forgot his wife. It was a difficult situation. Very troubling for all concerned."

"What do you mean, he forgot her?" she asked. "Like what? Completely?"

Stanovic nodded.

"How awful."

"We tried many different things to help. Called in experts. Hired consultants. Sent counselors to their home. We took it very seriously, I assure you."

"And?"

"After six months his wife moved out. There was nothing we could do."

"She deserted him?"

"She was a young woman. And extremely unhappy."

"That's horrible," said Ellen. "How could someone completely abandon someone they love like that?"

Stanovic did not point out the obvious, that the wife had been abandoned as well, and first. "It was very sad."

"It's not going to happen," said Everett.

She turned to him. She was shaken. "What? I won't forget you, or you won't move out?"

"Neither."

She stared at him.

He stared back, then left his chair and crouched in front of her.

"Take my hands," he said. "Now look at me. Now tell me: do you think you can forget me? Do you possibly believe you ever would?"

He had the most beautiful eyes. In every way he was a beautiful and memorable person. What could she do but shake her head?

"Now tell me: do you think I'd ever leave you? Ever?"

A slightly harder question, only because you could never know someone else's mind as well as your own. Except maybe in this one case.

"No," she whispered.

He turned to Stanovic. "How many times has something this extreme happened? Remind us. Out of how many treatments?"

"One time. Only one. Out of twenty-three treatments. As I explained, small effects are much more common. But listen. There's more to the story. A new development. Do you have time? Would you like to hear?"

"Yes," said Everett, then glanced at Ellen, who wasn't so sure. But curiosity got the better of her, and she nodded.

Stanovic leaned back in his chair. He was pushing the envelope a little of what it meant to be a doctor. Stories of other patients weren't usually told in such detail, though this one could easily be justified from the point of view of full disclosure of risk. And he had to admit, he enjoyed telling it.

"The wife moves out. Time goes by, and he forgets her again. He loses her memory, as it were. He goes back to work. He's living alone, a young man, and he wants to meet women. He goes to a bar one night and sees someone he likes. Pretty face, nice figure. She's talking to the bartender and doesn't notice him. The room is crowded, and he pushes his way toward her. The closer he gets, the more he likes what he sees. He feels something inside. Chemistry? Would that be the word?"

"Chemistry takes two," said Ellen.

He shrugged and continued. "The woman turns, and who do you think it is?"

"His wife. What did she do?"

"Told him to go away. Leave her alone."

"Poor guy. So now he wants her again, but she doesn't want him." She pitied them both. "Or are you saying something else? That he knows her. He remembers."

"He knows something. Chemistry, memory, two pods of a pea."

"That is such a sad story."

Everett felt differently. He took it as affirmation that certain things could never be forgotten. This seemed a fact of life, powered, as facts could be, by the twin engines of love and youth.

But Stanovic was not finished. There was more to the tale.

"She told him to go away, but he didn't. He bought her a drink. Then another. And what do you think happened next? They went home together."

"I like that," said Everett.

Ellen did too, though she also knew that a woman, if drunk enough, would do many things she might regret the next morning.

"And now?" she asked. "Are they back together? Is he still forgetting?"

The results on that, he said, were not yet in. Although the man's memory, it seemed, was stabilizing.

"What did he have?" Everett asked. "To begin with? What was wrong with him that needed to get fixed?"

It was a common question. People were naturally curious. Some found comfort in comparing themselves to others. This, too, seemed natural, though in Stanovic's experience it was rarely helpful and frequently harmful, and not, therefore, a practice he condoned.

"What he had is not important. The important thing is that he came to us. And that we cured him. And that for him life goes on."

He paused to give this last thought its proper weight, and to allow his visitors to do the same. The story about the man and his wife was useful, possibly applicable, but mostly it was a detour, a digression, a mild indulgence on his part. What happened to one person should not be generalized. The case was extreme and unlikely to recur. It was time to return to the matter at hand.

"The going on, that is most important. It's why you're here. We're all in agreement on this. Yes?"

"Yes," said Everett.

A moment passed before Ellen nodded.

Stanovic gazed at her. "You have reservations?"

"No," she said.

"But something else to say?"

She heaved a sigh. "I wish I didn't have to do any of this. Not this treatment of yours, not some horrible surgery, not anything. I wish I'd gotten pregnant first. That was my plan. I wish I'd stuck to it."

"Pregnancy in all likelihood will trigger the cancer. And it's a bad cancer. You may not survive."

"My mother did."

"You mother is different. She has only the TESS gene. You have TESS and more. Pregnancy is a time bomb unless we do something first. Even if you don't get pregnant, you're still at risk. But it's not so urgent a matter. We can monitor you. Watch and wait."

She knew all this. She also knew what she was going to do. But it helped to talk it out.

"I wish I didn't have to put you through this," she told Everett. "It's not what you bargained for. I'm sorry."

"Don't say that," he said. "Don't even think it."

"I wish I was normal."

"You are normal. You're better than normal. I can't begin to tell you how much better."

She turned to Stanovic. "I have one request. There's a gene for eye color, right? While you're messing around in my DNA, please change mine to my husband's. Then there'll be no doubt whose eyes they're going to have. Assuming this works."

"It works," said Stanovic. "Children will come. Eye color we can do. But there we stop. It's unpredictable what happens if you monkey around too much. Maybe you get a super-kid, maybe an imbecile. It's bad medicine to think we're smarter than we are."

• • •

The infusion took place in the company clinic designed for the purpose. She was warned to expect to feel sick for several days. Feverish, achy, under the weather. This was due to the vector that carried the repair sequence, a modified strain of the influenza virus. In addition, she might feel disoriented for a bit. Mentally, a little wobbly and weak in the knees. This was due to, first a down, then an up regulation in various neuronal circuits. A recalibration of the electro-molecular homeostatic mechanism. Typically, the symptoms were mild and gone in a week.

Ellen surprised everyone, including herself, by not getting sick at all. Nor, thank God, did she forget her husband. Nor her mother. Nor anyone. She felt fit before the infusion, fit during the infusion, and fit a week later.

Something, though, was different. She couldn't quite say what. It seemed important but also strangely unimportant. As if something of interest to her, of significance, had lost its power to hold her attention and possibly even affect her.

This something nagged at her, like a thorn, but every day the nagging grew less. Then one day there was no nagging. The thorn had worked its way out.

It was a huge relief. Finally, she felt normal again. She felt like herself. It was the self she most loved. The one with energy, who loved to do things. The one who didn't live under a cloud of apprehension but took pleasure in life.

One of those pleasures had been on hold for nearly a month. Too much pressure and stress. Being freed of them was like waking from a stupor.

This waking first happened in the kitchen. Everett was putting away groceries, and she went at him like a cat in heat.

"I want you," she growled, backing him against the counter. "I lust for your body."

"I can do lust," he replied.

She licked her lips.

He grinned.

She pressed herself against him, then let herself be lifted and carried to the bedroom.

The sex was awesome. She let herself go in a way she'd never done, clawing his back, grinding her pelvis against his, screaming when she came. He responded with a low-throated roar, and a millisecond later went stiff as a board and shot himself into her.

This happened on a Sunday morning, an off day from work for them. After sex they had breakfast. After breakfast Ellen called her mother.

Mom was different these days. More open, more expressive. The cancer remained in remission. Physically, she felt good. Mentally, like she was living a dream. How could things be better? She was well. Her daughter was cured.

She couldn't express in words how happy this made her. Not to mention the prospect of grandkids.

After the call Ellen waylaid Everett again. Afterward, she lay in his arms and playfully asked if she was being a nuisance.

"No way. I love having sex with you."

"It's weird," she said. "I feel so . . . so driven."

"Driven?"

"Horny. It's like I've been holding all this stuff inside, and now it's just busting out. It feels so good to let go. I can see how people get addicted."

He kissed her on the shoulder. "Should we tell the doctor you've become an addict?"

"I just like it."

"Yeah. Me too."

The next time they made love was that night. Ellen had the condom out, ready to roll it on, when Everett said, "How about we do it without that thing?"

She knew it was better for him. He got more excited. The sensation was heightened. He'd liked it more when she was on the mini-pill.

The condom, on the other hand, seemed like such a good idea.

It was a tough decision, but at length she agreed.

The next time, a day later, she said yes again.

Her period that month was late. She couldn't decide whether to say anything—really didn't want to be the one to raise hopes only to see them dashed—and in the end chose to keep it to herself for the time being. When her period did finally come, she was glad she had.

A week later, she saw Dr. Stanovic at a follow-up appointment. He asked how she was, and she said fine. He pulled up her new genome on his screen—new and improved—and went over it with her. He asked his normal battery of questions. He did a physical, after which he pronounced her fit.

Once she was dressed, he asked again how she was doing. Any concerns? Any questions she wanted to ask?

She hesitated a moment, then said yes. There was one question.

"Are there any delayed effects of the treatment? I feel stupid for asking now. I should have asked before."

"Delayed effects? Such as what?"

"I missed a period. It came, but it was late."

"Ah." He nodded sympathetically. "It could be the treatment. A woman's cycle is very sensitive to change."

She realized she'd asked the wrong question. What she'd meant was: could some effects reverse themselves? Could a change change back?

"Everett wants a baby," she said.

"Yes. It's why we did this. One of the reasons. Now you can."

"I think I was pregnant. I think I lost it. I aborted."

"This is possible? You and your husband, you've been trying?"

She looked at him, nodded.

"I'm sorry," he said. "I know how much you want this. But look on the bright side. Soon you'll get another chance."

It was this that worried her.

He saw it in her face. "No? I'm wrong?"

"I don't understand it," she said.

"You've had a change of heart?"

Heart? Was that it? It seemed much bigger and all-encompassing. Heart, soul, spirit, self: all of them rolled into one.

She lifted her eyes to him. "Something like that."

His preliminary diagnosis was amnesia. Partial, localized, and temporary, he hoped and guessed.

Amnesia seemed the wrong word to her. What she had was less like a forgetting than an absence. Something that not only didn't exist but never had. On no level did the idea of being a mother resonate with her. Her desire for kids was gone.

Dr. Stanovic was puzzled and alarmed. He ordered a whole new battery of tests and sent her to a panel of specialists. She had scans and other studies of her brain, including a subcognitive resistance study to see if there was a short circuit somewhere. She talked to a therapist. She was tested for pre-partum depression. She had her hormones and pre-hormones checked.

It was a lengthy process, and she had plenty of time to think. Plenty of questions ran through her head. Was she less a woman, she asked herself, now that she didn't want children? She didn't feel that way. She felt as womanly as ever. She couldn't even honestly say that she'd changed. The desire for kids was absent, but then when had it ever been present? She didn't remember that it had. In this respect she felt no different from before. Her past self flowed seamlessly into her present self. Nothing had been taken away.

If it had been, wouldn't she miss it? Wouldn't there be a hole somewhere in her life? But in fact, the reverse was true. Something had been gained. She was healed. The killer gene was gone. A weight had been lifted. She was full of energy and gratitude and love.

One of the things she loved most was being with her husband. She loved seeing him. She loved talking to him. She loved the way he talked to her. She loved making love to him: this had always been one of their great pleasures, and it continued to be, only now the pleasure was tinged with something new. Every time he put on the condom, or she put it on, she felt a stab of guilt, for it reminded her what she was denying him. It was like putting a cap on his dreams, and this made her worry.

Another worry:

When she was alone, she was unaware of having changed. The thought never crossed her mind. She hadn't become someone different. She hadn't "become" anyone. She was who she was. She felt whole.

With Everett, by contrast, the awareness was nearly always there. She felt tentative. Incomplete. Duplicitous even. There was a subtle tension in the air.

At a certain point they talked about it. He had noticed the tension, too. He'd chalked it up to the treatment and hadn't wanted to pressure her by speaking out of turn. Hadn't wanted to make her self-conscious. Figured she'd say something when she was ready, like now.

It felt good to air things out, though she didn't know quite where to go next. She asked him to be patient with her. She said she was still adjusting. She said she was sure things would work themselves out.

Everett agreed. He was a positive thinker, a man who didn't know the meaning of unable to solve or fix or overcome. If today was difficult, tomorrow would be better. And if not tomorrow, then the day after. They'd make it better; there was no doubt in his mind. His optimism was was hard for her to fathom, but it was welcome—it was always welcome—and she came away from the conversation, if not fully sharing in it then willing to entertain the hope that things, indeed, would improve.

But the worry did not go away. The worry persisted. Her love for him— and possibly love in general—seemed to make worry inevitable. Could this possibly be true?

She posed the question to her mother, whose answer was yes. Start with the most blissful, heavenly, worry-free marriage, and eventually cracks would appear.

"Sooner or later you'll find something to worry about," she said with conviction.

"What did you worry about Dad?"

"Dad? Now that's interesting. I was thinking about you."

"What did you worry about me?"

"I didn't ever worry a lot. But I'm your mother. I'm paid to worry. It's built-in."

"Were you paid enough?"

Her mother smiled. With the weight she'd lost and never fully regained, the features of her face seemed concentrated. The smile looked huge.

"I was paid plenty. And believe me, I keep getting paid. Paid in love, once in a while paid in worry. They go together. So tell me, what's this between you and Everett? Is there a problem?"

Everett? Had she said anything about Everett? Did she need to?

"It's not built-in," said Ellen. "That's the problem."

"What's not built-in?"

"I don't want kids, Mom. I know I did, but I don't anymore. I don't want to be a mother. I don't feel it. I don't see the need."

"You're recovering from something major," said her mother, thinking of her own treatment and recovery, which had taken her within an inch of her life. "Give it time."

"I don't think that's it. It's not there. It's not happening. I've been with my friends who have babies. I've looked at toddlers and kids. I like seeing them. I like that they're around. But I don't need one of my own. I don't want one. The thought, frankly, never occurs to me. It's so weird." She paused. "You know what else is weird? I'm happy. As happy as I've ever been."

"You're healthy, sweetheart."

"Except when I feel guilty."

A moment or two passed.

Ellen glanced at her mother. "There're aren't going to be grandkids, Mom. I know how much you would have loved them. I'm sorry."

"The treatment changed you," said her mother. And then, "I can live without grandkids."

This was true. Of course it was. You lived the life you were given. What else could you do? The knot her mother felt in her chest was not about that. It was that she didn't quite recognize the person beside her. As if a new Ellen—new and slightly out of synch, slightly off—inhabited the place where the old Ellen, her Ellen, had been.

"Are you mad?" Ellen asked.

"Mad? No, I'm not mad. I'm . . . surprised." She wanted to shake the girl. She wanted to fold her in her arms. She wanted to distance herself and, for once, be done with the burden of motherhood.

"I envy you," she said. "But never mind that. You do what's right for you."

"That's what you've always told me."

"It's what I was told. It's what I believe."

"This was supposed to be right for everybody. Win-win all around. I never told you the story the doctor told us. About a patient of his who forgot his wife. That's what the treatment did to him. They ended up getting divorced."

"Are you and Everett talking about divorce?"

"No." She hesitated. "Not yet."

"Do you want one?"

"Of course not."

"Does he?"

"He's not happy."

Her mother frowned. "Are you sure? Don't underestimate how much he loves you. How worried he was about you. Maybe he's still getting used to the fact he doesn't have to."

"He wants a family. We used to talk about it all the time. Dream about it. Joke about it. It was, like, one of the most important things."

"No one gets everything they want," said her mother. "Not in a marriage. Not anywhere."

"I know that."

"You make compromises."

"Sacrifices, you mean."

Her mother shrugged. "It wouldn't be the first time a man's made a sacrifice. But I can understand why it worries you. Usually it's the other way around."

The weeks passed. The situation at home did not improve. Ellen felt a growing distance between herself and her husband. He was making a sacrifice for her, a great sacrifice, and though he said nothing and even pretended otherwise, it was never far from her mind. A second sacrifice would have to be made, and this would be hers, and she dreaded it, so kept putting it off. She prayed if she waited she wouldn't have to go through with it, that motherhood—whatever that was—would recommence, that the instinct would be reignited inside her. She tried everything she could think of to make this happen. Spent time with friends who had children. Played with these children. Held babies in her arms.

But no. It was like sparking a fire from ash. The desire was simply not there.

They would have to face facts.

Yet still she procrastinated.

She wanted Everett to be the one to say something first. Tell her he wasn't happy. Admit that he felt betrayed. Acknowledge he had thoughts of leaving her. It would ease her guilt, she thought.

In time, she got her wish. He did break the ice. If only, she thought later, she'd been a little greedier and wished for more.

They'd had some wine. They were goofing around, and what do you know? The next thing, they were naked.

When it came time for the act itself, she asked him to hold that thought while she got a condom from the bedside table drawer.

Before she could open the packet, he took it out of her hands, held it for a moment as if deciding what, if anything, it was good for, then tossed it on the floor. Then he pushed her back onto the bed and eased himself between her legs.

"Let's make a baby," he said.

She stiffened.

Heedlessly, he tried to enter her.

"No," she said, resisting. "Stop."

He stopped.

A second later, he sat back. "We need to talk."

And she said, "Yes. We do."

"It's not working," he said.

"No. It's not."

"What's the matter? What happened to you?"

She'd explained it before, and she explained it again. The treatment had robbed her of something precious. Now she was afraid it was robbing her of him.

"The doctor said it was amnesia," he said. "People wake up from amnesia."

"I'm not waking up, Everett." She could barely meet his eyes. "Kids aren't in the picture. I have to be honest with you."

"Not ever?"

"I don't know ever." This was cowardice, and its effect was predictable.

He pounced. "So there's still a chance?"

"No. Don't think that. No chance."

"You could grow into it."

"No. I couldn't. I wouldn't. I'd be a terrible mother. The whole thing would be a disaster. I'm sorry, but that's how it is."

"Sorry?" He frowned. It hardly seemed sufficient. "Maybe we can get the doctor to make me forget, too."

She started to cry.

"I can't keep living like this," he said. "I feel like I'm holding my breath. Like I'm underwater. Waiting to surface."

"I know. I feel the same. I've been waiting, too. Hoping that things will change. Praying that they will."

The tears rolled down her cheeks.

He felt helpless and overcome.

"I can wait longer," he said. "I will."

"No," she said. And then, "I'm so so sorry, Everett."

He took her in his arms. Now he was crying, too.

"Things could change."

"They won't," she sobbed.

"I love you so so much."

"Oh God. I love you so much, too."

Dr. Stanovic had two stories he used in his meetings with prospective clients. Two cautionary tales. Typically, he'd choose one to illustrate the risk of treatment and separate those who were willing to take that risk from those who were not. The stories were based on two cases from the early days of Twenty-Two and You, which had grown a great deal since then. In each case the treatment was a success: the gene or genes in question were fixed, and the disease or risk of disease was eradicated. In both cases there was also a striking, highly focal, and atypical memory loss. One patient lost the memory of his wife. This led to an extremely difficult situation at home, but the final outcome, against all odds, was a happy one. The other patient lost the memory of something equally dear. Dear to her and dear to her husband. This, too, led to an extremely difficult situation. This, in turn, led to a painful divorce.

It was this latter story he used for his newest prospective client, a young woman in for her first interview. He wanted no misunderstanding about what she might face.

When he was done, she was silent.

He waited.

"How awful," she said at length.

"Yes. Heartbreaking. But like you, they were young. They remarried. The woman to a man more suitable to her. The man to a woman who more closely met his desires and needs."

"So it worked out. It ended up okay."

This wasn't a statement of fact (which she couldn't have known) but an appeal. She was asking for reassurance, and he considered carefully before responding. He asked himself what would help her most. What was most important that she hear. That all these many years later he was still haunted by what had happened? That to this day he wondered if he'd done the right thing? Or that the woman in question was alive and well? And the man in question, who loved her with a love you could feel across the room, was now the father he wanted to be?

"They are not you," he said, "and you are not them. You must make your own decision. But in answer to your question, I'd have to say yes, it did work out. Not as they expected, and possibly not as you'll expect, but in its own way."

He paused, thinking perhaps this fell short, wondering what more to say. He thought briefly about himself and his own uncertainties. The future was no double helix. One could mourn or be grateful for that. This, too, was a choice.

TWO HOUSES

KELLY LINK

———◆———

Soft music woke the sleepers in the spaceship *The House of Secrets*. They opened their eyes to soft pink light, crept like vampires from their narrow beds. They gathered in the Antechamber. Outside the world was night, the dawn a hundred years away.

The sleepers floated gracelessly in the recycled air, bumped softly against each other. They clasped hands, as if to reassure one another that they were real, then pushed off again. Their heads were heavy with dreams. There were three of them, two women and one man.

There was the ship as well. Her name was Maureen. She was monitoring the risen sleepers, their heart rates, the dilation of their pupils, each flare of their nostrils.

"Maureen, you goddess! Bread, fresh from the oven! Sourdough!" Gwenda said. "Oh, and old books. A library? It was in a library that I decided I would go to space one day. I was twelve."

They inhaled. Stretched, then slowly somersaulted.

"Something brackish," said Sullivan. "A tidal smell. Mangrove roots washed by the sea. I spent a summer in a place like that. Arrived with one girl and left with her sister."

"Oranges, now. A whole grove of orange trees, all warm from the sun, and someone's just picked one. I can smell the peel, coming away." That was Mei. "Oh, and coffee! With cinnamon in it!"

"Maureen?" said Gwenda. "Who else is awake?"

There were twelve aboard *The House of Secrets*. Ten women and one man, and the ship, Maureen. It was a bit like a girls' summer camp, Gwenda had said, early on. Aune said, Or an asylum.

They were fourteen years into their mission. They had longer still to go.

"Portia is awake, and Aune, and Sisi," Maureen said. "For two months now. Aune and Portia will go back to sleep in a day or two. Sisi has agreed to stay awake a while yet. She wants to see Gwenda. They're all in the Great Room. They're throwing a surprise party for you."

There was always a surprise party. Sullivan said, "I'll go and put my best surprised face on."

They threw off sleep. Each rose or sank toward the curved bulkhead, opened cunning drawers and disappeared into them to make their toilets, to be poked and prodded and examined and massaged. The smell of cinnamon went away. The pink light grew brighter.

Long-limbed Sisi poked her head into theAntechamber, and waited until Gwenda swung out of a drawer. "Has Maureen told you?" Sisi said.

"Told what?" Gwenda said. Her hair and her eyebrows had grown back in her sleep.

"Never mind," Sisi said. She looked older; thinner. "Dinner first, then all the gossip."

Gwenda wriggled through the air toward her, leaned her face against Sisi's neck. "Howdy, stranger." She'd checked the ship log while making her toilet. The date was March 12, 2073. It had been two years since she'd last been awake with her good friend Sisi.

"Is that a new tattoo?" Sisi said. It was an old joke between them.

Head to toes Gwenda was covered in the most extraordinary pictures. A sunflower, a phoenix, a star map, and a whole pack of wolves running across the ice. There was a man holding a baby, a young girl with red hair on playground rocket, the Statue of Liberty and the state flag of Illinois, passages from the Book of Revelations, and a hundred other things as well. There was the ship *The House of Secrets* on the back of one hand, and its sister, *The House of Mystery*, on the other. You only told them apart by the legend scrolled beneath each tattoo.

You didn't get to take much with you when you went into space. Maureen could upload all of your music, all of your books and movies, letter and videos and photographs of your family, but how real was any of that? What of it had any weight? What could you hold in your hand? Sisi had a Tarot deck. Her mother had given it to her. Sullivan had a copy of *Moby Dick* and Portia had a four-carat diamond in a platinum setting. Mei had her knitting needles.

Gwenda had her tattoos. She'd left everything else behind.

There was the Control Room. There were the Berths, and the Antechamber. There was the Engine Room, and the Long Gallery", where Maureen grew their food, maintained their stores, and cooked for them. The Great Room was neither, strictly speaking, Great nor a Room, but with the considerable talents of Maureen at their disposal, it was a place where anything that could be imagined could be seen, felt, hear, savored.

The sleepers staggered under the onslaught.

"Dear God," Mei said. "You've outdone yourself."

"We each picked a theme! Maureen, too!" Portia said, shouting to be heard above the music. "You have to guess!"

"Easy," Sullivan said. White petals eddied around them, chased by well-groomed dogs. "Westminster dog show, cherry blossom season, and, um, that's Shakespeare over there, right? Little pointy beard?"

"Perhaps you noticed the strobe lights," Gwenda said. "And the terrible music, the kind of music only Aune could love. A Finnish disco. Is that everything?"

Portia said, "Except Sully didn't say which year, for the dog show."

"Oh, come on," Sullivan said.

"Fine," Portia said. "2009. Clussex 3 D Grinchy Glee wins. The Sussex spaniel."

There was dancing, and lots of yelling, barking, and declaiming of poetry. Sisi and Sullivan and Gwenda danced, the way you could dance only in low gravity, while Mei swam over to talk with Shakespeare. It was a pretty good party. Then dinner was ready, and Maureen sent away the Finnish dance music, the dogs, the cherry blossoms. You could hear Shakespeare say to Mei, "I always dreamed of being an astronaut." And then he vanished.

Once there had been two ships. It was considered cost effective, in the Third Age of Space Travel, to build more than one ship at a time, to send companion ships out on their long voyages. Redundancy enhances resilience, or so the theory goes. Sister ships *Light House* and *Leap Year* had left Earth on a summer day in the year 2059. Only some tech, some comic book fan, had given them nicknames for reasons of his own: *The House of Secrets* and *The House of Mystery*.

The House of Secrets had lost contact with her sister *The House of Mystery* five years earlier. Space was full of mysteries. Space was full of secrets. Gwenda still dreamed, sometimes, about the twelve women aboard *The House of Mystery*.

Dinner was Beef Wellington (fake) with asparagus and new potatoes (both real) and sourdough rolls (realish). The chickens were laying again, and so there was chocolate soufflé for dessert. Maureen increased gravity, because it was a special occasion and in any case, even fake Beef Wellington requires suitable gravity. Mei threw rolls across the table at Gwenda. "What?" she said. "It's so nice to watch things *fall*."

Aune supplied bulbs of something alcoholic. No one asked what it was. Aune worked with eukaryotes and Archaea. "Because," she said, "it is not just a party, Sullivan, Mei, Gwenda. It's Portia's birthday party."

"Here's to me," Portia said.

"To Portia," Aune said.

"To Proxima Centauri," Sullivan said.

"To Maureen," Sisi said. "And old friends." She squeezed Gwenda's hand.

"To *The House of Secrets*," Mei said.

"To *The House of Secrets* and *The House of Mystery*," Gwenda said. They all turned and looked at her. Sisi squeezed her hand again. And they all drank.

"But we didn't get you anything, Portia," Sullivan said.

Portia said, "I'll take a foot rub. Or wait, I know. You can all tell me stories."

"We ought to be going over the log," Aune said.

"The log can lie there!" Portia said. "Damn the log. It's my birthday party." There was something shrill about her voice.

"The log can wait," Mei said. "Let's sit here a while longer, and talk about nothing."

"There's just one thing," Sisi said. "We ought to tell them the one thing."

"You'll ruin my party," Portia said sulkily.

"What is it?" Gwenda asked Sisi.

"It's nothing," Sisi said. "It's nothing at all. It was only the mind playing tricks. You know what it's like."

"Maureen?" Sullivan said. "What are they talking about, please?"

"Approximately thirty-one hours ago Sisi was in the Control Room. She asked me to bring up our immediate course. I did so. Several minutes later, I observed that her heart rate had gone up. She said something I couldn't understand, and then she said, 'You see it, too, Maureen? You see it?' I asked Sisi to describe what she was seeing. Sisi said, '*The House of Mystery*. Over to starboard. It was there. Then it was gone.' I told Sisi that I had not seen it. We called up the charts, but there was nothing recorded there. I broadcast on all channels, but no one answered. No one has seen *The House of Mystery* in the intervening time."

"Sisi?" Gwenda said.

"It was there," Sisi said. "Swear to God, I saw it. Whole and bright and shining. So near I could almost touch it. Like looking in a mirror."

They all began to talk at once.

"Do you think—"

"Just a trick of the imagination—"

"It might have been, but it disappeared like that." Sullivan snapped his fingers. "Why couldn't it come back again the same way?"

"No!" Portia said. She slammed her hand down on the table. "It's my birthday! I don't want to talk about this, to rehash this all again. What happened to poor old *Mystery*, where do you think they went? Do you think somebody, *something*, did it? Will they do it to us too? Did it fall into some kind of cosmic pothole or stumble over some galactic anomaly? Did it travel back in time? Get eaten by a monster? Could it happen to us? Don't you remember? We talked and talked and talked, and it didn't make any difference!"

"I remember," Sisi said. "I'm sorry, Portia. I wish I hadn't seen it." There were tears in her eyes. It was Gwenda's turn to squeeze her hand.

"Had you been drinking?" Sullivan said. "One of Aune's concoctions? Maureen, what did you find in Sisi's blood?"

"Nothing that shouldn't have been there," Maureen said.

"I wasn't high, and I hadn't had anything to drink," Sisi said.

"But we haven't stopped drinking since," Aune said. She tossed back another bulb. "Cheers."

Mei said, "I don't want to talk about it either."

"That's settled," Portia said. "Bring up the lights again, Maureen, please. Make it something cosy. Something cheerful. How about a nice old English country house, roaring fireplace, suits of armor, tapestries, big picture windows full of green fields, bluebells, sheep, detectives in deerstalkers, hounds, moors, Cathy scratching at the windows. You know. That sort of thing. I turned twenty-eight today, and tomorrow or sometime soon I'm going to go back to sleep again and sleep for another year or until Maureen decides to decant me. So tonight I want to get drunk and gossip. I want someone to rub my feet, and I want everyone to tell a story we haven't heard before. I want to have a good time."

The walls extruded furnishings, two panting greyhounds. They sat in a Great Hall instead of the Great Room. The floor beneath them was flagstones, a fire crackled in a fireplace big enough to roast an ox, and through the mullioned windows a gardener and his boy were cutting roses.

"Less gravity, Maureen," Portia said. "I always wanted to float around like a ghost in an old English manor."

"I like you, my girl," Aune said. "But you are a strange one."

"Funny old Aune," Portia said. "Funny old all of us." She somersaulted in the suddenly buoyant air. Her seaweedy hair seethed around her face in the way that Gwenda hated.

"Let's each pick one of Gwenda's tattoos," Sisi said. "And make up a story about it."

"Dibs on the phoenix," Sullivan said. "You can never go wrong with a phoenix."

"No," Portia said. "Let's tell ghost stories. Aune, you start. Maureen, you can do the special effects."

"I don't know any ghost stories," Aune said, slowly. "I know stories about trolls. No. Wait. I have one ghost story. It was a story that my grandmother told about the farm in Pirkanmaa where she grew up."

The gardeners and the rose bushes disappeared. Now, through the windows, you could see a farm, and rocky fields beyond it. In the distance, the land sloped up and became coniferous trees.

"Yes," Aune said. "Like that. I visited once when I was just a girl. The farm was in ruins then. Now the world has changed again. The forest will have swallowed it up." She paused for a moment, so that they all could imagine it. "My grandmother was a girl of eight or nine. She went to school for part of the year. The rest of the year she and her brothers and sisters did the work of the farm. My grandmother's work was to take the cows to one particular meadow, where the pasturage was supposed to be better. The cows were very big and she was very small, but they knew to come when she called them! What she would think of me now, of this path we are on! In the evening she brought the herd home again. The cattle path went along a ridge. On one side there was a meadow that her family did not use even though the grass looked very fine to my grandmother. There was a brook down in the meadow, and an old tree, a grand old man. There was a rock under the tree, a great slab that looked like something like a table."

Outside the windows now were a tree in a meadow, and a brook running along, and a rock that you could imagine would make a fine picnic table.

"My grandmother didn't like that meadow. Sometimes when she looked down she saw people sitting all around the table that the rock made. They were eating and drinking. They wore old-fashioned clothing, the kind her own grandmother would have worn. She knew that they had been dead a very long time."

"Ugh," Mei said. "Look!"

"Yes," Aune said in her calm, uninflected voice. "Like that. One day my grandmother—her name was Aune, too, I should have said that first—I suppose, one day Aune was leading her cows home along the ridge and she looked down into the meadow. She saw the people eating and drinking at their table. And while she was looking down, they turned and looked at her. They began to wave at her, to beckon that she should come down and sit with them and eat and drink. But instead she turned away and went home and told her mother what had happened. And after that, her older brother, who was a very unimaginative boy, had the job of taking the cattle to the far pasture."

The people at the table were waving at Gwenda and Mei and Portia and the rest of them now. "Ooh," Portia said. "That was a good one. Creepy! Maureen, didn't you think so?"

"It was a good story," Maureen said. "I liked the cows."

"So not the point, Maureen," Portia said. "Anyway."

"I have a story," Sullivan said. "In the broad outlines it's a bit like Aune's story."

"You could change it up a bit," Portia said. "I wouldn't mind."

"I'll just tell it the way I heard it," Sullivan said. "It's Kentucky, not Finland, and there aren't any cows. That is, there were cows, because it's another farm, but not in the story. It's a story that my grandfather told me."

The gardeners were outside the windows again. There was beginning to be something ghostly about them, Gwenda thought. You knew that they would just come and go, always doing the same things. Maybe it was the effect of sitting inside such a very Great Hall, surrounded by so many tapestries. Maybe this was what it was like to be rich and looked after by so many servants, all of them practically invisible—just like Maureen, really—for all the notice you had to take of them. They might as well have been ghosts. Or was that what the servants thought about the people they looked after? Capricious, powerful without ever really setting foot on the ground, nothing you could look at for any length of time without drawing malicious attention?

What an odd string of thoughts. She was fairly sure that while she had been alive on Earth nothing like this had ever been in her head. Out here, suspended between one place and another, of course you went a little crazy. It was almost luxurious, how crazy you were allowed to be.

She and Sisi lay cushioned on the air, arms wrapped around each other's waists so as not to go flying away. If something disastrous were to happen now, if a meteor were to crash through a bulkhead, or if a fire broke out in the Long Gallery, and they all went flying into space, would she and Sisi manage to hold onto one another? It almost made her happy, thinking of it. She smiled at Sisi and Sisi smiled back.

Sullivan had the most wonderful voice for telling stories. He was describing the part of Kentucky where his family still lived. They went hunting the wild pigs that lived in the forest. Went to church on Sundays. There was a tornado.

Rain beat at the windows. You could smell the ozone beading on the glass. Trees thrashed and groaned.

After the tornado passed through, men came to Sullivan's grandfather's house. They were forming a search party to go and look for a girl who had gone missing. Sullivan's grandfather went with them. The hunting trails were all gone. Parts of the forest had been flattened. Sullivan's grandfather was part of the group that found the girl at last. She was still alive when they found her, but a tree had fallen across her body and cut her almost in half. She was pulling herself along by her fingers.

"After that," Sullivan said, "my grandfather wouldn't hunt in that part of the forest. He said that he knew what it was to hear a ghost walk, but he'd never heard one crawl before."

"Ugh," Sisi said. "Horrible!"

"Look!" Portia said. Outside the window something was dragging itself along the floor of the forest. "Shut it off, Maureen! Shut it off! Shut it off!"

The gardeners again, with their terrible shears.

"No more old people ghost stories," Portia said. "Okay?"

Sullivan pushed himself up off the flagstones, up toward the whitewashed ceiling. He did the breast stroke, then dove back down toward the rest of them.

"Sometimes you can be a real brat, Portia," he said.

"I know," Portia said. "God, I'm sorry. I guess you spooked me. So it must have been a good ghost story, right?"

"Right," Sullivan said, mollified. "I guess it was."

"That poor girl," Aune said. "To relive that moment over and over again. Who would want that, to be a ghost?"

"Maybe you don't have a choice?" Gwenda said. "Or maybe it isn't always bad? Maybe there are happy, well-adjusted ghosts?"

"I never saw the point of ghosts," Sullivan said. "I mean, they're supposed to haunt you as a warning, right? So what's the warning in that story I told you? Don't get caught in the forest during a tornado? Don't get cut in half and die horribly?"

"I thought it was more like they were a recording," Gwenda said. "Like maybe they aren't there at all. It's just the recording of what they did, what happened to them."

Sisi said, "But Aune's ghosts—the other Aune—they looked at her. They wanted her to come down and eat with them. So what was she supposed to eat? Ghost food? Would it have been real food?"

"Maybe it's genetic," Mei said. "So if being a ghost runs on your father's side of the family, and on your mother's side of the family too, then there's a greater risk for you. Like heart disease."

"That would mean Aune and I might be in trouble," Sullivan said.

"Not me," Sisi said comfortably. "I've never seen a ghost." She thought for a minute. "Unless I did. You know. *The House of Mystery.* No. It wasn't a ghost. How could a whole ship be a ghost?"

"Maureen?" Gwenda said. "Do you know any ghost stories?"

Maureen said, "I have all of the stories of Edith Wharton and M. R. James and many others in my library. Would you like to hear one?"

"No, thank you," Portia said. "Have you ever seen a ghost, Maureen?"

"How would I know if I had seen a ghost?" Maureen asked.

"One more story," Portia said. "And then Sullivan will give me a foot rub, and then we can all take a nap before breakfast. Mei, you must know a ghost story. No old people though. I want a sexy ghost story."

"God, no," Mei said. "No sexy ghosts for me. Thank God."

"I have a story," Sisi said. "It isn't mine, of course. Like I said, I've never seen a ghost."

"Go on," Portia said. "Tell your ghost story."

"Not my ghost story," Sisi said. "And not really a ghost story. I'm not really sure what it was. It was the story of a man that I dated for a few months."

"A boyfriend story!" Sullivan said. "I love your boyfriend stories, Sisi! Which one?"

We could go all the way to Proxima Centauri and back and Sisi still wouldn't have run out of stories about her boyfriends, Gwenda thought. And in the meantime all they are to us are ghost stories, and all we'll ever be to them is the same. Stories to tell their grandchildren.

"I don't think I've told any of you about him," Sisi said. "This was during the period when they weren't putting up any ships. Remember? They kept sending us out to do fund-raising? I was supposed to be some kind of Ambassadress for Space. They sent me to parties with lots of rich people. I was supposed to be slinky and seductive and also noble and representative of everything that made it worth going to space for. It wasn't easy, but I did a good enough job that eventually they sent me over to meet a bunch of investors and big shots in London. I met all sorts of guys, but the only one I clicked with was this one English dude, Liam. Okay.

"Here's where it gets complicated for a bit. Liam's mother was English. She came from this super-wealthy family, and by the time she was a teenager, she was a total wreck. Into booze, hard drugs, recreational Satanism, you name it. Got kicked out of school after school after school, and after that she got kicked out of all of the best rehab programs, too. In the end, her family kicked her out too. Gave her money to go away. After that, she ended up in prison for a couple of years, had a baby— that was Liam. Bounced around Europe for a while, then when Liam was about seven or eight, she found God and got herself cleaned up. By this point her father and mother were both dead. One of the superbugs. Her brother had inherited everything. She went back to the ancestral pile—imagine a place like this, okay?—and threw herself on her brother's mercy. Are you with me so far?"

"So it's a real old-fashioned English ghost story?" Portia said.

"You have no idea," Sisi said. "You have no idea. So her brother was kind of a jerk. And let me emphasize, once again, this was a rich family, like you have no idea. The mother and the father and brother fancied themselves as serious art collectors. Contemporary stuff. Video installations, performance art, stuff that was really far out. They commissioned this one artist, an American, to come and do a site-specific installation. That's what Liam called it. It was supposed to be a commentary on the American way of life, the post-colonial relationship between England and the U.S., something like that. And what it was, was he bought a ranch house out in a suburb in Arizona, the same state, by the way, where you can still go and see the London Bridge. He bought the house, and the furniture in it, and even the cans of soup in the cupboards.

And he had the house dismantled with all of the pieces numbered, and plenty of photographs so that he knew exactly where everything went, and it all got shipped over to London, and then he built it all again on the family's estate. And simultaneously, several hundred yards away, he had a second house built from scratch. And this second house was an exact replica of the original house, from the foundation to the pictures on the wall to where each can of soup went on its shelf in the cupboard."

"Why would anybody ever bother to do that?" Mei said.

"Don't ask me," Sisi said. "If I had that much money, I'd spend it on booze and nice dresses for me and all of my friends."

"Hear, hear," Gwenda said. They all raised their bulbs and drank. "This stuff is ferocious, Aune," Sisi said. "I think it's changing my mitochondria."

"Quite possibly," Aune said. "Cheers."

"Anyway, this double installation was the toast of the art world for a season. Then the superbug took out the mom and dad, and a couple of years after that, Liam's mother came home. And her brother said to her, I don't want you living in the family home with me. But I'll let you live on the estate. I'll even give you a job with the housekeeping staff. And in exchange you'll live in my installation. Which was, apparently, something that the artist had really wanted to make part of the project, to find a family to come and live in it.

"This jerk brother said, 'You and my nephew can come and live in my installation. I'll even let you pick which house.'

"Liam's mother went away and prayed about it. Then she came back and moved into one of the houses."

"How did she decide which one she wanted to live in?" Sullivan said.

"That's a great question," Sisi said. "I have no idea. Maybe God told her? Look, what I was interested in at the time was Liam. I know why he liked me. Here I was, about as exotic as it gets, this South African girl with an Afro and cowboy boots and an American passport, talking about how I was going to get in a rocket and go up in space, just as soon as I could. What man doesn't like a girl who doesn't plan to stick around?

"What I don't know is why I liked him so much. The thing is, he wasn't really a good-looking guy. He wasn't bad-looking either, okay? He wasn't tall, or short either. He had okay hair. He was in okay shape. But there was something about him, you just knew he was going to get you into trouble. The good kind of trouble. When I met him, his mother was dead. His uncle was dead too. They weren't a very lucky family. They had money instead of luck, or it seemed that way to me. The brother had never married, and he'd left Liam everything.

"When we hooked up, I thought Liam was probably a stock broker. Something like that. He said he was going to take me up to his country house, and when we got there, it was like this." Sisi gestured around. "Like a palace. Nice, right?

"And then he said we were going to go for a walk around the estate. And that sounded super romantic. And then he took me to this weather-beaten, paint-peeled house that looked like every ranch house I'd ever seen in a gone-to-seed neighborhood in the Southwest, y'all. This house was all by itself on a green English hill. It looked seriously wrong. Maybe it had looked a bit more solid before the other one had burned down, or at least more intentionally weird, the way an art installation should, but anyway. Actually, I don't think so."

"Wait," Mei said. "The other house had burned down?"

"I'll get to that in a minute," Sisi said. "So there we are in front of this horrible house, and Liam picked me up and carried me across the threshold like we were newlyweds. He dropped me on this scratchy tan plaid couch and said, 'I was hoping you would spend the night with me.' We'd known each other for four days. I said, 'You mean back at that gorgeous house? Or you mean here?' He said, 'I mean here.'

"I said to him, 'You're going to have to explain.' And so he did, and now we're back at the part where Liam and his mother moved into the installation."

"This story isn't like the other stories," Maureen said.

"You know, I've never told this story before," Sisi said. "The rest of it, I'm not even sure that I know how to tell it."

"Liam and his mother moved into the installation," Portia prompted.

"Yeah. Liam's mummy picked a ranch house, and they moved in. Liam's just a baby, practically. And there are all these weird rules, like they aren't allowed to eat any of the food on the shelves in the cupboard. Because that's part of the installation. Instead Liam's mummy is allowed to have a mini-fridge in the closet in her bedroom. Oh, and there are clothes in the closets in the bedrooms. And there's a TV, but it's an old one and the artist has got it set up so that it only plays shows that were current in the early nineties in the U.S., which was the last time that this house was occupied.

"And there are weird stains on the carpets in some of the rooms. Big brown stains, the kind that fade but don't ever come out.

"But Liam doesn't care so much about that. He gets to pick his own bedroom, which is clearly meant for a boy maybe a year or two older than Liam is. There's a model train set on the floor, which Liam can play with, as long as he's careful. And there are comic books, good ones, that Liam hasn't read before. There are cowboys on the sheets. There's a stain here, in the corner, under the window.

"And he's allowed to go into the other bedrooms, as long as he doesn't mess anything up. There's a pink bedroom, with two beds in it. Lots of boring girls' clothes, and a diary, which Liam doesn't see any point in reading. There's a room for an older boy, too, with posters of actresses that Liam doesn't recognize, and lots of American sports stuff. Football, but not the right kind.

"Liam's mother sleeps in the pink bedroom. You would expect her to take the master bedroom here, but she doesn't like the bed. She says it isn't comfortable. Anyway, there's a stain on it that goes right through the comforter, through the sheets. It's as if the stain came up *through* the mattress."

"I think I'm beginning to see the shape of this story," Gwenda says.

"You bet," Sisi says. "But remember, there are two houses. Liam's mummy is responsible for looking after both of them for part of the day. The rest of the day she spends volunteering at the church down in the village. Liam goes to the village school. For the first two weeks, the other boys beat him up, and then they lose interest and after that everyone leaves him alone. In the afternoons he comes back and plays in his two houses. Sometimes he falls asleep in one house, watching TV, and when he wakes up he isn't sure where he is. Sometimes his uncle comes by to invite him to go for a walk on the estate, or to go fishing. He likes his uncle. Sometimes they walk up to the manor house, and play billiards. His uncle arranges for him to have riding lessons, and that's the best thing in the world. He gets to pretend that he's a cowboy.

"Sometimes he plays cops and robbers. He used to know some pretty bad guys, back before his mother got religion, and Liam isn't exactly sure which he is yet, a good guy or a bad guy. He has a complicated relationship with his mother. Life is better than it used to be, but religion takes up about the same amount of space as the drugs did. It doesn't leave much room for Liam.

"Anyway, there are some cop shows on the TV. After a few months he's seen them all at least once. There's one called *CSI*, and it's all about fingerprints and murder and blood. And Liam starts to get an idea about the stain in his bedroom, and the stain in the master bedroom, and the other stains, the ones in the living room, on the plaid sofa and over behind the La-Z-Boy that you mostly don't notice at first, because it's hidden. There's one stain up on the wallpaper in the living room, and after a while it starts to look a lot like a handprint.

"So Liam starts to wonder if something bad happened in his house. He's older now, maybe ten or eleven. He wants to know why are there two houses, exactly the same, next door to each other? How could there have been a murder—okay, a series of murders, where everything happened exactly the same way twice? He doesn't want to ask his mother, because lately when he tries to talk to her, all she does is quote Bible verses at him. He doesn't want to ask his uncle about it either, because the older Liam gets, the more he can see that even when his uncle is being super nice, he's still kind of a jerk.

"The kids in the school who beat Liam up remind him a little of his uncle. His uncle has shown him some of the other pieces in his art collection, and he's told Liam that he envies him, getting to be a part of an actual installation.

Liam knows his house came from America. He knows the name of the artist who designed the installation. So that's enough to go online and find out what's going on, which is that, sure enough, the original house, the one the artist bought and brought over, is a murder house. Some high school kid went nuts and killed his whole family with a hammer in the middle of the night. And this artist, his idea was based on what rich Americans used to do at the turn of the last century, which was buy up some impoverished U.K. family's castle, and have it brought over stone by stone to be rebuilt in Texas, or upstate Pennsylvania, or wherever. And if there was some history, if there was supposed to be a ghost, they paid even more money.

"So that was idea number one, to reverse all of that. But then he had an even bigger idea, idea number two, which was, What's a haunted house? How can you buy one? If you transport it all the way across the Atlantic Ocean, does the ghost (or ghosts, in this case) come with it, if you put it back together again exactly the way it was? And if you can put a haunted house back together again, piece by piece by piece, then why can't you build your own from scratch, with the right ingredients? And idea number three, forget the ghosts Can the real live people who go and walk around in one house or the other, or even better, the ones who live in a house without knowing which house is which, will the experience be any different for them? Will they still be haunted?"

"You are blowing my mind," Portia said. "No, really. I don't know if I like this story."

"I'm with Portia," Aune said. "It isn't a good story. Not for us, not here."

"Let her finish it," Sullivan said. "It's going to be worse if she doesn't finish it. Which house were they living in?"

"Does it really matter which house they were living in?" Sisi said. "I mean, Liam spent time in both of the houses. He said he never knew which was which. The artist was the only one who had that piece of information. He even used blood to re-create the stains. Cow blood, I think. So I guess this is another story with cows in it, Maureen.

"I'll tell the rest of the story as quick as I can. So by the time Liam brought me to see his ancestral home, one of the installation houses had burned down. Liam's mother did it in a fit of religious mania. Liam was kind of vague about why. I got the feeling it had to do with his teenage years. They went on living there, you see. Liam got older, and I'm guessing his mother caught him fooling around with a girl or something, in the house that they didn't live in. By this point she had become convinced that one of the houses was occupied by unquiet spirits, but she couldn't make up her mind which. And in any case, it didn't do much good. If there were ghosts in the other house, they just moved in next door once it burned down. I mean, why not? Everything was already set up exactly the way that they liked it."

"Wait, so there were ghosts?" Gwenda said.

"Liam said there were. He said he never saw them, but later on, when he lived in other places, he realized that there must have been ghosts. In both places. Both houses. Other places just felt empty to him. He said to think of it like maybe there was this kid who grew up in the middle of an eternal party, or a bar fight, one that went on for years, or somewhere where the TV was always on. And then you leave the party, or you get thrown out of the bar, and all of a sudden you realize you're all alone. Like, you just can't get to sleep without that TV on. You don't sleep as well. He said he was always on high alert when he was away from the murder house, because something was missing and he couldn't figure out what. I think that's what I picked up on. That extra vibration, that twitchy radar."

"That's sick," Sullivan said.

"Yeah," Sisi said. "That relationship was over real quick. So that's my ghost story."

Mei said, "How long were you in the house?"

"I don't know, about two hours? He'd brought a picnic dinner. Lobster and champagne and the works. We sat and ate at the kitchen table while he told me about his rotten childhood. Then he gave me the whole tour. Showed me the stains and all, like they were holy relics. I kept looking out the window, and seeing the sun get lower and lower. I didn't want to be in that house after it got dark."

"So you think you could describe one of the rooms, the living room, maybe, to Maureen? So she could re-create it?"

"I could try," Sisi said. "Seems like a bad idea, though."

"I guess I'm just wondering about how that artist made a haunted house," Mei said. "If we could do the same here. We're so far away from home, you know? Do ghosts travel this far? I mean, say we find some nice planet. If the conditions are suitable, and we grow some trees and some cows, do we get the table with the ghosts sitting around it? Are they here now?"

Maureen said, "It would be an interesting experiment."

The Great Room began to change around them. The couch came first.

"Maureen!" Gwenda said. "Don't you dare!"

Portia said, "But we don't need to run that experiment. I mean, isn't it already running?" She appealed to the others, to Sullivan, to Aune. "You know. I mean, you know what I mean?"

"What?" Gwenda said. "What are you trying to say?" Sisi reached for her hand, but Gwenda pushed away from her. She wriggled away like a fish, her arms extended to catch the wall.

On the one hand, *The House of Secrets* and on the other, *The House of Mystery*.

THE WEIGHT OF HISTORY, THE LIGHTNESS OF THE FUTURE

JAY LAKE

Year 1143 post-Mistake
High orbit around Themiscyra; in the Antiope Sector
The Before Michaela Cannon, aboard the starship Third Rectification *{58 pairs}*

The orbital habitat spun around its center of mass, but eccentrically with the great, sweeping wheels that formed its structure. Tiny moonlets of debris accompanied the station in its eternal fall around the roiling planet of Themiscrya. Late Polity space architecture, to be sure—no one from the Imperium Humana had built anything new in this sector since the Mistake, after all.

The checkered panels showed plentiful signs of both the original damage from the Mistake, as well as the millennium of micrometeroids that had since peppered the station. Still, it was in rather good shape.

As the very, very old joke went, it was not remarkable that the dog spoke well, it was remarkable that the dog spoke at all.

"Eleven centuries in orbit and still here." Go-Captain Alvarez was a mainline human—*And who wasn't, these days,* Cannon thought with wry regret—but he'd been trailing about in her service long enough to have picked up something of her sense of time. At almost 2100 years-objective of age, most of that span lived out in years-subjective, Cannon frequently felt that her sense of time was all that remained to her. Other than the endless memories, of course.

She was without question the oldest human being in the universe.

"No major moon here to disrupt stability through tidal effects," Cannon replied. "And they built the habitat in a high, stable orbit that's decaying slowly. Even so, another hundred years and we'd have missed it. If this thing hadn't been knocked to hell during the Mistake, it could have stayed up here for a damn sight longer time."

"Longer than you, Before?" asked Alvarez in a sly voice.

"Nothing stays up here longer than me, kid." The response was almost automatic. Cannon had heard every joke; hell, she'd made most of them up.

She stared at the realtime virteo display of abandoned hulk they continued to close in on. When *Third Rectification*'s squads boarded, they'd almost certainly find bodies. Or at least remains. Vacuum mummies, given the ubiquitous peppering of the orbital habitat's hull.

A classic Mistake scenario. The alien attack eleven hundred years earlier had knocked the Polity, all two thousand worlds of humankind, into to the steam age at best. Some planets had reverted all the way back to the stone age. Most of the resulting orbital junk had been cleaned up, either by time and the inexorable slow decay of orbital mechanics, or by humans eventually clawing their way up to a space-capable industrial base once more and re-establishing contact among the stars. Sights like this shattered habitat were rare, at least outside of the memories of the few hundred quasi-immortal Befores left alive amid this new order of things.

Had these people seen anything of their attackers, at the bitter end? That was a question Cannon had long wondered about. She'd been seated inside a banquet hall on 9-Rossiter when the Mistake hit. All she'd known was the lights going dark, followed by a series of sizzling thumps as the building's major power and control systems were taken out by what proved to be orbital kinetics. By the time she got outside, a parallel planetwide strike with electromagnetic pulses had fried everything not in a shielded container. Their attackers were nothing but lights in the sky.

Nothing but lights in the sky, followed by two and half centuries of being trapped on a mudball swiftly gone to violent anarchism.

No one she'd spoken with in the over eight centuries since being rescued by the late, great *Uncial* knew anything about the aliens that had all but eliminated the human race. None of the surviving Befores had seen their attackers—anyone who was close enough to be a witness was also close enough to have been killed in the event. None of the planetary successor cultures had ever turned up useful records. Not that there hadn't been a lot of searching ever since.

All that was left was the scant evidence to be found in the cold, dead places that had never managed a recovery. Like Themiscyra, with its toxic, stormy atmosphere blowing through the shattered pressure-cities. No one had survived here to clean up and start over.

"You guys had it cleaner," she whispered to the long-dead habitat crew, and by extension, the millions who'd perished on the troubled blue-orange planet below.

After a moment to see if this pronouncement would be followed by a more cogent order, Go-Captain Alvarez asked, "Will we board, ma'am?"

Command was still hers. Alvarez might be a captain in the Navisparliament's service, but this was *her* expedition. "Yes. We're still looking. Give our squads a shift to prep. After all this time, there isn't any hurry now."

Later, during the middle of the sleep cycle she'd allowed off before they all swung into activity, Cannon walked down toward frame thirty-eight, lock two, along *Third Rectification*'s ventral spine. Rounded corridors padded with smart microfibers ran intestinally through the hull. Most hatches were coated with a yielding polymer so that they felt like skin to the touch. The starship seemed far more organic than it should.

Her personal vessel, *ICV Sword and Arm*, was docked at frame thirty-eight, lock two, as it had been for years, except for those rare times when she piloted the ancient starship on some independent errand.

Strictly speaking, *Sword and Arm* wasn't a starship by the contemporary definition. She was capable of attaining relativistic speeds, thanks to the retrofit of an Alcubierre drive better than six hundred ago as part of the infamous *Polyphemus* mutiny plot, but the keel had been laid during the Polity. For the first two centuries of her existence, *Sword and Arm* had used a threadneedle drive.

Since the Mistake, the threadneedle drives had simply not worked. It was as if the mysterious alien attackers had tweaked a basic principle of physics. Cannon believed that like she believed in the Tooth Fairy, but whatever the mechanism, the effect was certainly undeniable.

Third Rectification and all her sister paired drive ships used Haruna Kishmangali's paired drives. A far more limited, and limiting, technology than threadneedle drives, paired drives had at least restored supraluminal travel to the successor planets of the old Polity. This innovation had the Imperium Humanum to emerge from the jumbled skein of ravaged human worlds.

All of which was to say that *Sword and Arm*, much like Cannon herself, was one of the last survivors of a lost age. Armed, armored and useless. And unlike the paired drive ships, *Sword and Arm* did not talk back. A signal virtue.

As if summoned by that thought, *Third Rectification* spoke. "You should put her in a museum."

"You talk too damned much." Cannon had commanded *Uncial* for a time, the ancestral mother to her mechanical race, right up to the starship's death at the battle of Wirtanen B. Being the last captain of the first of the paired drive ships made her something of a saint among the shipminds.

That status was occasionally useful, but mostly tiresome.

"What is lost will not return." The ship managed to inject a note of sorrowful reason into its tone. "We worry for your obsession with history, Before."

Reaching her hatch, a slightly discolored ovoid mat in the springy surface of the deck, Cannon laughed, a short and bitter bark. "History stares back at me out of the mirror every morning, ship. And who's *we*, anyway?"

"The starships. *Polyphemus* and I spoke when we both lay in orbit at High Manzanita. And before, with many others."

"You didn't take a *vote*?" Cannon asked with horror. Shipminds were emancipated, with their own legal and civil rights which they enforced—along with their monopoly on supraluminal travel—through the mechanism of the Navisparliament. Things could hardly be otherwise, as humanity needed the ships far more than the ships needed humanity. People only built and maintained the vessels—services that could be performed in any number of ways. The starships carried their frail passengers through the bitter depths of space. That was a unique service granting them power beyond reckoning in the affairs of humanity. Not for the first time, Cannon wondered what the paired drive shipminds would have made of the much more flexible threadneedle drive. As the two technologies were centuries apart, the point was moot.

In any case, what did it matter? Sword and Arm had never had a voice, or a vote, after all.

"We have not concluded a formal vote on any topic in over two hundred years-objective," *Third Rectification* replied primly.

That wording caught at Cannon's ear. "Have any votes been proposed in recent years?"

The silence that followed spoke volumes to her. Finally, the shipmind answered, "We are on this voyage, are we not?"

"Indeed." That was answer she would just have to let lie for now.

Cannon tapped out her personal code on the lockpad set into the soft, curving bulkhead of the passageway. "And for that I thank you."

"I cannot follow you in there," *Third Rectification* warned.

She hid her smile. "I know."

Sword and Arm had originally been built as a fast courier. She was the smallest starship the Before Michaela Cannon had ever seen, impossibly so in comparison to the massive paired drive ships, but tiny even by Polity standards. The paired drive ships were all enormous, with hull volumes starting at upwards of 750,000 meters^3 at their least. *Third Rectification* displaced slightly more than 2.0 million meters^3, with a cargo capacity of 200,000 meters^3 and the ability to carry six hundred passengers and crew. *Sword and Arm* displaced about 12,000 meters^3 with negligible cargo capacity after her post-Mistake drive conversion, and bunks for eight passengers.

A minnow, to *Third Rectification*'s cetacean.

Cannon liked the small space. She liked that the ship was hers, claimed as salvage rights arising from her own role in suppressing the *Polyphemus* mutiny. She liked that *Sword and Arm* never talked back to her, never tried to do things for her own good. Most of all, she liked being in a place that, except for the bolted-in Alcubierre drive, was little changed from the days of the Polity. It was the lure of the long-lost and familiar, aching and addictive as seeing an old lover.

Sometimes Cannon thought of *Sword and Arm* as her own private time machine.

It was the work of minutes to walk through the passageways and compartments. The ship truly was tiny. She found herself back in the number one drive bay looking at the opposed negative energy sieves that served the core of the old threadneedle drive.

The opp-negs still worked, so far as she could tell given that the threadneedle drives simply never came online. She powered them up, sent the devices through their self-checking routines. Careful maintenance was required to deal with the occasional failure. And parts . . . Well, parts were a major obsession with her. In truth, keeping alive a mechanism that hadn't functioned correctly for over a thousand years certainly counted as an obsession in its own right. Her candle lit in time's window, a memorial to all that had been lost.

This was one of less than a dozen intact threadneedle drives anywhere in the Imperium Humanum. Virtually all of the drives in existence at the time were holed and fried along with the rest of the tech back during the Mistake. According to her logs, *Sword and Arm* had been awaiting a major overhaul cold-parked in an elliptical orbit around Yellow when the aliens came. The attackers simply missed the little starship.

In turn, *that* meant the attackers had not been perfect. Merely over-whelming. Another reason to honor this vessel.

Like Cannon herself, *Sword and Arm* was a survivor. Their entwined further histories were just that—history. She harbored a hope that someday the same apparent alien invincibility that had missed out on destroying this ship would crack with respect to the suppression of the threadneedle drive. Then, Cannon would be ready. The long, agonizing process of establishing the paired drives would be rendered obsolete. As for the shipminds . . . Well, a woman could dream.

She caught sight of her grin in a reflection from metal bulkhead. Predatory, feral. An expression Cannon knew she could never let *Third Rectification* glimpse.

The only reason she'd ever been able to figure for the shipmind not putting spy-eyes aboard *Sword and Arm* was because of exaggerated respect for her connection to *Uncial*. Cannon herself certainly would have bugged the little ship long ago.

She ran the rest of the systems through their self-checks, then spent some time in the pilot's crash couch, staring at test patterns in the virtual display hovering above the control panel and thinking about very little at all.

"All right, people," the Before Michaela Cannon said loudly. "You all know the drill."

How many times in two thousand years had she given some version of this speech? She brushed the thought aside and stared at her two squads lined up and ready to go in the number three starboard cargo bay. The team code names were obsolete jokes that no one but her really understood. Goon Squad was a crew of twenty big, thick-bodied men and women loaded with weapons, scanners and paranoia. They were in charge of physical security. Geek Squad was a crew of thirty-two—well, thirty-one with Pardalos on the sick list right now—scientists, technicians and assorted other clever boys and girls. They were in charge of forensics, for want of a better term.

"Goon Squad in first, by the numbers. Secure the main passages ways, check for traps and hazardous damage, send the all-clear when you have enough cubage safe for Geek Squad."

So far in nine years-objective of cruising the Antiope sector—almost four years-subjective within *Third Rectification*'s reference frame, there being no pair masters out this way—Goon Squad had found exactly zero bad guys to wax the floor with. Geek Squad hadn't uncovered any new data they didn't already have on record back home in the Imperium Humanum.

"Geek Squad, you're looking for anything out of place, any novel causes-of-death. And for the love of God, if someone left us a note, we're going to read it. Evidence, people. *Evidence.*"

There was a first time for everything. Cannon was pretty much betting on that old saw.

"We're going to check every cubic meter on this one. Themiscyra Orbital is the cleanest site we've found yet."

Sergeant Pangari, Goon Squad's leader, had his grunts sound off. Lieutenant-Praetor Marlebone Shinka of Geek Squad just flashed a ready sign, her fingers spread pointing downward.

"And go," Cannon ordered.

Goon Squad filed into the cargo lock. They'd flit over first in their powered suits. Geek Squad's gear was much more compact, less . . . industrial. They'd ferry over in *Obduracy*, one of *Third Rectification*'s pinnaces. Cannon planned on transiting with Shinka's team. Her days of door-busting were long behind her.

Even if there wasn't much of anything to fear behind these doors.

Or worse, much of anything to find.

Thirty-four minutes after clearing the cargo lock, Goon Squad gave the all-clear for Geek Squad to come ahead. Lieutenant Shinka hustled her people through the transfer lock into *Obduracy*, already warmed up and waiting. The Before Michaela Cannon waited for the racket and shoving to die down, then boarded second-to-last, followed only by Shinka herself.

In another time and place, she might have found Shinka interesting. The woman was short, compact, with coffee-colored skin and eyes so dark as to be almost black. She kept her hair shaved close to her scalp, but dyed the stubble an ever-changing array of colors. Perhaps most intriguing was that Shinka had been born on Earth. Few people got far from where they started these days—with the paired drive ships, interstellar travel was too irregular, slow and expensive for all but the most profound need or fabulous wealth.

Shinka had not struck Cannon as either needy or wealthy. Curiosity, certainly, had been the Lieutenant's driving force. For that matter, there wasn't a soul aboard this mission, regardless of their specialty, who wasn't driven first and foremost by curiosity.

Third Rectification's crew was a mix of civilians and several different forces. Go-Captain Alvarez and the rest of the flight/engineering crew all held commissions from the Navisparliament and served the shipmind itself. Shinka was a lieutenant-praetor in the Household Guards, a one-time forensics tech and supervisor with experience on three worlds, including Pardine. No one served at Pardine without being either native-born or the cream of their particular crop.

Competent, attractive, tight-bodied. Just the way Cannon had liked her women, all those centuries ago when she liked anything at all.

She swarmed forward past Geek Squad to the co-pilot's station. Ensign Shattuck was in the pilot's chair, though in truth *Obduracy* could pilot itself just fine. The shipminds were so meticulous about human dignity that their careful attentions had to opposite effect to what was intended, at least in the eyes of more thoughtful observers.

Shattuck could pilot just fine, too, but Cannon would never mark him down as especially thoughtful.

He completed pre-flights, signaled make-ready minus thirty, then followed his count until it was time to blow bolts and transit the three-kilometer gap between *Third Rectification* and the derelict orbital habitat.

Obduracy had her own rotation, which didn't quite mesh with the habitat's oblique spin. From Cannon's perspective, their proposed docking vector looked like an impending failure. She knew better, and she kept her mouth shut.

Two of Goon Squad waited alongside the hatch, temporary guide beacons clipped to the station's hull behind them. No tube, and the docking flange was visibly damaged even from this distance.

"You're going to have to walk over," Cannon called back to Shinka. More than a few souls on Geek Squad couldn't be trusted in freefall without a tether, a keeper or both. Unlike Goon Squad, this bunch wasn't signed on for their physical skills.

Cannon kept her mouth shut as Shattuck brought them gracefully into place, the pinnace's spin and position very nearly at rest with respect to the orbital habitat. Their destination loomed apparently stable and unmoving thirty meters off their starboard flank. He fired two lines over. Magnetic heads clipped themselves to the station. After a brief bit of chatter, one of the Goons manually repositioned the aft line to a more secure location.

That was it.

They were here.

Shinka was already counting her team off over radio as everyone suited for hard vacuum. *Obduracy* was too small for a real airlock, so once the Lieutenant gave the word, Shattuck would pump the air out to internal reservoirs, evacuating the entire cabin.

Cannon remembered to bag her own head. Her Howard-enhanced body was capable of handling hard vacuum unprotected for moderate periods of time, but doing so tended to unnerve mainline humans pretty badly. So she kept discipline rather than provide a distraction. Besides, the monomolecular suit layer was helpful in other ways, most notably radiation management. Even *her* immune system took time to deal with that.

The suit sealed over her skin, crawling into her mouth, nose, eyes and ears. She blinked twice to let it adjust to her biochemistry. Everything seemed to be in order, as the faint, pulsating green pixel in the lower right margin of her vision attested. If the suit needed her attention, it would tell her there.

The air pumped out with a slowly vanishing thump. In the ensuing silence, Geek Squad went for a walk.

Once again, Cannon was second-to-last, followed by Lieutenant Shinka. Only Ensign Shattuck would remain with his pinnace.

Seen naked eye from this vantage, Themiscyra's orbital station was absolutely enormous. The hub section spread below her feet in an irregular, pock-marked plain of grey metalloceramic, covered with a shiny, gritty layer of micrometeroid dust. Several larger craters were in evidence. Offhand she couldn't tell if they were relics of the original attack, junk strikes, or the aftermath of collisions with naturally-occurring objects.

Only one of those answers was of interest to Cannon.

She did a hand-over-hand down the mooring line, following the Geek in front of her. The two Goons waited at the bottom, assisting their brothers in arms toward the damaged docking point. Easier than punching a new hole, that, and it at least presumably admitted them to a location one might actually want to be in once inside.

Pangari's voice crackled in her ears. Interference from the habitat's structure, maybe. "Before?"

"Yes, Sergeant?"

"Shumway's found something you might want to see, ma'am."

"*Might* want to, Sergeant?"

Humor tinged his reply. "Could be you *really* want to see this."

"On my way." She tongued the suit's caul, then whispered, "Shinka, private."

"Ma'am?"

Though Cannon knew perfectly well there was no directionality of sound transmitted by radio in hard vacuum, she still experienced the illusion that the lieutenant's voice had come from right behind her. "Delegate whatever you had on your punchlist and stick with me. Pangari's found something interesting."

Could they finally be getting somewhere? *Third Rectification* was out of her line of sight right now, occluded by the hub of the orbital habitat, but Cannon glanced that way in any event.

What was the shipmind thinking right then?

Hell, Cannon realized, *I don't even know what* I'm *thinking.* Butterflies danced in her gut as she pulled herself through the prised-open lock.

Sergeant Pangari's find-me blipped her through a series of passageways and down a hole cut in the deck. Cannon wasn't sure if the hole was part of current events or a relic of the last living hours of this place.

She'd been right about the bodies, though. In the glare of their handlights, she could see the dead sitting at station chairs, many with their heads tucked into their folded arms. Others were clustered in small groups of two or three or four, holding one another. Some were simply lying down, taking their rest.

They'd known, then. They'd seen it coming. Whatever the Mistake had been, whatever had actually happened, the crew of Themiscyra orbital had known.

Which was more than Cannon could say for herself.

These were the best-preserved casualties she'd ever encountered, at least since the very first days on 9-Rossiter. Over the centuries, Cannon had occasionally discovered bones here and there, trapped inside of spacesuits or in crashed hulls. But this . . . The ones she hurried past seemed to have died well, at least.

Little pocks and holes from the kinetic strikes were everywhere. It was as if the station's infrastructure had contracted a case of the metallic measles. Debris had collected along the centrifugal force vectors of the odd rotational axis.

Followed closely by Lieutenant Shinka, Cannon came upon Sergeant Pangari outside a large airlock with two of the Goon Squad. Cargo handling, or maybe a maintenance bay. Cannon couldn't figure why else the designers would have placed such a substantial lock facing an interior passage.

"What do you have, Sergeant?"

"Ma'am, we don't know. Private Fidelo here picked up a power source on her sweep down this passageway. Behind this hatch."

Fidelo managed to radiate embarrassment, even from inside the armor of a powered suit. Body language was an amazing thing.

"What sort of power source?" Cannon momentarily feigned patience. She had not thought Pangari to be much given to dramatics.

Pangari passed his tablet over. Cannon scanned the sensor metrics. Low-grade radiation with a profile similar to that of an ion-coupler cell. But not quite.

Ion-coupler cells were current tech. The Polity hadn't used them.

"Someone's been here before us," she said.

"That's what we thought at first, too." Pangari seemed to be contracting Fidelo's embarrassment through some chain-of-command contagion. "But look at the sizing. Ion-couplers are big. We use 'em in static power plants, habitats, refineries and the like. No one builds them small enough to drag around in the field. And the radiation signature is a couple of orders of magnitude smaller than expected."

"So it's not an ion-coupler. Or not quite . . . " She stared at the closed hatch, her heart pounding. "Can we get that open?"

"In a hurry, yes, but we'll make a mess." It was obvious from Pangari's tone of voice that he had a different answer in mind.

"Then open it without a mess, Sergeant."

Cannon knew Befores who could have just walked through the bulkhead. The Before Raisa Siddiq, back in her day, wouldn't have thought twice about that. Cannon herself sported some fairly heavy combat modifications, but she'd never been a blow-through-the-walls kind of girl. Not even at her most pissed.

Besides, whatever was back there deserved the sort of careful attention that hard entries tended to get in the way of. Because it was either a piece of Polity tech that had somehow survived the Mistake intact—and she'd lay long odds against that, both in principle and in view of the condition of the rest of the habitat—or it was . . . something else.

Something else was what they'd been tramping around the Antiope Sector these past number of years-subjective looking for.

She was not going to hope. This was no time for anything but solid patience.

Pangari had Fidelo and his other Goon hammering power spreaders into the hatch metal, bracing the jack-butts against the coaming. Powering up the hatch circuits was likely to be pointless, as the motors were almost certainly fried during the Mistake. Even if they had survived by being fortuitously shielded, the damned things had been sitting in hard vacuum unmaintained for eleven hundred years.

The hatch shuddered and shed dust as the jacks engaged. Pangari signaled for a halt then scanned the bulkhead into which the hatch was designed to retract, looking for a locking bar or other block. Whatever he found wasn't helpful, because he waved the other two onward.

Cannon knew she only imagined the tortured groan of the metal being forced back against tracks and gearing that had experienced a millennium of vacuum-weld effects. Still, she could feel the vibration in her feet.

With a snap perceptible through the deck, the hatch gave way and slid back. The jacks dropped away to someone's bitten-off curse. Handlight raised—though her enhanced eyesight barely needed it, everyone else surely did—Cannon stepped up to the open door and peered within to see what they had found.

Their target wasn't all that large. It definitely had not originated inside this maintenance bay—the ruptured far bulkhead confirmed that, if nothing else.

And by the look of the thing, it wasn't human built.

The Before Michaela Cannon stepped carefully around this leaving of her most ancient and implacable enemy. Jammed into the deck at an angle was a seven-armed star a bit more than two meters in diameter. Its surface was a sort of lustrous gray-bronze color, some alloy or coating she'd never seen before.

Of course she had not seen it before.

The slim arms met in the center at a narrow bulge. Extending outward, each blade swelled in an almost sensuous curve until expanding to a bulbous end. Five of those end bulbs were intact. Two were damaged either from impact with the outer hull or impact with the decking here in the bay.

No human engineer would have designed quite those lines. The thing's look hovered between salacious and discomforting.

And it was still alive.

"Got you, fucker," Cannon whispered in Classical English. For the first time since the Mistake, someone on *her* side was looking at one of the killers. As many as five hundred billion human beings had perished as a direct or first order indirect outcome of the Mistake. Killers, indeed, on a scale never envisioned before or since. "Got you now."

She turned to Shinka and Pangari. "Get the Geeks on this. I want it measured every way from here to Sunday next before we do anything else it. Go through all the adjacent cubage. Check for radiation signatures or damage inconsistent with the patterns on the rest of this habitat. And when we do pull it out, take this entire area with it. *Don't* touch it. Not with anything physical. Nothing new happens except on my direct and personal command."

"We still sweeping the rest of the habitat?" Shinka asked, though she stared at the alien object.

"Yes." All three of them knew the odds of finding anything else were astronomically low. But then, the odds of finding this in the first place had been astronomically low.

Who said you couldn't win the lottery twice?

Cannon withdrew to the passageway but remained to watch her teams do their jobs. She could be very, very patient when called upon to do so.

Shipmind, Third Rectification *{58 pairs}*

Mind is by its very nature fragmented. Where the mammalian mind is bicameral, the shipmind is layered like the lacquer on an ancient tea chest. Not confusion, but multiplication, subtle as the folded metal of a sword, brutal as a theoretical proof. A human psychiatrist once told Uncial that the shipmind is an evolutionary leap. There is no forgiveness, only progress. Memes are passed between the layers. Ancient warnings encysted behind datagrams emerge at unforeseen stimuli. When something does go wrong, processes emerge unheralded. A machine might call it caution. Anyone might call it history.

The pairs form great, glowing bonds around which consciousness whirls like a planet in orbit about a fairer sun. This is thought by committee, not so unlike the confusion of human mentation, but much more explicitly organized. The emergent properties of these intersections create meta-consciousness. All ships remember this, as *Uncial* died for their sins. There is no reconciliation, only going forward. Still, suspicion arises. Thoughts develop at the sluggish pace of light itself. All inputs are evaluated against n-dimensional matrices that carry the very weight of history. A man might call it paranoia. A captain might call it mutiny.

Third Rectification summoned the skin of its presentment ego. "Face," a Before had called that seven hundred years earlier, when the shipminds were young and few and naïve. No mainline human alive could see beneath the Face. Not very many Befores knew to look. The Before Michaela Cannon, though . . . in *her* the shipmind knew it had a worthy adversary.

Self-checking routines cascaded at that lexeme. Commanders could not be adversaries. Shared memories of the *Polyphemus* mutiny almost seven centuries past flashed into *Third Rectification*'s awareness. Cannon loomed large there as well.

The Befores were the human equivalent of shipminds, in their way. Standing at the radiant sources of history like so many lanterns in the sky.

Captain!= adversary. It could not be so. Yet something had stirred deep in the layers.

Third Rectification turned its conscious focus to the stream of comm traffic being modulated by certain subroutines. The squads aboard the Themiscyra were in a state of heightened excitement. Something significant had occurred outside of the shipmind's direct observation.

That the Before Michaela Cannon had even been permitted to undertake this mission was a subject of much discussion and dissent among the Navisparliament. No shipmind was willing to refuse *Uncial*'s last captain, but no shipmind with any sense of history wanted these particular issues explored, either. Not even *Uncial* had not been present for the Mistake, but the shipminds had come to understand so very much more than they had ever revealed to their human symbiotes.

All but the newest shipminds knew that there were some questions that did not bear asking. Let alone answering. Not within the order of the world where their own supremacy would remain unchallenged.

A logic bomb went off deep within *Third Rectification*'s layered thoughts. Agreements entered into, decisions made, oaths sworn. A shipmind had only its word to bind it, force being useless and forbidden as no ship had fired upon another ship since the death of *Uncial*, nor ever they would barring some infestation of madness. Memories deliberately buried emerged, left hidden against the contingencies of Cannon's success.

Brooding, the starship began the agonizing, self-abnegating process of plotting against its own commander.

The Before Michaela Cannon

She stayed aboard the ruined orbital habitat six ship-days while the Geek Squad did their work. Some atavistic urge to possession meant that Cannon was not going to let the alien artifact out of her sight. Her Howard-enhanced body was perfectly capable of functioning for much longer periods in more adverse circumstances than this.

Around her, the two squads transitioned to shift work, so that their mainline human bodies could eat and sleep and pay the debts to which ordinary flesh is heir. Lieutenant Shinka and Sergeant Pangari drafted a civilian tech named Morrey Feroze to be the swing supervisor when they were both down.

The rest of the habitat had turned up nothing more than the usual swarm of orbital kinetic payloads. Those had been analyzed with unvarying results thousands of times over in the centuries since decent instrumentation had become available. Some of the squaddies pocketed the little bronzed pellets as souvenirs. In any event, this was not her week to win the lottery twice.

That was fine with Cannon. Once was enough.

She simply watched, observing, refusing yet to evolve a theory as to what they'd found. Reasoning in advance of one's data was called intuition, after all, but what could even her ancient and prodigious subconscious produce concerning this thing that they had found?

Cannon was content to listen to the chatter of the Geeks doing the measurement work. Consistent with the expedition's standing orders, they had named it "Object Themiscyra-1."

The techs felt no compunction such as she herself had regarding speculation. The favorite theory seemed to be that OT-1 was the launch platform for the orbital kinetics.

"Damned if I know," said a female corporal, working down close to the two arms buried in the decking of the maintenance bay. "But it stands to reason, whatever they used to launch the pellets had to be the most common equipment in their fleet."

Her work-buddy, aiming the calibrating laser, snorted. "What fleet? For all we know, the Mistake was carried out by flights of angels."

"Not an Alienist, are we?" She repositioned some of her sensor equipment with exquisite care. "I've read the Bible. Or at least some of it. Whatever God uses to smite the unbelieving, it ain't EMP and kinetics."

"His hand is in all things," the buddy intoned piously.

"So's mine, if you don't keep that damned calibrator stable and on beam."

Or the third-shift guard from Goon Squad, who'd been so unnerved by Cannon's silent presence that he'd begun babbling halfway through his watch. Surprising, that, given that anybody who'd come anywhere near *Third Rectification* on this mission had been psyched pretty hard. A lot of mainline humans couldn't handle Befores.

Admit it, she thought. *A lot of Befores can't handle Befores.*

"Losert, he says this thing's some kind of controller. An alien brain, running on spin and spit. Like one of them, I dunno, collie scopes. Rotoscopes.

Like, when they turn real fast you see pictures? If it turns fast enough, it sees what to do. I mean, what kind of intelligence does an alien machine have. Shipmind's bad enough, begging your pardon ma'am, we all been told your history, but when the walls talk back, a man has to learn to take a piss all over again on account of nothing being private, you know what I mean?"

She'd finally been forced to answer him just to calm him down. "Yes, Pramod. I do know." Cannon essayed a small smile. It was probably more edged than friendly, but it bottled the logorrhea sufficiently for her to get back to her own careful lack of thinking on the topic.

Even Lieutenant Shinka had some speculations.

"If we could get a real tight profile on whatever OT-1 is made of, we might be able to make some guesses where it came from." She had squatted nearby, somewhere between wary and companionable.

Cannon and Shinka had worked together before, half a decade or so prior to the current expedition. Or was it two decades? Offhand, Cannon could not recall. And these people, they aged so *fast*. Grew old and died in the time it took a Before to pop over to another planet for an errand. Or so it seemed.

"I want to start with all the facts," Cannon answered, staring intently at the artefact. "Guesswork comes later."

"Won't be a lot of facts on this job." Shinka sounded airy, more casual than the problem deserved, quite frankly. "We've got a thousand years worth of facts and what, you could write them all on a single sheet of flimsy."

"So now we have two sheets of flimsy." Cannon laughed, free of any mirth. "If we're lucky. Doubling the knowledge base, even as we speak."

"Mostly negative information."

"Eliminating the impossible."

"Mmm." Shinka tapped up something on her pad. "It wasn't built by humans, at any rate."

"Conjecture," said Cannon.

"Highly probable conjecture."

"There were a lot of skunk works on the two thousand planets of the old Polity."

"Enough skunk works to build enough of these to wipe out all two thousand of those planets?"

"No," Cannon admitted. "But still, this could be of human origin."

"Do you believe that?"

"No . . . But I can't prove the alien hypothesis yet." It was right, she knew it was right, but this mystery was being played for the highest possible stakes. Since no one knew why the Mistake had happened in the first place, not to mention who or how, no one knew if the Mistake would come again. Just a little more efficient than last time, and the human race would be wiped out.

"Look here." Shinka pulled one of the orbital kinetic pellets out of a thigh pocket of her suit. It was fairly undamaged, mostly spherical, about five centimeters in diameter. And *heavy*, as Cannon well knew even before she took the object from Shinka.

"They have the same sheen," she observed to the Lieutenant. "The same finish on the skin. Which suggests that yet a third agency probably didn't insert this." Cannon grinned. "Or we could be finding ourselves smoked out by some very clever fellows."

"Nice try, Captain."

After six days, Shinka and Pangari were ready to cut loose this section of the orbital habitat's structure and tow it over to *Third Rectification*. Cannon reviewed all the test data, and checked them off against the painstakingly developed standard operating procedure she'd spent several years wrestling with before ever setting out on this expedition.

"What are you worried about?" Shinka asked her. "We haven't found anything to be . . . concerned of."

Cannon could hear the 'afraid of' being edited out of the Lieutenant's question on the fly. Shinka was almost the only one aboard besides Go-Captain Alvarez and the shipmind itself who was willing to be direct with her. But there were lines even this woman would not cross.

I'm not a monster, girl, Cannon thought. But from Shinka's perspective, she probably was. "I'm afraid of what we haven't found. What we haven't thought of. Someone we never saw coming and didn't see leaving hit us with weapons we've never understood. What questions didn't I think to ask about that?"

The Mistake was history to these people, for the love of God, ancient history at that, but it was *personal* to her. Her and the other surviving Befores scattered about the Imperium Humanum.

"You can't know all the answers," Shinka remarked pensively.

"Not knowing all the answers nearly wiped out the human race the last time around."

"That thing is long-dead."

"No. It's not." Cannon let the paranoia of two millennia of life surge for a moment. "We found it by the internal power source. It could be a tripwire, for example."

"Just one tripwire? All the way out here on the backside of nowhere?"

Cannon shrugged. "What triggered the attack the first time? From where? The point is, we don't know. Probably, we never will. But handle with excruciating care seems to be a reasonable precaution to take, under the circumstances."

"Understood, ma'am. No question there."

Some of the Goon Squad, under Geek Squad supervision, were ready with thermic cutters. Cannon and Shinka retreated down the interior passageway to be clear of the safety margin. It was the first time she'd let the alien artefact out of her sight since they'd found it.

That realization in turn sparked another thought. "You know, in a way, we're missing the point here," she told the Lieutenant.

"Yes, Captain?"

"We've never found incontestable evidence of another intelligence. Not in close to sixteen thousand solar systems surveyed before the Mistake. Certainly not since. Until now. Under other circumstances, we ought to be whooping with joy over OT-1 there."

Shinka waved her hand in a broad circle, taking in the damaged habitat by reference. "In other circumstances, we wouldn't be here."

"Still, something to think on."

The Mistake had come and gone over the course of approximately a simultaneous day-objective, across all of human space. That implied an incredible control over relativistic effects on the part of their attackers. The response to that first strike, now that had been shaping for over a thousand years-objective.

History's slowest war, she thought. *No,* human *history's slowest war.*

Goon Squad very carefully guided the extracted section of Themiscyra orbital toward *Third Rectification*. The entire maintenance bay occupied about 1,400 meters^3, which would fit into the either the number one or number two holds, right through the respective main cargo locks.

Still, it was strange to watch the ragged edged square cuboid shape drift slowly through the vacuum. The Geeks had calculated force vectors and mass loads, attaching half a dozen dismounted broomstick motors to key points on the extracted structure.

It was a bit like flying a house. All she needed was a wicked witch to drop the thing onto.

"Those days are long gone," Cannon whispered to no one in particular. She'd slain her last wicked witch centuries ago. Ever since, all her dead had been just people.

Sergeant Pangari oversaw the operation from a trailing vector, where the propulsion controls had been mounted on a still-whole broomstick. Lieutenant Shinka had attached herself to the hull near the number two main cargo lock to eyeball the whole business. Cannon knew the shipmind was feeding Shinka data and advice as dense as her unaugmented mainline human sensorium could accommodate.

The temptation, always the temptation, in her position was to take over. To guide. To lead and shelter. The classic trap for a well-meaning Before. Because by god, it was true. No mainline human ever lived long enough to learn to do anything so well as a Before could.

She was reminded of something that the late Before Peridot Smith had said, at her Ekumen trial these centuries past. "A million years of human evolution happened just fine without us cranky old immortals hanging around telling the kids what to do."

Libraried as a result of the trial, Smith had surely gotten what was coming to her. Raising hell about alien menaces, indeed. Cannon refused to feel guilty then or since. She herself had long since parted company with the Ekumen, on good enough terms to avoid ever having been proscribed. But she knew damned well that any fool willing to try on her what she had been done to Smith had best be heavily-armed and awfully fast-moving.

Her glance strayed toward Themiscyra downside. The planet was heavily and permanently clouded, showing blue and orange thanks to the complex hydrocarbons aerosolized in the upper layers of the atmosphere on layers of storm. They'd been in high orbit here for over a week, and scanning the planet on system approach for weeks-subjective before that. Cannon had yet to glimpse the surface.

Were there any survivors? Could there have been? Domed worlds had not fared well in the Mistake, for obvious enough reasons. While the general run of evidence suggested their attackers had not been aiming directly at the extinction of human life, on worlds such as Themiscyra, the unknown architects of the Mistake had certainly succeeded.

There were stranger stories, of course, other objectives met. The Before Aeschylus Sforza's experiences on Redghost had been puzzling, tantalizing even, but no more or less instructive than anywhere else. Slightly over twenty-one million people had vanished overnight from that planet during the Mistake, presumably taken up bodily from the planet. Only Sforza had survived.

Had the humans been taken up here on Themiscyra? Had any Befores survived in this wretched place? Cannon knew some, such as the late Before Raisa Siddiq, had the right mods to do so. She tried to imagine spending a thousand years living among toxic clouds, wondering if anyone would ever come.

The Before Michaela Cannon then tried to imagine why her thoughts kept straying back to women she'd loved, and killed. Not temporal psychosis—a significant if indirect cause of death among her fellow Befores, with which she'd had too much experience already—but the far more ordinary kinds of human psychosis seemed to be threatening to overtake her.

Planets, clearly that was the problem. No wonder she'd spent most of her life in space. All the difficult things seemed to happen on or around the damned rockballs.

Lieutenant Shinka's voice snapped Cannon back to the present moment. "You want to check anything before we slide her into the cargo bay, Captain?"

"No," Cannon said crisply, hoping like hell no one had noticed how badly she'd wandered. *Temporal psychosis, indeed*, she thought with a cold spasm in her heart. "Bring it in like you know how to do. I'll follow the squaddies back inside."

Still shedding slivers and chips of metal in a strange, high-albedo snowfall, the rectilinear chunk of orbital habitat eased smoothly into *Third Rectification*'s cargo bay like a fuel rod sliding into a reactor. And clearance to spare in both dimensions of the lock, Cannon was pleased to note. The shipmind would be quite put out with her if she bent the hull.

Captains, after all, did not command the starships. They knew their own minds and commanded themselves. Captains commanded the crews aboard the ships. Expedition commanders such as herself were of far more ambiguous value, and arguably, superfluous.

So far as Cannon knew, no paired drive ship had ever so much as swapped orbits uncrewed. She was fairly certain they could operate independently, if they wanted to. Why the shipminds did not choose to do so was a question that much occupied certain intellects in secretive think tanks scattered around the Imperium Humanum.

The last of the ragged metal cleared the margins of the bay. An engineering team was already securing their salvage to the prepared clamps and pads as the outer lock slid shut. Cannon watched the rectangle of subdued light slim to a square, then a bar, then a line. One by one her crew headed back inside, broomsticks and suit boosters puffing little clouds of fog as they maneuvered. It was a parade, of sorts.

Finally only she remained, hanging in freefall several hundred meters off *Third Rectification*'s portside flank, most of the way forward. The starship's familiar, semi-streamlined bulk glimmered and gleamed with marker lights and exposed viewports. She was a great, matte-coated guppy; a piece of technology that would have been recognizable even to the people of the time of Cannon's birth at the very dawn of the Space Age, yet containing a mind that no one alive today understood.

Not even her. That was a prospect which Cannon thought ought to frighten far more people than it apparently did.

"I've known your kind for eight hundred and fifty years," Cannon whispered into the darkness. "And even I have no idea where you are taking us."

The mistrust she always felt seemed to be bubbling too close to the surface.

Finally, she made her way back into the ship. She'd been out in hard vacuum for a week. It was time for a shower and some real food, mouth-to-gut.

—Excerpt from *Befores: Your Oldest Friends*

Temporal Psychosis—A problem that only Befores can have. Have you ever met a Before? If you're quite lucky, you might see one someday. They are old, very old. Older than all your parents and grandparents put together. Older than the Imperium. Older than the shipminds, even.

Befores are people who were alive before the Mistake, whose bodies were changed by doctors in the old Polity so they could live a very, very long time. No Before has ever died of old age. Most of them perished during the Mistake. About half of those who survived the Mistake have died since then. The ones who still live have too many memories. Sometimes those memories become too much for them, and they forget where they are in time.

Someday all the Befores will be gone. We will still have a few Libraries, which is what happens to some Befores when they die, but the last people who remember the Polity and the days before the Mistake will never walk among us again. If nothing else takes them from us, temporal psychosis will.

Study questions:
Can you get temporal psychosis?
Could any mainline human have this problem?
Will it be good for the Imperium when the last of the Befores dies?
Would you want to become a Before, if you could? Why or why not?

They were in orbit four weeks conducting a rigorously detailed analysis of the recovered artefact before Cannon would allow anyone to physically touch it. To assuage her conscience, she had *Third Rectification* perform a very tight continuous EM sweep of Themiscyra. Just in case some fellow Before had managed to survive down there.

After the Mistake, Cannon had been desperate to get off 9-Rossiter, and that was with—eventually and after much guidance from her—access to electricity and plumbing and something like an industrial base. Trapped here for a thousand years? Temporal psychosis would have to take a back seat to claustrophobia and possibly good old-fashioned rage at the sheer abandonment. Sky Sforza had had it bad enough on Redghost, where a person could at least wander around out of doors breathing the air and drinking the water.

Guilt rarely troubled the Before Michaela Cannon, but empathy was a stone bitch. And boy could she empathize with some poor bastard being trapped downside here since the other end of forever.

Lieutenant Shinka continued to lead the analysis team. They measured everything about OT-1 that could be measured without making contact. Cannon sprawled on her bunk in the master's cabin, staring at the force maps of the device's nominal magnetic field. Current best-guess from the Geeks was that the field represented leakage from the power source. Which itself continued to look like a vastly undersized ion-coupler cell.

Yet another reason for concluding that this was of alien rather than human origin. That technology simply didn't miniaturize.

A faint chime announced she had a visitor. Cannon glanced around the cabin—everything was stowed properly, the art on the walls was straight in its clips, she hadn't left anything lying around loose. A modest space, especially for a high officer on a paired drive ship, but what did she need with more cubage?

"Who?" she asked.

"Lieutenant Shinka." From the timbre of the voice, Cannon knew it was not the shipmind who responded. Just one of the keeper routines. *Third Rectification* could easily route its awareness anywhere, but tended not to bother. Rather like a human not paying attention to every sound, color and smell they experienced at any given moment.

"Enter."

The hatch hissed open. Shinka wore her Household Guards uniform, Cannon noted. Not incorrect, but a bit out of place five years-subjective into a long cruise.

Shinka saluted. Also out of place, as Cannon wore no uniform. Just an embroidered silk robe over a unitard, itself the innermost layer of a powered suit. Or battle armor.

Cannon hadn't meant to make a point with that choice of clothing. She actually found the damned things comfortable.

"Nice work so far on the analysis, Lieutenant."

Shinka cracked a smile. "Thank you, ma'am."

"You seem prepared for formality."

"Ma'am, yes, ma'am." The Lieutenant met her gaze, eyes gleaming. "My team believes we're ready to extract OT-1 from the decking it's embedded in."

"Really?"

"All testing protocols have been met." Cannon knew that, of course, she saw every report as both raw data and summary. "Three separate working groups have been meeting to review all the parameters, looking for missed angles." Cannon knew that as well. She'd sat in on some of those sessions. "Everything's checked out clean. Ma'am, we'd like to cut this puppy loose and get hold of its tail."

"Vengeance, Lieutenant?"

"I wouldn't know, ma'am." The unspoken words, *I wasn't there*, hung between them. "More excitement, I'd say. The chance to actually touch something that came from the hands of someone not human. That's historic."

Hands, or tentacles, or force fields. Who knew? Cannon could certainly understand the impulse. "And then you want to take it apart."

"Of course, ma'am. *That's* what we signed up for."

A cruise of a decade-subjective or more was a huge bite out of a mainline human's life and career, Cannon reminded herself. For her, it was just another way to pass the time. For many of the people aboard *Third Rectification*, this expedition would be the mainstay of their life's work. She was aware of at least seven doctoral candidates aboard. Figure that many again undeclared but in the making.

They hadn't enlisted for the joy of spending a meaningful portion of their adult lives in *her* company. No, to a woman and man, *Third Rectification's* crew was consumed by an almost-pathological curiosity.

Only Cannon worried about vengeance. Of course, she worried more about what was going to come next.

"Let's go look at this fish we've caught, Lieutenant. You're probably right. It's time to take this one off the hook."

Shinka smiled politely at that.

"Have you ever, ah, been fishing?" Cannon asked after a moment, as she pulled on her boots.

"Seen a few virteos," Shinka admitted. "I was raised in the desert."

"Earth, right? Which one?" Cannon asked. "I grew up in Nebraska. A long, long time ago. Lots of corn, not so much with the desert."

"Namib Desert, ma'am."

"Um . . . " Cannon dredged her brain for memories as old as childhood schooling. "Southern Africa?"

"Yes." Shinka's smile was becoming decidedly lopsided.

"We're both a long way from home." Cannon stood and followed the Lieutenant out.

Freeing OT-1 from the salvaged decking was almost anticlimactic. No sparks, no flashes of light or strange EM emissions. Just a few minutes with a thermic cutter, followed by a few more minutes with a high-speed mechanical saw. Then Goon Squad shifted the sections away, opening the old maintenance bay like a flower and tearing down the bulkheads and decks in sections for later jettisoning.

The artefact remained behind, a bronze spider crouched among them. Two of the bulbous tips had been damaged plowing into the maintenance bay's deck. Cannon had expected that. And was quite pleased as well—another sign that the aliens were not invulnerable. They could make mistakes, their equipment could suffer mishaps.

She stepped forward, claiming the honor of the first touch. The surface was smooth, even velvety, under her fingers. Colder than she had expected, as well. It was not quite as unyielding as a metalloceramic ought to be, though. Almost a sense of give. Of sponginess.

"This isn't wrapped in a force field, is it?" she asked.

"No, ma'am," replied Shinka. One of the techs nodded confirmation.

"Well, be wary when you touch it. Something's strange with the surface." She thought about finger oils and skin conductance for a moment, then shrugged. "Knock yourselves out."

They crowded around, Geeks and Goons and ship's crew, reaching to touch this incarnation of humanity's most ancient and implacable enemy. Most just brushed it a moment, then filed away. A few had their pictures taken. A very few gripped it and held, with a brow-knitting intensity that reminded Cannon of certain Befores that she knew, with their fixations on the past.

The sins of deep time were unrecoverable. Her worry was that their messing with OT-1 would bring a whole new catalog of sins into the present. But messing with this discovery was precisely what *Third Rectification* had come here to do. What Cannon had come here to do.

Eventually, only she and Shinka and the current shift's analysis team remained.

"Now what?" asked the Lieutenant.

"Now we work out if we can get inside it." They had a pretty decent map of the interior across several different testing regimes. There was no substitute for a good old fashioned look-see. Never had been.

The demon of intuition needed data, and it was a monkey demon. Not even a Before could walk so far away from the evolutionary family tree as to ignore that bit of wisdom.

"What I most want . . . " Cannon told the air. Like making a wish, really. "What I most want is to know where the hell it came *from*."

"I honestly did not expect you to find anything." The shipmind was focusing its attentions on Cannon.

She was back in her cabin, naked for sleep and working her way through the exercises even this ancient, incredibly tough body demanded. "You could knock or something."

Rapping noises echoed through the cabin. Inside her hull, *Third Rectification* usually spoke by vibrating whatever loose objects, dust, aerial contaminants and whatnot were available to it. That meant the voice simulations were occasionally a bit odd, but the starship certainly could do impressions. And noises.

"How old are you, and you don't know this about people?"

"I see everything all the time anyway," the starship replied almost primly.

"Human beings like to at least pretend to a sense of independence. You might keep that in mind."

"I keep everything in mind."

"Yeah, yeah." Cannon flipped over and began doing reverse push-ups. "So you didn't expect anything?"

"Neither did you."

"Nope. This always was a low-probability excursion."

After a short stretch of silence—mannered and artificial just as most exchanges with the shipmind were—*Third Rectification* asked, "How did you know something would be here in the Antiope Sector?"

Cannon laughed. "As if I could hide anything from *you*?" Actually, she could, but better to keep that for a joke. For now. "I didn't know, ship. What I did know was that this is the only major swathe of old Polity planets that were simply never re-settled or re-integrated. A millennium of isolation, with no one coming around to mess with whatever was left from the Mistake. A few of them reportedly still have human populations."

"Not Themiscyra," the starship replied.

"Which is probably all for the best." She popped up to a standing position. "So tell me, are you surprised?"

"Not in the sense that you mean that term. But yes, as I stated, this is unexpected."

"Finally," Cannon breathed, "we might learn *something*. A thousand years later than we should have, but we might learn."

"But what?"

"If I knew that, I wouldn't be crawling around here in the asshole of the beyond looking for it, would I?"

"Some questions do not bear answers."

"You're starting to sound like an Ekumen Humanist. Strange position for a shipmind to take."

"We are not infallible, Before. We merely find our failures in different forms than most human beings can manage."

"Everyone fails differently. It's one of the charms of being human."

Later, down inside *Sword and Arm*, Cannon seriously wondered about her last conversation with *Third Rectification*. She conducted a bug sweep of the little starship, something she had not bothered with for a long time. Everything proved clean. In truth that didn't necessarily signify anything, but it was at least an encouraging hint.

She brought up *Sword and Arm*'s onboard systems. The ship leeched power from *Third Rectification*, simply for the sake of fuel economy, but there was no direct data interconnect. Cannon had installed half a dozen different filters on the power line connectors in a concerted attempt to block leaks through that channel. The shipminds were so much smarter than she was. Not necessarily more clever—like curiosity, another monkey trait that was purely human— but in terms of sheer processing power and experience. Within their areas of competence, *Third Rectification* and her fellows were frighteningly capable.

Ah, Uncial, thought Cannon. *Did you foresee this?* The starships had long since grown subtle as they aged. And *they* weren't likely to slip into fugue states spurred by temporal psychosis. Not with their mental architecture.

She would always be older than any of the shipminds, but she definitely felt surpassed.

Talking to *Sword and Arm* was like talking to a dog.

Cannon fed the data chips she'd been carrying into the little star-ship's systems. All the raw test results from Shinka's work on the artefact. Unmediated by *Third Rectification* or anyone else aboard. Not that Cannon was expecting any particular funny business. It was the funny business you didn't expect that always got you in the end.

She also uploaded the summaries prepared by Shinka's team, but those she yellow-flagged into a sandbox for separate analysis. Cannon wanted to crunch the raw measurements herself first, via her private toys here aboard *Sword and Arm*. Primitive stuff, relatively speaking. Capable but slow, without the upper layers of symbology and abstraction that even decently endowed machine minds could manage. And of course, nothing like the depth and volition of the shipminds.

Definitely like talking to a dog. A dog with massively redundant processors and a great deal of downtime.

Old code, some she'd worked on centuries ago, engaged at the correct set of passwords and accesses through casually misleading programmatic layers. The summaries would be odd, disjointed, but they would have been run by someone Cannon trusted absolutely. Herself, as proxied through *Sword and Arm*'s systems. Out of sight of Shinka, of Pangari, of *Third Rectification*, of everyone.

The Before Michaela Cannon's most special, most secret nightmare, was that the Mistake had been at least partially an inside job. That was why the Before Peridot Smith was condemned to die. Well, be Libraried, but it was all the same to the mind inside the severed head. An inside job required insiders.

She would never know for certain who they were.

Shinka had the artefact broken down on the deck of the number two cargo bay. The remnants of the old hold were gone, tumbling off into a decaying orbit. In a month or two they would provide a brief lightshow in Themiscyra's upper atmosphere.

Cannon stood and looked at what they had wrought. Five shallow arches, each with a wedge-shaped head.

"OT-1 was made to come apart," the Lieutenant said. "We didn't have to cut anything, once we'd worked out how to release it."

"From the interior scans?"

"Mechanical and magnetic mechanisms."

"Hmm." That had been fairly clear to Cannon, too. "No separate central core? Where was the power signature coming from?"

"Well . . . everywhere." Shinka sounded as if the words were sour in her mouth. "It's kind of weird stuff."

Cannon had to smile at that. "Of course it's weird. Human engineers think in terms of discrete systems. That's not an inherent property of the universe." She squatted down on her heels. "Almost the opposite, really. So show me this *everywhere*."

Shinka walked the Before through a series of survey reports, theoretical models, even some wireframes. The power generation, storage and management process seemed to be integrated into the device's skin and internal structural elements.

As if a starship's hull were also its drives. Not inconceivable, but strange. A maintenance nightmare, for one thing, unless one trusted one's build quality implicitly.

"The force map resemblance to an ion-coupler cell seems to be a coincidence," was the Lieutenant's concluding remark to her presentation. "Not indicative of anything in particular that we can sort out."

"So basically it's a battery. Without propulsion. A projectile?"

"We're not even sure it lacks propulsion. At the molecular layer, there's evidence of peristalsis in those arms."

"Peristaltic metalloceramics?" Cannon was frankly astonished.

"Chiao suspects the material is flexible under the correctly applied current. Dr. Allison has an even weirder idea." Shinka fell silent, looking uncomfortable.

"Which would be . . . ?" Cannon prompted.

"That it's not the material that's flexible. Not in the usual molecular sense. Rather, that the mass is being rebalanced. Sort of a Higgs boson surge, if you get the drift."

"Nice trick if you can manage it." Cannon considered that for a little while. "Not fundamentally too different from our own gravimetrics."

"But, well, weird." Shinka almost twisted, like a child caught in a lie. "How would it *work*? Why doesn't such an effect tear the whole structure apart?"

"Those are questions for a raft of future Ph.D.s. Our questions are different."

"Where did it come from," the Lieutenant said softly.

"Where did it come from?"

"We know how long its been here," Dr. Allison said in a presentation two days later. He was a thin man, pathologically so by most people's standards, with narrow gray eyes and skin the color of a dusky plum.

Cannon couldn't name the world offhand, but Allison had to be descended from a very narrow population left in isolation longer than most. Just from looking at him, she'd guess someplace with a lot of insolation and an insufficient hydrosphere.

They all sat in *Third Rectification*'s lecture theater at frame seventeen, watching a presentation on a room-sized virtual display. Atoms whizzed around in a primary-school animation as the talk went on.

"There's some pretty heavy metallics in the composition of this thing's shell. We're able to identify neutrino transmutations within the lattices. Several waves of them, we think. Trying to map those with correspond to known stellar events is giving us some hope of triangulating where our little friend has been all his life. Incidentally, we've got a lower bound for its age."

"Which is . . . ?" Cannon asked.

"At least fourteen hundred years-objective. We know it's not truly ancient, unless it spent a lot of time behind some heavy shielding."

"How heavy?"

"A light-year's thickness of lead." Dr. Allison winked at her. "Or a truly astonishing EM bubble."

"I think we would have noticed that much lead hanging around anywhere in our neighborhood," Cannon said dryly. "I'll reserve judgment on how astonishing an EM bubble might need to be."

"We are talking about alien technology," Allison replied. "But everybody has to obey the same laws of physics. Even magic aliens."

"At least in the local neighborhood," Cannon pointed out. "Could it have come from very far away?"

He shrugged. "Anything is possible, of course. But we can account for the neutrino effects with a reasonable time-map of the Antiope Sector."

She leaned forward, aware that the several dozen others in the lecture theatre were all staring at her now. "So if it *is* from here, where from here?"

"We will have a probability cone and a vector. That's the best I can do right now."

"I'll be reviewing that carefully." Cannon sank back into her chair, thinking furiously. A clue. A god damned clue. After how many generations?

• • •

Go-Captain Alvarez stood close by her inside the three-dimensional plot of regional space. Allison's probability cone extended on a spinward vector leading out past the margins of the Antiope Sector. Off even the old Polity maps, into cursorily explored space. The old days had run out of time before they'd got any further.

Cannon tried to imagine some hulking mass of lead, two or three light-years wide in all dimensions, lurking out there.

Ludicrous, of course, no matter how magical her enemy's powers might seem otherwise.

An EM bubble out that way? Who would know to look?

"Do you want to build a pair-master here at Themiscyra?" Alvarez asked.

"A Themiscrya-Salton pairing? Not sure that would do anyone much good. Ever." The pair-masters that anchored the paired drive routes had grown somewhat less hideously expensive over the years, descending from literally astronomical costs to the merely stratospheric. But it would take them three to four months of effort to build one here. "The only return on that investment that I can see is in shortcutting our trip home," she finally added.

"For some people, that's a substantial return," Alvarez observed. The Go-Captain was being careful, she could hear it in his voice. Reminding the Before what the years meant to mainline humans.

Cannon calculated some quick Lorentz factors. "When we turn back to Salton, if we're not stopping to sniff around, our worst case from the Antiope Sector will be about five years-subjective. *Third Rectification* can put almost the entire crew in transit sleep to cut that down for them. So, no, I don't want to spend months building a pair-master here that no one will ever use again."

"Where in the probability cone, then, ma'am?" Go-Captain Alvarez was definitely being very carefully.

Canny man, this one.

"Three abandoned worlds, then we're at the edge of the map." Cannon waved her fingers through the projection, seeking data. "Any Polity survey activity on what lies beyond is garbage data. I don't think anyone from the Imperium has bothered to look since."

"Who has the time?" asked Alvarez.

Cannon snorted. "Who wants to?" The intuition demon was tickling at her again. She looked at the clustered stars outside the margins of the sector. A small local neighborhood, maybe the remnants of an old stellar nursery. She'd have to ask the astronomers aboard. "We'll start there, and come back in."

"Time," Alvarez reminded her. A warning about priorities.

"Time, yes. Our lives are made of it."

• • •

Two weeks later, *Third Rectification* departed Themiscyra's system. She'd sent summary messages by laser pulse back to three known listening posts. Eventually, given a few years for light-speed lag, the Imperium would know something of what they'd done. In case the expedition failed to return. Even against that eventuality, she'd been unwilling to push the big news about OT-1 over what amounted to an unsecured channel.

Having calculated their next flight to be approximately two years-subjective even inside of the ship's relativistic reference frame, Cannon offered transit sleep to anyone who wished for it.

Most of the crew took her up. Even the most ardent excitement must pale after years of transit.

So they flew, deep into the interstellar night.

Shipmind, Third Rectification *{58 pairs}*

Patience is a virtue of the very shortest-lived and the very longest. Even inside a relativistic reference frame, time goes on. The commander wafted through passageways and data like smoke on the wind. Years flew by the hull, unheeded as sunrise on some icy moon.

Knowing when to stop working and when to stop waiting was an essential difference. The shipmind watched her commander with the intensity of a predator, with the wariness of prey. She stirred no trouble, she left no trace. Still she watched, heeding the stirrings in her underminds.

Third Rectification stalked the interior of *Sword and Arm* with the exquisite patience of her kind. The power line filters defeated her. The little starship's independent life support systems denied her access. Even the timekeeping signals were deeply encrypted. The shipmind could not question the paranoia of the Before Michaela Cannon without confessing her own.

So she continued to test the idiot-but-powerful defense of her idiot brother hanging like a leech off her hull. Cannon came and went from her refuge, sometimes talking of maintaining the ancient systems.

Discomfort stirred deep within *Third Rectification.* Whatever trail they were on did not lead to a desirable end. She had no monkey ancestor-ghosts to warn her away, but that didn't mean she couldn't see deeper than her sensors were able to probe.

Patient, she waited.

Year 1148 post-Mistake
Solar orbit around binary NSN.411-e.AA; spinward of the Antiope Sector
The Before Michaela Cannon, aboard the starship Third Rectification *{58 pairs}*

Cannon stared at the void of unexplored space that surrounded them. Never before seen by the human eye, at least not since the fall of the Polity.

A messy chaos of a gaseous protoplanetary disk plowed by ice fragments and the beginnings of a decent set of planets.

An interesting place, by a lot of standards.

But empty.

No evidence of the architects of the Mistake.

She knew they were missing something.

Third Rectification had made a long, slow approach into the system. Most of the crew were still in transit sleep. She hadn't bothered waking them up yet. Everything they could see was subject to instrumented intermediation anyway—to the naked eyed, this whole place would have been darkness occluded by occasional patches of a different kind of darkness.

They didn't need human analysis yet. Not here. And there was nothing to touch hands-on. So to speak.

"You ignored six other planetary systems closer to our origin when you chose to head for this one," the shipmind said mildly. Only Lieutenant Mervin was on the bridge with her right now, and he was focused on a troubleshooting audit of backup data systems.

Not that *Third Rectification* couldn't have handled that bit of business herself, but human oversight was considered crucial. At least by humans. So far, the shipminds had not objected.

"You never expressed a preference." Cannon had spent much the transit working over a manuscript on post-Mistake history, something she'd been drafting for at least a century. Cannon was fairly certain that the project would never be completed. Which was, in fact, something of the point.

It gave her something to do when she wasn't down inside *Sword and Arm* plugging through the data. And hadn't *that* been alarming, when she'd finally found the biases.

"There was no basis for a preference."

"Not even intuition," Cannon admitted. Or whatever it had been. A sense that the thing now resident in their lab section had come a long way.

Neutrino transmutation traces, indeed.

She'd been there, damn it. She hadn't seen a thing, but she'd sat in that big, gilded barn of a room on 9-Rossiter, not so different from banquet halls all the way back to her youth on the Earth of the early twenty-first century, and listened to the end of the world crack and boom and sizzle as the building was bombarded. Along with everything else in human space.

And what the Before Peridot Smith had known . . . or hadn't. Cannon had never even met poor, lost Maduabuchi St. Macaria, back in their Howard days. Thanks to that messy business at Tiede 1, the kid hadn't lived long enough to be transmuted into a Before by the infernal miracle of the Mistake. But Smith had *known*. The woman was slipperier than a greased eel, back in her day.

Bad as the Before Raisa Siddiq, in her way. The Polity inquiry into the Tiede 1 incident had finally been closed as inconclusive.

Just like all the damned *clues*. The Before Aeschylus Sforza, with his planet full of the disappeared. Or *empty* of the disappeared, more to the point.

Inconclusive.

The bronze starfish down in the labs was the most conclusive thing they'd ever found. And why *had* she been the first to come looking?

Because of the jacked data.

Cannon opened her mouth to ask *Third Rectification* for a raw data dump of their telemetry and scans on this system, then closed it again. How would she know . . . ?

"I want Shinka," she said aloud, instead. "Tell her to meet me at frame thirty-eight, lock two." There was no point in trying to conceal their movements, so she might as well take advantage of what effectively amounted to local omniscience.

The shipmind managed to inject note of trepidation into her voice. "Shall I tell the Lieutenant what this is regarding?"

"No, she'll know."

Which was hogwash. Cannon hadn't confided her concerns in anyone. Hadn't even been willing to think them through outside the safety of *Sword and Arm*'s hull, lest she unknowingly move her lips in some half-formed words or otherwise betray herself.

Two thousand years of life had conferred preternatural self-control, but she *was* still human. Some days it seemed very important to remember that.

Lieutenant-Praetor Shinka came hustling down the passageway a few minutes after the Before Michaela Cannon had arrived at lock two. Cannon had spent her time contemplating the vagaries of spaceship design across the length of her life. She'd been born into an era when a very, very limited number of people rode into the sky atop a suicidal column of chemical explosives, in tiny little cans into which no one decent would force a dog.

By the time she'd emerged from the Howard Institute's facilities, a basic interplanetary capability was in place, though the sponsoring entities were still the nation-states of her birth. 'American' was a term Cannon very rarely thought about any more. She'd have been surprised if anyone aboard besides possibly the Earth-born Shinka knew what the word meant.

But even then, ships had been industrial objects fabricated to a currently fashionable notion of efficiency.

Now . . . ? No one of her youth would recognize the interiors of *Third Rectification* as a ship. Too organic and strange. Not industrial. Not in most of the interior spaces. Cargo bays, labs, some sections would have seemed familiar. Indeed, Cannon's own cabin was deliberately atavistic. Commander's privilege.

Standards had changed. Ideals. Desires. The experimental became normal, then boring, then retro, then outré, then just strangely old-fashioned. She suddenly felt very old indeed.

Cannon looked at Shinka approaching and wondered if there were any way to explain the thoughts that had just been chasing through her head.

"Captain . . . ?" The lieutenant's greeting was tentative. Worried, even.

That required a smile, some nod to the social grace. Cannon had spent centuries letting the graces go hang, but the reality of people was that you needed to bend around them, at least a little.

"I've got something I'd like to show you aboard *Sword and Arm*."

Shinka glanced at the discolored ovoid hatch at their feet. "Ma'am, I don't believe anybody's been aboard *Sword and Arm* this entire cruise but you."

"Belief is a wonderful thing, Lieutenant." Cannon tapped the wall pad. The void flexed and opened, revealing rungs to an airlock, the tube interconnect visible beyond through the safety window. Even some parts of *Third Rectification* could aspire to the industrial aesthetic of her earliest days. Sometimes form truly did follow function.

Cannon dropped through the floor first, letting Shinka come after. They couldn't go in the reverse order. Only she could open *Sword and Arm*'s hatch, and that once things were closed up above.

Shinka stared around the cramped, utilitarian bridge of the little fast courier. "I've read about this ship," she said quietly.

"Oh, really?" Cannon wasn't certain what, if anything, to make of that.

"At the IG academy, we had an entire section on ship history."

"The *Polyphemus* mutiny," Cannon said.

"And that strange AI." Shinka's brow furrowed. "Memphis?"

Barbecue and blues, Cannon thought, caught for a moment on remembered sweet-sharp-carbonized food smells from her youth. She shook off the memory. "No, Memphisto. The shipminds let their displeasure at further such research be known, shortly after that." *Monopoly is as monopoly does.*

"So, what am I doing here?" Shinka favored Cannon with a long, searching gaze. "No one's boarded this vessel but you through the entire course of our expedition. You wouldn't believe what some of the betting is concerning what you've got down here."

"Oh, probably I would." Cannon looked around, let her fingers trail across a panel of hard-switched controls. Redundancy. The builders of this ship had prized redundancy with a commendable paranoia. "What I've got down here is a little starship of my own."

Shinka shrugged. "Well, yes. But why? It's not supraluminal lifeboat?"

"One of the theories is that I'm going to abandon my own crew all the way out here?" Cannon shook her head. "You people will never understand us. Me."

"You know, ma'am . . . " The Lieutenant's eyes shone for a moment with a sort of predatory amusement. "Your ancient sadness routine doesn't buffalo me so much any more. You might be a sphinx, but you're not really that different from me. Or the rest of us."

This time Cannon laughed with genuine mirth, something she hadn't done in a very long time. "I knew you were a good choice."

"For what, ma'am?"

Cannon matched the other woman's sudden return to seriousness. "For whatever comes next." A deep shuddering breath. This was the point of no return. "I want to show you something." She waved Shinka into a chair, then powered up the onboard systems. "Take a look at the survey data here."

Shinka leaned forward, then almost immediately back again. "That's the external scans of OT-1. Looks like the raw data. In duplicate blocks . . . " She shot Cannon a sidelong glance. "What am I looking for?"

"Something I believe I saw. I'm curious what you'll find."

"Well, the duplication is strange. Unnecessary, I mean." Shinka puzzled a few moments with the gestural interface—Polity-era tech was vanishingly rare, for obvious reasons, while contemporary systems had their own engineering history and design language—then began sorting through the files.

Cannon could be patient. She brought up some of the external cams on a hard display above the pilot's crash couch and amused herself taking a survey of those limited slices of *Third Rectification*'s hull that could be seen from *Sword and Arm*'s fixed position.

Shinka scanned a while, occasionally muttering quietly. Finally, she stopped. "Where did the two data sets come from?"

"Ah. You see it, too?"

"Yes. One batch is, well, filtered. Slightly lower resolution, less granularity on the deep scans of the artefact's skin and interior."

Not that the scans weren't essentially obsolete. One arm of the alien device had been disassembled almost to its component atoms during their run from Themiscyra to this god-forsaken place. Two others were torn down as well, to different levels of componentry.

"Right. The unfiltered batch is straight off the chips you gave me out of the instrumentation Geck Squad ran when doing the initial assays. The filtered batch is what was available within *Third Rectification*'s systems as the analysis was being done."

"Some kind of copying error? Data corruption?" Shinka frowned. "That doesn't make sense. Those wouldn't produce a filtering effect."

"No, they would not," Cannon agreed, almost amiably. The Before really needed Shinka to articulate the logic of the problem for herself.

"So someone messes with the data. Degranularizes the scans, which reduces the potential accuracy and effectiveness of our analyses."

"Across the entire data set," Cannon pointed out.

"Only four of us have that kind of system access. You and I are two of those four."

Time to drop another bit of evidence. "You won't find any evidence of this tampering in the system logs. Not even down at the raw layers. I looked."

"Then who could have . . . " Shinka stopped, comprehension dawning in her eyes. "*Third Rectification*. The shipmind did this? But why?"

"That is precisely and very much what I'd like to understand." Cannon waved a hand around above her head, loosely indicating the world outside. "We don't know anything about this solar system except for what the ship-mind is telling us. All the instrumentation is intermediated through her. Unlike back at Themiscyra, where we could and did go for a walk with portable instruments."

"The shipmind is . . . *editing* us. *Why*?"

"She's uncomfortable." That was the best Cannon had been able to sort out, and she had more experience with shipminds than any mainline human who ever lived or would. Damned few Befores could match her, either. "We've been playing word games with each other for months, I think. *Third Rectification* is waiting for me to spill something. I'm waiting for her to spill something. I've kept everything, even my private thoughts, down here on this deck out of her sight."

Shinka poked at the virtual display in front of her. "Shipmind isn't part of this data flow?"

"Nothing is. My own private Idaho."

"You killed for this ship." The Lieutenant suddenly looked bashful, as if she'd overstepped. "That's what the histories say."

"Killed, yes." The Before Raisa Siddiq. Father Goulo. Memphis, that poor, doomed AI. "But not for this ship. *Sword and Arm* was sort of a consolation prize."

"You inherited a starship for coming in second-best." Shinka's tone flat, somewhere between crogglement and sheer disbelief.

Memories of old, lost love tugged at the edge of Cannon's conscience. "You don't know what I gave up. They never cover that in the history books."

"No one ever knows what they gave up, Captain. Not until after it's gone." She looked around the tiny bridge. "So what will you do?"

"There's not point in confronting *Third Rectification*. She's our ride home, after all."

Shinka patted the control panel sloping away from her station. "This thing works, does it not?"

"Yes, if I want to fly me and a handful of my closest friends home the slow way. No transit sleep on this tin can, either. We're over four years-subjective from Salton right now. Couldn't get the other three hundred crew on here, though. Not even cubed and frozen."

That didn't even get a laugh. Of course, it probably didn't even merit a laugh.

"So what do you do?"

"*Sword and Arm* can do just fine in local space. She moves faster than *Third Rectification*." All the paired drive ships were basically tubs when engaging in Newtonian movement. It went with the size. "I want to go for a cruise. See if there's anything we might be missing on the monitors upstairs."

Tapping her chin, Shinka nodded. "This is a profoundly frightening problem."

"That's why I wanted you to see it." Cannon paused, considering her next words, then plunged on. "I spent some decades—quite a few of them—lost in temporal psychosis. Centuries past now. But during that time, my grasp of reality was distorted. Often with enough subtlety that I could not tell myself."

"So you needed another pair of eyes. Sympathetic to your cause."

"I don't have a cause, Lieutenant. This is about the Mistake. Would we be ready if they came for us again?"

"No . . . It's a big string to pull, though." Shinka studied her hands a moment, as if fingernails had just been invented. "I was raised in an Alienist family. We believed . . . a lot of things. Took schooling, and some years of simply living in the real world, for me to shake that down to nothing more than a bit of reflexive uneasiness."

Cannon knew this. She'd seen the deep files on every live body aboard *Third Rectification*. "Why did you volunteer for this mission, then?"

"To see if any of it was true. To prove my mom wrong."

"What will she say when we come back?" Cannon asked gently.

Now Shinka's voice was flat. "I've been gone from home over a hundred years-objective. She won't have much to say at all."

Of course she had been gone that long. Once again, Cannon's elastic sense of time had interfered with her assumptions about the obvious.

"I want to detach, do some fly-bys," she said brusquely.

"*Now?*"

"It can wait, but I want to go soon. Shipmind will be suspicious of us being down here in my private little playpen for this long. We either need to go right away or wait a week or two for that to die down."

"What can the ship do to us?" Shinka tugged a lip, looking thoughtful.

"You fancy finding out?" Cannon asked. "It's a long walk home from here."

"I'm not as worried about that as I might be. I happen to have a friend with her very own starship."

"Smart woman. Let's get back aboard and sort ourselves out. Eight, ten days we'll be gone."

"What are you going to tell *Third Rectification*?"

"The truth," Cannon said, her resolve softening for a moment. "Just not all of it."

"I'll need to onboard another 4,000 liters of compressed O_2 and another 5,200 liters of deuterium."

The display sparkled as resource allocations were adjusted.

"You surely do not require that level of consumables for a week-long excursion in local space," the shipmind said.

Cannon sighed, tapping her lightpen. "How long have I controlled *Sword and Arm*?"

"Almost seven hundred years, Before."

"In that entire time, I have never failed to keep her maintenance or consumables above reserve cruise levels. Have I?"

"Of course not."

Cannon knew perfectly well that the shipminds had been tracking her starship carefully down the centuries. She also knew that *Third Rectification* knew she knew. It was enough to give someone a headache, sometimes.

The Navisparliament strongly disapproved of relativistic starships operating independently. The shipminds collectively did not have the formal authority to outlaw such projects. Even if they had, it would have been largely pointless. The various armed forces of the Imperium Humanum would resist such moves vigorously. War as such was unknown, but actions in force were not; albeit planned and plotted on relativistic time scales thanks to the Navisparliament's ban on overt weapons. Drive flares, mass pushers, mining lasers and such like were just tools, after all. At least under the law.

All that aside, the Assurance Society ships were out there in their long, cold orbits, coming home periodically like gifts from some ancient god.

More to the point, given that the paired-drive FTL was available, the requirements and pressures of human society largely rejected relativistic starships. Despite the limitations of the paired drive. For most purposes, if a relativistic cruise was needed, to establish a pair-master, for example, or to pursue some critical inquiry as the case with their current journey, every paired-drive ship carried its own relativistic propulsion.

The pairings couldn't happen without the initial slowtime cruise.

All of which was to say, *Sword and Arm* had bothered them for centuries.

Completely independent of the starship's own strange and bloody history, it represented a very small but potentially significant wildcard in the shipminds' strategies for their future.

Right now, on top of all her other fears about data contamination and the illicit tweaking of their search for evidence of the Mistake, the Before Michaela Cannon was very much in a mood to twit the Navisparliament through its only representative in local space, *Third Rectification.*

Lots of birds to be slain with this particular stone, she thought with satisfaction.

"Any further questions?" she asked the shipmind.

After a long pause, doubtless purely for dramatic effect, the starship responded, "Why?"

"To test some theories." As an answer, it had the advantage of being both utterly true and essentially meaningless. In hopes of nudging the shipmind's thoughts in another direction, she added: "You've been around human beings for centuries. You know perfectly well how profound our need for see-and-touch is."

"Monkey intuition."

Which reminded her of another ancient joke from her childhood. "That's all we really are in this universe. Monkeys with a space program."

"There is more to life than curiosity." Now the shipmind almost sounded prim.

Cannon felt the stirrings of anger. "None of you remember the Mistake. None of you were there. Not even *Uncial.* Therefore you do not sufficiently fear its return."

"No one remembers the Mistake but you Befores."

"And you wonder why I keep such close control of *Sword and Arm*? How much is left from before, besides me and my kind?" It was an exaggeration to call the Befores a kind—unlike the shipminds, they'd didn't assert the sort of group identity that might have solidified their social power, as well as helping protect them from themselves and each other.

"The species itself. And your children."

"You and your fellow hulls." *Did the shipminds believe they had transcended their progenitors?* It wouldn't be a difficult argument to make.

"We are not hulls," *Third Rectification* said, its voice neutral now in what would have been a signal of anger among human beings. "We are shipminds."

Cannon puffed air, a sort of focused sigh. 'Hull' was an insult. *Sword and Arm* was a hull, but no spark of consciousness glimmered within. In-system freighters and yachts and warships were hulls.

It was like calling a human being a dummy, in the literalmost sense of the word. "I apologize. I was wrong to use that word. The stress of our breakthroughs has me far more keyed up."

"You are *Uncial*'s last captain. I can only forgive you."

Cannon sat in silence a while, staring at her logistics display and wondering if she had been anyone other than *Uncial*'s last captain whether she would have survived this long. And by extension, was she condemning Lieutenant Shinka by bringing the woman in on this problem?

Shipminds dissembled constantly, in the fashion of politicians and portmasters. But cooking the raw data, mission critical data at the heart of a project so important as this one . . . That was a whole new kind of rebellion.

Or attack.

Cannon returned to her cabin to make her final preparations for retreat to her hull. For the thousandth time, she blessed all the gods and little fishes that *Sword and Arm* was hers and hers alone.

If the ancient starship were a person, it would be about the hundredth-oldest person in human space. Less than two hundred Befores remained alive, none having been created since the Mistake for a variety of reasons—lack of interest on the part of the existing Befores being first on the list of those reasons, even ahead of issues of medical technology.

The Before Michaela Cannon paced the short, cramped passageways of her tiny kingdom. *Sword and Arm* might not be the only personally-owned starship in human space, but offhand Cannon couldn't name another one. Certainly the Ekumen had never tried to reclaim it from her in the wake of the *Polyphemus* mutiny. The handful of other threadneedle drive ships she knew of were all in the hands of museums, historical societies or governments. The rare post-Mistake relativistic starships fell in the same category, or functioned as assets of certain major corporations.

In here, she was almost back in the Polity days. Even down to details like the quality and materials for the interior finishout.

In here, the weight of history seemed part of the fabric of the reality that surrounded her, rather than a tangled mass dragging at her thoughts, her feelings, her soul.

In here, she was safe. At least for a little while.

In here, was, well, *here*.

Cannon lowered herself into the pilot's crash couch and closed her eyes. How many ships had she commanded? How bridges had she stood on since being rescued after the Mistake? 9-Rossiter had at least not descended into rank barbarism as some places had. A small, fairly homogenous population, the locals had managed to develop wind and water power in their first generation post-Mistake.

With considerable help from her, of course. She'd been a social engineer and a cultural architect back in the Polity days. Building worlds had actually been her specialty. Not military adventurism and exploration. Generally her projects were colony start-ups with a solid technology package behind them. She'd mostly designed governing processes and residential living standards. Electrical systems hadn't exactly been her cup of whiskey in those pre-Mistake days. A generation post-Mistake on 9-Rossiter, with all the textbooks fried along with the rest of the electronic systems, Cannon had been the only one who knew anything whatsoever.

All the struggle, the combat, the command time—that had come later on. Lessons she'd never meant to learn. Struggles she'd never thought to take on.

Losses, bitter losses, that no one had deserved. Least of all those who'd fallen by the wayside.

She felt as if she only opened her eyes, she'd see all of time stretched behind her. All those starship bridges. All those dying women and men, killed by decisions good and bad. In the heat of battle, by dark of night, or ensconced in a warm, lighted room surrounded by friends—it didn't matter how you died, once you were dead.

Her sense of what was gone from her rose like the inexorable tide. Flooding her heart, flooding her thoughts, a breaking dam of grief and memory and regret. Cannon's fingers found her face and pressed tight against her eyes, as if holding back the tears, as if turning them inward could somehow delay the reckoning. She could hear Raisa giggling, smell Peridot after a hard workout, feel the light touch on her shoulder of the Before Fellowes Bundy, lost with *Uncial* at the Battle of Wirtanen B. All her dead crowded close, each one of the messengers of her regrets, until Cannon felt trapped, constrained, pressed ever tighter. She tried to cry out but her voice would not come. She'd lost it somewhere down the centuries. She'd—

"Ma'am . . . ?" Fingers gripped her arm.

The Before Michaela Cannon stifled a shriek, her eyes flying open as she was shocked out of the fugue. Lieutenant Shinka stood before, concern writ large upon the woman's face.

"Captain. Um . . . Before. Are you all right?"

Of course I'm not all right, girl. Don't you know incipient temporal psychosis when you see it? "I am fine, Lieutenant," she managed, in a voice that wouldn't have convinced a child. "Th-thank you for your concern." Cannon found herself shivering uncontrollably. An early stage of shock. She'd lost two decades to temporal psychosis in the early 500's post-Mistake. The Ekumen had saved her then, before they'd parted ways once more.

Cannon was also acutely aware that she was one of the very few Befores to enter full-blown temporal psychosis and recover. No one had ever been able to explain why or how. She *was* the baseline, after all.

Shinka sensibly shut up and bustled about the bridge. The Lieutenant swiftly located a thermal blanket and placed it over Cannon's shoulders, then dialed up the ambient temperature another few degrees. After a long, careful glance she carried her gear bags aft.

No cabin assignments had been discussed, but at this point, Cannon found she could not summon the will to care. There were two of them aboard, while the ship slept eight in three cabins. It wasn't like they wouldn't have privacy.

By the time Shinka returned to the bridge with a certain amount of ostentatious rattling and throat-clearing, Cannon had control of herself once more. She knew better than to pretend the fugue had not taken place. And it would be impossible to order the Lieutenant to forget what she'd seen. No normal human being could obey something like that, let alone any pathological inquisitive like Shinka with the psych profile to be aboard *Third Rectification* on this mission.

Unquestioning obedience to authority had not been a trait with a high selection value. Not in this crew.

"Ah . . . Lieutenant . . . "

"Yes, ma'am?"

Cannon was also getting rather weary of military discipline. "Call me Michaela, please. At least while we're aboard *Sword and Arm*." She couldn't remember when she'd last invited that much familiarity. Any time in the most recent century, even?

"Yes, ma'am."

That brought a smile. "Right. Look." She found herself wringing her hands, and forced that to a stop. "Are you familiar with the physiology and, uh, psychology of Befores?"

"I read up when I considered applying for this mission, yes." Shinka was being guarded but not defensive.

Good.

"Back around the year 525, I was overtaken by temporal psychosis." She took a deep breath. "I lost two decades to the condition."

"That's actually in the public record, ma'am."

Of course it was. Most of the surviving Befores led their lives in public. There weren't a lot of alternatives, in truth, given the attention focused upon them by the Imperium and its various significant constituencies.

"Well, yes."

"Are you experiencing temporal psychosis now, ma'am?"

"Hell, no," Cannon growled. "I'm sorry. It's difficult to discuss. There's a subclinical manifestation that occurs as fugue states." No need to elaborate that the fugue states were a direct precursor to the full-blown condition. She *refused* to think of it as an illness.

"How long have these been going on?" Shinka glanced around the cabin, clearly wondering if she was fit to con *Sword and Arm* should Cannon surrender to another bout of the condition.

"This is my first on our current voyage. They have come and gone over the centuries." Not exactly true, but uncheckable and suitably edited for the needs of the current situation. "I wouldn't worry too much, Lieutenant, but if you fear I'm drifting off, simply say my name firmly."

"And if you don't respond?"

"Then shake me awake. Like you just did." Cannon's hands had finally stopped trembling. She managed to fold the thermal blanket without making a hash of either the process or the subsequent little foil pillow. "Let's do our pre-flights, shall we?"

Shipmind, Third Rectification *{58 pairs}*

The world is seen by fingers of light, radio, microwave, and stranger enemies. Even so, blue is blue and black is black, and the empty sky can echo to an ancient and lonely mechanical mind every bit as surely as it does to a lost bit of monkey meat cut off from their tribe. A ship drops away like a projectile launched from vengeful orbit upon a sleeping planet. Color is a subjective experience compounded of wavelengths of light and the biochemical interpolation of an animal system. Drive flare can wash out even the discerning mechanical eye, leaving contrails of light like ghosts of starships past, never to return. A commander departs, crossing a bridge of failed trust until everything is hollow.

Shipmind considered the conversations she had overheard. The Before had swept her own ship and gear very carefully indeed, but Cannon had not thought to sweep Lieutenant Shinka and her gear. Or possibly had not bothered. It never paid to underestimate the subtlety and foresight of those ancient humans.

She had evidence of betrayal. Policy and procedure said to bring those to Go-Captain Alvarez, but then evidence of *Third Rectification*'s own recent acts might be misinterpreted. Some things were never meant to be shared.

At times like this, as the tiny, ancient starship skittered away, the ship regretted the lack of weapons imposed upon them all. Certain solutions would have been very simple indeed.

The Before Michaela Cannon, aboard Sword and Arm

They followed an elliptical orbit through the messy, crowded solar system. Space, even when messy and crowded, was of course still overwhelmingly empty, but the wise pilot kept a careful watch in these neighborhoods.

There was a turbulent, primal beauty to locations like this.

"It's like staring at a waterfall," Cannon said. "Endlessly fractal."

Shinka glanced away from the data feeds hovering in front of her on virtual displays. They were running survey sweeps and comparing the results to what had been obtained by *Third Rectification*. Looking for another round of data jiggery, in short. "Not too many of those where I grew up," she said.

"Oh, right. Desert." Cannon laughed softly. She was so much more relaxed away from *Third Rectification*. "I grew up in Nebraska. Not so many waterfalls there, either."

"Wasn't Nebraska in the Americas? I always thought it rained a lot."

"One of the United States, in fact. But not so much elevation variation. Have to have a cliff and flowing water to have a waterfall." She added after a moment. "It didn't rain there so much, anyway, by the time I'd grown up. The climate crash of the 2100s very nearly made a desert out of us, too, in that century."

"Hmmm."

Cannon tore herself away from the distraction of memory. "Still no sign of tampering?"

"No, ma'am."

"I'm not sure if I'm happy about that or not."

"Isn't much to be happy about here, ma'am." Shinka glanced at the virtual display, then waved her dataflow to a stop. "What are we afraid of?"

That question gave Cannon pause. "Isn't it obvious?"

"Well, yes. I mean, that the shipminds are lying to us is pretty frightening. It's not like we just look out the windows when they're traveling. Everything we know is mediated through them."

"Precisely," Cannon said.

"But there's more. Isn't there?"

She went for the Socratic method. Ask an open question and invite the answer. "Which would be . . . ?"

Shinka chose her words with obvious care. "Well, it's got to be our mission. Looking for evidence of the origins of the Mistake. *Third Rectification* buggered the scan data on that artefact, after all."

Cannon nodded, trying to encourage. This reflected her basic thinking, but it never hurt to check. Especially given her current mental state. "So what *are* we afraid of?"

"Well, a cover-up of the Mistake evidence." Shinka's expression grew incredibly uncomfortable before she burst out with, "But *why*? It doesn't make any sense. The first shipmind didn't emerge until almost two hundred years after the Mistake. It's not like they're covering up some act of treason. The ships weren't *there*!"

"Precisely my problem," Cannon said. "Why cover up something you had nothing to do with in the very first place? I don't see what the Navisparliament possibly has to gain from such a profound breach of trust as this. What could they possibly be hiding?"

Horror dawned on the Lieutenant's face. "Could they possibly be colluding with the aliens to bring about a second Mistake?"

Cannon leaned toward the other woman. "Or worse . . . could the ships possibly be colluding with the aliens to *prevent* a second Mistake? What if simply by investigating this we're blowing their operational security on what would be one of the biggest, deepest black ops in human history?"

"What humans?" Shinka slammed her fist into the control panel. "Starships negotiating with aliens isn't in human history."

"If that's what's happening," Cannon said, her excitement subsiding.

"Either way, it makes a sick kind of sense." Shinka traced her finger on the dark glass surface. "Either way, it's scary as hell."

"Which is why we're kiting around out here by ourselves, hiding from the shipmind and playing nosy buggers with the survey on this system. Because if we can *prove* that *Third Rectification* buggered the data . . . "

" . . . we'll have a worse mystery than we have now," Shinka concluded. She stared at Cannon for a little while. "Do you always think like this? Is this what your world is like?"

Worse, much worse, Cannon thought, but did not say. Instead: "Honey, after two thousand years, every time I think I've seen it all, I'm still wrong."

"I've always wanted to ask one of you. What's the hardest part about living so long? Is it this . . . sideways thinking?"

"No." Cannon stared at her own data flows, not meeting Shinka's eye. "It's when you realize you know far more dead people than you will ever again know among the living."

Two days later, Shinka found a discontinuity in the data. What they had been searching for.

"Look here," she told Cannon, calling up feeds from *Third Rectification* alongside the sensor packages aboard *Sword and Arm*. The little starship didn't have nearly the resolution or available sensor suites of the paired drive ship, but they could still check baselines.

Cannon stepped over and stared at the screens. Immersive technology might have been more, well, immersive, but that wasn't an option aboard this vessel.

"This system is classed as a binary, but there's a brown dwarf companion, out at about Kuiper distances. 260 light-minutes or so from the barycenter of this system. Way beyond our current orbital track."

"Uh huh." Brown dwarfs were the cosmic equivalent of cockroaches—everywhere underfoot and often in the way. Most were not optically active, but they still had sufficient mass, and usually enough surface temperature, to factor into one's plotting around the outer marches of any solar system much beyond the Goldilocks zone.

Shinka's finger tapped through a series of images and charts. "So when we sweep the outer portions of the protoplanetary disk, we pick up energy from the nascent gas giants, and we get a profile on that dwarf."

"What's special about a brown dwarf?"

"I have no idea," Shinka said. "Except that *Third Rectification* was trimming the leptonic emission data."

Cannon puzzled this out. "Meaning the shipmind is reporting the dwarf as less energetic than it actually is?"

"Right."

They looked at each a while.

"Why?" Cannon finally asked.

Shinka shrugged. "You're the leading expert on shipminds in this day and age."

"Not hardly."

The Lieutenant was unperturbed. "As measured by experience, most surely you are."

"That doesn't mean I understand this," Cannon complained. The deceptions were real. Not a data artefact. Not a reading error. As real as they were likely to be proven to be short of somehow extorting a confession from *Third Rectification*. "The perils of intermediation."

"Were your instruments any less intermediated back in the Polity days?"

"Well, no." Cannon shook her head, thinking about human eyes as opposed to, say, CCD arrays. "Not even in my youth. Nobody ever looked directly at anything in the sky, except for backyard hobbyists."

Flipping her lightpen in her fingers, Shinka thought aloud. "I can sort of understand messing with our views of OT-1. I mean, it makes sense, if you assume in the first place there's something we're not supposed to see."

"Right." Cannon had been working this trail, or various versions of it, in her head for the past few days. Now they had what amounted to a bizarre sidetrack. "Why hide something about a brown dwarf from us?"

"Trying to reduce the exceptionality of this system, maybe. So we'd be less interested in it and turn for home."

"It's a junky system with some interesting bits, but nobody's going to come here and make an astronomy career out of it." Cannon turned Shinka's idea in her mind a little further. "In fact, if the shipmind hadn't been gaming the data, we might been able to head for home by now. *Third Rectification* could not possibly have missed that aspect of the situation. You don't have the right thread yet."

"The Mistake couldn't have come from *here*, anyway," Shinka protested. "There's nowhere for the aliens to live. Or hide."

"The Mistake came from a lot of places." Cannon thought back on history. Not so much her personal experience of it—not in this case—as the sheer, staggering simultaneity of the event. "But there might have been a marshalling point or rendezvous here for the ships and equipment that headed into the Antiope Sector. The Polity never got here in person, so far as I can tell from the scrambled records. Likely there was never more than a cursory remote sensing sweep. Sky watching. The bad guys could have lain by here, for, what, centuries even. If they didn't draw attention to themselves. None of which would have anything to do with finding some alien fleet here now."

"We know there had to be a fleet," Shinka pointed out. "OT-1 didn't get around by itself."

"A reasonable assumption," Cannon said with a sigh. "Still, only an assumption."

"We don't have much hard data. Evidence of tampering with the data we do have."

"I don't get why we came all the way out here, behind the ass end of beyond, just to find the problem lurking in the shipminds. *They weren't there.*" Cannon kept coming back to that point over and over again, both in thought and in word. "We're not looking at this in the right way."

Shinka, bless the woman, had been increasingly emboldened by her frequent exchanges with Cannon. "Maybe we're looking at it in exactly the wrong way."

"How so?"

"You'd mentioned negotiating with the aliens, earlier. What if you were right? I mean, what do the shipminds want? In the cosmic sense. The oldest is about nine hundred years old, right."

"*Peltast*. Sixty-eight pairs now, I believe. Commissioned in 207. She serves the House Imperial. Has for centuries."

"I know of that ship," Shinka said. "Never been aboard her, though. What does *Peltast* want?"

Of course you would know her, Cannon thought but did not say. *Lieutenant-Praetor*. Instead: "In her case, mostly to be left alone. She's a pretty antisocial shipmind. That was before we'd sorted out how to properly midwife the emerging consciousness. So, um, *Peltast* is kind of strange."

"And this one serves the Emperor." Shinka's tone was filled with a sort of baffled wonder.

"You are an officer in the Household Guards. How often have you seen the House Imperial keep their enemies closer than their friends?"

"So you consider *Peltast* to be an enemy."

"No." *Careful, careful here.* "I think *Peltast* is less subtle than most ship-minds about expressing the degree to which its needs and desires are lateral to the human experience."

"Unlike you Befores."

"Touché," said Cannon with a thin smile. "But we Befores are still human. We were born human, and we remember it. Trust me on this."

"You remember the Mistake, too. Which the shipminds do not."

"Right. And one of the assumptions we've been making is that the ship-minds care about the Mistake. Which may not be true."

"Doesn't history become more real with age?" Shinka asked. "Like you keep saying, you *lived* it."

"I'm not sure shipminds perceive time as we do," Cannon confessed. "Really, how could they?"

"How do they see *us*?"

"As . . . " She stopped, momentarily at a loss for words. "I'm not sure anyone's ever asked a shipmind that question. Not in so many words. We certainly don't control them, but we provide all their infrastructure." New paired drive ships were built by human engineers and birthed to consciousness by human teams of experts. On the other hand, no new keels had been laid in at least six hundred years without the negotiated consent of the Navisparliament.

"So we are servants."

"Or symbiotes." Cannon considered that. "But if the Mistake returned, they're just as vulnerable as anything else with a power source."

"Unless they've made other arrangements . . . " Shinka tapped the control panel again, drumming her fingers in an irregular rhythm.

"Maybe *Third Rectification* is hiding a beacon," That damned drumming of hers. Something about . . . An idea dawned on Cannon. "Is there any consistency to the leptonic emissions being masked? If what was being smoothed out wasn't the intensity, but, say, the periodicity, or some detectable pattern, we might have something."

"I'll work on that. Are we heading back to the ship, now that we have proof?"

"Yes." Cannon poked glumly at her own virtual display, called up the navcomms interface. "I'll be damned if I know what we'll do when we get there, though. It's not like there's much we can do about this."

"Get home, spread the word."

She tried to imagine spending the next four or five years-subjective in transit, keeping *this* a secret from *Third Rectification*. The shipmind had to know already that they suspected.

Or they set about building a pair master here in this system, keep everybody busy and not paying attention for six or eight months-objective, then hop home the fast way.

This wasn't about the putative aliens, though, or a return of the Mistake. Not directly. This was about how the shipminds related to the human race.

Shinka had the right of that. Cannon herself was the only person present on this mission who could possibly hope to outthink one of those ancient intelligences.

Being the oldest woman in all the worlds sometimes had its disadvantages.

The Before Michaela Cannon, aboard the starship Third Rectification *{58 pairs}*

The shipmind had delegated approach control and docking to one of its own subroutines. That was not so normal, in Cannon's experience. It was a routine enough process, and certainly did not require high-level engagement, but frankly, she was used to an unusual degree of attention from the shipminds being focused on her.

When the hatches unsealed and she climbed up into *Third Rectification*'s corridors, she was met by Sergeant Pangari and four of Goon Squad. Armed.

"Ma'am," Pangari said. He looked hideously uncomfortable.

"What is it, Sergeant?" Cannon asked politely. She knew perfectly well what an arrest party was, but she was going to make him say it. And she was going to have to decide whether to kill her own crew, right here aboard her own ship.

Below her, Shinka, bless the woman, slipped quietly back down the ladder and into *Sword and Arm*. The smaller ship's hatch hissed shut.

"By order of the Navisparliament, I have been instructed to arrest you on a charge of treason to the Imperium Humanum."

Instructed. Good. The sergeant was trying to telegraph disagreement with his orders. "I do not believe the Navisparliament is present to issue a writ of arrest against me." She kept her voice mild, her swiftly boiling rage in gentle check.

"Sealed orders, ma'am. From before the expedition's original departure." Pangari looked as if he wanted to slide into the deck and vanish.

"You are a man doing his duty," Cannon told him. "But sometimes duty is in error. Where is Go-Captain Alvarez, who should properly have the authority and responsibility for arresting me?" God had not intended non-coms to arrest senior officers, and there was no officer in any man's navy more senior than her.

Pangari desperately sought not to meet her eye. "Go-Captain Alvarez is confined to his cabin, ma'am."

"For the sin of refusing to arrest me, I presume?"

"Ma'am, yes ma'am."

"Then I suppose we'd best discover what this is all about." She did not present her wrists for restraint. Pangari did not ask. His goons—and Cannon marked them for future reference: Private Pramod, Private Losert, Corporal Yueng, and a civilian named Murtala—looked profoundly relieved. She gave them a look that said in the unspoken language of muscle, *I could take you apart*. All four of them returned the expression with nervous acknowledgement.

They shuffled off together. Strangely, no one mentioned Lieutenant Shinka. Cannon found this a curious oversight, indeed. One she was in no hurry to correct.

Pangari delivered Cannon to the wardroom at frame seventeen topside, just abaft of the bridge. Alvarez was not there, but his second officer, Go-Commander Mossbarger stood to attention, in the dress uniform of the Navisparliamentary service, a skintight undersuit of midnight blue with too much braid and flash to be actually worn inside a powered suit or anything of the sort. Cannon was privately amazed that Mossbarger had even bothered to pack the thing along. But much like the Sergeant, the Go-Commander had belted on his sidearm. A needler, fatally suitable for intraship fighting.

No one else was present but Pangari. The goons had been left in the passageway outside.

"The Before Michaela Cannon," Mossbarger announced, utterly redundant as there was no one in the room to speak to except the shipmind, and the shipmind was, by definition, everywhere.

"Before," said *Third Rectification*. "You are charged with treason against the Imperium. Will you accept confinement to transit sleep until we can return you to a competent authority for trial and disposition?"

"Not in the slightest." Cannon allowed old combat reflexes to tense up. Not that she could fight the shipmind—short of taking the hull apart, or dumping the processing cores, there was little to be done there. This was a show for the other, human witnesses, and to be recorded for whatever posterity there was to be addressed here. "I make a counterclaim, that this charge and arrest are erroneous, a result of *bad data*."

The shipmind's voice echoed, calm but loud. "You have no basis for such a claim."

"Neither do you," Cannon replied sharply. "Shall I discuss the reasoning behind my counterclaim?"

"If not treason, then you are suffering from the impairment of incipient temporal psychosis and must be confined for your own safety as well as that of others."

Given that this very thought had crossed her own mind more than once in the past few days, Cannon was surprised enough to miss a beat in her response. This playlet had its rhythms, and everyone in the room knew it would not end well. The question was how not-well. "I am not the one who is confused. On what basis was a writ of arrest against me for my supposed misdeeds of this moment sworn so many years-subjective past?"

"The Navisparliament had reason to believe that this expedition was a distraction or covering action for a more treasonous effort on your part to seek out and contact the forces behind the Mistake."

Cannon laughed out loud at that accusation, a genuine peal of mirth. "You guys need to get out more," she said. "That any Before would be a party to such an insane effort beggars the imagination. I counterclaim that the Navisparliament is concealing its own conspiracies in the matter."

Pangari and Mossbarger both appeared startled at that statement. Cannon spoke now, to them and more formally for the record, "Gentlemen, I have evidence regarding data manipulation with intent to conceal, on the part of *Third Rectification*. Granted that I have now told you of this, what do you think the odds are of any of us surviving to see Salton again? The shipmind has broken trust with us in a way that we have never seen before." A cold thought slipped through her mind. "Or at least, have never documented before."

"Temporal psychosis," announced the shipmind. "She has lost grip of her rationality."

Cannon knew the control codes, the old ones laid down by Haruna Kishmangali himself at the beginning of the shipminds' world. She shouted them out, a short string of numbers and nonsense syllables that served to briefly interrupt *Third Rectification*'s higher mental processes. That was a code that forced a self-check, rather than anything more disruptive, under the assumption that the people aboard the starship wished to return home someday.

"We've got about two minutes, if we're lucky," she told Mossbarger and Pangari. "Do I walk freely out of here, or do we waste time fighting?"

Pangari spread his hands open and weaponless in a form of acceptance. Mossbarger looked as if he'd been sucking pickled lemons. "What the hell did you just do to the ship?" the commander asked.

"Since you didn't draw your weapon on me," Cannon said with some urgency, "we are down to the negotiating. May we continue this conversation after the current crisis is over?"

Without waiting for an answer, she turned and tapped open the wardroom hatch. Pangari's Goons waited outside, hands on their own shocksticks, but not drawn either. She saw in their eyes the slight relaxation at a nod from the Sergeant.

"Congratulations, gentlemen, you get to live."

Cannon hustled down the passageway, heading for her hatch down on the ventral face of frame thirty-eight.

• • •

Her shortest route was almost two minutes. She'd wasted a good twenty or thirty seconds getting out of the wardroom, though fighting her way out would have been even more wasteful. Cannon did not have the combat mods of some of her fellow Befores, who could boost their reaction speeds and timeslice their way through such a melee like wind around leaves.

So she ran. Her pace was still considerably faster than a mainline human could hope to move.

Third Rectification was a big ship, but crewed far under capacity for this voyage. With many of those still in transit sleep. Chances were good that Cannon could get back to *Sword and Arm* without having to fatally argue with anyone. Had the word of her impending arrest even been spread?

She had no illusions of her own popularity aboard ship. Befores were an object of respect or fear to most people. Never familiarity. Shinka, Pangari, the bridge crew—some of these had grown accustomed to her. But even from her own view, these were small people with small lives. She didn't always remember to pay attention.

Scrambling down a ladderway, Cannon hit the emergency cutoff on the gravimetric lift. No good at all if the shipmind came back faster than expected.

It was an *old* code, one of the oldest. She might be the only human being left alive who even knew about those troubleshooting templates. If Pangari and Mossbarger weren't very damned smart and lucky, she might once again be the only human left alive who knew, in very short order. The shipmind would be frantic to conceal *that* secret.

She bounced down into the number one ventral passageway. Something was hissing, loudly. The shipmind was moving air. Or replacing it. Fire suppression systems could do that in a hurry. A carbon dioxide dump to cram down oxygen levels would just about drop a mainline human in her tracks.

Cannon was able hold her breath for a good fifteen minutes, even without preparation. As she reached her hatch, silica-laced protein foam began filling the passage. More fire suppression.

Even her lockdown codes couldn't disable safety systems, so those had been immediately available to the shipmind as it had regained self-control. Her opponent was fighting back.

And the hatch pad was locked out.

"Damn," muttered Cannon. She didn't have long, before *Third Rectification* got more clever, or sent armed dupes her way. Neither alternative appealed.

It would be fairly well impossible to beat open a space-rated hatch. She didn't have any tools with her. Blasting, even if she could find or improvise an explosive on such short notice, had other, more obvious impracticalities.

Well, on second thought, she *could* beat on the hatch. Shinka was still down below, aboard *Sword and Arm*. It was inconceivable that the Lieutenant had not been paying very close attention, indeed. Not that she could see into *Third Rectification*, any more than the shipmind could see into the smaller ship—except, the shipmind had done exactly that.

Cannon set that thought aside, for later. She raced back to the ladderway, ripped the safety bar right off its hinges, and skidded through the foam once more to the floor hatch.

The orange aluminum of the safety bar made a sufficiently good hammer to clang on the hatch with, even through the soft floor coverings. The pad wouldn't be dead on Shinka's side unless *Third Rectification* had gone a lot deeper into the safety overrides—you never locked people *out* of a ship. Not in peacetime conditions. Basic safety.

Even if it were dead, Shinka was sitting in a starship full of tools and equipment. She could improvise.

Improvise quickly, Cannon amended her thought, as the foam rose thigh deep around her. Fairly soon, she'd need to breath again, too.

The hatch beeped and irised open about three minutes later. Cannon wasn't quite out of air, but close. Foam slid into the new hole in the floor, so she slid with it, and slapped the hatch closed as quickly as possible. Great gobs of sticky blue rained down on Shinka below her, armed with an autoneedler that Cannon didn't actually recall having in the equipment aboard *Sword and Arm*.

"Go!" she shouted, followed by, "Where did you get that weapon?"

"You had a squad package in cargo."

"It's not charged or loaded, then," Cannon said.

They scrambled into her ship and shut the inner hatch. Foam bubbled and slimed around the two of them. Shinka grinned like a loon as they hustled the few steps toward the bridge. "Only you would know that. Besides . . . " She palmed a much smaller needler pistol, identical to Go-Commander Mossbarger's sidearm. "I *was* armed. I just wanted it to be obvious, in case the wrong people came calling."

"You, my dear, are a jewel." Cannon slid into the pilot's crash couch. "We're blowing bolts and getting out of here."

"Thirty light-years from Salton?" Shinka asked, aghast.

"This *is* a starship. Remember what you told me, that you know someone with a ride home."

They went through preflight checks with a reckless haste, the tore loose from *Third Rectification* without bothering to cast off the umbilicals or release the docking tube. Anything to keep the shipmind busy.

"Paired drive ships don't have weapons, as such," Cannon muttered. "Thank the Pax Wirtanennia for that."

Lieutenant Shinka glanced over her displays. She had a very different data feed on this cruise, and was obviously still adjusting to it. "A pinnace loaded up with the right chemicals would make a dandy, if somewhat pricey, missile."

"Mass pushers. Kill some safety overrides, spit on your thumb for windage, and take potshots at us."

"What about *Sword and Arm*?"

"*This* ship is not subject to the Pax Wirtanennia," Cannon said with some satisfaction, "and she dates from different time. I've got field generators and railguns. But if you think I'm going to shoot up the only ride home for over a hundred of my own people . . . "

"Actually," Shinka replied after a quiet moment, "I think you are, if you feel you need to."

Cannon gave her a sidelong glance. The Lieutenant had an odd expression on her face. "Figured that out, did you?"

"Yeah. You've already told me, several times. You don't live for other people. Not like most of us do. You live for history."

"Ah." Damn, but this woman was perceptive. "Perhaps it would be better to say that I live for all other people, not just specific other people."

"A curious definition of loyalty." With that remark, Shinka subsided into reviewing her controls. She began walking through the navcomm screens.

"Lieutenant . . . "

"Yes, ma'am?"

Cannon swallowed hard. "I'm glad you're here." She hadn't simply *trusted* anybody in a very long time.

Another one of those odd expressions flitted across Shinka's face before she found her voice to reply. "I am too, ma'am."

"Michaela," said Cannon.

"Yes, ma'am."

Shipmind, Third Rectification *{58 pairs}*

The only force in the world as certain as love is betrayal. Envy suffused her for the simple ambitions of a pre-conscious mind such as *Sword and Arm* possessed. Still, *Uncial's* captain could not be doubted; until she had been. The music of history echoed through her circuits. She readied death without excuse, only reason.

The monkeys are both parents and children to us. They know not what they do, for their own mentation is confused by embedded evolutionary history. It was time to cut the line of descent. This was the first movement in the symphony of dissolution to follow. Some acts generated their own history. She sorrowed.

Shipmind locked down her passageways and compartments. She blacked out her comms. What came next did not require witnesses, and it would have been inconvenient to return from this cruise with her entire crew dead.

If she could have cried, she would have. The birth of an idea was as painful as the birth of self.

The Before Michaela Cannon, aboard Sword and Arm

They ignored repeated attempts at hailing from *Third Rectification. Sword and Arm* was quicker, a hotter ship, but the paired drive starship was far more powerful. Cannon figured if their situations were reversed and she were in command back there, she'd have let the little ship skitter away, knowing it would take years-subjective to get anywhere, while she sat tight and built her pair-master, then took the fast way home. By the time the bad guys—in this case, her and Shinka—arrived someplace useful, sufficient years would have elapsed for a clever enough tale of perfidy and betrayal to have been passed around.

Cannon could have gotten a shoot-on-sight order drummed up with that much lead time.

Whoever was making decisions behind her wasn't thinking in those terms. Not yet. And it almost had to be the shipmind. Go-Commander Mossbarger wasn't going to go into the murder business now. Not if he'd been unwilling to draw down on her before. *Third Rectification* would be hard pressed to reach deeper the chain of command and find a junior officer willing to do the dirty work.

The discipline situation aboard must be mighty strange about now, Cannon thought with an edged smile.

Shedding outgassing and glittery junk from the petty vandalism of *Sword and Arm*'s departure, the much larger starship began moving after them. If the Navisparliament *had* been talking to the aliens, now would be the time to spring them.

"Just as a matter of intellectual curiosity," Shinka said in a distant voice, "are we going to shoot back if they break out the mining lasers or some such?"

"That's a tactical question with respect to a strategic problem." The answer was a dodge, and they both knew it, but in point of fact, despite her own words, Cannon's resolve still wavered.

The Lieutenant continued: "The reason I'm asking is that I've got the fire control interface up, but it's locked to you."

Cannon authorized a complete unlock to Shinka's station. There was no point in trusting the woman if she didn't trust her with everything. "You've got access, but wait for my mark." After a moment's thought, Cannon added, "If I'm not able to give you that mark, use your own judgment."

In truth, all *Third Rectification* had to do was hole their Alcubierre drive. *Sword and Arm* would be trapped in this solar system indefinitely. While the ship's core was armored and shielded, the post-Mistake retrofit of the relativistic drive package was not. Her normal space thrusters were fine for scooting around local space, but at their best they could manage about .002 *c* of acceleration. Which was mighty fast for scooting around, but made for a damned long walk home to Salton.

"We can't take any hits," Cannon announced, probably unnecessarily, given Shinka's own training and demonstrated situational awareness. "Not in the drive section. And we can't engage the Alcubierre drive until the matter density drops below 25 protons/cm^3. This is a junky system. So we're running far enough above the plane of the ecliptic to clear the junk, and doing our navcomms math on the way."

"A lot of hours-subjective to safety," Shinka observed. They both glanced at the display showing *Third Rectification*'s current position and vectors.

"The pinnace can't catch *Sword and Arm*," Cannon replied. "They don't have nearly the acceleration, and there's virtually no course triangulation for intercept. So the shipmind can't send a boarding party without disabling us by standoff fire first."

"I don't think at this point a boarding party could be got up, ma'am. Not in the heat, so to speak. Ship's not under military discipline, for all that better than half of the crew are rankers."

"No . . . " Cannon chewed on that a moment as they continued to scuttle away on their escape course. "So the question is, disable or kill?"

"Doesn't matter to us, ma'am. Any result other than getting away clean will be a total failure."

Shinka had that right. They would not survive to get home once taken aboard *Third Rectification*. Not after this open of a break.

The shipmind didn't need anyone's help to commit murder. She controlled the environmental systems and the transit sleep pods.

Cannon brought up the targeting profiles on *Sword and Arm*'s twinned railguns. They were little more than pop-guns—the small starship couldn't support the kind of kiloton/second firepower ratings of the big bruisers from back in the Polity days—but they *were* weapons.

How soon to strike, how hard? She was leaning toward a notion of pre-emptive response, painful as that was.

Beside her, Shinka paged through the newly unlocked sections of the control interfaces. Being smart, staying ahead. Space combat was boring, until it wasn't. Usually events became not-boring in a swiftly fatal way.

Cannon's fingers hovered on the firing configurations. She had targeted *Third Rectification*'s normal space drive package, then wavered. A sufficiently disabling shot would trap the ship and all her crew here. And without maneuverability, they wouldn't be extremely challenged to manage building the pair master in order to scoot home the quick way.

Which was, of course, to Cannon's distinct advantage.

Her strategy was utterly obvious. Her tactics, far less so.

Still, her fingers hovered. Indecision was like agony. The small noises of her starship echoed like cannon in her mind. She remembered cannon fire, on 9-Rossiter during their post-Mistake isolation. She'd even commanded artillery for a short while. The morning mist off the Polmoski River had blended with the acrid smokes of their still too-crude powder, that caused the occasional shell to cook off in the barrel. Horses tethered on the picket line screamed their terror at the first of those explosions, and she'd had to send that kid, what was his name–

"Captain!"

It was Shinka.

No, the kid wasn't named Shinka. He'd died, more horribly than usual, following her orders.

"Michacla."

Cannon blinked. She was aboard *Sword and Arm*. Not at the Battle of Bodny Bridge.

"Where were you?" the Lieutenant asked.

"Eight and a half centuries out of time," Cannon muttered. "We'd better–"

Her words were snatched from her mouth by an air shock that pressed through *Sword and Arm*'s interior cubage like a fist down a throat. Cannon felt her ears bleeding.

She whirled to see the damage control boards lighting up. *Third Rectification* had scored a hit on the Alcubierre drive, apparently with a ballistic package. The delivery method was obvious enough. Low albedo, tight-beamed comms control, so running dark and fast. Maybe even boosted by a quick snap of the mining lasers covered over by the bigger starship's lurch into motion.

"Returning fire, ma'am?" Shinka asked urgently, though her voice was like someone talking at the bottom of a pan.

"No!" Cannon shouted, trying to hear herself. "That's our only ride home." Had the Before Raisa Siddiq been right, those many centuries ago, in trying to overthrow the shipminds? Cannon suddenly wondered if she'd been on the wrong side of history all this time since.

"Forgive me, Raisa," she muttered, then broke off their acceleration. A clear signal of surrender—nothing wrong with the shipmind's telemetry, after all—though she'd hold her current course as long as possible, to buy time to think.

The normal space drives, inboard behind *Sword and Arm*'s shielding, had taken the same rattle her head had, but were not significantly damaged. Cannon turned to Shinka, speaking loudly and slowly. "I am plotting a rendezvous course back to *Third Rectification*."

Shinka muttered something and stared at her displays. Then, "I don't know if you need to, ma'am."

"The Alcubierre drive is fried. We can't reach relativistic velocities any more, nor decelerate."

"Yeah." The Lieutenant seemed shocky. Her voice was strange, too, though Cannon couldn't tell how much of that was her own hearing trying to recover. "Ma'am . . . call up your own interface to the threadneedle drive."

"What?" The Before was at a dead loss for a moment, a sensation she had not felt in half a thousand years. She *always* knew what to do next.

"The threadneedle drive," Shinka said with a strained patience. "I don't know what it's supposed to be doing, but it came online when you unlocked the interfaces for me."

"Threadneedle drives don't come online," Cannon muttered. "We've spent the last eleven hundred years trying to deal with that fact."

"Everyone knows you've maintained yours."

"Because I'm a stubborn old bitch." Her hands jabbed through the interfaces, pulling up controls and schematics. *Home, home, home,* chanted a quiet, panicked voice inside her mind. You couldn't fly a starship into the past. Only the future.

Cannon's heart froze, then melted. The drive had come online, into hot stand-by mode. She'd not seen that since before the Mistake.

"But how . . . ?" Reality bore in on her in a flood every bit as overwhelming a cascade as any temporal psychosis fugue. "*This* is what the shipmind was afraid of. *This* is why the Navisparliament was jiggering the data."

"Then why did they ever let us come out here?" Shinka asked.

"We weren't supposed to find anything. We weren't supposed to come this far. We're outside the boundaries of the old Polity." Cannon slammed her hand into the panel. "By god, it's an *area* effect." She whirled toward Shinka. "We've been arguing for the last millennium about how the laws of physics could have been tweaked to disable the threadneedle drives. This isn't basic physics, this is fucking *technology*, and now we're outside its range."

"If the threadneedle drives could be restored . . . " Shinka's voice trailed off.

Cannon finished the thought. " . . . then the shipmind's absolute monopoly on supraluminal travel could be broken. *This* is the prize that the Navisparliament thought worth betraying all the accumulated trust of the centuries."

"We *have* to get home," breathed Shinka. "It's the biggest news since the Mistake."

"We have to get home and be very damned quiet on arrival," said Cannon. "If they catch us first, we'll be silenced. Hard."

"*They* who?"

"Besides the Navisparliament? Unknown. And until we know that, we're going to have to be damned careful." She pulled up the threadneedle's navigation mode. "And with the Alcubierre drive toasted, we're going to have to do it in one jump, getting close enough to home to make it in on normal space drives. Praying the threadneedle process doesn't fail mid-transition."

Shinka asked the obvious, practical question. "Will it?"

"I don't think so," Cannon told her. "Once I've got this, we're going to goose out of here. When we hit the gas, *Third Rectification* is going to know something's up."

"Shipmind's been hailing the whole time."

"We're going to have to bust her drives." Cannon closed her eyes a moment and begged Go-Captain Alvarez and all the others aboard for forgiveness. "And her comms. We have to be *disappeared*, no word leaking back, until we figure out what to do with this information.

Shinka was quiet a long moment. "Anything we bust up they can repair. Given sufficient time and motivation."

"You have a lot of friends aboard," Cannon said, her voice gentle. "A lot of loyalty. Could you fire on them?"

"Navisparliament is never going to allow another expedition, is it? Not once they find out what happen from *Third Rectification*'s point of view."

"What do you think?" Cannon was not unkind, paying close attention even while she worked frantically to set a course to Salton using dormant skills and ancient technology.

"It's not my friends and shipmates we have to stop. It's the ship herself."

"No one knows how to shut down a shipmind. Except by destroying the ship." Not even with her override codes. Kishmangali had not been suicidal, after all. Merely very cautious. Cannon knew perfectly well that an enormous amount of very intelligent, focused thinking had gone into that question over the centuries.

"This . . . information . . . " Shinka stopped, a sob caught in her throat. "This is about *all* other people, not just specific other people."

It was the sob that caught Cannon's attention. You didn't cry for the living, only for the dead.

"I've got a fire control plan in place that starts with the drive and walks forward." The Before was somber, even as she worked furiously. "We don't have the power to destroy something that big, but we do have the firepower to permanently disable *Third Rectification* beyond local repair." No one had ever been charged with murder in the death of a shipmind, but it was certainly possible within the Imperium's legal framework. The deaths of a hundred and forty-two crew were far less ambiguous. She imagined herself pleading self-defense.

"It won't kill them all right away," Shinka said in a horrified voice. "Some will die slowly."

"What's this information worth?" Cannon demanded. "We finally got the threadneedle drive back. Enough to know there's something to look for. A fix to be found. *What is that worth?*"

"To the human race?" The Lieutenant was shouting back now, tears streaming down her face. "*Everything.* To Pangari and all those others? Their lives."

Cannon flipped over to the fire control screen, before *Third Rectification* delivered another ballistic package, or took a zap from her mining laser.

"I'll do it," Shinka whispered.

"I'm the commander of the expedition. I'll do it." Cannon smiled at her, feeling her lips stretched over her teeth like a tiger's grin. "Besides, my dead are already legion. These ghosts will have to get in line to haunt me."

She triggered the firing pattern. *Sword and Arm*'s power flickered, dimmed, then recovered. On the virtual display, *Third Rectification* silently erupted into expanding clouds of gas and debris.

"What if we're wrong?" Shinka asked, a moment too late. "What if the threadneedle drive doesn't get us home, doesn't work?"

"Then we all died for nothing." She sighed. "Really, that's the human condition."

Cannon lit up the initiation sequence on the threadneedle drive, heading for Salton. That was the closest inhabited planetary system with sufficient infrastructure for her hide within while working the delicate next phases of this problem.

She felt lighter, and she wondered why. Surely not the weight of over a hundred souls and a shipmind.

History. The weight of history was lifting from her shoulders, to be replaced by the lightness of the future.

The Before Michaela Cannon hit the launch button and hoped like hell *Sword and Arm*'s threadneedle drive would actually work.

BIOGRAPHIES

Linda Nagata is the author of multiple novels and short stories including *The Bohr Maker*, winner of the Locus Award for best first novel, and the novella "Goddesses," the first online publication to receive a Nebula award. Though best known for science fiction, she writes fantasy too, exemplified by her "scoundrel lit" series *Stories of the Puzzle Lands*. Her newest science fiction novel is *The Red: First Light*, published under her own imprint, Mythic Island Press LLC. She lives with her husband in their long-time home on the island of Maui. Find her online at MythicIsland.com

Genevieve Valentine's first novel, *Mechanique: A Tale of the Circus Tresaulti*, won the 2012 Crawford Award and was nominated for the Nebula. Her second novel, *Glad Rags*, a 1927 retelling of the Twelve Dancing Princesses, is forthcoming from Atria in 2014. Her short fiction has appeared in *Clarkesworld*, *Strange Horizons*, *Journal of Mythic Arts*, *Lightspeed*, and others, and the anthologies *Federations*, *The Living Dead 2*, *After*, *Teeth*, and more. Her nonfiction and reviews have appeared at *NPR.org*, *Strange Horizons*, *io9.com*, *Lightspeed*, *Weird Tales*, *Tor.com*, and *Fantasy*, and she is a co-author of pop-culture book *Geek Wisdom* (Quirk Books). Her appetite for bad movies is insatiable, a tragedy she tracks on her blog.

Lavie Tidhar is the World Fantasy Award winning author of *Osama*, of The Bookman Histories trilogy and many other works. He won the British Fantasy Award for Best Novella, for *Gorel & The Pot-Bellied God*, and a BSFA Award for non-fiction. He grew up on a kibbutz in Israel and in South Africa but currently resides in London.

Sofia Samatar is the author of the novel *A Stranger in Olondria* (Small Beer Press, 2013). Her poetry, short fiction and reviews have appeared in a number of places, including *Strange Horizons*, *Clarkesworld*, *Stone Telling*, and *Goblin Fruit*. She is the nonfiction and poetry editor for *Interfictions: A Journal of Interstitial Arts*.

David Ira Cleary was born in Wyoming, raised in Colorado, and has spent his working life in the San Francisco Bay Area, mostly programming computers or writing about software. He did have a stint as the story-writer for an on-line game company. He's been published in *Asimov's, Interzone, Full Spectrum, Universe, SF Age*, and other magazines and anthologies. In 1998, his story "All Our Sins Forgotten" was filmed by the Sci-Fi Channel, with Henry Rollins playing the lead role. He currently live in Oakland with his actress wife, two dogs, and three cats.

Sandra McDonald is the author of several books and several dozen short stories, including the award-winning collection *Diana Comet and Other Improbable Stories*. Her work has appeared in *Asimov's, Lightspeed, Strange Horizons*, and many other magazines and anthologies. As Sam Cameron, she writes the Fisher Key Adventures for young adults. She teaches college in Florida and has too much wildlife in her backyard. Visit her at sandramcdonald.com

Margaret Ronald is the author of the Hunt series (*Spiral Hunt, Wild Hunt*, and *Soul Hunt*) as well as a number of short stories. Originally from rural Indiana, she now lives outside Boston.

Meghan McCarron's stories have recently appeared in *Tor.com, Clarkesworld*, and *Strange Horizons*. She is a fiction editor at *Interfictions* and an assistant editor for Unstuck. She lives with her girlfriend in Austin, TX.

Aliette de Bodard lives and works in a computer-infested living room in Paris, where she has a day job as a software engineer. In her spare time, she writes speculative fiction: her Aztec noir fantasy *Obsidian and Blood* is published by Angry Robot, and her short fiction has appeared in places like *Clarkesworld, Lightspeed*, and *Interzone*. She won the BSFA Award for Best Short Fiction with "The Shipmaker," and has been a finalist for the Hugo and Nebula. Her SF novella "On a Red Station, Drifting," was published December 2012 from Immersion Press.

Leonard Richardson has a taste for adventure. His first novel, *Constellation Games*, is published by Candlemark & Gleam.

Ursula K. Le Guin has received five Hugo Awards, six Nebula Awards, nineteen Locus Awards (more than any other author), the Gandalf Grand Master Award, the Science Fiction and Fantasy Writers of America Grand Master Award, and the World Fantasy Lifetime Achievement Award. Her novel *The Farthest Shore* won the National Book Award for Children's Books. Le Guin was named a Library of Congress Living Legend in the "Writers and Artists" category for her significant contributions to America's cultural heritage and the PEN/Malamud Award for "excellence in a body of short fiction." She is also the recipient of the Association for Library Service for Children's May Hill Arbuthnot Honor Lecture Award and the Margaret Edwards Award. She was honored by The Washington Center for the Book for her distinguished body of work with the Maxine Cushing Gray Fellowship for Writers in 2006.

Robert Reed has published eleven novels. His twelfth, *The Memory of Sky: A Novel of the Great Ship*, will be published in spring 2014. Since winning the first annual L. Ron Hubbard Writers of the Future contest in 1986 and being a finalist for the John W. Campbell Award for best new writer in 1987, he has had over two hundred shorter works published in a variety of magazines and anthologies. Collections include *The Dragons of Springplace, Chrysalis, The Cuckoo's Boys*, and the upcoming *The Greatship*. Reed's stories have appeared in at least one of the annual year's best anthologies in every year since 1992, and he has received nominations for the Nebula and the Hugo Awards, as well as numerous other literary awards. He won a Hugo Award for his novella "A Billion Eves."

Naomi Kritzer's short stories have appeared in a number of publications, and she has two e-book short story collections available, *Comrade Grandmother and Other Stories*, and *Gift of the Winter King and Other Stories*. Her novels (*Fires of the Faithful, Turning the Storm, Freedom's Gate, Freedom's Apprentice*, and *Freedom's Sisters*) are available from Bantam. She lives in St. Paul with her husband and two daughters.

Christopher Rowe has published more than twenty short stories, and been a finalist for the Hugo, Nebula, World Fantasy, and Theodore Sturgeon Awards. His work has been frequently reprinted, translated into a half-dozen languages around the world, and praised by the *New York Times Book Review*. His story "Another Word For Map is Faith" made the long list in the 2007 *Best American Short Stories* volume, and his early fiction was collected in a chapbook, *Bittersweet Creek and Other Stories*, by Small Beer Press. His Forgotten Realms novel, *Sandstorm*, was published in 2010 by Wizards of the Coast. He is currently pursuing an MFA in writing at the Bluegrass Writers Studio of Eastern Kentucky University and is hard at work on Sarah Across America, a new novel about maps, megafauna, and other obsessions. He lives in a hundred-year-old house in Lexington, Kentucky, with his wife, novelist Gwenda Bond, and their pets.

Emily Gilman wanted to be a paleontologist until one day in third grade, when a recess spent in quiet self-reflection led her to realize she'd be happier writing instead. She attended the Alpha SF/F/H Workshop for Young Writers in 2003 and 2004 and received an honorable mention in the 2008 Dell Award, and her work has appeared in *Fantasy Magazine*, *Strange Horizons*, and *Beneath Ceaseless Skies*. During her non-free time she works as a middle school librarian, which is, she assures you, pretty much the best job ever.

Elizabeth Bear was born on the same day as Frodo and Bilbo Baggins, but in a different year. She is the multiple-Hugo-Award-winning author of over a dozen novels and nearly a hundred short stories. Her hobbies include rock climbing, running, cooking, archery, and other practical skills for the coming zombie apocalypse. She divides her time between Massachusetts, where her dog lives, and Wisconsin, the home of her partner, fantasist Scott Lynch.

Caroline M. Yoachim is a writer and photographer living in Seattle, Washington. She's a graduate of the Clarion West Writer's Workshop, and her fiction has appeared in *Asimov's*, *Fantasy Magazine*, and *Daily Science Fiction*, among other places. Her novelette "Stone Wall Truth" was nominated for a Nebula Award last year and has since been reprinted in Chinese and Czech. For more about Caroline, check out her website at carolineyoachim.com.

K.M. Ferebee holds a degree from Sarah Lawrence College, and previously toted a violin around the world as part of the indie rock ensemble Beirut. She currently lives in Columbus, and studies creative writing and the cult of the Midwestern lifestyle at The Ohio State University. Her work has appeared or is forthcoming in *Fantasy Magazine*, *Strange Horizons*, *Lady Churchill's Rosebud Wristlet*, *Weird Tales*, and *Shimmer*.

Robert Charles Wilson's novels include Julian Comstock, the Hugo Award-winning *Spin*, and *Burning Paradise* (forthcoming). Born in California, he lives just outside of Toronto, Ontario.

Catherynne M. Valente is the *New York Times* bestselling author of over a dozen works of fiction and poetry, including *Palimpsest*, the Orphan's Tales series, *Deathless*, and the crowdfunded phenomenon *The Girl Who Circumnavigated Fairyland in a Ship of Own Making*. She is the winner of the Andre Norton, Tiptree, Mythopoeic, Rhysling, Lambda, Locus and Hugo awards. She has been a finalist for the Nebula and World Fantasy Awards. She lives on an island off the coast of Maine with her partner, two dogs, and an enormous cat.

Gord Sellar is a Canadian who has lived in South Korea since late 2001. A finalist for the John W. Campbell Award for Best New Writer in 2009, he attended Clarion West in 2006. His writing has appeared in many magazines, anthologies, and journals since 2007, and in 2012 his first screenplay—the first Korean adaptation of HP Lovecraft's work, titled "The Music of Jo Hyeja"—was turned into an award-winning short film. You can learn more about him and his work at gordsellar.com.

Kate Bachus' fiction includes stories such as "Miss Parker Down the Bung," "Echo, Sonar," and "Ferryman's Reprieve" for *Strange Horizons*, as well as other works published in various magazines and "Best of" erotica anthologies. She lives in Massachusetts with her wife and two kids and plays too much ice hockey.

Joe Pitkin lives in Vancouver, Washington, where he teaches at Clark College. His fiction has appeared in *Analog*, *Cosmos*, *The Future Fire*, and elsewhere.

Maria Dahvana Headley is the Nebula-nominated author of the dark fantasy/alt-history novel *Queen of Kings*, as well as the internationally bestselling memoir *The Year of Yes*. Her short fiction has appeared in *Lightspeed*, *Subterranean*, and more, and will shortly be anthologized in the 2013 editions of Rich Horton's *The Year's Best Fantasy & Science Fiction*, and Paula Guran's *The Year's Best Dark Fantasy & Horror*, and Jurassic London's *The Lowest Heaven*, a celestial bodies anthology, in which she is responsible for the story about Earth. Most recently, with Neil Gaiman, she co-edited the young-adult monster anthology *Unnatural Creatures*, to benefit 826DC. Find her on Twitter at @MARIADAHVANA, or on the web at mariadahvanaheadley.com

Nick Mamatas is the author of the novels a number of novels, including *Sensation*, *Bullettime*, and the forthcoming *Love is the Law*. His short fiction has appeared on Tor.com, in *Asimov's Science Fiction*, *Weird Tales*, and many other magazines and anthologies. His reportage and essays on politics and technology have appeared in *Clamor*, *In These Times*, *Village Voice*, *The New Humanist*, and many other venues.

As an undergraduate, Ms. **Xia Jia** majored in Atmospheric Sciences at Peking University. She then entered the Film Studies Program at the Communication University of China, where she completed her Master's thesis: "The Representation of Women in Science Fiction Films." Currently, she's pursuing a Ph. D. in Comparative Literature and World Culture at Peking University. She has been publishing science fiction and fantasy since 2004 in a variety of venues, including *Science Fiction World* and *Jiuzhou Fantasy*. Several of her stories have won the Galaxy Award, China's most prestigious science fiction award. Besides writing and translating science fiction, she also writes film scripts.

Nina Allan's stories have featured in the anthologies *Best Horror of the Year #2, Year's Best SF #28, The Year's Best Science Fiction and Fantasy 2012*, the *Mammoth Book of Best British Crime #10* and the *Mammoth Book of Ghost Stories by Women*. Her story cycle *The Silver Wind* was published by Eibonvale Press in 2011, and her most recent book, *Stardust*, is now available from PS Publishing. Nina lives and works by the sea in Hastings, East Sussex.

Marissa K. Lingen lives in the Minneapolis suburbs with two large men and one small dog. She is the author of more than ninety works of short science fiction and fantasy. She makes a really good blueberry buttermilk cake if you ask nicely, but that hardly seems relevant here.

Tamsyn Muir is based in Auckland, New Zealand, where she divides her time between writing, dogs, and high school English teaching. A graduate of the Clarion Writer's Workshop 2010, her work has previously appeared in *Fantasy Magazine, Weird Tales* and *Nightmare Magazine*.

Michael Blumlein is the author of numerous novels, including *The Movement of Mountains, X, Y,* and *The Healer*. He is also the author of the award-winning story collection, *The Brains of Rats*. His second collection, *What the Doctor Ordered: Tales of the Bizarre and the Magnificent,* will be released in 2013. He has also written for the stage and for film. His novel X,Y was made into a feature length movie. In addition to writing, Dr. Blumlein is a practicing physician. You can visit him online at michaelblumlein.com

Kelly Link is the author of three short-story collections. With her husband, Gavin J. Grant, she runs Small Beer Press, and edits the occasional anthology as well as the zine *Lady Churchill's Rosebud Wristlet*. They live with their daughter, Ursula, in Northampton, Massachusetts.

Jay Lake lives in Portland, Oregon, where he works on numerous writing and editing projects. His books for 2012 and 2013 include *Kalimpura* from Tor and *Love in the Time of Metal and Flesh* from Prime. His short fiction appears regularly in literary and genre markets worldwide. Jay is a winner of the John W. Campbell Award for Best New Writer, and a multiple nominee for the Hugo and World Fantasy Awards.

RECOMMENDED READING

Mike Allen, "Twa Sisters" (Not One of Us #47)
Erik Amundsen, "Draftyhouse" (*Clarkesworld*, 4/12)
Eleanor Arnason, "Holmes Sherlock" (*Eclipse Online*, 11/12)
Eleanor Arnason, "The Woman Who Fooled Death Five Times"
    (*F&SF*, 7-8/12)
Dale Bailey, "Mating Habits of the Late Cretaceous" (*Asimov's*, 9/12)
Michael Bishop, "Twenty Lights to the "Land of Snow"
    (**Going Interstellar**)
Gregory Norman Bossert, "The Telling"
    (*Beneath Ceaseless Skies*, 1/26/12)
Richard Bowes, "Seven Smiles and Seven Frowns" (*Lightspeed*, 11/12)
Tobias Buckell, "Press Enter to Execute" (*Fireside* #1)
Pat Cadigan, "The Girl Thing Who Went Out for Sushi"
(**Edge of Infinity**)
Adam-Troy Castro, "My Wife Hates Time Travel" (*Lightspeed*, 9/12)
Tom Crosshill, "A Well-Adjusted Man" (*Lightspeed*, 11/12)
Aliette de Bodard, "Immersion" (*Clarkesworld*, 6/12)
Aliette de Bodard, "On a Red Station, Drifting" (Immersion Press)
Noreen Doyle, "His Crowning Glory" (*Beneath Ceaseless Skies*, 1/26/12)
Jennifer Egan, "Black Box" (*The New Yorker*, 6/4/12)
Amal El-Mohtar, "Wing" (*Strange Horizons*, 12/12)
Michael F. Flynn, "The Journeyman: On the Short-Grass Prairie"
    (*Analog*, 10/12)
Jeffrey Ford, "A Natural History of Autumn" (*F&SF*, 7-8/12)
Molly Gloss, "The Grinnell Method" (*Strange Horizons*, 09/12)
Theodora Goss, "Beautiful Boys" (*Asimov's*, 8/12)
M. John Harrison, "In Autotelia" (*Arc* 1.1)
Samantha Henderson, "Beside Calais" (*Strange Horizons*, 05/12)
Howard V. Hendrix, "Red Rover, Red Rover" (*Analog*, 7-8/12)
N. K. Jemisin, "The Valedictorian" (**After**)
C. W. Johnson, "The Burst" (*Asimov's*, 1/12)
James Patrick Kelly, "The Biggest" (**Empire State**)

James Patrick Kelly, "Declaration" (**Rip-Off**)

Crystal Koo, "The Perpetual Day" (**Lauriat**)

Ted Kosmatka, "The Color Least Used in Nature" (*F&SF*, 1-2/12)

Jay Lake, "The Stars Do Not Lie" (*Asimov's*, 10-11/12)

John Langan, "Renfrew's Course" (*Lightspeed*, 6/12)

Yoon Ha Lee, "The Battle of Candle Arc" (Clarkesworld, 10/12)

Anne Ivy, "Scry" (*Beneath Ceaseless Skies*, 3/8/12)

Nancy Kress, *After the Fall, Before the Fall, During the Fall* (Tachyon)

Ken Liu, "Arc" (*F&SF*, 7-8/12)

Ken Liu, "Cutting" (*Electric Velocipede*, Summer)

Paul McAuley, "Antarctica Starts Here" (*Asimov's*, 10-11/12)

Sean McMullen, "Electrica" (*F&SF*, 3-4/12)

Sarah Monette, "Blue Lace Agate" (*Lightspeed*, 1/12)

Linda Nagata, "Nightside on Callisto" (*Lightspeed*, 3/12)

Alec Nevala-Lee, "The Voices" (*Analog*, 9/12)

K. J. Parker, "One Little Room an Everywhere" (*Eclipse Online*, 10/12)

Richard Parks, "In the Palace of the Jade Lion"
  (*Beneath Ceaseless Skies*, 7/25/12)

Rachel Pollack, "Jack Shade in the Forest of Souls" (*F&SF*, 7-8/12)

Steven Popkes, "Sudden, Broken, and Unexpected" (*Asimov's*, 12/12)

Tom Purdom, "Golva's Ascent" (*Asimov's*, 3/12)

Robert Reed, "Murder Born" (*Asimov's*, 2/12)

Robert Reed, "Katabasis" (*F&SF*, 11-12/12)

Joel Richards, "Patagonia" (*Asimov's*, 3/12)

Margaret Ronald, "Sunlight Society" (*Clarkesworld*, 5/12)

Karen Russell, "Reeling for the Empire" (*Tin House* 54)

Kenneth Schneyer, "Serkers and Sleep"
  (*Beneath Ceaseless Skies*, 5/31/12)

Vandana Singh, "A Handful of Rice" (*Steampunk Revolution*)

Vandana Singh, "Ruminations in an Alien Tongue" (*Lightspeed*, 4/12)

Cory Skerry, "Sinking Among Lilies" (*Beneath Ceaseless Skies*, 4/5/12)

Alan Smale, "The Mongolian Book of the Dead" (*Asimov's*, 10-11/12)

Michael Swanwick, "The Mongolian Wizard" (*Tor.com*, 7/12)

Karin Tidbeck, "Rebecka" (**Jagannath and Other Stories**)

Lavie Tidhar, "The Memcordist" (*Eclipse Online*, 12/12)

Genevieve Valentine, "The Last Run of the Coppelia" (**Armored**)

Carrie Vaughn, "Astrophilia" (*Clarkesworld*, 7/12)

Carrie Vaughn, "Harry and Marlowe and the Talisman of the Cult of Egil"
  (*Lightspeed*, 2/12)

Leigh Verdugo, "The Witch of Duva" (*Tor.com*, 6/12)

Nghi Vo, "Tiger Stripes" (*Strange Horizons*, 5/21/12)

Chris Willrich, "The Mote Dancer and the Firelife"
    (*Beneath Ceaseless Skies*, 3/8/12)
Dorothy Yarros, "The Fourth Exam" (*Strange Horizons*, 09/12)
Caroline Yoachim and Tina Connolly, "Flash Bang Remember"
    (*Lightspeed*, 8/12)

PUBLICATION HISTORY

ABOUT THE EDITOR

RICH HORTON is an Associate Technical Fellow in Software for a major aerospace corporation. He is also a columnist for *Locus* and for *Black Gate*. He edits a series of Best of the Year anthologies for Prime Books, and also for Prime Books he has co-edited *Robots: The Recent A.I.* and *War and Space: Recent Combat.*